THE FOURTH AGATHA CHRISTIE COMPANION

The three books in this volume are reproduced
by arrangement with William Collins Sons & Co. Ltd.
This edition published 1982 by Book Club Associates

The Body in the Library

The Moving Finger

Nemesis

Printed in Great Britain
by Mackays of Chatham Limited

THE FOURTH AGATHA CHRISTIE COMPANION

The Body in the Library

The Moving Finger

Nemesis

BOOK CLUB ASSOCIATES LONDON

CONTENTS

The Body in the Library

AGATHA
CHRISTIE

DEC '84

To My Friend Nan

Chapter 1

i

MRS. BANTRY was dreaming. Her sweet peas had just taken a First at the flower show. The vicar, dressed in cassock and surplice, was giving out the prizes in church. His wife wandered past, dressed in a bathing-suit, but as is the blessed habit of dreams this fact did not arouse the disapproval of the parish in the way it would assuredly have done in real life. . . .

Mrs. Bantry was enjoying her dream a good deal. She usually did enjoy those early-morning dreams that were terminated by the arrival of early-morning tea. Somewhere in her inner consciousness was an awareness of the usual early-morning noises of the household. The rattle of the curtain-rings on the stairs as the housemaid drew them, the noises of the second housemaid's dustpan and brush in the passage outside. In the distance the heavy noise of the front-door bolt being drawn back.

Another day was beginning. In the meantime she must extract as much pleasure as possible from the flower show—for already its dream-like quality was becoming apparent. . . .

Below her was the noise of the big wooden shutters in the drawing-room being opened. She heard it, yet did not hear it. For quite half an hour longer the usual household noises would go on, discreet, subdued, not disturbing because they were so familiar. They would culminate in a swift, controlled sound of footsteps along the passage, the rustle of a print dress, the subdued chink of tea-things as the tray was deposited on the table outside, then the soft knock and the entry of Mary to draw the curtains.

In her sleep Mrs. Bantry frowned. Something disturbing was penetrating through to the dream state, something out of its time. Footsteps along the passage, footsteps that were too hurried and too soon. Her ears listened unconsciously for the chink of china, but there was no chink of china.

The knock came at the door. Automatically from the depths of her dream Mrs. Bantry said: "Come in." The door opened—now there would be the chink of curtain-rings as the curtains were drawn back.

But there was no chink of curtain-rings. Out of the dim green light Mary's voice came—breathless, hysterical: "Oh, m'am, oh, m'am, *there's a body in the library*."

And then with a hysterical burst of sobs she rushed out of the room again.

ii

Mrs. Bantry sat up in bed.

Either her dream had taken a very odd turn or else—or else Mary had really rushed into the room and had said (incredible! fantastic!) that there was a body in the library.

"Impossible," said Mrs. Bantry to herself. "I must have been dreaming."

But even as she said it, she felt more and more certain that she had not been dreaming, that Mary, her superior self-controlled Mary, had actually uttered those fantastic words.

Mrs. Bantry reflected a minute and then applied an urgent conjugal elbow to her sleeping spouse.

"Arthur, Arthur, wake up."

Colonel Bantry grunted, muttered, and rolled over on his side.

"Wake up, Arthur. Did you hear what she said?"

"Very likely," said Colonel Bantry indistinctly. "I quite agree with you, Dolly," and promptly went to sleep again.

Mrs. Bantry shook him.

"You've got to listen. Mary came in and said that there was a body in the library."

"Eh, what?"

"A *body* in the *library*."

"Who said so?"

"Mary."

Colonel Bantry collected his scattered faculties and proceeded to deal with the situation. He said:

"Nonsense, old girl; you've been dreaming."

"No, I haven't. I thought so, too, at first. But I haven't. She really came in and said so."

"Mary came in and said there was a body in the library?"

"Yes."

"But there couldn't be," said Colonel Bantry.

"No—no, I suppose not," said Mrs. Bantry doubtfully.

Rallying, she went on.

"But then why did Mary say there was?"

"She can't have."

"She did."

"You must have imagined it."

"I didn't imagine it."

Colonel Bantry was by now thoroughly awake and prepared to deal with the situation on its merits. He said kindly:

"You've been dreaming, Dolly, that's what it is. It's that detective story you were reading—*The Clue of the Broken Match*. You know—Lord Edgbaston finds a beautiful blonde dead on the library hearthrug. Bodies are always being found in libraries in books. I've never known a case in real life."

"Perhaps you will now," said Mrs. Bantry. "Anyway, Arthur, you've got to get up and see."

"But really, Dolly, it *must* have been a dream. Dreams often do seem wonderfully vivid when you first wake up. You feel quite sure they're true."

"I was having quite a different sort of dream—about a flower show and the vicar's wife in a bathing-dress—something like that."

With a sudden burst of energy Mrs. Bantry jumped out of bed and pulled back the curtains. The light of a fine autumn day flooded the room.

"I did *not* dream it," said Mrs. Bantry firmly. "Get up at once, Arthur, and go downstairs and see about it."

"You want me to go downstairs and ask if there's a body in the library? I shall look a damned fool."

"You needn't ask anything," said Mrs. Bantry. "If there *is* a body—and of course it's just possible that Mary's gone mad and thinks she sees things that aren't there—well, somebody will tell you soon enough. *You* won't have to say a word."

Grumbling, Colonel Bantry wrapped himself in his dressing-gown and left the room. He went along the passage and down the staircase. At the foot of it was a little knot of huddled servants, some of them were sobbing. The butler stepped forward impressively.

"I'm glad you have come, sir. I have directed that nothing should be done until you came. Will it be in order for me to ring up the police, sir?"

"Ring 'em up about what?"

The butler cast a reproachful glance over his shoulder at the tall young woman who was weeping hysterically on the cook's shoulder.

"I understood, sir, that Mary had already informed you. She said she had done so."

Mary gasped out:

"I was so upset I don't know what I said. It all came over me again and my legs gave way and my inside turned over. Finding it like that—oh, oh, oh!"

She subsided again on to Mrs. Eccles, who said: "There, there, my dear," with some relish.

"Mary is naturally somewhat upset, sir, having been the one to make the gruesome discovery," explained the butler. "She went into the library as usual, to draw the curtains, and—and almost stumbled over the body."

"Do you mean to tell me," demanded Colonel Bantry, "that there's a dead body in my library—*my* library?"

The butler coughed.

"Perhaps, sir, you would like to see for yourself."

iii

"Hallo, 'allo, 'allo. Police station here. Yes, who's speaking?"

Police-Constable Palk was buttoning up his tunic with one hand while the other held the receiver.

"Yes, yes, Gossington Hall. Yes? Oh, good-morning, sir." Police-Constable Palk's tone underwent a slight modification. It became less impatiently official, recognizing the generous patron of the police sports and the principal magistrate of the district.

"Yes, sir? What can I do for you?—I'm sorry, sir, I didn't quite catch—a *body*, did you say?—yes?—yes, if you please, sir—that's right, sir—young woman not known to you, you say?—quite, sir. Yes, you can leave it all to me."

Police-Constable Palk replaced the receiver, uttered a long-drawn whistle and proceeded to dial his superior officer's number.

Mrs. Palk looked in from the kitchen whence proceeded an appetizing smell of frying bacon.

"What is it?"

"Rummest thing you ever heard of," replied her husband. "Body of a young woman found up at the Hall. In the Colonel's library."

"Murdered?"

"Strangled, so he says."

"Who was she?"

"The Colonel says he doesn't know her from Adam."

"Then what was she doing in 'is library?"

Police-Constable Palk silenced her with a reproachful glance and spoke officially into the telephone.

"Inspector Slack? Police-Constable Palk here. A report has just come in that the body of a young woman was discovered this morning at seven-fifteen——"

iv

Miss Marple's telephone rang when she was dressing. The sound of it flurried her a little. It was an unusual hour for her telephone to ring. So well ordered was her prim spinster's life that unforeseen telephone calls were a source of vivid conjecture.

"Dear me," said Miss Marple, surveying the ringing instrument with perplexity. "I wonder who that can be?"

Nine o'clock to nine-thirty was the recognized time for the village to make friendly calls to neighbours. Plans for the day, invitations and so on were always issued then. The butcher had been known to ring up just before nine if some crisis in the meat trade had occurred. At intervals during the day spasmodic calls might occur, though it was considered bad form to ring up after nine-thirty at night. It was true that Miss Marple's nephew, a writer, and therefore erratic, had been known to ring up at the most peculiar times, once as late as ten minutes to midnight. But whatever Raymond West's eccentricities, early rising was not one of them. Neither he nor any one of Miss Marple's acquaintance would be likely to ring up before eight in the morning. Actually a quarter to eight.

Too early even for a telegram, since the post office did not open until eight.

"It must be," Miss Marple decided, "a wrong number."

Having decided this, she advanced to the impatient instrument and quelled its clamour by picking up the receiver. "Yes?" she said.

"Is that you, Jane?"

Miss Marple was much surprised.

"Yes, it's Jane. You're up very early, Dolly."

Mrs. Bantry's voice came breathless and agitated over the wires.

"The most awful thing has happened."

"Oh, my dear."

"We've just found a body in the library."

For a moment Miss Marple thought her friend had gone mad.

"You've found a *what*?"

"I know. One doesn't believe it, does one? I mean, I thought they only happened in books. I had to argue for hours with Arthur this morning before he'd even go down and see."

Miss Marple tried to collect herself. She demanded breathlessly: "But whose body is it?"

"It's a blonde."

"A what?"

"A blonde. A beautiful blonde—like books again. None of us have ever seen her before. She's just lying there in the library, dead. That's why you've got to come up at once."

"You want *me* to come up?"

"Yes, I'm sending the car down for you."

Miss Marple said doubtfully:

"Of course, dear, if you think I can be of any comfort to you——"

"Oh, I don't want comfort. But you're so good at bodies."

"Oh no, indeed. My little successes have been mostly theoretical."

"But you're very good at murders. She's been murdered, you see, strangled. What I feel is that if one has got to have a murder actually happening in one's house, one might as well enjoy it, if you know what I mean. That's why I want you to come and help me find out who did it and unravel the mystery and all that. It really *is* rather thrilling, isn't it?"

"Well, of course, my dear, if I can be of any *help* to you."

"Splendid! Arthur's being rather difficult. He seems to think I shouldn't enjoy myself about it at all. Of course, I do know it's very sad and all that, but then I don't know the girl—and when you've seen her you'll understand what I mean when I say she doesn't look *real* at all."

V

A little breathless, Miss Marple alighted from the Bantrys' car, the door of which was held open for her by the chauffeur.

Colonel Bantry came out on the steps, and looked a little surprised.

"Miss Marple?—er—very pleased to see you."

"Your wife telephoned to me," explained Miss Marple.

"Capital, capital. She ought to have someone with her. She'll crack up otherwise. She's putting a good face on things at the moment, but you know what it is——"

At this moment Mrs. Bantry appeared, and exclaimed:

"Do go back into the dining-room and eat your breakfast, Arthur. Your bacon will get cold."

"I thought it might be the Inspector arriving," explained Colonel Bantry.

"He'll be here soon enough," said Mrs. Bantry. "That's why it's important to get your breakfast first. You need it."

"So do you. Much better come and eat something, Dolly——"

"I'll come in a minute," said Mrs. Bantry. "Go on, Arthur."

Colonel Bantry was shooed back into the dining-room rather like a recalcitrant hen.

"*Now!*" said Mrs. Bantry with an intonation of triumph. "Come on."

She led the way rapidly along the long corridor to the east of the house. Outside the library door Constable Palk stood on guard. He intercepted Mrs. Bantry with a show of authority.

"I'm afraid nobody is allowed in, madam. Inspector's orders."

"Nonsense, Palk," said Mrs. Bantry. "You know Miss Marple perfectly well."

Constable Palk admitted to knowing Miss Marple.

"It's very important that she should see the body," said Mrs. Bantry. "Don't be stupid, Palk. After all, it's *my* library, isn't it?"

Constable Palk gave way. His habit of giving in to the gentry was lifelong. The Inspector, he reflected, need never know about it.

"Nothing must be touched or handled in any way," he warned the ladies.

"Of course not," said Mrs. Bantry impatiently. "We know *that*. You can come in and watch, if you like."

Constable Palk availed himself of this permission. It had been his intention anyway.

Mrs. Bantry bore her friend triumphantly across the library to the big old-fashioned fireplace. She said, with a dramatic sense of climax: "There!"

Miss Marple understood then just what her friend had meant when she said the dead girl wasn't real. The library was a room very typical of its owners. It was large and shabby and untidy. It had big sagging arm-chairs, and pipes and books and estate papers laid out on the big table. There were one or two good old family portraits on the walls, and some bad Victorian water-colours, and some would-be-funny hunting scenes. There was a big vase of Michaelmas daisies in the corner. The whole room was dim and mellow and casual. It spoke of long occupation and familiar use and of links with tradition.

And across the old bearskin hearthrug there was sprawled something new and crude and melodramatic.

The flamboyant figure of a girl. A girl with unnaturally fair hair dressed up off her face in elaborate curls and rings. Her thin body was dressed in a backless evening-dress of white spangled satin. The face was heavily made-up, the powder standing out grotesquely on its blue swollen surface, the mascara of the lashes lying thickly on the distorted cheeks, the scarlet of the lips looking like a gash. The finger-nails were enamelled in a deep blood-red and so were the toenails in their cheap silver sandal shoes. It was a cheap, tawdry, flamboyant figure—almost incongruous in the solid old-fashioned comfort of Colonel Bantry's library.

Mrs. Bantry said in a low voice:

"You see what I mean? It just isn't *true*!"

The old lady by her side nodded her head. She looked down long and thoughtfully at the huddled figure.

She said at last in a gentle voice:

"She's very young."

"Yes—yes—I suppose she is." Mrs. Bantry seemed almost surprised—like one making a discovery.

Miss Marple bent down. She did not touch the girl. She looked at the fingers that clutched frantically at the front of the girl's dress, as though she had clawed it in her last frantic struggle for breath.

There was the sound of a car scrunching on the gravel outside. Constable Palk said with urgency:

"That'll be the Inspector. . . ."

True to his ingrained belief that the gentry didn't let you down, Mrs. Bantry immediately moved to the door. Miss Marple followed her. Mrs. Bantry said:

"That'll be all right, Palk."

Constable Palk was immensely relieved.

vi

Hastily downing the last fragments of toast and marmalade with a drink of coffee, Colonel Bantry hurried out into the hall and was relieved to see Colonel Melchett, the Chief Constable of the county, descending from a car with Inspector Slack in attendance. Melchett was a friend of the Colonel's. Slack he had never much taken to—an energetic man who belied his name and who accompanied his bustling manner with a good deal of disregard for the feelings of any one he did not consider important.

"Morning, Bantry," said the Chief Constable. "Thought I'd better come along myself. This seems an extraordinary business."

"It's—it's——" Colonel Bantry struggled to express himself. "It's *incredible—fantastic*!"

"No idea who the woman is?"

"Not in the slightest. Never set eyes on her in my life."

"Butler know anything?" asked Inspector Slack.

"Lorrimer is just as taken aback as I am."

"Ah," said Inspector Slack. "I wonder."

Colonel Bantry said:

"There's breakfast in the dining-room, Melchett, if you'd like anything?"

"No, no—better get on with the job. Haydock ought to be here any minute now—ah, here he is."

Another car drew up and big, broad-shouldered Doctor Haydock, who was also the police surgeon, got out. A second police car had disgorged two plain-clothes men, one with a camera.

"All set—eh?" said the Chief Constable. "Right. We'll go along. In the library, Slack tells me."

Colonel Bantry groaned.

"It's incredible! You know, when my wife insisted this morning that the housemaid had come in and said there was a body in the library, I just wouldn't believe her."

"No, no, I can quite understand that. Hope your missus isn't too badly upset by it all?"

"She's been wonderful—really wonderful. She's got old Miss Marple up here with her—from the village, you know."

"Miss Marple?" The Chief Constable stiffened. "Why did she send for her?"

"Oh, a woman wants another woman—don't you think so?"

Colonel Melchett said with a slight chuckle:

"If you ask me, you wife's going to try her hand at a little amateur detecting. Miss Marple's quite the local sleuth. Put it over us properly once, didn't she, Slack?"

Inspector Slack said: "That was different."

"Different from what?"

"That was a local case, that was sir. The old lady knows everything that goes on in the village, that's true enough. But she'll be out of her depth here."

Melchett said dryly: "You don't know very much about it yourself yet, Slack."

"Ah, you wait, sir. It won't take me long to get down to it."

vii

In the dining-room Mrs. Bantry and Miss Marple, in their turn, were partaking of breakfast.

After waiting on her guest, Mrs. Bantry said urgently:

"Well, Jane?"

Miss Marple looked up at her, slightly bewildered.

Mrs. Bantry said hopefully:

"Doesn't it *remind* you of anything?"

For Miss Marple had attained fame by her ability to link up trivial village happenings with graver problems in such a way as to throw light upon the latter.

"No," said Miss Marple thoughtfully, "I can't say that it does—not at the moment. I was reminded a little of Mrs. Chetty's youngest—Edie, you know—but I think that was just because this poor girl bit her nails and her front teeth stuck out a little. Nothing more than that. And of course," went on Miss Marple, pursuing the parallel further, "Edie was fond of what I call cheap finery, too."

"You mean her dress?" said Mrs. Bantry.

"Yes, a very tawdry satin—poor quality."

Mrs. Bantry said:

"I know. One of those nasty little shops where everything is a guinea." She went on hopefully:

"Let me see, what happened to Mrs. Chetty's Edie?"

"She's just gone into her second place—and doing very well, I believe."

Mrs. Bantry felt slightly disappointed. The village parallel didn't seem to be exactly hopeful.

"What I can't make out," said Mrs. Bantry, "is what she could possibly be doing in Arthur's study. The window was forced, Palk tells me. She might have come down here with a burglar and then they quarrelled—but that seems such nonsense, doesn't it?"

"She was hardly dressed for burglary," said Miss Marple thoughtfully.

"No, she was dressed for dancing—or a party of some kind. But there's nothing of that kind down here—or anywhere near."

"N-n-o," said Miss Marple doubtfully.

Mrs. Bantry pounced.

"Something's in your mind, Jane."

"Well, I was just wondering——"

"Yes?"

"Basil Blake."

Mrs. Bantry cried impulsively: "Oh, no!" and added as though in explanation, "I know his mother."

The two women looked at each other.

Miss Marple sighed and shook her head.

"I quite understand how you feel about it."

"Selina Blake is the nicest woman imaginable. Her herbaceous borders are simply marvellous—they make me green with envy. And she's frightfully generous with cuttings."

Miss Marple, passing over these claims to consideration on the part of Mrs. Blake, said:

"All the same, you know, there has been a lot of *talk*."

"Oh, I know—I know. And of course Arthur goes simply livid when he hears Basil Blake mentioned. He was really *very* rude to Arthur, and since then Arthur won't hear a good word for him. He's got that silly slighting way of talking that these boys have nowadays—sneering at people sticking up for their school or the Empire or that sort of thing. And then, of course, the *clothes* he wears!

"People say," continued Mrs. Bantry, "that it doesn't matter what you wear in the country. I never heard such nonsense. It's just in the country that every one notices." She paused, and added wistfully: "He was an adorable baby in his bath."

"There was a lovely picture of the Cheviot murderer as a baby in the paper last Sunday," said Miss Marple.

"Oh, but Jane, you didn't think *he*——"

"No, no, dear. I didn't mean that at all. That would indeed be jumping to conclusions. I was just trying to account for the young woman's presence down here. St. Mary Mead is such an unlikely place. And then it seemed to me that the only possible explanation was Basil Blake. He *does* have parties. People came down from London and from the studios—you remember last July? Shouting and singing—the most *terrible* noise—every one very drunk, I'm afraid—and the mess and the broken glass next morning simply unbelievable—so old Mrs. Berry told me—and a young woman asleep in the bath with practically *nothing on*!"

Mrs. Bantry said indulgently:

"I suppose they were film people."

"Very likely. And then—what I expect you've heard—several week-ends lately he's brought down a young woman with him—a platinum blonde."

Mrs. Bantry exclaimed:

"You don't think it's *this* one?"

"Well—I wondered. Of course, I've never seen her close to—only just getting in and out of the car—and once in the cottage garden when she was sunbathing with just some shorts and a brassière. I never really saw her *face*. And all those girls with their make-up and their hair and their nails look so alike."

"Yes. Still, it *might* be. It's an idea, Jane."

Chapter 2

i

IT WAS an idea that was being at that moment discussed by Colonel Melchett and Colonel Bantry.

The Chief Constable, after viewing the body and seeing his subordinates set to work on their routine tasks, had adjourned with the master of the house to the study in the other wing of the house.

Colonel Melchett was an irascible-looking man with a habit of tugging at his short red moustache. He did so now, shooting a perplexed sideways glance at the other man. Finally, he rapped out:

"Look here, Bantry, got to get this off my chest. Is it a fact that you don't know from Adam who this girl is?"

The other's answer was explosive, but the Chief Constable interrupted him.

"Yes, yes, old man, but look at it like this. Might be deuced awkward for you. Married man—fond of your missus and all that. But just between ourselves—if you *were* tied up with this girl in any way, better say so *now*. Quite natural to want to suppress the fact—should feel the same myself. But it won't do. Murder case. Facts bound to come out. Dash it all, I'm not suggesting *you* strangled the girl—not the sort of thing you'd do—*I* know that. But, after all, she came here—to this house. Put it she broke in and was waiting to see you, and some bloke or other followed her down and did her in. Possible, you know. See what I mean?"

"Damn it all, Melchett, I tell you I've never set eyes on that girl in my life! I'm not that sort of man."

"That's all right, then. Shouldn't blame you, you know. Man of the world. Still, if you say so— Question is, what was she doing down here? She doesn't come from these parts—that's quite certain."

"The whole thing's a nightmare," fumed the angry master of the house.

"The point is, old man, what was she doing in your library?"

"How should I know? *I* didn't ask her here."

"No, no. But she *came* here, all the same. Looks as though she wanted to see you. You haven't had any odd letters or anything?"

"No, I haven't."

Colonel Melchett inquired delicately:

"What were you doing yourself last night?"

"I went to the meeting of the Conservative Association. Nine o'clock, at Much Benham."

"And you got home when?"

"I left Much Benham just after ten—had a bit of trouble on the way home, had to change a wheel. I got back at a quarter to twelve."

"You didn't go into the library?"

"No."

"Pity."

"I was tired. I went straight up to bed."

"Any one waiting up for you?"

"No. I always take the latchkey. Lorrimer goes to bed at eleven unless I give orders to the contrary."

"Who shuts up the library?"

"Lorrimer. Usually about seven-thirty this time of year."

"Would he go in there again during the evening?"

"Not with my being out. He left the tray with whisky and glasses in the hall."

"I see. What about your wife?"

"I don't know. She was in bed when I got home and fast asleep. She may have sat in the library yesterday evening or in the drawing-room. I forgot to ask her."

"Oh well, we shall soon know all the details. Of course, it's possible one of the servants may be concerned, eh?"

Colonel Bantry shook his head.

"I don't believe it. They're all a most respectable lot. We've had 'em for years."

Melchett agreed.

"Yes, it doesn't seem likely that they're mixed up in it. Looks more as though the girl came down from town—perhaps with some young fellow. Though why they wanted to break into this house—"

Bantry interrupted.

"London. That's more like it. We don't have goings on down here—at least——"

"Well, what is it?"

"Upon my word!" exploded Colonel Bantry. "Basil Blake!"

"Who's he?"

"Young fellow connected with the film industry. Poisonous young brute. My wife sticks up for him because she was at school with his mother, but of all the decadent useless young jackanapes! Wants his behind kicked! He's taken that cottage on the Lansham Road—you know—ghastly bit of building. He has parties there, shrieking, noisy crowds, and he has girls down for the week-end."

"Girls?"

"Yes, there was one last week—one of these platinum blondes——"

The Colonel's jaw dropped.

"A platinum blonde, eh?" said Melchett reflectively.

"Yes. I say, Melchett, you don't think——"

The Chief Constable said briskly:

"It's a possibility. It accounts for a girl of this type being in St. Mary Mead. I think I'll run along and have a word with this young fellow—Braid—Blake—what did you say his name was?"

"Blake. Basil Blake."

"Will he be at home, do you know?"

"Let me see. What's to-day—Saturday? Usually gets here some time Saturday morning."

Melchett said grimly:

"We'll see if we can find him."

ii

Basil Blake's cottage, which consisted of all modern conveniences enclosed in a hideous shell of half timbering and sham Tudor, was known to the postal authorities, and to William Brooker, builder, as "Chatsworth"; to Basil and his friends as "The Period Piece," and to the village of St. Mary Mead at large as "Mr. Booker's new house."

It was little more than a quarter of a mile from the village proper, being situated on a new building estate that had been bought by the enterprising Mr. Booker just beyond the Blue Boar, with frontage on what had been a particularly unspoilt country lane. Gossington Hall was about a mile farther on along the same road.

Lively interest had been aroused in St. Mary Mead when news went round that "Mr. Booker's new house" had been bought by a film star. Eager watch was kept for the first appearance of the legendary creature in the village, and it may be said that as far as appearances went Basil Blake was all that could be asked for. Little by little, however, the real facts leaked out. Basil Blake was *not* a film star—not even a film actor. He was a very junior person, rejoicing in the title of about fifteenth in the list of those responsible for Set Decorations at Lenville Studios, headquarters of British New Era Films. The village maidens lost interest, and the ruling class of censorious spinsters took exception to Basil Blake's way of life. Only the landlord of the Blue Boar continued to be enthusiastic about Basil and Basil's friends. The revenues of the Blue Boar had increased since the young man's arrival in the place.

The police car stopped outside the distorted rustic gate of Mr. Booker's fancy, and Colonel Melchett, with a glance of distaste at the excessive half timbering of Chatsworth, strode up to the front door and attacked it briskly with the knocker.

It was opened much more promptly than he had expected. A young man with straight, somewhat long, black hair, wearing orange corduroy trousers and a royal-blue shirt, snapped out: "Well, what do you want?"

"Are you Mr. Basil Blake?"

"Of course I am."

"I should be glad to have a few words with you, if I may, Mr. Blake?"

"Who are you?"

"I am Colonel Melchett, the Chief Constable of the County."

Mr. Blake said insolently:

"You don't say so; how amusing!"

And Colonel Melchett, following the other in, understood what Colonel Bantry's reactions had been. The toe of his own boot itched.

Containing himself, however, he said with an attempt to speak pleasantly:

"You're an early riser, Mr. Blake."

"Not at all. I haven't been to bed yet."

"Indeed."

"But I don't suppose you've come here to inquire into my hours of bedgoing—or if you have it's rather a waste of the county's time and money. What is it you want to speak to me about?"

Colonel Melchett cleared his throat.

"I understand, Mr. Blake, that last week-end you had a visitor—a—er—fair-haired young lady."

Basil Blake stared, threw back his head and roared with laughter.

"Have the old cats been on to you from the village? About my morals? Damn it all, morals aren't a police matter. *You* know that."

"As you say," said Melchett dryly, "your morals are no concern of mine. I have come to you because the body of a fair-haired young woman of slightly—er—exotic appearance has been found—murdered."

"Strewth!" Blake stared at him. "Where?"

"In the library at Gossington Hall."

"At Gossington? At old Bantry's? I say, that's pretty rich. Old Bantry? The dirty old man!"

Colonel Melchett went very red in the face. He said sharply through the renewed mirth of the young man opposite him: "Kindly control your tongue, sir. I came to ask you if you can throw any light on this business."

"You've come round to ask me if I've missed a blonde? Is that it? Why should—hallo, 'allo, 'allo, what's this?"

A car had drawn up outside with a scream of brakes. Out of it tumbled a young woman dressed in flapping black-and-white pyjamas. She had scarlet lips, blackened eyelashes, and a platinum-blonde head. She strode up to the door, flung it open, and exclaimed angrily:

"Why did you run out on me, you brute?"

Basil Blake had risen.

"So there you are! Why shouldn't I leave you? I told you to clear out and you wouldn't."

"Why the hell should I because you told me to? I was enjoying myself."

"Yes—with that filthy brute Rosenberg. You know what *he's* like."

"You were jealous, that's all."

"Don't flatter yourself. I hate to see a girl I like who can't hold her drink and lets a disgusting Central European paw her about."

"That's a damned lie. You were drinking pretty hard yourself—and going on with the black-haired Spanish bitch."

"If I take you to a party I expect you to be able to behave yourself."

"And I refuse to be dictated to, and that's that. You said we'd go to the party and come on down here afterwards. I'm not going to leave a party before I'm ready to leave it."

"No—and that's why I left you flat. I was ready to come down here and I came. I don't hang round waiting for any fool of a woman."

"Sweet, polite person you are!"

"You seem to have followed me down all right!"

"I wanted to tell you what I thought of you!"

"If you think you can boss me, my girl, you're wrong!"

"And if you think you can order me about, you can think again!"

They glared at each other.

It was at this moment that Colonel Melchett seized his opportunity, and cleared his throat loudly.

Basil Blake swung round on him.

"Hallo, I forgot you were here. About time you took yourself off, isn't it? Let me introduce you—Dinah Lee—Colonel Blimp of the County Police. And now, Colonel, that you've seen my blonde is alive and in good condition, perhaps you'll get on with the good work concerning old Bantry's little bit of fluff. Good-morning!"

Colonel Melchett said:

"I advise you to keep a civil tongue in your head, young man, or you'll let yourself in for trouble," and stamped out, his face red and wrathful.

Chapter 3

i

IN HIS office at Much Benham, Colonel Melchett received and scrutinized the reports of his subordinates.

". . . so it all seems clear enough, sir," Inspector Slack was concluding: "Mrs. Bantry sat in the library after dinner and went to bed just before ten. She turned out the lights when she left the room and, presumably, no one entered the room afterwards. The servants went to bed at half-past ten and Lorrimer, after putting the drinks in the hall, went to bed at a quarter to eleven. Nobody heard anything out of the usual except the third housemaid, and she heard too much! Groans and a blood-curdling yell and sinister footsteps and I don't know what. The second housemaid who shares a room with her says the other girl slept all night through without a sound. It's those ones that make up things that cause us all the trouble."

"What about the forced window?"

"Amateur job, Simmons says; done with a common chisel—ordinary pattern—wouldn't have made much noise. Ought to be a chisel about the house but nobody can find it. Still, that's common enough where tools are concerned."

"Think any of the servants know anything?"

Rather unwillingly Inspector Slack replied:

"No, sir, I don't think they do. They all seemed very shocked and upset. I had my suspicions of Lorrimer—reticent, he was, if you know what I mean—but I don't think there's anything in it."

Melchett nodded. He attached no importance to Lorrimer's reticence. The energetic Inspector Slack often produced that effect on people he interrogated.

The door opened and Dr. Haydock came in.

"Thought I'd look in and give you the rough gist of things."

"Yes, yes, glad to see you. Well?"

"Nothing much. Just what you'd think. Death was due to strangulation. Satin waistband of her own dress, which was passed round the neck and crossed at the back. Quite easy and simple to do. Wouldn't have needed great strength—that is, if the girl were taken by surprise. There are no signs of a struggle."

"What about time of death?"

"Say, between ten o'clock and midnight."

"You can't get nearer than that?"

Haydock shook his head with a slight grin.

"I won't risk my professional reputation. Not earlier than ten and not later than midnight."

"And your own fancy inclines to which time?"

"Depends. There was a fire in the grate—the room was warm—all that would delay rigor and cadaveric stiffening."

"Anything more you can say about her?"

"Nothing much. She was young—about seventeen or eighteen, I should say. Rather immature in some ways but well developed muscularly. Quite a healthy specimen. She was virgo intacta, by the way."

And with a nod of his head the doctor left the room.

Melchett said to the Inspector:

"You're quite sure she'd never been seen before at Gossington?"

"The servants are positive of that. Quite indignant about it. They'd have remembered if they'd ever seen her about in the neighbourhood, they say."

"I expect they would," said Melchett. "Any one of that type sticks out a mile round here. Look at that young woman of Blake's."

"Pity it wasn't her," said Slack; "then we should be able to get on a bit."

"It seems to me this girl must have come down from London," said the Chief Constable thoughtfully. "Don't believe there will be any local leads. In that case, I suppose, we should do well to call in the Yard. It's a case for them, not for us."

"Something must have brought her down here, though," said Slack. He added tentatively: "Seems to me, Colonel and Mrs. Bantry *must* know something—of course, I know they're friends of yours, sir——"

Colonel Melchett treated him to a cold stare. He said stiffly:

"You may rest assured that I'm taking every possibility into account. *Every* possibility." He went on: "You've looked through the list of persons reported missing, I suppose?"

Slack nodded. He produced a typed sheet.

"Got 'em here. Mrs. Saunders, reported missing a week ago, dark-haired, blue eyed, thirty-six. 'Tisn't her—and, anyway, every one knows except her husband that she's gone off with a fellow from Leeds—commercial. Mrs. Barnard—she's sixty-five. Pamela Reeves, sixteen, missing from her home last night, had attended Girl Guide rally, dark-brown hair in pigtail, five feet five—"

Melchett said irritably:

"Don't go on reading idiotic details, Slack. This wasn't a schoolgirl. In my opinion——"

He broke off as the telephone rang. "Hallo—yes—yes, Much Benham Police Headquarters—what? Just a minute——"

He listened, and wrote rapidly. Then he spoke again, a new tone in his voice:

"Ruby Keene, eighteen, occupation professional dancer, five feet four inches, slender, platinum-blonde hair, blue eyes, *retroussé* nose, believed to be wearing white diamante evening-dress, silver sandal shoes. Is that right? What? Yes, not a doubt of it, I should say. I'll send Slack over at once."

He rang off and looked at his subordinate with rising excitement. "We've got it, I think. That was the Glenshire Police (Glenshire was the adjoining county). Girl reported missing from the Majestic Hotel, Danemouth."

"Danemouth," said Inspector Slack. "That's more like it."

Danemouth was a large and fashionable watering-place on the coast not far away.

"It's only a matter of eighteen miles or so from here," said the Chief Constable. "The girl was a dance hostess or something at the Majestic. Didn't come on to do her turn last night and the management were very fed up about it. When she was still missing this morning one of the other girls got the wind up about her, or someone else did. It sounds a bit obscure. You'd better go over to Danemouth at once, Slack. Report there to Superintendent Harper, and co-operate with him."

ii

Activity was always to Inspector Slack's taste. To rush off in a car, to silence rudely those people who were anxious to tell him things, to cut short conversations on the plea of urgent necessity. All this was the breath of life to Slack.

In an incredibly short time, therefore, he had arrived at Danemouth, reported at police headquarters, had a brief interview with a distracted and apprehensive hotel manager, and, leaving the latter with the doubtful comfort of— "got to make sure it *is* the girl, first, before we start raising the wind" — was driving back to Much Benham in company with Ruby Keene's nearest relative.

He had put through a short call to Much Benham before leaving Danemouth, so the Chief Constable was prepared for his arrival, though not perhaps for the brief introduction of: "This is Josie, sir."

Colonel Melchet stared at his subordinate coldly. His feeling was that Slack had taken leave of his senses.

The young woman who had just got out of the car came to the rescue.

"That's what I'm known as professionally," she explained with a momentary flash of large, handsome white teeth. "Raymond and Josie, my partner and I call ourselves, and, of course, all the hotel know me as Josie. Josephine Turner's my real name."

Colonel Melchett stared at his subordinate coldly. His feeling Miss Turner to sit down, meanwhile casting a swift, professional glance over her.

She was a good-looking young woman of perhaps nearer thirty than twenty, her looks depending more on skilful grooming than actual features. She looked competent and good-tempered, with plenty of common sense. She was not the type that would ever be described as glamorous, but she had nevertheless plenty of attraction. She was discreetly made-up and wore a dark tailor-made suit. Though she looked anxious and upset she was not, the Colonel decided, particularly grief-stricken.

As she sat down she said: "It seems too awful to be true. Do you really think it's Ruby?"

"That, I'm afraid, is what we've got to ask you to tell us. I'm afraid it may be rather unpleasant for you."

Miss Turner said apprehensively:

"Does she—does she—look very terrible?"

"Well—I'm afraid it may be rather a shock to you." He handed her his cigarette-case and she accepted one gratefully.

"Do—do you want me to look at her right away?"

"It would be best, I think, Miss Turner. You see, it's not much good asking you questions until we're sure. Best get it over, don't you think?"

"All right."

They drove down to the mortuary.

When Josie came out after a brief visit, she looked rather sick.

"It's Ruby all right," she said shakily. "Poor kid! Goodness, I do feel queer. There isn't"—she looked round wistfully—"any gin?"

Gin was not available, but brandy was, and after gulping a little down Miss Turner regained her composure. She said frankly:

"It gives you a turn, doesn't it, seeing anything like that? Poor litte Rube! What swine men are, aren't they?"

"You believe it was a man?"

Josie looked slightly taken aback.

"Wasn't it? Well, I mean—I naturally thought——"

"Any special man you were thinking of?"

She shook her head vigorously.

"No—not me. I haven't the least idea. Naturally Ruby wouldn't have let on to me if——"

"If what?"

Josie hesitated.

"Well—if she'd been—going about with any one."

Melchett shot her a keen glance. He said no more until they

were back at his office. Then he began:

"Now, Miss Turner, I want all the information you can give me."

"Yes, of course. Where shall I begin?"

"I'd like the girl's full name and address, her relationship to you and all you know about her."

Josephine Turner nodded. Melchett was confirmed in his opinion that she felt no particular grief. She was shocked and distressed but no more. She spoke readily enough.

"Her name was Ruby Keene—her professional name, that is. Her real name was Rosy Legge. Her mother was my mother's cousin. I've known her all my life, but not particularly well, if you know what I mean. I've got a lot of cousins—some in business, some on the stage. Ruby was more or less training for a dancer. She had some good engagements last year in panto and that sort of thing. Not really classy, but good provincial companies. Since then she's been engaged as one of the dancing partners at the Palais de Danse in Brixwell—South London. It's a nice respectable place and they look after the girls well, but there isn't much money in it." She paused.

Colonel Melchett nodded.

"Now this is where I come in. I've been dance and bridge hostess at the Majestic in Danemouth for three years. It's a good job, well paid and pleasant to do. You look after people when they arrive—size them up, of course—some like to be left alone and others are lonely and want to get into the swing of things. You try to get the right people together for bridge and all that, and get the young people dancing with each other. It needs a bit of tact and experience."

Again Melchett nodded. He thought that this girl would be good at her job; she had a pleasant, friendly way with her and was, he thought, shrewd without being in the least intellectual.

"Besides that," continued Josie, "I do a couple of exhibition dances every evening with Raymond. Raymond Starr—he's the tennis and dancing pro. Well, as it happens, this summer I slipped on the rocks bathing one day and gave my ankle a nasty turn."

Melchett had noticed that she walked with a slight limp.

"Naturally that put the stop to dancing for a bit and it was rather awkward. I didn't want the hotel to get someone else in my place. That's always a danger"—for a minute her good-natured blue eyes were hard and sharp; she was the female fighting for existence—"that they may queer your pitch, you see. So I thought of Ruby and suggested to the manager that I should get her down. I'd carry on with the hostess business and the bridge and all that. Ruby would just take on the dancing. Keep it in the family, if you see what I mean?"

Melchett said he saw.

"Well, they agreed, and I wired to Ruby and she came down. Rather a chance for her. Much better class than anything she'd ever done before. That was about a month ago."

Colonel Melchett said:

"I understand. And she was a success?"

"Oh, yes," Josie said carelessly, "she went down quite well. She doesn't dance as well as I do, but Raymond's clever and carried her through, and she was quite nice-looking, you know—slim and fair and baby-looking. Overdid the make-up a bit—I was always on at her about that. But you know what girls are. She was only eighteen, and at that age they always go and overdo it. It doesn't do for a good-class place like the Majestic. I was always ticking her off about it and getting her to tone it down."

Melchett asked: "People liked her?"

"Oh, yes. Mind you, Ruby hadn't got much comeback. She was a bit dumb. She went down better with the older men than with the young ones."

"Had she got any special friend?"

The girl's eyes met his with complete understanding.

"Not in the way *you* mean. Or, at any rate, not that *I* knew about. But then, you see, she wouldn't tell me."

Just for a moment Melchett wondered why not—Josie did not give the impression of being a strict disciplinarian. But he only said: "Will you describe to me now when you last saw your cousin."

"Last night. She and Raymond do two exhibition dances—one at 10.30 and the other at midnight. They finished the first one. After it, I noticed Ruby dancing with one of the young men staying in the hotel. I was playing bridge with some people in the lounge. There's a glass panel between the lounge and the ballroom. That's the last time I saw her. Just after midnight Raymond came up in a terrible taking, said where was Ruby, she hadn't turned up, and it was time to begin? I *was* vexed, I can tell you! That's the sort of silly things girls do and get the management's backs up and then they get the sack! I went up with him to her room, but she wasn't there. I noticed that she'd changed. The dress she'd been dancing in—sort of pink, foamy thing with full skirts—was lying over a chair. Usually she kept the same dress on unless it was the special dance night—Wednesdays, that is.

"I'd no idea where she'd got to. We got the band to play one more foxtrot—still no Ruby, so I said to Raymond *I*'d do the exhibition dance with him. We chose one that was easy on my ankle and made it short—but it played up my ankle pretty badly all the same. It's all swollen this morning. Still Ruby didn't show up. We sat about waiting up for her until two o'clock. Furious with her, I was."

Her voice vibrated slightly. Melchett caught the note of real anger in it. Just for a moment he wondered. The reaction seemed a little more intense than was justified by the facts. He had a feeling of something deliberately left unsaid. He said:

"And this morning, when Ruby Keene had not returned and her bed had not been slept in, you went to the police?"

He knew from Slack's brief telephone message from Danemouth that that was not the case. But he wanted to hear what Josephine Turner would say.

She did not hesitate. She said: "No, *I* didn't."

"Why not, Miss Turner?"

Her eyes met his frankly. She said:

"*You* wouldn't—in my place!"

"You think not?"

Josie said:

"I've got my job to think about. The one thing a hotel doesn't want is scandal—especially anything that brings in the police. I didn't think anything had happened to Ruby. Not for a minute! I thought she'd just made a fool of herself about some young man. I thought she'd turn up all right—and I was going to give her a good dressing down when she did! Girls of eighteen are such fools."

Melchett pretended to glance through his notes.

"Ah, yes, I see it was a Mr. Jefferson who went to the police. One of the guests staying at the hotel?"

Josephine Turner said shortly:

"Yes."

Colonel Melchett asked:

"What made this Mr. Jefferson do that?"

Josie was stroking the cuff of her jacket. There was a constraint in her manner. Again Colonel Melchett had a feeling that something was being withheld. She said rather sullenly:

"He's an invalid. He—he gets all het up rather easily. Being an invalid, I mean."

Melchett passed on from that. He asked:

"Who was the young man with whom you last saw your cousin dancing?"

"His name's Bartlett. He'd been there about ten days."

"Were they on very friendly terms?"

"Not specially, I should say. Not that *I* knew, anyway."

Again a curious note of anger in her voice.

"What does he have to say?"

"Said that after their dance Ruby went upstairs to powder her nose."

"That was when she changed her dress?"

"I suppose so."

"And that is the last thing you know? After that she just——"

"Vanished," said Josie. "That's right."

"Did Miss Keene know anybody in St. Mary Mead? Or in this neighbourhood?"

"I don't know. She may have done. You see, quite a lot of young men came in to Danemouth to the Majestic from all round about. I wouldn't know where they lived unless they happened to mention it."

"Did you ever hear your cousin mention Gossington?"

"Gossington?" Josie looked patently puzzled.

"Gossington Hall."

She shook her head.

"Never heard of it." Her tone carried conviction. There was curiosity in it too.

"Gossington Hall," explained Colonel Melchett, "is where her body was found."

"Gossington Hall?" She stared. "How extraordinary!"

Melchett thought to himself: "Extraordinary's the word!" Aloud he said:

"Do you know a Colonel or Mrs. Bantry?"

Again Josie shook her head.

"Or a Mr. Basil Blake?"

She frowned slightly.

"I think I've heard that name. Yes, I'm sure I have—but I don't remember anything about him.

The diligent Inspector Slack slid across to his superior officer a page torn from his note-book. On it was pencilled:

"*Col. Bantry dined at Majestic last week.*"

Melchett looked up and met the Inspector's eye. The Chief Constable flushed. Slack was an industrious and zealous officer and Melchett disliked him a good deal. But he could not disregard the challenge. The Inspector was tacitly accusing him of favouring his own class—of shielding an "old school tie."

He turned to Josie.

"Miss Turner, I should like you, if you do not mind, to accompany me to Gossington Hall."

Coldly, defiantly , almost ignoring Josie's murmur of assent, Melchett's eyes met Slack's.

Chapter 4

i

ST. MARY MEAD was having the most exciting morning it had known for a long time.

Miss Wetherby, a long-nosed, acidulated spinster, was the first to spread the intoxicating information. She dropped in upon her friend and neighbour Miss Hartnell.

"Forgive me coming so early, dear, but I thought, perhaps, you mightn't have heard the *news*."

"What news?" demanded Miss Hartnell. She had a deep bass voice and visited the poor indefatigably, however hard they tried to avoid her ministrations.

"About the body in Colonel Bantry's library—a *woman*'s body——"

"In Colonel Bantry's *library*?"

"Yes. Isn't it *terrible*?"

"His *poor* wife." Miss Hartnell tried to disguise her deep and ardent pleasure.

"Yes, indeed. I don't suppose she had any idea."

Miss Hartnell observed censoriously:

"She thought too much about her garden, and not enough about her husband. You've got to keep an eye on a man—all the time—all the time." repeated Miss Hartnell fiercely.

"I know. I know. It's really too dreadful."

"I wonder what Jane Marple will say. Do you think she knew anything about it? She's so sharp about these things."

"Jane Marple has gone up to Gossington."

"What? This morning?"

"Very early. Before breakfast."

"But really! I do think! Well, I mean, I think that is carrying things *too* far. We all know Jane likes to poke her nose into things—but I call this—indecent!"

"Oh, but Mrs. Bantry sent for her."

"Mrs. Bantry *sent* for her?"

"Well, the car came—with Muswell driving it."

"Dear me! How very peculiar. . . ."

They were silent a minute or two digesting the news.

"Whose body?" demanded Miss Hartnell.

"You know that dreadful woman who comes down with Basil Blake?"

"That terrible peroxide blonde?" Miss Hartnell was slightly behind the times. She had not yet advanced from peroxide to platinum. "The one who lies about in the garden with practically nothing on?"

"Yes, my dear. There she was—on the hearthrug *strangled*!"

"But what do you mean—at *Gossington*?"

Miss Wetherby nodded with infinite meaning.

"Then—Colonel Bantry *too*——?"

Again Miss Wetherby nodded.

"Oh!"

There was a pause as the ladies savoured this new addition to village scandal.

"What a wicked woman!" trumpeted Miss Hartnell with righteous wrath.

"Quite, quite abandoned, I'm afraid!"

"And Colonel Bantry—such a nice quiet man——"

Miss Wetherby said zestfully:

"Those quiet ones are often the worst. Jane Marple always says so."

ii

Mrs. Price Ridley was among the last to hear the news.

A rich and dictatorial widow, she lived in a large house next door to the vicarage. Her informant was her little maid Clara.

"A *woman*, you say, Clara? *Found dead on Colonel Bantry's hearthrug.*"

"Yes, mum. And they say, mum, as she hadn't anything on at all, mum, not a stitch!"

"That will do, Clara. It is not necessary to go into details."

"No, mum, and they say, mum, that at first they thought it was Mr. Blake's young lady—what comes down for the week-ends with 'im to Mr. Booker's new 'ouse. But now they say it's quite a different young lady. And the fishmonger's young man, he says he'd never have believed it of Colonel Bantry—not with him handing round the plate on Sundays and all."

"There is a lot of wickedness in the world, Clara," said Mrs. Price Ridley. "Let this be a warning to you."

"Yes, mum. Mother, she never *will* let me take a place where there's a gentleman in the 'ouse."

"That will *do*, Clara," said Mrs. Price Ridley.

iii

It was only a step from Mrs. Price Ridley's house to the vicarage.

Mrs. Price Ridley was fortunate enough to find the vicar in his study.

The vicar, a gentle, middle-aged man, was always the last to hear anything.

"Such a *terrible* thing," said Mrs. Price Ridley, panting a little, because she had come rather fast. "I felt I must have your advice, your counsel about it, dear vicar."

Mr. Clement looked mildly alarmed. He said:

"Has anything happened?"

"Has anything *happened*?" Mrs. Price Ridley repeated the question dramatically. "The most terrible scandal! None of us had any idea of it. An abandoned woman, completely unclothed, strangled on Colonel Bantry's hearthrug."

The vicar stared. He said:

"You—you are feeling quite well?"

"No wonder you can't believe it! *I* couldn't at first. The hypocrisy of the man! All these years!"

"Please tell me exactly what all this is about."

Mrs. Price Ridley plunged into a full-swing narrative. When she had finished Mr. Clement said mildly:

"But there is nothing, is there, to point to Colonel Bantry's being involved in this?"

"Oh, dear vicar, you are so unworldly! But I must tell you a little story. Last Thursday—or was it the Thursday before? well, it doesn't matter—I was going up to London by the cheap day train. Colonel Bantry was in the same carriage. He looked, I thought, very abstracted. And nearly the whole way he buried himself behind *The Times*. As though, you know, he didn't want to *talk*."

The vicar nodded with complete comprehension and possible sympathy.

"At Paddington I said goodbye. He had offered to get me a taxi, but I was taking the bus down to Oxford Street—but he got into one, and I distinctly heard him tell the driver to go to—*where do you think*?"

Mr. Clement looked inquiring.

"An address in *St. John's Wood*!"

Mrs. Price Ridley paused triumphantly.

The vicar remained completely unenlightened.

"That, I consider, *proves* it," said Mrs. Price Ridley.

iv

At Gossington, Mrs. Bantry and Miss Marple were sitting in the drawing-room.

"You know," said Mrs. Bantry, "I can't help feeling glad they've taken the body away. It's not *nice* to have a body in one's house."

Miss Marple nodded.

"I know, dear. I know just how you feel."

"You can't," said Mrs. Bantry; "not until you've had one. I know you had one next door once, but that's not the same thing. I only hope," she went on, "that Arthur won't take a dislike to the library. We sit there so much. What are you doing, Jane?"

For Miss Marple, with a glance at her watch, was rising to her feet.

"Well, I was thinking I'd go home. If there's nothing more I can do for you?"

"Don't go yet," said Mrs. Bantry. "The finger-print men and the photographers and most of the police have gone, I know, but I still feel something might happen. You don't want to miss anything."

The telephone rang and she went off to answer. She returned with a beaming face.

"I told you more things would happen. That was Colonel Melchett. He's bringing the poor girl's cousin along."

"I wonder why," said Miss Marple.

"Oh, I suppose, to see where it happened and all that."

"More than that, I expect," said Miss Marple.

"What do you mean, Jane?"

"Well, I think—perhaps—he might want her to meet Colonel Bantry."

Mrs. Bantry said sharply:

"To see if she recognizes him? I suppose—oh yes, I suppose they're bound to suspect Arthur."

"I'm afraid so."

"As though Arthur could have anything to do with it!"

Miss Marple was silent. Mrs. Bantry turned on her accusingly.

"And don't quote old General Henderson—or some frightful old man who kept his housemaid—at me. Arthur isn't like that."

"No, no, of course not."

"No, but he *really* isn't. He's just—sometimes—a little bit silly about pretty girls who come to tennis. You know—rather fatuous and avuncular. There's no harm in it. And why shouldn't he? After all," finished Mrs. Bantry rather obscurely, "I've got the garden."

Miss Marple smiled.

"You must not worry, Dolly," she said.

"No, I don't mean to. But all the same I do a little. So does Arthur. It's upset him. All these policemen prowling about. He's gone down to the farm. Looking at pigs and things always soothes him if he's been upset. Hallo, here they are."

The Chief Constable's car drew up outside.

Colonel Melchett came in accompanied by a smartly dressed young woman.

"This is Miss Turner, Mrs. Bantry. The cousin of the—er—victim."

"How do you do," said Mrs. Bantry, advancing with outstretched hand. "All this must be rather awful for you."

Josephine Turner said frankly: "Oh, it is. None of it seems *real*, somehow. It's like a bad dream."

Mrs. Bantry introduced Miss Marple.

Melchett said casually: "Your good man about?"

"He had to go down to one of the farms. He'll be back soon."

"Oh——" Melchett seemed rather at a loss.

Mrs. Bantry said to Josie: "Would you like to see where—where it happened? Or would you rather not?"

Josephine said after a moment's pause:

"I think I'd like to see."

Mrs. Bantry led her to her library with Miss Marple and Melchett following behind.

"She was there," said Mrs. Bantry, pointing dramatically; "on the hearthrug."

"Oh!" Josie shuddered. But she also looked perplexed. She said, her brow creased: "I just *can't* understand it! I *can't*!"

"Well, *we* certainly can't," said Mrs. Bantry.

Josie said slowly:

"It isn't the sort of place——" and broke off.

Miss Marple nodded her head gently in agreement with the unfinished sentiment.

"That," she murmured, "is what makes it so very interesting."

"Come now, Miss Marple," said Colonel Melchett good-humouredly, "haven't you got an explanation?"

"Oh yes, I've got an *explanation*," said Miss Marple. "Quite a feasible one. But of course it's only my own *idea*. Tommy Bond," she continued, "and Mrs. Martin, our new schoolmistress. She went to wind up the clock and a frog jumped out."

Josephine Turner looked puzzled. As they all went out of the room she murmured to Mrs. Bantry: "Is the old lady a bit funny in the head?"

"Not at all," said Mrs. Bantry indignantly.

Josie said: "Sorry, I thought perhaps she thought she *was* a frog or something."

Colonel Bantry was just coming in through the side door. Melchett hailed him, and watched Josephine Turner as he introduced them to each other. But there was no sign of interest or recognition in her face. Melchett breathed a sigh of relief. Curse Slack and his insinuations!

In answer to Mrs. Bantry's questions Josie was pouring out the story of Ruby Keene's disappearance.

"Frightfully worrying for you, my dear," said Mrs. Bantry.

"I was more angry than worried," said Josie. "You see, I didn't know then that anything had happened to her."

"And yet," said Miss Marple, "you went to the police. Wasn't that—excuse me—rather *premature*?"

Josie said eagerly:

"Oh, but I didn't. That was Mr. Jefferson——"

Mrs. Bantry said: "Jefferson?"

"Yes, he's an invalid."

"Not *Conway* Jefferson? But I know him well. He's an old friend of ours. Arthur, listen—Conway Jefferson. He's staying at the Majestic, and it was he who went to the police! Isn't that a coincidence?"

Josephine Turner said:

"Mr. Jefferson was here last summer too."

"Fancy! And we never knew. I haven't seen him for a long time." She turned to Josie. "How—how is he, nowadays?"

Josie considered.

"I think he's wonderful, really—quite wonderful. Considering, I mean. He's always cheerful—always got a joke."

"Are the family there with him?"

"Mr. Gaskell, you mean? And young Mrs. Jefferson? And Peter? Oh, yes."

There was something inhibiting Josephine Turner's usual attractive frankness of manner. When she spoke of the Jeffersons there was something not quite natural in her voice.

Mrs. Bantry said: "They're both very nice, aren't they? The young ones, I mean."

Josie said rather uncertainly:

"Oh, yes—yes, they are. I—we—yes, they are, *really*."

V

"And what," demanded Mrs. Bantry as she looked through the window at the retreating car of the Chief Constable, "did she mean by that? 'They are, *really*.' Don't you think, Jane, that there's something——"

Miss Marple fell upon the words eagerly.

"Oh, I do—indeed I do. It's quite *unmistakable*! Her manner changed *at once* when the Jeffersons were mentioned. She had seemed quite natural up to then."

"But what do you think it *is*, Jane?'

"Well, my dear, *you* know them. All I feel is that there is *something*, as you say, about them which is worrying that young woman. Another thing, did you notice that when you asked her if she wasn't anxious about the girl being missing, she said that she was *angry*! And she *looked* angry—*really* angry! That strikes me as *interesting*, you know. I have a feeling—perhaps I'm wrong—that that's her main reaction to the fact of the girl's death. She didn't care for her, I'm sure. She's not grieving in any way. But I do think, very definitely, that the thought of that girl, Ruby Keene, makes her *angry*. And the interesting point is—*why*?"

"We'll find out!" said Mrs. Bantry. "We'll go over to Danemouth and stay at the Majestic—yes, Jane, you too. I need a change for my nerves after what has happened here. A few days at the Majestic—that's what we need. And you'll meet Conway Jefferson. He's a dear—a perfect dear. It's the saddest story imaginable. Had a son and a daughter, both of whom he loved dearly. They were both married, but they still spent a lot of time at home. His wife, too, was the sweetest woman, and he was devoted to her. They were flying home one year from France and there was an accident. They were all killed: the pilot, Mrs. Jefferson, Rosamund and Frank. Conway had both legs so badly injured they had to be amputated. And he's been wondeful—his courage, his pluck! He was a very active man and now he's a helpless cripple, but he never complains. His daughter-in-law lives with him—she was a widow when Frank Jefferson married her and she had a son by her first marriage—Peter Carmody. They both live with Conway. And Mark

Gaskell, Rosamund's husband, is there too most of the time. The whole thing was the most awful tragedy."

"And now," said Miss Marple, "there's another tragedy——"

Mrs. Bantry said: "Oh yes—yes—but it's nothing to do with the Jeffersons."

"Isn't it?" said Miss Marple. "It was Mr. Jefferson who went to the police."

"So he did. . .You know, Jane, that *is* curious. . . ."

Chapter 5

i

COLONEL MELCHETT was facing a much annoyed hotel manager. With him was Superintendent Harper of the Glenshire Police and the inevitable Inspector Slack—the latter rather disgruntled at the Chief Constable's wilful usurpation of the case.

Superintendent Harper was inclined to be soothing with the almost tearful Mr. Prestcott—Colonel Melchett tended towards a blunt brutality.

"No good crying over spilt milk," he said sharply. "The girl's dead—strangled. You're lucky that she wasn't strangled in your hotel. This puts the inquiry in a different county and lets your establishment down extremely lightly. But certain inquiries have got to be made, and the sooner we get on with it the better. You can trust us to be discreet and tactful. So I suggest you cut the cackle and come to the horses. Just what exactly do you know about the girl?"

"I know nothing of her—nothing at all. Josie brought her here."

"Josie's been here some time?"

"Two years—no, three."

"And you like her?"

"Yes, Josie's a good girl—a nice girl. Competent. She gets on with people, and smoothes over differences—bridge, you know, is a touchy sort of game——" Colonel Melchett nodded feelingly. His wife was a keen but an extremely bad bridge player. Mr. Prestcott went on: "Josie was very good at calming down unpleasantnesses. She could handle people well—sort of bright and firm, if you know what I mean."

Again Melchett nodded. He knew now what it was Miss

Josephine Turner had reminded him of. In spite of the make-up and the smart turnout there was a distinct touch of the nursery governess about her.

"I depend upon her," went on Mr. Prestcott. His manner became aggrieved. "What does she want to go playing about on slippery rocks in that damn fool way? We've got a nice beach here. Why couldn't she bathe from that? Slipping and falling and breaking her ankle. It wasn't fair on *me*! I pay her to dance and play bridge and keep people happy and amused—not to go bathing off rocks and breaking her ankle. Dancers ought to be careful of their ankles—not take risks. I was very annoyed about it. It wasn't fair to the hotel."

Melchett cut the recital short.

"And then she suggested this girl—her cousin—coming down?"

Prestcott assented grudgingly.

"That's right. It sounded quite a good idea. Mind you, I wasn't going to pay anything extra. The girl could have her keep; but as for salary, that would have to be fixed up between her and Josie. That's the way it was arranged. *I* didn't know anything about the girl."

"But she turned out all right?"

"Oh yes, there wasn't anything wrong with her—not to look at, anyway. She was very young, of course—rather cheap in style, perhaps, for a place of this kind, but nice manners—quiet and well-behaved. Danced well. People liked her."

"Pretty?"

It had been a question hard to answer from a view of the blue swollen face.

Mr. Prestcott considered.

"Fair to middling. Bit weaselly, if you know what I mean. Wouldn't have been much without make-up. As it was she managed to look quite attractive."

"Many young men hanging about after her?"

"I know what you're trying to get at, sir," Mr. Prestcott became excited. "*I* never saw anything. Nothing special. One or two of the boys hung around a bit—but all in the day's work, so to speak. Nothing in the strangling line, I'd say. She got on well with the older people, too—had a kind of prattling way with her—seemed quite a kid, if you know what I mean. It amused them."

Superintendent Harper said in a deep melancholy voice:

"Mr. Jefferson, for instance?"

The manager agreed.

"Yes, Mr. Jefferson was the one I had in mind. She used to sit with him and his family a lot. He used to take her out for drives sometimes. Mr. Jefferson's very fond of young people and very good to them. I don't want to have any misunderstanding. Mr. Jefferson's a cripple; he can't get about much—only where his wheel-chair will take him. But he's always keen on seeing young people enjoy themselves—watches the tennis and the bathing and all that—and gives parties for young people here. He likes youth—and there's nothing bitter about him as there might well be. A very popular gentleman and, I'd say, a very fine character."

Melchett asked:

"And he took an interest in Ruby Keene?"

"Her talk amused him, I think."

"Did his family share his liking for her?"

"They were always very pleasant to her."

Harper said:

"And it was he who reported the fact of her being missing to the police?"

He contrived to put into the words a significance and a reproach to which the manager instantly responded.

"Put yourself in my place, Mr. Harper. *I* didn't dream for a minute anything was wrong. Mr. Jefferson came along to my office, storming, and all worked up. The girl hadn't slept in her room. She hadn't appeared in her dance last night. She must have gone for a drive and had an accident, perhaps. The police must be informed at once! Inquiries made! In a state, he was, and quite high-handed. He rang up the police station then and there."

"Without consulting Miss Turner?"

"Josie didn't like it much. I could see that. She was very annoyed about the whole thing—annoyed with Ruby, I mean. But what could she say?"

"I think," said Melchett, "we'd better see Mr. Jefferson. Eh,

Harper?"

Superintendent Harper agreed.

ii

Mr. Prestcott went up with them to Conway Jefferson's suite. It was on the first floor, overlooking the sea. Melchett said carelessly:

"Does himself pretty well, eh? Rich man?"

"Very well off indeed, I believe. Nothing's ever stinted when he comes here. Best rooms reserved—food usually *à la carte*, expensive wines—best of everything."

Melchett nodded.

Mr. Prestcott tapped on the outer door and a woman's voice said: "Come in."

The manager entered, the others behind him.

Mr. Prestcott's manner was apologetic as he spoke to the woman who turned her head at their entrance from her seat by the window.

"I am so sorry to disturb you, Mrs. Jefferson, but these gentlemen are—from the police. They are very anxious to have a word with Mr. Jefferson. Er—Colonel Melchett—Superintendent Harper, Inspector—er—Slack—Mrs. Jefferson."

Mrs. Jefferson acknowledged the introduction by bending her head.

A plain woman, was Melchett's first impression. Then, as a slight smile came to her lips and she spoke, he changed his opinion. She had a singularly charming and sympathetic voice and her eyes, clear hazel eyes, were beautiful. She was quietly but not unbecomingly dressed and was, he judged, about thirty-five years of age.

She said:

"My father-in-law is asleep. He is not strong at all, and this affair has been a terrible shock to him. We had to have the doctor, and the doctor gave him a sedative. As soon as he wakes he will, I know, want to see you. In the meantime, perhaps I can help you? Won't you sit down?"

Mr. Prestcott, anxious to escape, said to Colonel Melchett: "Well—er—if that's all I can do for you?" and thankfully received permission to depart.

With his closing of the door behind him, the atmosphere took on a mellow and more social quality. Adelaide Jefferson had the power of creating a restful atmosphere. She was a woman who never seemed to say anything remarkable but who succeeded in stimulating other people to talk and in setting them at their ease. She struck now the right note when she said:

"This business has shocked us all very much. We saw quite a lot of the poor girl, you know. It seems quite unbelievable. My father-in-law is terribly upset. He was very fond of Ruby."

Colonel Melchett said:

"It was Mr. Jefferson, I understand, who reported her disappearance to the police?"

He wanted to see exactly how she would react to that. There was a flicker—just a flicker—of—annoyance? concern?—he could not say what exactly, but there was *something*, and it seemed to him she had definitely to brace herself, as though to an unpleasant task, before going on.

She said:

"Yes, that is so. Being an invalid, he gets easily upset and worried. We tried to persuade him that it was all right, that there was some natural explanation, and that the girl herself would not like the police being notified. He insisted. Well"—she made a slight gesture—"he was right and we were wrong."

Melchett asked: "Exactly how well did you know Ruby Keene, Mrs. Jefferson?"

She considered.

"It's difficult to say. My father-in-law is very fond of young people and likes to have them round him. Ruby was a new type to him—he was amused and interested by her chatter. She sat with us a good deal in the hotel and my father-in-law took her out for drives in the car."

Her voice was quite non-committal. Melchett thought to himself: "She could say more if she chose."

He said: "Will you tell me what you can of the course of events last night?"

"Certainly, but there is very little that will be useful, I'm afraid. After dinner Ruby came and sat with us in the lounge. She remained even after the dancing had started. We had arranged to play bridge later, but we were waiting for Mark, that is Mark Gaskell, my brother-in-law—he married Mr. Jefferson's daughter, you know—who had some important letters to write, and also for Josie. She was going to make a fourth with us."

"Did that often happen?"

"Quite frequently. She's a first-class player, of course, and very nice. My father-in-law is a keen bridge player and whenever possible liked to get hold of Josie to make the fourth instead of an outsider. Naturally, as she has to arrange the fours, she can't always play with us, but she does whenever she can, and as"—her eyes smiled a little—"my father-in-law spends a lot of money in the hotel, the management are quite pleased for Josie to favour us."

Malchett asked:

"You like Josie?"

"Yes, I do. She's always good-humoured and cheerful, works hard and seems to enjoy her job. She's shrewd, though not well educated, and—well—never pretends about anything. She's natural and unaffected."

"Please go on, Mrs. Jefferson."

"As I say, Josie had to get her bridge fours arranged and Mark was writing, so Ruby sat and talked with us a little longer than usual. Then Josie came along, and Ruby went off to do her first solo dance with Raymond—he's the dance and tennis professional. She came back to us afterwards just as Mark joined us. Then she went off to dance with a young man and we four started our bridge."

She stopped, and made a slight insignificant gesture of helplessness.

"And that's all I know! I just caught a glimpse of her once dancing, but bridge is an absorbing game and I hardly glanced through the glass partition at the ballroom. Then, at midnight, Raymond came along to Josie very upset and asked where Ruby was. Josie, naturally, tried to shut him up but——"

Superintendent Harper interrupted. He said in his quiet voice: "Why '*naturally*,' Mrs. Jefferson?"

"Well"—she hesitated, looked, Melchett thought, a little put out—"Josie didn't want the girl's absence made too much of. She considered herself responsible for her in a way. She said Ruby was probably up in her bedroom, said the girl had talked about having a headache earlier—I don't think that was true, by the way; Josie just said it by way of excuse. Raymond went off and telephoned up to Ruby's room, but apparently there was no answer, and he came back in rather a state—temperamental, you know. Josie went off with him and tried to soothe him down, and in the end she danced with him instead of Ruby. Rather plucky of her, because you could see afterwards it had hurt her ankle. She came back to us when the dance was over and tried to calm down Mr. Jefferson. He had got worked up by then. We persuaded him in the end to go to bed, told him Ruby had probably gone for a spin in a car and that they'd had a puncture. He went to bed worried, and this morning he began to agitate at once." She paused. "The rest you know."

"Thank you, Mrs. Jefferson. Now I'm going to ask you if you've any idea who could have done this thing?"

She said immediately: "No idea whatever. I'm afraid I can't help you in the slightest."

He pressed her. "The girl never said anything? Nothing about jealousy? About some man she was afraid of? Or intimate with?"

Adelaide Jefferson shook her head to each query.

There seemed nothing more that she could tell them.

The Superintendent suggested that they should interview young George Bartlett and return to see Mr. Jefferson later. Colonel Melchett agreed, and the three men went out, Mrs. Jefferson promising to send word as soon as Mr. Jefferson was awake.

"Nice woman," said the Colonel, as they closed the door behind them.

"A very nice lady indeed," said Superintendent Harper.

iii

George Bartlett was a thin, lanky youth with a prominent

Adam's apple and an immense difficulty in saying what he meant. He was in such a state of dither that it was hard to get a calm statement from him.

"I say, it is awful, isn't it? Sort of thing one reads about in the Sunday papers—but one doesn't feel it really happens, don't you know?"

"Unfortunately there is no doubt about it, Mr. Bartlett," said the Superintendent.

"No, no, of course not. But it seems so rum somehow. And miles from here and everything—in some country house, wasn't it? Awfully county and all that. Created a bit of a stir in the neighbourhood—what?"

Colonel Melchett took charge.

"How well did you know the dead girl, Mr. Bartlett?"

George Bartlett looked alarmed.

"Oh, n-n-n-ot well at all, s-s-sir. No, hardly at all—if you know what I mean. Danced with her once or twice—passed the time of day—bit of tennis—*you* know."

"You were, I think, the last person to see her alive last night?"

"I suppose I was—doesn't it sound awful? I mean, she was perfectly all right when I saw her—absolutely."

"What time was that, Mr. Bartlett?"

"Well, you know, I never know about time—wasn't very late, if you know what I mean."

"You danced with her?"

"Yes—as a matter of fact—well, yes, I did. Early on in the evening, though. Tell you what, it was just after her exhibition dance with the pro. fellow. Must have been ten, half-past, eleven, I don't know."

"Never mind the time. We can fix that. Please tell us exactly what happened."

"Well, we danced, don't you know. Not that *I'm* much of a dancer."

"How you dance is not really relevant, Mr. Bartlett."

George Bartlett cast an alarmed eye on the Colonel and stammered:

"No—er—n-n-n-o, I suppose it isn't. Well, as I say, we danced, round and round, and I talked, but Ruby didn't say very much and she yawned a bit. As I say, I don't dance awfully well, and so girls—well—inclined to give it a miss, if you know what I mean. She said she had a headache—I know where I get off, so I said righty ho, and that was that."

"What was the last you saw of her?"

"She went off upstairs."

"She said nothing about meeting any one? Or going for a drive? Or—or—having a date?" The Colonel used the colloquial expression with a slight effort.

Bartlett shook his head.

"Not to me." He looked rather mournful. "Just gave me the push."

"What was her manner? Did she seem anxious, abstracted, anything on her mind?"

George Bartlett considered. Then he shook his head.

"Seemed a bit bored. Yawned, as I said. Nothing more."

Colonel Melchett said:

"And what did you do, Mr. Bartlett?"

"Eh?"

"What did you do when Ruby Keene left you?"

George Bartlett gaped at him.

"Let's see now—what *did* I do?"

"We're waiting for you to tell us."

"Yes, yes—of course. Jolly difficult, remembering things, what? Let me see. Shouldn't be surprised if I went into the bar and had a drink."

"*Did* you go into the bar and have a drink?"

"That's just it. I *did* have a drink. Don't think it was just then. Have an idea I wandered out, don't you know? Bit of air. Rather stuffy for September. Very nice outside. Yes, that's it. I strolled around a bit, then I came in and had a drink and then I strolled back to the ballroom. Wasn't much doing. Noticed what's-her-name—Josie—was dancing again. With the tennis fellow. She'd been on the sick list—twisted ankle or something."

"That fixes the time of your return at midnight. Do you intend us to understand that you spent over an hour walking about outside?"

"Well, I had a drink, you know. I was—well, I was thinking of things."

This statement received more incredulity than any other.

Colonel Melchett said sharply:

"What were you thinking about?"

"Oh, I don't know. Things," said Mr. Bartlett vaguely.

"You have a car, Mr. Bartlett?"

"Oh, yes, I've got a car."

"Where was it, in the hotel garage?"

"No, it was in the courtyard, as a matter of fact. Thought I might go for a spin, you see."

"Perhaps you did go for a spin?"

"No—no, I didn't. Swear I didn't."

"You didn't, for instance, take Miss Keene for a spin?"

"Oh, I say. Look here, what are you getting at? I didn't—I swear I didn't. Really, now."

"Thank you, Mr. Bartlett, I don't think there is anything more at present. *At present*," repeated Colonel Melchett with a good deal of emphasis on the words.

They left Mr. Bartlett looking after them with a ludicrous expression of alarm on his unintellectual face.

"Brainless young ass," said Colonel Melchett. "Or isn't he?"

Superintendent Harper shook his head.

"We've got a long way to go," he said.

Chapter 6

i

NEITHER THE night porter nor the barman proved helpful. The night porter remembered ringing up to Miss Keene's room just after midnight and getting no reply. He had not noticed Mr. Bartlett leaving or entering the hotel. A lot of gentlemen and ladies were strolling in and out, the night being fine. And there were side doors off the corridor as well as the one in the main hall. He was fairly certain Miss Keene had not gone out by the main door, but if she had come down from her room, which was on the first floor, there was a staircase next to it and a door out at the end of the corridor, leading on to the side terrace. She could have gone out of that unseen easily enough. It was not locked until the dancing was over at two o'clock.

The barman remembered Mr. Bartlett being in the bar the preceding evening but could not say when. Somewhere about the middle of the evening, he thought. Mr. Bartlett had sat against the wall and was looking rather melancholy. He did not know how long he was there. There were a lot of outside guests coming and going in the bar. He had noticed Mr. Bartlett but he couldn't fix the time in any way.

ii

As they left the bar, they were accosted by a small boy of about nine years old. He burst immediately into excited speech.

"I say, are you the detectives? I'm Peter Carmody. It was my grandfather, Mr. Jefferson, who rang up the police about Ruby. Are you from Scotland Yard? You don't mind my speaking to you, do you?"

Colonel Melchett looked as though he were about to return a short answer, but Superintendent Harper intervened. He spoke benignly and heartily.

"That's all right, my son. Naturally interests you, I expect?"

"You bet it does. Do you like detective stories? I do. I read them all, and I've got autographs from Dorothy Sayers and Agatha Christie and Dickson Carr and H.C. Bailey. Will the murder be in the papers?"

"It'll be in the papers all right," said Superintendent Harper grimly.

"You see, I'm going back to school next week and I shall tell them all that I knew her—really knew her *well*."

"What did you think of her, eh?"

Peter considered.

"Well, I didn't like her much. I think she was rather a stupid sort of girl. Mum and Uncle Mark didn't like her much either. Only Grandfather. Grandfather wants to see you, by the way. Edwards is looking for you."

Superintendent Harper murmured encouragingly:

"So your mother and your Uncle Mark didn't like Ruby Keene much? Why was that?"

"Oh, I don't know. She was always butting in. And they didn't like Grandfather making such a fuss of her. I expect," said Peter cheerfully, "that they're glad she's dead."

Superintendent Harper looked at him thoughtfully. He said:

"Did you hear them—er—say so?"

"Well, not exactly. Uncle Mark said: 'Well, it's one way out, anyway,' and Mums said: 'Yes, but such a horrible one,' and Uncle Mark said it was no good being hypocritical."

The men exchanged glances. At that moment a respectable, clean-shaven man, neatly dressed in blue serge, came up to them.

"Excuse me, gentlemen. I am Mr. Jefferson's valet. He is awake now and sent me to find you, as he is very anxious to see you."

Once more they went up to Conway Jefferson's suite. In the sitting-room Adelaide Jefferson was talking to a tall, restless man who was prowling nervously about the room. He swung round sharply to view the new-comers.

"Oh, yes. Glad you've come. My father-in-law's been asking for you. He's awake now. Keep him as calm as you can, won't you? His health's not too good. It's a wonder, really, that this shock didn't do for him."

Harper said:

"I'd no idea his health was as bad as that."

"He doesn't know it himself," said Mark Gaskell. "It's his heart, you see. The doctor warned Addie that he mustn't be over-excited or startled. He more or less hinted that the end might come any time, didn't he, Addie?"

Mrs. Jefferson nodded. She said:

"It's incredible that he's rallied the way he has."

Melchett said dryly:

"Murder isn't exactly a soothing incident. We'll be as careful as we can."

He was sizing up Mark Gaskell as he spoke. He didn't much care for the fellow. A bold, unscrupulous, hawk-like face. One of those men who usually get their own way and whom women frequently admire.

"But not the sort of fellow I'd trust," the Colonel thought to himself.

Unscrupulous—that was the word for him.

The sort of fellow who wouldn't stick at anything. . . .

iii

In the big bedroom overlooking the sea, Conway Jefferson was sitting in his wheeled-chair by the window.

No sooner were you in the room with him than you felt the power and magnetism of the man. It was as though the injuries which had left him a cripple had resulted in concentrating the vitality of his shattered body into a narrower and more intense focus.

He had a fine head, the red of the hair slightly grizzled. The face was rugged and powerful, deeply sun-tanned, and the eyes were a startling blue. There was no sign of illness or feebleness about him. The deep lines on his face were the lines of suffering, not the lines of weakness. Here was a man who would never rail against fate but accept it and pass on to victory.

He said: "I'm glad you've come." His quick eyes took them in. He said to Melchett: "You're the Chief Constable of Radfordshire? Right. And you're Superintendent Harper? Sit down. Cigarettes on the table beside you."

They thanked him and sat down. Melchett said:

"I understand, Mr. Jefferson, that you were interested in the dead girl?"

A quick, twisted smile flashed across the lined face.

"Yes—they'll all have told you that! Well, it's no secret. How much has my family said to you?"

He looked quickly from one to the other as he asked the question.

It was Melchett who answered.

"Mrs Jefferson told us very little beyond the fact that the girl's chatter amused you and that she was by way of being a protégée. We have only exchanged half a dozen words with Mr. Gaskell."

Conway Jefferson smiled.

"Addie's a discreet creature, bless her. Mark would probably have been more outspoken. I think, Melchett, that I'd better tell you some facts rather fully. It's important, in order that you should understand my attitude. And, to begin with, it's necessary that I go back to the big tragedy of my life. Eight years ago I lost my wife, my son and my daughter in an aeroplane accident. Since then I've been like a man who's lost half himself—and I'm not speaking of my physical plight! I was a family man. My daughter-in-law and my son-in-law have been very good to me. They've done all they can to take the place of my flesh and blood. But I've realized—especially of late, that they have, after all, their own lives to live.

"So you must understand that, essentially, I'm a lonely man. I like young people. I enjoy them. Once or twice I've played with the idea of adopting some girl or boy. During this last month I got very friendly with the child who's been killed. She was absolutely natural—completely naïve. She chattered on about her life and her experiences—in pantomime, with touring companies, with Mum and Dad as a child in cheap lodgings. Such a different life from any I've known! Never complaining, never seeing it as sordid. Just a natural, uncomplaining, hard-working child, unspoilt and charming. Not a lady, perhaps, but, thank God, neither vulgar nor—abominable word—'ladylike.'

"I got more and more fond of Ruby. I decided, gentlemen, to adopt her legally. She would become—by law—my daughter. That, I hope, explains my concern for her and the steps I took when I heard of her unaccountable disappearance."

There was a pause. Then Superintendent Harper, his unemotional voice robbing the question of any offence, asked: "May I ask what your son-in-law and daughter-in-law said to that?"

Jefferson's answer came back quickly:

"What could they say? They didn't, perhaps, like it very much. It's the sort of thing that arouses prejudice. But they behaved very well—yes, very well. It's not as though, you see, they were dependent on me. When my son Frank married I turned over half my worldly goods to him then and there. I believe in that. Don't let your children wait until you're dead. They want the money when they're young, not when they're middle-aged. In the same way when my daughter Rosamund insisted on marrying a poor man, I settled a big sum of money on her. That sum passed to him at her death. So, you see, that simplified the matter from the financial angle."

"I see, Mr. Jefferson," said Superintendent Harper.

But there was a certain reserve in his tone. Conway Jefferson pounced upon it.

"But you don't agree, eh?"

"It's not for me to say, sir, but families, in my experience, don't always act reasonably."

"I dare say you're right, Superintendent, but you must remember that Mr. Gaskell and Mrs. Jefferson aren't, strictly speaking, my *family*. They're not blood relations."

"That, of course, makes a difference," admitted the Superintendent.

For a moment Conway Jefferson's eyes twinkled. He said: "That's not to say that they didn't think me an old fool! That *would* be the average person's reaction. But I wasn't being a fool. I know character. With education and polishing, Ruby Keene could have taken her place anywhere."

Melchett said:

"I'm afraid we're being rather impertinent and inquisitive, but it's important that we should get at all the facts. You proposed to make full provision for the girl—that is, settle money upon her, but you hadn't already done so?"

Jefferson said:

"I understand what you're driving at—the possibility of someone's benefiting by the girl's death? But nobody could. The necessary formalities for legal adoption were under way, but they hadn't yet been completed."

Melchett said slowly:

"Then, if anything happened to you——?"

He left the sentence unfinished, as a query. Conway Jefferson was quick to respond.

"Nothing's likely to happen to me! I'm a cripple, but I'm not an invalid. Although doctors *do* like to pull long faces and give advice about not overdoing things! Not overdoing things! I'm as strong as a horse! Still, I'm quite aware of the fatalities of life—my God, I've good reason to be! Sudden death comes to the strongest man—especially in these days of road casualties. But I'd provided for that. I made a new will about ten days ago."

"Yes?" Superintendent Harper leaned forward.

"I left the sum of fifty thousand pounds to be held in trust for Ruby Keene until she was twenty-five, when she would come into the principal."

Superintendent Harper's eyes opened. So did Colonel Melchett's. Harper said in an almost awed voice:

"That's a very large sum of money, Mr. Jefferson."

"In these days, yes, it is."

"And you were leaving it to a girl you had only known a few weeks?"

Anger flashed into the vivid blue eyes.

"Must I go on repeating the same thing over and over again? I've no flesh and blood of my own—no nieces or nephews or distant cousins, even! I might have left it to charity. I prefer to leave it to an individual." He laughed "Cinderella turned into a princess overnight! A fairy-godfather instead of a fairy-godmother. Why not? It's *my* money. *I* made it."

Colonel Melchett asked: "Any other bequests?"

"A small legacy to Edwards, my valet—and the remainder to

Mark and Addie in equal shares."

"Would—excuse me—the residue amount to a large sum?"

"Probably not. It's difficult to say exactly, investments fluctuate all the time. The sum involved, after death duties and expenses had been paid, would probably have come to something between five and ten thousand pounds net."

"I see."

"And you needn't think I was treating them shabbily. As I said, I divided up my estate at the time my children married. I left myself, actually, a very small sum. But after—after the tragedy—I wanted something to occupy my mind. I flung myself into business. At my house in London I had a private line put in connecting my bedroom with my office. I worked hard—it helped me not to think, and it made me feel that my—my mutilation had not vanquished me. I threw myself into work"—his voice took on a deeper note, he spoke more to himself than to his audience— "and, by some subtle irony, everything I did prospered! My wildest speculations succeeded. If I gambled, I won. Everything I touched turned to gold. Fate's ironic way of righting the balance, I suppose."

The lines of suffering stood out on his face again.

Recollecting himself, he smiled wryly at them.

"So you see, the sum of money I left Ruby was indisputably mine to do with as my fancy dictated."

Melchett said quickly:

"Undoubtedly, my dear fellow, we are not questioning that for a moment."

Conway Jefferson said: "Good. Now I want to ask some questions in my turn, if I may. I want to hear—more about this terrible business. All I know is that she—that little Ruby was found strangled in a house some twenty miles from here."

"That is correct. At Gossington Hall."

Jefferson frowned.

"Gossington? But that's——"

"Colonel Bantry's house."

"Bantry! *Arthur Bantry?* But I know him. Know him and his wife! Met them abroad some years ago. I didn't realize they lived in this part of the world. Why it's——"

He broke off. Superintendent Harper slipped in smoothly:

"Colonel Bantry was dining in the hotel here Tuesday of last week. You didn't see him?"

"Tuesday? Tuesday? No, we were back late. Went over to Harden Head and had dinner on the way back."

Melchett said:

"Ruby Keene never mentioned the Bantrys to you?"

Jefferson shook his head.

"Never. Don't believe she knew them. Sure she didn't. She didn't know anybody but the theatrical folk and that sort of thing." He paused and then asked abruptly:

"What's Bantry got to say about it?"

"He can't account for it in the least. He was out at a Conservative meeting last night. The body was discovered this morning. He says he's never seen the girl in his life."

Jefferson nodded. He said:

"It certainly seems fantastic."

Superintendent Harper cleared his throat. He said:

"Have you any idea at all, sir, who can have done this?"

"Good God, I wish I had!" The veins stood out on his forehead. "It's incredible, unimaginable! I'd say it couldn't have happened, if it hadn't happened!"

"There's no friend of hers—from her past life—no man hanging about—or threatening her?"

"I'm sure there isn't. She'd have told me if so. She's never had a regular 'boy-friend.' She told me so herself."

Superintendent Harper thought:

"Yes, I dare say that's what *she* told you! But that's as may be!"

Conway Jefferson went on:

"Josie would know better than any one if there had been some man hanging about Ruby or pestering her. Can't she help?"

"She says not."

Jefferson said frowning:

"I can't help feeling it must be the work of some maniac—the brutality of the method—breaking into a country house—the whole thing so unconnected and senseless. There are men of that type, men outwardly sane, but who decoy girls—sometimes children—away and kill them. Sexual crimes really, I suppose."

Harper said:

"Oh, yes, there are such cases, but we've no knowledge of any one of that kind operating in this neighbourhood."

Jefferson went on:

"I've thought over all the various men I've seen with Ruby. Guests here and outsiders—men she'd danced with. They all seem harmless enough—the usual type. She had no special friend of any kind."

Superintendent Harper's face remained quite impassive, but unseen by Conway Jefferson there was still a speculative glint in his eye.

It was quite possible, he thought, that Ruby Keene might have had a special friend even though Conway Jefferson did not know about it.

He said nothing, however. The Chief Constable gave him a glance of inquiry and then rose to his feet. He said:

"Thank you, Mr. Jefferson. That's all we need for the present."

Jefferson said:

"You'll keep me informed of your progress?"

"Yes, yes, we'll keep in touch with you."

The two men went out.

Conway Jefferson leaned back in his chair.

His eyelids came down and veiled the fierce blue of his eyes. He looked suddenly a very tired man.

Then, after a minute or two, the lids flickered. He called: "Edwards?"

From the next room the valet appeared promptly. Edwards knew his master as no one else did. Others, even his nearest, knew only his strength. Edwards knew his weakness. He had seen Conway Jefferson tired, discouraged, weary of life, momentarily defeated by infirmity and loneliness.

"Yes, sir?"

Jefferson said:

"Get on to Sir Henry Clithering. He's at Melborne Abbas. Ask him, from me, to get here to-day if he can, instead of to-morrow. Tell him it's urgent."

Chapter 7

i

WHEN THEY were outside Jefferson's door, Superintendent Harper said:

"Well, for what it's worth, we've got a motive, sir."

"H'm," said Melchett. "Fifty thousand pounds, eh?"

"Yes, sir. Murder's been done for a good deal less than that."

"Yes, but——"

Colonel Melchett left the sentence unfinished. Harper, however, understood him.

"You don't think it's likely in this case? Well, I don't either, as far as that goes. But it's got to be gone into, all the same."

"Oh, of course."

Harper went on:

"If, as Mr. Jefferson says, Mr. Gaskell and Mrs. Jefferson are already well provided for and in receipt of a comfortable income, well, it's not likely they'd set out to do a brutal murder."

"Quite so. Their financial standing will have to be investigated, of course. Can't say I like the appearance of Gaskell much—looks a sharp, unscrupulous sort of fellow—but that's a long way from making him out a murderer."

"Oh, yes, sir, as I say, I don't think it's *likely* to be either of them, and from what Josie said I don't see how it would have been humanly possible. They were both playing bridge from twenty minutes to eleven until midnight. No, to my mind there's another possibility much more likely."

Melchett said: "Boy friend of Ruby Keene's?"

"That's it, sir. Some disgruntled young fellow—not too strong in the head, perhaps. Someone, I'd say, she knew before she came here. This adoption scheme, if he got wise to it, may just have put the lid on things. He saw himself losing her, saw her being removed to a different sphere of life altogether, and he went mad and blind with rage. He got her to come out and meet him last night, had a row with her over it, lost his head completely and did her in."

"And how did she come to be in Bantry's library?"

"I think that's feasible. They were out, say, in his car at the time. He came to himself, realized what he'd done, and his first thought was how to get rid of the body. Say they were near the gates of a big house at the time. The idea comes to him that if she's found there the hue and cry will centre round the house and its occupants and will leave him comfortably out of it. She's a little bit of a thing. He could easily carry her. He's got a chisel in the car. He forces a window and plops her down on the hearthrug. Being a strangling case, there's no blood or mess to give him away in the car. See what I mean, sir?"

"Oh, yes, Harper, it's all perfectly possible. But there's still one thing to be done. *Cherchez l'homme*."

"What? Oh, very good, sir."

Superintendent Harper tactfully applauded his superior's joke, although, owing to the excellence of Colonel Melchett's French accent he almost missed the sense of the words.

ii

"Oh—er—I say—er—c-c-could I speak to you a minute?"

It was George Bartlett who thus waylaid the two men.

Colonel Melchett, who was not attracted to Mr. Bartlett and who was anxious to see how Slack had got on with the investigation of the girl's room and the questioning of the chambermaids, barked sharply:

"Well, what is it—what is it?"

Young Mr. Bartlett retreated a step or two, opening and shutting his mouth and giving an unconscious imitation of a fish in a tank.

"Well—er—probably isn't important, don't you know—thought I ought to tell you. Matter of fact, can't find my car."

"What do you mean, can't find your car?"

Stammering a good deal, Mr. Bartlett explained that what he

meant was that he couldn't find his car.

Superintendent Harper said:

"Do you mean it's been stolen?"

George Bartlett turned gratefully to the more placid voice.

"Well, that's just it, you know. I mean, one can't tell, can one? I mean someone may just have buzzed off in it, not meaning any harm, if you know what I mean."

"When did you last see it, Mr. Bartlett?"

"Well, I was tryin' to remember. Funny how difficult it is to remember anything, isn't it?"

Colonel Melchett said coldly:

"Not, I should think to a normal intelligence. I understood you to say just now that it was in the courtyard of the hotel last night——"

Mr. Bartlett was bold enough to interrupt. He said:

"That's just it—was it?"

"What do you mean by 'was it'? You said it *was*."

"Well—I mean I *thought* it was. I mean—well, I didn't go out and look, don't you see?"

Colonel Melchett sighed. He summoned all his patience. He said:

"Let's get this quite clear. When was the last time you saw—actually *saw* your car? What make is it, by the way?"

"Minoan 14."

"And you last saw it—when?"

George Bartlett's Adam's apple jerked convulsively up and down.

"Been trying to think. Had it before lunch yesterday. Was going for a spin in the afternoon. But somehow, you know how it is, went to sleep instead. Then, after tea, had a game of squash and all that, and a bathe afterwards."

"And the car was then in the courtyard of the hotel?"

"Suppose so. I mean, that's where I'd put it. Thought, you see, I'd take someone for a spin. After dinner, I mean. But it wasn't my lucky evening. Nothing doing. Never took the old bus out after all."

Harper said:

"But, as far as you knew, the car was still in the courtyard?"

"Well, naturally. I mean, I'd put it there—what?"

"Would you have noticed if it had *not* been there?"

Mr. Bartlett shook his head.

"Don't think so, you know. Lots of cars going and coming and all that. Plenty of Minoans."

Superintendent Harper nodded. He had just cast a casual glance out of the window. There were at that moment no less than eight Minoan 14s in the courtyard—it was the popular cheap car of the year.

"Aren't you in the habit of putting your car away at night?" asked Colonel Melchett.

"Don't usually bother," said Mr. Bartlett. "Fine weather and all that, you know. Such a fag putting a car away in a garage."

Glancing at Colonel Melchett, Superintendent Harper said: "I'll join you upstairs, sir. I'll just get hold of Sergeant Higgins and he can take down particulars from Mr. Bartlett."

"Right, Harper."

Mr. Bartlett murmured wistfully:

"Thought I ought to let you know, you know. Might be important, what?"

iii

Mr. Prestcott had supplied his additional dancer with board and lodging. Whatever the board, the lodging was the poorest the hotel possessed.

Josephine Turner and Ruby Keene had occupied rooms at the extreme end of a mean and dingy little corridor. The rooms were small, faced north on to a portion of the cliff that backed the hotel, and were furnished with the odds and ends of suites that had once, some thirty years ago, represented luxury and magnificence in the best suites. Now, when the hotel had been modernized and the bedrooms supplied with built-in receptacles for clothes, these large Victorian oak and mahogany wardrobes were relegated to those rooms occupied by the hotel's resident staff, or given to guests in the height of the season when all the rest of the hotel was full.

As Melchett saw at once, the position of Ruby Keene's room was ideal for the purpose of leaving the hotel without being observed, and was particularly unfortunate from the point of view of throwing light on the circumstances of that departure.

At the end of the corridor was a small staircase which led down to an equally obscure corridor on the ground floor. Here there was a glass door which led out on to the side terrace of the hotel, an unfrequented terrace with no view. You could go from it to the main terrace in front, or you could go down a winding path and come out in a lane that eventually rejoined the cliff road farther along. Its surface being bad, it was seldom used.

Inspector Slack had been busy harrying chambermaids and examining Ruby's room for clues. He had been lucky enough to find the room exactly as it had been left the night before.

Ruby Keene had not been in the habit of rising early. Her usual procedure, Slack discovered, was to sleep until about ten or half-past and then ring for breakfast. Consequently, since Conway Jefferson had begun his representations to the manager very early, the police had taken charge of things before the chambermaids had touched the room. They had actually not been down that corridor at all. The other rooms there, at this season of the year, were only opened and dusted once a week.

"That's all to the good as far as it goes," Slack explained gloomily. "It means that if there *were* anything to find we'd find it, but there isn't anything."

The Glenshire police had already been over the room for finger-prints, but there were none unaccounted for. Ruby's own, Josie's, and the two chambermaids—one on the morning and one on the evening shift. There were also a couple of prints made by Raymond Starr, but these were accounted for by his story that he had come up with Josie to look for Ruby when she did not appear for the midnight exhibition dance.

There had been a heap of letters and general rubbish in the pigeonholes of the massive mahogany desk in the corner. Slack had just been carefully sorting through them. But he had found nothing of a suggestive nature. Bills, receipts, theatre programmes, cinema stubs, newspaper cuttings, beauty hints torn from magazines. Of the letters there were some from "Lil", apparently a friend from the Palais de Danse, recounting various affairs and gossip, saying they "missed Rube a lot. Mr. Findeison asked after you ever so often! Quite put out he is!

Young Reg has taken up with May now you've gone. Barny asks after you now and then. Things going much as usual. Old Grouser still as mean as ever with us girls. He ticked off Ada for going about with a fellow."

Slack had carefully noted all the names mentioned. Inquiries would be made—and it was possible some useful information might come to light. To this Colonel Melchett agreed; so did Superintendent Harper, who had joined them. Otherwise the room had little to yield in the way of information.

Across a chair in the middle of the room was the foamy pink dance frock Ruby had worn early in the evening with a pair of pink satin high-heeled shoes kicked off carelessly on the floor. Two sheer silk stockings were rolled into a ball and flung down. One had a ladder in it. Melchett recalled that the dead girl had had bare feet and legs. This Slack learned, was her custom. She used make-up on her legs instead of stockings and only sometimes wore stockings for dancing, by this means saving expense. The wardrobe door was open and showed a variety of rather flashy evening-dresses and a row of shoes below. There was some soiled underwear in the clothes-basket, some nail-parings, soiled face-cleaning tissue and bits of cotton wool stained with rouge and nail-polish in the waste-paper basket—in fact, nothing out of the ordinary! The facts seemed plain to read. Ruby Keene had hurried upstairs, changed her clothes and hurried off again—*where?*

Josephine Turner, who might be supposed to know most of Ruby's life and friends, had proved unable to help. But this, as Inspector Slack pointed out, might be natural.

"If what you tell me is true, sir—about this adoption business, I mean—well, Josie would be all for Ruby breaking with any old friends she might have and who might queer the pitch, so to speak. As I see it, this invalid gentleman gets all worked up about Ruby Keene being such a sweet, innocent, childish little piece of goods. Now, supposing Ruby's got a tough boy friend—that won't go down so well with the old boy. So it's Ruby's business to keep that dark. Josie doesn't know much about the girl anyway—not about her friends and all that. But one thing she wouldn't stand for—Ruby's messing up things by carrying on with some undesirable fellow. So it stands to reason that Ruby (who, as I see it, was a sly little piece!) would keep very dark about seeing any old friend. She wouldn't let on to Josie anything about it—otherwise Josie would say: 'No, you don't, my girl.' But you know what girls are—especially young ones—always ready to make a fool of themselves over a tough guy. Ruby wants to see him. He comes down here, cuts up rough about the whole business, and wrings the girl's neck."

"I expect you're right, Slack," said Colonel Melchett, disguising his usual repugnance for the unpleasant way Slack had of putting things. "If so, we ought to be able to discover this tough friend's identity fairly easily."

"You leave it to me, sir," said Slack with his usual confidence. "I'll get hold of this 'Lil' girl at that Palais de Danse place and turn her right inside out. We'll soon get at the truth."

Colonel Melchett wondered if they would. Slack's energy and activity always made him feel tired.

"There's one other person you might be able to get a tip from, sir," went on Slack, "and that's the dance and tennis pro. fellow. He must have seen a lot of her and he'd know more than Josie would. Likely enough she'd loosen her tongue a bit to him."

"I have already discussed that point with Superintendent Harper."

"Good, sir. *I*'ve done the chambermaids pretty thoroughly! They don't know a thing. Looked down on these two, as far as I can make out. Scamped the service as much as they dared. Chambermaid was in here last at seven o'clock last night, when she turned down the bed and drew the curtains and cleared up a bit. There's a bathroom next door, if you'd like to see it?"

The bathroom was situated between Ruby's room and the slightly larger room occupied by Josie. It was unilluminating. Colonel Melchett silently marvelled at the amount of aids to beauty that women could use. Rows of jars of face cream, cleansing cream, vanishing cream, skin-feeding cream! Boxes of different shades of powder. An untidy heap of every variety of lipstick. Hair lotions and "brightening" applications. Eyelash black, mascara, blue stain for under the eyes, at least twelve different shades of nail varnish, face tissues, bits of cotton wool, dirty powder-puffs. Bottles of lotions—astringent, tonic, soothing, etc.

"Do you mean to say?" he murmured feebly, "that women use all these things?"

Inspector Slack, who always knew everything, kindly enlightened him.

"In private life, sir, so to speak, a lady keeps to one or two distinct shades, one for evening, one for day. They know what suits them and they keep to it. But these professional girls, they have to ring a change, so to speak. They do exhibition dances, and one night it's a tango and the next a crinoline Victorian dance and then a kind of Apache dance and then just ordinary ball-room, and, of course, the make-up varies a good bit."

"Good Lord!" said the Colonel. "No wonder the people who turn out these creams and messes make a fortune."

"Easy money, that's what it is," said Slack. "Easy money. Got to spend a bit in advertisement, of course."

Colonel Melchett jerked his mind away from the fascinating and age-long problem of woman's adornments. He said to Harper, who had just joined them:

"There's still this dancing fellow. Your pigeon, Superintendent?"

"I suppose so, sir."

As they went downstairs Harper asked:

"What did you think of Mr. Bartlett's story, sir?"

"About his car? I think, Harper, that that young man wants watching. It's a fishy story. Supposing that he did take Ruby Keene out in that car last night, after all?"

iv

Superintendent Harper's manner was slow and pleasant and absolutely non-committal. These cases where the police of two counties had to collaborate were always difficult. He liked Colonel Melchett and considered him an able Chief Constable, but he was nevertheless glad to be tackling the present interview by himself. Never do too much at once, was Superintendent Harper's rule. Bare routine inquiry for the first time. That left the persons you were interviewing relieved and predisposed them to be more unguarded in the next interview you had with them.

Harper already knew Raymond Starr by sight. A fine-looking specimen, tall, lithe and good-looking, with very white teeth in a deeply-bronzed face. He was dark and graceful. He had a pleasant, friendly manner and was very popular in the hotel.

"I'm afraid I can't help you much, Superintendent. I knew Ruby quite well, of course. She'd been here over a month and we had practised our dances together and all that. But there's really very little to say. She was quite a pleasant and rather stupid girl."

"It's her friendships we're particularly anxious to know about. Her friendships with men."

"So I suppose. Well, *I* don't know anything! She'd got a few young men in tow in the hotel, but nothing special. You see, she was nearly always monopolized by the Jefferson family."

"Yes, the Jefferson family." Harper paused meditatively. He shot a shrewd glance at the young man.

"What did you think of that business, Mr. Starr?"

Raymond Starr said coolly: "What business?"

Harper said: "Did you know that Mr. Jefferson was proposing to adopt Ruby Keene legally?"

This appeared to be news to Starr. He pursed up his lips and whistled. He said:

"The clever little devil! Oh, well, there's no fool like an old fool."

"That's how it strikes you, is it?"

"Well—what else can one say? If the old boy wanted to adopt someone, why didn't he pick upon a girl of his own class?"

"Ruby Keene never mentioned the matter to you?"

"No, she didn't. I knew she was elated about something, but I didn't know what it was."

"And Josie?"

"Oh, I think Josie must have know what was in the wind. Probably she was the one who planned the whole thing. Josie's no fool. She's got a head on her, that girl."

Harper nodded. It was Josie who had sent for Ruby Keene. Josie, no doubt, who had encouraged the intimacy. No wonder she had been upset when Ruby had failed to show up for her dance that night and Conway Jefferson had begun to panic. She was envisaging her plans going awry.

He asked:

"Could Ruby keep a secret, do you think?"

"As well as most. She didn't talk about her own affairs much."

"Did she ever say anything—anything at all—about some friend of hers—someone from her former life who was coming to see her here, or whom she had had difficulty with—you know the sort of thing I mean, no doubt."

"I know perfectly. Well, as far as I'm aware, there was no one of the kind. Not by anything she ever said."

"Thank you, Mr. Starr. Now will you just tell me in your own words exactly what happened last night?"

"Certainly. Ruby and I did our ten-thirty dance together—"

"No signs of anything unusual about her then?"

Raymond considered.

"I don't think so. I didn't notice what happened afterwards. I had my own partners to look after. I do remember noticing she wasn't in the ball-room. At midnight she hadn't turned up. I was very annoyed and went to Josie about it. Josie was playing bridge with the Jeffersons. She hadn't any idea where Ruby was, and I think she got a bit of a jolt. I noticed her shoot a quick, anxious glance at Mr. Jefferson. I persuaded the band to play another dance and I went to the office and got them to ring up to Ruby's room. There wasn't any answer. I went back to Josie. She suggested that Ruby was perhaps asleep in her room. Idiotic suggestion really, but it was meant for the Jeffersons, of course! She came away with me and said we'd go up together."

"Yes, Mr. Starr. And what did she say when she was alone with you?"

"As far as I can remember, she looked very angry and said: 'Damned little fool. She can't do this sort of thing. It will ruin all her chances. Who's she with, do you know?'

"I said that I hadn't the least idea. The last I'd seen of her was dancing with young Bartlett. Josie said: 'She wouldn't be with *him*. What *can* she be up to? She isn't with that film man, is she?' "

Harper said sharply: "*Film man?* Who was he?"

Raymond said: "I don't know his name. He's never stayed here. Rather an unusual-looking chap—black hair and theatrical-looking. He has something to do with the film industry, I believe—or so he told Ruby. He came over to dine here once or twice and danced with Ruby afterwards, but I don't think she knew him at all well. That's why I was surprised when Josie mentioned him. I said I didn't think he'd been here to-night. Josie said: 'Well, she must be out with *someone*. What on earth am I going to say to the Jeffersons?' I said what did it matter to the Jeffersons? And Josie said it *did* matter. And she said too, that she'd never forgive Ruby if she went and messed things up.

"We'd got to Ruby's room by then. She wasn't there, of course, but she'd been there, because the dress she had been wearing was lying across a chair. Josie looked in the wardrobe and said she thought she'd put on her old white dress. Normally she'd have changed into a black velvet dress for our Spanish dance. I was pretty angry by this time at the way Ruby had let me down. Josie did her best to soothe me and said she'd dance herself so that old Prestcott shouldn't get after us all. She went away and changed her dress and we went down and did a tango—exaggerated style and quite showy but not really too exhausting upon the ankles. Josie was very plucky about it—for it hurt her, I could see. After that she asked me to help her soothe the Jeffersons down. She said it was important. So, of course, I did what I could."

Superintendent Harper nodded. He said:

"Thank you, Mr. Starr."

To himself he thought: "It was important, all right! Fifty thousand pounds!"

He watched Raymond Starr as the latter moved gracefully away. He went down the steps of the terrace, picking up a bag of tennis balls and a racket on the way. Mrs. Jefferson, also carrying a racket, joined him and they went towards the tennis courts.

"Excuse me, sir."

Sergeant Higgins, rather breathless, stood at Harper's side.

The Superintendent, jerked from the train of thought he was following, looked startled.

"Message just come through for you from headquarters, sir. Labourer reported this morning saw glare as of fire. Half an hour ago they found a burnt-out car in a quarry. Venn's Quarry—about two miles from here. Traces of a charred body inside."

A flush came over Harper's heavy features. He said:

"What's come to Glenshire? An epidemic of violence? Don't tell me we're going to have a Rouse case now!"

He asked: "Could they get the number of the car?"

"No, sir. But we'll be able to identify it, of course, by the engine number. A Minoan 14, they think it is."

Chapter 8

i

SIR HENRY CLITHERING, as he passed through the lounge of the Majestic, hardly glanced at its occupants. His mind was preoccupied. Nevertheless, as is the way of life, something registered in his subconscious. It waited its time patiently.

Sir Henry was wondering as he went upstairs just what had induced the sudden urgency of his friend's message. Conway Jefferson was not the type of man who sent out urgent summonses to any one. Something quite out of the usual must have occurred, decided Sir Henry.

Jefferson wasted no time in beating about the bush. He said:

"Glad you've come. Edwards, get Sir Henry a drink. Sit down, man. You've not heard anything, I suppose? Nothing in the papers yet?"

Sir Henry shook his head, his curiosity aroused.

"What's the matter?"

"Murder's the matter. I'm concerned in it and so are your friends the Bantrys."

"Arthur and Dolly Bantry?" Clithering sounded incredulous.

"Yes, you see, the body was found in their house."

Clearly and succinctly Conway Jefferson ran through the facts. Sir Henry listened without interrupting. Both men were accustomed to grasping the gist of a matter. Sir Henry, during his term as Commissioner of the Metropolitan Police, had been renowned for his quick grip on essentials.

"It's an extraordinary business," he commented when the other had finished. "How do the Bantrys come into it, do you think?"

"That's what worries me. You see, Henry, it looks to me as though possibly the fact that I know them might have a bearing on the case. That's the only connection I can find. Neither of them, I gather, ever saw the girl before. That's what they say, and there's no reason to disbelieve them. It's most unlikely they *should* know her. Then isn't it possible that she was decoyed away and her body deliberately left in the house of friends of mine?"

Clithering said:

"I think that's far fetched."

"It's possible, though," persisted the other.

"Yes, but unlikely. What do you want *me* to do?"

Conway Jefferson said bitterly:

"I'm an invalid. I disguise the fact—refuse to face it—but now it comes home to me. I can't go about as I'd like to, asking questions, looking into things. I've got to stay here meekly grateful for such scraps of information as the police are kind enough to dole out to me. Do you happen to know Melchett, by the way, the Chief Constable of Radfordshire?"

"Yes, I've met him."

Something stirred in Sir Henry's brain. A face and figure noted unseeingly as he passed through the lounge. A straight-backed old lady whose face was familiar. It linked up with the last time he had seen Melchett. . . .

He said:

"Do you mean you want me to be a kind of amateur sleuth? That's not my line."

Jefferson said:

"You're *not* an amateur, that's just it."

"I'm not a professional any more. I'm on the retired list now."

Jefferson said: "That simplifies matters."

"You mean that if I were still at Scotland Yard I couldn't butt in? That's perfectly true."

"As it is," said Jefferson, "your experience qualifies you to take an interest in the case, and any co-operation you offer will be welcomed."

Clithering said slowly:

"Etiquette permits, I agree. But what do you really want, Conway? To find out who killed this girl?"

"Just that."

"You've no idea yourself?"

"None whatever."

Sir Henry said slowly:

"You probably won't believe me, but you've got an expert at solving mysteries sitting downstairs in the lounge at this minute. Someone who's better than I am at it, and who in all probability *may* have some local dope."

"What are you talking about?"

"Downstairs in the lounge, by the third pillar from the left, there sits an old lady with a sweet, placid, spinsterish face, and a mind that has plumbed the depths of human iniquity and taken it as all in the day's work. Her name's Miss Marple. She comes from the village of St. Mary Mead, which is a mile and a half from Gossington, she's a friend of the Bantrys—and where crime is concerned she's the goods, Conway."

Jefferson stared at him with thick, puckered eyebrows. He said heavily:

"You're joking."

"No, I'm not. You spoke of Melchett just now. The last time I saw Melchett there was a village tragedy. Girl supposed to have drowned herself. Police quite rightly suspected that it wasn't suicide, but murder. They thought they knew who did it. Along to me comes old Miss Marple, fluttering and dithering. She's afraid, she says, they'll hang the wrong person. She's got no evidence, but she knows who did do it. Hands me a piece of paper with a name written on it. And, by God, Jefferson, she was right!"

Conway Jefferson's brows came down lower than ever. He grunted disbelievingly:

"Woman's intuition, I suppose," he said sceptically.

"No, she doesn't call it that. Specialised knowledge is her claim."

"And what does that mean?"

"Well, you know, Jefferson, *we* use it in police work. We get a burglary and we usually know pretty well who did it—of the regular crowd, that is. We know the sort of burglar who acts in a particular sort of way. Miss Marple has an interesting, though occasionally trivial, series of parallels from village life."

Jefferson said sceptically:

"What is she likely to know about a girl who's been brought up in a theatrical milieu and probably never been in a village in her life?"

"I think," said Sir Henry Clithering firmly, "that she might have ideas."

ii

Miss Marple flushed with pleasure as Sir Henry bore down upon her.

"Oh, Sir Henry, this is indeed a great piece of luck meeting you here."

Sir Henry was gallant. He said:

"To me it is a great pleasure."

Miss Marple murmured, flushing: "So kind of you."

"Are you staying here?"

"Well, as a matter of fact, we are."

"*We?*"

"Mrs. Bantry's here too." She looked at him sharply. "Have you heard yet? Yes, I can see you have. It is terrible, is it not?"

"What's Dolly Bantry doing here? Is her husband here too?"

"No. Naturally, they both reacted quite differently. Colonel Bantry, poor man, just shuts himself up in his study, or goes down to one of the farms, when anything like this happens. Like tortoises, you know, they draw their heads in and hope nobody will notice them. Dolly, of course, is *quite* different."

"Dolly, in fact," said Sir Henry, who knew his old friend fairly well, "is almost enjoying herself, eh?"

"Well—er—yes. Poor dear."

"And she's brought you along to produce the rabbits out of the hat for her?"

Miss Marple said composedly:

"Dolly thought that a change of scene would be a good thing and she didn't want to come alone." She met his eye and her own gently twinkled. "But, of course, your way of describing it is quite true. It's rather embarrassing for me, because, of course, I am no use at all."

"No ideas? No village parallels?"

"I don't know very much about it all yet."

"I can remedy that, I think. I'm going to call you into consultation, Miss Marple."

He gave a brief recital of the course of events. Miss Marple listened with keen interest.

"Poor Mr. Jefferson," she said. "What a very sad story. These terrible accidents. To leave him alive, crippled, seems more cruel than if he had been killed too."

"Yes, indeed. That's why all his friends admire him so much for the resolute way he's gone on, conquering pain and grief and physical disabilities."

"Yes, it is splendid."

"The only thing I can't understand is this sudden outpouring of affection for this girl. She may, of course, have had some remarkable qualities."

"Probably not," said Miss Marple placidly.

"You don't think so?"

"I don't think her qualities entered into it."

Sir Henry said:

"He isn't just a nasty old man, you know."

"Oh, no, no!" Miss Marple got quite pink. "I wasn't implying that for a minute. What I was trying to say was—very badly, I know—that he was just looking for a nice bright girl to take his dead daughter's place—and then this girl saw her opportunity and played it for all she was worth! That sounds rather uncharitable, I know, but I have seen so many cases of the kind. The young maid-servant at Mr. Harbottle's, for instance. A *very* ordinary girl, but quiet with nice manners. His sister was called away to nurse a dying relative and when she got back she found the girl completely above herself, sitting down in the drawing-room laughing and talking and not wearing her cap or apron. Miss Harbottle spoke to her very sharply and the girl was impertinent, and then old Mr. Harbottle left her quite dumbfounded by saying that he thought she had kept house for him long enough and that he was making other arrangements.

"Such a scandal as it created in the village, but poor Miss Harbottle had to go and live *most* uncomfortably in rooms in Eastbourne. People *said* things, of course, but I believe there was no familiarity of any kind—it was simply that the old man found it much pleasanter to have a young, cheerful girl telling him how clever and amusing he was than to have his sister continually pointing out his faults to him, even if she *was* a good economical manager."

There was a moment's pause, and then Miss Marple resumed.

"And there was Mr. Badger who had the chemist's shop. Made a lot of fuss over the young lady who worked in his toilet section. Told his wife they must look on her as a daughter and have her to live in the house. Mrs. Badger didn't see it that way at all."

Sir Henry said: "If she'd only been a girl in his own rank of life—a friend's child——"

Miss Marple interrupted him.

"Oh! but that wouldn't have been nearly as satisfactory from his point of view. It's like King Cophetua and the beggar maid. If you're really rather a lonely, tired old man, and if, perhaps, your own family have been neglecting you"—she paused for a second—"well, to befriend someone who will be overwhelmed with your magnificence—(to put it rather melodramatically, but I hope you see what I mean)—well, that's much more interesting. It makes you feel a much greater person—a beneficent monarch! The recipient is more likely to be dazzled, and that, of course, is a pleasant feeling for you." She paused and said: "Mr. Badger, you know, bought the girl in his shop some really fantastic presents, a diamond bracelet and a most expensive radio-gramophone. Took out a lot of his savings to do it. However, Mrs. Badger, who was a much more astute woman than poor Miss Harbottle (marriage, of course, *helps*), took the trouble to find out a few things. And when Mr. Badger discovered that the girl was carrying on with a *very* undesirable young man connected with the racecourses, and had actually pawned the bracelet to give him the money—well, he was completely disgusted and the affair passed over quite safely. And he gave Mrs. Badger a diamond ring the following Christmas."

Her pleasant, shrewd eyes met Sir Henry's. He wondered if what she had been saying was intended as a hint. He said:

"Are you suggesting that if there had been a young man in Ruby Keene's life, my friend's attitude towards her might have altered?"

"It probably would, you know. I dare say, in a year or two, he might have liked to arrange for her marriage himself—though more likely he wouldn't—gentlemen are usually rather selfish. But I certainly think that if Ruby Keene had had a young man she'd have been careful to keep very quiet about it."

"And the young man might have resented that?"

"I suppose that *is* the most plausible solution. It struck me, you know, that her cousin, the young woman who was at Gossington Hall this morning, looked definitely *angry* with the dead girl. What you've told me explains *why*. No doubt she was looking forward to doing very well out of the business."

"Rather a cold-blooded character, in fact?"

"That's too harsh a judgment, perhaps. The poor thing has had to earn her living, and you can't expect her to sentimentalize because a well-to-do man and woman—as you have described Mr. Gaskell and Mrs. Jefferson—are going to be done out of a further large sum of money to which they have really no particular moral right. I should say Miss Turner was a hard-headed, ambitious young woman, with a good temper and considerable *joie de vivre*. A little," added Miss Marple, "like Jessie Golden, the baker's daughter."

"What happened to her?" asked Sir Henry.

"She trained as a nursery governess and married the son of the house, who was home on leave from India. Made him a very good wife, I believe."

Sir Henry pulled himself clear of these fascinating side issues. He said:

"Is there any reason, do you think, why my friend Conway Jefferson should suddenly have developed this 'Cophetua complex,' if you like to call it that?"

"There might have been."

"In what way?"

Miss Marple said, hesitating a little:

"I should think—it's only a suggestion, of course—that perhaps his son-in-law and daughter-in-law *might* have wanted to get married again."

"Surely he couldn't have objected to that?"

"Oh, no, not *objected*. But, you see, you must look at it from *his* point of view. He had a terrible shock and loss—so had they. The three bereaved people live together and the *link* between them is the loss they have all sustained. But Time, as my dear mother used to say, is a great healer. Mr. Gaskell and Mrs. Jefferson are young. Without knowing it themselves, they may have begun to feel restless, to resent the bonds that tied them to their past sorrow. And so, feeling like that, old Mr. Jefferson would have become conscious of a sudden lack of sympathy without knowing its cause. It's usually that. Gentlemen so *easily* feel neglected. With Mr. Harbottle it was Miss Harbottle going away. And with the Badgers it was Mrs. Badger taking such an interest in Spiritualism and always going out to séances."

"I must say," said Sir Henry ruefully, "that I do dislike the way you reduce us all to a General Common Denominator."

Miss Marple shook her head sadly.

"Human nature is very much the same anywhere, Sir Henry."

Sir Henry said distastefully:

"Mr. Harbottle! Mr. Badger! And poor Conway! I hate to intrude the personal note, but have you any parallel for *my* humble self in your village?"

"Well, of course, there is Briggs."

"Who's Briggs?"

"He was the head gardener up at Old Hall. *Quite* the best man they ever had. Knew *exactly* when the under-gardeners were slacking off—quite uncanny it was! He managed with only three men and a boy and the place was kept better than it had been with six. And took several firsts with his sweet peas. He's retired now."

"Like me," said Sir Henry.

"But he still does a little jobbing—if he likes the people."

"Ah," said Sir Henry. "Again like me. That's what I'm doing now—jobbing—to help an old friend."

"Two old friends."

"Two?" Sir Henry looked a little puzzled.

Miss Marple said:

"I suppose you meant Mr. Jefferson. But I wasn't thinking of him. I was thinking of Colonel and Mrs. Bantry."

"Yes—yes—I see——" He asked sharply: "Was that why you alluded to Dolly Bantry as 'poor dear' at the beginning of our conversation?"

"Yes. She hasn't begun to realize things yet. *I* know because I've had more experience. You see, Sir Henry, it seems to me that there's a great possibility of this crime being the kind of crime that never *does* get solved. Like the Brighton trunk murders. But if that happens it will be absolutely disastrous for the Bantrys. Colonel Bantry, like nearly all retired military men, is really *abnormally* sensitive. He reacts very quickly to public opinion. He won't notice it for some time, and then it will begin to go home to him. A slight here, and a snub there, and invitations that are refused, and excuses that are made—and then, little by little, it will dawn upon him and he'll retire into his shell and get terribly morbid and miserable."

"Let me be sure I understand you rightly, Miss Marple. You mean that, because the body was found in his house, people will think that *he* had something to do with it?"

"Of course they will! I've no doubt they're saying so already. They'll say so more and more. And people will cold shoulder the Bantrys and avoid them. That's why the truth has got to be found out and why I was willing to come here with Mrs. Bantry. An open accusation is one thing—and quite easy for a soldier to meet. He's indignant and he has a chance of fighting. But this other *whispering* business will break him—will break them both. So you see, Sir Henry, we've *got* to find out the truth."

Sir Henry said:

"Any ideas as to why the body should have been found in his house? There must be an explanation of that. Some connection."

"Oh, of course."

"The girl was last seen here about twenty minutes to eleven. By midnight, according to the medical evidence, she was dead. Gossington's about eighteen miles from here. Good road for sixteen of those miles until one turns off the main road. A powerful car could do it in well under half an hour. Practically *any* car could average thirty-five. But why any one should either kill her here and take her body out to Gossington or should take her out to Gossington and strangle her there, I don't know."

"Of course you don't, because it didn't happen."

"Do you mean that she was strangled by some fellow who took her out in a car and he then decided to push her into the first likely house in the neighbourhood?"

"I don't think anything of the kind. I think there was a very careful plan made. What happened was that the plan went wrong."

Sir Henry stared at her.

"Why did the plan go wrong?"

Miss Marple said rather apologetically:

"Such curious things happen, don't they? If I were to say that this particular plan went wrong because human beings are so much more vulnerable and sensitive than any one thinks, it wouldn't sound sensible, would it? But that's what I believe—and——"

She broke off. "Here's Mrs. Bantry now."

Chapter 9

MRS. BANTRY was with Adelaide Jefferson. The former came up to Sir Henry and exclaimed: "*You?*"

"I, myself." He took both her hands and pressed them warmly. "I can't tell you how distressed I am at all this, Mrs. B."

Mrs. Bantry said mechanically:

"*Don't call me Mrs. B!*" and went on: "Arthur isn't here. He's taking it all rather seriously. Miss Marple and I have come here to sleuth. Do you know Mrs. Jefferson?"

"Yes, of course."

He shook hands. Adelaide Jefferson said:

"Have you seen my father-in-law?"

"Yes, I have."

"I'm glad. We're anxious about him. It was a terrible shock."

Mrs. Bantry said:

"Let's come out on the terrace and have drinks and talk about it all."

The four of them went out and joined Mark Gaskell, who was sitting at the extreme end of the terrace by himself.

After a few desultory remarks and the arrival of the drinks Mrs. Bantry plunged straight into the subject with her usual zest for direct action.

"We can talk about it, can't we?" she said. "I mean, we're all old friends—except Miss Marple and she knows all about crime. And she wants to help."

Mark Gaskell looked at Miss Marple in a somewhat puzzled fashion. He said doubtfully:

"Do you—er—write detective stories?"

The most unlikely people, he knew, wrote detective stories.

And Miss Marple, in her old-fashioned spinster's clothes, looked a singularly unlikely person.

"Oh no, I'm not clever enough for *that.*"

"She's wonderful," said Mrs. Bantry impatiently. "I can't explain now, but she is. Now, Addie, I want to know all about things. What was she really like, this girl?"

"Well——" Adelaide Jefferson paused, glanced across at Mark, and half laughed. She said: "You're so direct."

"Did you like her?"

"No, of course I didn't"

"What was she really like?" Mrs. Bantry shifted her inquiry to ask Mark Gaskell. Mark said deliberately:

"Common or garden gold-digger. And she knew her stuff. She'd got her hooks into Jeff all right."

Both of them called their father-in-law Jeff.

Sir Henry thought, looking disapprovingly at Mark:

"Indiscreet fellow. Shouldn't be so outspoken."

He had always disapproved a little of Mark Gaskell. The man had charm but he was unreliable—talked too much, was occasionally boastful—not quite to be trusted, Sir Henry thought. He had sometimes wondered if Conway Jefferson thought so too.

"But couldn't you *do* something about it?" demanded Mrs. Bantry.

Mark said dryly:

"We might have—if we'd realized it in time."

He shot a glance at Adelaide and she coloured faintly. There had been reproach in that glance.

She said:

"Mark thinks I ought to have seen what was coming."

"You left the old boy alone too much, Addie. Tennis lessons and all the rest of it."

"Well, I had to have some exercise." She spoke apologetically. "Anyway, I never dreamed——"

"No," said Mark, "neither of us ever dreamed. Jeff has always been such a sensible, level-headed old boy."

Miss Marple made a contribution to the conversation.

"Gentlemen," she said with her old-maid's way of referring to the opposite sex as though it were a species of wild animal, "are frequently not as level-headed as they seem."

"I'll say you're right," said Mark. "Unfortunately, Miss Marple, we didn't realize that. We wondered what the old boy saw in that rather insipid and meretricious little bag of tricks. But we were pleased for him to be kept happy and amused. We thought there was no harm in her. No harm in her! I wish I'd wrung her neck!"

"Mark," said Addie, "you really *must* be careful what you say."

He grinned at her engagingly.

"I suppose I must. Otherwise people will think I actually *did* wring her neck. Oh well, I suppose I'm under suspicion, anyway. If any one had an interest in seeing that girl dead it was Addie and myself."

"Mark," cried Mrs. Jefferson, half laughing and half angry, "you really *mustn't*!"

"All right, all right," said Mark Gaskell pacifically. "But I do like speaking my mind. Fifty thousand pounds our esteemed father-in-law was proposing to settle upon that half-baked nitwitted little slypuss."

"Mark, you mustn't—she's dead."

"Yes, she's dead, poor little devil. And after all, why shouldn't she use the weapons that Nature gave her? Who am I to judge? Done plenty of rotten things myself in my life. No, let's say Ruby was entitled to plot and scheme and we were mugs not to have tumbled to her game sooner."

Sir Henry said:

"What did you say when Conway told you he proposed to adopt the girl?"

Mark thrust out his hands.

"What could we say? Addie, always the little lady, retained her self-control admirably. Put a brave face upon it. I endeavoured to follow her example."

"*I* should have made a fuss!" said Mrs. Bantry.

"Well, frankly speaking, we weren't entitled to make a fuss. It was Jeff's money. We weren't his flesh and blood. He'd always been damned good to us. There was nothing for it but to bite on the bullet." He added reflectively: "But we didn't love little Ruby."

Adelaide Jefferson said:

"If only it had been some other kind of girl. Jeff had two godchildren, you know. If it had been one of them—well, one would have *understood* it." She added, with a shade of resentment: "And Jeff's always seemed so fond of Peter."

"Of course," said Mrs. Bantry. "I always have known Peter was your first husband's child—but I'd quite forgotten it. I've always thought of him as Mr. Jefferson's grandson."

"So have I," said Adelaide. Her voice held a note that made Miss Marple turn in her chair and look at her.

"It was Josie's fault," said Mark. "Josie brought her here."

Adelaide said:

"Oh, but surely you don't think it was deliberate, do you? Why, you've always liked Josie so much."

"Yes, I did like her. I thought she was a good sport."

"It was sheer accident her bringing the girl down."

"Josie's got a good head on her shoulders, my girl."

"Yes, but she couldn't foresee——"

Mark said:

"No, she couldn't. I admit it. I'm not really accusing her of planning the whole thing. But I've no doubt she saw which way the wind was blowing long before we did and kept very quiet about it."

Adelaide said with a sigh:

"I suppose one can't blame her for that."

Mark said:

"Oh, we can't blame any one for anything!"

Mrs. Bantry asked:

"Was Ruby Keene very pretty?"

Mark stared at her. "I though you'd seen——"

Mrs. Bantry said hastily:

"Oh yes, I saw her—her body. But she'd been strangled, you know, and one couldn't tell——" She shivered.

Mark said, thoughtfully:

"I don't think she was really pretty at all. She certainly wouldn't have been without any make-up. A thin ferrety little face, not much chin, teeth running down her throat, nondescript sort of nose——"

"It sounds revolting," said Mrs. Bantry.

"Oh no, she wasn't. As I say, with make-up she managed to give quite an effect of good looks, don't you think so, Addie?"

"Yes, rather chocolate-box, pink and white business. She had nice blue eyes."

"Yes, innocent baby stare, and the heavily-blacked lashes brought out the blueness. Her hair was bleached, of course. It's true, when I come to think of it, that in colouring—artifical colouring, anyway—she had a kind of spurious resemblance to Rosamund—my wife, you know. I dare say that's what attracted the old man's attention to her."

He sighed.

"Well, it's a bad business. The awful thing is that Addie and I can't help being glad, really, that she's dead——"

He quelled a protest from his sister-in-law.

"It's no good, Addie; I know what you feel. I feel the same. And I'm not going to pretend! But, at the same time, if you know what I mean, I really am most awfully concerned for Jeff about the whole business. It's hit him very hard. I——"

He stopped, and stared towards the doors leading out of the lounge on to the terrace.

"Well, well—see who's here. What an unscrupulous woman you are, Addie."

Mrs. Jefferson looked over her shoulder, uttered an exclamation and got up, a slight colour rising in her face. She walked quickly along the terrace and went up to a tall middle-aged man with a thin brown face, who was looking uncertainly about him.

Mrs. Bantry said: "Isn't that Hugo McLean?"

Mark Gaskell said:

"Hugo McClean it is. Alias William Dobbin."

Mrs. Bantry murmured:

"He's very faithful, isn't he?"

"Dog-like devotion," said Mark. "Addie's only got to whistle and Hugo comes trotting from any odd corner of the globe. Always hopes that some day she'll marry him. I dare say she will."

Miss Marple looked beamingly after them. She said:

"I see. A romance?"

"One of the good old-fashioned kind," Mark assured her. "It's being going on for years. Addie's that kind of woman."

He added meditatively: "I suppose Addie telephoned him this morning. She didn't tell me she had."

Edwards came discreetly along the terrace and paused at Mark's elbow.

"Excuse me, sir. Mr. Jefferson would like you to come up."

"I'll come at once." Mark sprang up.

He nodded to them, said: "See you later," and went off.

Sir Henry leant forward to Miss Marple. He said:

"Well, what do you think of the principal beneficiaries of the crime?"

Miss Marple said thoughtfully, looking at Adelaide Jefferson as she stood talking to her old friend:

"I should think, you know, that she was a very devoted mother."

"Oh, she is," said Mrs. Bantry. "She's simply devoted to Peter."

"She's the kind of woman," said Miss Marple, "that every one likes. The kind of woman that could go on getting married again and again. I don't mean a *man's* woman—that's quite different."

"I know what you mean," said Sir Henry.

"What you both mean," said Mrs. Bantry, "is that she's a good listener."

Sir Henry laughed. He said:

"And Mark Gaskell?"

"Ah," said Miss Marple, "he's a downy fellow."

"Village parallel, please?"

"Mr. Cargill, the builder. He bluffed a lot of people into having things done to their houses they never meant to do. And how he charged them for it! But he could always explain his bill away plausibly. A downy fellow. He married money. So did Mr. Gaskell, I understand."

"You don't like him."

"Yes, I do. Most women would. But he can't take me in. He's a very attractive person, I think. But a little unwise, perhaps, to *talk* as much as he does."

"Unwise is the word," said Sir Henry. "Mark will get himself into trouble if he doesn't look out."

A tall dark young man in white flannels came up the steps to the terrace and paused just for a minute, watching Adelaide Jefferson and Hugo McClean.

"And that," said Sir Henry obligingly, "is X, whom we might describe as an interested party. He is the tennis and dancing pro.—Raymond Starr, Ruby Keene's partner."

Miss Marple looked at him with interest. She said:

"He's very nice looking, isn't he?"

"I suppose so."

"Don't be absurd, Sir Henry," said Mrs. Bantry; "there's no supposing about it. He *is* good looking."

Miss Marple murmured:

"Mrs. Jefferson has been taking tennis lessons, I think she said."

"Do you mean anything by that, Jane, or don't you?"

Miss Marple had no chance of replying to this downright question. Young Peter Carmody came across the terrace and joined them. He addressed himself to Sir Henry:

"I say, are you a detective, too? I saw you talking to the Superintendent—the fat one is a superintendent, isn't he?"

"Quite right, my son."

"And somebody told me you were a frightfully important detective from London. The head of Scotland Yard or something like that."

"The head of Scotland Yard is usually a complete dud in books, isn't he?"

"Oh no, not nowadays. Making fun of the police is very old-fashioned. Do you know who did the murder yet?"

"Not yet, I'm afraid."

"Are you enjoying this very much, Peter." asked Mrs. Bantry.

"Well, I am, rather. It makes a change, doesn't it? I've been hunting round to see if I could find any clues, but I haven't been lucky. I've got a souvenir, though. Would you like to see it? Fancy, mother wanted me to throw it away. I do think one's parents are rather trying sometimes."

He produced from his pocket a small matchbox. Pushing it open, he disclosed the precious contents.

"See, *it's a finger-nail. Her finger-nail!* I'm going to label it *Finger-nail of the Murdered Woman* and take it back to school.

It's a good souvenir, don't you think?"

"Where did you get it?" asked Miss Marple.

"Well, it was a bit of luck, really. Because, of course, I didn't know she was going to be murdered *then*. It was before dinner last night. Ruby caught her nail in Josie's shawl and it tore it. Mums cut it off for her and gave it to me and said put it in the wastepaper basket, and I meant to, but I put it in my pocket instead, and this morning I remembered and looked to see if it was still there and it was, so now I've got it as a souvenir."

"Disgusting," said Mrs. Bantry.

Peter said politely: "Oh, do you think so?"

"Got any other souvenirs?" asked Sir Henry.

"Well, I don't know. I've got something that might be."

"Explain yourself, young man."

Peter looked at him thoughtfully. Then he pulled out an envelope. From the inside of it he extracted a piece of brown tapey substance.

"It's a bit of that chap George Bartlett's shoe-lace," he explained. "I saw his shoes outside the door this morning and I bagged a bit just in case."

"In case what?"

"In case he should be the murderer, of course. He was the last person to see her and that's always frightfully suspicious, you know. Is it nearly dinner-time, do you think? I'm frightfully hungry. It always seems such a long time between tea and dinner. Hallo, there's Uncle Hugo. I didn't know mums had asked *him* to come down. I suppose she sent for him. She always does if she's in a jam. Here's Josie coming. Hi, Josie!"

Josephine Turner, coming along the terrace, stopped and looked rather startled to see Mrs. Bantry and Miss Marple.

Mrs. Bantry said pleasantly:

"How d'you do, Miss Turner. We've come to do a bit of sleuthing!"

Josie cast a guilty glance around. She said, lowering her voice:

"It's awful. Nobody knows yet. I mean, it isn't in the papers yet. I suppose every one will be asking me questions and it's so awkward. I don't know what I ought to say."

Her glance went rather wistfully towards Miss Marple, who said: "Yes, it will be a very difficult situation for you, I'm afraid."

Josie warmed to this sympathy.

"You see, Mr. Prestcott said to me: 'Don't talk about it.' And that's all very well, but every one is sure to ask me, and you can't offend people, can you? Mr. Prestcott said he hoped I'd feel able to carry on as usual—and he wasn't very nice about it, so of course I want to do my best. And I really don't see why it should all be blamed on me."

Sir Henry said:

"Do you mind me asking you a frank question, Miss Turner?"

"Oh, do ask me anything you like," said Josie, a little insincerely.

"Has there been any unpleasantness between you and Mrs. Jefferson and Mr. Gaskell over all this?"

"Over the murder, do you mean?"

"No, I don't mean the murder."

Josie stood twisting her fingers together. She said rather sullenly:

"Well, there has and there hasn't, if you know what I mean. Neither of them have *said* anything. But I think they blamed it on me—Mr. Jefferson taking such a fancy to Ruby, I mean. It wasn't my fault, though, was it? These things happen, and I never dreamt of such a thing happening beforehand, not for a moment. I—I was quite dumbfounded."

Her words rang out with what seemed undeniable sincerity.

Sir Henry said kindly:

"I'm quite sure you were. But once it *had* happened?"

Josie's chin went up.

"Well, it was a piece of luck, wasn't it? Every one's got the right to have a piece of luck sometimes."

She looked from one to the other of them in a slightly defiant questioning manner and then went on across the terrace and into the hotel.

Peter said judicially:

"I don't think *she* did it."

Miss Marple murmured:

"It's interesting, that piece of finger-nail. It had been worrying me, you know—how to account for her nails."

"Nails?" asked Sir Henry.

"The dead girl's nails," explained Mrs. Bantry. "They were quite *short*, and now that Jane says so, of course it *was* a little unlikely. A girl like that usually has absolute talons."

Miss Marple said:

"But of course if she tore one off, then she might clip the others close, so as to match. Did they find nail parings in her room, I wonder?"

Sir Henry looked at her curiously. He said:

"I'll ask Superintendent Harper when he gets back."

"Back from where?" asked Mrs. Bantry. "He hasn't gone over to Gossington, has he?"

Sir Henry said gravely:

"No. There's been another tragedy. Blazing car in a quarry——"

Miss Marple caught her breath.

"Was there someone in the car?"

"I'm afraid so—yes."

Miss Marple said thoughtfully:

"I expect that will be the Girl Guide who's missing—Patience—no, Pamela Reeves."

Sir Henry stared at her.

"Now why on earth do you think that, Miss Marple?"

Miss Marple got rather pink.

"Well, it was given out on the wireless that she was missing from her home—since last night. And her home was Daneleigh Vale; that's not very far from here. And she was last seen at the Girl-Guide Rally up on Danebury Downs. That's very close indeed. In fact, she'd have to pass through Danemouth to get home. So it does rather fit in, doesn't it? I mean, it looks as though she might have seen—or perhaps heard—something that no one was supposed to see and hear. If so, of course, she'd be a source of danger to the murderer and she'd have to be—removed. Two things like that *must* be connected, don't you think?"

Sir Henry said, his voice dropping a little:

"You think—a second murder?"

"Why not?" Her quiet placid gaze met his. "When any one has committed one murder, they don't shrink from another, do they. Nor even from a third."

"A third? You don't think there will be a *third* murder?"

"I think it's just possible. . . .Yes, I think it's highly possible."

"Miss Marple," said Sir Henry, "you frighten me. Do you know who is going to be murdered?"

Miss Marple said: "I've a very good idea."

Chapter 10

i

SUPERINTENDENT HARPER stood looking at the charred and twisted heap of metal. A burnt-up car was always a revolting object, even without the additional gruesome burden of a charred and blackened corpse.

Venn's Quarry was a remote spot, far from any human habitation. Though actually only two miles as the crow flies from Danemouth, the approach to it was by one of those narrow, twisted, rutted roads, little more than a cart track, and which led nowhere except to the quarry itself. It was a long time now since the quarry had been worked, and the only people who came along the lane were the casual visitors in search of blackberries. As a spot to dispose of a car it was ideal. The car need not have been found for weeks but for the accident of the glow in the sky having been seen by Albert Biggs, a labourer, on his way to work.

Albert Biggs was still on the scene, though all he had to tell had been heard some time ago, but he continued to repeat the thrilling story with such embellishments as occurred to him.

"Why, dang my eyes, I said, whatever be that? Proper glow it was, up in the sky. Might be a bonfire, I says, but who's be having bonfire over to Venn's Quarry? No, I says, 'tis some mighty big fire, to be sure. But whatever would it be, I says? There's no house or farm to that direction. 'Tis over by Venn's, I says, that's where it is, to be sure. Didn't rightly know what I ought to do about it, but seeing as Constable Gregg comes along just then on his bicycle, I tells him about it. 'Twas all died down by then, but I tells him just where 'twere. 'Tis over that direction, I says. Big glare in the sky, I says. Mayhap as it's a rick, I says. One of them tramps, as likely as not, set alight of it. But I did never think as how it might be a car—far less as someone was being burnt up alive in it. 'Tis a teribble tragedy to be sure."

The Glenshire police had been busy. Cameras had clicked and the position of the charred body had been carefully noted before the police surgeon had started his own investigation.

The latter came over now to Harper, dusting black ash off his hands, his lips set grimly together.

"A pretty thorough job," he said. "Part of one foot and the shoe are about all that has escaped. Personally I myself couldn't say if the body was a man's or a woman's at the moment, though we'll get some indication from the bones, I expect. But the shoe is one of the black strapped affairs—the kind schoolgirls wear."

"There's a schoolgirl missing from the next county," said Harper; "quite close to here. Girl of sixteen or so."

"Then it's probably her," said the doctor. "Poor kid."

Harper said uneasily: "She wasn't alive when——"

"No, no, I don't think so. No signs of her having tried to get out. Body just slumped down on the seat—with the foot sticking out. She was dead when she was put there, I should say. Then the car was set fire to in order to try and get rid of the evidence."

He paused, and asked:

"Want me any longer?"

"I don't think so, thank you."

"Right, I'll be off."

He strode away to his car. Harper went over to where one of his sergeants, a man who specialized in car cases, was busy.

The latter looked up.

"Quite a clear case, sir. Petrol poured over the car and the whole thing deliberately set light to. There are three empty cans in the hedge over there."

A little further away another man was carefully arranging small objects picked out of the wreckage. There was a scorched black leather shoe and with it some scraps of scorched and blackened material. As Harper approached, his subordinate looked up and exclaimed:

"Look at this, sir. This seems to clinch it."

Harper took the small object in his hand. He said:

"Button from a Girl Guide's uniform?"

"Yes, sir."

"Yes," said Harper, "that does seem to settle it."

A decent, kindly man, he felt slightly sick. First Ruby Keene and now this child, Pamela Reeves.

He said to himself, as he had said before:

"What's come to Glenshire?"

His next move was first to ring up his own Chief Constable, and afterwards to get in touch with Colonel Melchett. The disappearance of Pamela Reeves had taken place in Radfordshire though her body had been found in Glenshire.

The next task set him was not a pleasant one. He had to break the news to Pamela Reeves's father and mother. . . .

ii

Superintendent Harper looked up consideringly at the façade of Braeside as he rang the front door bell.

Neat little villa, nice garden of about an acre and a half. The sort of place that had been built fairly freely all over the countryside in the last twenty years. Retired Army men, retired Civil Servants—that type. Nice decent folk; the worst you could say of them was that they might be a bit dull. Spent as much money as they could afford on their children's education. Not the kind of people you associated with tragedy. And now tragedy had come to them. He sighed.

He was shown at once into a lounge where a stiff man with a grey moustache and a woman whose eyes were red with weeping both sprang up. Mrs. Reeves cried out eagerly:

"You have some news of Pamela?"

Then she shrank back, as though the Superintendent's commiserating glance had been a blow.

Harper said:

"I'm afraid you must prepare yourself for bad news."

"Pamela——" faltered the woman.

Major Reeves said sharply:

"Something's happened—to the child?"

"Yes, sir."

"Do you mean she's dead?"

Mrs. Reeves burst out:

"Oh no, no," and broke into a storm of weeping. Major Reeves put his arm round his wife and drew her to him. His lips trembled but he looked inquiringly at Harper, who bent his head.

"An accident?"

"Not exactly, Major Reeves. She was found in a burnt-out car which had been abandoned in a quarry."

"In a car? In a quarry?"

His astonishment was evident.

Mrs. Reeves broke down altogether and sank down on the sofa, sobbing violently.

Superintendent Harper said:

"If you'd like me to wait a few minutes?"

Major Reeves said sharply:

"What does this mean? Foul play?"

"That's what it looks like, sir. That's why I'd like to ask you some questions if it isn't too trying for you."

"No, no, you're quite right. No time must be lost if what you suggest is true. But I can't believe it. Who would want to harm a child like Pamela?"

Harper said stolidly:

"You've already reported to your local police the circumstances of your daughter's disappearance. She left here to attend a Guides' rally and you expected her home for supper. That is right?"

"Yes."

"She was to return by bus?"

"Yes."

"I understand that, according to the story of her fellow Guides, when the rally was over Pamela said she was going into Danemouth to Woolworth's, and would catch a later bus home. That strikes you as quite a normal proceeding?"

"Oh yes. Pamela was very fond of going to Woolworth's. She often went into Danemouth to shop. The bus goes from the main road, only about a quarter of a mile from here.

"And she had no other plans, so far as you know?"

"None.

"She was not meeting anybody in Danemouth?"

"No, I'm sure she wasn't. She would have mentioned it if so.

We expected her back for supper. That's why, when it got so late and she hadn't turned up, we rang up the police. It wasn't like her not to come home."

"Your daughter had no undesirable friends—that is, friends that you didn't approve of?"

"No, there was never any trouble of that kind."

Mrs. Reeves said tearfully:

"Pam was just a child. She was very young for her age. She liked games and all that. She wasn't precocious in any way."

"Do you know a Mr. George Bartlett who is staying at the Majestic Hotel in Danemouth?"

Major Reeves stated.

"Never heard of him."

"You don't think your daughter knew him?"

"I'm quite sure she didn't."

He added sharply: "How does he come into it?"

"He's the owner of the Minoan 14 car in which your daughter's body was found."

Mrs. Reeves cried: "But then he must——"

Harper said quickly:

"He reported his car missing early to-day. It was in the courtyard of the Majestic Hotel at lunch time yesterday. Anybody might have taken the car."

"But didn't someone see who took it?"

The Superintendent shook his head.

"Dozens of cars going in and out all day. And a Minoan 14 is one of the commonest makes."

Mrs. Reeves cried:

"But aren't you doing something? Aren't you trying to find the—the devil who did this? My little girl—oh, my little girl! She wasn't burnt alive, was she? Oh, Pam, Pam. . .!"

"She didn't suffer, Mrs. Reeves. I assure you she was already dead when the car was set alight."

Reeves asked stiffly:

"How was she killed?"

Harper gave him a significant glance.

"We don't know. The fire has destroyed all evidence of that kind."

He turned to the distraught woman on the sofa.

"Believe me, Mrs. Reeves, we're doing everything we can. It's a matter of checking up. Sooner or later we shall find someone who saw your daughter in Danemouth yesterday, and saw whom she was with. It all takes time, you know. We shall have dozens, hundreds of reports coming in about a Girl Guide who was seen here, there, and everywhere. It's a matter of selection and of patience—but we shall find out the truth in the end, never you fear."

Mrs. Reeves asked:

"Where—where is she? Can I go to her?"

Again Superintendent Harper caught the husband's eye. He said:

"The medical officer is attending to all that. I'd suggest that your husband comes with me now and attends to all the formalities. In the meantime, try and recollect anything Pamela may have said—something, perhaps, that you didn't pay attention to at the time but which might throw some light upon things. You know what I mean—just some chance word or phrase. That's the best way you can help us."

As the two men went towards the door, Reeves said, pointing to a photograph:

"There she is."

Harper looked at it attentively. It was a hockey group. Reeves pointed out Pamela in the centre of the team.

"A nice kid," Harper thought, as he looked at the earnest face of the pigtailed girl.

His mouth set in a grim line as he thought of the charred body in the car.

He vowed to himself that the murder of Pamela Reeves should not remain one of the Glenshire's unsolved mysteries.

Ruby Keene, so he admitted privately, might have asked for what was coming to her, but Pamela Reeves was quite another story. A nice kid, if he ever saw one. He'd not rest until he'd hunted down the man or woman who'd killed her.

Chapter 11

A DAY or two later Colonel Melchett and Superintendent Harper looked at each other across the former's big desk. Harper had come over to Much Benham for a consultation.

Melchett said gloomily:

"Well, we know where we are—or rather where we aren't!"

"Where we aren't expresses it better, sir."

"We've got two deaths to take into account," said Melchett. "Two murders. Ruby Keene and the child Pamela Reeves. Not much to identify her by, poor kid, but enough. That shoe that escaped burning has been identified positively as hers by her father, and there's this button from her Girl Guide uniform. A fiendish business, Superintendent."

Superintendent Harper said very quietly:

"I'll say you're right, sir."

"I'm glad it's quite certain she was dead before the car was set on fire. The way she was lying, thrown across the seat, shows that. Probably knocked on the head, poor kid."

"Or strangled, perhaps," said Harper.

Melchett looked at him sharply.

"You think so?"

"Well, sir, there are murderers like that."

"I know. I've seen the parents—the poor girl's mother's beside herself. Damned painful, the whole thing. The point for us to settle is—are the two murders connected?"

"I'd say definitely yes."

"So would I."

The Superintendent ticked off the points on his fingers.

"Pamela Reeves attended rally of Girl Guides on Danebury Downs. Stated by companions to be normal and cheerful. Did not return with three companions by the bus to Medchester. Said to them that she was going into Danemouth to Woolworth's and would take the bus home from there. The main road into Danemouth from the downs does a big round inland. Pamela Reeves took a short-cut over two fields and a footpath and lane which would bring her into Danemouth near the Majestic Hotel. The lane, in fact, actually passes the hotel on the west side. It's possible, therefore, that she overheard or saw something—something concerning Ruby Keene—which would have proved dangerous to the murderer—say, for instance, that she heard him arranging to meet Ruby Keene at eleven that evening. He realizes that this schoolgirl has overheard, and he has to silence her."

Colonel Melchett said:

"That's presuming, Harper, that the Ruby Keene crime was premeditated—not spontaneous."

Superintendent Harper agreed.

"I believe it was, sir. It looks as though it would be the other way—sudden violence, a fit of passion or jealousy—but I'm beginning to think that that's not so. I don't see otherwise how you can account for the death of the Reeves child. If she was a witness of the actual crime, it would be late at night, round about eleven p.m., and what would she be doing round about the Majestic at that time? Why, at nine o'clock her parents were getting anxious because she hadn't returned."

"The alternative is that she went to meet someone in Danemouth unknown to her family and friends, and that her death is quite unconnected with the other death."

"Yes, sir, and I don't believe that's so. Look how even the old lady, old Miss Marple, tumbled to it at once that there was a connection. She asked at once if the body in the burnt car was the body of the missing Girl Guide. Very smart old lady, that. These old ladies are sometimes. Shrewd, you know. Put their fingers on the vital spot."

"Miss Marple has done that more than once," said Colonel Melchett dryly.

"And besides, sir, there's the car. That seems to me to link up her death definitely with the Majestic Hotel. It was Mr. George Bartlett's car."

Again the eyes of the two men met. Melchett said:

"George Bartlett? Could be! What do you think?"

Again Harper methodically recited various points.

"Ruby Keene was last seen with George Bartlett. He says she went to her room (borne out by the dress she was wearing being found there), but did she go to her room and change *in order to go out with him*? Had they made a date to go out together earlier—discussed it, say, before dinner, and did Pamela Reeves happen to overhear?"

Melchett said: "He didn't report the loss of his car until the following morning, and he was extremely vague about it then, pretended he couldn't remember exactly when he had last noticed it."

"That might be cleverness, sir. As I see it, he's either a very clever gentleman pretending to be a silly ass, or else—well, he is a silly ass."

"What we want," said Melchett, "is motive. As it stands, he had no motive whatever for killing Ruby Keene."

"Yes—that's where we're stuck every time. Motive. All the reports from the Palais de Danse at Brixwell are negative, I understand?"

"Absolutely! Ruby Keene had no special boy friend. Slack's been into the matter thoroughly—give Slack his due, he *is* thorough."

"That's right, sir. Thorough's the word."

"If there was anything to ferret out, he'd have ferreted it out. But there's nothing there. He got a list of her most frequent dancing partners—all vetted and found correct. Harmless fellows, and all able to produce alibis for that night."

"Ah," said Superintendent Harper. "Alibis. That's what we're up against."

Melchett looked at him sharply. "Think so? I've left that side of the investigation to you."

"Yes, sir. It's been gone into—very thoroughly. We applied to London for help over it."

"Well?"

"Mr. Conway Jefferson may think that Mr. Gaskell and young Mrs. Jefferson are comfortably off, but that is not the case. They're both extremely hard up."

"Is that true?"

"Quite true, sir. It's as Mr. Conway Jefferson said, he made over considerable sums of money to his son and daughter when they married. That was over ten years ago, though. Mr. Frank Jefferson fancied himself as knowing good investments. He didn't invest in anything absolutely wild cat, but he was unlucky and showed poor judgment more than once. His holdings have gone steadily down. I should say the widow found it difficult to make both ends meet and send her son to a good school."

"But she hasn't applied to her father-in-law for help?"

"No, sir. As far as I can make out she lives with him, and consequently has no household expenses."

"And his health is such that he wasn't expected to live long?"

"That's right, sir. Now for Mr. Mark Gaskell. He's a gambler, pure and simple. Got through his wife's money very soon. Has got himself tangled up rather critically just at present. He needs money badly—and a good deal of it."

"Can't say I liked the looks of him much," said Colonel Melchett. "Wild-looking sort of fellow—what? And he's got a motive all right. Twenty-five thousand pounds it meant to him getting that girl out of the way. Yes, it's a motive all right."

"They both had a motive."

"I'm not considering Mrs. Jefferson."

"No, sir, I know you're not. And, anyway, the alibi holds for both of them. They *couldn't* have done it. Just that."

"You've got a detailed statement of their movements that evening?"

"Yes, I have. Take Mr. Gaskell first. He dined with his father-in-law and Mrs. Jefferson, had coffee with them afterwards when Ruby Keene joined them. Then he said he had to write letters and left them. Actually he took his car and went for a spin down to the front. He told me quite frankly he couldn't stick playing bridge for a whole evening. The old boy's mad on it. So he made letters an excuse. Ruby Keene remained with the others. Mark Gaskell returned when she was dancing with Raymond. After the dance Ruby came and had a drink with them, then she went off with young Bartlett, and Gaskell and the others cut for partners and started their bridge. That was at twenty minutes to eleven—and he didn't leave the table until after midnight. That's quite certain, sir. Every one says so. The family, the waiters, every one. Therefore *he* couldn't have done it. And Mrs. Jefferson's alibi is the same. She, too, didn't leave the table. They're out, both of them—out."

Colonel Melchett leaned back, tapping the table with a paper cutter.

Superintendent Harper said:

"That is, assuming the girl was killed before midnight."

"Haydock said she was. He's a very sound fellow in police work. If he says a thing, it's so."

"There might be reasons—health, physical idiosyncrasy or something."

"I'll put it to him." Melchett glanced at his watch, picked up the telephone receiver and asked for a number. He said: "Haydock ought to be at home at this time. Now, assuming that she was killed *after* midnight?"

Harper said:

"Then there might be a chance. There was some coming and going afterwards. Let's assume that Gaskell had asked the girl to meet him outside somewhere—say at twenty-past twelve. He slips away for a minute or two, strangles her, comes back and disposes of the body later—in the early hours of the morning."

Melchett said:

"Takes her by car thirty-odd miles to put her in Bantry's library? Dash it all, it's not a likely story."

"No, it isn't," the Superintendent admitted at once.

The telephone rang. Melchett picked up the receiver.

"Hallo, Haydock, is that you? Ruby Keene. Would it be possible for her to have been killed *after* midnight?"

"I told you she was killed between ten and midnight."

"Yes, I know, but one could stretch it a bit—what?"

"No, you couldn't stretch it. When I say she was killed before midnight I mean before midnight, and don't try to tamper with the medical evidence."

"Yes, but couldn't there be some physiological what-not? You know what I mean."

"I know that you don't know what you're talking about. The girl was perfectly healthy and not abnormal in any way—and I'm not going to say she was just to help you fit a rope round the neck of some wretched fellow whom you police wallahs have got your knife into. Now don't protest. I know your ways. And, by the way, the girl wasn't strangled willingly—that is to say, she was drugged first. Powerful narcotic. She died of strangulation but she was drugged first." Haydock rang off.

Melchett said gloomily: "Well, that's that."

Harper said:

"Thought I'd found another likely starter—but it petered out."

"What's that? Who?"

"Strictly speaking, he's your pigeon, sir. Name of Basil Blake. Lives near Gossington Hall."

"Impudent young jackanapes!" The Colonel's brow darkened as he remembered Basil Blake's outrageous rudeness. "How's he mixed up in it?"

"Seems he knew Ruby Keene. Dined over at the Majestic quite often—danced with the girl. Do you remember what Josie said to Raymond when Ruby was discovered to be missing? 'She's not with that film fellow, is she?' I've found out it was Blake she meant. He's employed with the Lemville Studios, you know. Josie has nothing to go upon except a belief that Ruby was rather keen on him."

"Very promising, Harper, very promising."

"Not so good as it sounds, sir. Basil Blake was at a party at the studios that night. You know the sort of thing. Starts at eight with cocktails and goes on and on until the air's too thick to see through and every one passes out. According to Inspector Slack, who's questioned him, he left the show round about midnight. At midnight Ruby Keene was dead."

"Any one bear out his statement?"

"Most of them, I gather, sir, were rather—er—far gone. The —er—young woman now at the bungalow—Miss Dinah Lee—says his statement is correct."

"Doesn't mean a thing!"

"No, sir, probably not. Statements taken from other members of the party bear Mr. Blake's statement out on the whole, though ideas as to time are somewhat vague."

"Where are these studios?"

"Lemville, sir, thirty miles south-west of London."

"H'm—about the same distance from here?"

"Yes, sir."

Colonel Melchett rubbed his nose. He said in a rather dissatisfied tone:

"Well, it looks as though we could wash him out."

"I think so, sir. There is no evidence that he was seriously attracted by Ruby Keene. In fact"—Superintendent coughed primly—"he seems fully occupied with his own young lady."

Melchett said:

"Well, we are left with 'X,' an unknown murderer—so unknown Slack can't find a trace of him! Or Jefferson's son-in-law, who might have wanted to kill the girl—but didn't have a chance to do so. Daughter-in-law ditto. Or George Bartlett, who has no alibi—but unfortunately no motive either. Or with young Blake, who has an alibi and no motive. And that's the lot! No, stop, I suppose we ought to consider the dancing fellow—Raymond Starr. After all, he saw a lot of the girl."

Harper said slowly:

"Can't believe he took much interest in her—or else he's a thundering good actor. And, for all practical purposes, he's got an alibi too. He was more or less in view from twenty minutes to eleven until midnight, dancing with various partners. I don't see that we can make a case against him."

"In fact," said Colonel Melchett, "we can't make a case against anybody."

"George Bartlett's our best hope. If we could only hit on a motive."

"You've had him looked up?"

"Yes, sir. Only child. Coddled by his mother. Came into a good deal of money on her death a year ago. Getting through it fast. Weak rather than vicious."

"May be mental," said Melchett hopefully.

Superintendent Harper nodded. He said:

"Has it struck you, sir—that that may be the explanation of the whole case?"

"Criminal lunatic, you mean?"

"Yes, sir. One of those fellows who go about strangling young girls. Doctors have a long name for it."

"That would solve all our difficulties," said Melchett.

"There's only one thing I don't like about it," said Superintendent Harper.

"What?"

"It's too easy."

"H'm—yes—perhaps. So, as I said at the beginning, where are we?"

"Nowhere, sir," said Superintendent Harper.

Chapter 12

i

CONWAY JEFFERSON stirred in his sleep and stretched. His arms were flung out, long, powerful arms into which all the strength of his body seemed to be concentrated since his accident.

Through the curtains the morning light glowed softly.

Conway Jefferson smiled to himself. Always, after a night of rest, he woke like this, happy, refreshed, his deep vitality renewed. Another day!

So for a minute he lay. Then he pressed the special bell by his hand. And suddenly a wave of remembrance swept over him.

Even as Edwards, deft and quiet-footed, entered the room, a groan was wrung from his master.

Edwards paused with his hand on the curtains. He said: "You're not in pain, sir?"

Conway Jefferson said harshly:

"No. Go on, pull 'em."

The clear light flooded the room. Edwards, understanding, did not glance at his master.

His face grim, Conway Jefferson lay remembering and thinking. Before his eyes he saw again the pretty, vapid face of Ruby. Only in his mind he did not use the adjective vapid. Last night he would have said innocent. A naîve, innocent child! And now?

A great weariness came over Conway Jefferson. He closed his eyes. He murmured below his breath:

"Margaret. . ."

It was the name of his dead wife. . . .

ii

"I like your friend," said Adelaide Jefferson to Mrs. Bantry.

The two women were sitting on the terrace.

"Jane Marple's a very remarkable woman," said Mrs. Bantry.

"She's nice too," said Addie, smiling.

"People call her a scandalmonger," said Mrs. Bantry, "but she isn't really."

"Just a low opinion of human nature?"

"You could call it that."

"It's rather refreshing," said Adelaide Jefferson, "after having had too much of the other thing."

Mrs. Bantry looked at her sharply.

Addie explained herself.

"So much high-thinking—idealization of an unworthy object!"

"You mean Ruby Keene?"

Addie nodded.

"I don't want to be horrid about her. There wasn't any harm in her. Poor little rat, she had to fight for what she wanted. She wasn't bad. Common and rather silly and quite good-natured, but a decided little gold-digger. I don't think she schemed or planned. It was just that she was quick to take advantage of a possibility. And she knew just how to appeal to an elderly man who *was*—lonely."

"I suppose," said Mrs. Bantry thoughtfully, "that Conway *was* lonely?"

Addie moved restlessly. She said:

"He was—this summer." She paused and then burst out: "Mark will have it that it was all my fault. Perhaps it was, I don't know."

She was silent for a minute, then, impelled by some need to talk, she went on speaking in a difficult, almost reluctant way.

"I—I've had such an odd sort of life. Mike Carmody, my first husband, died so soon after we were married—it—it knocked me out. Peter, as you know, was born after his death. Frank Jefferson was Mike's great friend. So I came to see a lot of him. He was Peter's godfather—Mike had wanted that. I got very fond of him—and—oh! sorry for him too."

"Sorry?" queried Mrs. Bantry with interest.

"Yes, just that. It sounds odd. Frank had always had everything he wanted. His father and his mother couldn't have been nicer to him. And yet—how can I say it?—you see, old Mr. Jefferson's personality is so strong. If you live with it, you can't somehow have a personality of your own. Frank felt that.

"When we were married he was very happy—wonderfully so. Mr. Jefferson was very generous. He settled a large sum of money on Frank—said he wanted his children to be independent and not have to wait for his death. It was so nice of him—so generous. But it was much too sudden. He ought really to have accustomed Frank to independence little by little.

"It went to Frank's head. He wanted to be as good a man as his father, as clever about money and business, as far-seeing and successful. And, of course, he wasn't. He didn't exactly speculate with the money, but he invested in the wrong things at the wrong time. It's frightening, you know, how soon money goes if you're not clever about it. The more Frank dropped, the more eager he was to get it back by some clever deal. So things went from bad to worse."

"But, my dear," said Mrs. Bantry, "couldn't Conway have advised him?"

"He didn't want to be advised. The one thing he wanted was to do well on his own. That's why we never let Mr. Jefferson know. When Frank died there was very little left—only a tiny income for me. And I-I didn't let his father know either. You see——"

She turned abruptly.

"It would have felt like betraying Frank to him. Frank would have hated it so. Mr. Jefferson was ill for a long time. When he got well he assumed that I was a very-well-off widow. I've never undeceived him. It's been a point of honour. He knows I'm very careful about money—but he approves of that, thinks I'm a thrifty sort of woman. And, of course, Peter and I have lived with him practically ever since, and he's paid for all our living expenses. So I've never had to worry."

She said slowly:

"We've been like a family all these years—only—only—you see (or don't you see?) I've never been Frank's *widow* to him—

I've been Frank's *wife*."

Mrs. Bantry grasped the implication.

"You mean he's never accepted their deaths?"

"No. He's been wonderful. But he's conquered his own terrible tragedy by refusing to recognize death. Mark is Rosamund's husband and I'm Frank's wife—and though Frank and Rosamund aren't exactly here with us—they are still existent."

Mrs. Bantry said softly:

"It's a wonderful triumph of faith."

"I know. We've gone on, year after year. But suddenly—this summer—something went wrong in me. I felt—I felt rebellious. It's an awful thing to say, but I didn't want to think of Frank any more! All that was over—my love and companionship with him, and my grief when he died. It was something that had been and wasn't any longer.

"It's awfully hard to describe. It's like wanting to wipe the slate clean and start again. I wanted to be me—Addie, still reasonably young and strong and able to play games and swim and dance—just a *person*. Even Hugo—(you know Hugo McLean?) he's a dear and wants to marry me, but, of course, I've never really thought of it—but this summer I *did* begin to think of it—not seriously—only vaguely. . ."

She stopped and shook her head.

"And so I suppose it's true. *I neglected Jeff*. I don't mean *really* neglected him, but my mind and thoughts weren't with him. When Ruby, as I saw, amused him, I was rather glad. It left me freer to go and do my own things. I never dreamed—of course I never dreamed—that he would be so—so—*infatuated* by her!"

Mrs. Bantry asked:

"And when you did find out?"

"I was dumbfounded—absolutely dumbfounded! And, I'm afraid, angry too."

"*I*'d have been angry," said Mrs. Bantry.

"There was Peter, you see. Peter's whole future depends on Jeff. Jeff practically looked on him as a grandson, or so I thought, but, of course, he wasn't a grandson. He was no relation at all. And to think that he was going to be—disinherited!" Her firm, well-shaped hands shook a little where they lay in her lap. "For that's what it felt like—and for a vulgar, gold-digging little simpleton——Oh! I could have killed her!"

She stopped, stricken. Her beautiful hazel eyes met Mrs. Bantry's in a pleading horror. She said:

"*What an awful thing to say!*"

Hugo McLean, coming quietly up behind them, asked:

"What's an awful thing to say?"

"Sit down, Hugo. You know Mrs. Bantry, don't you?"

McLean had already greeted the older lady. He said now in a slow, persevering way:

"What was an awful thing to say?"

Addie Jefferson said:

"That I'd like to have killed Ruby Keene."

Hugo McLean reflected a minute or two. Then he said:

"No, I wouldn't say that if I were you. Might be misunderstood."

His eyes—steady, reflective, grey eyes—looked at her meaningly.

He said:

"*You've got to watch your step, Addie.*"

There was a warning in his voice.

iii

When Miss Marple came out of the hotel and joined Mrs. Bantry a few minutes later, Hugo McLean and Adelaide Jefferson were walking down the path to the sea together.

Seating herself, Miss Marple remarked:

"He seems very devoted."

"He's been devoted for years! One of those men."

"I know. Like Major Bury. He hung around an Anglo-Indian widow for quite ten years. A joke among her friends! In the end she gave in—but unfortunately ten days before they were to have been married she ran away with the chauffeur! Such a nice woman, too, and usually so well balanced."

"People do do very odd things," agreed Mrs. Bantry. "I wish you'd been here just now, Jane. Addie Jefferson was telling me all about herself—how her husband went through all his money but they never let Mr. Jefferson know. And then, this summer, things felt different to her——"

Miss Marple nodded.

"Yes. She rebelled, I suppose, against being made to live in the past? After all, there's a time for everything. You can't sit in the house with the blinds down for ever. I suppose Mrs. Jefferson just pulled them up and took off her widow's weeds, and her father-in-law, of course, didn't like it. Felt left out in the cold, though I don't suppose for a minute he realized who put her up to it. Still, he certainly wouldn't like it! And so, of course, like old Mr. Badger when his wife took up Spiritualism, he was just ripe for what happened. Any fairly nice-looking young girl who listened prettily would have done."

"Do you think," said Mrs. Bantry, "that that cousin, Josie, got her down here deliberately—that it was a family plot?"

Miss Marple shook her head.

"No, I don't think so at all. I don't think Josie has the kind of mind that could foresee people's reactions. She's rather dense in that way. She's got one of those shrewd, limited, practical minds that never do foresee the future and are usually astonished by it."

"It seems to have taken every one by surprise," said Mrs. Bantry. "Addie—and Mark Gaskell too, apparently."

Miss Marple smiled.

"I dare say he had his own fish to fry. A bold fellow with a roving eye! Not the man to go on being a sorrowing widower for years, no matter how fond he may have been of his wife. I should think they were both restless under old Mr. Jefferson's yoke of perpetual remembrance."

"Only," added Miss Marple cynically, "it's easier for gentlemen, of course."

iv

At that very moment Mark was confirming this judgment on himself in a talk with Sir Henry Clithering.

With characteristic candour Mark had gone straight to the

heart of things.

"It's just dawned on me," he said, "that I'm Favourite Suspect No. 1 to the police! They've been delving into my financial troubles. I'm broke, you know, or very nearly. If dear old Jeff dies according to schedule in a month or two, and Addie and I divide the dibs also according to schedule, all will be well. Matter of fact, I owe rather a lot. . . . If the crash comes it will be a big one! If I can stave it off, it will be the other way round—I shall come out on top and be a very rich man."

Sir Henry Clithering said:

"You're a gambler, Mark."

"Always have been. Risk everything—that's my motto! Yes, it's a lucky thing for me that somebody strangled that poor kid. I didn't do it. I'm not a strangler. I don't really think I could ever murder anybody. I'm too easy going. But I don't suppose I can ask the police to believe *that*! I must look to them like the answer to the criminal investigator's prayer! I had a motive, was on the spot, I am not burdened with high moral scruples! I can't imagine why I'm not in jug already! That Superintendent's got a very nasty eye."

"You've got that useful thing, an alibi."

"An alibi is the fishiest thing on God's earth! No innocent person ever has an alibi! Besides, it all depends on the time of death, or something like that, and you may be sure if three doctors say the girl was killed at midnight, at least six will be found who will swear positively that she was killed at five in the morning—and where's my alibi then?"

"At anyrate, you are able to joke about it."

"Damned bad taste, isn't it?" said Mark cheerfully. "Actually, I'm rather scared. One is—with murder! And don't think I'm not sorry for old Jeff. I am. But it's better this way—bad as the shock was—than if he'd found her out."

"What do you mean, found her out?"

Mark winked.

"Where did she go off to last night? I'll lay you any odds you like she went to meet a man. Jeff wouldn't have liked that. He wouldn't have liked it at all. If he'd found she was deceiving him—that she wasn't the prattling little innocent she seemed—well—my father-in-law is an odd man. He's a man of great self-control, but that self-control can snap. And then—look out!"

Sir Henry glanced at him curiously.

"Are you fond of him or not?"

"I'm very fond of him—and at the same time I resent him. I'll try and explain. Conway Jefferson is a man who likes to control his surroundings. He's a benevolent despot, kind, generous, and affectionate—but his is the tune, and the others dance to his piping."

Mark Gaskell paused.

"I loved my wife. I shall never feel the same for any one else. Rosamund was sunshine and laughter and flowers, and when she was killed I felt just like a man in the ring who's had a knock-out blow. But the referee's been counting a good long time now. I'm a man, after all. I like women. I don't want to marry again—not in the least. Well, that's all right. I've had to be discreet—but I've had my good times all right. Poor Addie hasn't. Addie's a really nice woman. She's the kind of woman men want to marry, not to sleep with. Give her half a chance and she would marry again—and be very happy and make the chap happy too. But old Jeff saw her always as Frank's wife—and hypnotized her into seeing herself like that. He doesn't know it, but we've been in prison. I broke out, on the quiet, a long time ago. Addie broke out this summer—and it gave him a shock. It split up his world. Result—Ruby Keene."

Irrepressibly he sang:

> *"But she is dead and in her grave,*
> *And, oh, the difference to me!*

"Come and have a drink, Clithering."

It was hardly surprising, Sir Henry reflected, that Mark Gaskell should be an object of suspicion to the police.

Chapter 13

i

DR. METCALF was one of the best-known physicians in Danemouth. He had no aggressive bedside manner, but his presence in the sick room had an invariably cheering effect. He was middle-aged, with a quiet pleasant voice.

He listened carefully to Superintendent Harper and replied to his questions with gentle precision.

Harper said:

"Then I can take it, Doctor Metcalf, that what I was told by Mrs. Jefferson is substantially correct?"

"Yes, Mr. Jefferson's health is in a precarious state. For several years now the man has been driving himself ruthlessly. In his determination to live like other men, he has lived at a far greater pace than the normal man of his age. He has refused to rest, to take things easy, to go slow—or any of the other phrases with which I and his other medical advisers have tendered our opinion. The result is that the man is an overworked engine. Heart, lungs, blood pressure—they're all overstrained."

"You say Mr. Jefferson has absolutely refused to listen?"

"Yes. I don't know that I blame him. It's not what I say to my patients, Superintendent, but a man may as well wear out as rust out. A lot of my colleagues do that, and take it from me it's not a bad way. In a place like Danemouth one sees most of the other thing: invalids clinging to life, terrified of over-exerting themselves, terrified of a breath of draughty air, of a stray germ, of an injudicious meal!"

"I expect that's true enough," said Superintendent Harper. "What it amounts to, then, is this: Conway Jefferson is strong enough, physically speaking—or, I suppose I mean, muscularly speaking. Just what can he do in the active line, by the way?"

"He has immense strength in his arms and shoulders. He was a powerful man before his accident. He is extremely dexterous in his handling of his wheeled chair, and with the aid of crutches he can move himself about a room—from his bed to the chair, for instance."

"Isn't it possible for a man injured as Mr. Jefferson was to have artificial legs?"

"Not in his case. There was a spine injury."

"I see. Let me sum up again. Jefferson is strong and fit in the muscular sense. He feels well and all that?"

Metcalf nodded.

"But his heart is in a bad condition. Any overstrain or exertion, or a shock or sudden fright, and he might pop off. Is that it?"

"More or less. Over-exertion is killing him slowly, because he won't give in when he feels tired. That aggravates the cardiac condition. It is unlikely that exertion would kill him suddenly. But a sudden shock or fright might easily do so. That is why I expressly warned his family."

Superintendent Harper said slowly:

"But in actual fact a shock *didn't* kill him. I mean, doctor, that there couldn't have been a much worse shock than this business, and he's still alive?"

Dr. Metcalf shrugged his shoulders.

"I know. But if you'd had my experience, Superintendent, you'd know that case history shows the impossibility of prognosticating accurately. People who *ought* to die of shock and exposure *don't* die of shock and exposure, etc., etc. The human frame is tougher than one can imagine possible. Moreover, in my experience, a physical shock is more often fatal than a *mental* shock. In plain language, a door banging suddenly would be more likely to kill Mr. Jefferson than the discovery that a girl he was fond of had died in a particularly horrible manner."

"Why is that, I wonder?"

"The breaking of a piece of bad news nearly always sets up a defence reaction. It numbs the recipient. They are unable—at first—to take it in. Full realization takes a little time. But the banged door, someone jumping out of a cupbaord, the sudden onslaught of a motor as you cross a road—all those things are immediate in their action. The heart gives a terrified leap—to put it in layman's language."

Superintendent Harper said slowly:

"But as far as any one would know, Mr. Jefferson's death might easily have been caused by the shock of the girl's death?"

"Oh, easily." The doctor looked curiously at the other. "You don't think——"

"I don't know what I think," said Superintendent Harper vexedly.

ii

"But you'll admit, sir, that the two things would fit in very prettily together," he said a little later to Sir Henry Clithering. "Kill two birds with one stone. First the girl—and the fact of her death takes off Mr. Jefferson too—before he's had any opportunity of altering his will."

"Do you think he will alter it?"

"You'd be more likely to know that, sir, than I would. What do you say?"

"I don't know. Before Ruby Keene came on the scene I happen to know that he had left his money between Mark Gaskell and Mrs. Jefferson. I don't see why he should now change his mind about that. But of course he might do so. Might leave it to a Cats' Home, or to subsidize young professional dancers."

Superintendent Harper agreed.

"You never know what bee a man is going to get in his bonnet—especially when he doesn't feel there's any moral obligation in the disposal of his fortune. No blood relations in this case.

Sir Henry said:

"He is fond of the boy—of young Peter."

"D'you think he regards him as a grandson? You'd know better than I would, sir."

Sir Henry said slowly:

"No, I don't think so."

"There's another thing I'd like to ask you, sir. It's a thing I can't judge for myself. But they're friends of yours and so you'd know. I'd like very much to know just how fond Mr. Jefferson is of Mr. Gaskell and young Mrs. Jefferson."

Sir Henry frowned.

"I'm not sure if I understand you, Superintendent?"

"Well, it's this way, sir. How fond is he of them as *persons*—apart from his relationship to them?"

"Ah, I see what you mean."

"Yes, sir. Nobody doubts that he was very attached to them both—but he was attached to them, as I see it, because they were, respectively, the husband and the wife of his daughter and his son. But supposing, for instance, one of them had married again?

Sir Henry reflected. He said:

"It's an interesting point you raise there. I don't know. I'm inclined to suspect—this is a mere opinion—that it would have altered his attitude a good deal. He would have wished them well, borne no rancour, but I think, yes, I rather think that he would have taken very little more interest in them."

"In both cases, sir?"

"I think so, yes. In Mr. Gaskell's, almost certainly, and I rather think in Mrs. Jefferson's also, but that's not nearly so certain. I think he *was* fond of her for her own sake."

"Sex would have something to do with that," said Superintendent Harper sapiently. "Easier for him to look on her as a daughter than to look on Mr. Gaskell as a son. It works both ways. Women accept a son-in-law as one of the family easily enough, but there aren't many times when a woman looks on her son's wife as a daughter."

Superintendent Harper went on:

"Mind if we walk along this path, sir, to the tennis court? I see Miss Marple's sitting there. I want to ask her to do something for me. As a matter of fact I want to rope you both in."

"In what way, Superintendent?"

"To get at stuff that I can't get at myself. I want you to tackle Edwards for me, sir."

"Edwards? What do you want from him?"

"Everything you can think of! Everything he knows and what he thinks! About the relations between the various members of the family, his angle on the Ruby Keene business. Inside stuff. He knows better than any one the state of affairs—you bet he does! And he wouldn't tell *me*. But he'll tell *you*. Because you're a gentleman and a friend of Mr. Jefferson's. And something *might* turn up from it. That is, of course, if you don't object?"

Sir Henry said grimly:

"I don't object. I've been sent for, urgently, to get at the truth. I mean to do my utmost."

He added:

"How do you want Miss Marple to help you?"

"With some girls. Some of those Girl Guides. We've rounded up half a dozen or so, the ones who were most friendly with Pamela Reeves. It's possible that they may know something. You see, I've been thinking. It seems to me that if that girl was really going to Woolworth's she would have tried to persuade one of the other girls to go with her. Girls usually like to shop with someone."

"Yes, I think that's true."

"So I think it's possible that Woolworth's was only an excuse. I want to know where the girl was really going. She may have let slip something. If so, I feel Miss Marple's the person to get it out of these girls. I'd say she knows a thing or two about girls—more than I do. And, anyway, they'd be scared of the police."

"It sounds to me the kind of village domestic problem that is right up Miss Marple's street. She's very sharp, you know."

The Superintendent smiled. He said:

"I'll say you're right. Nothing much gets past her."

Miss Marple looked up at their approach and welcomed them eagerly. She listened to the Superintendent's request and at once acquiesced.

"I should like to help you very much, Superintendent, and I think perhaps I *could* be of some use. What with the Sunday School, you know, and the Brownies, and our Guides, and the Orphanage quite near—I'm on the committee, you know, and often run in to have a little talk with Matron—and then *servants*—I usually have very young maids. Oh, yes, I've quite a lot of experience in when a girl is speaking the truth and when she is holding something back."

"In fact, you're an expert," said Sir Henry.

Miss Marple flashed him a reproachful glance and said:

"Oh, *please* don't laugh at me, Sir Henry."

"I shouldn't dream of laughing at you. You've had the laugh of me too many times."

"One does see so much evil in a village," murmured Miss Marple in an explanatory voice.

"By the way," said Sir Henry, "I've cleared up one point you asked me about. The Superintendent tells me that there were nail clippings in Ruby's wastepaper-basket."

Miss Marple said thoughtfully:

"There were? Then that's that. . . ."

"Why did you want to know, Miss Marple?" asked the Superintendent.

Miss Marple said:

"It was one of things that—well, that seemed *wrong* when I looked at the body. The hands were wrong, somehow, and I couldn't at first think *why*. Then I realized that girls who are very much made-up, and all that, usually have very long finger-nails. Of course, I know that girls everywhere do bite their nails—it's one of those habits that are very hard to break oneself of. But vanity often does a lot to help. Still, I presumed that this girl *hadn't* cured herself. And then the little boy—Peter, you know—he said something which showed that her nails *had* been long, only she caught one and broke it. So then, of course, she might have trimmed off the rest to make an even appearance, and I asked about clippings and Sir Henry said he'd find out."

Sir Henry remarked:

"You said just now, '*one* of the things that seemed wrong when you looked at the body.' Was there something else?"

Miss Marple nodded vigorously.

"Oh yes!" she said. "There was the dress. The dress was *all* wrong."

Both men looked at her curiously.

"Now why?" said Sir Henry.

"Well, you see, it was an old dress. Josie said so, definitely, and I could see for myself that it was shabby and rather worn. Now that's all wrong."

"I don't see why?"

Miss Marple got a little pink.

"Well, the idea is, isn't it, that Ruby Keene changed her dress and went off to meet someone on whom she presumably had what my young nephews call a 'crush'?"

The Superintendent's eyes twinkled a little.

"That's the theory. She'd got a date with someone—a boy friend, as the saying goes."

"Then why," demanded Miss Marple, "was she wearing an old dress?"

The Superintendent scratched his head thoughtfully. He said:

"I see your point. You think she'd wear a new one?"

"I think she'd wear her best dress. Girls do."

Sir Henry interposed.

"Yes, but look here, Miss Marple. Suppose she was going outside to this *rendezvous*. Going in an open car, perhaps, or walking in some rough going. Then she'd not want to risk messing a new frock and she'd put on an old one."

"That would be the sensible thing to do," agreed the Superintendent.

Miss Marple turned on him. She spoke with animation.

"The sensible thing to do would be to change into trousers and a pullover, or into tweeds. That, of course (I don't want to be snobbish, but I'm afraid it's unavoidable), that's what a girl of—of our class would do.

"A well-bred girl," continued Miss Marple, warming to her subject, "is always very particular to wear the right clothes for the right occasion. I mean, however hot the day was, a well-bred girl would never turn up at a point-to-point in a silk flowered frock."

"And the correct wear to meet a lover?" demanded sir Henry.

"If she were meeting him inside the hotel or somewhere evening dress was worn, she'd wear her best evening frock, of course—but *outside* she'd feel she'd look ridiculous in evening dress and she'd wear her most attractive sports wear."

"Granted, Fashion Queen, but the girl Ruby——"

Miss Marple said:

"Ruby, of course, wasn't—well, to put it bluntly—Ruby *wasn't* a lady. She belonged to the class that wear their best clothes however unsuitable to the occasion. Last year, you know, we had a picnic outing at Scrantor Rocks. You'd be surprised at the unsuitable clothes the girls wore. Foulard dresses and patent shoes and quite elaborate hats, some of them. For climbing about over rocks and in gorse and heather. And the young men in their best suits. Of course, hiking's different again. That's practically a uniform—and girls don't seem to realize that shorts are very unbecoming unless they are very slender."

The Superintendent said slowly:

"And you think that Ruby Keene——"

"I think that she'd have kept on the frock she was wearing—her best pink one. She'd only have changed it if she'd had something newer still."

Superintendent Harper said:

"And what's your explanation, Miss Marple?"

Miss Marple said:

"I haven't got one—yet. But I can't help feeling that it's important. . . ."

iii

Inside the wire cage, the tennis lesson that Raymond Starr was giving had come to an end.

A stout middle-aged woman uttered a few appreciative squeaks, picked up a sky-blue cardigan and went off towards the hotel.

Raymond called out a few gay words after her.

Then he turned towards the bench where the three onlookers were sitting. The balls dangled in a net in his hand, his racket was under one arm. The gay, laughing expression on his face was wiped off as though by a sponge from a slate. He looked tired and worried.

Coming towards them, he said: "*That's* over."

Then the smile broke out again, that charming, boyish, expressive smile that went so harmoniously with his suntanned face and dark lithe grace.

Sir Henry found himself wondering how old the man was. Twenty-five, thirty, thirty-five? It was impossible to say.

Raymond said, shaking his head a little:

"*She*'ll never be able to play, you know."

"All this must be very boring for you," said Miss Marple.

Raymond said simply:

"It is, sometimes. Especially at the end of the summer. For a time the thought of the pay buoys you up, but even that fails to stimulate imagination in the end!"

Superintendent Harper got up. He said abruptly:

"I'll call for you in half an hour's time, Miss Marple, if that will be all right?"

"Perfectly, thank you. I shall be ready."

Harper went off. Raymond stood looking after him. Then he said: "Mind if I sit here for a bit?"

"Do," said Sir Henry. "Have a cigarette?" He offered his case, wondering as he did so why he had a slight feeling of prejudice against Raymond Starr. Was it simply because he was a professional tennis coach and dancer? If so, it wasn't the tennis—it was the dancing. The English, Sir Henry decided, had a distrust for any man who danced too well! This fellow moved with too much grace! Ramon—Raymond—which was his name? Abruptly, he asked the question.

The other seemed amused.

"Ramon was my original professional name. Ramon and Josie—Spanish effect, you know. Then there was rather a prejudice against foreigners—so I became Raymond—very British——"

Miss Marple said:

"And is your real name something quite different?"

He smiled at her.

"Actually my real name is Ramon. I had an Argentine grandmother, you see——" (And that accounts for that swing from the hips, thought Sir Henry parenthetically.) "But my first name is Thomas. Painfully prosaic."

He turned to Sir Henry.

"You come from Devonshire, don't you, sir? From Stane? My people lived down that way. At Alsmonston."

Sir Henry's face lit up.

"Are you one of the Alsmonston Starrs? I didn't realize that."

"No—I don't suppose you would."

There was a slight bitterness in his voice.

Sir Henry said awkwardly:

"Bad luck—er—all that."

"The place being sold up after it had been in the family for three hundred years? Yes, it was rather. Still, our kind have to go, I suppose. We've outlived our usefulness. My elder brother went to New York. He's in publishing—doing well. The rest of us are scattered up and down the earth. I'll say it's hard to get a job nowadays when you've nothing to say for yourself except that you've had a public-school education! Sometimes, if you're lucky, you get taken on as a reception clerk at an hotel. The tie and the manner are an asset there. The only job I could get was showman in a plumbing establishment. Selling superb peach and lemon-coloured porcelain baths. Enormous showrooms, but as I never knew the price of the damned things or how soon we could deliver them—I got fired.

"The only things I *could* do were dance and play tennis. I got taken on at an hotel on the Riviera. Good pickings there. I suppose I was doing well. Then I overheard an old Colonel, real old Colonel, incredibly ancient, British to his backbone and always talking about Poona. He went up to the manager and said at the top of voice:

"'Where's the *gigolo*? I want to get hold of the *gigolo*. My wife and daughter want to dance, yer know. Where is the feller? What does he sting yer for? It's the *gigolo* I want.'"

Raymond went on:

"Silly to mind—but I did. I chucked it. Came here. Less pay but pleasanter work. Mostly teaching tennis to rotund women who will never, never, never be able to play. That and dancing with the neglected wallflower daughters of rich clients. Oh well, it's life, I suppose. Excuse to-day's hard-luck story!"

He laughed. His teeth flashed out white, his eyes crinkled up at the corners. He looked suddenly healthy and happy and very much alive.

Sir Henry said:

"I'm glad to have a chat with you. I've been wanting to talk with you."

"About Ruby Keene? I can't help you, you know. I don't know who killed her. I knew very little about her. She didn't confide in me."

Miss Marple said: "Did you like her?"

"Not particularly. I didn't dislike her."

His voice was careless, uninterested.

Sir Henry said:

"So you've no suggestions to offer?"

"I'm afraid not. . . .I'd have told Harper if I had. It just seems to me one of those things! Petty, sordid little crime—no clues, no motive."

"Two people had a motive," said Miss Marple.

Sir Henry looked at her sharply.

"Really?" Raymond looked surprised.

Miss Marple looked insistently at Sir Henry and he said rather unwillingly:

"Her death probably benefits Mrs. Jefferson and Mr. Gaskell to the amount of fifty thousand pounds."

"What?" Raymond looked really startled—more than startled—upset. "Oh, but that's absurd—absolutely absurd—Mrs. Jefferson—neither of them—could have had anything to do with it. It would be incredible to think of such a thing."

Miss Marple coughed. She said gently:

"I'm afraid, you know, you're rather an idealist."

"I?" he laughed. "Not me! I'm a hard-boiled cynic."

"Money," said Miss Marple, "is a very powerful motive."

"Perhaps," Raymond said hotly. "But that either of those two would strangle a girl in cold blood——" He shook his head.

Then he got up.

"Here's Mrs. Jefferson now. Come for her lesson. She's late." His voice sounded amused. "Ten minutes late!"

Adelaide Jefferson and Hugo McLean were walking rapidly down the path towards them.

With a smiling apology for her lateness, Addie Jefferson went on to the court. McLean sat down on the bench. After a polite inquiry whether Miss Marple minded a pipe, he lit it and puffed for some minutes in silence, watching critically the two white figures about the tennis court.

He said at last:

"Can't see what Addie wants to have lessons for. Have a game, yes. No one enjoys it better than I do. But why *lessons*?"

"Wants to improve her game," said Sir Henry.

"She's not a bad player," said Hugo. "Good enough, at all events. Dash it all, she isn't aiming to play at Wimbledon."

He was silent for a minute or two. Then he said:

"Who *is* this Raymond fellow. Where do they come from, these pros.? Fellow looks like a dago to me."

"He's one of the Devonshire Starrs," said Sir Henry.

"What? Not really?"

Sir Henry nodded. It was clear that this news was unpleasing to Hugo McLean. He scowled more than ever.

He said: "Don't know why Addie sent for *me*. She seems not to have turned a hair over this business! Never looked better. Why send for me?"

Sir Henry asked with some curiosity:

"When did she send for you?"

"Oh—er—when all this happened."

"How did you hear? Telephone or telegram?"

"Telegram."

"As a matter of curiosity, when was it sent off?"

"Well—I don't know exactly."

"What time did you receive it?"

"I didn't exactly receive it. It was telephoned on to me—as a matter of fact."

"Why, where were you?"

"Fact is, I'd left London the afternoon before. I was staying at Danebury Head."

"What—quite near here?"

"Yes, rather funny, wasn't it? Got the message when I got in from a round of golf and came over here at once."

Miss Marple gazed at him thoughtfully. He looked hot and uncomfortable. She said: "I've heard it's very pleasant at Danebury Head, and not very expensive."

"No, it's not expensive. I couldn't afford it if it was. It's a nice little place."

"We must drive over there one day," said Miss Marple.

"Eh? What? Oh—er—yes, I should." He got up. "Better take some exercise—get an appetite."

He walked away stiffly.

"Women," said Sir Henry, "treat their devoted admirers

very badly."

Miss Marple smiled but made no answer.

"Does he strike you as rather a dull dog?" asked Sir Henry. "I'd be interested to know."

"A little limited in his ideas, perhaps," said Miss Marple. "But with possibilities, I think—oh, definitely possibilities."

Sir Henry in his turn got up.

"It's time for me to go and do my stuff. I see Mrs. Bantry's on her way to keep you company."

iv

Mrs. Bantry arrived breathless and sat down with a gasp.

She said:

"I've been talking to chambermaids. But it isn't any good. I haven't found out a thing more! Do you think that girl can really have been carrying on with someone without everybody in the hotel knowing all about it?"

"That's a very interesting point, dear. I should say, definitely *not*. *Somebody* knows, depend upon it, if it's true! But she must have been very clever about it."

Mrs. Bantry's attention had strayed to the tennis court. She said approvingly:

"Addie's tennis is coming on a lot. Attractive young man, that tennis pro. Addie's looking quite nice looking. She's still an attractive woman—I shouldn't be at all surprised if she married again.

"She'll be a rich woman, too, when Mr. Jefferson dies," said Miss Marple.

"Oh, don't always have such a nasty mind, Jane! Why haven't you solved this mystery yet? We don't seem to be getting on at all. I thought you'd know *at once*." Mrs. Bantry's tone held reproach.

"No, no, dear. I didn't know at once—not for some time."

Mrs. Bantry turned startled and incredulous eyes on her.

"You mean you know *now* who killed Ruby Keene?"

"Oh yes," said Miss Marple, "I know *that*!"

"But Jane, who is it? Tell me at once."

Miss Marple shook her head very firmly and pursed up her lips.

"I'm sorry, Dolly, but that wouldn't do at all."

"Why wouldn't it do?"

"Because you're so indiscreet. You would go round telling every one—or, if you didn't tell, you'd *hint*."

"No, I wouldn't. I wouldn't tell a soul."

"People who use that phrase are always the last to live up to it. It's no good, dear. There's a long way to go yet. A great many things that are quite obscure. You remember when I was so against letting Mrs. Partridge collect for the Red Cross, and I couldn't say *why*. The reason was that her nose had twitched in just the same way that that maid of mine, Alice, twitched *her* nose when I sent her out to pay the books. Always paid them a shilling or so short, and said 'it could go on to the next week's account,' which, of course, was *exactly* what Mrs. Partridge did, only on a much larger scale. Seventy-five pounds it was *she* embezzled."

"Never mind Mrs. Partridge," said Mrs. Bantry.

"But I had to explain to you. And if you care I'll give you a *hint*. The trouble in this case is that everybody has been much too *credulous* and *believing*. You simply cannot *afford* to believe everything that people tell you. When there's anything fishy about, I never believe any one at all! You see, I know human nature so well."

Mrs. Bantry was silent for a minute or two. Then she said in a different tone of voice:

"I told you, didn't I, that I didn't see why I shouldn't enjoy myself over this case. A real murder in my own house! The sort of thing that will never happen again."

"I hope not," said Miss Marple.

"Well, so do I, really. Once is enough. But it's *my* murder, Jane; I want to enjoy myself over it."

Miss Marple shot a glance at her.

Mrs. Bantry said belligerently:

"Don't you believe that?"

Miss Marple said sweetly:

"Of course, Dolly, if you tell me so."

"Yes, but you never believe what people tell you, do you?

You've just said so. Well, you're quite right." Mrs. Bantry's voice took on a sudden bitter note. She said: "I'm not altogether a fool. You may think, Jane, that I don't know what they're saying all over St. Mary Mead—all over the county! They're saying, one and all, that there's no smoke without fire, that if the girl was found in Arthur's library, then Arthur must know something about it. They're saying that the girl was Arthur's mistress—that she was his illegitimate daughter—that she was blackmailing him. They're saying anything that comes into their damned heads! And it will go on like that! Arthur won't realize it at first—he won't know what's wrong. He's such a dear old stupid that he'd never believe people would think things like that about him. He'll be cold-shouldered and looked at askance (whatever *that* means!) and it will dawn on him little by little and suddenly he'll be horrified and cut to the soul, and he'll fasten up like a clam and just *endure*, day after day, in misery.

"It's because of all that's going to happen to him that I've come here to ferret out every single thing about it that I can! This murder's *got* to be solved! If it isn't, then Arthur's whole life will be wrecked—and I won't have that happen. I won't! I won't! I won't!"

She paused for a minute and said:

"I *won't* have the dear old boy go through hell for something he didn't do. That's the only reason I came to Danemouth and left him alone at home—to find out the truth."

"I know, dear," said Miss Marple. "That's why I'm here too."

Chapter 14

i

IN A QUIET hotel room Edwards was listening deferentially to Sir Henry Clithering.

"There are certain questions I would like to ask you, Edwards, but I want you first to understand quite clearly my position here. I was at one time Commissioner of Police at Scotland Yard. I am now retired into private life. Your master sent for me when this tragedy occurred. He begged me to use my skill and experience in order to find out the truth."

Sir Henry paused.

Edwards, his pale intelligent eyes on the other's face, inclined his head. He said: "Quite so, Sir Henry."

Clithering went on slowly and deliberately:

"In all police cases there is necessarily a lot of information that is held back. It is held back for various reasons—because it touches on a family skeleton, because it is considered to have no bearing on the case, because it would entail awkwardness and embarrassment to the parties concerned."

Again Edwards said:

"Quite so, Sir Henry."

"I expect, Edwards, that by now you appreciate quite clearly the main points of this business. The dead girl was on the point of becoming Mr. Jefferson's adopted daughter. Two people had a motive in seeing that this should not happen. Those two people are Mr. Gaskell and Mrs. Jefferson."

The valet's eyes displayed a momentary gleam. He said: "May I ask if they are under suspicion, sir?"

"They are in no danger of arrest, if that is what you mean. But the police are bound to be suspicious of them and will continue to be so *until the matter is cleared up*."

"An unpleasant position for them, sir."

"Very unpleasant. Now to get at the truth one must have *all* the facts of the case. A lot depends, *must* depend, on the reactions, the words and gestures, of Mr. Jefferson and his family. How did they feel, what did they show, what things were said? I am asking you, Edwards, for inside information—the kind of inside information that only you are likely to have. You know your master's moods. From observation of them you probably know what caused them. I am asking this, not as a policeman, but as a friend of Mr. Jefferson's. That is to say, if anything you tell me is not, in my opinion, relevant to the case, I shall not pass it on to the police."

He paused. Edwards said quietly:

"I understand you, sir. You want me to speak quite frankly—to say things that in the ordinary course of events I should not say—and that, excuse me, sir, *you* wouldn't dream of listening to."

Sir Henry said:

"You're a very intelligent fellow, Edwards. That's exactly what I *do* mean."

Edwards was silent for a minute or two, then he began to speak.

"Of course I know Mr. Jefferson fairly well by now. I've been with him quite a number of years. And I see him in his 'off' moments, not only in his 'on' ones. Sometimes, sir, I've questioned in my own mind whether it's good for any one to fight fate in the way Mr. Jefferson has fought. It's taken a terrible toll of him, sir. If, sometimes, he could have given way, been an unhappy, lonely, broken old man—well, it might have been better for him in the end. But he's too proud for that! He'll go down fighting—that's his motto.

"But that sort of thing leads, Sir Henry, to a lot of nervous reaction. He looks a good-tempered gentleman. I've seen him in violent rages when he could hardly speak for passion. And the one thing that roused him, sir, was deceit. . . ."

"Are you saying that for any particular reason, Edwards?"

"Yes, sir, I am. You asked me, sir, to speak quite frankly?"

"That is the idea."

"Well, then, Sir Henry, in my opinion the young woman that

Mr. Jefferson was so taken up with wasn't worth it. She was, to put it bluntly, a common little piece. And she didn't care tuppence for Mr. Jefferson. All that play of affection and gratitude was so much poppycock. I don't say there was any harm in her—but she wasn't, by a long way, what Mr. Jefferson thought her. It was funny, that, sir, for Mr. Jefferson was a shrewd gentleman; he wasn't often deceived over people. But there, a gentleman isn't himself in his judgment when it comes to a young woman being in question. Young Mrs. Jefferson, you see, whom he'd always depended upon a lot for sympathy, had changed a good deal this summer. He noticed it and he felt it badly. He was fond of her, you see. Mr. Mark he never liked much."

Sir Henry interjected:

"And yet he had him with him constantly?"

"Yes, but that was for Miss Rosamund's sake. Mrs. Gaskell that was. She was the apple of his eye. He adored her. Mr. Mark was Miss Rosamund's husband. He always thought of him like that."

"Supposing Mr. Mark had married someone else?"

"Mr. Jefferson, sir, would have been furious."

Sir Henry raised his eyebrows. "As much as that?"

"He wouldn't have shown it, but that's what it would have been."

"And if Mrs. Jefferson had married again?"

"Mr. Jefferson wouldn't have like that either, sir."

"Please go on, Edwards."

"I was saying, sir, that Mr. Jefferson fell for this young woman. I've often seen it happen with the gentlemen I've been with. Comes over them like a kind of disease. They want to protect the girl, and shield her, and shower benefits upon her—and nine times out of ten the girl is very well able to look after herself and has a good eye to the main chance."

"So you think Ruby Keene was a schemer?"

"Well, Sir Henry, she was quite inexperienced, being so young, but she had the makings of a very fine schemer indeed when she'd once got well into her swing, so to speak! In another five years she'd have been an expert at the game!"

Sir Henry said:

"I'm glad to have your opinion of her. It's valuable. Now, do you recall any incident in which this matter was discussed between Mr. Jefferson and his family?"

"There was very little discussion, sir. Mr. Jefferson announced what he had in mind and stifled any protests. That is, he shut up Mr. Mark, who was a bit outspoken. Mrs. Jefferson didn't say much—she's a quiet lady—only urged him not to do anything in a great hurry."

Sir Henry nodded.

"Anything else? What was the girl's attitude?"

With marked distaste the valet said:

"I should describe it, sir, as jubilant."

"Ah—jubilant, you say? You had no reason to believe, Edwards, that"—he sought about for a phrase suitable to Edwards—"that—er—her affections were engaged elsewhere?"

"Mr. Jefferson was not proposing marriage, sir. He was going to adopt her."

"Cut out the 'elsewhere' and let the question stand."

The valet said slowly: "There *was* one incident, sir. I happened to be a witness of it."

"That is gratifying. Tell me."

"There is probably nothing in it, sir. It was just that one day the young woman, chancing to open her handbag, a small snapshot fell out. Mr. Jefferson pounced on it and said: 'Hallo, Kitten, who's this, eh?'

"It was a snapshot, sir, of a young man, a dark young man with rather untidy hair and his tie very badly arranged.

"Miss Keene pretended that she didn't know anything about it. She said: 'I've no idea, Jeffie. No idea at all. I don't know how it could have got into my bag. *I* didn't put it there!'

"Now, Mr. Jefferson, sir, wasn't quite a fool. That story wasn't good enough. He looked angry, his brows came down heavy, and his voice was gruff when he said:

"'Now then, Kitten, now then. *You* know who it is right enough.'

"She changed her tactics quick, sir. Looked frightened. She said: 'I do recognize him now. He comes here sometimes and I've danced with him. I don't know his name. The silly idiot must have stuffed his photo into my bag one day. These boys are too silly for anything!' She tossed her head and giggled and passed it off. But it wasn't a likely story, was it? And I don't think Mr. Jefferson quite believed it. He looked at her once or twice after that in a sharp way, and sometimes, if she'd been out, he asked her where she'd been."

Sir Henry said: "Have you ever seen the original of the photo about the hotel?"

"Not to my knowledge, sir. Of course, I am not much downstairs in the public apartments."

Sir Henry nodded. He asked a few more questions, but Edwards could tell him nothing more.

ii

In the police station at Danemouth, Superintendent Harper was interviewing Jessie Davis, Florence Small, Beatrice Henniker, Mary Price, and Lilian Ridgeway.

They were girls much of an age, differing slightly in mentality. They ranged from "county" to farmers' and shopkeepers' daughters. One and all they told the same story—Pamela Reeves had been just the same as usual, she had said nothing to any of them except that she was going to Woolworth's and would go home by a later bus.

In the corner of Superintendent Harper's office sat an elderly lady. The girls hardly noticed her. If they did, they may have wondered who she was. She was certainly no police matron. Possibly they assumed that she, like themselves, was a witness to be questioned.

The last girl was shown out. Superintendent Harper wiped his forehead and turned round to look at Miss Marple. His glance was inquiring, but not hopeful.

Miss Marple, however, spoke crisply.

"I'd like to speak to Florence Small."

The Superintendent's eyebrows rose, but he nodded and touched a bell. A constable appeared.

Harper said: "Florence Small."

The girl reappeared, ushered in by the constable. She was the daughter of a well-to-do farmer—a tall girl with fair hair, a rather foolish mouth, and frightened brown eyes. She was twisting her hands and looked nervous.

Superintendent Harper looked at Miss Marple, who nodded.

The Superintendent got up. He said:

"This lady will ask you some questions."

He went out, closing the door behind him.

Florence shot an uneasy glance at Miss Marple. Her eyes looked rather like one of her father's calves.

Miss Marple said: "Sit down, Florence."

Florence Small sat down obediently. Unrecognized by herself, she felt suddenly more at home, less uneasy. The unfamiliar and terrorizing atmosphere of a police station was replaced by something more familiar, the accustomed tone of command of somebody whose business it was to give orders. Miss Marple said:

"You understand, Florence, that it's of the utmost importance that everything about poor Pamela's doings on the day of her death should be known?"

Pamela murmured that she quite understood.

"And I'm sure you want to do your best to help?"

Florence's eyes were wary as she said, of course she did.

"To keep back any piece of information is a very serious offence," said Miss Marple.

The girl's fingers twisted nervously in her lap. She swallowed once or twice.

"I can make allowances," went on Miss Marple, "for the fact that you are naturally alarmed at being brought into contact with the police. You are afraid, too, that you may be blamed for not having spoken sooner. Possibly you are afraid that you may also be blamed for not stopping Pamela at the time. But you've got to be a brave girl and make a clean breast of things. If you refuse to tell what you know now, it will be a very serious matter indeed—*very* serious—practically *perjury*, and for that, as you know, you can be sent to prison."

"I—I don't——"

Miss Marple said sharply:

"Now don't prevaricate, Florence! Tell me all about it at once! Pamela wasn't going to Woolworth's, was she?"

Florence licked her lips with a dry tongue and gazed imploringly at Miss Marple like a beast about to be slaughtered.

"Something to do with the films, wasn't it?" asked Miss Marple.

A look of intense relief mingled with awe passed over Florence's face. Her inhibitions left her. She gasped:

"Oh, *yes*!"

"I thought so," said Miss Marple. "Now I want all the details, please."

Words poured from Florence in a gush.

"Oh! I've been ever so worried. I promised Pam, you see, I'd never say a word to a soul. And then when she was found all burnt up in the car—oh! it was horrible and I thought I should *die*—I felt it was all my fault. I ought to have stopped her. Only I never thought, not for a minute, that it wasn't all right. And then I was asked if she'd been quite as usual that day and I said 'Yes' before I'd had time to think. And not having said anything then I didn't see how I could say anything later. And, after all, I didn't know anything—not really—only what Pam told me."

"What did Pam tell you?"

"It was as we were walking up the lane to the bus—on the way to the rally. She asked me if I could keep a secret, and I said 'Yes,' and she made me swear not to tell. She was going into Danemouth for a film test after the rally! She'd met a film producer—just back from Hollywood, he was. He wanted a certain type, and he told Pam she was just what he was looking for. He warned her, though, not to build on it. You couldn't tell, he said, not until you saw how a person photographed. It might be no good at all. It was a kind of Bergner part, he said. You had to have someone quite young for it. A schoolgirl, it was, who changes places with a revue artist and has a wonderful career. Pam's acted in plays at school and she's awfully good. He said he could see she could act, but she'd have to have some intensive training. It wouldn't be all beer and skittles, he told her, it would be damned hard work. Did she think she could stick it?"

Florence Small stopped for breath. Miss Marple felt rather sick as she listened to the glib rehash of countless novels and screen stories. Pamela Reeves, like most other girls, would have been warned against talking to strangers—but the glamour of the films would obliterate all that.

"He was absolutely businesslike about it all," continued Florence. "Said if the test was successful she'd have a contract, and he said that as she was young and inexperienced she ought to let a lawyer look at it before she signed it. But she wasn't to pass on that *he'd* said that. He asked her if she'd have trouble with her parents, and Pam said she probably would, and he said: 'Well, of course, that's always a difficulty with any one as young as you are, but I think if it was put to them that this was a wonderful chance that wouldn't happen once in a million times, they'd see reason.' But, anyway, he said, it wasn't any good going into that until they knew the result of the test. She mustn't be disappointed if it failed. He told her about Hollywood and about Vivien Leigh—how she'd suddenly taken London by storm—and how these sensational leaps into fame did happen. He himself had come back from America to work with the Lemville Studios and put some pep into the English film companies."

Miss Marple nodded.

Florence went on:

"So it was all arranged. Pam was to go into Danemouth after the rally and meet him at his hotel and he'd take her along to the studios (they'd got a small testing studio in Danemouth, he told her). She'd have her test and she could catch the bus home afterwards. She could say she'd been shopping, and he'd let her know the result of the test in a few days, and if it was favourable Mr. Harmsteiter, the boss, would come along and talk to her parents.

"Well, of course, it sounded too wonderful! I was green with envy! Pam got through the rally without turning a hair—we always call her a regular poker face. Then, when she said she was going into Danemouth to Woolworth's she just winked at me.

"I saw her start off down the footpath." Florence began to cry. "I ought to have stopped her. I ought to have stopped her. . . .I ought to have known a thing like that couldn't be true. I ought to have told someone. Oh dear, I wish I was *dead*!"

"There, there." Miss Marple patted her on the shoulder. "It's quite all right. No one will blame you. You've done the right thing in telling me."

She devoted some minutes to cheering the child up.

Five minutes later she was telling the story to Superintendent

Harper. The latter looked very grim.

"The clever devil!" he said. "By God, I'll cook his goose for him. This puts rather a different aspect on things."

"Yes, it does."

Harper looked at her sideways.

"It doesn't surprise you?"

I expected something of the kind."

Superintendent Harper said curiously:

"What put you on to this particular girl? They all looked scared to death and there wasn't a pin to choose between them as far as I could see."

Miss Marple said gently:

"You haven't had as much experience with girls telling lies as I have. Florence looked at you very straight, if you remember, and stood very rigid and just fidgeted with her feet like the others. But you didn't watch her as she went out of the door. I knew at once then that she'd got something to hide. They nearly always relax too soon. My little maid Janet always did. She'd explain quite convincingly that the mice had eaten the end of a cake and give herself away by smirking as she left the room."

"I'm very grateful to you," said Harper.'

He added thoughtfully: "Lemville Studios, eh?"

Miss Marple said nothing. She rose to her feet.

"I'm afraid," she said, "I must hurry away. So glad to have been able to help you."

"Are you going back to the hotel?"

"Yes—to pack up. I must go back to St. Mary Mead as soon as possible. There's a lot for me to do there."

Chapter 15

i

MISS MARPLE passed out through the french windows of her drawing-room, tripped down her neat garden path, through a garden gate, in through the vicarage garden gate, across the vicarage garden, and up to the drawing-room window, where she tapped gently on the pane.

The vicar was busy in his study composing his Sunday sermon, but the vicar's wife, who was young and pretty, was admiring the progress of her offspring across the hearthrug.

"Can I come in, Griselda?"

"Oh, do, Miss Marple. Just *look* at David! He gets so angry because he can only crawl in reverse. He wants to get to something and the more he tries the more he goes backwards into the coal-box!"

"He's looking very bonny, Griselda."

"He's not bad, is he?" said the young mother, endeavouring to assume an indifferent manner. "Of course I don't *bother* with him much. All the books say a child should be left alone as much as possible."

"Very wise, dear," said Miss Marple. "Ahem, I came to ask if there was anything special you are collecting for at the moment?"

The vicar's wife turned somewhat astonished eyes upon her.

"Oh, heaps of things," she said cheerfully. "There always are."

She ticked them off on her fingers.

"There's the Nave Restoration Fund, and St. Giles's Mission, and our Sale of Work next Wednesday, and the Unmarried Mothers, and a Boy Scouts' Outing, and the Needlework Guild, and the Bishop's Appeal for Deep Sea Fishermen."

"Any of them will do," said Miss Marple. "I thought I might make a little round—with a book, you know—if you would authorize me to do so?"

"Are you up to something? I believe you are. Of course I authorize you. Make it the Sale of Work; it would be lovely to get some real money instead of those awful sachets and comic pen-wipers and depressing children's frocks and dusters all done up to look like dolls.

"I suppose," continued Griselda, accompanying her guest to the window, "you wouldn't like to tell me what it's all about?"

"Later, my dear," said Miss Marple, hurrying off.

With a sigh the young mother returned to the hearthrug and, by way of carrying out her principles of stern neglect, butted her son three times in the stomach so that he caught hold of her hair and pulled it with gleeful yells. They then rolled over and over in a grand rough-and-tumble until the door opened and the vicarage maid announced to the most influential parishioner (who didn't like children):

"Missus is in here."

Whereupon Griselda sat up and tried to look dignified and more what a vicar's wife should be.

ii

Miss Marple, clasping a small black book with pencilled entries in it, walked briskly along the village street until she came to the crossroads. Here she turned to the left and walked past the *Blue Boar* until she came to Chatsworth, alias "Mr. Booker's new house."

She turned in at the gate, walked up to the front door and knocked briskly.

The door was opened by the blonde young woman named Dinah Lee. She was less carefully made-up than usual, and in fact looked slightly dirty. She was wearing grey slacks and an emerald jumper.

"Good-morning," said Miss Marple briskly and cheerfully. "May I just come in for a minute?"

She pressed forward as she spoke, so that Dinah Lee, who was somewhat taken aback at the call, had no time to make up her mind.

"Thank you so much," said Miss Marple, beaming amiably at her and sitting down rather gingerly on a "period" bamboo chair.

"Quite warm for the time of year, is it not?" went on Miss Marple, still exuding geniality.

"Yes, rather. Oh, quite," said Miss Lee.

At a loss how to deal with the situation, she opened a box and offered it to her guest. "Er—have a cigarette?"

"Thank you so much, but I don't smoke. I just called, you know, to see if I could enlist your help for our Sale of Work next week."

"Sale of Work?" said Dinah Lee, as one who repeats a phrase in a foreign language.

"At the vicarage," said Miss Marple. "Next Wednesday."

"Oh!" Miss Lee's mouth fell open. "I'm afraid I couldn't——"

"Not even a small subscription—half a crown perhaps?"

Miss Marple exhibited her little book.

"Oh—er—well, yes, I dare say I could manage that."

The girl looked relieved and turned to hunt in her handbag.

Miss Marple's sharp eyes were looking round the room.

She said:

"I see you've no hearthrug in front of the fire."

Dinah Lee turned round and stared at her. She could not but be aware of the very keen scrutiny the old lady was giving her, but it aroused in her no other emotion than slight annoyance. Miss Marple recognized that. She said:

"It's rather dangerous, you know. Sparks fly out and mark the carpet."

"Funny old Tabby," thought Dinah, but she said quite amiably if somewhat vaguely:

"There used to be one. I don't know where it's got to."

"I suppose," said Miss Marple, "it was the fluffy woolly kind?"

"Sheep," said Dinah. "That's what it looked like."

She was amused now. An eccentric old bean, this.

She held out a half-crown. "Here you are," she said.

"Oh, thank you, my dear."

Miss Marple took it and opened the little book.

"Er–what name shall I write down?"

Dinah's eyes grew suddenly hard and contemptuous.

"Nosey old cat," she thought, "that's all she came for—prying around for scandal!"

She said clearly and with malicious pleasure:

"Miss Dinah Lee."

Miss Marple looked at her steadily.

She said:

"This is Mr. Basil Blake's cottage, isn't it?

"Yes, and *I*'m Miss Dinah Lee!"

Her voice rang out challengingly, her head went back, her blue eyes flashed.

Very steadily Miss Marple looked at her. She said:

"Will you allow me to give you some advice, even though you may consider it impertinent?"

"I *shall* consider it impertinent. You had better say nothing."

"Nevertheless," said Miss Marple, "I am going to speak. I want to advise you, very strongly, not to continue using your maiden name in the village."

Dinah stared at her. She said:

"What—what do you mean?"

Miss Marple said earnestly:

"In a very short time you may need all the sympathy and goodwill you can find. It will be important to your husband, too, that he shall be thought well of. There is a prejudice in old-fashioned country districts against people living together who are not married. It has amused you both, I dare say, to pretend that that is what you are doing. It kept people away, so that you weren't bothered with what I expect you would call 'old frumps.' Nevertheless, old frumps have their uses."

Dinah demanded:

"How did you know we are married?"

Miss Marple smiled a deprecating smile.

"Oh, my dear," she said.

Dinah persisted.

"No, but how *did* you know? You didn't—you didn't go to Somerset House?"

A momentary flicker showed in Miss Marple's eyes.

"Somerset House? Oh, no. But it was quite easy to *guess*. Everything, you know, gets round in a village. The—er—the kind of quarrels you have—typical of early days of marriage. Quite—*quite* unlike an illicit relationship. It has been said, you know (and, I think, quite truly), that you can only really get under anybody's skin if you are married to them. When there is no—no *legal* bond, people are much more careful, they have to keep assuring themselves how happy and halcyon everything is. They have, you see, to *justify* themselves. They dare not quarrel! Married people, I have noticed, quite enjoy their battles and the—er—appropriate reconciliations."

She paused, twinkling benignly.

"Well, I——" Dinah stopped and laughed. She sat down and lit a cigarette. "You're absolutely marvellous!" she said.

Then she went on:

"But why do you want us to own up and admit to respectability?"

Miss Marple's face was grave. She said:

"Because, any minute now, *your husband may be arrested for murder*."

iii

For several moments Dinah stared at her. Then she said incredulously:

"Basil? Murder? Are you joking?"

"No, indeed. Haven't you seen the papers?"

Dinah caught her breath.

"You mean—that girl at the Majestic Hotel. Do you mean they suspect Basil of killing her?"

"Yes."

"But it's nonsense!"

There was a whirr of a car outside, the bang of a gate. Basil Blake flung open the door and came in, carrying some bottles. He said:

"Got the gin and the vermouth. Did you——"

He stopped and turned incredulous eyes on the prim, erect visitor.

Dinah burst out breathlessly:

"Is she mad? She says you're going to be arrested for the murder of that girl Ruby Keene."

"Oh, God!" said Basil Blake. The bottles dropped from his arms on to the sofa. He reeled to a chair and dropped down in it and buried his face in his hands. He repeated: "Oh, my God! Oh, my God!"

Dinah darted over to him. She caught his shoulders.

"Basil, look at me! It isn't true! I know it isn't true! I don't believe it for a moment!"

His hand went up and gripped hers.

"Bless you, darling."

"But why should they think—— You didn't even *know* her, did you?"

"Oh, yes, he knew her," said Miss Marple.

Basil said fiercely:

"Be quiet, you old hag. Listen, Dinah darling, I hardly knew her at all. Just ran across her once or twice at the Majestic. That's all, I swear that's all."

Dinah said, bewildered:

"I don't understand. Why should any one suspect you, then?"

Basil groaned. He put his hands over his eyes and rocked to and fro.

Miss Marple said:

"What did you do with the hearthrug?"

His reply came mechanically:

"I put it in the dustbin."

Miss Marple clucked her tongue vexedly.

"That was stupid—very stupid. People don't put good hearthrugs in dustbins. It had spangles in it from her dress, I suppose?"

"Yes, I couldn't get them out."

Dinah cried: "But what are you both talking about?"

Basil said sullenly:

"Ask her. She seems to know all about it."

"I'll tell you what I think happened, if you like," said Miss Marple. "You can correct me, Mr. Blake, if I go wrong. I think that after having had a violent quarrel with your wife at a party and after having had, perhaps, rather too much—er—to drink, you drove down here. I don't know what time you arrived——"

Basil Blake said sullenly:

"About two in the morning. I meant to go up to town first, then when I got to the suburbs I changed my mind. I thought Dinah might come down here after me. So I drove down here. The place was all dark. I opened the door and turned on the light and I saw—and I saw——"

He gulped and stopped. Miss Marple went on:

"You saw a girl lying on the hearthrug—a girl in a white evening-dress—strangled. I don't know whether you recognized her then——"

Basil Blake shook his head violently.

"I couldn't look at her after the first glance—her face was all blue—swollen. She'd been dead some time and she was *there*—in *my* room!"

He shuddered.

Miss Marple said gently:

"You weren't, of course, quite yourself. You were in a fuddled state and your nerves are not good. You were, I think, panic-stricken. You didn't know what to do——"

"I thought Dinah might turn up any minute. And she'd find me there with a dead body—a girl's dead body—and she'd think I'd killed her. Then I got an idea—it seemed, I don't know why, a good idea at the time—I thought: I'll put her in old Bantry's library. Damned pompous old stick, always looking down his nose, sneering at me as artistic and effeminate. Serve the pompous old brute right, I thought. He'll look a fool when a dead lovely is found on his hearthrug." He added, with a pathetic eagerness to explain: "I was a bit drunk, you know, at the time. It really seemed positively *amusing* to me. Old Bantry with a dead blonde."

"Yes, yes," said Miss Marple. "Little Tommy Bond had very much the same idea. Rather a sensitive boy with an inferiority complex, he said teacher was always picking on him. He put a frog in the clock and it jumped out at her.

"You were just the same," went on Miss Marple, "only, of course, bodies are more serious matters than frogs."

Basil groaned again.

"By the morning I'd sobered up. I realized what I'd done. I was scared stiff. And then the police came here—another damned pompous ass of a Chief Constable. I was scared of him—and the only way I could hide it was by being abominably rude. In the middle of it all Dinah drove up."

Dinah looked out of the window.

She said:

"There's a car driving up now. . . .there are men in it."

"The police, I think," said Miss Marple.

Basil Blake got up. Suddenly he became quite calm and resolute. He even smiled. He said:

"So I'm for it, am I? All right, Dinah sweet, keep your head. Get on to old Sims—he's the family lawyer—and go to mother and tell her about our marriage. She won't bite. And don't worry. *I didn't do it.* So it's bound to be all right, see, sweetheart?"

There was a tap on the cottage door. Basil called "Come in." Inspector Slack entered with another man. He said:

"Mr. Basil Blake?"

"Yes."

"I have a warrant here for your arrest on the charge of murdering Ruby Keene on the night of September 21st last. I warn you that anything you say may be used at your trial. You will please accompany me now. Full facilities will be given you for communicating with your solicitor."

Basil nodded.

He looked at Dinah, but did not touch her. He said:

"So long, Dinah."

"Cool customer," thought Inspector Slack.

He acknowledged the presence of Miss Marple with a half bow and a "Good-morning," and thought to himself:

"Smart old Pussy, *she's* on to it! Good job we've got that hearthrug. That and finding out from the car-park man at the studio that he left that party at *eleven* instead of midnight. Don't think those friends of his meant to commit perjury. They were bottled and Blake told 'em firmly the next day it was twelve o'clock when he left and they believed him. Well, *his* goose is cooked good and proper! Mental, I expect! Broadmoor, not hanging. First the Reeves kid, probably strangled her, drove her out to the quarry, walked back into Danemouth, picked up his own car in some side lane, drove to this party, then back to Danemouth, brought Ruby Keene out here, strangled her, put her in old Bantry's libary, then probably got the wind up about the car in the quarry, drove there, set it on fire, and got back here. Mad—sex and blood lust—lucky *this* girl's escaped. What they call recurring mania, I expect."

Alone with Miss Marple, Dinah Blake turned to her. She said:

"I don't know who you are, but you've got to understand this—*Basil didn't do it.*"

Miss Marple said:

"I know he didn't. I know who *did* do it. But it's not going to be easy to prove. I've an idea that something you said—just now—may help. It gave me an idea—the *connection* I'd been trying to find—now what *was* it?"

Chapter 16

i

"I'M HOME, Arthur!" declared Mrs. Bantry, announcing the fact like a Royal Proclamation as she flung open the study door.

Colonel Bantry immediately jumped up, kissed his wife, and declared heartily: "Well, well, that's splendid!"

The words were unimpeachable, the manner very well done, but an affectionate wife of as many years' standing as Mrs. Bantry was not deceived. She said immediately:

"Is anything the matter?"

"No, of course not, Dolly. What should be the matter?"

"Oh, I don't know," said Mrs. Bantry vaguely. "Things are so queer, aren't they?"

She threw off her coat as she spoke and Colonel Bantry picked it up carefully and laid it across the back of the sofa.

All exactly as usual—yet not as usual. Her husband, Mrs. Bantry thought, seemed to have shrunk. He looked thinner, stooped more; there were pouches under his eyes and those eyes were not ready to meet hers.

He went on to say, still with that affectation of cheerfulness:

"Well, how did you enjoy your time at Danemouth?"

"Oh! it was great fun. You ought to have come, Arthur."

"Couldn't get away, my dear. Lot of things to attend to here."

"Still, I think the change would have done you good. And you like the Jeffersons?"

"Yes, yes, poor fellow. Nice chap. All very sad."

"What have you been doing with yourself since I've been away?"

"Oh, nothing much. Been over the farms, you know. Agreed that Anderson shall have a new roof—can't patch it up any longer."

"How did the Radfordshire Council meeting go?"

"I—well—as a matter of fact I didn't go."

"Didn't *go*? But you were taking the chair?"

"Well, as a matter of fact, Dolly—seems there was some mistake about that. Asked me if I'd mind if Thompson took it instead."

"I *see*," said Mrs. Bantry.

She peeled off a glove and threw it deliberately into the waste-paper basket. Her husband went to retrieve it, and she stopped him, saying sharply:

"Leave it. I hate gloves."

Colonel Bantry glanced at her uneasily.

Mrs. Bantry said sternly:

"Did you go to dinner with the Duffs on Thursday?"

"Oh, that! It was put off. Their cook was ill."

"Stupid people," said Mrs. Bantry. She went on: "Did you go to the Naylors' yesterday?"

"I rang up and said I didn't feel up to it, hoped they'd excuse me. They quite understood."

"They did, did they?" said Mrs. Bantry grimly.

She sat down by the desk and absent-mindedly picked up a pair of gardening scissors. With them she cut off the fingers, one by one, of her second glove.

"What *are* you doing, Dolly?"

"Feeling destructive," said Mrs. Bantry.

She got up. "Where shall we sit after dinner, Arthur? In the libary?"

"Well—er—I don't think so—eh? Very nice in here—or the drawing-room."

"I think," said Mrs. Bantry, "that we'll sit in the library!"

Her steady eye met his. Colonel Bantry drew himself up to his full height. A sparkle came into his eye.

He said:

"You're right, my dear. We'll sit in the library!"

ii

Mrs. Bantry put down the telephone receiver with a sigh of

annoyance. She had rung up twice, and each time the answer had been the same: Miss Marple was out.

Of a naturally impatient nature, Mrs. Bantry was never one to acquiesce in defeat. She rang up in rapid succession the vicarage, Mrs. Price Ridley, Miss Hartnell, Miss Wetherby, and, as a last resort, the fishmonger, who, by reason of his advantageous geographical position, usually knew where everybody was in the village.

The fishmonger was sorry, but he had not seen Miss Marple at all in the village that morning. She had not been her usual round.

"Where *can* the woman be?" demanded Mrs. Bantry impatiently aloud.

There was a deferential cough behind her. The discreet Lorrimer murmured:

"You were requiring Miss Marple, madam? I have just observed her approaching the house."

Mrs. Bantry rushed to the front door, flung it open, and greeted Miss Marple breathlessly:

"I've been trying to get you *everywhere*. Where have you been?" She glanced over her shoulder. Lorrimer had discreetly vanished. "Everything's *too* awful! People are beginning to cold-shoulder Arthur. He looks *years* older. We *must* do something, Jane. *You* must do something!"

Miss Marple said:

"You needn't worry, Dolly," in a rather peculiar voice.

Colonel Bantry appeared from the study door.

"Ah, Miss Marple. Good-morning. Glad you've come. My wife's been ringing you up like a lunatic."

"I thought I'd better bring you the news," said Miss Marple, as she followed Mrs. Bantry into the study.

"News?"

"Basil Blake has just been arrested for the murder of Ruby Keene."

"Basil Blake?" cried the Colonel.

"But he didn't do it," said Miss Marple.

Colonel Bantry took no notice of this statement. It is doubtful if he even heard it.

"Do you mean to say he strangled that girl and then brought

her along and put her in *my* library?"

"He put her in your library," said Miss Marple. "But he didn't kill her."

"Nonsense! If he put her in my library, of course he killed her! The two things go together."

"Not necessarily. He found her dead in his own cottage."

"A likely story," said the Colonel derisively. "If you find a body, why, you ring up the police—naturally—if you're an honest man."

"Ah," said Miss Marple, "but we haven't all got such iron nerves as you have, Colonel Bantry. You belong to the old school. This younger generation is different."

"Got no stamina," said the Colonel, repeating a well-worn opinion of his.

"Some of them," said Miss Marple, "have been through a bad time. I've heard a good deal about Basil. He did A.R.P. work, you know, when he was only eighteen. He went into a burning house and brought out four children, one after another. He went back for a dog, although they told him it wasn't safe. The building fell in on him. They got him out, but his chest was badly crushed and he had to lie in plaster for nearly a year and was ill for a long time after that. That's when he got interested in designing."

"Oh!" The Colonel coughed and blew his nose. "I—er—never knew that."

"He doesn't talk about it," said Miss Marple.

"Er—quite right. Proper spirit. Must be more in the young chap than I thought. Always thought he'd shirked the war, you know. Shows you ought to be careful in jumping to conclusions."

Colonel Bantry looked ashamed.

"But, all the same"—his indignation revived—"what did he mean trying to fasten a murder on *me*?"

"I don't think he saw it like that," said Miss Marple. "He thought of it more as a—as a joke. You see, he was rather under the influence of alcohol at the time."

"Bottled, was he?" said Colonel Bantry, with an Englishman's sympathy for alcoholic excess. "Oh, well, can't judge a fellow by what he does when he's drunk. When I was at

Cambridge, I remember I put a certain utensil—well, well, never mind. Deuce of a row there was about it."

He chuckled, then checked himself sternly. He looked piercingly at Miss Marple with eyes that were shrewd and appraising. He said: "*You* don't think he did the murder, eh?"

"I'm sure he didn't"

"And you think you know who did?"

Miss Marple nodded.

Mrs. Bantry, like an ecstatic Greek chorus, said: "Isn't she wonderful?" to an unhearing world.

"Well, who was it?"

Miss Marple said:

"I was going to ask you to help me. I think, if we went up to Somerset House we should have a very good idea."

Chapter 17

i

SIR HENRY'S face was very grave.

He said:

"I don't like it."

"I am aware," said Miss Marple, "that it isn't what you call orthodox. But it *is* so important, isn't it, to be quite *sure*—'to make assurance doubly sure,' as Shakespeare has it. I think, if Mr. Jefferson would agree——"

"What about Harper? Is he to be in on this?"

"It might be awkward for him to know too much. But there might be a hint from you. To watch certain persons—have them trailed, you know."

Sir Henry said slowly:

"Yes, that would meet the case. . . ."

ii

Superintendent Harper looked piercingly at Sir Henry Clithering.

"Let's get this quite clear, sir. You're giving me a hint?"

Sir Henry said:

"I'm informing you of what my friend has just informed me—he didn't tell me in confidence—that he proposes to visit a solicitor in Danemouth to-morrow for the purpose of making a new will."

The Superintendent's bushy eyebrows drew downwards over his steady eyes. He said:

"Does Mr. Conway Jefferson propose to inform his son-in-law and daughter-in-law of that fact?"

"He intends to tell them about it this evening."

"I see."

The Superintendent tapped his desk with a pen-holder. He repeated again: "I see. . . ."

Then the piercing eyes bored once more into the eyes of the other man. Harper said:

"So you're not satisfied with the case against Basil Blake?"

"Are you?"

The Superintendent's moustaches quivered. He said:

"Is Miss Marple?"

The two men looked at each other.

Then Harper said:

"You can leave it to me. I'll have men detailed. There will be no funny business, I can promise you that."

Sir Henry said:

"There is one more thing. You'd better see this."

He unfolded a slip of paper and pushed it across the table.

This time the Superintendent's calm deserted him. He whistled:

"So that's it, is it? That puts an entirely different complexion on the matter. How did you come to dig up this?"

"Women," said Sir Henry, "are eternally interested in marriages."

"Especially," said the Superintendent, "elderly single women."

iii

Conway Jefferson looked up as his friend entered.

His grim face relaxed into a smile.

He said:

"Well I told 'em. They took it very well."

"What did you say?"

"Told 'em that, as Ruby was dead, I felt that the fifty thousand I'd originally left her should go to something that I could associate with her memory. It was to endow a hostel for young girls working as professional dancers in London. Damned silly way to leave your money—surprised they swallowed it. As though *I*'d do a thing like that!"

He added meditatively:

"You know, I made a fool of myself over that girl. Must be turning into a silly old man. I can see it now. She was a pretty kid—but most of what I saw in her I put there myself. I pretended she was another Rosamund. Same colouring, you know. But not the same heart or mind. Hand me that paper—rather an interesting bridge problem."

iv

Sir Henry went downstairs. He asked a question of the porter.

"Mr. Gaskell, sir? He's just gone off in his car. Had to go to London."

"Oh! I see. Is Mrs. Jefferson about?"

"Mrs. Jefferson, sir, has just gone up to bed."

Sir Henry looked into the lounge and through to the ballroom. In the lounge Hugo McLean was doing a crossword puzzle and frowning a good deal over it. In the ballroom Josie was smiling valiantly into the face of a stout, perspiring man as her nimble feet avoided his destructive tread. The stout man was clearly enjoying his dance. Raymond, graceful and weary, was dancing with an anaemic-looking girl with adenoids, dull brown hair, and an expensive and exceedingly unbecoming dress.

Sir Henry said under his breath:

"*And so to bed*," and went upstairs.

v

It was three o'clock. The wind had fallen, the moon was shining over the quiet sea.

In Conway Jefferson's room there was no sound except his own heavy breathing as he lay, half propped up on pillows.

There was no breeze to stir the curtains at the window, but they stirred. . . . For a moment they parted, and a figure was silhouetted against the moonlight. Then they fell back into place. Everything was quiet again, but there was someone else inside the room.

Nearer and nearer to the bed the intruder stole. The deep breathing on the pillow did not relax.

There was no sound, or hardly any sound. A finger and thumb were ready to pick up a fold of skin, in the other hand the hypodermic was ready.

And then, suddenly, out of the shadows a hand came and closed over the hand that held the needle, the other arm held the figure in an iron grasp.

An unemotional voice, the voice of the law, said:

"No, you don't. I want that needle!"

The light switched on and from his pillows Conway Jefferson looked grimly at the murderer of Ruby Keene.

Chapter 18

i

Sir Henry Clithering said:

"Speaking as Watson, I want to know your methods Miss Marple."

Superintendent Harper said:

"*I*'d like to know what put you on to it first."

Colonel Melchett said:

"You've done it again, by Jove! I want to hear all about it from the beginning."

Miss Marple smoothed the puce silk of her best evening-gown. She flushed and smiled and looked very self-conscious.

She said: "I'm afraid you'll think my 'methods,' as Sir Henry calls them, are terribly amateurish. The truth is, you see, that most people—and I don't exclude policemen—are far too trusting for this wicked world. They believe what is told them. I never do. I'm afraid I always like to prove a thing for myself."

"That is the scientific attitude," said Sir Henry

"In this case," continued Miss Marple, "certain things were taken for granted from the first—instead of just confining oneself to the facts. The facts, as I noted them, were that the victim was quite young and that she bit her nails and that her teeth stuck out a little—as young girls' so often do if not corrected in time with a plate—(and children are very naughty about their plates and taking them out when their elders aren't looking).

"But that is wandering from the point. Where was I? Oh, yes, looking down at the dead girl and feeling sorry, because it is always sad to see a young life cut short, and thinking that whoever had done it was a very wicked person. Of course it was all very confusing her being found in Colonel Bantry's library, altogether too like a book to be *true*. In fact, it made the wrong pattern. It wasn't, you see, *meant*, which confused us a lot. The *real* idea had been to plant the body on poor young Basil Blake (a *much* more likely person), and his action in putting it in the Colonel's library delayed things considerably, and must have been a source of great annoyance to the *real* murderer.

"Originally, you see, Mr. Blake would have been the first object of suspicion. They'd have made inquiries in Danemouth, found he knew the girl, then found he had tied himself up with another girl, and they'd have assumed that Ruby came to blackmail him, or something like that, and that he'd strangled her in a fit of rage. Just an ordinary, sordid, what I call *night-club* type of crime!

"But that, of course, *all went wrong*, and interest became focused much too soon on the Jefferson family—to the great annoyance of *a certain person*.

"As I've told you, I've got a very suspicious mind. My nephew Raymond tells me (in fun, of course, and quite affectionately) that I have a mind like a *sink*. He says that most Victorians have. All I can say is that the Victorians knew a good deal about human nature.

"As I say, having this rather insanitary—or surely *sanitary*?—mind, I looked at once at the *money* angle of it. Two people stood to benefit by this girl's death—you couldn't get away from that. Fifty thousand pounds is a lot of money—especially when you are in financial difficulties, as both these people were. Of course they both seemed very nice, agreeable people—they didn't seem *likely* people—but one never can tell, can one?

"Mrs. Jefferson, for instance—every one liked her. But it did seem clear that she had become very restless that summer, and that she was tired of the life she led, completely dependent on her father-in-law. She knew, because the doctor had told her, that he couldn't live long—so *that* was all right—to put it callously—or it *would* have been all right if Ruby Keene hadn't come along. Mrs. Jefferson was passionately devoted to her son, and some women have a curious idea that crimes committed for the sake of their offspring are almost morally justified. I have come across that attitude once or twice in the village. 'Well, 'twas all for Daisy, you see, miss,' they say, and seem to think that

that makes doubtful conduct quite all right. Very *lax* thinking.

"Mr. Mark Gaskell, of course, was a much more likely starter, if I may use such a sporting expression. He was a gambler and had not, I fancied, a very high moral code. But, for certain reasons, I was of the opinion that a *woman* was concerned in this crime.

"As I say, with my eye on motive, the money angle seemed *very* suggestive. It was annoying, therefore, to find that both these people had alibis for the time when Ruby Keene, according to the medical evidence, had met her death.

"But soon afterwards there came the discovery of the burnt-out car with Pamela Reeve's body in it, and then the whole thing leaped to the eye. The alibis, of course, were worthless.

"I now had two *halves* of the case, and both quite convincing, but they did not fit. There must *be* a connection, but I could not find it. The one person whom I *knew* to be concerned in the crime hadn't got a motive.

"It was stupid of me," said Miss Marple meditatively. "If it hadn't been for Dinah Lee I shouldn't have thought of it—the most obvious thing in the world. Somerset House! Marriage! It wasn't a question of only Mr. Gaskell or Mrs. Jefferson—there was the further possibility of *marriage*. If either of those two was married, or even was *likely* to marry, *then the other party to the marriage contract was involved too*. Raymond, for instance, might think he had a pretty good chance of marrying a rich wife. He had been very assiduous to Mrs. Jefferson, and it was his charm, I think, that awoke her from her long widowhood. She had been quite content just being a daughter to Mr. Jefferson—like Ruth and Naomi—only Naomi, if you remember, took a lot of trouble to arrange a suitable marriage for Ruth.

"Besides Raymond there was Mr. McLean. She liked him very much and it seemed highly possible that she would marry him in the end. *He* wasn't well off—and he was not far from Danemouth on the night in question. So it seemed, didn't it," said Miss Marple, "as though *any one* might have done it?

"But, of course, really, in my own mind, I *knew*. You couldn't get away, could you, from those bitten nails?"

"Nails?" said Sir Henry. "But she tore her nail and cut the others."

"Nonsense," said Miss Marple. "*Bitten* nails and close *cut* nails are quite different! Nobody could mistake them who knew anything about girls' nails—very ugly, bitten nails, as I always tell the girls in my class. Those nails, you see, were a *fact*. And they could only mean one thing. *The body in Colonel Bantry's library wasn't Ruby Keene at all.*

"And that brings you straight to the one person who must be concerned. *Josie!* Josie identified the body. She knew, she *must* have known, that it wasn't Ruby Keene's body. She said it was. She was puzzled, completely puzzled, at finding that body where it was. She practically betrayed that fact. Why? Because *she* knew, none better, where it ought to have been found! In Basil Blake's cottage. Who directed our attention to Basil? Josie, by saying to Raymond that Ruby might have been with the film man. And before that, by slipping a snapshot of him into Ruby's handbag. Who cherished such bitter anger against the dead girl that she couldn't hide it even when she looked down at her dead? Josie! Josie, who was shrewd, practical, hard as nails, and *all out for money*.

"That is what I meant about believing too readily. Nobody thought of disbelieving Josie's statement that the body was Ruby Keene's. Simply because it didn't seem at the time that she could have any motive for lying. Motive was always the difficulty—Josie was clearly involved, but Ruby's death seemed, if anything, contrary to her interests. It was not till Dinah Lee mentioned Somerset House that I got the connection.

"Marriage! If Josie and Mark Gaskell were actually married—then the whole thing was clear. As we know now, Mark and Josie were married a year ago. They were keeping it dark until Mr. Jefferson died.

"It was really quite interesting, you know, tracing out the course of events—seeing exactly how the plan had worked out. Complicated and yet simple. First of all the selection of the poor child, Pamela, the approach to her from the film angle. A screen test—of course the poor child couldn't resist it. Not when it was put up to her as plausibly as Mark Gaskell put it. She comes to the hotel, he is waiting for her, he takes her in by the side door and introduces her to Josie—one of their make-up experts! That poor child, it makes me quite sick to think of it! Sitting in Josie's bathroom while Josie bleaches her hair and makes up her face and varnishes her finger-nails and toe-nails. During all this, the drug was given. In an ice-cream soda, very likely. She goes off into a coma. I imagine that they put her into one of the empty rooms opposite—they were only cleaned once a week, remember.

"After dinner Mark Gaskell went out in his car—to the sea-front, *he* said. That is when he took Pamela's body to the cottage dressed in one of Ruby's old dresses and arranged it on the hearthrug. She was still unconscious, but not dead, when he strangled her with the belt of the frock. . . .Not nice, no—but I hope and pray she knew nothing about it. Really, I feel quite pleased to think of him being hanged. . . .That must have been just after ten o'clock. Then he drove back at top speed and found the others in the lounge where Ruby Keene, *still alive*, was dancing her exhibition dance with Raymond.

"I should imagine that Josie had given Ruby intructions beforehand. Ruby was accustomed to doing what Josie told her. She was to change, go into Josie's room and wait. She, too, was drugged, probably in after-dinner coffee. She was yawning, remember, when she talked to young Bartlett.

"Josie came up later to 'look for her'—*but nobody but Josie went into Josie's room.* She probably finished the girl off then—with an injection, perhaps, or a blow on the back of the head. She went down, danced with Raymond, debated with the Jeffersons where Ruby could be, and finally went up to bed. In the early hours of the morning she dressed the girl in Pamela's clothes, carried the body down the side stairs—she was a strong muscular young woman—fetched George Bartlett's car, drove two miles to the quarry, poured petrol over the car and set it alight. Then she walked back to the hotel, probably timing her arrival there for eight or nine o'clock—up early in her anxiety about Ruby!"

"An intricate plot," said Colonel Melchett.

"Not more intricate than the steps of a dance," said Miss Marple.

"I suppose not."

"She was very thorough," said Miss Marple. "She even foresaw the discrepancy of the nails. That's why she managed to break one of Ruby's nails on her shawl. It made an excuse for pretending that Ruby had clipped her nails close."

Harper said: "Yes, she thought of everything. And the only real proof you had, Miss Marple, was a schoolgirl's bitten nails."

"More than that," said Miss Marple. "People *will* talk too much. Mark Gaskell talked too much. He was speaking of Ruby and he said 'her teeth ran down her throat.' But the dead girl in Colonel Bantry's library had teeth that stuck *out*."

Conway Jefferson said rather grimly:

"And was the last dramatic *finale* your idea, Miss Marple?"

Miss Marple confessed. "Well, it *was*, as a matter of fact. It's so nice to be *sure*, isn't it?"

"Sure is the word," said Conway Jefferson grimly.

"You see," said Miss Marple, "once Mark and Josie knew that you were going to make a new will, they'd *have* to do something. They'd already committed *two* murders on account of the money. So they might as well commit a third. Mark, of course, must be absolutely clear, so he went off to London and established an alibi by dining at a restaurant with friends and going on to a night club. Josie was to do the work. They still wanted Ruby's death to be put down to Basil's account, so Mr. Jefferson's death must be thought due to his heart failing. There was digitalin, so the Superintendent tells me, in the syringe. Any doctor would think death from heart trouble quite natural in the circumstances. Josie had loosened one of the stone balls on the balcony and she was going to let it crash down afterwards. His death would be put down to the shock of the noise."

Melchett said: "Ingenious devil."

Sir Henry said: "So the third death you spoke of was to be Conway Jefferson?'

Miss Marple shook her head.

"Oh no—I meant Basil Blake. They'd have got him hanged if they could."

"Or shut up in Broadmoor," said Sir Henry.

Conway Jefferson grunted. He said:

"Always knew Rosamund had married a rotter. Tried not to admit it to myself. She was damned fond of him. Fond of a murderer! Well, he'll hang as well as the woman. I'm glad he went to pieces and gave the show away."

Miss Marple said:

"She was always the strong character. It was her plan throughout. The irony of it is that she got the girl down here herself, never dreaming that she would take Mr. Jefferson's fancy and ruin all her own prospects."

Jefferson said:

"Poor lass. Poor little Ruby. . . ."

Adelaide Jefferson and Hugo McLean came in. Adelaide looked almost beautiful to-night. She came up to Conway Jefferson and laid a hand on his shoulder. She said, with a little catch in her breath:

"I want to tell you something, Jeff. At once. I'm going to marry Hugo."

Conway Jefferson looked up at her for a moment. He said gruffly:

"About time you married again. Congratulations to you both. By the way, Addie, I'm making a new will to-morrow."

She nodded. "Oh yes. I know."

Jefferson said:

"No, you don't. I'm settling ten thousand pounds on you. Everything else I have goes to Peter when I die. How does that suit you, my girl?"

"Oh, *Jeff*!" Her voice broke. "You're *wonderful*!"

"He's a nice lad. I'd like to see a good deal of him—in the time I've got left."

"Oh, you shall!"

"Got a great feeling for crime, Peter has," said Conway Jefferson meditatively. "Not only has he got the finger-nail of the murdered girl—one of the murdered girls, anyway—but he was lucky enough to have a bit of Josie's shawl caught in with the nail. So he's got a souvenir of the murderess too! That makes him *very* happy!"

ii

Hugo and Adelaide passed by the ballroom. Raymond came

up to them.

Adelaide said, rather quickly:

"I must tell you my news. We're going to be married."

The smile on Raymond's face was perfect—a brave, pensive smile.

"I hope," he said, ignoring Hugo and gazing into her eyes, "that you will be very, very happy. . . ."

They passed on and Raymond stood looking after them.

"A nice woman," he said to himself. "A very nice woman. And she would have had money too. The trouble I took to mug up that bit about the Devonshire Starrs. . . .Oh well, my luck's out. Dance, dance, little gentleman!"

And Raymond returned to the ballroom.

THE MOVING FINGER

The Moving Finger

AGATHA CHRISTIE

TO MY FRIENDS
SYDNEY AND MARY SMITH

1

i

WHEN AT last I was taken out of the plaster, and the doctors had pulled me about to their hearts' content, and nurses had wheedled me into cautiously using my limbs, and I had been nauseated by their practically using baby talk to me, Marcus Kent told me I was to go and live in the country.

"Good air, quiet life, nothing to do—that's the prescription for you. That sister of yours will look after you. Eat, sleep and imitate the vegetable kingdom as far as possible."

I didn't ask him if I'd ever be able to fly again. There are questions that you don't ask because you're afraid of the answers to them. In the same way during the last five months I'd never ask if I was going to be condemned to lie on my back all my life. I was afraid of a bright hypocritical reassurance from Sister. "Come now, *what* a question to ask! We don't let our patients go talking in *that* way!"

So I hadn't asked—and it had been all right. I wasn't to be a helpless cripple. I could move my legs, stand on them, finally walk a few steps—and if I did feel rather like an adventurous baby learning to toddle, with wobbly knees and cotton wool soles to my feet—well, that was only weakness and disuse and would pass.

Marcus Kent, who is the right kind of doctor, answered what I hadn't said.

"You're going to recover completely," he said. "We weren't sure until last Tuesday when you had that final overhaul, but I can tell you so authoritatively now. But—it's going to be a long business. A long and, if I may say so, a wearisome business. When it's a question of healing nerves and muscles, the brain must help the body. Any impatience, any fretting, will throw you back. And whatever you do, don't 'will yourself to get well quickly.' Anything of that kind and you'll find yourself back in a nursing home. You've got to take life slowly and easily, the *tempo* is marked *Legato*. Not only has your body got to recover, but your nerves have been weakened by the necessity of keeping you under drugs for so long.

"That's why I say, go down to the country, take a house, get interested in local politics, in local scandal, in village gossip. Take an inquisitive and violent interest in your neighbours. If I may make a suggestion, go to a part of the world where you haven't got any friends scattered about."

I nodded. "I had already," I said, "thought of that."

I could think of nothing more insufferable than members of one's own gang dropping in full of sympathy and their own affairs.

"But Jerry, you're looking marvellous—isn't he? Absolutely. Darling, I must tell you—What do you think Buster has done now?"

No, none of that for me. Dogs are wise. They crawl away into a quiet corner and lick their wounds and do not rejoin the world until they are whole once more.

So it came about that Joanna and I, sorting wildly through house-agents' glowing eulogies of properties all over the British Isles, selected Little Furze, Lymstock, as one of the "possibles" to be viewed, mainly because we had never been to Lymstock, and knew no one in that neighbourhood.

And when Joanna saw Little Furze she decided at once that it was just the house we wanted.

It lay about half a mile out of Lymstock on the road leading up to the moors. It was a prim low white house, with a sloping Victorian veranda painted a faded green. It had a pleasant view over a slope of heather-covered land with the church spire of Lymstock down below to the left.

It had belonged to a family of maiden ladies, the Misses Barton, of whom only one was left, the youngest, Miss Emily.

Miss Emily Barton was a charming little old lady who matched her house in an incredible way. In a soft apologetic voice she explained to Joanna that she had never let her house before, indeed would never have thought of doing so, "but you see, my dear, things are so different nowadays—*taxation*, of course, and then my stocks and shares, so *safe*, as I always imagined, and indeed the bank manager *himself* recommended some of them, but they seem to be paying *nothing* at all these days—*foreign*, of course! And really it makes it all so *difficult*. One does not (I'm sure you will understand me, my dear, and not take offence, you look so kind) *like* the idea of letting one's house to strangers—but something must be done, and really, having seen you, I shall be quite *glad* to think of you being here—it needs, you know, *young life*. And I must confess I did shrink from the idea of having *Men* here!"

At this point, Joanna had to break the news of me. Miss Emily rallied well.

"Oh dear, I see. How sad! A flying accident? So brave these young men. Still, your brother will be practically an invalid—"

The thought seemed to soothe the gently little lady. Presumably I should not be indulging in those grosser masculine activities which Emily Barton feared. She inquired diffidently if I smoked.

"Like a chimney," said Joanna. "But then," she pointed out, "so do I."

"Of course, of course. So stupid of me. I'm afraid, you know, I haven't moved with the times. My sisters were all older than myself, and my dear mother lived to be ninety-seven—just fancy!—and was most particular. Yes, yes, everyone smokes now. The only thing is, there are no ash-trays in the house."

Joanna said that we would bring lots of ash-trays, and she added with a smile, "We won't put down cigarette ends on your nice furniture, that I do promise you. Nothing makes me so mad myself as to see people do that."

So it was settled and we took Little Furze for a period of six months, with an option of another three, and Emily Barton explained to Joanna that she herself was going to be very comfortable because she was going into rooms kept by an old parlourmaid, "my faithful Florence," who had married "after being with us for fifteen years. *Such* a nice girl, and her husband is in the building trade. They have a nice house in the High Street and two beautiful rooms on the top floor where I shall be *most* comfortable, and Florence so pleased to have me."

So everything seemed to be most satisfactory, and the agreement was signed and in due course, Joanna and I arrived and settled in, and Miss Emily Barton's maid Partridge having consented to remain, we were well looked after with the assistance of a "girl" who came in every morning and who seemed to be half-witted but amiable.

Partridge, a gaunt, dour female of middle age, cooked admirably, and though disapproving of late dinner (it having been Miss Emily's custom to dine lightly off a boiled egg) nevertheless accommodated herself to our ways and went so far as to admit that she could see I needed my strength building up.

When we had settled in and been at Little Furze a week Miss Emily Barton came solemnly and left cards. Her example was followed by Mrs. Symmington, the lawyer's wife, Miss Griffith, the doctor's sister, Mrs. Dane Calthrop, the vicar's wife, and Mr. Pye of Prior's End.

Joanna was much impressed.

"I didn't know," she said in an awestruck voice, "that people really *called*—with *cards*."

"That is because, my child," I said, "you know nothing about the country."

"Nonsense. I've stayed away for heaps of week-ends with people."

"That is not at all the same thing," I said.

I am five years older than Joanna. I can remember as a child the big white shabby untidy house we had with the fields running down to the river. I can remember creeping under the nets of raspberry canes unseen by the gardener, and the smell of white dust in the stable yard and an orange cat crossing it, and the sound of horse hoofs kicking something in the stables.

But when I was seven and Joanna two, we went to live in London with an aunt, and thereafter our Christmas and Easter holidays were spent there with pantomimes and theatres and cinemas and excursions to Kensington Gardens with boats, and later to skating rinks. In August we were taken to an hotel by the seaside somewhere.

Reflecting on this, I said thoughtfully to Joanna, and with a feeling of compunction as I realised what a selfish, self-centred invalid I had become:

"This is going to be pretty frightful for you, I'm afraid. You'll miss everything so."

For Joanna is very pretty and very gay, and she likes dancing and cocktails, and love affairs and rushing about in high-powered cars.

Joanna laughed and said she didn't mind at all.

"As a matter of fact, I'm glad to get away from it all. I really was fed up with the whole crowd, and although you won't be sympathetic, I was really very cut up about Paul. It will take me a long time to get over it."

I was sceptical over this. Joanna's love affairs always run the same course. She has a mad infatuation for some completely spineless young man who is a misunderstood genius. She listens to his endless complaints and works like anything to get him recognition. Then, when he is ungrateful, she is deeply wounded and says her heart is broken—until the next gloomy young man comes along, which is usually about three weeks later!

So I did not take Joanna's broken heart very seriously. But I did see that living in the country was like a new game to my attractive sister.

"At any rate," she said, "I look all right, don't I?"

I studied her critically and was not able to agree.

Joanna was dressed (by Mirotin) for *le Sport*. That is to say she was wearing a skirt of outrageous and preposterous checks. It was skin-tight, and on her upper half she had a ridiculous little short-sleeved jersey with a Tyrolean effect. She had sheer silk stockings and some irreproachable but brand new brogues.

"No," I said, "you're all wrong. You ought to be wearing a very old tweed skirt, preferably of dirty green or faded brown. You'd wear a nice cashmere jumper matching it, and perhaps a cardigan coat, and you'd have a felt hat and thick stockings and old shoes. Then, and only then, you'd sink into the background of Lymstock High Street, and not stand out as you do at present." I added: "Your face is all wrong, too."

"What's wrong with that? I've got on my Country Tan Make-up No. 2."

'Exactly," I said. "If you lived in Lymstock, you would have on just a little powder to take the shine off the nose, and possibly a *soupçon* of lipstick—not very well applied—and you would almost certainly be wearing all your eyebrows instead of only a quarter of them."

Joanna gurgled and seemed much amused.

"Do you think they'll think I'm awful?" she said.

"No," I said. "Just queer."

Joanna had resumed her study of the cards left by our callers. Only the vicar's wife had been so fortunate, or possibly unfortunate, as to catch Joanna at home.

Joanna murmured:

"It's rather like Happy Families, isn't it? Mrs. Legal the lawyer's wife, Miss Dose the doctor's daughter, etc." She added with enthusiasm: "I do think this is a nice place, Jerry! So sweet and funny and old-world. You just can't think of anything nasty happening here, can you?"

And although I knew what she said was really nonsense, I agreed with her. In a place like Lymstock nothing nasty could happen. It is odd to think that it was just a week later that we got the first letter.

ii

I see that I have begun badly. I have given no description of Lymstock and without understanding what Lymstock is like, it is impossible to understand my story.

To begin with, Lymstock has its roots in the past. Somewhere about the time of the Norman Conquest, Lymstock was a place of importance. That importance was chiefly ecclesiastical. Lymstock had a priory, and it had a long succession of ambitious and powerful priors. Lords and barons in the surrounding countryside made themselves right with Heaven by leaving certain of their lands to the priory. Lymstock Priory waxed rich and important and was a power in the land for many centuries. In due course, however, Henry the Eighth caused it to share the fate of its contemporaries. From then on a castle dominated the town. It was still important. It had rights and privileges and wealth.

And then, somewhere in seventeen hundred and something

the tide of progress swept Lymstock into a back-water. The castle crumbled. Neither railways nor main roads came near Lymstock. It turned into a little provincial market town, unimportant and forgotten, with a sweep of moorland rising behind it and placid farms and fields ringing it round.

A market was held there once a week, on which day one was apt to encounter cattle in the lanes and roads. It had a small race meeting twice a year which only the most obscure horses attended. It had a charming High Street with dignified houses set flat back, looking slightly incongruous with their ground-floor windows displaying buns or vegetables or fruit. It had a long straggling draper's shop, a large and portentous iron-monger's, a prententious post office, and a row of straggly indeterminate shops, two rival butchers and an International Stores. It had a doctor, a firm of solicitors, Messrs. Galbraith, Galbraith and Symmington, a beautiful and unexpectedly large church dating from fourteen hundred and twenty, with some Saxon remains incorporated in it, a new and hideous school, and two pubs.

Such was Lymstock, and urged on by Emily Barton, anybody who was anybody came to call upon us, and in due course Joanna, having bought a pair of gloves and assumed a velvet beret rather the worse for wear, sallied forth to return them.

To us, it was all quite novel and entertaining. We were not there for life. It was, for us, an interlude. I prepared to obey my doctor's instructions and get interested in my neighbours.

Joanna and I found it all great fun.

I remembered, I suppose, Marcus Kent's instructions to enjoy the local scandals. I certainly didn't suspect how those scandals were going to be introduced to my notice.

The odd part of it was that the letter, when it came, amused us more than anything else.

It arrived, I remember, at breakfast. I turned it over, in the idle way one does when time goes slowly and every event must be spun out to its full extent. It was, I saw, a local letter with a typewritten address.

I opened it before the two with London postmarks, since one of them was a bill and the other from a rather tiresome cousin.

Inside, printed words and letters had been cut out and

gummed to a sheet of paper. For a minute or two I stared at the words without taking them in. Then I gasped.

Joanna, who was frowning over some bills, looked up.

"Hallo," she said, "what is it? You look quite startled."

The letter, using terms of the coarsest character, expressed the writer's opinion that Joanna and I were not brother and sister.

"It's a particularly foul anonymous letter," I said.

I was still suffering from shock. Somehow one didn't expect that kind of thing in the placid backwater of Lymstock.

Joanna at once displayed lively interest.

"*No?* What does it say?"

In novels, I have noticed, anonymous letters of a foul and disgusting character are never shown, if possible, to women. It is implied that women must at all cost be shielded from the shock it might give their delicate nervous systems.

I am sorry to say it never occurred to me not to show the letter to Joanna. I handed it to her at once.

She vindicated my belief in her toughness by displaying no emotion but that of amusement.

"What an awful bit of dirt! I've always heard about anonymous letters, but I've never seen one before. Are they always like this?"

"I can't tell you," I said. "It's my first experience, too."

Joanna began to giggle.

"You must have been right about my make-up, Jerry. I suppose they think I just *must* be an abandoned female!"

"That," I said, "coupled with the fact that our father was a tall, dark lantern-jawed man and our mother a fair-haired blue-eyed little creature, and that I take after him and you take after her."

Joanna nodded thoughtfully.

"Yes, we're not a bit alike. Nobody would take us for brother and sister."

"Somebody certainly hasn't," I said with feeling.

Joanna said she thought it was frightfully funny.

She dangled the letter thoughtfully by one corner and asked what we were to do with it.

"The correct procedure, I believe," I said, "is to drop it into the fire with a sharp exclamation of disgust."

I suited the action to the word, and Joanna applauded.

"You did that beautifully," she added. "You ought to have been on the stage. It's lucky we still have fires, isn't it?"

"The waste-paper basket would have been much less dramatic," I agreed. "I could of course, have set light to it with a match and slowly watched it burn—or watched it slowly burn."

'Things never burn when you want them to," said Joanna. "They go out. You'd probably have had to strike match after match."

She got up and went towards the window. Then, standing there, she turned her head sharply.

"I wonder," she said, "who wrote it?"

"We're never likely to know," I said.

"No—I suppose not." She was silent a moment, and then said: "I don't know when I come to think of it that it is so funny after all. You know, I thought they—they *liked* us down here."

"So they do," I said. "This is just some half-crazy brain on the borderline."

'I suppose so. Ugh— Nasty!"

As she went out into the sunshine I thought to myself as I smoked my after-breakfast cigarette that she was quite right. It was nasty. Someone resented our coming here—someone resented Joanna's bright young sophisticated beauty—someone wanted to *hurt*. To take it with a laugh was perhaps the best way—but deep down it wasn't funny. . . .

Dr. Griffith came that morning. I had fixed up for him to give me a weekly overhaul. I liked Owen Griffith. He was dark, ungainly, with awkward ways of moving and deft, very gentle hands. He had a jerky way of talking and was rather shy.

He reported progress to be encouraging. Then he added:

"You're feeling all right, aren't you? Is it my fancy, or are you a bit under the weather this morning?"

"Not really," I said. "A particularly scurrilous anonymous letter arrive with the morning coffee, and it's left rather a nasty taste in the mouth."

He dropped his bag on the floor. His thin dark face was excited.

"Do you mean to say that *you've* had one of them?"

I was interested.

"They've been going about, then?"

"Yes. For some time."

"Oh," I said, "I see. I was under the impression that our presence as strangers was resented here."

"No, no, it's nothing to do with that. It's just—" He paused and then asked, "What did it say? At least—" he turned suddenly red and embarrassed—"perhaps I oughtn't to ask?"

"I'll tell you with pleasure," I said. "It just said that the fancy tart I'd brought down with me wasn't my sister—not 'alf! And that, I may say, is a Bowdlerized version."

His dark face flushed angrily.

"How damnable! Your sister didn't—she's not upset, I hope?"

"Joanna," I said, "looks a little like the angel off the top of the Christmas tree, but she's eminently modern and quite tough. She found it highly entertaining. Such things haven't come her way before."

"I should hope not, indeed," said Griffith warmly.

"And anyway," I said firmly. "That's the best way to take it, I think. As something utterly ridiculous."

"Yes," said Owen Griffiths. "Only—"

He stopped, and I chimed in quickly:

"Quite so," I said. "Only is the word!"

"The trouble is," he said, "that this sort of thing, once it starts, grows."

"So I should imagine."

"It's pathological, of course."

I nodded. "Any idea who's behind it?" I asked.

"No, I wish I had. You see, the anonymous letter pest arises from one of two causes. Either it's *particular*—directed at one particular person or set of people, that is to say it's *motivated,* it's someone who's got a definite grudge (or thinks they have) and who chooses a particularly nasty and underhand way of working it off. It's mean and disgusting but it's not necessarily crazy, and it's usually fairly easy to trace the writer—a discharged servant, a jealous woman—and so on. But if it's *general,* and not particular, then it's more serious. The letters are sent indiscriminately and serve the purpose of working off some frustration in the writer's mind. As I say, it's definitely pathological. And the craze grows. In the end, of course, you track down the person in question—it's often someone extremely unlikely, and that's that. There was a bad outburst of the kind over the other side of the country last year—turned out to be the head of the millinery department in a big draper's establishment. Quiet, refined woman—had been there for years. I remember something of the same kind in my last practice up north—but that turned out to be purely personal spite. Still, as I say, I've seen something of this kind of thing, and, quite frankly, it frightens me!"

"Has it been going on long?" I asked.

"I don't think so. Hard to say, of course, because people who get these letters don't go round advertising the fact. They put them in the fire."

He paused.

"I've had one myself. Symmington, the solicitor, he's had one. And one or two of my poorer patients have told me about them."

"All much the same sort of thing?"

"Oh yes. A definite harping on the sex theme. That's always a feature." He grinned. "Symmington was accused of illicit relations with his lady clerk—poor old Miss Ginch, who's forty at least, with pince-nez and teeth like a rabbit. Symmington took it straight to the police. My letters accused me of violating professional decorum with my lady patients, stressing the details. They're all quite childish and absurd, but horribly venomous." His face changed, grew grave. "But all the same, I'm *afraid*. These things can be dangerous, you know."

"I suppose they can."

"You see," he said, "crude, childish spite though it is, sooner or later one of these letters will hit the mark. And then, God knows what may happen! I'm afraid, too, of the effect upon the slow, suspicious uneducated mind. If they see a thing written, they believe it's true. All sorts of complications may arise."

"It was an illiterate sort of letter," I said thoughtfully, "written by somebody practically illiterate, I should say."

"Was it?" said Owen, and went away.

Thinking it over afterwards, I found that "Was it?" rather disturbing.

2

i

I AM not going to pretend that the arrival of our anonymous letter did not leave a nasty taste in the mouth. It did. At the same time, it soon passed out of my mind. I did not, you see, at that point, take it seriously. I think I remember saying to myself that these things probably happen fairly often in out-of-the-way villages. Some hysterical woman with a taste for dramatising herself was probably at the bottom of it. Anyway, if the letters were as childish and silly as the one we had got, they couldn't do much harm.

The next *incident*, if I may put it so, occurred about a week later, when Partridge, her lips set tightly together, informed me, that Beatrice, the daily help, would not be coming to-day.

"I gather, sir," said Partridge, "that the girl has been Upset."

I was not very sure what Partridge was implying, but I diagnosed (wrongly) some stomachic trouble to which Partridge was too delicate to allude more directly. I said I was sorry and hoped she would soon be better.

"The girl is perfectly well, sir," said Partridge. "She is Upset in her Feelings."

"Oh ," I said rather doubtfully.

"Owing," went on Partridge, 'to a letter she has received. Making, I understand, Insinuations."

The grimness of Partridge's eye, coupled with the obvious capital I of Insinuations, made me apprehensive that the insinuations were concerned with me. Since I would hardly have recognised Beatrice by sight if I had met her in the town, so unaware of her had I been—I felt a not unnatural annoyance. An invalid hobbling about on two sticks is hardly cast for the role of deceiver of village girls. I said irritably:

"What nonsense!"

"My very words, sir, to the girl's mother," said Partridge. " 'Goings On in this house,' I said to her, 'there never have been and never will be while I am in charge. As to Beatrice,' I said, 'girls are difficult nowadays, and as to Goings On elsewhere I can say nothing.' But the truth is, sir, that Beatrice's friend from the garage as she walks out with got one of them nasty letters too, and he isn't acting reasonable at all."

"I have never heard anything so preposterous in my life," I said angrily.

"It's my opinion, sir," said Partridge, "that we're well rid of the girl. What I say is, she wouldn't take on so if there wasn't *something* she didn't want found out. No smoke without fire, that's what I say."

I had no idea how horribly tired I was going to get of that particular phrase.

ii

That morning, by way of adventure, I was to walk down to the village. (Joanna and I always called it the village, although technically we were incorrect, and Lymstock would have been annoyed to hear us.)

The sun was shining, the air was cool and crisp with the sweetness of spring in it. I assembled my sticks and started off, firmly refusing to permit Joanna to accompany me.

"No," I said, "I will not have a guardian angel teetering along beside me and uttering encouraging chirrups. A man travels fastest who travels alone, remember. I have much business to transact. I shall go to Galbraith, Galbraith and Symmington, and sign that transfer of shares, I shall call in at the baker's and complain about the current loaf, and I shall return that book we borrowed. I have to go to the bank, too. Let me away, woman, the morning is all too short."

It was arranged that Joanna should pick me up with the car and drive me back up the hill in time for lunch.

"That ought to give you time to pass the time of day with everyone in Lymstock."

"I have no doubt," I said, "that I shall have seen anybody who is anybody by then."

For morning in the High Street was a kind of rendezvous for shoppers, when news was exchanged.

I did not, after all, walk down to the town unaccompanied. I had gone about two hundred yards, when I heard a bicycle bell behind me, then a scrunching of brakes, and then Megan Hunter more or less fell off her machine at my feet.

"Hallo," she said breathlessly as she rose and dusted herself off.

I rather liked Megan and always felt oddly sorry for her.

She was Symmington the lawyer's step-daughter, Mrs. Symmington's daughter by a first marriage. Nobody talked much about Mr. (or Captain) Hunter, and I gathered that he was considered best forgotten. He was reported to have treated Mrs. Symmington very badly. She had divorced him a year or two after the marriage. She was a woman with means of her own and had settled down with her little daughter in Lymstock "to forget," and had eventually married the only eligible bachelor in the place, Richard Symmington. There were two boys of the second marriage to whom their parents were devoted, and I fancied that Megan sometimes felt odd man out in the establishment. She certainly did not resemble her mother, who was a small anaemic woman, fadedly pretty, who talked in a thin melancholy voice of servant difficulties and her health.

Megan was a tall awkward girl, and although she was actually twenty, she looked more like a schoolgirlish sixteen. She had a shock of untidy brown hair, hazel green eyes, a thin bony face, and an unexpected charming one-sided smile. Her clothes were drab and unattractive and she usually had on lisle thread stockings with holes in them.

She looked, I decided this morning, much more like a horse than a human being. In fact she would have been a very nice horse with a little grooming.

She spoke, as usual, in a kind of breathless rush.

"I've been up to the farm—you know, Lasher's—to see if they'd got any duck's eggs. They've got an awfully nice lot of little pigs. Sweet! Do you like pigs? I do. I even like the smell."

"Well-kept pigs shouldn't smell," I said.

"Shouldn't they? They all do round here. Are you walking down to the town? I saw you were alone, so I thought I'd stop and walk with you, only I stopped rather suddenly."

"You've torn your stocking," I said.

Megan looked rather ruefully at her right leg.

"So I have. But it's got two holes already, so it doesn't matter very much, does it?"

"Don't you ever mend your stockings, Megan?"

"Rather. When Mummy catches me. But she doesn't notice awfully what I do—so it's lucky in a way, isn't it?"

"You don't seem to realise you're grown up," I said.

"You mean I ought to be more like your sister? All dolled up?"

I rather resented this description of Joanna.

"She looks clean and tidy and pleasing to the eye," I said.

"She's awfully pretty," said Megan. "She isn't a bit like you, is she? Why not?"

"Brothers and sisters aren't always alike."

"No. Of course I'm not very like Brian or Colin. And Brian and Colin aren't like each other." She paused and said, "It's very rum, isn't it?"

"What is?"

Megan replied briefly: "Families."

I said thoughtfully, "I suppose they are."

I wondered just what was passing in her mind. We walked on in silence for a moment or two, then Megan said in a rather shy voice:

"You fly, don't you?"

"Yes."

"That's how you got hurt?"

"Yes, I crashed."

Megan said:

"Nobody down here flies."

"No," I said. "I suppose not. Would you like to fly, Megan?"

"Me?" Megan seemed surprised. "Goodness, no. I should be sick. I'm sick in a train even."

She paused, and then asked with that directness which only a child usually displays:

"Will you get all right and be able to fly again, or will you always be a bit of a crock?"

"My doctor says I shall be quite all right."

"Yes, but is he the kind of man who tells lies?"

"I don't think so," I replied. "In fact, I'm quite sure of it. I trust him."

"That's all right then. But a lot of people do tell lies."

I accepted this undeniable statement of fact in silence.

Megan said in a detached judicial kind of way:

"I'm glad. I was afraid you looked bad tempered because you were crocked up for life—but if it's just natural, it's different."

"I'm not bad tempered," I said coldly.

"Well, irritable, then."

"I'm irritable because I'm in a hurry to get fit again—and these things can't be hurried."

"Then why fuss?"

I began to laugh.

"My dear girl, aren't you ever in a hurry for things to happen?"

Megan considered the question. She said:

"No. Why should I be? There's nothing to be in a hurry about. Nothing ever happens."

I was struck by something forlorn in the words. I said gently: "What do you do with yourself down here?"

She shrugged her shoulders.

"What is there to do?"

"Haven't you got any hobbies? Do you play games? Have you got friends round about?"

"I'm stupid at games. And I don't like them much. There aren't many girls round here, and the ones there are I don't like. They think I'm awful."

"Nonsense. Why should they?"

Megan shook her head.

"Didn't you go to school at all?"

"Yes, I came back a year ago."

"Did you enjoy school?"

"It wasn't bad. They taught you things in an awfully silly way, though."

"How do you mean?"

"Well—just bits and pieces. Chopping and changing from

one thing to the other. It was a cheap school, you know, and the teachers weren't very good. They could never answer questions properly."

"Very few teachers can," I said.

"Why not? They ought to."

I agreed.

"Of course I'm pretty stupid," said Megan. "And such a lot of things seem to me such rot. History, for instance. Why, it's quite different out of different books!"

"That is its real interest," I said.

"And grammar," went on Megan. "And silly compositions. And all the blathering stuff Shelley wrote, twittering on about skylarks, and Wordsworth going all potty over some silly daffodils. And Shakespeare."

"What's wrong with Shakespeare?" I inquired with interest.

"Twisting himself up to say things in such a difficult way that you can't get at what he means. Still, I like *some* Shakespeare."

"He would be gratified to know that, I'm sure," I said.

Megan suspected no sarcasm. She said, her face lighting up:

"I like Goneril and Regan, for instance."

"Why these two?"

"Oh, I don't know. They're *satisfactory*, somehow. Why do you think they were like that?"

"Like what?"

"Like they were. I mean *something* must have made them like that?"

For the first time I wondered. I had always accepted Lear's elder daughters as two nasty bits of goods and had let it go at that. But Megan's demand for a first cause interested me.

"I'll think about it," I said.

"Oh, it doesn't really matter. I just wondered. Anyway, it's only English Literature, isn't it?"

"Quite, quite. Wasn't there any subject you enjoyed?"

"Only Maths."

"Maths?" I said, rather surprised.

Megan's face had lit up.

"I loved Maths. But it wasn't awfully well taught. I'd like to be taught Maths really well. It's heavenly. I think there's something heavenly about numbers, anyway, don't you?"

"I've never felt it," I said truthfully.

We were now entering the High Street. Megan said sharply:

"Here's Miss Griffith. Hateful woman."

"Don't you like her?"

"I loathe her. She's always at me to join her foul Guides. I hate Guides. Why dress yourself up and go about in clumps, and put badges on yourself for something you haven't really learnt to do properly. I think it's all rot."

On the whole, I rather agreed with Megan. But Miss Griffith had descended on us before I could voice my assent.

The doctor's sister, who rejoiced in the singularly inappropriate name of Aimée, had all the positive assurance that her brother lacked. She was a handsome woman in a masculine weather-beaten way, with a deep hearty voice.

"Hallo, you two," she bayed at us. "Gorgeous morning, isn't it? Megan, you're just the person I wanted to see. I want some help addressing envelopes for the Conservative Association."

Megan muttered something elusive, propped up her bicycle against the kerb and dived in a purposeful way into the International Stores.

"Extraordinary child," said Miss Griffith, looking after her. "Bone lazy. Spends her time mooning about. Must be a great trial to poor Mrs. Symmington. I know her mother's tried more than once to get her to take up something—shorthand-typing, you know, or cookery, or keeping Angora rabbits. She needs an *interest* in life."

I thought that was probably true, but felt that in Megan's place I should have withstood firmly any of Aimée Griffith's suggestions for the simple reason that her aggressive personality would have put my back up.

"I don't believe in idleness," went on Miss Griffith. "And certainly not for young people. It's not as though Megan was pretty or attractive or anything like that. Sometimes I think the girl's half-witted. A great disappointment to her mother. The father, you know," she lowered her voice slightly, "was definitely a wrong 'un. Afraid the child takes after him. Painful for her mother. Oh, well, it takes all sorts to make a world, that's what I say."

"Fortunately," I responded.

Aimée Griffith gave a "jolly" laugh.

"Yes, it wouldn't do if we were all made to one pattern. But I don't like to see any one not getting all they can out of life. I enjoy life myself and I want everyone to enjoy it too. People say to me you must be bored to death living down there in the country all the year round. Not a bit of it, I say. I'm always busy, always happy! There's always something going on in the country. My time's taken up, what with my Guides, and the Institute and various committees—to say nothing of looking after Owen."

At this minute, Miss Griffith saw an acquaintance on the other side of the street, and uttering a bay of recognition she leaped across the road, leaving me free to pursue my course to the bank.

I always found Miss Griffith rather overwhelming, though I admired her energy and vitality, and it was pleasant to see the beaming contentment with her lot in life which she always displayed, and which was a pleasant contrast to the subdued complaining murmurs of so many woman.

My business at the bank transacted satisfactorily, I went on to the offices of Messrs. Galbraith, Galbraith and Symmington. I don't know if there were any Galbraiths extant. I never saw any. I was shown into Richard Symmington's inner office which had the agreeable mustiness of a long-established legal firm.

Vast numbers of deed boxes, labelled Lady Hope, Sir Everard Carr, William Yatesby-Hoares, Esq., Deceased, etc., gave the required atmosphere of decorous county families and legitimate long-established business.

Studying Mr. Symmington as he bent over the documents I had brought, it occurred to me that if Mrs. Symmington had encountered disaster in her first marriage, she had certainly played it safe in her second. Richard Symmington was the acme of calm respectability, the sort of man who would never give his wife a moment's anxiety. A long neck with a pronounced Adam's apple, a slightly cadaverous face and a long thin nose. A kindly man, no doubt, a good husband and father, but not one to set the pulses madly racing.

Presently Mr. Symmington began to speak. He spoke clearly and slowly, delivering himself of much good sense and shrewd acumen. We settled the matter in hand and I rose to go, remarking as I did so:

"I walked down the hill with your step-daughter."

For a moment Mr. Symmington looked as though he did not know who his step-daughter was, then he smiled.

"Oh yes, of course, Megan. She—er—has been back from school some time. We're thinking about finding her something to do—yes, to do. But of course she's very young still. And backward for her age, so they say. Yes, so they tell me."

I went out. In the outer office was a very old man on a stool writing slowly and laboriously, a small cheeky looking boy and a middle-aged woman with frizzy hair and pince-nez who was typing with some speed and dash.

If this was Miss Ginch I agreed with Owen Griffith that tender passages between her and her employer were exceedingly unlikely.

I went into the baker's and said my piece about the currant loaf. It was received with the exclamations and incredulity proper to the occasion, and a new currant loaf was thrust upon me in replacement—"fresh from the oven this minute"—as its indecent heat pressed against my chest proclaimed to be no less than truth.

I came out of the shop and looked up and down the street hoping to see Joanna with the car. The walk had tired me a good deal and it was awkward getting along with my sticks and the currant loaf.

But there was no sign of Joanna as yet.

Suddenly my eyes were held in glad and incredulous surprise.

Along the pavement towards me there came floating a goddess. There is really no other word for it.

The perfect features, the crisply curling golden hair, the tall exquisitely shaped body! And she walked like a goddess, without effort, seeming to swim nearer and nearer. A glorious, an incredible, a breath-taking girl!

In my intense excitement something had to go. What went was the currant loaf. It slipped from my clutches. I made a dive after it and lost my stick, which clattered to the pavement, and I slipped and nearly fell myself.

It was the strong arm of the goddess that caught and held me. I began to stammer:

"Th-thanks awfully, I'm f-f-frightfully sorry."

She had retrieved the currant loaf and handed it to me together with the stick. And then she smiled kindly and said cheerfully:

"Don't mention it. No trouble, I assure you," and the magic died completely before the flat competent voice.

A nice healthy-looking well set-up girl, no more.

I fell to reflecting what would have happened if the Gods had given Helen of Troy exactly those flat accents. How strange that a girl could trouble your inmost soul so long as she kept her mouth shut, and that the moment she spoke the glamour could vanish as though it had never been.

I had known the reverse happen, though. I had seen a little sad monkey-faced woman whom no one would turn to look at twice. Then she had opened her mouth and suddenly enchantment had lived and bloomed and Cleopatra had cast her spell anew.

Joanna had drawn up at the kerb beside me without my noticing her arrival. She asked if there was anything the matter.

"Nothing," I said, pulling myself together. "I was reflecting on Helen of Troy and others."

"What a funny place to do it," said Joanna. "You looked *most* odd, standing there clasping currant bread to your breast with your mouth wide open."

"I've had a shock," I said. "I have been transplanted to Ilium and back again."

"Do you know who that is?" I added, indicating a retreating back that was swimming gracefully away.

Peering after the girl Joanna said that it was the Symmingtons' nursery governess.

"Is that what struck you all of a heap?" she asked. "She's good-looking, but a bit of a wet fish."

"I know." I said. "Just a nice kind girl. And I'd been thinking her Aphrodite."

Joanna opened the door of the car and I got in.

"It's funny, isn't it?" she said. "Some people have lots of looks and absolutely no S.A. That girl has. It seems such a pity."

I said that if she was a nursery governess it was probably just as well.

3

i

THAT AFTERNOON we went to tea with Mr. Pye.

Mr. Pye was an extremely ladylike plump little man, devoted to his *petit point* chairs, his Dresden shepherdesses and his collection of bric-à-brac. He lived at Prior's Lodge in the grounds of which were the ruins of the old Priory.

Prior's Lodge was certainly a very exquisite house and under Mr. Pye's loving care it showed to its best advantage. Every piece of furniture was polished and set in the exact place most suited to it. The curtains and cushions were of exquisite tone and colour, and of the most expensive silks.

It was hardly a man's house, and it did strike me that to live there would be rather like taking up one's abode in a Period room at a museum. Mr. Pye's principal enjoyment in life was taking people round his house. Even those completely insensitive to their surroundings could not escape. Even if you were so hardened as to consider the essentials of living a radio, a cocktail bar, a bath and a bed surrounded by the necessary walls, Mr. Pye did not despair of leading you to better things.

His small plump hands quivered with sensibility as he described his treasures, and his voice rose to a falsetto squeak as he narrated the exciting circumstances under which he had brought his Italian bedstead home from Verona.

Joanna and I being both fond of antiquities and of period furniture, met with approval.

"It is really a pleasure, a great pleasure, to have such an acquisition to our little community. The dear good people down her, you know, so painfully bucolic—not to say *provincial*. They don't know anything. Vandals—absolute vandals! And the inside of their houses—it would make you weep, dear lady, I assure you it would make you weep. Perhaps it has done so?"

Joanna said that she hadn't gone quite as far as that.

"But you see what I mean? They mix things so terribly! I've seen with my own eyes a most delightful little Sheraton piece—delicate, perfect—a collector's piece, absolutely—and next to it a Victorian occasional table, or quite possibly a fumed oak revolving bookcase—yes, even that—*fumed oak*."

He shuddered—and murmured plaintively:

"Why are people so blind? You agree—I'm sure you agree, that beauty is the only thing worth living for."

Hypnotised by his earnestness, Joanna said, yes, yes, that was so.

"Then why," demanded Mr. Pye, "do people surround themselves with ugliness?"

Joanna said it was very odd.

"Odd? It's *criminal*! That's what I call it—criminal! And the excuses they give! They say something is *comfortable*. Or that it is *quaint*. Quaint! Such a horrible word.

"The house you have taken," went on Mr. Pye, "Miss Emily Barton's house. Now that is charming, and she has some quite nice pieces. Quite nice. One or two of them are really first class. And she has taste, too—although I'm not quite so sure of that as I was. Sometimes, I am afraid, I think it's really sentiment. She likes to keep things as they were—but not for *le bon motif*—not because of the resultant harmony—but because it is the way her mother had them."

He transferred his attention to me, and his voice changed. It altered from that of the rapt artist to that of the born gossip.

"You didn't know the family at all? No, quite so—yes, through house agents. But, my dears, you *ought* to have known that family! When I came here the old mother was still alive. An incredible person—quite incredible! A *monster*, if you know what I mean. Positively a monster. The old-fashioned Victorian monster, devouring her young. Yes, that's what it amounted to. She was monumental, you know, must have weighed seventeen stone, and all the five daughters revolved round her. 'The girls'! That's how she always spoke of them. The girls! And the eldest was well over sixty then. 'Those stupid girls!' she used to call them sometimes. Black slaves, that's all they were, fetching and carrying and agreeing with her. Ten o'clock they had to go to bed and they weren't allowed a fire in their bedroom, and as for asking their own friends to the house, that would have been unheard of. She despised them, you know, for not getting married, and yet so arranged their lives that it was practically impossible for them to meet anybody. I believe Emily, or perhaps it was Agnes, did have some kind of affair with a curate. But his family wasn't good enough and Mamma soon put a stop to *that*!"

"It sounds like a novel," said Joanna.

"Oh, my dear, it was. And then the dreadful old woman died, but of course it was far too late *then*. They just went on living there and talking in hushed voices about what poor Mamma would have wished. Even re-papering her bedroom they felt to be quite sacrilegious. Still they did enjoy themselves in the parish in a quiet way. . . . But none of them had much stamina, and they just died off one by one. Influenza took off Edith, and Minnie had an operation and didn't recover and poor Mabel had a stroke—Emily looked after her in the most devoted manner. Really that poor woman has done nothing but nursing for the last ten years. A charming creature, don't you think. Like a piece of Dresden. So sad for her having financial anxieties—but of course all investments have depreciated."

"We feel rather awful being in her house," said Joanna.

"No, no, my dear young lady. You mustn't feel that way. Her dear good Florence is devoted to her and she told me herself how happy she was to have got such nice tenants." Here Mr. Pye made a little bow. "She told me she thought she had been most fortunate."

"The house," I said, "has a very soothing atmosphere."

Mr. Pye darted a quick glance at me.

"Really? You feel that? Now, that's very interesting. I wondered, you know. Yes, I wondered."

"What do you mean, Mr. Pye?" asked Joanna.

Mr. Pye spread out his plump hands.

"Nothing, nothing. One wondered, that is all. I do believe in atmosphere, you know. People's thoughts and feelings. They give their impression to the walls and the furniture."

I did not speak for a moment or two. I was looking round me

and wondering how I would describe the atmosphere of Prior's Lodge. It seemed to me that the curious thing was that it hadn't any atmosphere! That was really very remarkable.

I reflected on this point so long that I heard nothing of the conversation going on between Joanna and her host. I was recalled to myself, however, by hearing Joanna uttering farewell preliminaries. I came out of my dream and added my quota.

We all went out into the hall. As we came towards the front door a letter came through the box and fell on the mat.

"Afternoon post," murmured Mr. Pye as he picked it up. "Now, my dear young people, you will come again, won't you? Such a pleasure to meet some broader minds, if you understand me. Someone with an appreciation of Art. Really you know, these dear good people down here, if you mention the Ballet, it conveys to them pirouetting toes, the *tulle* skirts and old gentlemen with opera glasses in the Naughty Nineties. It does indeed. Fifty years behind the times—that's what I put them down as. A wonderful country, England. It has, you know, *pockets*. Lymstock is one of them. Interesting from a collector's point of view—I always feel I have voluntarily put myself under a glass shade when I am here. The peaceful backwater where nothing ever happens."

Shaking hands with us twice over, he helped me with exaggerated care into the car. Joanna took the wheel, she negotiated with some care the circular sweep round a plot of unblemished grass, then with a straight drive ahead, she raised a hand to wave good-bye to our host where he stood on the steps of the house. I leaned forward to do the same.

But our gesture of farewell went unheeded. Mr. Pye had opened his mail.

He was standing staring down at the open sheet in his hand.

Joanna has described him once as a plump pink cherub. He was still plump, but he was not looking like a cherub now. His face was a dark congested purple, contorted with rage and surprise.

And at that moment I realised that there had been something familiar about the look of that envelope. I had not realised it at the time—indeed it had been one of those things that you note unconsciously without knowing that you do note them.

"Goodness," said Joanna. "What's bitten the poor pet?"

"I rather fancy," I said, "that it's the Hidden Hand again."

She turned an astonished face towards me and the car swerved.

"Careful, wench," I said.

Joanna refixed her attention on the road. She was frowning.

"You mean a letter like the one you got?"

"That's my guess."

"What is this place?" asked Joanna. "It looks the most innocent sleepy harmless little bit of England you can imagine—"

"Where to quote Mr. Pye, nothing ever happens," I cut in. "He chose the wrong minute to say that. Something has happened."

"But who writes these things, Jerry?"

I shrugged my shoulders.

"My dear girl, how should I know? Some local nitwit with a screw loose, I suppose."

"But why? It seems so idiotic."

"You must read Freud and Jung and that lot to find out. Or ask our Dr. Owen."

Joanna tossed her head.

"Dr. Owen doesn't like me."

"He's hardly seen you."

"He's seen quite enough, apparently, to make him cross over if he sees me coming along the High Street."

"A most unusual reaction," I said sympathetically. "And one you're not used to."

Joanna was frowning again.

"No, but seriously, Jerry, why *do* people write anonymous letters?"

"As I say, they've got a screw loose. It satisfies some urge, I suppose. If you've been snubbed, or ignored, or frustrated, and your life's pretty drab and empty, I suppose you get a sense of power from stabbing in the dark at people who are happy and enjoying themselves."

Joanna shivered. "Not nice."

"No, not nice. I should imagine the people in these country places tend to be inbred—and so you would get a fair amount of queers."

"Somebody, I suppose, quite uneducated and inarticulate? With better education—"

Joanna did not finish her sentence, and I said nothing. I have never been able to accept the easy belief that education is a panacea for every ill.

As we drove through the town before climbing up the hill road, I looked curiously at the few figures abroad in the High Street. Was one of those sturdy country-woman going about with a load of spite and malice behind her placid brow, planning perhaps even now a further outpouring of vindictive spleen?

But I still did not take the thing seriously.

ii

Two days later we went to a bridge party at the Symmingtons'.

It was a Saturday afternoon—the Symmingtons always had their bridge parties on a Saturday, because the office was shut then.

There were two tables. The players were the Symmingtons, ourselves, Miss Griffith, Mr. Pye, Miss Barton and a Colonel Appleton whom we had not yet met and who lived at Combeacre, a village some seven miles distant. He was a perfect specimen of the Blimp type, about sixty years of age, liked playing what he called a "plucky game" (which usually resulted in enormous sums above the line being scored by his opponents) and was so intrigued by Joanna that he practically never took his eyes off her the whole afternoon.

I was forced to admit that my sister was probably the most attractive thing that had been seen in Lymstock for many a long day.

When we arrived, Elsie Holland, the children's governess, was hunting for some extra bridge scorers in an ornate writing desk. She glided across the floor with them in the same celestial way I had first noticed, but the spell could not be cast a second time. Exasperating that it should be so—a waste of a perfectly lovely form and face. But I noticed now only too clearly the exceptionally large white teeth like tombstones, and the way she showed her gums when she laughed. She was, unfortunately, one of your prattling girls.

"Are these the ones, Mrs. Symmington? It's ever so stupid of me not to remember where we put them away last time. It's my fault, too, I'm afraid. I had them in my hand and then Brian called out his engine had got caught, and I ran out and what with one thing and another I must have just stuffed them in somewhere stupid. These aren't the right ones, I see now, they're a bit yellow at the edges. Shall I tell Agnes tea at five? I'm taking the kiddies to Long Barrow so there won't be any noise."

A nice kind bright girl. I caught Joanna's eye. She was laughing. I stared at her coldly. Joanna always knows what is passing in my mind, curse her.

We settled down to bridge.

I was soon to know to a nicety the bridge status of everyone in Lymstock. Mrs. Symmington was an exceedingly good bridge player and was quite a devotee of the game. Like many definitely unintellectual women, she was not stupid and had a considerable natural shrewdness. Her husband was a good sound player, slightly over-cautious. Mr. Pye can best be described as brilliant. He had an uncanny flair for psychic bidding. Joanna and I, since the party was in our honour, played at a table with Mrs. Symmington and Mr. Pye. It was Symmington's task to pour oil on troubled waters and by the exercise of tact to reconcile the three other players at his table. Colonel Appleton, as I have said, was wont to play "a plucky game." Little Miss Barton was without exception the worst bridge player I have ever come across and always enjoyed herself enormously. She did manage to follow suit, but had the wildest ideas as to the strength of her hand, never knew the score, repeatedly led out of the wrong hand and was quite unable to count trumps and often forgot what they were. Aimée Griffith's play can be summed up in her own words.

"I like a good game of bridge with no nonsense—and I don't play any of these rubbishy conventions. I say what I mean. And no post-mortems! After all, it's only a game!" It will be seen, therefore, that their host had not too easy a task.

Play proceeded fairly harmoniously, however, with occasional forgetfulness on the part of Colonel Appleton as he stared across at Joanna.

Tea was laid in the dining-room, round a big table. As we were finishing, two hot and excited little boys rushed in and were introduced, Mrs. Symmington beaming with maternal pride, as was their father.

Then, just as we were finishing, a shadow darkened my plate, and I turned my head to see Megan standing in the french window.

"Oh," said her mother. "Here's Megan."

Her voice held a faintly surprised note, as though she had forgotten that Megan existed.

The girl came in and shook hands, awkwardly and without any grace.

"I'm afraid I forgot about your tea, dear," said Mrs. Symmington. "Miss Holland and the boys took theirs out with them, so there's no nursery tea to-day. I forgot you weren't with them."

Megan nodded.

"That's all right. I'll go to the kitchen."

She slouched out of the room. She was untidily dressed as usual and there were potatoes in both heels.

Mrs. Symmington said with a little apologetic laugh:

"My poor Megan. She's just at that awkward age, you know. Girls are always shy and awkward when they've just left school before they're properly grown up."

I saw Joanna's fair head jerk backwards in what I knew to be a warlike gesture.

"But Megan's twenty, isn't she?" she said.

"Oh, yes, yes. She is. But of course she's very young for her age. Quite a child still. It's so nice, I think, when girls don't grow up too quickly." She laughed again. "I expect all mothers want their children to remain babies."

"I can't think why," said Joanna. "After all, it would be a bit awkward if one had a child who remained mentally six while his body grew up."

"Oh, you mustn't take things so literally, Miss Burton," said Mrs. Symmington.

It occurred to me at that moment that I did not much care for Mrs. Symmington. That anaemic, slighted, faded prettiness concealed, I thought, a selfish and grasping nature. She said, and I disliked her a little more still:

"My poor Megan. She's rather a difficult child, I'm afraid. I've been trying to find something for her to do—I believe there are several things one can learn by correspondence. Designing and dressmaking—or she might try and learn shorthand and typing."

The red glint was still in Joanna's eye. She said as we sat down again at the bridge table:

"I suppose she'll be going to parties and all that sort of thing. Are you going to give a dance for her?"

"A dance?" Mrs. Symmington seemed surprised and amused. "Oh, no, we don't do things like that down here."

"I see. Just tennis parties and things like that."

"Our tennis court has not been played on for years. Neither Richard nor I play. I suppose, later, when the boys grow up—Oh, Megan will find plenty to do. She's quite happy just pottering about, you know. Let me see, did I deal? Two No Trumps."

As we drove home, Joanna said with a vicious pressure on the accelerator pedal that made the car leap forward:

"I feel awfully sorry for that girl."

"Megan?"

"Yes. Her mother doesn't like her."

"Oh, come now, Joanna, it's not as bad as that."

"Yes, it is. Lots of mothers don't like their children. Megan, I should imagine, is an awkward sort of creature to have about the house. She disturbs the pattern—the Symmington pattern. It's a complete unit without her—and that's a most unhappy feeling for a sensitive creature to have—and she *is* sensitive."

"Yes," I said, "I think she is."

I was silent for a moment.

Joanna suddenly laughed mischievously.

"Bad luck for you about the governess."

"I don't know what you mean," I said with dignity.

"Nonsense. Masculine chagrin was written on your face every time you looked at her. I agree with you. It is a waste."

"I don't know what you're talking about."

"But I'm delighted, all the same. It's the first sign of reviving life. I was quite worried about you at the nursing home. You never even looked at that remarkably pretty nurse you had. An attractive minx, too—absolutely God's gift to a sick man."

"Your conversation, Joanna, I find low."

My sister continued without paying the least attention to my remarks.

"So I was much relieved to see you'd still got an eye for a nice bit of skirt. She *is* a good looker. Funny that the S.A. should have been left out so completely. It is odd, you know, Jerry. What *is* the thing that some women have and others haven't. What is it that makes one woman, even if she only says 'Foul weather' so attractive that every man within range wants to come over and talk about the weather with her? I suppose Providence makes a mistake every now and then when sending out the parcel. One Aphrodite face and form, one temperament ditto. And something goes astray and the Aphrodite temperament goes to some little plain-faced creature, and then all the other women go simply mad and say, 'I can't think what the men see in her. She isn't even good-looking!' "

"Have you quite finished, Joanna?"

"Well, you do agree, don't you?"

I grinned. "I'll admit to disappointment."

"And I don't see who else there is here for you. You'll have to fall back upon Aimée Griffith."

"God forbid," I said.

"She's quite good-looking, you know."

"Too much of an Amazon for me."

"She seems to enjoy her life all right," said Joanna. "Absolutely disgustingly hearty, isn't she? I shouldn't be at all surprised if she had a cold bath every morning."

"And what are you going to do for yourself?" I asked.

"Me?"

"Yes. You'll need a little distraction down here if I know you."

"Who's being low now? Besides, you forget Paul." Joanna heaved up a not very convincing sigh.

"I shan't forget him nearly as quickly as you will. In about ten days you'll be saying, 'Paul? Paul Who? I never knew a Paul.' "

"You think I'm completely fickle," said Joanna.

"When people like Paul are in question, I'm only too glad that you should be."

"You never did like him. But he really was a bit of a genius."

"Possibly, though I doubt it. Anyway, from all I've heard, geniuses are people to be heartily disliked. One thing, you won't find any geniuses down here."

Joanna considered for a moment, her head on one side.

"I'm afraid not," she said regretfully.

"You'll have to fall back upon Owen Griffith," I said. "He's the only unattached male in the place. Unless you count old Colonel Appleton. He was looking at you like a hungry bloodhound most of the afternoon."

Joanna laughed.

"He was, wasn't he? It was quite embarrassing."

"Don't pretend. You're never embarrassed."

Joanna drove in silence through the gate and round to the garage.

She said then:

"There may be something in that idea of yours."

"What idea?"

Joanna replied:

"I don't see why any man should deliberately cross the street to avoid me. It's rude, apart from anything else."

"I see," I said. "You're going to hunt the man down in cold blood."

"Well, I don't like being avoided."

I got slowly and carefully out of the car, and balanced my sticks. Then I offered my sister a piece of advice.

"Let me tell you this, girl. Owen Griffith isn't any of your tame whining artistic young men. Unless you're careful you'll stir up a hornet's nest about your ears. That man could be dangerous."

"Oh, do you think so?" demanded Joanna with every symptom of pleasure at the prospect.

"Leave the poor devil alone," I said sternly.

"How dare he cross the street when he saw me coming?"

"All you women are alike. You harp on one theme. You'll have Sister Aimée gunning for you, too, if I'm not mistaken."

"She dislikes me already," said Joanna. She spoke meditatively, but with a certain satisfaction.

"We have come down here," I said sternly, "for peace and quiet, and I mean to see we get it."

But peace and quiet were the last things we were to have.

4

i

IT WAS, I think, about a week later, that Partridge informed me that Mrs. Baker would like to speak to me for a minute or two if I would be so kind.

The name Mrs. Baker conveyed nothing at all to me.

"Who is Mrs. Baker?" I said, bewildered—"Can't she see Miss Joanna?"

But it appeared that I was the person with whom an interview was desired. It further transpired that Mrs. Baker was the mother of the girl Beatrice.

I had forgotten Beatrice. For a fortnight now, I had been conscious of a middle-aged woman with wisps of grey hair, usually on her knees retreating crablike from bathroom and stairs and passages when I appeared, and I knew, I suppose, that she was our new Daily Woman. Otherwise the Beatrice complication had faded from my mind.

I could not very well refuse to see Beatrice's mother, especially as I learned that Joanna was out, but I was, I must confess, a little nervous at the prospect. I sincerely hoped that I was not going to be accused of having trifled with Beatrice's affections. I cursed the mischievous activities of anonymous letter writers to myself at the same time as, aloud, I commanded that Beatrice's mother should be brought to my presence.

Mrs. Baker was a big broad weather-beaten woman with a rapid flow of speech. I was relieved to notice no signs of anger or accusation.

"I hope, sir," she said, beginning at once when the door had closed behind Partridge, "that you'll excuse the liberty I've taken in coming to see you. But I thought, sir, as you was the proper person to come to, and I should be thankful if you could see your way to telling me what I ought to do in the circumstances, because in my opinion, sir, something ought to be done, and I've never been one to let the grass grow under my feet, and what I say is, no use moaning and groaning, but 'Up and doing' as vicar said in his sermon only the week before last."

I felt slightly bewildered and as though I had missed something essential in the conversation.

"Certainly," I said. "Won't you—er—sit down, Mrs. Baker? I'm sure I shall be glad to—er help you in any way I can——"

I paused expectantly.

"Thank you, sir." Mrs. Baker sat down on the edge of a chair. "It's very good of you, I'm sure. And glad I am that I came to you, I said to Beatrice, I said, and her howling and crying on her bed, Mr. Burton will know what to do, I said, being a London gentleman. And something must be done, what with young men being so hot-headed and not listening to reason the way they are, and not listening to a word a girl says, and anyway, if it was *me*, I says to Beatrice I'd give him as good as I got, and what about that girl down at the mill?"

I felt more than ever bewildered.

"I'm sorry," I said. "But I don't quite understand. What has happened?"

"It's the letters, sir. Wicked letters—indecent, too, using such words and all. Worse than I've ever seen in the Bible, even"

Passing over an interesting side-line here, I said desperately:

"Has your daughter been having more letters?"

"Not her, sir. She had just the one. That one as was the occasion of her leaving here."

"There was absolutely no reason—" I began, but Mrs. Baker firmly and respectfully interrupted me:

"There is no need to tell me, sir, that what was wrote was all wicked lies. I had Miss Partridge's word for that—and indeed I would have known it for myself. You aren't that type of gentleman, sir, that I well know, and you an invalid and all. Wicked untruthful lies it was, but all the same I says to Beatrice as she'd better leave because you know what talk is, sir. No smoke without fire, that's what people say. And a girl can't be too careful. And besides the girl herself felt bashful like after what had been written, so I says, 'Quite right,' to Beatrice when she said she wasn't coming up here again, though I'm sure we both regretted the inconvenience being such——"

Unable to find her way out of this sentence, Mrs. Baker took a deep breath and began again.

"And that, I hoped, would be the end of any nasty talk. But now George, down at the garage, him what Beatrice is going with, he's got one of them. Saying awful things about our Beatrice, and how she's going on with Fred Ledbetter's Tom—and I can assure you, sir, the girl has been no more than civil to him and passing the time of day so to speak."

My head was now reeling under this new complication of Mr. Ledbetter's Tom.

"Let me get this straight," I said. "Beatrice's—er—young man has had an anonymous letter making accusations about her and another young man?"

"That's right, sir, and not nicely put at all—horrible words used, and it drove young George mad with rage, it did, and he came round and told Beatrice he wasn't going to put up with that sort of thing from her, and he wasn't going to have her go behind his back with other chaps—and she says it's all a lie—and he says no smoke without fire, he says, and rushes off being hot-like in his temper, and Beatrice she took on ever so, poor girl, and I said I'll put my hat on and come straight up to you, sir."

Mrs. Baker paused and looked at me expectantly, like a dog waiting for reward after doing a particularly clever trick.

"But why come to me?" I demanded.

"I understood, sir, that you'd had one of these nasty letters yourself, and I thought, sir, that being a London gentlemen, you'd know what to do about them."

"If I were you," I said, "I should go to the police. This sort of thing ought to be stopped."

Mrs. Baker looked deeply shocked.

"Oh, no, sir, I couldn't go to the police."

"Why not?"

"I've never been mixed up with the police, sir. None of us ever have."

"Probably not. But the police are the only people who can deal with this sort of thing. It's their business."

"Go to Bert Rundle?"

Bert Rundle was the constable, I knew.

"There's a sergeant, or an inspector, surely, at the police station."

"Me, go into the police station?"

Mrs. Baker's voice expressed reproach and incredulity. I began to feel annoyed.

"That's the only advice I can give you."

Mrs. Baker was silent, obviously quite unconvinced. She said wistfully and earnestly:

"These letters ought to be stopped, sir, they did ought to be stopped. There'll be mischief done sooner or later."

"It seems to me there is mischief done now," I said.

"I mean *violence,* sir. These young fellows, they get violent in their feelings—and so do the older ones."

I asked:

"Are a good many of these letters going about?"

Mrs. Baker nodded.

"It's getting worse and worse, sir. Mr. and Mrs. Beadle at the Blue Boar—very happy they've always been—and now these letters comes and it sets him thinking things—things that aren't so, sir."

I leaned forward:

"Mrs. Baker," I said, "have you any idea, any idea at all, who is writing these abominable letters?"

To my great surprise she nodded her head.

"We've got our idea, sir. Yes, we've all got a very fair idea."

"Who is it?"

I had fancied she might be reluctant to mention a name, but she replied promptly:

"'Tis Mrs. Cleat—that's what we all think, sir. 'Tis Mrs. Cleat for sure."

I had heard so many names this morning that I was quite bewildered. I asked:

"Who is Mrs. Cleat?"

Mrs. Cleat, I discovered, was the wife of an elderly jobbing gardener. She lived in a cottage on the road leading down to the Mill. My further questions only brought unsatisfactory answers. Questioned as to why Mrs. Cleat should write these letters, Mrs. Baker would only say vaguely that "'Twould be like her."

In the end, I let her go, reiterating once more my advice to go to the police, advice which I could see Mrs. Baker was not going to act upon. I was left with the impression that I had disappointed her.

I thought over what she had said. Vague as the evidence was, I decided that if the village was all agreed that Mrs. Cleat was the culprit, then it was probably true. I decided to go and consult Griffith about the whole thing. Presumably he would know this Cleat woman. If he thought advisable, he or I might suggest to the police that she was at the bottom of this growing annoyance.

I timed my arrival for about the moment I fancied Griffith would have finished his "Surgery." When the last patient had left, I went into the surgery.

"Hallo, it's you, Burton."

"Yes. I want to talk to you."

I outlined my conversation with Mrs. Baker, and passed on to him the conviction that this Mrs. Cleat was responsible. Rather to my disappointment, Griffith shook his head.

"It's not so simple as that," he said.

"You don't think this Cleat woman is at the bottom of it?"

"She may be. But I think it most unlikely."

"Then why do they all think it is her?"

He smiled.

"Oh," he said, "you don't understand. Mrs. Cleat is the local witch."

"Good gracious!" I exclaimed.

"Yes, sounds rather strange nowadays, nevertheless that's what it amounts to. The feeling lingers you know, that there are certain people, certain families, for instance, whom it isn't wise to offend. Mrs. Cleat came from a family of 'wise women.' And I'm afraid she's taken pains to cultivate the legend. She's a queer woman with a bitter and sardonic sense of humour. It's been easy enough for her, if a child cuts its finger, or had a bad fall, or sickened with mumps, to nod her head and say, 'Yes, he stole my apples last week' or 'He pulled my cat's tail.' Soon enough mothers pulled their children away, and other women brought honey or a cake they'd baked to give to Mrs. Cleat so as to keep on the right side of her so that she shouldn't 'ill wish' them. It's superstitious and silly, but it happens. So naturally, now, they think she's at the bottom of this."

"But she isn't?"

"Oh, no. She isn't the type. It's—it's not so simple as that."

"Have you any idea?" I looked at him curiously.

He shook his head, but his eyes were absent.

"No," he said. "I don't know at all. But I don't like it, Burton—some harm is going to come of this."

ii

When I got back to the house I found Megan sitting on the veranda steps, her chin resting on her knees.

She greeted me with her usual lack of ceremony.

"Hallo," she said. "Do you think I could come to lunch?"

"Certainly," I said.

"If it's chops, or anything difficult like that and they won't go round, just tell me," shouted Megan as I went round to apprise Partridge of the fact that there would be three to lunch.

I fancy that Partridge sniffed. She certainly managed to convey without saying a word of any kind, that she didn't think much of that Miss Megan.

I went back to the veranda.

"Is it quite all right?" asked Megan anxiously.

"Quite all right," I said. "Irish stew."

"Oh well, that's rather like dogs' dinner anyway, isn't it? I mean it's mostly potato and flavour."

"Quite," I said.

I took out my cigarette case and offered it to Megan. She flushed.

"How nice of you."

"Won't you have one?"

"No, I don't think I will, but it was very nice of you to offer it to me—just as though I was a real person."

"Aren't you a real person?" I said, amused.

Megan shook her head, then, changing the subject, she stretched out a long dusty leg for my inspection.

"I've darned my stockings," she announced proudly.

I am not an authority on darning, but it did occur to me that the strange puckered blot of violently contrasting wool was perhaps not quite a success.

"It's much more uncomfortable than the hole," said Megan.

"It looks as though it might be," I agreed.

"Does your sister darn well?"

I tried to think if I had ever observed any of Joanna's handiwork in this direction.

"I don't know," I had to confess.

"Well, what does she do when she gets a hole in her stocking?"

"I rather think," I said reluctantly, "that she throws them away and buys another pair."

"Very sensible," said Megan. "But I can't do that. I get an allowance now—forty pounds a year. You can't do much on that."

I agreed.

"If only I wore black stockings, I could ink my legs," said Megan sadly. "That's what I always did at school. Miss Batworthy, the mistress who looked after our mending was like her name—blind as a bat. It was awfully useful."

"It must have been," I said.

We were silent while I smoked my pipe. It was quite a companionable silence.

Megan broke it by saying suddenly and violently:

"I suppose you think I'm awful, like everyone else?"

I was so startled that my pipe fell out of my mouth. It was a meerschaum, just colouring nicely, and it broke. I said angrily to Megan:

"Now, see what you've done."

That most unaccountable of children, instead of being upset, merely grinned broadly.

"I do like you," she said.

It was a most warming remark. It is the remark that one fancies, perhaps erroneously, that one's dog would say if he could talk. It occurred to me that Megan, for all she looked like a horse had the disposition of a dog. She was certainly not quite human.

"What did you say before the catastrophe?" I asked, carefully picking up the fragments of my cherished pipe.

"I said I supposed you thought me awful," said Megan, but not at all in the same tone she had said it before.

"Why should I?"

Megan said gravely:

"Because I am."

I said sharply:

"Don't be stupid."

Megan shook her head.

"That's just it. I'm not really stupid. People think I am. They don't know that inside I know just what they're like, and that all the time I'm hating them."

"*Hating* them?"

"Yes," said Megan.

Her eyes, those melancholy, unchildlike eyes stared straight into mine, without blinking. It was a long mournful gaze.

"You would hate people if you were like me," she said. "If you weren't wanted."

"Don't you think you're being rather morbid?" I asked.

"Yes," said Megan. "That's what people always say when you're saying the truth. And it is true. I'm not wanted and I can quite see why. Mummie doesn't like me a bit. I remind her, I think, of my father, who was cruel to her and pretty dreadful from all I can hear. Only mothers can't say they don't want their children and just go away. Or eat them. Cats eat the kittens they don't like. Awfully sensible, I think. No waste or mess. But human mothers have to keep their children, and look after them. It hasn't been so bad while I could be sent away to school—but you see what Mummie would really like is to be just herself and my stepfather and the boys."

I said slowly:

"I still think you're morbid, Megan, but accepting some of what you say is true, why don't you go away and have a life of your own?"

She gave me an unchildlike smile.

"You mean take up a career. Earn my living?"

"Yes."

"What at?"

"You could train for something, I suppose. Shorthand

typing—book-keeping."

"I don't believe I could. I am stupid about doing things. And besides—"

"Well?"

She had turned her face away, now she turned it slowly back again. It was crimson and there were tears in her eyes. She spoke now with all the childishness back in her voice.

"Why should I go away? And be made to go away? They don't want me, but I'll *stay*. I'll stay and make everyone sorry. I'll make them all sorry. Hateful pigs! I hate everyone here in Lymstock. They all think I'm stupid and ugly. I'll show them. I'll show them. I'll——"

It was a childish, oddly pathetic rage.

I heard a step on the gravel round the corner of the house.

"Get up," I said savagely. "Go into the house through the drawing-room. Go up to the first floor to the bathroom. End of the passage. Wash your face. Quick."

She sprang awkwardly to her feet and darted through the window as Joanna came round the corner of the house.

"Gosh, I'm hot," she called out. She sat down beside me and fanned her face with the Tyrolean scarf that had been round her head. "Still I think I'm educating these damned brogues now. I've walked miles. I've learnt one thing, you shouldn't have these fancy holes in your brogues. The gorse prickles go through. Do you know, Jerry, I think we ought to have a dog?"

"So do I," I said. "By the way, Megan is coming to lunch."

"Is she? Good."

"You like her?" I asked.

"I think she's a changeling," said Joanna. "Something left on a doorstep, you know, while the fairies take the right one away. It's very interesting to meet a changeling. Oof, I must go up and wash."

"You can't yet," I said, "Megan is washing."

"Oh, she's been foot-slogging too, has she?"

Joanna took out her mirror and looked at her face long and earnestly. "I don't think I like this lipstick," she announced presently.

Megan came out through the window. She was composed, moderately clean, and showed no signs of the recent storm. She looked doubtfully at Joanna.

"Hallo," said Joanna, still preoccupied by her face. "I'm so glad you've come to lunch. Good gracious, I've got a freckle on my nose. I must do something about it. Freckles are so earnest and Scottish."

Partridge came out and said coldly that luncheon was served.

"Come on," said Joanna, getting up. "I'm starving."

She put her arm through Megan's and they went into the house together.

5

i

I SEE that there has been one omission in my story. So far I have made little or no mention of Mrs. Dane Calthrop, or indeed of the Rev. Caleb Dane Calthrop.

And yet both the vicar and his wife were distinct personalities. Dane Calthrop himself was perhaps a being more remote from everyday life than any one I have ever met. His existence was in his books and in his study, and in his intimate knowledge of early Church history. Mrs. Dane Calthrop, on the other hand, was quite terrifyingly on the spot. I have perhaps purposely put off mentioning her, because I was from the first a little afraid of her. She was a woman of character and of almost Olympian knowledge. She was not in the least the typical vicar's wife—but that, as I set it down, makes me ask myself, what do I know of vicars' wives?

The only one I remember well was a quiet nondescript creature, devoted to a big strong husband with a magnetic way of preaching, she had so little general conversation that it was a puzzle to know how to sustain a conversation with her.

Otherwise I was depending on the fictional presentment of vicars' wives, caricatures of females poking their noses everywhere, and uttering platitudes. Probably no such type exists.

Mrs. Dane Calthrop never poked her nose in anywhere, yet she had an uncanny power of knowing things and I soon discovered that almost everyone in the village was slightly afraid of her. She gave no advice and never interfered, yet she represented, to any uneasy conscience, the Deity personified.

I have never seen a woman more indifferent to her material surroundings. On hot days she would stride about clad in Harris tweed, and in rain or even sleet, I have seen her absent-mindedly race down the village street in a cotton dress of printed poppies.

She had a long thin well-bred face like a greyhound, and a most devastating sincerity of speech.

She stopped me in the High Street the day after Megan had come to lunch. I had the usual feeling of surprise, because Mrs. Dane Calthrop's progress resembled coursing more than walking, and her eyes were always fixed on the distant horizon so that you felt sure her real objective was about a mile and a half away.

"Oh," she said, "Mr. Burton!"

She said it rather triumphantly, as someone might who had solved a particularly clever puzzle.

I admitted that I was Mr. Burton and Mrs. Dane Calthrop stopped focusing on the horizon and seemed to be trying to focus on me instead.

"Now what," she said, "did I want to see you about?"

I could not help her there. She stood frowning, deeply perplexed.

"Something rather nasty," she said.

"I'm sorry about that," I said, startled.

"Ah," cried Mrs. Dane Calthrop. "I hate my love with an A. That's it. Anonymous letters! What this story you've brought down here about anonymous letters?"

"I didn't bring it," I said. "It was here already."

"Nobody got any until you came, though," said Mrs. Dane Calthrop accusingly.

"But they did, Mrs. Dane Calthrop. The trouble had already started."

"Oh dear," said Mrs. Dane Calthrop. "I don't like that."

She stood there, her eyes absent and far away again. She said:

"I can't help feeling it's all *wrong*. We're not like that here. Envy, of course, and malice, and all the mean spiteful little sins—but I didn't think there was any one who would do that—No, I really didn't. And it distresses me, you see, because *I* ought to know."

Her fine eyes came back from the horizon and met mine. They were worried, and seemed to hold the honest bewilderment of a child.

"How should you know?" I said.

"I usually do. I've always felt that's my function. Caleb preaches good sound doctrine and administers the sacraments.

That's a priest's duty, but if you admit marriage at all for a priest, then I think his wife's duty is to know what people are feeling and thinking, even if she can't do anything about it. And I haven't the least idea whose mind is——"

She broke off, adding absently:

"They are such silly letters, too."

"Have you—er—had any yourself?"

I was a little diffident of asking, but Mrs. Dane Calthrop replied perfectly naturally, her eyes opening a little wider:

"Oh yes, two—no, three. I forget exactly what they said. Something very silly about Caleb and the schoolmistress, I think. Quite absurb, because Caleb has absolutely no taste for fornication. He never has had. So lucky, being a clergyman."

"Quite," I said. "Oh, quite."

"Caleb would have been a saint," said Mrs. Dane Calthrop, "if he hadn't been just a little too intellectual."

I did not feel qualified to answer this criticism, and anyway Mrs. Dane Calthrop went on, leaping back from her husband to the letters in rather a puzzling way.

"There are so many things the letters might say, but don't. That's what is so curious."

"I should hardly have thought they erred on the side of restraint," I said bitterly.

"But they don't seem to *know* anything. None of the real things."

"You mean?"

Those fine vague eyes met mine.

"Well, of course. There's plenty of adultery here—and everything else. Any amount of shameful secrets. Why doesn't the writer use those?" She paused and then asked abruptly, "What did they say in your letters?"

"They suggested that my sister wasn't my sister."

"And she is?"

Mrs. Dane Calthrop asked the question with unembarrassed friendly interest.

"Certainly Joanna is my sister."

Mrs. Dane Calthrop nodded her head.

"That just shows you what I mean. I dare say there are other things——"

Her clear uninterested eyes looked at me thoughtfully, and I suddenly understood why Lymstock was afraid of Mrs. Dane Calthrop.

In everybody's life there are hidden chapters which they hope may never be known. I felt that Mrs. Dane Calthrop knew them.

For once in my life, I was positively delighted when Aimée Griffith's hearty voice boomed out:

"Hallo, Maud. Glad I've just caught you. I want to suggest an alteration of date for the Sale of Work. Morning, Mr. Burton."

She went on:

"I must just pop into the grocer's and leave my order, then I'll come along to the Institute if that suits you?"

"Yes, yes, that will do quite well," said Mrs. Dane Calthrop.

Aimée Griffith went into the International Stores.

Mrs. Dane Calthrop said: "Poor thing."

I was puzzled. Surely she could not be pitying Aimée?

She went on, however:

"You know, Mr. Burton, I'm rather afraid——"

"About this letter business?"

"Yes, you see it means—it must mean—" She paused lost in thought, her eyes screwed up. Then she said slowly, as one who solves a problem, "Blind hatred . . . yes, blind hatred. But even a blind man might stab to the heart by pure chance. . . . And what would happen then, Mr. Burton?"

We were to know that before another day had passed.

ii

It was Partridge who brought the news of the tragedy. Partridge enjoys calamity. Her nose always twitches ecstatically when she has to break bad news of any kind.

She came into Joanna's room with her nose working overtime, her eyes bright, and her mouth pulled down into an exaggerated gloom. "There's terrible news, this morning, miss," she observed as she drew up the blinds.

It takes a minute or two for Joanna, with her London habits, to become fully conscious in the morning. She said, "Er ah," and rolled over without real interest.

Partridge placed her early tea beside her and began again.

"Terrible it is. Shocking! I couldn't hardly believe it when I heard."

"What's terrible? said Joanna, struggling into wakefulness.

"Poor Mrs. Symmington." She paused dramatically. "Dead."

"Dead?" Joanna sat up in bed, now wide awake.

"Yes, miss, yesterday afternoon, and what's worse, took her own life."

"Oh no, Partridge?"

Joanna was really shocked—Mrs. Symmington was not, somehow, the sort of person you associated with tragedies.

"Yes, miss, it's the truth. Did it deliberate. Not but what she was drove to it, poor soul."

"Drove to it?" Joanna had an inkling of the truth then. "Not——?"

Her eyes questioned Partridge and Partridge nodded.

"That's right, miss. One of them nasty letters!"

"What did it say?"

But that, to Partridge's regret, she had not succeeded in learning.

"They're beastly things," said Joanna. "But I don't see why they should make one want to kill oneself."

Partridge sniffed and then said with meaning:

"Not unless they were *true*, miss."

"Oh," said Joanna.

She drank her tea after Partridge had left the room, then she threw on a dressing-gown and came in to me to tell me the news.

I thought of what Owen Griffith had said. Sooner or later the shot in the dark went home. It had done with Mrs. Symmington. She, apparently the most unlikely of women, had had a secret. . . . It was true, I reflected, that for all her shrewdness she was not a woman of much stamina. She was the anaemic clinging type that crumples easily.

Joanna nudged me and asked me what I was thinking about.

I repeated to her what Owen had said.

"Of course," said Joanna waspishly, "he would know all about it. The man thinks he knows everything."

"He's clever," I said.

"He's conceited," said Joanna. She added, "Abominably conceited!"

After a minute or two she said:

"How awful for her husband—and for the girl. What do you think Megan will feel about it?"

I hadn't the slightest idea and said so. It was curious that one could never gauge what Megan would think or feel.

Joanna nodded and said:

"No, one never does know with changelings."

After a minute or two she said:

"Do you think—would you like—I wonder if she'd like to come and stay with us for a day or two? It's rather a shock for a girl that age."

"We might go along and suggest it," I agreed.

"The children are all right," said Joanna. "They've got that governess woman. But I expect she's just the sort of creature who would drive someone like Megan mad."

I thought that was very possible. I could imagine Elsie Holland uttering platitude after platitude and suggesting innumerable cups of tea. A kindly creature, but not, I thought, the person for a sensitive girl.

I had thought myself of bringing Megan away, and I was glad that Joanna had thought of it spontaneously without prompting from me.

We went down to the Symmingtons' house after breakfast.

We were a little nervous, both of us. Our arrival might look like sheer ghoulish curiosity. Luckily we met Owen Griffith just coming out through the gate. He looked worried and preoccupied.

He greeted me, however, with some warmth.

"Oh, hallo, Burton. I'm glad to see you. What I was afraid would happen sooner or later has happened. A damnable business!"

"Good morning, Dr. Griffith," said Joanna, using the voice she keeps for one of our deafer aunts.

Griffith started and flushed.

"Oh—oh, good morning, Miss Burton."

"I thought perhaps," said Joanna, "that you didn't see me."

Owen Griffith got redder still. His shyness enveloped him like a mantle.

"I'm—I'm so sorry—preoccupied—I didn't."

Joanna went on mercilessly: "After all, I *am* life size."

"Merely kit-kat," I said in a stern aside to her. Then I went on:

"My sister and I, Griffith, wondered whether it would be a good thing if the girl came and stopped with us for a day or two? What do you think? I don't want to butt in—but it must be rather grim for the poor child. What would Symmington feel about it, do you think?"

Griffith turned the idea over in his mind for a moment or two.

"I think it would be an excellent thing." he said at last. "She's a queer nervy sort of girl, and it would be good for her to get away from the whole thing. Miss Holland is doing wonders—she's an excellent head on her shoulders, but she really has quite enought to do with the two children and Symmington himself. He's quite broken up—bewildered."

"It was—" I hesitated—"suicide?"

Griffith nodded.

"Oh yes. No question of accident. She wrote, 'I can't go on' on a scrap of paper. The letter must have come by yesterday afternoon's post. The envelope was down on the floor by her chair and the letter itself was screwed up into a ball and thrown into the fireplace."

"What did——"

I stopped, rather horrified at myself.

"I beg your pardon," I said.

Griffith gave a quick unhappy smile.

"You needn't mind asking. That letter will have to be read at the inquest. No getting out of it, more's the pity. It was the usual kind of thing—couched in the same foul style. The specific accusation was that the second boy, Colin, was not Symmington's child."

"Do you think that was true?" I exclaimed incredulously.

Griffith shrugged his shoulders.

"I've no means of forming a judgment. I've only been here five years. As far as I've ever seen, the Symmingtons were a placid, happy couple devoted to each other and their children.

It's true that the boy doesn't particularly resemble his parents—he's got bright red hair for one thing—but a child often throws back in appearance to a grandfather or grandmother."

"That lack of resemblance might have been what prompted the particular accusation. A foul and quite uncalled-for bow at a venture."

"Very likely. In fact, probably. There's not been much accurate knowledge behind these poisen pen letters, just unbridled spite and malice."

"But it happened to hit the bull's eye," said Joanna. 'After all, she wouldn't have killed herself otherwise would she?"

Griffith said doubtfully:

"I'm not quite sure. She's been ailing in health for some time, neurotic, hysterical. I've been treating her for a nervous condition. It's possible, I think, that the shock of receiving such a letter, couched in those terms, may have induced such a state of panic and despondency that she may have decided to take her life. She may have worked herself up to feel that her husband might not believe her if she denied the story, and the general shame and disgust might have worked upon her so powerfully as to temporarily unbalance her judgment."

"Suicide whilst of unsound mind," said Joanna.

"Exactly. I shall be quite justified, I think, in putting forward that point of view at the inquest."

"I see," said Joanna.

There was something in her voice which made Owen say:

"Perfectly justified!" in an angry voice. He added, "You don't agree, Miss Burton?"

"Oh yes, I do," said Joanna. "I'd do exactly the same in your place."

Owen looked at her doubtfully, then moved slowly away down the street. Joanna and I went on into the house.

The front door was open and it seemed easier than ringing the bell, especially as we heard Elsie Holland's voice inside.

She was talking to Mr. Symmington who, huddled in a chair, was looking completely dazed.

"No, but really, Mr. Symmington, you must take something. You haven't had any breakfast, not what I call a proper breakfast, and nothing to eat last night, and what with the shock and all, you'll be getting ill yourself, and you'll need all your strength. The doctor said so before he left."

Symmington said in a toneless voice:

"You're very kind, Miss Holland, but—"

"A nice cup of hot tea," said Elsie Holland, thrusting the beverage on him firmly.

Personally I should have given the poor devil a stiff whisky and soda. He looked as though he needed it. However, he accepted the tea, and looking up at Elsie Holland:

"I can't thank you for all you've done and are doing, Miss Holland. You've been perfectly splendid."

This girl flushed and looked pleased.

"It's nice of you to say that, Mr. Symmington. You must let me do all I can to help. Don't worry about the children—I'll see to them, and I've got the servants calmed down, and if there's anything I can do, letter-writing or telephoning, don't hesitate to ask me."

"You're very kind," Symmington said again.

Elsie Holland, turning, caught sight of us and came hurrying out into the hall.

"Isn't it terrible?" she said in a hushed whisper.

I thought, as I looked at her, that she was really a very nice girl. Kind, competent, practical in an emergency. Her magnificent blue eyes were just faintly rimmed with pink, showing that she had been soft-hearted enough to shed tears for her employer's death.

"Can we speak to you a minute?" asked Joanna. "We don't want to disturb Mr. Symmington."

Elsie Holland nodded comprehendingly and led the way into the dining-room on the other side of the hall.

"It's been awful for him," she said. "Such a shock. Who ever would have thought a thing like this could happen? But of course, I do realise now that she had been queer for some time. Awfully nervy and weepy. I thought it was her health, though Dr. Griffith always said there was nothing really wrong with her. But she was snappy and irritable and some days you wouldn't know just how to take her."

"What we really came for," said Joanna, "was to know whether we could have Megan for a few days—that is, if she'd like to come."

Elsie Holland looked rather surprised.

"Megan?" she said doubtfully. "I don't know, I'm sure. I mean, it's ever so kind of you, but she's such a queer girl. One never knows what she's going to say or feel about things."

Joanna said rather vaguely:

"We thought it might be a help, perhaps."

"Oh well, as far as that goes, it would. I mean, I've got the boys to look after (they're with cook just now) and poor Mr. Symmington—he really needs looking after as much as any one, and such a lot to do and see to. I really haven't had time to see much of Megan. I think she's upstairs in the old nursery at the top of the house. She seems to want to get away from everyone. I don't know if——"

Joanna gave me the faintest of looks. I slipped quickly out of the room and upstairs.

The old nursery was at the top of the house. I opened the door and went in. The room downstairs had given on to the garden behind and the blinds had not been down there. But in this room which faced the road they were decorously drawn down.

Through a dim grey gloom I saw Megan. She was crouching on a divan set against the far wall, and I was reminded at once of some terrified animal, hiding. She looked petrified with fear.

"Megan," I said.

I came forward, and unconsciously I adopted the tone one does adopt when you want to reassure a frightened animal. I'm really surprised I didn't hold out a carrot or a piece of sugar. I felt like that.

She stared at me, but she did not move, and her expression did not alter.

"Megan," I said again. "Joanna and I have come to ask you if you would like to come and stay with us for a little."

Her voice came hollowly out of the dim twilight.

"Stay with you? In your house?"

"Yes."

"You mean, you'll take me away from here?"

"Yes, my dear."

Suddenly she began to shake all over. It was frightening and very moving.

"Oh, do take me away! Please do. It's so awful, being here, and feeling so wicked."

I came over to her and her hands fastened on my coat sleeve.

"I'm an awful coward. I didn't know what a coward I was."

"It's all right, funny face," I said. "These things are a bit shattering. Come along."

"Can we go at once? Without waiting a minute?"

"Well, you'll have to put a few things together, I suppose."

"What sort of things? Why?"

"My dear girl," I said. "We can provide you with a bed and a bath and the rest of it, but I'm damned if I'll lend you my toothbrush."

She gave a very faint weak little laugh.

"I see. I think I'm stupid to-day. You mustn't mind. I'll go and pack some things. You—you won't go away? You'll wait for me?"

"I'll be on the mat."

"Thank you. Thank you very much. I'm sorry I'm so stupid. But you see it's rather dreadful when your mother dies."

"I know," I said.

I gave her a friendly pat on the back and she flashed me a grateful look and disappeared into a bedroom. I went on downstairs.

"I found Megan," I said. "She's coming."

"Oh now, that *is* a good thing," exclaimed Elsie Holland. "It will take her out of herself. She's rather a nervy girl, you know. Difficult. It will be a great relief to feel I haven't got her on my mind as well as everything else. It's very kind of you, Miss Burton. I hope she won't be a nuisance. Oh dear, there's the telephone. I must go and answer it. Mr. Symmington isn't fit."

She hurried out of the room. Joanna said:

"Quite the ministering angel!"

"You said that rather nastily," I observed. "She's a nice kind girl, and obviously most capable."

"Most. And she knows it."

"This is unworthy of you, Joanna," I said.

"Meaning why shouldn't the girl do her stuff?"

"Exactly."

"I never can stand seeing people pleased with themselves,"

said Joanna. "It arouses all my worst instincts. How did you find Megan?"

"Crouching in a darkened room looking rather like a stricken gazelle."

"Poor kid. She was quite willing to come?"

"She leapt at it."

A series of thuds out in the hall announced the descent of Megan and her suitcase. I went out and took it from her. Joanna, behind me, said urgently:

"Come on. I've already refused some nice hot tea twice."

We went out to the car. It annoyed me that Joanna had to sling the suitcase in. I could get along with one stick now, but I couldn't do any athletic feats.

"Get in," I said to Megan.

She got in, I followed her. Joanna started the car and we drove off.

We got to Little Furze and went into the drawing-room.

Megan dropped into a chair and burst into tears. She cried with the hearty fervour of a child—bawled, I think, is the right word. I left the room in search of a remedy. Joanna stood by feeling rather helpless, I think.

Presently I heard Megan say in a thick choked voice:

"I'm sorry for doing this. It seems idiotic."

Joanna said kindly, "Not at all. Have another handkerchief."

I gather she supplied the necessary article. I re-entered the room and handed Megan a brimming glass.

"What is it?"

"A cocktail," I said.

"Is it? Is it really?" Megan's tears were instantly dried. "I've never drunk a cocktail."

"Everything has to have a beginning," I said.

Megan sipped her drink gingerly, then a beaming smile spread over her face, she tilted her head back and gulped it down at a draught.

"It's lovely," she said. "Can I have another?"

"No," I said.

"Why not?"

"In about ten minutes you'll probably know."

"Oh!"

Megan transferred her attention to Joanna.

"I really am awfully sorry for having made such a nuisance of myself howling away like that. I can't think why. It seems awfully silly when I'm so glad to be here."

"That's all right," said Joanna. "We're very pleased to have you."

"You can't be, really. It's just kindness on your part. But I am grateful."

"Please don't be grateful," said Joanna. "It will embarrass me. I was speaking the truth when I said we should be glad to have you. Jerry and I have used up all our conversation. We can't think of any more things to say to each other."

"But now," I said, "we shall be able to have all sorts of interesting discussions—about Goneril and Regan and things like that."

Megan's face lit up.

"I've been thinking about that, and I think I know the answer. It was because that awful old father of theirs always insisted on such a lot of sucking up. When you've always got to be saying thank you and how kind and all the rest of it, it would make you go a bit rotten and queer inside, and you'd just long to be able to be beastly for a change—and when you got the chance, you'd probably find it went to your head and you'd go too far. Old Lear was pretty awful, wasn't he? I mean, he did deserve the snub Cordelia gave him."

"I can see," I said, "that we are going to have many interesting discussions about Shakespeare."

"I can see you two are going to be very highbrow," said Joanna. "I'm afraid I always find Shakespeare terribly dreary. All those long scenes where everybody is drunk and it's supposed to be funny."

"Talking of drink," I said turning to Megan. "How are you feeling?"

"Quite all right, thank you."

"Not at all giddy? You don't see two of Joanna or anything like that?"

"No. I just feel as though I'd like to talk rather a lot."

"Splendid," I said. "Obviously you are one of our natural drinkers. That is to say, if that really was your first cocktail."

"Oh, it was."

"A good strong head is an asset to any human being." I said.

Joanna took Megan upstairs to unpack.

Partridge came in, looking sour, and said she had made two cup custards for lunch and what should she do about it?

6

i

THE INQUEST was held three days later. It was all done as decorously as possible, but there was a large attendance and, as Joanna observed, the beady bonnets were wagging.

The time of Mrs. Symmington's death was put at between three and four o'clock. She was alone in the house, Symmington was at his office, the maids were having their day out, Elsie Holland and the children were out walking and Megan had gone for a bicycle ride.

The letter must have come by the afternoon post. Mrs. Symmington must have taken it out of the box, read it—and then in a state of agitation she had gone to the potting shed, fetched some of the cyanide kept there for taking wasps' nests, dissolved it in water and drunk it after writing those last agitated words, "I can't go on . . ."

Owen Griffith gave medical evidence and stressed the view he had outlined to us of Mrs. Symmington's nervous condition and poor stamina. The coroner was suave and discreet. He spoke with bitter condemnation of people who write those despicable things, anonymous letters. Whoever had written that wicked, and lying letter was morally guilty of murder, he said. He hoped the police would soon discover the culprit and take action against him or her. Such a dastardly and malicious piece of spite deserved to be punished with the utmost rigour of the law. Directed by him, the jury brought in the inevitable verdict. Suicide whilst temporarily insane.

The coroner had done his best—Owen Griffith also, but afterwards, jammed in the crowd of eager village women, I heard the same hateful sibilant whisper I had begun to know so well, "No smoke without fire, that's what *I* say!" "Must 'a been something in it for certain sure. She wouldn't never have done it otherwise . . ."

Just for a moment I hated Lymstock and its narrow boundaries, and its gossiping whispering women.

ii

It is difficult to remember things in their exact chronological order. The next landmark of importance, of course, was Superintendent Nash's visit. But it was before that, I think, that we received calls from various members of the community, each of which was interesting in its way and shed some light on the characters and personalities of the people involved.

Aimée Griffith came on the morning after the inquest. She was looking, as always, radiant with health and vigour and succeeded, also as usual, in putting my back up almost immediately. Joanna and Megan were out, so I did the honours.

"Good morning," said Miss Griffith. "I hear you've got Megan Hunter here?"

"We have."

"Very good of you, I'm sure. It must be rather a nuisance to you. I came up to say she can come to us if you like. I dare say I can find ways of making her useful about the house."

I looked at Aimée Griffith with a good deal of distaste.

"How good of you," I said. "But we like having her. She potters about quite happily."

"I dare say. Much too fond of pottering, that child. Still, I suppose she can't help it, being practically half-witted."

"I think she's rather an intelligent girl," I said.

Aimée Griffith gave me a hard stare.

"First time I've ever heard any one say that of her," she remarked. "Why, when you talk to her, she looks through you as though she doesn't understand what you are saying!"

"She probably just isn't interested," I said.

"If so, she's extremely rude," said Aimée Griffith.

"That may be. But not half-witted."

Miss Griffith declared sharply:

"At best, it's wool-gathering. What Megan needs is good hard work—something to give her an interest in life. You've no idea what a difference that makes to a girl. I know a lot about girls. You'd be surprised at the difference even becoming a Guide makes to a girl. Megan's much too old to spend her time lounging about and doing nothing."

"It's been rather difficult for her to do anything else so far," I said. "Mrs. Symmington alway seemed under the impression that Megan was about twelve years old."

Miss Griffith snorted.

"I know. I had no patience with that attitude of hers. Of course she's dead now, poor woman, so one doesn't want to say much, but she was a perfect example of what I call the unintelligent domestic type. Bridge and gossip and her children—and even there that Holland girl did all the looking after them. I'm afraid I never thought very much of Mrs. Symmington, although of course I never suspected the truth."

"The truth?" I said sharply.

Miss Griffith flushed.

"I was terribly sorry for Dick Symmington its all having to come out as it did at the inquest," she said. "It was awful for him."

"But surely you heard him say that there was not a word of truth in that letter—that he was quite sure of that?"

"Of course he *said* so. Quite right. A man's got to stick up for his wife. Dick would." She paused and then explained:

"You see, I've known Dick Symmington a long time."

I was a little surprised.

"Really?" I said. "I understand from your brother that he only bought this practice a few years ago."

"Oh yes, but Dick Symmington used to come and stay in our part of the world up north. I've known him for years."

Women jump to conclusions that men do not. Nevertheless, the suddenly softened tone of Aimée Griffith's voice put, as our old nurse would have expressed it, ideas into my head.

I looked at Aimée curiously. She went on—still in that softened tone:

"I know Dick very well. . . . He's a proud man, and very reserved. But he's the sort of man who could be very jealous."

"That would explain," I said deliberately, "why Mrs.

Symmington was afraid to show him or tell him about the letter. She was afraid that, being a jealous man, he might not believe her denials."

Miss Griffith looked at me angrily and scornfully.

"Good Lord," she said, "do you think any woman would go and swallow a lot of cyanide of potassium for an accusation that wasn't true?"

"The coroner seemed to think it was possible. Your brother, too—"

Aimée interrupted me.

"Men are all alike. All for preserving the decencies. But you don't catch *me* believing that stuff. If an innocent woman gets some foul anonymous letter, she laughs and chucks it away. That's what I——" she paused suddenly, and then finished, "would do."

But I had noticed the pause. I was almost sure that what she had been about to say was "That's what I did."

I decided to take the war into the enemy's country.

"I see," I said pleasantly, "so you've had one, too?"

Aimée Griffith was the type of woman who scorns to lie. She paused a minute—flushed, then said:

"Well, yes. But I didn't let it worry me!"

"Nasty?" I inquired sympathetically, as a fellow-sufferer.

"Naturally. These things always are. The ravings of a lunatic. I read a few words of it, realised what it was and chucked it straight into the waste-paper basket."

"You didn't think of taking it to the police?"

"Not then. Least said soonest mended—that's what I felt."

An urge came over me to say solemnly: "No smoke without fire!" but I restrained myself. To avoid temptation I reverted to Megan.

"Have you any idea of Megan's financial position?" I asked. "It's not idle curiosity on my part. I wondered if it would actually be necessary for her to earn her living."

"I don't think it's strictly *necessary*. Her grandmother, her father's mother, left her a small income, I believe. And in any case Dick Symmington would always give her a home and provide for her, even if her mother hasn't left her anything outright. No, it's the *principle* of the thing."

"What principle?"

"Work, Mr. Burton. There's nothing like work, for men and women. The one unforgivable sin is idleness."

"Sir Edward Grey," I said, "afterwards our foreign minister, was sent down from Oxford for incorrigible idleness. The Duke of Wellington, I have heard, was both dull and inattentive at his books. And has it every occurred to you, Miss Griffith, that you would probably not be able to take a good express train to London if little Georgie Stephenson had been out with his youth movement instead of lolling about, bored, in his mother's kitchen until the curious behaviour of the kettle lid attracted the attention of his idle mind?"

Aimée merely snorted.

"It is a theory of mine," I said, warming to my theme, "that we owe most of our great inventions and most of the achievements of genius to idleness—either enforced or voluntary. The human mind prefers to be spoon-fed with the thoughts of others, but deprived of such nourishment it will reluctantly, begin to think for itself—and such thinking, remember, is original thinking and may have valuable results.

"Besides," I went on, before Aimée could get in another sniff, "there is the artistic side."

I got up and took from my desk where it always accompanied me a photograph of my favourite Chinese picture. It represents an old man sitting beneath a tree playing cat's cradle with a piece of string on his fingers and toes.

"It was in the Chinese exhibition," I said. "It fascinated me. Allow me to introduce you. It is called 'Old Man enjoying the Pleasures of Idleness.' "

Aimée Griffith was unimpressed by my lovely picture. She said: "Oh well, we all know what the Chinese are like!"

"It doesn't appeal to you?" I asked.

"Frankly, no. I'm not very interested in art, I'm afraid. Your attitude, Mr. Burton, is typical of that of most men. You dislike the idea of women working—of their competing——"

I was taken aback. I had come up against the Feminist. Aimée was well away, her cheeks flushed.

"It is incredible to you that women should want a career. It was incredible to my parents. I was anxious to study for a doctor. They would not hear of paying the fees. But they paid them readily for Owen. Yet I should have made a far better doctor than my brother."

I'm sorry about that," I said. "It was tough on you. If one wants to do a thing——"

She went on quickly:

"Oh, I've got over it now. I've plenty of will-power. My life is busy and active. I'm one of the happiest people in Lymstock. Plenty to do. But I do go up in arms against the silly old-fashioned prejudice that women's place is always the home."

"I'm sorry if I offended you," I said. "And that wasn't really my point. I don't see Megan in a domestic role at all."

"No, poor child. She'll be a misfit anywhere, I'm afraid." Aimée had calmed down. She was speaking quite normally again. "Her father, you know——"

She paused and I said bluntly: "I *don't* know. Everyone says 'her father' and drops their voice, and that is that. What did the man *do*? Is he alive still?"

"I really don't know. And I'm rather vague myself, I'm afraid. But he was definitely a bad lot. Prison, I believe. And a streak of very strong abnormality. That's why it wouldn't surprise me if Megan was a bit 'wanting.' "

"Megan," I said, "is in full possession of her senses, and as I said before, I consider her an intelligent girl. My sister thinks so too. Joanna is very fond of her."

Aimée said:

"I'm afraid your sister must find it very dull down here."

And as she said it, I learnt something else. Aimée Griffith disliked my sister. It was there in the smooth conventional tones of her voice.

"We've all wondered how you could both bear to bury yourselves in such an out-of-the-way spot."

It was a question and I answered it.

"Doctor's orders. I was to come somewhere very quiet where nothing ever happened." I paused and added, "Not quite true of Lymstock now."

"No, no, indeed."

She sounded worried and got up to go. She said then:

"You know—it's got to be put a stop to—all this beastliness!

We can't have it going on."

"Aren't the police doing anything?"

"I suppose so. But I think we ought to take it in hand *ourselves*."

"We're not as well equipped as they are."

"Nonsense! We probably have far more sense and intelligence! A little determination is all that is needed."

She said good-bye abruptly and went away.

When Joanna and Megan came back from their walk I showed Megan my Chinese picture. Her face lighted up. She said, "It's heavenly, isn't it?"

"That *is* rather my opinion."

Her forehead was crinkling in the way I knew so well.

"But it would be difficult, wouldn't it?"

"To be idle."

"No, not to be idle—but to enjoy the pleasures of it. You'd have to be very old——"

She paused. I said: "He *is* an old man."

"I don't mean old that way. Not *age*. I mean old in—in . . ."

"You mean," I said, "that one would have to attain a very high state of civilisation for the thing to present itself to you in that way—a fine point of sophistication? I think I shall complete your education, Megan, by reading to you one hundred poems translated from the Chinese."

iii

I met Symmington in the town later in the day.

"Is it quite all right for Megan to stay on with us for a bit?" I asked. "It's company for Joanna—she's rather lonely sometimes with none of her own friends."

"Oh—er—Megan? Oh yes, very good of you."

I took a dislike to Symmington then which I never quite overcame. He had so obviously forgotten all about Megan. I wouldn't have minded if he had actively disliked the girl—a man may sometimes be jealous of a first husband's child—but he didn't dislike her, he just hardly noticed her. He felt towards her much as a man who doesn't care much for dogs would feel about a dog in the house. You notice it when you fall over it and swear at it, and you give it a vague pat sometimes when it presents itself to be patted. Symmington's complete indifference to his stepdaughter annoyed me very much.

I said: "What are you planning to do with her?"

"With Megan?" He seemed rather startled. "Well, she'll go on living at home. I mean, naturally, it is her home."

My grandmother, of whom I had been very fond, used to sing old-fashioned songs to her guitar. One of them, I remembered, ended thus:

Oh maid, most dear, I am not here
I have no place, no part,
No dwelling more, by sea nor shore,
But only in your heart.

I went home humming it.

iv

Emily Barton came just after tea had been cleared away.

She wanted to talk about the garden. We talked garden for about half an hour. Then we turned back towards the house.

It was then that lowering her voice, she murmured:

"I do hope that that child—that she hasn't been too much *upset* by all this dreadful business?"

"Her mother's death, you mean?"

"That, of course. But I really meant, the—the unpleasantness *behind* it."

I was curious. I wanted Miss Barton's reaction.

"What do you think about that? Was it true?"

"Oh, no, no, surely not. I'm quite sure that Mrs. Symmington never—that he wasn't"—little Emily Barton was pink and confused—"I mean it's quite untrue—although of course it may have been a judgment."

"A judgment?" I said, staring.

Emily Barton was very pink, very Dresden china shepherdess-like.

"I cannot help feeling that all these dreadful letters, all the sorrow and pain they have caused, may have been sent for a *purpose*."

"They were sent for a purpose, certainly," I said grimly.

"No, no, Mr. Burton, you misunderstand me. I'm not talking of the misguided creature who wrote them— someone quite abandoned that must be. I mean that they have been permitted—by Providence! To awaken us to a sense of our shortcomings."

"Surely," I said, "the Almighty could choose a less unsavoury weapon."

Miss Emily murmured that God moved in a mysterious way.

"No," I said. "There's too much tendency to attribute to God the evils that man does of his own free will. I might concede you the Devil. God doesn't really need to punish us, Miss Barton. We're so very busy punishing ourselves."

"What I can't make out is *why* should any one want to do such a thing?"

I shrugged my shoulders.

"A warped mentality."

"It seems very sad."

"It doesn't seem to me sad. It seems to me just damnable. And I don't apologise for the word. I mean just that."

The pink had gone out of Miss Barton's cheeks. They were very white.

"But why, Mr. Burton, *why*? What pleasure can any one get out of it?"

"Nothing you and I can understand, thank goodness."

Emily Barton lowered her voice.

"They say that *Mrs. Cleat*—but I really cannot believe it."

I shook my head. She went on in an agitated manner:

"Nothing of this kind has ever happened before—never in my memory. It has been such a happy little community. What would my dear mother have said? Well, one must be thankful that she has been spared."

I thought from all I had heard that old Mrs. Barton had been sufficiently tough to have taken anything, and would probably have enjoyed this sensation.

Emily went on:

"It distresses me deeply."

"You've not—er—had anything yourself?"

She flushed crimson.

"Oh, no—oh, no, indeed. Oh! that would be dreadful."

I apologised hastily, but she went away looking rather upset.

I went into the house. Joanna was standing by the drawing-room fire which she had just lit, for the evenings were still chilly.

She had an open letter in her hand.

She turned her head quickly as I entered.

"Jerry! I found this in the letter box—dropped in by hand. It begins, 'You painted trollop . . .' "

"What else does it say?"

Joanna gave a wide grimace.

"Same old muck."

She dropped it on to the fire. With a quick gesture that hurt my back I jerked it off again just before it caught.

"Don't," I said. "We may need it."

"Need it?"

"For the police."

V

Superintendent Nash came to see me the following morning. From the first moment I saw him I took a great liking to him. He was the best type of C.I.D. country superintendent. Tall, soldierly, with quiet reflective eyes and a straightforward unassuming manner.

He said: "Good morning, Mr. Burton, I expect you can guess what I've come to see you about."

"Yes, I think so. This letter business."

He nodded.

"I understand you had one of them?"

"Yes, soon after we got here."

"What did it say exactly?"

I thought a minute, then conscientiously repeated the wording of the letter as closely as possible.

The superintendent listened with an immovable face, showing no signs of any kind of emotion. When I had finished, he said:

"I see. You didn't keep the letter, Mr. Burton?"

"I'm sorry. I didn't. You see, I thought it was just an isolated instance of spite against newcomers to the place."

The superintendent inclined his head comprehendingly.

He said briefly: "A pity."

"However," I said, "my sister got one yesterday. I just stopped her putting it in the fire."

"Thank you, Mr. Burton, that was thoughtful of you."

I went across to my desk and unlocked the drawer in which I had put it. It was not, I thought, very suitable for Partridge's eyes. I gave it to Nash.

He read it through. Then he looked up and asked me:

"Is this the same in appearance as the last one?"

"I think so—as far as I can remember."

"The same difference between the envelope and the text?"

"Yes," I said. "The envelope was typed. The letter itself had printed words pasted on to a sheet of paper."

Nash nodded and put it in his pocket. Then he said:

"I wonder, Mr. Burton, if you would mind coming down to the station with me? We could have a conference there and it would save a good deal of time and overlapping."

"Certainly," I said. "You would like me to come now?"

"If you don't mind."

There was a police car at the door. We drove down in it.

I said:

"Do you think you'll be able to get to the bottom of this?"

Nash nodded with easy confidence.

"Oh yes, we'll get to the bottom of it all right. It's a question of time and routine. They're slow, these cases, but they're pretty sure. It's a matter of narrowing things down."

"Elimination?" I said.

"Yes. And general routine."

"Watching post boxes, examining typewriters, fingerprints, all that?"

He smiled. "As you say."

At the police station I found Symmington and Griffith were already there. I was introduced to a tall lantern-jawed man in plain clothes, Inspector Graves.

"Inspector Graves," explained Nash, "has come down from

London to help us. He's an expert on anonymous letter cases."

Inspector Graves smiled mournfully. I reflected that a life spent in the pursuit of anonymous letter writers must be singularly depressing. Inspector Graves, however, showed a kind of melancholy enthusiasm.

"They're all the same, these cases," he said in a deep lugubrious voice like a depressed bloodhound. "You'd be surprised. The wording of the letters and the things they say."

"We had a case just on two years ago," said Nash. "Inspector Graves helped us then."

Some of the letters, I saw, were spread out on the table in front of Graves. He had evidently been examining them.

"Difficulty is," said Nash, "to get hold of the letters. Either people put them in the fire, or they won't admit to having received anything of the kind. Stupid, you see, and afraid of being mixed up with the police. They're a backward lot here."

"Still, we've got a fair amount to get on with," said Graves. Nash took the letter I had given him from his pocket and tossed it over to Graves.

The latter glanced through it, laid it with others and observed approvingly:

"Very nice—very nice indeed."

It was not the way I should have chosen to describe the epistle in question, but experts, I suppose, have their own point of view. I was glad that that screed of vituperative and obscene abuse gave *somebody* pleasure.

"We've got enough, I think, to go on with," said Inspector Graves, "and I'll ask all you gentlemen, if you should get any more, to bring them along at once. Also, if you hear of someone else getting one—(you, in particular, doctor, among your patients) do your best to get them to come along here with them. I've got—" he sorted with deft fingers among his exhibits, "one to Mr. Symmington, received as far back as two months ago, one to Dr. Griffith, one to Miss Ginch, one written to Mrs. Mudge, the butcher's wife, one to Jennifer Clark, barmaid at the Three Crowns, the one received by Mrs. Symmington, this one now to Miss Burton—oh yes, and one from the bank manager."

"Quite a representative collection," I remarked.

"And not one I couldn't match from other cases! This one here is as near as nothing to one written by that milliner woman. This one is the dead spit of an outbreak we had up in Northumberland—written by a schoolgirl, they were. I can tell you, gentlemen, I'd like to see something *new* sometimes, instead of the same old treadmill."

"There is nothing new under the sun," I murmured.

"Quite so, sir. You'd know that if you were in our profession."

Nash sighed and said, "Yes, indeed."

Symmington asked:

"Have you come to any definite opinion as to the writer?"

Graves cleared his throat and delivered a small lecture.

"There are certain similarities shared by all these letters. I shall enumerate them, gentlemen, in case they suggest anything to your minds. The text of the letters is composed of words made up from individual letters cut out of a printed book. It's an old book, printed, I should say, about the year 1830. This has obviously been done to avoid the risk of recognition through handwriting which is, as most people know nowadays, a fairly easy matter . . . the so-called disguising of a hand not amounting to much when faced with expert tests. There are no fingerprints on the letters and envelopes of a distinctive character. That is to say, they have been handled by the postal authorities, the recipient, and there are other stray fingerprints, but no set common to all, showing therefore that the person who put them together was careful to wear gloves. The envelopes are typewritten by a Windsor 7 machine, well worn, with the a and the t out of alignment. Most of them have been posted locally, or put in the box of a house by hand. It is therefore evident that they are of local provenance. They were written by a woman, and in my opinion a woman of middle age or over, and probably, though not certainly, unmarried."

We maintained a respectful silence for a minute or two. Then I said:

"The typewriter's your best bet, isn't it? That oughtn't to be difficult in a little place like this."

Inspector Graves shook his head sadly and said:

"That's where you're wrong, sir."

"The typewriter," said Superintendent Nash, "is unfortunately too easy. It's an old one from Mr. Symmington's office, given by him to the Women's Institute where, I may say, it's fairly easy of access. The ladies here all often go into the Institute."

"Can't you tell something definite from the—er—the touch, don't you call it?"

Again Graves nodded.

"Yes, that can be done—but these envelopes have all been typed by someone using one finger."

"Someone then unused to the typewriter?"

"No, I wouldn't say that. Someone, say, who can type but doesn't want us to know the fact."

"Whoever writes these things has been very cunning," I said slowly.

"She is, sir, she is," said Graves. "Up to every trick of the trade."

"I shouldn't have thought one of these bucolic women down here would have had the brains," I said.

Graves coughed.

"I haven't made myself plain, I'm afraid. Those letters were written by an educated woman."

"What, by a lady?"

The word slipped out involuntarily. I hadn't used the term "lady" for ten years. But now it came automatically to my lips, re-echoed from days long ago, and my grandmother's faint unconsciously arrogant voice saying, "Of course, she isn't a *lady*, dear."

Nash understood at once. The word lady still meant something to him.

"Not necessarily a lady," he said. "But certainly not a village woman. They're mostly pretty illiterate down here, can't spell, and certainly can't express themselves with fluency."

I was silent, for I had had a shock. The community was so small. Unconsciously I had visualised the writer of the letters as a Mrs. Cleat or her like, some spiteful, cunning half-wit.

Symmington put my thoughts into words. He said sharply:

"But that narrows it down to about half a dozen people in the whole place!"

"That's right."

"I can't believe it."

Then, with a slight effort, and looking straight in front of him as though the mere sound of his own words was distasteful, he said:

"You have heard what I stated at the inquest. In case you may have thought that that statement was actuated by a desire to protect my wife's memory, I should like to repeat now that I am firmly convinced that the subject matter of the letter my wife received was absolutely false. I *know* it was false. My wife was a very sensitive woman, and—er—well, you might call it *prudish* in some respects. Such a letter would have been a great shock to her, and she was in poor health."

Graves responded instantly.

"That's quite likely to be right, sir. None of these letters show any signs of intimate knowledge. They're just blind accusations. There's been no attempt to blackmail. And there doesn't seem to be any religious bias—such as we sometimes get. It's just sex and spite! And that's going to give us quite a good pointer towards the writer."

Symmington got up. Dry and unemotional as the man was, his lips were trembling.

"I hope you find the devil who writes these soon. She murdered my wife as surely as if she'd put a knife into her." He paused. "How does she feel now, I wonder?"

He went out, leaving that question unanswered.

"How does she feel, Griffith?" I asked. It seemed to me the answer was in his province.

"God knows. Remorseful, perhaps. On the other hand, it may be that she's enjoying her power. Mrs. Symmington's death may have fed her mania."

"I hope not," I said, with a slight shiver. "Because if so, she'll——"

I hesitated and Nash finished the sentence for me.

"She'll try it again? That, Mr. Burton, would be the best thing that could happen, for us. The pitcher goes to the well once too often, remember."

"She'd be mad to go on with it," I exclaimed.

"She'll go on," said Graves. "They always do. It's a vice, you know, they can't let it alone."

I shook my head with a shudder. I asked if they needed me any longer, I wanted to get out into the air. The atmosphere seemed tinged with evil.

"There's nothing more, Mr. Burton," said Nash. "Only keep your eyes open, and do as much propaganda as you can—that is to say, urge on everyone that they've got to report any letter they recieve."

I nodded.

"I should think everyone in the place has had one of the foul things by now," I said.

"I wonder," said Graves. He put his sad head a little on one side and asked, "You don't know, definitely, of any one who *hasn't* had a letter?"

"What an extraordinary question! The population at large isn't likely to take me into their confidence."

"No, no, Mr. Burton, I didn't mean that. I just wondered if you knew of any one person who quite definitely, to your certain knowledge, has not received an anonymous letter."

"Well, as a matter of fact," I hesitated, "I do, in a way."

And I repeated my conversation with Emily Barton and what she had said.

Graves received the information with a wooden face and said: "Well, that may come in useful. I'll note it down."

I went out into the afternoon sunshine with Owen Griffith. Once in the street, I swore aloud.

"What kind of place is this for a man to come to to lie in the sun and heal his wounds? It's full of festering poison, this place, and it looks as peaceful and as innocent as the Garden of Eden."

"Even there," said Owen dryly, "there was one serpent."

"Look here, Griffith, do they know anything? Have they got any idea?"

"I don't know. They've got a wonderful technique, the police. They're seemingly so frank, and they tell you nothing."

"Yes. Nash is a nice fellow."

"And a very capable one."

"If anyone's batty in this place, *you* ought to know it," I said accusingly.

Griffith shook his head. He looked discouraged. But he

looked more than that—he looked worried. I wondered if he had an inkling of some kind.

We had been walking along the High Street. I stopped at the door of the house agents.

"I believe my second instalment of rent is due—in advance. I've got a good mind to pay it and clear out with Joanna right away. Forfeit the rest of the tenancy."

"Don't go," said Owen.

"Why not?"

He didn't answer. He said slowly after a minute or two.

"After all—I dare say you're right. Lymstock isn't healthy just now. It might—it might harm you or—or your sister."

"Nothing harms Joanna," I said. "She's tough. I'm the weakly one. Somehow this business makes me sick."

"It makes *me* sick," said Owen.

I pushed the door of the house agents half-open.

"But I shan't go," I said. "Vulgar curiosity is stronger than pusillanimity. I want to know the solution."

I went in.

A woman who was typing got up and came towards me. She had frizzy hair and simpered, but I found her more intelligent than the spectacled youth who had previously held sway in the outer office.

A minute or two later something familiar about her penetrated through to my consciousness. It was Miss Ginch, lately Symmington's lady clerk. I commented on the fact.

"You were with Galbraith and Symmington, weren't you?" I said.

"Yes. Yes, indeed. But I thought it was better to leave. This is quite a good post, though not quite so well paid. But there are things that are more valuable than money, don't you think so?"

"Undoubtedly," I said.

"Those awful letters," breathed Miss Ginch in a sibilant whisper. "I got a dreadful one. About me and Mr. Symmington—oh, terrible it was, saying the most *awful* things! I knew my duty and I took it to the police, though of course it wasn't exactly *pleasant* for me, was it?"

"No, no, most unpleasant."

"But they thanked me and said I had done quite right. But I

felt that, after that, if people were talking—and evidently they *must* have been, or where did the writer get the idea from?—then I must avoid even the appearance of evil, though there has never been anything at all *wrong* between me and Mr. Symmington."

I felt rather embarrassed.

"No, no, of course not."

"But people have such evil minds. Yes, alas, such evil minds!"

Nervously trying to avoid it, I nevertheless met her eye, and I made a most unpleasant discovery.

Miss Ginch was thoroughly enjoying herself.

Already once to-day I had come across someone who reacted pleasurably to anonymous letters. Inspector Graves's enthusiasm was professional. Miss Ginch's enjoyment I found merely suggestive and disgusting.

An idea flashed across my startled mind.

Had Miss Ginch written these letters herself?

7

i

WHEN I got home I found Mrs. Dane Calthrop sitting talking to Joanna. She looked, I thought, grey and ill.

"This has been a terrible shock to me, Mr. Burton," she said. "Poor thing, poor thing."

"Yes," I said. "It's awful to think of someone being driven to the stage of taking their own life."

"Oh, you mean Mrs. Symmington?"

"Didn't you?"

Mrs. Dane Calthrop shook her head.

"Of course one is sorry for her, but it would have been bound to happen anyway, wouldn't it?"

"Would it?" said Joanna dryly.

Mrs. Dane Calthrop turned to her.

"Oh, I think so, dear. If suicide is your idea of escape from trouble then it doesn't very much matter what the trouble is. Whenever some very unpleasant shock had to be faced, she'd have done the same thing. What it really comes down to is that she was that kind of woman. Not that one would have guessed it. She always seemed to me a selfish rather stupid woman, with a good firm hold on life. Not the kind to panic, you would think—but I'm beginning to realise how little I really know about any one."

"I'm still curious as to whom you meant when you said 'Poor thing'," I remarked.

She stared at me.

"The woman who wrote the letters, of course."

"I don't think," I said dryly, "I shall waste sympathy on her."

Mrs. Dane Calthrop leaned forward. She laid a hand on my knee.

"But don't you realise—can't you *feel*? Use your imagination. Think how desperately, violently unhappy any one must be to sit down and write these things. How lonely, how cut off from human kind. Poisoned through and through, with a dark stream of poison that finds its outlet in this way. That's why I feel so self-reproachful. Somebody in this town has been racked with that terrible unhappiness, and I've had no idea of it. I should have had. You can't interfere with actions—I never do. But that black inward unhappiness—like a septic arm physically, all black and swollen. If you could cut it and let the poison out it would flow away harmlessly. Yes, poor soul, poor soul."

She got up to go.

I did not feel like agreeing with her. I had no sympathy for our anonymous letter writer whatsoever. But I did ask curiously:

"Have you any idea at all, Mrs. Calthrop, who this woman is?"

She turned her fine perplexed eyes on me.

"Well, I can guess," she said. "But then I might be wrong, mightn't I?"

She went swiftly out through the door, popping her head back to ask:

"Do tell me, why have you never married, Mr. Burton?"

In any one else it would have been impertinence, but with Mrs. Dane Calthrop you felt that the idea had suddenly come into her head and she had really wanted to know.

"Shall we say," I said, rallying, "that I have never met the right woman?"

"We can say so," said Mrs. Dane Calthrop, "but it wouldn't be a very good answer, because so many men have obviously married the wrong woman."

This time she really departed.

Joanna said:

"You know I really do think she's mad. But I like her. The people in the village here are afraid of her."

"So am I, a little."

"Because you never know what's coming next?"

"Yes. And there's a careless brilliancy about her guesses."

Joanna said slowly: "Do you really think whoever wrote those letters is very unhappy?"

"I don't know what the damned hag is thinking or feeling! And I don't care. It's her victims I'm sorry for."

It seems odd to me now that in our speculations about Poison Pen's frame of mind, we missed the most obvious one. Griffith had pictured her as possibly exultant. I had envisaged her as remorseful—appalled by the result of her handiwork. Mrs. Dane Calthrop had seen her as suffering.

Yet the obvious, the inevitable reaction we did not consider—or perhaps I should say, I did not consider. That reaction was Fear.

For with the death of Mrs. Symmington, the letters had passed out of one category into another. I don't know what the legal position was—Symmington knew, I suppose, but it was clear that with a death resulting, the position of the writer of the letters was much more serious. There could now be no question of passing it off as a joke if the identity of the writer was discovered. The police were active, a Scotland Yard expert called in. It was vital now for the anonymous author to remain anonymous.

And granted that Fear was the principal reaction, other things followed. Those possibilities also I was blind to. Yet surely they should have been obvious.

ii

Joanna and I came down rather late to breakfast the next morning. That is to say, late by the standards of Lymstock. It was nine-thirty, an hour at which, in London, Joanna was just unclosing an eyelid, and mine would probably be still tight shut. However when Partridge had said "Breakfast at half-past eight, or nine o'clock?" neither Joanna nor I had had the nerve to suggest a later hour.

To my annoyance, Aimée Griffith was standing on the door-step talking to Megan.

She gave tongue with her usual heartiness at the sight of us.

"Hallo, there, slackers! I've been up for hours."

That, of course, was her own business. A doctor, no doubt, has to have early breakfast, and a dutiful sister is there to pour out his tea, or coffee. But it is no excuse for coming and butting in on one's more somnolent neighbours. Nine-thirty is not the time for a morning call.

Megan slipped back into the house and into the dining-room, where I gathered she had been interrupted in her breakfast.

"I said I wouldn't come in," said Aimée Griffith—though why it is more of a merit to force people to come and speak to you on the doorstep, than to talk to them inside the house I do not know. "Just wanted to ask Miss Burton if she'd any vegetables to spare for our Red Cross stall on the main road. If so, I'd get Owen to call for them in the car."

"You're out and about very early," I said.

"The early bird catches the worm," said Aimée. "You have a better chance of finding people in this time of the day. I'm off to Mr. Pye's next. Got to go over to Brenton this afternoon. Guides."

"Your energy makes me quite tired," I said, and at that moment the telephone rang and I retired to the back of the hall to answer it, leaving Joanna murmuring rather doubtfully something about rhubarb and french beans and exposing her ignorance of the vegetable garden.

"Yes?" I said into the telephone mouthpiece.

A confused noise of deep breathing came from the other end of the wire and a doubtful female voice said "Oh!"

"Yes?" I said again encouragingly.

"Oh," said the voice again, and then it inquired adenoidally, "Is that—what I mean—is that Little Furze?"

"This is Little Furze."

"Oh!" This was clearly a stock beginning to every sentence. The voice inquired cautiously, "Could I speak to Miss Partridge just a minute?"

"Certainly," I said. "Who shall I say?"

"Oh. Tell her it's Agnes, would you? Agnes Waddle."

"Agnes Waddle?"

"That's right."

Resisting the temptation to say, "Donald Duck to you," I put down the telephone receiver and called up the stairs to where I could hear the sound of Partridge's activities overhead.

"Partridge. Partridge."

Partridge appeared at the head of the stairs, a long mop in one hand, and a look of "What is it *now*?" clearly discernible behind her invariably respectful manner.

"Yes, sir?"

"Agnes Waddle wants to speak to you on the telephone."

"I beg your pardon, sir?"

I raised my voice. "Agnes Waddle."

I have spelt the name as it presented itself to my mind. But I will now spell it as it was actually written.

"Agnes Woddell—whatever can she want now?"

Very much put out of countenance Partridge relinquished her mop and rustled down the stairs, her print dress crackling with agitation.

I beat an unobtrusive retreat into the dining-room where Megan was wolfing down kidneys and bacon. Megan, unlike Aimée Griffith, was displaying no "glorious morning face." In fact she replied very gruffly to my morning salutations and continued to eat in silence.

I opened the morning paper and a minute or two later Joanna entered looking somewhat shattered.

"Whew!" she said. "I'm so tired. And I think I've exposed my utter ignorance of what grows when. Aren't there runner beans this time of year?"

"August," said Megan.

"Well, one has them any time in London," said Joanna defensively.

"Tins, sweet fool," I said. "And cold storage on ships from the far-flung limits of empire."

"Like ivory, apes and peacocks?" asked Joanna.

"Exactly."

"I'd rather have peacocks," said Joanna thoughtfully.

"I'd like a monkey of my own as a pet," said Megan.

Meditatively peeling an orange, Joanna said:

"I wonder what it would feel like to be Aimée Griffith, all bursting with health and vigour and enjoyment of life. Do you think she's ever tired, or depressed, or—or wistful?"

I said I was quite certain Aimée Griffith was never wistful, and followed Megan out of the open french window on to the veranda.

Standing there, filling my pipe, I heard Partridge enter the dining-room from the hall and heard her voice say grimly:

"Can I speak to you a minute, miss?"

"Dear me," I thought. "I hope Partridge isn't going to give notice. Emily Barton will be very annoyed with us if so."

Partridge went on: "I must apologise, miss, for being rung up on the telephone. That is to say, the young person who did so should have known better. I have never been in the habit of using the telephone or of permitting my friends to ring me up on it, and I'm very sorry indeed that it should have occurred, and the master taking the call and everything."

"Why, that's quite all right, Partridge," said Joanna soothingly, "why shouldn't your friends use the phone if they want to speak to you?"

Partridge's face, I could feel, though I could not see it, was more dour than ever as she replied coldly:

"It is not the kind of thing that has ever been done in this house. Miss Emily would never permit it. As I say, I am sorry it occurred, but Agnes Woddell the girl who did it was upset and she's young too, and doesn't know what's fitting in a gentleman's house."

"That's one for you, Joanna," I thought gleefully.

"This Agnes who rung me up, miss," went on Partridge, "she used to be in service here under me. Sixteen she was, then, and come straight from the orphanage. And you see, not having a home, or a mother or any relations to advise her, she's been in the habit of coming to me. I can tell her what's what, you see."

"Yes?" said Joanna and waited. Clearly there was more to follow.

"So I am taking the liberty of asking you, miss, if you would allow Agnes to come here to tea this afternoon in the kitchen. It's her day out, you see, and she's got something on her mind she wants to consult me about. I wouldn't dream of suggesting such a thing in the usual way."

Joanna said bewildered:

"But why shouldn't you have any one to tea with you?"

Partridge drew herself up at this, so Joanna said afterwards and really looked most formidable, as she replied:

"It has never been the custom of This House, miss. Old Mrs.

Barton never allowed visitors in the kitchen, excepting as it should be our own day out, in which case we were allowed to entertain friends here instead of going out, but otherwise, on ordinary days, no. And Miss Emily she keeps to the old ways."

Joanna is very nice to servants and most of them like her but she has never cut any ice with Partridge.

"It's no good, my girl," I said when Partridge had gone and Joanna had joined me outside. "You sympathy and leniency are not appreciated. The good old overbearing ways for Partridge and things done the way they should be done in a gentleman's house."

"I never heard of such tyranny as not allowing them to have their friends to see them," said Joanna. "It's all very well, Jerry, but they can't *like* being treated like black slaves."

"Evidently they do," I said. "At least the Partridges of this world do."

"I can't imagine why she doesn't like me. Most people do."

"She probably despises you as an inadequate housekeeper. You never draw your hand across a shelf and examine it for traces of dust. You don't look under the mats. You don't ask what happened to the remains of the chocolate soufflé, and you never order a nice bread pudding."

"Ugh!" said Joanna.

She went on sadly. "I'm a failure all round to-day. Despised by our Aimée for ignorance of the vegetable kingdom. Snubbed by Partridge for being a human being. I shall now go out into the garden and eat worms."

"Megan's there already," I said.

For Megan had wandered away a few minutes previously and was now standing aimlessly in the middle of a patch of lawn looking not unlike a meditative bird waiting for nourishment.

She came back, however, towards us and said abruptly:

"I say, I must go home to-day."

"What?" I was dismayed.

She went on, flushing, but speaking with nervous determination.

"It's been awfully good of you having me and I expect I've been a fearful nuisance, but I have enjoyed it awfully, only now I must go back, because after all, well, it's my home and one can't stay away for ever, so I think I'll go this morning."

Both Joanna and I tried to make her change her mind, but she was quite adamant, and finally Joanna got out the car and Megan went upstairs and came down a few minutes later with her belongings packed up again.

The only person pleased seemed to be Partridge, who had almost a smile on her grim face. She had never liked Megan much.

I was standing in the middle of the lawn when Joanna returned.

She asked me if I thought I was a sundial.

"Why?"

"Standing there like a garden ornament. Only one couldn't put on you the motto of only marking the sunny hours. You looked like thunder!"

"I'm out of humour. First Aimée Griffith. ('Gracious!' murmured Joanna in parenthesis, 'I must speak about those vegetables!) and then Megan beetling off. I'd thought of taking her for a walk up to Legge Tor."

"With a collar and lead, I suppose," said Joanna.

"What?"

Joanna repeated loudly and clearly as she moved off round the corner of the house to the kitchen garden:

"I said, 'With a collar and lead I suppose?' Master's lost his dog, that's what's the matter with you!"

iii

I was annoyed, I must confess, at the abrupt way in which Megan had left us. Perhaps she had suddenly got bored with us.

After all, it wasn't a very amusing life for a girl. At home she'd got the kids and Elsie Holland.

I heard Joanna returning and hastily moved in case she should make more rude remarks about sundials.

Owen Griffith called in his car just before lunch-time, and the gardener was waiting for him with the necessary garden produce.

Whilst Old Adams was stowing it in the car I brought Owen

indoors for a drink. He wouldn't stay to lunch.

When I came in with the sherry I found Joanna had begun doing her stuff.

No signs of animosity now. She was curled up in the corner of the sofa and was positively purring, asking Owen questions about his work, if he liked being a G.P., if he wouldn't rather have specialised? She thought doctoring was one of the most fascinating things in the world.

Say what you will of her, Joanna is a lovely, a heaven-born listener. And after listening to so many would-be geniuses telling her how they had been unappreciated, listening to Owen Griffith was easy money. By the time we had got to the third glass of sherry, Griffith was telling her about some obscure reaction or lesion in such scientific terms that nobody could have understood a word of it except a fellow medico.

Joanna was looking intelligent and deeply interested.

I felt a moment's qualm. It was really too bad of Joanna. Griffith was too good a chap to be played fast and loose with. Women really were devils.

Then I caught a sideways view of Griffith, his long purposeful chin and the grim set of his lips, and I was not so sure that Joanna was going to have it her own way after all. And anyway, a man has no business to let himself be made a fool of by a woman. It's his own look-out if he does.

Then Joanna said:

"Do change your mind and stay to lunch with us, Dr. Griffith," and Griffith flushed a little and said he would, only his sister would be expecting him back——

"We'll ring her up and explain," said Joanna quickly and went back into the hall and did so.

I thought Griffith looked a little uneasy, and it crossed my mind that he was probably a little afraid of his sister.

Joanna came back smiling and said that that was all right.

And Owen Griffith stayed to lunch and seemed to enjoy himself. We talked about books and plays and world politics, and about music and painting and modern architecture.

We didn't talk about Lymstock at all, or about anonymous letters, or Mrs. Symmington's suicide.

We got right away from everything, and I think Owen

Griffith was happy. His dark sad face lighted up, and he revealed an interesting mind.

When he had gone I said to Joanna:

"That fellow's too good for your tricks."

Joanna said:

"That's what you say! You men all stick together!"

"Why are you out after his hide, Joanna? Wounded vanity?"

"Perhaps," said my sister.

iv

That afternoon we were to go to tea with Miss Emily Barton at her rooms in the village.

We strolled down there on foot, for I felt strong enough now to manage the hill back again.

We must actually have allowed too much time and got there early, for the door was opened to us by a tall rawboned fierce-looking woman who told us that Miss Barton wasn't in yet.

"But she's expecting you, I know, so if you'll come up and wait, please."

This was evidently Faithful Florence.

We followed her up the stairs and she threw open a door and showed us into what was quite a comfortable sitting-room, though perhaps a little over-furnished. Some of the things, I suspected, had come from Little Furze.

The woman was clearly proud of her room.

"It's nice, isn't it?" she demanded.

"Very nice," said Joanna warmly.

"I make her as comfortable as I can. Not that I can do for her as I'd like to and in the way she ought to have. She ought to be in her own house, properly, not turned out into rooms."

Florence, who was clearly a dragon, looked from one to the other of us reproachfully. It was not, I felt, our lucky day. Joanna had been ticked off by Aimée Griffith and Partridge and now we were both being ticked off by the dragon Florence.

"Parlourmaid I was for fifteen years there," she added.

Joanna, goaded by injustice, said:

"Well, Miss Barton wanted to let the house. She put it down

at the house agents."

"Forced to it," said Florence. "And she living so frugal and careful. But even then, the government can't leave her alone! Has to have its pound of flesh just the same."

I shook my head sadly.

"Plenty of money there was in the old lady's time," said Florence. "And then they all died off one by one, poor dears. Miss Emily nursing of them one after the other. Wore herself out she did, and always so patient and uncomplaining. But it told on her, and then to have worry about money on top of it all! Shares not bringing in what they used to, so she says, and why not, I should like to know? They ought to be ashamed of themselves. Doing down a lady like her who's got no head for figures and can't keep up to their tricks."

"Practically everyone has been hit that way," I said, but Florence remained unsoftened.

"It's all right for some as can look after themselves, but not for *her*. She needs looking after, and as long as she's with me I'm going to see no one imposes on her or upsets her in any way. I'd do anything for Miss Emily."

And glaring at us for some moments in order to drive that point thoroughly home, the indomitable Florence left the room, carefully shutting the door behind her.

"Do you feel like a blood-sucker, Jerry?" inquired Joanna. "Because I do. What's the matter with us?"

"We don't seem to be going down very well," I said. "Megan gets tired of us, Partridge disapproves of you, faithful Florence disapproves of both of us."

Joanna murmured: "I wonder why Megan *did* leave?"

"She got bored."

"I don't think she did at all. I wonder—do you think, Jerry, it could have been something that Aimée Griffith said?"

"You mean this morning, when they were talking on the doorstep."

"Yes. There wasn't much time, of course, but——"

I finished the sentence.

"But that woman's got the tread of a cow elephant! She might have——"

The door opened and Miss Emily came in. She was pink and a

little out of breath and seemed excited. Her eyes were very blue and shining.

She chirruped at us in quite a distracted manner.

"Oh dear, I'm so sorry I'm late. Just doing a little shopping in the town, and the cakes at the Blue Rose didn't seem to me quite fresh, so I went on to Mrs. Lygon's. I always like to get my cakes the last thing, then one gets the newest batch just out of the oven, and one isn't put off with the day before's. But I am so distressed to have kept you waiting— really unpardonable——"

Joanna cut in.

"It's our fault, Miss Barton. We're early. We walked down and Jerry strides along so fast now that we arrive everywhere too soon."

"Never too soon, dear. Don't say that. One cannot have too much of a good thing, you know."

And the old lady patted Joanna affectionately on the shoulder.

Joanna brightened up. At last, so it seemed, she was being a success. Emily Barton extended her smile to include me, but with a slight timidity in it, rather as one might approach a man-eating tiger guaranteed for the moment harmless.

"It's very good of you to come to such a feminine meal as tea, Mr. Burton."

Emily Barton, I think, has a mental picture of men as interminably consuming whiskies and soda and smoking cigars, and in the intervals dropping out to do a few seductions of village maidens, or to conduct a liaison with a married woman.

When I said this to Joanna later, she replied that it was probably wishful thinking, that Emily Barton would have liked to come across such a man, but alas, had never done so.

In the meantime Miss Emily was fussing round the room, arranging Joanna and myself with little tables, and carefully providing ashtrays, and a minute later the door opened and Florence came in bearing a tray of tea with some fine Crown Derby cups on it which I gathered Miss Emily had brought with her. The tea was china and delicious and there were plates of sandwiches and thin bread and butter, and a quantity of little cakes.

Florence was beaming now, and looked at Miss Emily with a

kind of maternal pleasure, as at a favourite child enjoying a doll's tea party.

Joanna and I ate far more than we wanted, our hostess pressed us so earnestly. The little lady was clearly enjoying her tea party and I perceived that, to Emily Barton, Joanna and I were a big adventure, two people from the mysterious world of London and sophistication. Miss Barton spoke warmly of Dr. Griffith, his kindness and his cleverness as a doctor. Mr. Symmington, too, was a very clever lawyer, and had helped Miss Barton to get some money back from the income tax which she would never have known about. He was so nice to his children, too, devoted to them and to his wife—she caught herself up. "Poor Mrs. Symmington, it's so dreadfully sad, with those young children left motherless. Never, perhaps, a very strong woman—and her health had been bad of late. A brain storm, that is what it must have been. I read about such a thing in the paper. People really do not know what they are doing under those circumstances. And she can't have known what she was doing or else she would have remembered Mr. Symmington and the children."

"That anonymous letter must have shaken her up very badly," said Joanna.

Miss Barton flushed. She said, with a tinge of reproof in her voice:

"Not a very nice thing to discuss, do you think, dear? I know there have been—er—letters, but we won't talk about them. Nasty things. I think they are better just ignored."

Well, Miss Barton might be able to ignore them, but for some people it wasn't so easy. However I obediently changed the subject and we discussed Aimée Griffith.

"Wonderful, quite wonderful," said Emily Barton. "Her energy and her organising powers are really splendid. She's so good with girls too. And she's so practical and up-to-date in every way. She really runs this place. And absolutely devoted to her brother. It's very nice to see such devotion between brother and sister."

"Doesn't he ever find her a little overwhelming?" asked Joanna.

Emily Barton stared at her in a startled fashion.

"She has sacrificed a great deal for his sake," she said with a touch of reproachful dignity.

I saw a touch of Oh Yeay! in Joanna's eyes and hastened to divert the conversation to Mr. Pye.

Emily Barton was a little dubious about Mr. Pye.

All she could say was, repeated rather doubtfully, that he was very kind—yes, very kind. Very well off, too, and most generous. He had very strange visitors sometimes, but then, of course, he had travelled a lot.

We agreed that travel not only broadened the mind, but occasionally resulted in the forming of strange acquaintances.

"I have often wished myself, to go on a cruise," said Emily Barton wistfully. "One reads about them in the papers and they sound so attractive."

"Why don't you go?" asked Joanna.

This turning of a dream into a reality seemed to alarm Miss Emily. "Oh, no, no, that would be *quite* impossible."

"But why? They're fairly cheap."

"Oh, it's not only the expense. But I shouldn't like to go alone. Travelling alone would look very peculiar, don't you think?"

"No," said Joanna.

Miss Emily looked at her doubtfully.

"And I don't know how I would manage about my luggage—and going shore at foreign ports—and all the different currencies——"

Innumerable pitfalls seemed to rise up before the little lady's affrighted gaze, and Joanna hastened to calm her by a question about an approaching garden fête and sale of work. This led us quite naturally to Mrs. Dane Calthrop.

A faint spasm showed for a minute on Miss Barton's face.

"You know, dear," she said, "she is really a very *odd* woman. The things she says sometimes."

I asked what things.

"Oh, I don't know. Such very *unexpected* things. And the way she looks at you, as though you weren't there but somebody else was—I'm expressing it badly but it is so hard to convey the impression I mean. And then she won't—well, *interfere* at all. There are so many cases where a vicar's wife could advise and—perhaps *admonish*. Pull people up, you know, and make them mend their ways. Because people would listen to her, I'm sure of that, they're all quite in awe of her. But she insists on being aloof and far away, and has such a curious habit of feeling sorry for the most unworthy people."

"That's interesting," I said, exchanging a quick glance with Joanna.

"Still, she is a very well-bred woman. She was a Miss Farroway of Bellpath, very good family, but these old families sometimes *are* a little peculiar, I believe. But she is devoted to her husband who is a man of very fine intellect—wasted, I am sometimes afraid, in this country circle. A good man, and most sincere, but I always find his habit of quoting Latin a little confusing."

"Hear, hear," I said fervently.

"Jerry had an expensive public school eduction, so he doesn't recognise Latin when he hears it," said Joanna.

This led Miss Barton to a new topic.

"The schoolmistress here is a most unpleasant young woman," she said. "Quite *Red*, I'm afraid." She lowered her voice over the word "Red."

Later, as we walked home up the hill, Joanna said to me:

"She's rather sweet."

V

At dinner that night, Joanna said to Partridge that she hoped her tea-party had been a success.

Partridge got rather red in the face and held herself even more stiffly.

"Thank you, miss, but Agnes never turned up after all."

"Oh, I'm sorry."

"It didn't matter to *me*," said Partridge.

She was so swelling with grievance that she condescended to pour it out to us.

"It wasn't me who thought of asking her! She rang up herself, said she'd something on her mind and could she come here, it being her day off. And I said, yes, subject to your permission which I obtained. And after that, not a sound or sign of her! And no word of apology either, though I should hope I'll get a postcard to-morrow morning. These girls nowadays—don't know their place—no idea of how to behave."

Joanna attempted to soothe Partridge's wounded feelings.

"She mayn't have felt well. You didn't ring up to find out?"

Partridge drew herself up again.

"No, I did *not*, miss. No, indeed. If Agnes likes to behave rudely that's her look-out, but I shall give her a piece of my mind when we meet."

Partridge went out of the room still stiff with indignation and Joanna and I laughed.

"Probably a case of 'Advice from Aunt Nancy's Column'," I said. "*'My boy is very cold in his manner to me, what shall I do about it?'* Failing Aunt Nancy, Partridge was to be applied to for advice, but instead there has been a reconciliation and I expect at this minute that Agnes and her boy are one of those speechless couples locked in each other's arms that you come upon suddenly standing by a dark hedge. They embarrass you horribly, but you don't embarrass them."

Joanna laughed and said she expected that was it.

We began talking of the anonymous letters and wondered how Nash and the melancholy Graves were getting on.

"It's a week to-day exactly," said Joanna, "since Mrs. Symmington's suicide. I should thing they must have got on to something by now. Fingerprints, or handwriting, or *something*."

I answered her absently. Somewhere behind my conscious mind, a queer uneasiness was growing. It was connected in some way with the phrase that Joanna had used, "a week exactly."

I ought, I dare say, to have put two and two together earlier. Perhaps, unconsciously, my mind was already suspicious.

Anyway the leaven was working now. The uneasiness was growing—coming to a head.

Joanna noticed suddenly that I wasn't listening to her spirited account of a village encounter.

"What's the matter, Jerry?"

I did not answer because my mind was busy piecing things together.

Mrs. Symmington's suicide. . . .She was alone in the house

that afternoon. . . .Alone in the house *because the maids were having their day out*. . . . A week ago exactly. . . .

"Jerry, what——"

I interrupted.

"Joanna, maids have days out once a week, don't they?"

"And alternate Sundays," said Joanna. "What on——"

"Never mind Sundays. They go out the same day every week?"

"Yes. That's the usual thing."

Joanna was staring at me curiously. Her mind had not taken the track mine had done.

I crossed the room and rang the bell. Partridge came.

"Tell me," I said, "this Agnes Woddell. She's in service?"

"Yes, sir. At Mrs. Symmington's. At Mr. Symmington's, I should say now."

I drew a deep breath. I glanced at the clock. It was half-past ten.

"Would she be back now, do you think?"

Partridge was looking disapproving.

"Yes, sir. The maids have to be in by ten there. They're old-fashioned."

I said: "I'm going to ring up."

I went out to the hall. Joanna and Partridge followed me. Partridge was clearly furious. Joanna was puzzled. She said, as I was trying to get the number:

"What are you going to do, Jerry?"

"I'd like to be sure that the girl has come in all right."

Partridge snifffed. Just sniffed, nothing more. But I did not care twopence about Partridge's sniffs.

Elsie Holland answered the telephone the other end.

"Sorry to ring you up," I said. "This is Jerry Burton speaking. Is—has—your maid Agnes come in?"

It was not until after I had said it that I suddenly felt a bit of a fool. For if the girl had come in and it was all right, how on earth was I going to explain my ringing up and asking. It would have been better if I had let Joanna ask the question, though even that would need a bit of explaining. I foresaw a new trail of gossip started in Lymstock, with myself and the unknown Agnes Woddell as its centre.

Elsie Holland sounded, not unnaturally, very much surprised.

"Agnes? Oh, she's sure to be in by now."

I felt a fool but I went on with it.

"Do you mind just seeing if she has come in, Miss Holland?"

There is one thing to be said for a nursery governess; she is used to doing things when told. Hers not to reason why! Elsie Holland put down the receiver and went off obediently.

Two minutes later I heard her voice.

"Are you there, Mr. Burton?"

"Yes."

"Agnes isn't in yet, as a matter of fact."

I knew then that my hunch had been right.

I heard a noise of voices vaguely from the other end, then Symmington himself spoke.

"Hallo, Burton, what's the matter?

"Your maid Agnes isn't back yet."

"No. Miss Holland has just been to see. What's the matter? There's not been an accident, has there?"

"Not an *accident*," I said.

"Do you mean you have reason to believe something has happened to the girl?"

I said grimly: "I shouldn't be surprised."

8

i

I SLEPT badly that night. I think that, even then, there were pieces of the puzzle floating about in my mind. I believe that if I had given my mind to it, I could have solved the whole thing then and there. Otherwise why did those fragments tag along so persistently?

How much do we know at any time? Much more, or so I believe, than we know we know! But we cannot break through to that subterranean knowledge. It is there, but we cannot reach it.

I lay on my bed, tossing uneasily, and only vague bits of the puzzle came to torture me.

There *was* a pattern if only I could get hold of it. I ought to know who wrote those damned letters. There was a trail somewhere if only I could follow it. . . .

As I dropped off to sleep, words danced irritatingly through my drowsy mind.

"No smoke without fire." No fire without smoke. Smoke . .Smoke? Smoke screen. . .No, that was the war—a war phrase. War. Scrap of paper. . . .Only a scrap of paper. Belgium—Germany. . . .

I fell asleep. I dreamt that I was taking Mrs. Dane Calthrop who had turned into a greyhound, for a walk with a collar and lead.

ii

It was the ringing of the telephone that roused me. A

persistent ringing.

I sat up in bed, glanced at my watch. It was half-past seven. I had not yet been called. The telephone was ringing in the hall downstairs.

I jumped out of bed, pulled on a dressing-gown, and raced down. I beat Partridge coming through the back door from the kitchen by a short head. I picked up the receiver.

"Hallo?"

"Oh——" It was a sob of relief. "It's *you*!" Megan's voice. Megan's voice indescribably forlorn and frightened. "Oh, please do come—*do* come. Oh, please do! Will you?"

"I'm coming at once," I said. "Do you hear? *At once*."

I took the stairs two at a time and burst in on Joanna.

"Look here, Jo, I'm going off to the Symmingtons'."

Joanna lifted a curly blonde head from the pillow and rubbed her eyes like a small child.

"Why—what's happened?"

"I don't know. It was the child—Megan. She sounded all in."

"What do you think it is?"

"The girl Agnes, unless I'm very much mistaken."

As I went out of the door, Joanna called after me:

"Wait. I'll get up and drive you down."

"No need. I'll drive myself."

"You can't drive the car."

"Yes, I can."

I did, too. It hurt, but not too much. I'd washed, shaved, dressed, got the car out and driven to the Symmingtons' in half an hour. Not bad going.

Megan must have been watching for me. She came out of the house at a run and clutched me. Her poor little face was white and twitching.

"Oh, you've come—you've *come*!"

"Hold up, funny face," I said. "Yes, I've come. Now what is it?"

She began to shake. I put my arm round her.

"I—I found her."

"You found Agnes? Where?"

The trembling grew.

"Under the stairs. There's a cupboard there. It has fishing-rods and golf clubs and things. You know."

I nodded. It was the usual cupboard.

Megan went on.

"She was there—all huddled up—and—and *cold*—horribly cold. She was—she was *dead*, you know!"

I asked curiously. "What made you look there?"

"I—I don't know. You telephoned last night. And we all began wondering where Agnes was. We waited up some time, but she didn't come in, and at last we went to bed. I didn't sleep very well and I got up early. There was only Rose (the cook, you know) about. She said she was very cross about Agnes not having come back. She said she'd been before somewhere when a girl did a flit like that. I had some milk and bread and butter in the kitchen—and then suddenly Rose came in looking queer and she said that Agnes's outdoor things were still in her room. Her best ones that she goes out in. And I began to wonder if—if she'd ever left the house, and I started looking round, and I opened the cupboard under the stairs and—and she was there. . ."

"Somebody's rung up the police, I suppose?"

"Yes, they're here now. My stepfather rang them up straightaway. And then I—I felt I couldn't bear it, and I rang *you* up. You don't mind?"

"No," I said. "I don't mind."

I looked at her curiously.

"Did anybody give you some brandy, or some coffee, or some tea after—after you found her?"

Megan shook her head.

I cursed the whole Symmington *ménage*. That stuffed shirt, Symmington, thought of nothing but the police. Neither Elsie Holland nor the cook seemed to have thought of the effect on the sensitive child who had made that gruesome discovery.

"Come on, slabface," I said. "We'll go to the kitchen."

We went round the house to the back door and into the kitchen. Rose, a plump pudding-faced woman of forty, was drinking strong tea by the kitchen fire. She greeted us with a flow of talk and her hand to her heart.

She'd come all over queer, she told me, awful the palpitations were! Just think of it, it might have been *her*, it might have been any of them, murdered in their beds they might have been.

"Dish out a good strong cup of that tea for Miss Megan," I said. "She's had a shock, you know. Remember it was she who found the body."

The mere mention of a body nearly sent Rose off again, but I quelled her with a stern eye and she poured out a cup of inky fluid.

"There you are, young woman." I said to Megan. "You drink that down. You haven't got any brandy, I suppose, Rose?"

Rose said rather doubtfully that there was a drop of cooking brandy left over from the Christmas puddings.

"That'll do," I said, and put a dollop of it into Megan's cup. I saw by Rose's eye that she thought it a good idea.

I told Megan to stay with Rose.

"I can trust you to look after Miss Megan?" I said, and Rose replied in a gratified way, "Oh yes, sir."

I went through into the house. If I knew Rose and her kind, she would soon find it necessary to keep her strength up with a little food, and that would be good for Megan too. Confound these people, why couldn't they look after the child?

Fuming inwardly I ran into Elsie Holland in the hall. She didn't seem surprised to see me. I suppose that the gruesome excitement of the discovery made one oblivious of who was coming and going. The constable, Bert Rundle, was by the front door.

Elsie Holland gasped out:

"Oh, Mr. Burton, isn't it *awful*? Whoever can have done such a dreadful thing?"

"It *was* murder, then?"

"Oh, yes. She was struck on the back of the head. It's all blood and hair—oh! it's *awful*—and bundled into that cupboard. Who can have done such a wicked thing? And *why*? Poor Agnes, I'm sure she never did anyone any harm."

"No," I said. "Somebody saw to that pretty promptly."

She stared at me. Not, I thought, a quick-witted girl. But she had good nerves. Her colour was as usual, slightly heightened by excitement, and I even fancied that in a macabre kind of way, and in spite of a naturally kind heart, she was enjoying the drama.

She said apologetically: "I must go up to the boys. Mr. Symmington is so anxious that they shouldn't get a shock. He wants me to keep them right away."

"Megan found the body, I hear," I said. "I hope somebody is looking after her?"

I will say for Elsie Holland that she looked conscience stricken.

"Oh dear," she said. "I forgot all about her. I do hope she's all right. I've been so rushed, you know, and the police and everything—but it was remiss of me. Poor girl, she must be feeling bad. I'll go and look for her at once."

I relented.

"She's all right," I said. "Rose is looking after her. You get along to the kids."

She thanked me with a flash of white tombstone teeth and hurried upstairs. After all, the boys were her job, and not Megan—Megan was nobody's job. Elsie was paid to look after Symmington's blinking brats. One could hardly blame her for doing so.

As she flashed round the corner of the stairs, I caught my breath. For a minute I caught a glimpse of a Winged Victory, deathless and incredibly beautiful, instead of a conscientious nursery governess.

Then a door opened and Superintendent Nash stepped out into the hall with Symmington behind him.

"Oh, Mr. Burton," he said. "I was just going to telephone you. I'm glad you are here."

He didn't ask me—then—why I was here.

He turned his head and said to Symmington:

"I'll use this room if I may."

It was a small morning-room with a window on the front of the house.

"Certainly, certainly."

Symmington's poise was pretty good, but he looked desperately tired. Superintendent Nash said gently:

"I should have some breakfast if I were you, Mr. Symmington. You and Miss Holland and Miss Megan will feel much better after coffee and eggs and bacon. Murder is a nasty business on an empty stomach."

He spoke in a comfortable family doctor kind of way.

Symmington gave a faint attempt at a smile and said:

"Thank you, superintendent, I'll take your advice."

I followed Nash into the little morning-room and he shut the door. He said then:

"You've got here very quickly? How did you hear?"

I told him that Megan had rung me up. I felt well disposed towards Superintendent Nash. He, at any rate, had not forgotten that Megan, too, would be in need of breakfat.

"I hear that you telephoned last night, Mr. Burton, asking about this girl? Why was that?"

I suppose it did seem odd. I told him about Agnes's telephone call to Partridge and her non-appearance. He said, "Yes, I see. . ."

He said it slowly and reflectively, rubbing his chin.

Then he sighed:

"Well," he said. "It's murder now, right enough. Direct physical action. The question is, what did the girl know? Did she say anything to this Partridge? Anything definite?"

"I don't think so. But you can ask her."

"Yes. I shall come up and see her when I've finished here."

"What happened exactly?" I asked. "Or don't you know yet?"

"Near enough. It was the maids' day out——"

"Both of them?"

"Yes, it seems that there used to be two sisters here who liked to go out together, so Mrs. Symmington arranged it that way. Then when these two came, she kept to the same arrangement. They used to leave cold supper laid out in the dining-room, and Miss Holland used to get tea."

"I see."

"It's pretty clear up to a point. The cook, Rose, comes from Nether Mickford, and in order to get there on her day out she has to catch the half-past two bus. So Agnes has to finish clearing up lunch always. Rose used to wash up the supper things in the evenings to even things up.

"That's what happened yesterday. Rose went off to catch the bus at two twenty-five, Symmington left for his office at five-and-twenty to three. Elsie Holland and the children went out at a quarter to three. Megan Hunter went out on her bicycle about five minutes later. Agnes would then be alone in the house. As far as I can make out, she normally left the house between three o'clock and half-past three."

"The house being then left empty?"

"Oh, they don't worry about that down here. There's not much locking up done in these parts. As I say, at ten minutes to three Agnes was alone in the house. That she never left it is clear, for she was in her cap and apron still when we found her body."

"I suppose you can tell roughly the time of death?"

"Doctor Griffith won't commit himself. Between two o'clock and four-thirty, is his official medical verdict."

"How was she killed?"

"She was first stunned by a blow on the back of the head. Afterwards an ordinary kitchen skewer, sharpened to a fine point, was thrust into the base of the skull, causing instantaneous death."

I lit a cigarette. It was not a nice picture.

"Pretty cold blooded," I said.

"Oh yes, yes, that was indicated."

I inhaled deeply.

"Who did it?" I said. "And why?"

"I don't suppose," said Nash slowly, "that we shall ever know exactly why. But we can guess."

"She knew something?"

"She knew something."

"She didn't give any one here a hint?"

"As far as I can make out, no. She's been upset, so the cook says, ever since Mrs. Symmington's death, and according to this Rose, she's been getting more and more worried, and kept saying she didn't know what she ought to do."

He gave a short exasperated sigh.

"It's always the way. They won't come to us. They've got that deep-seated prejudice against 'being mixed up with the police.' If she'd come along and told us what was worrying her, she'd be alive to-day."

"Didn't she give the other woman *any* hint?"

"No, or so Rose says, and I'm inclined to believe her. For if she had, Rose would have blurted it out at once with a good many fancy embellishments of her own."

"It's maddening," I said, "not to know."

"We can still guess, Mr. Burton. To begin with, it can't be anything very definite. It's got to be the sort of thing that you can think over, and as you think it over, your uneasiness grows. You see what I mean?"

"Yes."

"Actually, I think I know what it was."

I looked at him with respect.

"That's good work superintendent."

"Well, you see, Mr. Burton, I know something that you don't. On the afternoon that Mrs. Symmington committed suicide both maids were supposed to be out. It was their day out. But actually Agnes came back to the house."

"You know that?"

"Yes. Agnes has a boy friend—young Rendell from the fish shop. Wednesday is early closing and he comes along to meet Agnes and they go for a walk, or to the pictures if it's wet. That Wednesday they had a row practically as soon as they met. Our letter writer had been active, suggesting that Agnes had other fish to fry, and young Fred Rendell was all worked up. They quarrelled violently and Agnes bolted back home and said she wasn't coming out unless Fred said he was sorry."

"Well?"

"Well, Mr. Burton, the kitchen faces the back of the house but the pantry looks out where we are looking now. There's only one entrance gate. You come through it and either up to the front door, or else along the path at the side of the house to the back door."

He paused.

"Now I'll tell you something. That letter that came to Mrs. Symmington that afternoon *didn't come by post*. It had a used stamp affixed to it, and the postmark faked quite convincingly in lamp-black, so that it would seem to have been delivered by the postman with the afternoon letters. But actually *it had not been through the post*. You see what that means?"

I said slowly: "It means that it was left *by hand*, pushed through the letter box some time before the afternoon post was delivered, so that it should be amongst the other letters."

"Exactly. The afternoon post comes round about a quarter to four. My theory is this. The girl was in the pantry looking through the window (it's masked by shrubs but you can see through them quite well) watching out for her young man to turn up and apologise."

I said: "*And she saw whoever it was deliver that note?*"

"That's my guess, Mr. Burton. I may be wrong, of course."

"I don't think you are. . . .It's simple—and convincing—and it means that Agnes knew *who the anonymous letter writer was.*"

"Yes."

"But then why didn't she——"

I paused, frowning.

Nash said quickly:

"As I see it, the girl *didn't realise what she had seen*. Not at first. Somebody had left a letter at the house, yes—but that somebody was nobody she would dream of connecting with the anonymous letters. It was somebody, from that point of view, quite above suspicion.

"But the more she thought about it, the more uneasy she grew. Ought she, perhaps, to tell someone about it? In her perplexity she thinks of Miss Barton's Partridge who, I gather, is a somewhat dominant personality and whose judgment Agnes would accept unhesitatingly. She decides to ask Partridge what she ought to do."

"Yes," I said thoughtfully. "It fits well enough. And somehow or other, Poison Pen found out. How did she find out, superintendent?"

"You're not used to living in the country, Mr. Burton. It's a kind of miracle how things get around. First of all, there's the telephone call. Who overheard it your end?"

I reflected.

"I answered the telephone originally. Then I called up the stairs to Partridge."

"Mentioning the girl's name?"

"Yes—yes, I did."

"Anyone overhear you?"

"My sister or Miss Griffith might have done so."

"Ah, Miss Griffith. What was she doing up there?"

I explained.

"Was she going back to the village?"

"She was going to Mr. Pye first."

Superintendent Nash sighed.

"That's two ways it could have gone all over the place."

I was incredulous.

"Do you mean that either Miss Griffith or Mr. Pye would bother to repeat a meaningless little bit of information like that?"

"Anything's news in a place like this. You'd be surprised. If the dressmaker's mother has got a bad corn everybody hears about it! And then there is this end. Miss Holland, Rose—they could have heard what Agnes said. And there's Fred Rendell. It may have gone round through him that Agnes went back to the house that afternoon."

I gave a slight shiver. I was looking out of the window. In front of me was a neat square of grass and a path and the low prim gate.

Someone had opened the gate, had walked very correctly and quietly up to the house, and had pushed a letter through the letter box. I saw, hazily, in my mind's eye, that vague woman's shape. The face was blank—but it must be a face that I knew. . . .

Superintendent Nash was saying:

"All the same, this narrows things down. That's always the way we get 'em in the end. Steady, patient elimination. There aren't so very many people it could be now."

"You mean——?"

"It knocks out any women clerks who were at their work all yesterday afternoon. It knocks out the schoolmistress. She was teaching. And the district nurse. I know where she was yesterday. Not that I ever thought it was any of *them*, but now we're *sure*. You see, Mr. Burton, we've got two definite times now on which to concentrate—yesterday afternoon, and the week before. On the day of Mrs. Symmington's death from, say, a quarter-past three (the earliest possible time at which Agnes could have been back in the house after her quarrel) and four o'clock when the post must have come (but I can get that fixed more accurately with the postman). And yesterday from ten minutes to three (when Miss Megan Hunter left the house) until half-past three or more probably a quarter-past three as Agnes hadn't begun to change."

"What do you think happened yesterday?"

Nash made a grimace.

"What do I think? I think a certain lady walked up to the front door and rang the bell, quite calm and smiling, the afternoon caller. . . .Maybe she asked for Miss Holland, or for Miss Megan, or perhaps she had brought a parcel. Anyway Agnes turns round to get a salver for cards, or to take the parcel in, and our lady-like caller bats her on the back of her unsuspecting head."

"With what?"

Nash said:

"The ladies round here usually carry large sizes in handbags. No saying what mightn't be inside it."

"And then stabs her through the back of the neck and bundles her into the cupboard? Wouldn't that be a hefty job for a woman?"

Superintendent Nash looked at me with rather a queer expression.

"The woman we're after isn't normal—not by a long way—and that type of mental instability goes with surprising strength. Agnes wasn't a big girl."

He paused and then asked: "What made Miss Megan Hunter think of looking in that cupboard?"

"Sheer instinct," I said.'

Then I asked: "Why drag Agnes into the cupboard? What was the point?"

"The longer it was before the body was found, the more difficult it would be to fix the time of death accurately. If Miss Holland, for instance, fell over the body as soon as she came in, a doctor might be able to fix it within ten minutes or so—which might be awkward for our lady friend."

I said, frowning:

"But if Agnes were suspicious of this person——"

Nash interrupted me.

"She wasn't. Not to the pitch of definite suspicion. She just thought it 'queer.' She was a slow-witted girl, I imagine, and she was only vaguely suspicious with a feeling that something was wrong. She certainly didn't suspect that she was up against a woman who would do murder."

"Did you suspect that?" I asked.

Nash shook his head. He said, with feeling:

"I ought to have known. That suicide business, you see, frightened Poison Pen. She got the wind up. Fear, Mr. Burton, is an incalculable thing."

Yes, fear. That was the thing we ought to have foreseen. Fear—in a lunatic brain. . .

"You see," said Superintendent Nash, and somehow his words made the whole thing seem absolutely horrible. "We're up against someone who's respected and thought highly of—someone, in fact, of good social position!"

iii

Presently Nash said that he was going to interview Rose once more. I asked him, rather diffidently, if I might come too. Rather to my surprise he assented cordially.

"I'm very glad of your co-operation, Mr. Burton, if I may say so."

"That sounds suspicious," I said. "In books when a detective welcomes someone's assistance, that someone is usually the murderer."

Nash laughed shortly. He said: "You're hardly the type to write anonymous letters, Mr. Burton."

He added: "Frankly, you can be useful to us."

"I'm glad, but I don't see how."

"You're a stranger down here, that's why. You've got no preconceived ideas about the people here. But at the same time, you've got the opportunity of getting to know things in what I may call a social way."

"The murderer is a person of good social position," I murmured.

"Exactly."

"I'm to be the spy within the gates?"

"Have you any objection?"

I thought it over.

"No," I said, "frankly I haven't. If there's a dangerous lunatic about driving inoffensive women to suicide and hitting miserable little maidservants on the head, then I'm not averse to doing a bit of dirty work to put that lunatic under restraint."

"That's sensible of you, sir. And let me tell you, the person we're after is dangerous. She's about as dangerous as a rattle-snake and a cobra and a black mamba rolled into one."

I gave a slight shiver. I said:

"In fact, we've got to make haste?"

"That's right. Don't think we're inactive in the force. We're not. We're working on several different lines."

He said it grimly.

I had a vision of a fine far-flung spider's web. . . .

Nash wanted to hear Rose's story again, so he explained to me, because she had already told him two different versions, and the more versions he got from her, the more likely it was that a few grains of truth might be incorporated.

We found Rose washing up breakfast, and she stopped at once and rolled her eyes and clutched her heart and explained again how she'd been coming over queer all the morning.

Nash was patient with her but firm. He'd been soothing the first time, so he told me, and peremptory the second, and he now employed a mixture of the two.

Rose enlarged pleasurably on the details of the past week, of how Agnes had gone about in deadly fear, and had shivered and said, "Don't ask me," when Rose had urged her to say what was the matter. "It would be death if she told me," that's what she said, finished Rose, rolling her eyes happily.

Had Agnes given no hint of what was troubling her?

No, except that she went in fear of her life.

Superintendent Nash sighed and abandoned the theme, contenting himself with extracting an exact account of Rose's own activities the preceding afternoon.

This, put baldly, was that Rose had caught the 2.30 bus and had spent the afternoon and evening with her family, returning by the 8.40 bus from Nether Mickford. The recital was complicated by the extraordinary presentiments of evil Rose had had all the afternoon and how her sister had commented on it and how she hadn't been able to touch a morsel of seed cake.

From the kitchen we went in search of Elsie Holland, who was superintending the children's lessons. As always, Elsie Holland was competent and obliging. She rose and said:

"Now, Colin, you and Brian will do these three sums and have the answers ready for me when I come back."

She then led us into the night nursery. "Will this do? I thought it would be better not to talk before the children."

"Thank you, Miss Holland. Just tell me, once more, are you *quite* sure that Agnes never mentioned to you being worried over anything—since Mrs. Symmington's death, I mean?"

"No, she never said anything. She was a very quiet girl, you know, and didn't talk much."

"A change from the other one, then!"

"Yes, Rose talks much too much. I have to tell her not to be impertinent sometimes."

"Now, will you tell me exactly what happened yesterday afternoon? Everything you can remember."

"Well, we had lunch as usual. One o'clock, and we hurry just a little. I don't let the boys dawdle. Let me see. Mr. Symmington went back to the office, and I helped Agnes by laying the table for supper—the boys ran out in the garden till I was ready to take them."

"Where did you go?"

"Towards Combeacre, by the field path—the boys wanted to fish. I forgot their bait and had to go back for it."

"What time was that?"

"Let me see, we started about twenty to three—or just after. Megan was coming but changed her mind. She was going out on her bicycle. She's got quite a craze for bicycling."

"I mean what time was it when you went back for the bait? Did you go into the house?"

"No. I'd left it in the conservatory at the back. I don't know what time it was then—about ten minutes to three, perhaps."

"Did you see Megan or Agnes?"

"Megan must have started, I think. No, I didn't see Agnes. I didn't see anyone."

"And after that you went fishing?"

"Yes, we went along by the stream. We didn't catch anything. We hardly ever do, but the boys enjoy it. Brian got rather wet. I had to change his things when we got in."

"You attend to tea on Wednesdays?"

"Yes. It's all ready in the drawing-room for Mr. Symmington. I just make the tea when he comes in. The children and I have ours in the schoolroom—and Megan, of course. I have my own tea things and everything in the cupboard up there."

"What time did you get in?"

"At ten minutes to five. I took the boys up and started to lay tea. Then when Mr. Symmington came in at five I went down to make his but he said he would have it with us in the schoolroom. The boys were so pleased. We played Animal Grab afterwards. It seems so awful to think of now—with that poor girl in the cupboard all the time."

"Would anybody go to that cupboard normally?"

"Oh no, it's only used for keeping junk. The hats and coats hang in the little cloakroom to the right of the front door as you come in. No one might have gone to the other cupboard for months."

"I see. And you noticed nothing unusual, nothing abnormal at all when you came back?"

The blue eyes opened very wide.

"Oh no, inspector, nothing at all. Everything was just the same as usual. That's what was so awful about it."

"And the week before?"

"You mean the day Mrs. Symmington——"

"Yes."

"Oh, that was terrible—terrible!"

"Yes, yes, I know. You were out all that afternoon also?"

"Oh yes, I always take the boys out in the afternoon—if it's fine enough. We do lessons in the morning. We went up to the moor, I remember—quite a long way. I was afraid I was late back because as I turned in at the gate I saw Mr. Symmington coming from his office at the other end of the road, and I hadn't even put the kettle on, but it was just ten minutes to five."

"You didn't go up to Mrs. Symmington?"

"Oh no. I never did. She always rested after lunch. She had

attacks of neuralgia—and they used to come on after meals. Dr. Griffith had given her some cachets to take. She used to lie down and try to sleep."

Nash said in a casual voice:

"So no one would take her up the post?"

"The afternoon post? No, I'd look in the letter box and put the letters on the hall table when I came in. But very often Mrs. Symmington used to come down and get it herself. She didn't sleep all the afternoon. She was usually up again by four."

"You didn't think anything was wrong because she wasn't up that afternoon?"

"Oh, no, I never dreamed of such a thing. Mr. Symmington was hanging up his coat in the hall and I said, 'Tea's not quite ready, but the kettle's nearly boiling,' and he nodded and called out, 'Mona, Mona!'—and then as Mrs. Symmington didn't answer he went upstairs to her bedroom, and it must have been the most terrible shock to him. He called me and I came, and he said, 'Keep the children away,' and then he phoned Dr. Griffith and we forgot all about the kettle and it burnt the bottom out! Oh dear, it *was* dreadful, and she'd been so happy and cheerful at lunch."

Nash said abruptly: "What is your own opinion of that letter she received, Miss Holland?"

Elsie Holland said indignantly:

"Oh, I think it was wicked—wicked!"

"Yes, yes, I don't mean that. Did you think it was true?"

Elsie Holland said firmly:

"No, indeed I don't. Mrs. Symmington was very sensitive—very sensitive indeed. She had to take all sorts of things for her nerves. And she was very—well, *particular*." Elsie flushed. "Anything of that sort—*nasty*, I mean—would have given her a great shock."

Nash was silent for a moment, then he asked:

"Have you had any of these letters, Miss Holland?"

"No. No, I haven't had any."

"Are you sure? Please"—he lifted a hand–"don't answer in a hurry. They're not pleasant things to get, I know. And sometimes people don't like to admit they've had them. But it's very important in this case that we should know. We're quite aware that the statements in them are just a tissue of lies, so you needn't feel embarrassed."

"But I haven't, superintendent. Really I haven't. Not anything of the kind."

She was indignant, almost tearful, and her denials seemed genuine enough.

When she went back to the children, Nash stood looking out of the window.

"Well," he said, "that's that! She says she hasn't received any of these letters. And she sounds as though she's speaking the truth."

"She did certainly. I'm sure she was."

"H'm," said Nash. "Then what I want to know is, why the devil hasn't she?"

He went on rather impatiently, as I stared at him.

"She's a pretty girl, isn't she?"

"Rather more than pretty."

"Exactly. As a matter of fact, she's uncommonly good looking. And she's young. In fact she's just the meat an anonymous letter writer would like. Then why has she been left out?"

I shook my head.

"It's interesting, you know. I must mention it to Graves. He asked if we could tell him definitely of any one who hadn't had one."

"She's the second person," I said. "There's Emily Barton, remember."

Nash gave a faint chuckle.

"You shouldn't believe everything you're told, Mr. Burton. Miss Barton had one all right—more than one."

"How do you know?"

"That devoted dragon she's lodging with told me—her late parlourmaid or cook. Florence Elford. Very indignant she was about it. Would like to have the writer's blood."

"Why did Miss Emily say she hadn't had any?"

"Delicacy. Their language isn't nice. Little Miss Barton has spent her life avoiding the coarse and unrefined."

"What did the letters say?"

"The usual. Quite ludicrous in her case. And incidentally insinuated that she poisoned off her old mother and most of her sisters!"

I said incredulously:

"Do you mean to say there's really this dangerous lunatic going about and we can't spot her right away?"

"We'll spot her," said Nash, and his voice was grim. "She'll write just one letter too many."

"But, my goodness, man, she won't go on writing these things—not now."

He looked at me.

"Oh yes, she will. You see, *she can't stop now*. It's a morbid craving. The letters will go on, make no mistake about that."

9

i

I WENT and found Megan before leaving the house. She was in the garden and seemed almost back to her usual self. She greeted me quite cheerfully.

I suggested that she should come back to us again for a while, but after a momentary hesitation she shook her head.

"It's nice of you—but I think I'll stay here. After all, it is—well, I suppose it's my home. And I dare say I can help with the boys a bit."

"Well," I said, "it's as you like."

"Then I think I'll stay. I could—I could——"

"Yes?" I prompted.

"If—if anything awful happened, I could ring you up, couldn't I, and you'd come."

I was touched. "Of course. But what awful thing do you think might happen?"

"Oh, I don't know." She looked vague. "Things seem rather like that just now, don't they?"

"For God's sake," I said. "Don't go nosing out any more bodies! It's not good for you."

She gave me a brief flash of a smile.

"No, it isn't. It made me feel awfully sick."

I didn't much like leaving her there, but after all, as she had said, it was her home. And I fancied that now Elsie Holland wold feel more responsible for her.

Nash and I went up together to Little Furze. Whilst I gave Joanna an account of the morning's doings, Nash tackled Partridge. He rejoined us looking discouraged.

"Not much help there. According to this woman, the girl only said she was worried about something and didn't know what to do and that she'd like Miss Partridge's advice."

"Did Partridge mention the fact to any one?" asked Joanna.

Nash nodded, looking grim.

"Yes, she told Mrs. Emory—your daily woman—on the lines, as far as I can gather, that there were *some* young women who were willing to take advice from their elders and didn't think they could settle everything for themselves off-hand! Agnes mightn't be very bright, but she was a nice respectful girl and knew her manners."

"Partridge preening herself, in fact," murmured Joanna. "And Mrs. Emory could have passed it round the town?"

"That's right, Miss Burton."

"There's one thing rather surprises me," I said. "Why were my sister and I included amongst the recipients of the anonymous letters? We were strangers down here—nobody could have had a grudge against us."

"You're failing to allow for the mentality of a Poison Pen—all is grist that comes to their mill. Their grudge, you might say, is against humanity."

"I suppose," said Joanna thoughtfully, "that that is what Mrs. Dane Calthrop meant."

Nash looked at her inquiringly, but she did not enlighten him. The superintendent said:

"I don't know if you happened to look closely at the envelope of the letter you got, Miss Burton. If so, you may have noticed that it was actually addressed to Miss Barton and the *a* altered to a *u* afterwards."

That remark, properly interpreted, ought to have given us a clue to the whole busines. As it was, none of us saw any significance in it.

Nash went off, and I was left with Joanna. She actually said: "You don't think that letter can really have been meant for Miss Emily, do you?"

"It would hardly have begun, 'You painted trollop'," I pointed out, and Joanna agreed.

Then she suggested that I should go down to the town. "You ought to hear what everyone is saying. It will be *the* topic this morning!"

I suggested that she should come too, but rather to my

surprise Joanna refused. She said she was going to mess about in the garden.

I paused in the doorway and said, lowering my voice:

"I suppose Partridge is all right?"

"Partridge!"

The amazement in Joanna's voice made me feel ashamed of my idea. I said apologetically: "I just wondered. She's rather 'queer' in some ways—a grim spinster—the sort of person who might have religious mania."

"This isn't religious mania—or so you told me Graves said."

"Well, sex mania. They're very closely tied up together, I understand. She's repressed and respectable, and has been shut up here with a lot of elderly women for years."

"What put the idea into your head?"

I said slowly:

"Well, we've only her word for it, haven't we, as to what the girl Agnes said to her? Suppose Agnes asked Partridge to tell her why Partridge came and left a note that day—and Partridge said she'd call round that afternoon and explain."

"And then camouflaged it by coming to us and asking if the girl could come here?"

"Yes,"

"But Partridge never went out that afternoon."

"We don't know that. We were out ourselves, remember."

"Yes, that's true. It's possible, I suppose." Joanna turned it over in her mind. "But I don't think so, all the same. I don't think Partridge has the mentality to cover her tracks over the letters. To wipe off fingerprints, and all that. It isn't only cunning you want—it's knowledge. I don't think she's got that. I suppose——" Joanna hesitated, then said slowly, "they are sure it is a woman, aren't they?"

"You don't think it's a man? I exclaimed incredulously.

"Not—not an ordinary man—but a certain kind of man. I'm thinking, really, of Mr. Pye."

"So Pye is your selection?"

"Don't you feel yourself that he's a possibility? He's the sort of person who might be lonely—and unhappy— and spiteful. Everyone, you see, rather laughs at him. Can't you see him secretly hating all the normal happy people, and taking a queer perverse artistic pleasure in what he was doing?"

"Graves said a middle-aged spinster."

"Mr. Pye," said Joanna, "*is* a middle-aged spinster."

"A misfit," I said slowly.

"Very much so. He's rich, but money doesn't help. And I do feel he might be unbalanced. He is, really, rather a *frightening* little man."

"He got a letter himself, remember."

"We don't know that," Joanna pointed out. "We only thought so. And anyway, he might have been putting on an act."

"For our benefit?"

"Yes. He's clever enough to think of that—and not to overdo it."

"He must be a first-class actor."

"But of course, Jerry, whoever is doing this *must* be a first-class actor. That's partly where the pleasure comes in."

"For God's sake, Joanna, don't speak so understandingly! You make me feel that you—that you understand the mentality."

"I think I do. I can—just—get into the mood. If I weren't Joanna Burton, if I weren't young and reasonably attractive and able to have a good time, if I were—how shall I put it?—behind bars, watching other people enjoy life, would a black evil tide rise in me, making me want to hurt, to torture—even to destroy?"

"Joanna!" I took her by the shoulders and shook her. She gave a little sigh and shiver, and smiled at me.

"I frightened you, didn't I, Jerry? But I have a feeling that that's the right way to solve this problem. You've got to be the person, knowing how they feel and what makes them act, and then—and then perhaps you'll know what they're going to do next."

"Oh, hell!" I said. "And I came down here to be a vegetable and get interested in all the dear little local scandals. Dear little local scandals! Libel, vilification, obscene language and murder!"

ii

Joanna was quite right. The High Street was full of interested groups. I was determined to get everyone's reactions in turn.

I met Griffith first. He looked terribly ill and tired. So much so that I wondered. Murder is not, certainly, all in the day's work to a doctor, but his profession does equip him to face most things including suffering, the ugly side of human nature, and the fact of death.

"You look all in," I said.

"Do I?" He was vague. "Oh! I've had some worrying cases lately."

"Including our lunatic at large?"

"That, certainly." He looked away from me across the street. I saw a fine nerve twitching in his eyelid.

"You've no suspicions as to—*who*?"

"No. No. I wish to God I had."

He asked abruptly after Joanna, and said, hesitatingly, that he had some photographs she'd wanted to see.

I offered to take them to her.

"Oh, it doesn't matter. I shall be passing that way actually later in the morning."

I began to be afraid that Griffith had got it badly. Curse Joanna! Griffith was too good a man to be dangled as a scalp.

I let him go, for I saw his sister coming and I wanted, for once, to talk to her.

Aimée Griffith began, as it were, in the middle of a conversation.

"Absolutely shocking!" she boomed. "I hear you were there—quite early?"

There was a question in the words, and her eyes glinted as she stressed the world "early." I wasn't going to tell her that Megan had rung me up. I said instead:

"You see, I was a bit uneasy last night. The girl was due to tea at our house and didn't turn up."

"And so you feared the worst? Damned smart of you!"

"Yes," I said. "I'm quite the human bloodhound."

"It's the first murder we've ever had in Lymstock. Excitement is terrific. Hope the police can handle it all right."

"I shouldn't worry," I said. "they're an efficient body of men."

"Can't even remember what the girl looked like, although I suppose she's opened the door to me dozens of times. Quiet, insignificant little thing. Knocked on the head and then stabbed through the back of the neck, so Owen tells me. Looks like a boy friend to me. What do you think?"

"That's your solution?"

"Seems the most likely one. Had a quarrel, I expect. They're very inbred round here—bad heredity, a lot of them." She paused, and then went on, "I hear Megan Hunter found the body? Must have given her a bit of a shock."

I said shortly:

"It did."

"Not too good for her, I should imagine. In my opinion she's not too strong in the head—and a thing like this might send her completely off her onion."

I took a sudden resolution. I had to know something.

"Tell me, Miss Griffith, was it you who persuaded Megan to return home yesterday?"

"Well, I wouldn't say exactly persuaded."

I stuck to my guns.

"But you did say something to her?"

Aimée Griffith planted her feet firmly and stared at me in the eyes. She was, just slightly, on the defensive. She said:

"It's no good that young woman shirking her responsibilities. She's young and she doesn't know how tongues wag, so I felt it my duty to give her a hint."

"Tongues——?" I broke off because I was too angry to go on.

Aimée Griffith continued with that maddeningly complacent confidence in herself which was her chief characteristic:

"Oh, I dare say *you* don't hear all the gossip that goes round. I do! I know what people are saying. Mind you, I don't for a minute think there's anything in it—not for a minute! But you know what people are—if they can say something ill-natured, they do! And it's rather hard lines on the girl when she's got her living to earn."

"Her living to earn?" I said puzzled.

Aimée went on:

"It's a difficult position for her, naturally. And I think she did the right thing. I mean, she couldn't go off at a moment's notice and leave the children with no one to look after them. She's been splendid—absolutely splendid. I say so to everybody! But there it is, it's an invidious position, and people will talk."

"Who are you talking about?" I asked.

"Elsie Holland, of course," said Aimée Griffith impatiently. "In my opinion, she's a thoroughly nice girl, and has only been doing her duty."

"And what are people saying?"

Aimée Griffith laughed. It was, I thought, rather an unpleasant laugh.

"They're saying that she's already considering the possibility of becoming Mrs. Symmington No. 2—that she's all out to console the widower and make herself indispensible."

"But, good God," I said, shocked, "Mrs. Symmington's only been dead a week!"

Aimée Griffith shrugged her shoulders.

"Of course. It's absurd! But you know what people are! The Holland girl is young and she's good looking—that's enough. And mind you, being a nursry governess isn't much of a prospect for as girl. I wouldn't blame her if she wanted a settled home and a husband and was playing her cards accordingly.

"Of course," she went on. "Poor Dick Symmington hasn't the least idea of all this! He's still completely knocked out by Mona Symmington's death. But you know what men are! If the girl is always there, making him comfortable, looking after him, being obviously devoted to the children—well, he gets to be dependent on her."

I said quietly:

"So you do think that Elsie Holland is a designing hussy?"

Aimée Griffith flushed.

"Not at all. I'm sorry for the girl—with people saying nasty things! That's why I more or less told Megan that she ought to go home. It looks better than having Dick Symmington and the girl alone in the house."

I began to understand things.

Aimée Griffith gave her jolly laugh.

"You're shocked, Mr. Burton, at hearing what our gossiping little town thinks. I can tell you this—they always think the worst!"

She laughed and nodded and strode away.

iii

I came upon Mr. Pye by the church. He was talking to Emily Barton, who looked pink and excited.

Mr. Pye greeted me with every evidence of delight.

"Ah, Burton, good-morning, good-morning! How is your charming sister?"

I told him that Joanna was well.

"But not joining our village parliament? We are all agog over the news. Murder! Real Sunday newspaper murder in our midst! Not the most interesting of crimes, I fear. Somewhat sordid. The brutal murder of a little serving maid. No finer points about the crime, but still undeniably, news."

Miss Barton said tremulously:

"It is shocking—quite shocking."

Mr. Pye turned to her.

"But you enjoy it, dear lady, you enjoy it. Confess it now. You disapprove, you deplore, but there *is* the thrill. I insist, there *is* the thrill!"

"Such a nice girl," said Emily Barton. "She came to me from St. Clotilde's Home. Quite a raw girl. But most teachable. She turned into such a nice little maid. Partridge was very pleased with her."

I said quickly:

"She was coming to tea with Partridge yesterday afternoon." I turned to Pye. "I expect Aimée Griffith told you."

My tone was quite casual. Pye responded apparently quite unsuspiciously: "She did mention it, yes. She said, I remember, that it was something quite new for servants to ring up on their employers' telephones."

"Partridge would never dream of doing such a thing," said Miss Emily, "and I am really surprised at Agnes doing so."

"You are behind the times, dear lady," said Mr. Pye. "My

two terrors use the telephone constantly and smoked all over the house until I objected. But one daren't say too much. Prescott is a divine cook, though temperamental, and Mrs. Prescott is an admirable house-parlourmaid."

"Yes, indeed, we all think you're very lucky."

I intervened, since I did not want the conversation to become purely domestic.

"The news of the murder has got round very quickly," I said.

"Of course, of course," said Mr. Pye. "The butcher, the baker, the candlestick maker. Enter Rumour, painted full of tongues! Lymstock, alas! is going to the dogs. Anonymous letters, murders, any amount of criminal tendencies."

Emily Barton said nervously: "They don't think—there's no idea—that—that the two are connected."

Mr. Pye pounced on the idea.

"An interesting speculation. The girl knew something, therefore she was murdered. Yes, yes, most promising. How clever of you to think of it."

"I—I can't bear it."

Emily Barton spoke abruptly and turned away, walking very fast.

Pye looked after her. His cherubic face was pursed up quizzically.

He turned back to me and shook his head gently.

"A sensitive soul. A charming creature, don't you think? Absolutely a period piece. She's not, you know, of her own generation, she's of the generation before that. The mother must have been a woman of a very strong character. She kept the family ticking at about 1870, I should say. The whole family preserved under a glass case. I do like to come across that sort of thing."

I did not want to talk about period pieces.

"What do you really think about all this business?" I asked.

"Meaning by that?"

"Anonymous letters, murder. . ."

"Our local crime wave? What do you?"

"I asked you first," I said pleasantly.

Mr. Pye said gently:

"I'm a student, you know, of abnormalities. They interest

me. Such apparently unlikely people do the most fantastic things. Take the case of Lizzie Borden. There's not really a reasonable explanation of that. In this case, my advice to the police would be—study *character*. Leave your fingerprints and your measuring of handwriting and your microscopes. Notice instead what people do with their hands, and their little tricks of manner, and the way they eat their food, and if they laugh sometimes for no apparent reason."

I raised my eyebrows. "Mad?" I said.

"Quite, quite mad," said Mr. Pye, and added, "but you'd never know it!"

"Who?"

His eyes met mine. He smiled.

"No, no, Burton, that would be slander. We can't add slander to all the rest of it."

He fairly skipped off down the street.

iv

As I stood staring after him the church door opened and the Rev. Caleb Dane Calthrop came out.

He smiled vaguely at me.

"Good—good-morning, Mr.—er—er——"

I helped him. "Burton."

"Of course, of course, you mustn't think I don't remember you. Your name had just slipped my memory for the moment. A beautiful day."

"Yes," I said rather shortly.

He peered at me.

"But something—something—ah, yes, that poor unfortunate child who was in service at the Symmingtons'. I find it hard to believe, I must confess, that we have a murderer in our midst, Mr.—er—Burton."

"It does seem a bit fantastic," I said.

"Something else has just reached my ears." He leaned towards me. "I learn that there have been anonymous letters going about. Have you heard any rumour of such things?"

"I have heard," I said.

"Cowardly and dastardly things." He paused and quoted an enormous stream of Latin. "Those words of Horace are very applicable, don't you think?" he said.

"Absolutely," I said.

V

There didn't seem any one more I could profitably talk to, so I went home, dropping in for some tobacco and for a bottle of sherry, so as to get some of the humbler opinions on the crime.

"A narsty tramp," seemed to be the verdict.

"Come to the door, they do, and whine and ask for money, and then if it's a girl alone in the house, they turn narsty. My sister Dora, over to Combeacre, she had a narsty experience one day—Drunk, he was, and selling those little printed poems. . ."

The story went on, ending with the intrepid Dora courageously banging the door in the man's face and taking refuge and barricading herself in some vague retreat, which I gathered from the delicacy in mentioning it must be the lavatory. "And there she stayed till her lady came home!"

I reached Little Furze just a few minutes before lunch time. Joanna was standing in the drawing-room window doing nothing at all and looking as though her thoughts were miles away.

"What have you been doing with yourself?" I asked.

"Oh, I don't know. Nothing particular."

I went out on the verandah. Two chairs were drawn up to an iron table and there were two empty sherry glasses. On another chair was an object at which I looked with bewilderment for some time.

"What on earth is this?"

"Oh," said Joanna, "I think it's a photograph of a diseased spleen or something. Dr. Griffith seemed to think I'd be interested to see it."

I looked at the photograph with some interest. Every man has his own ways of courting the female sex. I should not, myself, choose to do it with photographs of spleens, diseased or otherwise. Still no doubt Joanna had asked for it!

"It looks most unpleasant," I said.

Joanna said it did, rather.

"How was Griffith?" I asked.

"He looked tired and very unhappy. I think he's got something on his mind."

"A spleen that won't yield to treatment?"

"Don't be silly. I mean something real."

"I should say the man's got *you* on his mind. I wish you'd lay off him, Joanna."

"Oh, do shut up. I haven't done anything."

"Women always say that."

Joanna whirled angrily out of the room.

The diseased spleen was beginning to curl up in the sun. I took it by one corner and brought it into the drawing-room. I had no affection for it myself, but I presumed it was one of Griffith's treasures.

I stooped down and pulled out a heavy book from the bottom shelf of the bookcase in order to press the photograph flat again between its leaves. It was a ponderous volume of somebody's sermons.

The book came open in my hand in rather a surprising way. In another minute I saw why. *From the middle of it a number of pages had been neatly cut out.*

vi

I stood staring at it. I looked at the title page. It had been published in 1840.

There could be no doubt at all. I was looking at the book from the pages of which the anonymous letters had been put together. Who had cut them out?

Well, to begin with, it could be Emily Barton herself. She was, perhaps, the obvious person to think of. Or it could have been Partridge.

But there were other possibilities. The pages could have been cut out by anyone who had been alone in this room, any visitor, for instance, who had sat there waiting for Miss Emily. Or even anyone who called on business.

No, that wasn't so likely. I had noticed that when, one day, a clerk from the bank had come to see me, Partridge had shown him into the little study at the back of the house. That was clearly the house routine.

A visitor, then? Someone "of good social position." Mr. Pye? Aimée Griffith? Mrs. Dane Calthrop?

vii

The gong sounded and I went in to lunch. Afterwards, in the drawing-room I showed Joanna my find.

We discussed it from every aspect. Then I took it down to the police station.

They were elated at the find, and I was patted on the back for what was, after all, the sheerest piece of luck.

Graves was not there, but Nash was, and rang up the other man. They would test the book for fingerprints, though Nash was not hopeful of finding anything. I may say that he did not. There were mine, Partridge's and nobody else's, merely showing that Partridge dusted conscientiously.

Nash walked back with me up the hill. I asked how he was getting on. "We're narrowing it down, Mr. Burton. We've eliminated the people it couldn't be."

"Ah," I said. "And who remains?"

"Miss Ginch. She was to meet a client at a house yesterday afternoon by appointment. The house was situated not far along the Combeacre Road, that's the road that goes past the Symmingtons'. She would have to pass the house both going and coming. . . .the week before, the day the anonymous letter was delivered, and Mrs. Symmington committed suicide, was her last day at Symmington's office. Mr. Symmington thought at first she had not left the office at all that afternoon. He had Sir Henry Lushington with him all the afternoon and rang several times for Miss Ginch. I find, however, that she did leave the office between three and four. She went out to get some high denomination of stamp of which they had run short. The office boy could have gone, but Miss Ginch elected to go, saying she had a headache and would like the air. She was not gone long."

"But long enough?"

"Yes, long enough to hurry along to the other end of the village, slip the letter in the box and hurry back. I must say, however, that I cannot find anybody who saw her near the Symmingtons' house."

"Would they notice?"

"They might and they might not."

"Who else is in your bag?"

Nash looked very straight ahead of him.

"You'll understand that we can't exclude anybody—anybody at all."

"No," I said. "I see that."

He said gravely: "Miss Griffith went to Brenton for a meeting of Girl Guides yesterday. She arrived rather late."

"You don't think——"

"No, I don't think. But I don't *know*. Miss Griffith seems an eminently sane healthy-minded woman—but I say, I don't *know*."

"What about the previous week? Could she have slipped the letter in the box?"

"It's possible. She was shopping in the town that afternoon." He paused. "The same applies to Miss Emily Barton. She was out shopping early yesterday afternoon and she went for a walk to see some friends on the road past the Symmingtons' house the week before."

I shook my head unbelievingly. Finding the cut book in Little Furze was bound, I knew, to direct attention to the owner of that house, but when I remembered Miss Emily coming in yesterday so bright and happy and excited. . .

Damn it all—excited. . .Yes, excited—pink cheeks—shining eyes—surely not because—not because——

I said thickly: "This business is bad for one! One sees things—one imagines things——"

"Yes, it isn't very pleasant to look upon the fellow creatures one meets as possible criminal lunatics."

He paused for a moment, then went on:

"And there's Mr. Pye——"

I said sharply: "So you have considered him?"

Nash smiled.

"Oh, yes, we've considered him all right. A very curious

character—not, I should say, a very nice character. He's got no alibi. He was in his garden, alone, on both occasions."

"So you're not only suspecting women?"

"I don't think a man wrote the letters—in fact I'm sure of it—and so is Graves—always excepting our Mr. Pye, that is to say, who's got an abnormally female streak in his character. But we've checked up on *everybody* for yesterday afternoon. That's a murder case, you see. *You're* all right," he grinned, "and so's your sister, and Mr. Symmington didn't leave his office after he got there and Dr. Griffith was on a round in the other direction, and I've checked up on his visits."

He paused, smiled again, and said, "You see, we *are* thorough."

I said slowly, "So your case is eliminated down to those four—Miss Ginch, Mr. Pye, Miss Griffith and little Miss Barton?"

"Oh, no, we've got a couple more—besides the vicar's lady."

"You've thought of *her*?"

"We've thought of *everybody*, but Mrs. Dane Calthrop is a little too openly mad, if you know what I mean. Still, she *could* have done it. She was in a wood watching birds yesterday afternoon—and the birds can't speak for her."

He turned sharply as Owen Griffith came into the police station.

"Hallo, Nash. I heard you were round asking for me this morning. Anything important?"

"Inquest on Friday, if that suits you, Dr. Griffith."

"Right. Moresby and I are doing the P.M. to-night."

Nash said:

"There's just one other thing, Dr. Griffith. Mrs. Symmington was taking some cachets, powders or something that you prescribed for her——"

He paused. Owen Griffith said interrogatively:

"Yes?"

"Would an overdose of those cachets have been fatal?"

Griffith said dryly:

"Certainly not. Not unless she'd taken about twenty-five of them!"

"But you once warned her about exceeding the dose, so Miss

Holland tells me."

"Oh that, yes. Mrs. Symmington was the sort of woman who would go and overdo anything she was given—fancy that to take twice as much would do her twice as much good, and you don't want anyone to overdo even phenacetin or aspirin—bad for the heart. And anyway there's absolutely no doubt about the cause of death. It was cyanide."

"Oh, I know that—you don't get my meaning. I only thought that when committing suicide you'd prefer to take an overdose of a soporific rather than to feed yourself prussic acid."

"Oh quite. On the other hand, prussic acid is more dramatic and is pretty certain to do the trick. With barbiturates, for instance, you can bring the victim round if only a short time has elapsed."

"I see, thank you, Dr. Griffith."

Griffith departed, and I said goodbye to Nash. I went slowly up the hill home. Joanna was out—at least there was no sign of her, and there was an enigmatical memorandum scribbled on the telephone block presumably for the guidance of either Partridge or myself.

"*If Dr. Griffith rings up, I can't go on Tuesday, but could manage Wednesday or Thursday.*"

I raised my eyebrows and went into the drawing-room. I sat down in the most comfortable arm-chair—(none of them were very comfortable, they tended to have straight backs and were reminiscent of the late Mrs. Barton)—stretched out my legs and tried to think the whole thing out.

With sudden annoyance I remembered that Owen's arrival had interrupted my conversation with the inspector, and that he had just mentioned two other people as being possibilities.

I wondered who they were.

Partridge, perhaps, for one? After all, the cut book had been found in this house. And Agnes could have been struck down quite unsuspecting by her guide and mentor. No, you couldn't eliminate Partridge.

But who was the other?

Somebody, perhaps, that I didn't know? Mrs. Cleat? The original suspect?

I closed my eyes. I considered four people, strangely unlikely people, in turn. Gentle, frail little Emily Barton? What points were there actually against her? A starved life? Dominated and repressed from early childhood? Too many sacrifices asked of her? Her curious horror of discussing anything "not quite nice"? Was that actually a sign of inner preoccupation with just these themes? Was I getting too horribly Freudian? I remembered a doctor once telling me that the mutterings of gentle maiden ladies when going off under an anaesthetic were a revelation. "You wouldn't think they knew such words!"

Aimée Griffith?

Surely nothing repressed or "inhibited" about her. Cheery, mannish, successful. A full, busy life. Yet Mrs. Dane Calthrop had said, "Poor thing!"

And there was something—something—some remembrance. . .Ah! I'd got it. Owen Griffith saying something like, "We had an outbreak of anonymous letters up North where I had a practice."

Had that been Aimée Griffith's work too? Surely rather a coincidence. Two outbreaks of the same thing.

Stop a minute, they'd tracked down the author of those. Griffith had said so. A schoolgirl.

Cold it was suddenly—must be a draught, from the window. I turned uncomfortably in my chair. Why did I suddenly feel so queer and upset?

Go on thinking . . .Aimée Griffith? Perhaps it was Aimée Griffith, *not* that other girl? And Aimée had come down here and started her tricks again. And that was why Owen Griffith was looking so unhappy and hag ridden. He suspected. Yes, he suspected. . .

Mr. Pye? Not, somehow, a very nice little man. I could imagine him staging the whole business. . .laughing. . .

That telephone message on the telephone pad in the hall. . .why did I keep thinking of it? Griffith and Joanna—he was falling for her. . . .No, that wasn't why the message worried me. It was something else. . .

My senses were swimming, sleep was very near. I repeated idiotically to myself, "No smoke without fire. No smoke without fire. . .That's it. . .it all links up together. . .

And then I was walking down the street with Megan and Elsie

Holland passed. She was dressed as a bride, and people were murmuring:

"She's going to marry Dr. Griffith at last. Of course they've been engaged secretly for years. . ."

There we were, in the church, and Dane Calthrop was reading the service in Latin.

And in the middle of it Mrs. Dane Calthrop jumped up and cried energetically:

"It's got to be stopped, I tell you. It's got to be stopped!"

For a minute or two I didn't know whether I was asleep or awake. Then my brain cleared, and I realised I was in the drawing-room of Little Furze and that Mrs. Dane Calthrop had just come through the window and was standing in front of me saying with nervous violence:

"It has got to be *stopped*, I tell you."

I jumped up. I said: "I beg your pardon. I'm afraid I was asleep. What did you say?"

Mrs. Dane Calthrop beat one fist fiercely on the palm of her other hand.

"It's got to be stopped. These letters! Murder! You can't go on having poor innocent children like Agnes Woddell *killed*!"

"You're quite right," I said. "But how do you propose to set about it?"

Mrs. Dane Calthrop said:

"We've got to do something!"

I smiled, perhaps in rather a superior fashion.

"And what do you suggest that we should do?"

"Get the whole thing cleared up! I said this wasn't a wicked place. I was wrong. It is."

I felt annoyed. I said, not too politely:

"Yes, my dear woman, but what are you going to *do*?"

Mrs. Dane Calthrop said: "Put a stop to it all, of course."

"The police are doing their best."

"If Agnes could be killed yesterday, their best isn't good enough."

"So you know better than they do?"

"Not at all. *I* don't know anything at all. That's why I'm going to call in an expert."

I shook my head.

"You can't do that. Scotland Yard will only take over on a demand from the chief constable of the county. Actually they *have* sent Graves."

"I don't mean *that* kind of an expert. I don't mean someone who knows about anonymous letters or even about murder. I mean someone who knows *people*. Don't you see? We want someone who knows a great deal about *wickedness*!"

It was a queer point of view. But it was, somehow, stimulating.

Before I could say anything more, Mrs. Dane Calthrop nodded her head at me and said in a quick, confident tone:

"I'm going to see about it right away."

And she went out of the window again.

10

i

THE NEXT week, I think, was one of the queerest times I have ever passed through. It had an odd dream quality. Nothing seemed real.

The inquest on Agnes Woddell was held and the curious of Lymstock attended *en masse*. No new facts came to light and the only possible verdict was returned, "Murder by person or persons unknown."

So poor little Agnes Woddell, having had her hour of limelight, was duly buried in the quiet old churchyard and life in Lymstock went on as before.

No, that last statement is untrue. Not as before. . .

There was a half-scared, half-avid gleam in almost everybody's eye. Neighbour looked at neighbour. One thing had been brought out clearly at the inquest—it was most unlikely that any stranger had killed Agnes Woddell. No tramps nor unknown men had been noticed or reported in the district. Somewhere, then, in Lymstock, walking down the High Street, shopping, passing the time of day, was a person who had cracked a defenceless girl's skill and driven a sharp skewer home to her brain.

And no one knew who that person was.

As I say, the days went by in a kind of dream. I looked at everyone I met in a new light, the light of a possible murderer. It was not an agreeable sensation!

And in the evenings, with the curtain drawn, Joanna and I sat talking, talking, arguing, going over in turn all the various possibilities that still seemed so fantastic and incredible.

Joanna held firm to her theory of Mr. Pye. I, after wavering a little, had gone back to my original suspect, Miss Ginch. But we went over the possible names again and again.

Mr. Pye?

Miss Ginch?

Mrs. Dane Calthrop?

Aimée Griffith?

Emily Barton?

Partridge?

And all the time, nervously, apprehensively, we waited for something to happen.

But nothing did happen. Nobody, as far as we knew, received any more letters. Nash made periodic appearances in the town but what he was doing and what traps the police were setting, I had no idea. Graves had gone again.

Emily Barton came to tea. Megan came to lunch. Owen Griffith went about his practice. We went and drank sherry with Mr. Pye. And we went to tea at the vicarage.

I was glad to find Mrs. Dane Calthrop displayed none of the militant ferocity she had shown on the occasion of our last meeting. I think she had forgotten all about it.

She seemed principally concerned with the destruction of white butterflies so as to preserve cauliflower and cabbage plants.

Our afternoon at the vicarage was really one of the most peaceful we had spent. It was an attractive old house and had a big shabby comfortable drawing-room with faded rose cretonne. The Dane Calthrops had a guest staying with them, an amiable elderly lady who was knitting something with white fleecy wool. We had very good hot scones for tea, the vicar came in, and beamed placidly on us whilst he pursued his gentle erudite conversation. It was very pleasant.

I don't mean that we got away from the topic of the murder, because we didn't.

Miss Marple, the guest, was naturally thrilled by the subject. As she said apologetically: "We have so little to talk about in the country!" She had made up her mind that the dead girl must have been just like her Edith.

"Such a nice little maid, and so willing, but sometimes just a *little* slow to take in things."

Miss Marple also had a cousin whose niece's sister-in-law had a great deal of annoyance and trouble over some anonymous letters, so the letters, also, were very interesting to the charming old lady.

"But tell me, dear," she said to Mrs. Dane Calthrop, "what do the village people—I mean the townspeople—say? What do *they* think?"

"Mrs. Cleat still, I suppose," said Joanna.

"Oh no," said Mrs. Dane Calthrop. "Not *now*."

Miss Marple asked who Mrs. Cleat was.

Joanna said she was the village witch.

"That's right, isn't it, Mrs. Dane Calthrop?"

The vicar murmured a long Latin quotation about, I think, the evil power of witches, to which we all listened in respectful and uncomprehending silence.

"She's a very silly woman," said his wife. "Likes to show off. Goes out to gather herbs and things at the full of the moon and takes care that everybody in the place knows about it."

"And silly girls go and consult her, I suppose?" said Miss Marple.

I saw the vicar getting ready to unload more Latin on us and I asked hastily: "But why shouldn't people suspect her of the murder now? They thought the letters were her dong."

Miss Marple said: "Oh! But the girl was killed with a *skewer*, so I hear—(very unpleasant!). Well, naturally, that takes *all* suspicion away from this Mrs. Cleat. Because, you see, she could ill-wish her, so that the girl would waste away and die from natural causes."

"Strange how those old beliefs linger," said the vicar. "In early Christian times, local superstitions were wisely incorporated with Christian doctrine and their more unpleasant attributes gradually eliminated."

"It isn't superstition we've got to deal with here," said Mrs. Dane Calthrop, "but *facts*."

"And very unpleasant facts," I said.

"As you say, Mr. Burton," said Miss Marple. "Now *you*—excuse me if I am being too personal—are a stranger here, and have a knowledge of the world and of various aspects of life. It seems to me that you ought to be able to find a solution to this distasteful problem."

I smiled. "The best solution I have had was a dream. In my dream it all fitted in and panned out beautifully. Unfortunately when I woke up the whole thing was nonsense!"

"How interesting, though. Do tell me how the nonsense went?"

"Oh, it all started with the silly phrase, 'No smoke without fire.' People have been saying that *ad nauseum*. And then I got it mixed up with war terms. Smoke screen, scrap of paper, telephone messages—No, that was another dream."

"And what was that dream?"

The old lady was so eager about it, that I felt sure she was a secret reader of Napoleon's Book of Dreams, which had been the great stand-by of my old nurse.

"Oh! only Elsie Holland—the Symmingtons' nursery governess, you know, was getting married to Dr. Griffith and the vicar here was reading the service in Latin—('Very appropriate, dear,' murmured Mrs. Dane Calthrop to her spouse) and then Mrs. Dane Calthrop got up and forbade the banns and said it had got to be stopped!"

"But that part," I added with a smile, "was true. I woke up and found you standing over me saying it."

"And I was quite right," said Mrs. Dane Calthrop—but quite mildly, I was glad to note.

"But where did a telephone message come in?" asked Miss Marple, crinkling her brows.

"I'm afraid I'm being rather stupid. That wasn't in the dream. It was just before it. I came through the hall and noticed Joanna had written down a message to be given to someone if they rang up. . . ."

Miss Marple leaned forward. There was a pink spot in each cheek. "Will you think me *very* inquisitive and *very* rude if I ask just what that message was?" She cast a glance at Joanna. "I *do* apologise, my dear."

Joanna, however, was highly entertained.

"Oh, I don't mind," she assured the old lady. "I can't remember anything about it myself, but perhaps Jerry can. It must have been something quite trivial."

Solemnly I repeated the message as best I could remember it, enormously tickled at the old lady's rapt attention.

I was afraid the actual words were going to disappoint her, but perhaps she had some sentimental idea of a romance, for she nodded her head and smiled and seemed pleased.

"I see," she said. "I thought it might be something like that."

Mrs. Dane Calthrop said sharply: "Like what, Jane?"

"Something quite ordinary," said Miss Marple.

She looked at me thoughtfully for a moment or two, then she said unexpectedly:

"I can see you are a very clever young man—but not quite enough confidence in yourself. You ought to have!"

Joanna gave a loud hoot.

"For goodness' sake don't encourage him to feel like that. He thinks quite enough of himself as it is."

"Be quiet, Joanna," I said. "Miss Marple understands me."

Miss Marple had resumed her fleecy knitting. "You know," she observed pensively. "To commit a successful murder must be very much like bringing off a conjuring trick."

"The quickness of the hand deceives the eye?"

"Not only that. You've got to make people look at the wrong thing and in the wrong place—Misdirection, they call it, I believe."

"Well," I remarked. "So far everybody seems to have looked in the wrong place for our lunatic at large."

"I should be inclined, myself," said Miss Marple, "to look for somebody very sane."

"Yes," I said thoughtfully. "That's what Nash said. I remember he stressed respectability too."

"Yes," agreed Miss Marple. "That's *very* important."

Well, we all seemed agreed.

I addressed Mrs. Calthrop. "Nash thinks," I said, "that there will be more anonymous letters. What do you think?"

She said slowly: "There may be, I suppose."

"If the police think that, there will have to be, no doubt," said Miss Marple.

I went on doggedly to Mrs. Dane Calthrop.

"Are you still sorry for the writer?"

She flushed. "Why not?"

"I don't think I agree with you, dear," said Miss Marple. "Not in this case."

I said hotly: "They've driven one woman to suicide, and caused untold misery and heartburnings!"

"Have you had one, Miss Burton?" asked Miss Marple of Joanna.

Joanna gurgled, "Oh yes! It said the most frightful things."

"I'm afraid," said Miss Marple, "that the people who are young and pretty are apt to be singled out by the writer."

"That's why I certainly think it's odd that Elsie Holland hasn't had any," I said.

"Let me see," said Miss Marple, "Is that the Symmingtons' nursery governess—the one you dreamt about, Mr. Burton?"

"Yes."

"She's probably had one and won't say so," said Joanna.

"No," I said, "I believe her. So does Nash."

"Dear me," said Miss Marple. "Now that's *very* interesting. That's the most interesting thing I've heard yet."

ii

As we were going home Joanna told me that I ought not to have repeated what Nash said about letters coming.

"Why not?"

"Because Mrs. Dane Calthrop might be It."

"You don't really believe that!"

"I'm not sure. She's a queer woman."

We began our discussion of probables all over again.

It was two nights later that I was coming back in the car from Exhampton. I had had dinner there and then started back and it was already dark before I got into Lymstock.

Something was wrong with the car lights, and after slowing up and switching them on and off, I finally got out to see what I could do. I was some time fiddling, but I managed to fix them up finally.

The road was quite deserted. Nobody in Lymstock is about after dark. The first few houses were just ahead, amongst them the ugly gabled building of the Women's Institute. It loomed up in the dim starlight and something impelled me to go and have a look at it. I don't know whether I had caught a faint glimpse of a stealthy figure flitting through the gate—if so, it must have been so indeterminate that it did not register in my conscious mind, but I did suddenly feel a kind of overweening curiosity about the place.

The gate was slightly ajar, and I pushed it open and walked in. A short path and four steps led up to the door.

I stood there a moment hesitating. What was I really doing there? I didn't know, and then, suddenly, just near at hand, I caught the sound of a rustle. It sounded like a woman's dress. I took a sharp turn and went round the corner of the building towards where the sound had come from.

I couldn't see anybody. I went on and again turned a corner. I was at the back of the house now and suddenly I saw, only two feet away from me, an open window.

I crept up to it and listened. I could hear nothing, but somehow or other I felt convinced that there was someone inside.

My back wasn't too good for acrobatics yet, but I managed to hoist myself up and drop over the sill inside. I made rather a noise unfortunately.

I stood just inside the window listening. Then I walked forward, my hands outstretched. I heard then the faintest sound ahead of me to my right.

I had a torch in my pocket and I switched it on.

Immediately a low, sharp voice said: "Put that out."

I obeyed instantly, for in that brief second I had recognised Superintendent Nash.

I felt him take my arm and propel me through a door and into a passage. Here, where there was no window to betray our presence to anyone outside, he switched on a lamp and looked at me more in sorrow than in anger.

"You *would* have to butt in just that minute, Mr. Burton."

"Sorry," I apologised. "But I got a hunch that I was on to something."

"And so you were probably. Did you see anyone?"

I hesitated. "I'm not sure," I said slowly. "I've got a vague feeling I saw someone sneak in through the front gate but I didn't really *see* anyone. Then I heard a rustly round the side of the house."

Nash nodded.

"That's right. Somebody came round the house before you. They hesitated by the window, then went on quickly—heard *you*, I expect."

I apologised again. "What's the big idea?" I asked.

Nash said:

"I'm banking on the fact that an anonymous letter writer can't stop writing letters. She may know it's dangerous, but she'll have to do it. It's like a craving for drink or drugs."

I nodded.

"Now you see, Mr. Burton, I fancy whoever it is will want to keep the letters looking the same as much as possible. She's got the cut-out pages of that book, and can go on using letters and words cut out of them. But the envelopes present a difficulty. She'll want to type them on the same machine. She can't risk using another typewriter or her own handwriting."

"Do you really think she'll go on with the game?" I asked incredulously.

"Yes, I do. And I'll bet you anything you like she's full of confidence. They're always vain as hell, these people! Well,then, I figured out that whoever it was would come to the Institute after dark so as to get at the typewriter."

"Miss Ginch," I said.

"Maybe."

"You don't know yet?"

"I don't *know*."

"But you suspect?"

"Yes. But somebody's very cunning, Mr. Burton. Somebody knows all the tricks of the game."

I could imagine some of the network that Nash had spread abroad. I had no doubt that every letter written by a suspect and posted or left by hand was immediately inspected. Sooner or later the criminal would slip up, would grow careless.

For the third time I apologised for my zealous and unwanted presence.

"Oh well," said Nash philosophically. "It can't be helped. Better luck next time."

I went out into the night. A dim figure was standing beside my car. To my astonishment I recognised Megan.

"Hallo!" she said. "I thought this was your car. What have

you been doing?"

"What are you doing is much more to the point?" I asked.

"I'm out for a walk. I like walking at night. Nobody stops you and says silly things, and I like the stars, and things smell better, and everyday things look all mysterious."

"All of that I grant you freely," I said. "But only cats and witches walk in the dark. They'll wonder about you at home."

"No, they won't. They never wonder where I am or what *I'm* doing."

"How are you getting on?" I asked.

"All right, I suppose."

"Miss Holland look after you and all that?"

"Elsie's all right. She can't help being a perfect fool."

"Unkind—but probably true," I said. "Hop in and I'll drive you home."

It was not quite true that Megan was never missed.

Symmington was standing on the doorstep as we drove up.

He peered towards us. "Hallo, is Megan there?"

"Yes," I said. "I've brought her home.

Symmington said sharply:

"You mustn't go off like this without telling us, Megan. Miss Holland has been quite worried about you."

Megan muttered something and went past him into the house. Symmington sighed.

"A grown-up girl is a great responsibility with no mother to look after her. She's too old for school, I suppose."

He looked towards me rather suspiciously.

"I suppose you took her for a drive?"

I thought it best to leave it like that.

11

i

ON THE following day I went mad. Looking back on it, that is really the only explanation I can find.

I was due for my monthly visit to Marcus Kent. . . .I went up by train. To my intense surprise Joanna elected to stay behind. As a rule she was eager to come and we usually stayed up for a couple of days.

This time, however, I proposed to return the same day by the evening train, but even so I was astonished at Joanna. She merely said enigmatically that she'd got plenty to do, and why spend hours in a nasty stuffy train when it was a lovely day in the country?

That, of course, was undeniable, but sounded very unlike Joanna.

She said she didn't want the car, so I was to drive it to the station and leave it parked there against my return.

The station of Lymstock is situated, for some obscure reason known to railway companies only, quite half a mile from Lymstock itself. Half-way along the road I overtook Megan shuffling along in an aimless manner. I pulled up.

"Hallo, what are you doing?"

"Just out for a walk."

"But not what is called a good brisk walk, I gather. You were crawling along like a dispirited crab."

"Well, I wasn't going anywhere particular."

"Then you'd better come and see me off at the station." I opened the door of the car and Megan jumped in.

"Where are you going?" she asked.

"London. To see my doctor."

"Your back's not worse, is it?"

"No, it's practically all right again. I'm expecting him to be very pleased about it."

Megan nodded.

We drew up at the station. I parked the car and went in and bought my ticket at the booking office. There were very few people on the platform and nobody I knew.

"You wouldn't like to lend me a penny, would you?" said Megan. "Then I'd get a bit of chocolate out of the slot machine."

"Here you are, baby," I said, handing her the coin in question. "Sure you wouldn't like some clear gums or some throat pastilles as well?"

"I like chocolate best," said Megan without suspecting sarcasm.

She went off to the chocolate machine, and I looked after her with a feeling of mounting irritation.

She was wearing trodden over shoes, and coarse unattractive stockings and a particularly shapeless jumper and skirt. I don't why all this should have infuriated me, but it did.

I said angrily as she came back:

"Why do you wear those disgusting stockings?"

Megan looked down at them, surprised.

"What's the matter with them?"

"Everything's the matter with them. They're loathsome. And why wear a pullover like a decayed cabbage?"

"It's all right, isn't it? I've had it for years."

"So I should imagine. And why do you——"

At this minute the train came in and interrupted my angry lecture.

I got into an empty first-class carriage, let down the window and leaned out to continue the conversation.

Megan stood below me, her face upturned. She asked me why I was so cross.

"I'm not cross," I said untruly. "It just infuriates me to see you so slack, and not caring how you look."

"I couldn't look nice, anyway, so what does it matter?"

"My God," I said. "I'd like to see you turned out properly. I'd like to take you to London and outfit you from tip to toe."

"I wish you could," said Megan.

The train began to move. I looked down into Megan's upturned, wistful face.

And then, as I have said, madness came upon me.

I opened the door, grabbed Megan with one arm and fairly hauled her into the carriage.

There was an outraged shout from a porter, but all he could do was dexterously to bang shut the door again. I pulled Megan up from the floor where my impetuous action had landed her.

"What on earth did you do that for?" she demanded, rubbing one knee.

"Shut up," I said. "You're coming to London with me and when I've done with you you won't know yourself. I'll show you what you can look like if you try. I'm tired of seeing you mooch about down at heel and all anyway."

"Oh!" said Megan in an ecstatic whisper.

The ticket collector came along and I bought Megan a return ticket. She sat in her corner looking at me in a kind of awed respect.

"I say," she said when the man had gone. "You are sudden, aren't you?"

"Very," I said. "It runs in our family."

How explain to Megan the impulse that had come over me? She had looked like a wistful dog being left behind. She now had on her face the incredulous pleasure of the dog who has been taken on the walk after all.

"I suppose you don't know London very well?" I said to Megan.

"Yes, I do," said Megan. "I always went through it to school. And I've been to the dentist there and to a pantomime."

"This," I said darkly, "will be a different London."

We arived with half an hour to spare before my appointment in Harley Street.

I took a taxi and we drove straight to Mirotin, Joanna's dressmaker. Mirotin is, in the flesh, an unconventional and breezy woman of forty-five, Mary Grey. She is a clever woman and very good company. I have always liked her.

I said to Megan. "You're my cousin."

"Why?"

"Don't argue," I said.

Mary Grey was being firm with a stout Jewess who was enamoured of a skin-tight powder-blue evening dress. I detached her and took her aside.

"Listen," I said. "I've brought a little cousin of mine along. Joanna was coming up but was prevented. But she said I could leave it all to you. You see what the girl looks like now?"

"My God, I do," said Mary Grey with feeling.

"Well, I want her turned out right in every particular from head to foot. *Carte blanche*. Stockings, shoes, undies, everything! By the way, the man who does Joanna's hair is close round here, isn't he?"

"Antoine? Round the corner. I'll see to that too."

"You're a woman in a thousand."

"Oh, I shall enjoy it—apart from the money—and that's not to be sneezed at these days—half my damned brutes of women never pay their bills. But as I say, I shall enjoy it." She shot a quick professional glance at Megan standing a little way away. "She's got a lovely figure."

"You must have X-ray eyes," I said. "She looks completely shapeless to me."

Mary Grey laughed.

"It's these schools," she said. "They seem to take a pride in turning out girls who preen themselves on looking like nothing on earth. They call it being sweet and unsophisticated. Sometimes it takes a whole season before a girl can pull herself together and look human. Don't worry, leave it all to me."

"Right," I said. "I'll come back and fetch her about six."

ii

Marcus Kent was pleased with me. He told me that I surpassed his wildest expectations.

"You must have the constitution of an elephant," he said, "to make a come-back like this. Oh well, wonderful what country air and no late hours or excitements will do for a man if he can only stick it."

"I grant you your first two," I said. "But don't think that the country is free from excitements. We've had a good deal in my part."

"What sort of excitement?"

"Murder," I said.

Marcus Kent pursed up his mouth and whistled.

"Some bucolic love tragedy? Farm lad kills his lass?"

"Not at all. A crafty, determined lunatic killer."

"I haven't read anything about it. When did they lay him by the heels?"

"They haven't, and it's a she!"

"Whew! I'm not sure that Lymstock's quite the right place for you, old boy."

I said firmly:

"Yes, it is. And you're not going to get me out of it."

Marcus Kent has a low mind. He said at once?

"So that's it! Found a blonde?"

"Not at all," I said, with a guilty thought of Elsie Holland. "It's merely that the psychology of crime interests me a good deal."

"Oh, all right. It certainly hasn't done you any harm so far, but just make sure that your lunatic killer doesn't obliterate *you*."

"No fear of that," I said.

"What about dining with me this evening? You can tell me all about your revolting murder."

"Sorry. I'm booked."

"Date with a lady—eh? Yes, you're definitely on the mend."

"I suppose you could call it that," I said, rather tickled at the idea of Megan in the role.

I was at Mirotin's at six o'clock when the establishment was officially closing. Mary Grey came to meet me at the top of the stairs outside the showroom. She had a finger to her lips.

"You're going to have a shock! If I say it myself, I've put in a good bit of work."

I went into the big showroom. Megan was standing looking at herself in a long mirror. I give you my word I hardly recognised her! For a minute it took my breath away. Tall and slim as a willow with delicate ankles and feet shown off by sheer silk stockings and well-cut shoes. Yes, lovely feet and hands, small bones—quality and distinction in every line of her. Her hair had been trimmed and shaped to her head and it was glowing like a glossy chestnut. They'd had the sense to leave her face alone.

She was not made up, or if she was it was so light and delicate that it did not show. Her mouth needed no lipstick.

Moreover there was about her something that I had never seen before, a new innocent pride in the arch of her neck. She looked at me gravely with a small shy smile.

"I do look—rather nice, don't I?" said Megan.

"Nice?" I said. "Nice isn't the word! Come on out to dinner and if every second man doesn't turn round to look at you I'll be surprised. You'll knock all the other girls into a cocked hat."

Megan was not beautiful, but she was unusual and striking looking. She had personality. She walked into the restaurant ahead of me and, as the head waiter hurried towards us, I felt the thrill of idiotic pride that a man feels when he has got something out of the ordinary with him.

We had cocktails first and lingered over them. Then we dined. And later we danced. Megan was keen to dance and I didn't want to disappoint her, but for some reason or other I hadn't thought she would dance well. But she did. She was light as a feather in my arms, and her body and feet followed the rhythm perfectly.

"Gosh!" I said. "You can dance!"

She seemed a little surprised. "Well, of course I can. We had dancing class every week at school."

"It takes more than dancing class to make a dancer," I said.

We went back to our table.

"Isn't this food lovely?" said Megan. "And everything!"

She heaved a delighted sigh.

"Exactly my sentiments," I said.

It was a delirious evening. I was still mad. Megan brought me down to earth when she said doubtfully:

"Oughtn't we to be going home?"

My jaw dropped. Yes, definitely I was mad. I had forgotten everything! I was in a world divorced from reality, existing in it with the creature I had created.

"Good Lord!" I said.

I realised that the last train had gone.

"Stay there," I said. "I'm going to telephone."

I rang up the Llewellyn Hire people and ordered their biggest and fastest car to come round as soon as possible.

I came back to Megan. "The last train has gone," I said. "So we're going home by car."

"Are we? What fun!"

What a nice child she was, I thought. So pleased with everything, so unquestioning, accepting all my suggestions without fuss or bother.

The car came, and it was large and fast, but all the same it was very late when we came into Lymstock.

Suddenly conscious-stricken, I said, "They'll have been sending out search parties for you!"

But Megan seemed in an equable mood. She said vaguely:

"Oh, I don't think so. I often go out and don't come home for lunch."

"Yes, my dear child, but you've been out for tea and dinner too."

However, Megan's lucky star was in the ascendent. The house was dark and silent. On Megan's advice, we went round to the back and threw stones at Rose's window.

In due course Rose looked out and with many suppressed exclamations and palpitations came down to let us in.

"Well now, and I saying you were asleep in your bed. The master and Miss Holland"—(slight sniff after Miss Holland's name)—"had early supper and went for a drive. I said I'd keep an eye to the boys. I thought I heard you come in when I was up in the nursery trying to quiet Colin, who was playing up, but you weren't about when I came down so I thought you'd gone up to bed. And that's what I said when the master came in and asked for you."

I cut short the conversation by remarking that that was where Megan had better go now.

"Good night," said Megan, "and thank you *awfully*. It's been the loveliest day I've ever had."

I drove home slightly light-headed still, and tipped the chauffeur handsomely, offering him a bed if he liked. But he preferred to drive back through the night.

The hall door had opened during our colloquy and as he drove away it was flung wide and Joanna said:

"So it's you at last, is it?"

"Were you worried about me?" I asked, coming in and

shutting the door.

Joanna went into the drawing-room and I followed her. There was a coffee pot on the trivet and Joanna made herself coffee whilst I helped myself to a whisky and soda.

"Worried about you? No, of course not. I thought you'd decided to stay in town and have a binge."

"I've had a binge—of a kind."

I grinned and then began to laugh.

Joanna asked what I was laughing at and I told her.

"But Jerry, you must have been mad—quite mad!"

"I suppose I was."

"But, my dear boy, you can't do things like that—not in a place like this. It will be all round Lymstock to-morrow."

"I suppose it will. But, after all, Megan's only a child."

"She isn't. She's twenty. You can't take a girl of twenty to London and buy her clothes without a most frightful scandal. Good gracious, Jerry, you'll probably have to marry the girl."

Joanna was half-serious, half-laughing.

It was at that moment that I made a very important discovery. "Damn it all," I said. "I don't mind if I do. In fact—I should like it."

A very funny expression came over Joanna's face. She got up and said dryly, as she went towards the door:

"Yes, I've known that for some time. . ."

She left me standing, glass in hand, aghast at my new discovery.

12

i

I DON'T KNOW what the usual reactions are of a man who goes to propose marriage.

In fiction his throat is dry and his collar feels too tight and he is in a pitiable state of nervousness.

I didn't feel at all like that. Having thought of a good idea I just wanted to get it all settled as soon as possible. I didn't see any particular need for embarrassment.

I went along to the Symmingtons' house about eleven o'clock. I rang the bell and when Rose came, I asked for Miss Megan. It was the knowing look that Rose gave me that first made me feel slightly shy.

She put me in the little morning-room and whilst waiting there I hoped uneasily that they hadn't been upsetting Megan.

When the door opened and I wheeled round, I was instantly relieved. Megan was not looking shy or upset at all. Her head was still like a glossy chestnut, and she wore that air of pride and self-respect that she had acquired yesterday. She was in her old clothes again but she had managed to make them look different. It's wonderful what knowledge of her own attractiveness will do for a girl. Megan, I realised suddenly, had grown up.

I suppose I must really have been rather nervous, otherwise I should not have opened the conversation by saying affectionately, "Hallo, catfish!" It was hardly, in the circumstances, a lover-like greeting.

It seemed to suit Megan. She grinned and said, "Hallo!"

"Look here," I said. "You didn't get into a row about yesterday, I hope?"

Megan said with assurance, "Oh *no*," and then blinked and said vaguely, "Yes, I believe I did. I mean, they said a lot of things and seemed to think it had been very odd—but then you know what people are and what fusses they make all about nothing."

I was relieved to find that shocked disapproval had slipped off Megan like water off a duck's back.

"I came round this morning," I said, "because I've a suggestion to make. You see I like you a lot, and I think you like me——"

"Frightfully," said Megan with rather disquieting enthusiasm.

"And we get on awfully well together, so I think it would be a good idea if we got married."

"Oh," said Megan.

She looked surprised. Just that. Not startled. Not shocked. Just mildly surprised.

"You mean you really want to marry me?" she asked with the air of one getting a thing perfectly clear.

"More than anything in the world," I said—and I meant it.

"You mean, you're in love with me?"

"I'm in love with you."

Her eyes were steady and grave. She said:

"I think you're the nicest person in the world—but I'm not in love with you."

"I'll make you love me."

"That wouldn't do. I don't want to be *made*."

She paused and then said gravely: "I'm not the sort of wife for you. I'm better at hating than at loving."

She said it with a queer intensity.

I said, "Hate doesn't last. Love does."

"Is that true?"

"It's what I believe."

Again there was a silence. Then I said:

"So it's 'no,' is it?"

"Yes, it's no."

"And you don't encourage me to hope?"

"What would be the good of that?"

"None whatever," I agreed. "Quite redundant, in fact—because I'm going to hope whether you tell me to or not."

ii

Well, that was that. I walked away from the house feeling slightly dazed but irritatingly conscious of Rose's passionately interested gaze following me.

Rose had had a good deal to say before I could escape.

That she'd never felt the same since that awful day! That she wouldn't have stayed except for the children and being sorry for poor Mr. Symmington. That she wasn't going to stay unless they got another maid quick—and they wouldn't be likely to do that when there had been a murder in the house! That it was all very well for that Miss Holland to say she'd do the housework in the meantime. Very sweet and obliging she was—Oh yes, but it was mistress of the house that she was fancying herself going to be one fine day! Mr. Symmington, poor man, never saw anything—but one knew what a widower was, a poor helpless creature made to be the prey of a designing woman. And that it wouldn't be for want of trying if Miss Holland didn't step into the dead mistress's shoes!

I assented mechanically to everything, yearning to get away and unable to do so because Rose was holding firmly on to my hat whilst she indulged in her flood of spite.

I wondered if there was any truth in what she said. Had Elsie Holland envisaged the possibility of becoming the second Mrs. Symmington? Or was she just a decent kind-hearted girl doing her best to look after a bereaved household?

The result could quite likely be the same in either case. And why not? Symmington's young children needed a mother—Elsie was a decent soul—besides being quite indecently beautiful—a point which a man might appreciate—even such a stuffed fish as Symmington!

I thought all this, I know, because I was trying to put off thinking about Megan.

You may say that I gone to ask Megan to marry me in an absurdly complacent frame of mind and that I deserved what I got—but it was not really like that. It was because I felt so assured, so certain, that Megan belonged to me—that she was my business, that to look after her and make her happy and keep her from harm was the only natural right way of life for me, that

I had expected her to feel, too, that she and I belonged to each other.

But I was not giving up. Oh no! Megan was my woman and I was going to have her.

After a moment's thought, I went to Symmington's office. Megan might pay no attention to strictures on her conduct, but I would like to get things straight.

Mr. Symmington was disengaged, I was told, and I was shown into his room. By a pinching of the lips, and an additional stiffness of manner, I gathered that I was not exactly popular at the moment.

"Good morning," I said. "I'm afraid this isn't a professional call, but a personal one. I'll put it plainly. I dare say you'll have realised that I'm in love with Megan. I've asked her to marry me and she has refused. But I'm not taking that as final."

I saw Symmington's expression change, and I read his mind with ludicrous ease. Megan was a disharmonious element in his house. He was, I felt sure, a just and kindly man, and he would never have dreamed of not providing a home for his dead wife's daughter. But her marriage to me would certainly be a relief. The frozen halibut thawed. He gave me a pale cautious smile.

"Frankly, you know, Burton, I had no idea of such a thing. I know you've taken a lot of notice of her, but we've always regarded her as a child."

"She's not a child," I said shortly.

"No, no, not in years."

"She can be her age any time she's allowed to be," I said, still slightly angry. "She's not twenty-one, I know, but she will be in a month or two. I'll let you have all the information about myself you want. I'm well off and have led quite a decent life. I'll look after her and do all I can to make her happy."

"Quite—quite. Still, it's up to Megan herself."

"She'll come round in time," I said. "But I just thought I'd like to get straight with you about it."

He said he appreciated that, and we parted amicably.

iii

I ran into Miss Emily Barton outside. She had a shopping basket on her arm.

"Good morning, Mr. Burton, I hear you went to London yesterday."

Yes, she had heard all right. Her eyes were, I thought, kindly, but full of curiosity, too.

"I went to see my doctor," I said.

Miss Emily smiled.

That smile made little of Marcus Kent. She murmured:

"I hear Megan nearly missed the train. She jumped in when it was going."

"Helped by me," I said. "I hauled her in."

"How lucky you were there. Otherwise there might have been an accident."

It is extraordinary how much of a fool one gentle inquisitive old maiden lady can make a man feel!

I was saved further suffering by the onslaught of Mrs. Dane Calthrop. She had her own tame elderly maiden lady in tow, but she herself was full of direct speech.

"Good morning," she said. "I hear you've made Megan buy herself some decent clothes? Very sensible of you. It takes a man to think of something really practical like that. I've been so worried about that girl for a long time. Girls with brains are so liable to turn into morons, aren't they?"

With which remarkable statement, she shot into the fish shop.

Miss Marple, left standing by me, twinkled a little and said:

"Mrs. Dane Calthrop is a very remarkable woman, you know. She's nearly always right."

"It makes her rather alarming," I said.

"Sincerity has that effect," said Miss Marple.

Mrs. Dane Calthrop shot out of the fish shop again and rejoined us. She was holding a large red lobster.

"Have you ever seen anything so unlike Mr. Pye?" she said—"very virile and handsome, isn't it?"

iv

I was a little nervous of meeting Joanna but I found when I got home that I needn't have worried. She was out and she did not return for lunch. This aggrieved Partridge a good deal, who said sourly as she proffered two loin chops in an entrée dish: "Miss Burton said specially as she was going to be *in*."

I ate both chops in an attempt to atone for Joanna's lapse. All the same, I wondered where my sister was. She had taken to be very mysterious about her doings of late.

It was half-past three when Joanna burst into the drawing-room. I had heard a car stop outside and I half expected to see Griffith, but the car drove on and Joanna came in alone.

Her face was very red and she seemed upset. I perceived that something had happened.

"What's the matter?" I asked.

Joanna opened her mouth, closed it again, sighed, plumped herself down in a chair and stared in front of her.

She said:

"I've had the most awful day."

"What's happened?"

"I've done the most incredible things. It was awful——"

"But what——"

"I just started out for a walk, an ordinary walk—I went up over the hill and on to the moor. I walked miles—I felt like it. Then I dropped down into a hollow. There's a farm there—a God-forsaken lonely sort of spot. I was thirsty and I wondered if they'd got any milk or something. So I wandered into the farmyard and then the door opened and Owen came out."

"Yes?"

"He thought it might be the district nurse. There was a woman in there having a baby. He was expecting the nurse and he'd sent word to her to get hold of another doctor. It—things were going wrong."

"Yes?"

"So he said—to *me*, 'Come on, you'll do—better than nobody.' I said I couldn't, and he said what did I mean? I said I'd never done anything like that, that I didn't know anything—

"He said what the hell did that matter? And then he was

awful. He turned on me. He said, 'You're a woman, aren't you? I suppose you can do your durnedest to help another woman?' And he went on at me—said I'd talked as though I was interested in doctoring and had said I wished I was a nurse. 'All pretty talk, I suppose! You didn't mean anything real by it, but this *is* real and you're going to behave like a decent human being and not like a useless ornamental nit-wit!'

"I've done the most incredible things, Jerry. Held instruments and boiled them and handed things. I'm so tired I can hardly stand up. It was dreadful. But he saved her—and the baby. It was born alive. He didn't think at one time he could save it. Oh dear!"

Joanna covered her face with her hands.

I contemplated her with a certain amount of pleasure and mentally took my hat off to Owen Griffith. He'd brought Joanna slap up against reality for once.

I said, "There's a letter for you in the hall. From Paul, I think."

"Eh?" She paused for a minute and then said, "I'd no idea, Jerry, what doctors had to *do*. The nerve they've got to have!"

I went out into the hall and brought Joanna her letter. She opened it, glanced vaguely at its contents, and let it drop.

"He was really rather wonderful. The way he fought—the way he wouldn't be beaten! He was rude and horrible to *me*—but he *was* wonderful.

I observed Paul's disregarded letter with some pleasure. Plainly, Joanna was cured of Paul.

13

i

THINGS NEVER come when they are expected.

I was full of Joanna's and my personal affairs and was quite taken aback the next morning when Nash's voice said over the telephone: "*We've got her*, Mr. Burton!"

I was so startled I nearly dropped the receiver.

"You mean the——"

He interrupted.

"Can you be overheard where you are?"

"No, I don't think so—well, perhaps——"

It seemed to me that the baize door to the kitchen had swung open a trifle.

"Perhaps you'd care to come down to the station?"

"I will. Right away."

I was at the police station in next to no time. In an inner room Nash and Sergeant Parkins were together. Nash was wreathed in smiles.

"It's been a long chase," he said. "But we're there at last."

He flicked a letter across the table. This time it was all typewritten. It was, of its kind, fairly mild.

"*It's no use thinking you're going to step into a dead woman's shoes. The whole town is laughing at you. Get out now. Soon it will be too late. This is a warning. Remember what happened to that other girl. Get out and stay out.*"

It finished with some mildly obscene language.

"That reached Miss Holland this morning," said Mash.

"Thought it was funny she hadn't had one before," said Sergeant Parkin.

"Who wrote it?" I asked.

Some of the exultation faded out of Nash's face.

"I'm sorry about it, because it will hit a decent man hard, but there it is. Perhaps he's had his suspicions already."

"Who wrote it?" I reiterated.

"Miss Aimée Griffith."

ii

Nash and Parkins went to the Griffiths' house that afternoon with a warrent.

By Nash's invitation I went with them.

"The doctor," he said, "is very fond of you. He hasn't many friends in this place. I think if it is not too painful to you, Mr. Burton, that you might help him to bear up under the shock."

I said I would come. I didn't relish the job, but I thought I might be some good.

We rang the bell and asked for Miss Griffith and we were shown into the drawing-room. Elsie Holland, Megan and Symmington were there having tea.

Nash behaved very circumspectly.

He asked Aimée if he might have a few words with her privately.

She got up and came towards us. I thought I saw just a faint hunted look in her eye. If so, it went again. She was perfectly normal and hearty.

"Want me? Not in trouble over my car lights again, I hope?"

She led the way out of the drawing-room and across the hall into a small study.

As I closed the drawing-room door, I saw Symmington's head jerk up sharply. I supposed his legal training had brought him in contact with police cases, and he had recognised something in Nash's manner. He half rose.

That is all I saw before I shut the door and followed the others.

Nash was saying his piece. He was very quiet and correct. He cautioned her and then told her that he must ask her to accompany him. He had a warrant for her arrest and he read out the charge——

I forget now the exact legal term. It was the letters, not

murder yet.

Aimée Griffith flung up her head and bayed with laughter. She boomed out: "What ridiculous nonsense! As though I'd write a packet of indecent stuff like that. You must be mad. I've never written a word of the kind.

Nash produced the letter to Elsie Holland. He said:

"Do you deny having written this, Miss Griffith?"

If she hesitated it was only for a split second.

"Of course I do. I've never seen it before."

Nash said quietly: "I must tell you, Miss Griffith, that you were observed to type that letter on the machine at the Women's Institute between eleven and eleven-thirty p.m. on the night before last. Yesterday you entered the post office with a bunch of letters in your hand——"

"I never posted this."

"No, *you* did not. Whilst waiting for stamps, you dropped it inconspicuously on the floor, so that somebody should come along unsuspectingly and pick it up and post it."

"I never——"

The door opened and Symmington came in. He said sharply: "What's going on? Aimée, if there is anything wrong, you ought to be legally represented. If you wish me——"

She broke then. Covered her face with her hands and staggered to a chair. She said:

"Go away, Dick, go away. Not you. Not *you*!"

"You need a solicitor, my dear girl."

"Not you. I—I—couldn't bear it. I don't want you to know—all this."

He understood then, perhaps. He said quietly:

"I'll get hold of Mildmay, of Exhampton. Will that do?"

She nodded. She was sobbing now.

Symmington went out of the room. In the doorway he collided with Owen Griffith.

"What's this?" said Owen violently. "My sister——"

"I'm sorry, Dr. Griffith. Very sorry. But we have no alternative."

"You think she—was responsible for those letters?"

"I'm afraid there is no doubt of it, sir," said Nash—he turned to Aimée, "You must come with us now, please, Miss Griffith—

you shall have every facility for seeing a solicitor, you know."

Owen cried: "Aimée?"

She brushed past him without looking at him.

She said: "Don't talk to me. Don't say anything. And for God's sake don't *look* at me!"

They went out. Owen stood like a man in a trance.

I waited a bit, then I came up to him.

"If there's anything I can do, Griffith, tell me."

He said like a man in a dream:

"Aimée? I don't believe it."

"It may be a mistake," I suggested feebly.

He said slowly: "She wouldn't take it like that if it were. But I would never have believed it. I *can't* believe it."

He sank down on a chair. I made myself useful by finding a stiff drink and bringing it to him. He swallowed it down and it seemed to do him good.

He said: "I couldn't take it in at first. I'm all right now. Thanks, Burton, but there's nothing you can do. Nothing *anyone* can do."

The door opened and Joanna came in. She was very white.

She came over to Owen and looked at me.

She said: "Get out, Jerry. This is my business."

As I went out of the door, I saw her kneel down by his chair.

iii

I can't tell you coherently the events of the next twenty-four hours. Various incidents stand out, unrelated to other incidents.

I remember Joanna coming home, very white and drawn, and of how I tried to cheer her up, saying:

"Now who's being a ministering angel?"

And of how she smiled in a pitiful twisted way and said:

"He says he won't have me, Jerry. He's very, *very* proud and stiff!"

We sat there for a while, Joanna saying at last:

"The Burton family isn't exactly in demand at the moment!"

I said: "Never mind, my sweet, we still have each other," and

Joanna said, "Somehow or other, Jerry, that doesn't comfort me much just now. . ."

iv

Owen came the next day and rhapsodied in the most fulsome way about Joanna. She was wonderful, marvellous! The way she'd come to him, the way she was willing to marry him—at once if he liked. But he wasn't going to let her do that. No, she was too good, too fine to be associated with the kind of muck that would start as soon as the papers got hold of the news.

I was fond of Joanna, and knew she was the kind who's all right when standing by in trouble, but I got rather bored with all this high-falutin' stuff. I told Owen rather irritably not to be so damned noble.

I went down to the High Street and found everybody's tongues wagging nineteen to the dozen. Emily Barton was saying that she had never really trusted Aimée Griffith. The grocer's wife was saying with gusto that she'd always thought Miss Griffith had a queer look in her eye——

They had completed the case against Aimée, so I learnt from Nash. A search of the house had brought to light the cut pages of Emily Barton's book—in the cupboard under the stairs, of all places, wrapped up in an old roll of wallpaper.

"And a jolly good place too," said Nash appreciatively. "You never know when a prying servant won't tamper with a desk or a locked drawer—but those junk cupboards full of last year's tennis balls and old wallpaper are never opened except to shove something more in."

"The lady would seem to have had a *penchant* for that particular hiding-place," I said.

"Yes. The criminal mind seldom has much variety. By the way, talking of the dead girl, we've got one fact to go upon. There's a large heavy pestle missing from the doctor's dispensary. I'll bet anything you like that's what she was stunned with."

"Rather an awkward thing to carry about," I objected.

"Not for Miss Griffith. She was going to the Guides that afternoon, but she was going to leave flowers and vegetables at the Red Cross stall on the way, so she'd got a whopping great basket with her."

"You haven't found the skewer?"

"No, and I shan't. The poor devil may be mad, but she wasn't mad enough to keep a blood-stained skewer just to make it easy for us, when all she'd got to do was to wash it and return it to a kitchen drawer."

"I suppose," I conceded, "that you can't have everything."

The vicarage had been one of the last places to hear the news. Old Miss Marple was very much distressed by it. She spoke to me very earnestly on the subject.

"It isn't *true*, Mr. Burton. I'm sure it isn't true."

"It's true enough, I'm afraid. They were lying in wait, you know. They actually *saw* her type that letter."

"Yes, yes—perhaps they did. Yes, I can understand *that*."

"And the printed pages from which the letters were cut were found where she'd hidden them in her house."

Miss Marple stared at me. Then she said, in a very low voice: "But that is horrible—really *wicked*."

Mrs. Dane Calthrop came up with a rush and joined us and said: "What's the matter, Jane?"

Miss Marple was murmuring helplessly:

"Oh dear, oh dear, what can one *do*?"

"What's upset you, Jane?"

Miss Marple said: "There must be *something*. But I am so old and ignorant, and I am afraid, so foolish."

I felt rather embarrassed and was glad when Mrs. Dane Calthrop took her friend away.

I was to see Miss Marple again that afternoon, however. Much later when I was on my way home.

She was standing near the little bridge at the end of the village, near Mrs. Cleat's cottage, and talking to Megan of all people.

I wanted to see Megan. I had been wanting to see her all day. I quickened my pace. But as I came up to them, Megan turned on her heel and went off in the other direction.

It made me angry and I would have followed her, but Miss

Marple blocked my way.

She said: "I wanted to speak to you. No, don't go after Megan now. It wouldn't be wise."

I was just going to make a sharp rejoinder when she disarmed me by saying:

"That girl has great courage—a very high order of courage."

I still wanted to go after Megan, but Miss Marple said:

"Don't try and see her now. I do know what I am talking about. She must keep her courage intact."

There was something about the old lady's assertion that chilled me. It was as though she knew something that I didn't.

I was afraid and didn't know why I was afraid.

I didn't go home. I went back into the High Street and walked up and down aimlessly. I don't know what I was waiting for, nor what I was thinking about. . . .

I got caught by that awful old bore Colonel Appleton. He asked after my pretty sister as usual and then went on:

"What's all this about Griffith's sister being mad as a hatter? They say she's been at the bottom of this anonymous letter business that's been such a confounded nuisance to everybody? Couldn't believe it at first, but they say it's quite true."

I said it was true enough.

"Well, well—I must say our police force is pretty good on the whole. Give 'em time, that's all, give 'em time. Funny business this anonymous letter stunt—these desiccated old maids are always the ones who go in for it—though the Griffith woman wasn't bad-looking even if she was a bit long in the tooth. But there aren't any decent-looking girls in this part of the world. Except that governess girl of the Symmingtons. She's worth looking at. Pleasant girl, too. Grateful if one does any little thing for her. Came across her having a picnic or something with those kids not long ago. They were romping about in the heather and she was knitting—ever so vexed she'd run out of wool. 'Well,' I said, 'like me to run you into Lymstock? I've got to call for a rod of mine there. I shan't be more than ten minutes getting it, then I'll run you back again.' She was a bit doubtful about leaving the boys. 'They'll be all right,' I said. 'Who's to harm them?' Wasn't going to have the boys along, no fear! So I ran her in, dropped her at the wool shop, picked her up again later and that was that. Thanked me very prettily. Grateful and all that. Nice girl."

I managed to get away from him.

It was after that, that I caught sight of Miss Marple for the third time. She was coming out of the police-station.

V

Where do one's fears come from? Where do they shape themselves? Where do they hide before coming out into the open?

Just one short phrase. Heard and noted and never quite put aside:

"Take me away—it's so awful being here—feeling so wicked. . ."

Why had Megan said that? What had she to feel wicked about?

There could be nothing in Mrs. Symmington's death to make Megan feel wicked.

Why had the child felt wicked? Why? Why?

Could it be because she felt responsible in any way?

Megan? Impossible! *Megan* couldn't have had anything to do with those letters—those foul obscene letters.

Owen Griffith had known a case up North—a schoolgirl. . .

What had Inspector Graves said?

Something about an *adolescent mind*. . .

Innocent middle-aged ladies on operating tables babbling words they hardly knew. Little boys chalking up things on walls.

No, no, not *Megan*.

Heredity? Bad blood? An unconscious inheritance of something abnormal? Her misfortune, not her fault, a curse laid upon her by a past generation?

"I'm not the wife for you. I'm better at hating than loving."

Oh, my Megan, my little child. Not *that*! Anything but that. And that old Tabby is after you, she suspects. She says you have courage. Courage to do *what*?

It was only a brainstorm. It passed. But I wanted to see Megan—I wanted to see her badly.

At half-past nine that night I left the house and went down to the town and along to the Symmingtons'.

It was then that an entirely new idea came into my mind. The idea of a woman whom nobody had considered for a moment.

(Or had Nash considered her?)

Wildly unlikely, wildly improbable, and I would have said up to to-day, impossible, too. But that was not so. No, not *impossible*.

I passed through the Symmingtons' gate and up to the house. It was a dark overcast night. A little rain was beginning to fall. The visibility was bad.

I saw a line of light from one of the windows. The little morning-room?

I hesitated a moment or two, then instead of going up to the front door, I swerved and crept very quietly up to the window, skirting a big bush and keeping low.

The light came from a chink in the curtains which were not quite drawn. It was easy to look through and see.

It was a strangely peaceful and domestic scene. Symmington in a big arm-chair, and Elsie Holland, her head bent, busily patching a boy's torn shirt.

I could hear as well as see for the window was open at the top.

Elsie Holland was speaking.

"But I do think, really, Mr. Symmington, that the boys are quite old enough to go to boarding school. Not that I shan't hate leaving them because I shall. I'm ever so fond of them both."

Symmington said: "I think perhaps you're right about Brian, Miss Holland. I've decided that he shall start next term at Winhays—my old prep. school. But Colin is a little young yet. I'd prefer him to wait another year."

"Well of course I see what you mean. And Colin is perhaps a little young for his age——"

Quiet domestic talk—quiet domestic scene—and a golden head bent over needlework.

Then the door opened and Megan came in.

She stood very straight in the doorway, and I was aware at once of something tense and strung up about her. The skin of her face was tight and drawn and her eyes bright and resolute. There was no diffidence about her to-night and no childishness.

She said, addressing Symmington, but giving him no title

(and I suddenly reflected that I never had heard her call him anything. Did she address him as father or as Dick or what?):

"I would like to speak to you, please. Alone."

Symmington looked surprised and, I fancied, not best pleased. He frowned, but Megan carried her point with a determination unusual in her.

She turned to Elsie Holland and said:

"Do you mind, Elsie?"

"Oh, of course not." Elsie Holland jumped up. She looked startled and a little flurried.

She went to the door and Megan came farther in so that Elsie passed her.

Just for a moment Elsie stood motionless in the doorway looking over her shoulder.

Her lips were closed, she stood quite still, one hand stretched out, the other clasping her needlework to her.

I caught my breath, overwhelmed suddenly by her beauty.

When I think of her now, I always think of her like that—in arrested motion, with that matchless deathless perfection that belonged to ancient Greece.

Then she went out shutting the door.

Symmington said rather fretfully:

"Well, Megan, what is it? What do you want?"

Megan had come right up to the table. She stood there looking down at Symmington. I was struck anew by the resolute determination of her face and by something else—a hardness new to me.

Then she opened her lips and said something that startled me to the core.

"I want some money," she said.

The request didn't improve Symmington's temper. He said sharply:

"Couldn't you have waited until to-morrow morning? What's the matter, do you think your allowance is inadequate?"

A fair man, I thought even then, open to reason, though not to emotional appeal.

Megan said: "I want a good deal of money."

Symmington sat up straight in his chair. He said coldly:

"You will come of age in a few months' time. Then the money

left you by your grandmother will be turned over to you by the public trustee."

Megan said:

"You don't understand. I want money from *you*." She went on, speaking faster. "Nobody's ever talked much to me about my father. They've not wanted me to know about him. But I do know that he went to prison and I know why. It was for blackmail!"

She paused.

"Well, I'm his daughter. And perhaps I take after him. Anyway, I'm asking you to give me money because—if you don't"—she stopped and then went on very slowly and evenly—"if you don't—*I shall say what I saw you doing to the cachet that day in my mother's room*."

There was a pause. Then Symmington said in a completely emotionless voice:

"I don't know what you mean."

Megan said: "I think you do."

And she smiled. It was not a nice smile.

Symmington got up. He went over to the writing-desk. He took a cheque-book from his pocket and wrote out a cheque. He blotted it carefully and then came back. He held it out to Megan.

"You're grown up now," he said. "I can understand that you may feel you want to buy something rather special in the way of clothes and all that. I don't know what you're talking about. I didn't pay attention. But here's a cheque."

Megan looked at it, then she said:

"Thank you. That will do to go on with."

She turned and went out of the room. Symmington stared after her and at the closed door, then he turned round and as I saw his face I made a quick uncontrolled movement forward.

It was checked in the most extraordinary fashion. The big bush that I had noticed by the wall stopped being a bush. Superintendent Nash's arms went round me and Superintendent Nash's voice just breathed in my ear:

"Quiet, Burton. For God's sake."

Then, with infinite caution he beat a retreat, his arm impelling me to accompany him.

Round the side of the house he straightened himself and

wiped his forehard.

"Of course," he said "You *would* have to butt in!"

"That girl isn't safe," I said urgently. "You saw his face? We've got to get her out of here."

Nash took a firm grip of my arm.

"Now, look here, Mr. Burton, you've got to *listen*."

vi

Well, I listened.

I didn't like it—but I gave in.

But I insisted on being on the spot and I swore to obey orders implicitly.

So that is how I came with Nash and Parkins into the house by the back door which was already unlocked.

And I waited with Nash on the upstairs landing behind the velvet curtain masking the window alcove until the clocks in the house struck two, and Symmington's door opened and he went across the landing and into Megan's room.

I did not stir or make a move for I knew that Sergeant Parkins was inside masked by the opening door, and I knew that Parkins was a good man and knew his job, and I knew that I couldn't have trusted myself to keep quiet and not break out.

And waiting there, with my heart thudding, I saw Symmington come out with Megan in his arms and carry her downstairs, with Nash and myself a discreet distance behind him.

He carried her through to the kitchen and he had just arranged her comfortably with her head in the gas-oven and had turned on the gas when Nash and I came through the kitchen door and switched on the light.

And that was the end of Richard Symmington. He collapsed. Even while I was hauling Megan out and turning off the gas I saw the collapse. He didn't even try to fight. He knew he'd played and lost.

vii

Upstairs I sat by Megan's bed waiting for her to come round and occasionally cursing Nash.

"How do you know she's all right? It was too big a risk."

Nash was very soothing.

"Just a soporific in the milk she always had by her bed. Nothing more. It stands to reason, he couldn't risk her being poisoned. As far as he's concerned the whole business is closed with Miss Griffith's arrest. He can't afford to have any mysterious death. No violence, no poison. But if a rather unhappy type of girl broods over her mother's suicide, and finally goes and puts her head in the gas oven—well, people just say that she was never quite normal and the shock of her mother's death finished her."

I said, watching Megan:

"She's a long time coming round."

"You heard what Dr. Griffith said? Heart and pulse quite all right—she'll just sleep and wake naturally. Stuff he gives a lot of his patients, he says."

Megan stirred. She murmured something.

Superintendent Nash unobtrusively left the room.

Presently Megan opened her eyes. "Jerry."

"Hello, sweet."

"Did I do it well?"

"You might have been blackmailing ever since your cradle!"

Megan closed her eyes again. Then she murmured:

"Last night—I was writing to you—in case anything went—went wrong. But I was too sleepy to finish. It's over there."

I went across to the writing-table. In a shabby little blotter I found Megan's unfinished letter.

"My dear Jerry," it began primly:

"I was reading my school Shakespeare and the sonnet that begins:

'So are you to my thoughts as food to life

Or as sweet-season'd showers are to the ground.'

and I see that I am in love with you after all, because that is what I feel. . . ."

14

i

"SO YOU see," said Mrs. Dane Calthrop, "I was quite right to call in an expert."

I stared at her. We were all at the vicarage. The rain was pouring down outside and there was a pleasant log fire, and Mrs. Dane Calthrop had just wandered round, beat up a sofa cushion and put it for some reason of her own on the top of the grand piano.

"But did you?" I said, surprised. "Who was it? What did he do?"

"It wasn't a he," said Mrs. Dane Calthrop.

With a sweeping gesture she indicated Miss Marple. Miss Marple had finished the fleecy knitting and was now engaged with a crochet hook and a ball of cotton.

"That's my expert," said Mrs. Dane Calthrop. "Jane Marple. Look at her well. I tell you, that woman knows more about the different kinds of human wickedness than anyone I've ever known."

"I don't think you should put it quite like that, dear," murmured Miss Marple.

"But you do."

"One sees a good deal of human nature living in a village all the year round," said Miss Marple placidly. Then, seeming to feel it was expected of her, she laid down her crochet, and delivered a gentle old-maidish dissertation on murder.

"The great thing is in these cases to keep an absolutely open mind. Most crimes, you see, are so absurdly simple. This one was. Quite sane and straightforward—and quite understandable—in an unpleasant way, of course."

"Very unpleasant!"

"The truth was really so very obvious. *You* saw it, you know, Mr. Burton."

"Indeed, I did not."

"But you did. You indicated the whole thing to me. You saw perfectly the relationship of one thing to the other, but you just hadn't enough self-confidence to see what those feelings of yours meant. To begin with, that tiresome phrase 'No smoke without fire.' It irritated you, but you proceeded quite correctly to label it for what it was—a smoke screen. Misdirection, you see—everybody looking at the wrong thing—the anonymous letters, but the whole point was that there *weren't* any anonymous letters!"

"But my dear Miss Marple, I can assure you that there *were*. I had one."

"Oh yes, but they weren't real at all. Dear Maud here tumbled to that. Even in peaceful Lymstock there are plenty of scandals, and I can assure you any *woman* living in the place would have known about them and used them. But a man, you see, isn't interested in gossip in the same way—especially a detached logical man like Mr. Symmington. A genuine woman writer of those letters would have made her letters much more to the point.

"So you see that if you disregard the smoke and come to the fire you know where you are. You just come down to the actual facts of what happened—Mrs. Symmington died.

"So then, naturally, one thinks of who might have wanted Mrs. Symmington to die, and of course the very person one thinks of in such a case is, I am afraid, the *husband*. And one asks onself is there any *reason*?—any *motive*?—for instance, *any other woman*?

"And the very first thing I hear is that there is a very attractive young governess in the house. So clear, isn't it? Mr. Symmington, a rather dry repressed unemotional man, tied to a querulous and neurotic wife and then suddenly this radiant young creature comes along."

"I'm afraid, you know, that gentlemen, when they fall in love at a certain age, get the disease very badly. It's quite a madness. And Mr. Symmington, as far as I can make out, was never actually a *good* man—he wasn't very kind or affectionate or very sympathetic—his qualities were all negative—so he hadn't really the strength to fight his madness. And in a place like this, only his wife's death would solve his problem. He wanted to marry the girl, you see. She's very respectable and so is he. And besides, he's devoted to his children and didn't want to give them up. He wanted everything, his home, his children, his respectability and Elsie. And the price he would have to pay for that was murder.

"He chose, I do think, a very clever way. He knew so well from his experience of criminal cases how soon suspicion falls on the husband if a wife dies unexpectedly—and the possibility of exhumation in the case of poison. So he created a death which seemed only incidental to something else. He created a non-existent anonymous letter-writer. And the clever thing was that the police were certain to suspect a *woman*—and they were quite right in a way. All the letters *were* a woman's letters; he cribbed them very cleverly from the letters in the case last year and from a case Dr. Griffith told him about. I don't mean that he was so crude as to reproduce any letter verbatim, but he took phrases and expressions from them and mixed them up, and the net result was that the letters definitely represented a woman's mind—a half-crazy repressed personality.

"He knew all the tricks that the police use, handwriting, typewriting tests, etc. He's been preparing his crime for some time. He typed all the envelopes before he gave away the typewriter to the Woman's Institute, and he cut the pages from the book at Little Furze probably quite a long time ago when he was waiting in the drawing-room one day. People don't open books of sermons much!

"And finally, having got his false Poison Pen well established, he staged the real thing. A fine afternoon when the governess and the boys and his stepdaughter would be out, and the servants having their regular day out. He couldn't foresee that the little maid Agnes would quarrel with her boy and come back to the house."

Joanna asked:

"But what did she *see*? Do you know that?

"I don't *know*. I can only guess. My guess would be that she didn't see anything."

"That it was all a mare's nest?"

"No, no, my dear, I mean that she stood at the pantry window all the afternoon waiting for the young man to come and make it up and that—quite literally—she saw *nothing*. That is, *no one* came to the house at all, not the postman, nor anybody else.

"It would take her some time, being slow, to realise that that was very odd—because apparently Mrs. Symmington *had* received an anonymous letter that afternoon."

"Didn't she receive one?" I asked puzzled.

"But of course not! As I say, this crime is so simple. Her husband just put the cyanide in the top cachet of the ones she took in the afternoon when her sciatica came on after lunch. All Symmington had to do was to get home before, or at the same time as Elsie Holland, call his wife, get no answer, go up to her room, drop a spot of cyanide in the plain glass of water she had used to swallow the cachet, toss the crumpled-up anonymous letter into the grate, and put by her hand the scrap of paper with '*I can't go on*' written on it."

Miss marple turned to me.

"You were quite right about that, too, Mr. Burton. A 'scrap of paper' was all wrong. People don't leave suicide notes on small torn scraps of paper. They use a *sheet* of paper—and very often an envelope too. Yes, the scrap of paper was wrong and you knew it."

"You are rating me too high," I said, "I knew nothing."

"But you did, you really *did*, Mr. Burton. Otherwise why were you immediately impressed by the message your sister left scribbled on the telephone pad?"

I repeated slowing, "Say that '*I can't go on* Friday'—I see! *I can't go on*?"

Miss Marple beamed on me.

"Exactly. Mr. Symmington came across such a message and saw its possibilities. He tore off the words he wanted for when the time came—a message genuinely in his wife's handwriting."

"Was there any further brilliance on my part?" I asked.

Miss Marple twinkled at me.

"You put me on the track, you know. You assembled those facts together for me—in sequence—and on top of it you told me the most important thing of all—that Elsie Holland had never received any anonymous letters."

"Do you know," I said, "last night I thought that *she* was the letter writer and that that was why there had been no letters written to her?"

"Oh dear me, no. . . .The person who writes anonymous letters practically always sends them to herself as well. That's part of the—well, the excitement, I suppose. No, no, the fact interested me for *quite* another reason. It was really, you see, Mr. Symmington's one weakness. He couldn't bring himself to write a foul letter to the girl he loved. It's a very interesting sidelight on human nature—and a credit to him, in a way—but it's where he gave himself away."

Joanna said:

"And he killed Agnes? But surely that was quite unnecessary?"

"Perhaps it was, but what you don't realise, my dear (not having killed anyone), is that your judgment is distorted afterwards and everything seems exaggerated. No doubt he heard the girl telephoning to Partridge, saying she'd been worried every since Mrs. Symmington's death, that there was something she didn't understand. He can't take any chances—this stupid, foolish girl has seen *something*, knows something."

"Yet apparently he was at his office all that afternoon?"

"I should imagine he killed her before he went. Miss Holland was in the dining-room and kitchen. He just went out into the hall, opened and shut the front door as though he had gone out, then slipped into the little cloakroom. When only Agnes was left in the house, he probably rang the front-door bell, slipped back into the cloakroom, came out behind her and hit her on the head as she was opening the front door, and then after thrusting the body into the cupboard, he hurried along to his office, arriving just a little late if anyone had happened to notice it, but they probably didn't. You see, no one was suspecting a *man*."

"Abominable brute," said Mrs. Dane Calthrop.

"You're not sorry for him, Mrs. Dane Calthrop?" I inquired.

"Not in the least. Why?"

"I'm glad to hear it, that's all."

Joanna said:

"But why Aimée Griffith. I know that the police have found

the pestle taken from Owen's dispensary—and the skewer too. I suppose it's not so easy for a man to return things to kitchen drawers. And guess where they were? Superintendent Nash only told me just now when I met him on my way here. In one of those musty old deed-boxes in his office. Estate of Sir Jasper Harrington-West, deceased."

"Poor Jasper," said Mrs. Dane Calthrop. "He was a cousin of mine. Such a correct old boy. He would have had a fit!"

"Wasn't it madness to keep them?" I asked.

"Probably madder to throw them away," said Mrs. Dane Calthrop. "No one had any suspicions about Symmington."

"He didn't strike her with the pestle," said Joanna. "There was a clock weight there, too, with hair and blood on it. He pinched the pestle, they think, on the day Aimée was arrested, and hid the book pages in her house. And that brings me back to my original question. What about Aimée Griffith? The police actually *saw* her write that letter."

"Yes, of course," said Miss Marple. "She did write *that* letter."

"But why?"

"Oh, my dear, surely you have realised that Miss Griffith has been in love with Symmington all her life?"

"Poor thing!" said Mrs. Dane Calthrop mechanically.

"They'd always been good friends, and I dare say she thought, after Mrs. Symmington's death, that some day, perhaps—well——" Miss Marple coughed delicately. "And then the gossip began spreading about Elsie Holland and I expect that upset her badly. She thought of the girl as a designing minx worming her way into Symmington's affections and quite unworthy of him. And so, I think, she succumbed to temptation. Why not add one more anonymous letter, and frighten the girl out of the place? It must have seemed quite safe to her and she took, as she thought, every precaution."

"Well?" said Joanna. "Finish the story."

"I should imagine," said Miss Marple slowly, "that when Miss Holland showed that letter to Symmington he realised at once who had written it, and he saw a chance to finish the case once and for all, and make himself safe. Not very nice, no, not very nice, but he was frightened, you see. The police wouldn't be satisfied until they'd got the anonymous letter-writer. When he took the letter down to the police and he found they'd actually seen Aimée writing it, he felt he'd got a chance in a thousand of finishing the whole thing.

"He took the family to tea there that afternoon and as he came from the office with his attaché case, he could easily bring the torn-out book pages to hide under the stairs and clinch the case. Hiding them under the stairs was a neat touch. It recalled the disposal of Agnes's body, and, from the practical point of view, it was very easy for him. When he followed Aimée and the police, just a minute or two in the hall passing through would be enough."

"All the same," I said, "there's one thing I can't forgive you for, Miss Marple—roping in Megan."

Miss Marple put down her crochet which she had resumed. She looked at me over her spectacles and her eyes were stern.

"My dear young man, *something* had to be done. There was no evidence against this very clever and unscrupulous man. I needed someone to help me, someone of high courage and good brains. I found the person I needed."

"It was very dangerous for her."

"Yes, it was dangerous, but we are not put into this world, Mr. Burton, to avoid danger when an innocent fellow-creature's life is at stake. You understand me?"

I understood.

15

MORNING IN the High Street.

Miss Emily Barton comes out of the grocer's with her shopping bag. Her cheeks are pink and her eyes are excited.

"Oh, dear, Mr. Burton, I really am in such a flutter. To think I really am going on a cruise at last!"

"I hope you'll enjoy it."

"Oh, I'm sure I shall. I should never have dared to go by myself. It does seem so *providential* the way everything has turned out. For a long time I've felt that I ought to part with Little Furze, that my means were really *too* straitened but I couldn't bear the idea of *strangers* there. But now that you have bought it and are going to live there with Megan—it is quite different. And then dear Aimée, after her terrible ordeal, not quite knowing what to do with herself, and her brother getting married (how nice to think you have *both* settled down with us!) and agreeing to come with me. We mean to be away quite a long time. We might even"—Miss Emily dropped her voice—"*go round the world*! And Aimée is so splendid and so practical. I really do think, don't you, that everything turns out for the *best*?"

Just for a fleeting moment I thought of Mrs. Symmington and Agnes Woddell in their graves in the churchyard and wondered if they would agree, and then I remembered that Agnes's boy hadn't been very fond of her and that Mrs. Symmington hadn't been very nice to Megan and, what the hell? we've all got to die some time! And I agreed with happy Miss Emily that everything was for the best in the best of possible worlds.

I went along the High Street and in at the Symmingtons' gate and Megan came out to meet me.

It was not a romantic meeting because an outsize Old English sheepdog came out with Megan and nearly knocked me over with his ill-timed exuberance.

"Isn't he *adorable*?" said Megan.

"A little overwhelming. Is he ours?"

"Yes, he's a wedding present from Joanna.. We *have* had nice wedding presents, haven't we? That fluffy woolly thing that we don't know what it's for from Miss Marple, and the lovely Crown Derby tea-set from Mr. Pye, and Elsie sent me a toast-rack——"

"How typical," I interjected.

"And she's got a post with a dentist and is very happy. And—where was I?"

"Enumerating wedding presents. Don't forget if you change your mind you'll have to send them all back."

"I shan't change my mind. What else have we got? Oh, yes, Mrs. Dane Calthrop has sent an Egyptian scarab."

"Original woman," I said.

"Oh! Oh! but you don't know the best. *Partridge* has actually sent me a present. It's the most hideous teacloth you've ever seen. But I think she *must* like me now because she says she embroidered it all with her own hands."

"In a design of sour grapes and thistles, I suppose?"

"No, true lovers' knots."

"Dear, dear," I said. "Partridge *is* coming on."

Megan had dragged me into the house.

She said:

"There's just one thing I can't make out. Besides the dog's own collar and lead, Joanna has sent an extra collar and lead. What do you think that's for?"

"That," I said, "is Joanna's little joke."

NEMESIS

Nemesis

AGATHA
CHRISTIE

To Daphne Honeybone

Contents

1. *Overture*

IN THE afternoons it was the custom of Miss Jane Marple to unfold her second newspaper. Two newspapers were delivered at her house every morning. The first one Miss Marple read while sipping her early morning tea, that is, if it was delivered in time. The boy who delivered the papers was notably erratic in his management of time. Frequently, too, there was either a new boy or a boy who was acting temporarily as a stand-in for the first one. And each one would have ideas of his own as to the geographical route that he should take in delivering. Perhaps it varied monotony for him. But those customers who were used to reading their paper early so that they could snap up the more saucy items in the day's news before departing for their bus, train or other means of progress to the day's work were annoyed if the papers were late, though the middle-aged and elderly ladies who resided peacefully in St Mary Mead often preferred to read a newspaper propped up on their breakfast table.

Today, Miss Marple had absorbed the front page and a few other items in the daily paper that she had nicknamed "the Daily All-Sorts", this being a slightly satirical allusion to the fact that her paper, the *Daily Newsgiver*, owing to a change of proprietor, to her own and to other of her friends' great annoyance, now provided articles on men's tailoring, women's dress, female heart-throbs, competitions for children, and complaining letters from women and had managed pretty well to shove any real news off any part of it but the front page, or to some obscure corner where it was impossible to find it. Miss Marple, being old-fashioned, preferred her newspapers to *be* newspapers and give you news.

In the afternoon, having finished her luncheon, treated herself to twenty minutes' nap in a specially purchased, upright armchair which catered for the demands of her rheumatic back, she had opened *The Times* which lent itself still to a more leisurely perusal. Not that *The Times* was what it used to be. The maddening thing about *The Times* was that you couldn't *find* anything any more. Instead of going through from the front page and knowing where everything else was so that you passed easily to any special articles on subjects in which you were interested, there were now extraordinary interruptions in this time-honoured programme. Two pages were suddenly devoted to travel in Capri with illustrations. Sport appeared with far more prominence than it had ever had in the old days. Court news and obituaries were a little more faithful to routine. The births, marriages and deaths which had at one time occupied Miss Marple's attention first of all owing to their prominent position had migrated to a different part of *The Times*, though of late, Miss Marple noted, they had come almost permanently to rest on the back page.

Miss Marple gave her attention first to the main news on the front page. She did not linger long on that because it was equivalent to what she had already read this morning, though possibly couched in a slightly more dignified manner. She cast her eye down the table of contents. Articles, comments, science, sport; then she pursued her usual plan, turned the paper over and had a quick run down the births, marriages and deaths, after which she proposed to turn to the page given to correspondence, where she nearly always found something to enjoy; from that she passed on to the Court Circular, on which page today's news from the Sale Rooms could also be found. A short article on Science was often placed there but she did not propose to read that. It seldom made sense to her.

Having turned the page over as usual to the births, marriages and deaths, Miss Marple thought to herself, as so often before—

"It's sad really, but nowadays one is only interested in the *deaths*!"

People had babies, but the people who had babies were not likely to be even known by name to Miss Marple. If there had been a column dealing with babies labelled as grandchildren, there might have been some chance of a pleasurable recognition.

She might have thought to herself,

"Really, Mary Prendergast has had a *third* granddaughter!", though even that perhaps might have been a bit remote.

She skimmed down Marriages, also with not a very close survey, because most of her old friends' daughters or sons had married some years ago already. She came to the Deaths column and gave that her more serious attention. Gave it enough, in fact, so as to be sure she would not miss a name. Alloway, Angopastro, Arden, Barton, Bedshaw, Burgoweisser—(dear me, what a *German* name, but he seemed to be late of Leeds). Carpenter, Camperdown, Clegg. Clegg? Now was that one of the Cleggs she knew? No, it didn't seem to be. Janet Clegg. Somewhere in Yorkshire. McDonald, McKenzie, Nicholson, Nicholson? No. Again not a Nicholson she knew. Ogg, Ormerod,—that must be one of the aunts, she thought. Yes, probably so. Linda Ormerod. No, she hadn't known her. Quantril? Dear me, that must be Elizabeth Quantril. Eighty-five. Well, really! She had thought Elizabeth Quantril had died some years ago. Fancy her having lived so long! So delicate she'd always been, too. Nobody had expected *her* to make old bones. Race, Radley, Rafiel. Rafiel? Something stirred. That name was familiar. Rafiel. Belford Park, Maidstone. Belford Park, Maidstone. No, she couldn't recall that address. No flowers. Jason Rafiel. Oh well, an unusual name. She supposed she'd just heard it somewhere. Ross-Perkins. Now that might be—no, it wasn't. Ryland? Emily Ryland. No. No, she'd never known an Emily Ryland. *Deeply loved by her husband and children*. Well, very nice or very sad. Whichever way you liked to look at it.

Miss Marple laid down her paper, glancing idly through the crossword while she puzzled to remember why the name Rafiel was familiar to her.

"It will come to me," said Miss Marple, knowing from long experience the way old people's memories worked.

"It'll come to me, I have no doubt."

She glanced out of the window towards the garden, withdrew her gaze and tried to put the garden out of her mind. Her garden had been the source of great pleasure and also a great deal of hard work to Miss Marple for many, many years. And now, owing to the fussiness of doctors, working in the garden was forbidden to her. She'd once tried to fight this ban, but had come to the conclusion that she had, after all, better do as she was told. She had arranged her chair at such an angle as not to be easy to look out in the garden unless she definitely and clearly wished to see something in particular. She sighed, picked up her knitting bag and took out a small child's woolly jacket in process of coming to a conclusion. The back was done and the front. Now she would have to get on with the sleeves. Sleeves were always boring. Two sleeves, both alike. Yes, very boring. Pretty coloured pink wool, however. Pink wool. Now wait a minute, where did that fit in? Yes—yes—it fitted in with that name she'd just read in the paper. Pink wool. A blue sea. A Caribbean sea. A sandy beach. Sunshine. Herself knitting and—why, of course, Mr Rafiel. That trip she had made to the Caribbean. The island of St Honoré. A treat from her nephew Raymond. And she remembered Joan, her niece-in-law, Raymond's wife, saying:

"Don't get mixed up in any more murders, Aunt Jane. It isn't good for you."

Well, she hadn't *wished* to get mixed up in any murders, but it just happened. That was all. Simply because of an elderly Major with a glass eye who had insisted on telling her some very long and boring stories. Poor Major—now what was *his* name? She'd forgotten that now. Mr Rafiel and his secretary, Mrs—Mrs Walters, yes, Esther Walters, and his masseur-attendant, Jackson. It all came back. Well, well. Poor Mr Rafiel. So Mr Rafiel was dead. He had known he was going to die before very long. He had practically told her so. It seemed as though he had lasted longer than the doctors had thought. He was a strong man, an obstinate man—a very rich man.

Miss Marple remained in thought, her knitting needles working regularly, but her mind not really on her knitting. Her mind was on the late Mr Rafiel, and remembering what she could remember about him. Not an easy man to forget, really. She could conjure his appearance up mentally quite well. Yes, a very definite personality, a difficult man, an irritable man, shockingly rude sometimes. Nobody ever resented his being rude, though. She remembered that also. They didn't resent his being rude because he was so rich. Yes, he had been very rich. He had had his secretary with him and a valet attendant, a qualified masseur. He had not been able to get about very well without help.

Rather a doubtful character that nurse-attendant had been, Miss Marple thought. Mr Rafiel had been very rude to him sometimes. He had never seemed to mind. And that, again, of course was because Mr Rafiel was so rich.

"Nobody else would pay him half what I do," Mr Rafiel had said, "and he knows it. He's good at his job, though."

Miss Marple wondered whether Jackson?—Johnson? had stayed on with Mr Rafiel. Stayed on for what must have been—another year? A year and three or four months. She thought probably not. Mr Rafiel was one who liked a change. He got tired of people, tired of their ways, tired of their faces, tired of their voices.

Miss Marple understood that. She had felt the same sometimes. That companion of hers, that nice, attentive, maddening woman with her cooing voice.

"Ah," said Miss Marple, "what a change for the better since—" oh dear, she'd forgotten *her* name now—Miss—Miss Bishop?—no, not Miss Bishop, of course not. Why had she thought of the name Bishop. Oh dear, how difficult it was.

Her mind went back to Mr Rafiel and to—no, it wasn't Johnson, it had been Jackson, Arthur Jackson.

"Oh, dear," said Miss Marple again, "I always get *all* the names wrong. And of course, it was Miss *Knight* I was thinking of. Not Miss *Bishop*. Why do I think of her as Miss Bishop?" The answer came to her. Chess, of course. A chess piece. A knight. A bishop.

"I shall be calling her Miss Castle next time I think of her, I suppose, or Miss Rook. Though, really, she's not the sort of person who would ever rook anybody. No, indeed. And now what was the name of that nice secretary that Mr Rafiel had. Oh yes, Esther Walters. That was right. I wonder what has happened to Esther Walters? She'd inherited money? She would probably inherit money now,"

Mr Rafiel, she remembered, had told her something about that, or she had—oh, dear, what a muddle things were when you tried to remember with any kind of exactitude. Esther Walters. It had hit her badly, that business in the Caribbean, but she would have got over it. She'd been a widow, hadn't she? Miss Marple hoped that Esther Walters had married again, some nice, kindly, reliable man. It seemed faintly unlikely. Esther Walters, she thought, had had rather a genius for liking the wrong kind of men to marry.

Miss Marple went back to thinking about Mr Rafiel. No flowers, it had said. Not that she herself would have dreamed of sending flowers to Mr Rafiel. He could buy up all the nurseries in England if he'd wanted to. And anyway, they hadn't been on those terms. They hadn't been—friends, or on terms of affection. They had been—what was the word she wanted?—allies. Yes, they had been allies for a very short time. A very exciting time. And he had been an ally worth having. She had known so. She'd known it as she had gone running through a dark, tropical night in the Caribbean and had come to him. Yes, she remembered, she'd been wearing that pink wool—what used they to call them when she was young?—a fascinator. That nice pink wool kind of shawl-scarf that she'd put round her head, and he had looked at her and laughed, and later when she had said—she smiled at the remembrance—one word she had used and he had laughed, but he hadn't laughed in the end. No, he'd done what she asked him and therefore—"Ah!" Miss Marple sighed, it had been, she had to admit it, all very exciting. And she'd never told her nephew or dear Joan about it because, after all, it was what they'd told her not to do, wasn't it? Miss Marple nodded her head. Then she murmured softly,

"Poor Mr Rafiel, I hope he didn't—suffer."

Probably not. Probably he'd been kept by expensive doctors under sedatives, easing the end. He had suffered a great deal in those weeks in the Caribbean. He'd nearly always been in pain.

A brave man. She was sorry he was dead because she thought that though he'd been elderly and an invalid and ill, the world had lost something through his going. She had no idea what he could have been like in business. Ruthless, she thought, and rude and over-mastering and aggressive. A great attacker. But—but a good friend, she thought. And somewhere in him a deep kind of kindness that he was very careful never to show on the surface. A man she admired and respected. Well, she was sorry he was gone and she hoped he hadn't minded too much and that his passing had been easy. And now he would be cremated no doubt and put in some large, handsome marble vault. She didn't even know if he'd been married. He had never mentioned a wife, never mentioned children. A lonely man? Or had his life been so full that he hadn't needed to feel lonely. She wondered.

She sat there quite a long time that afternoon, wondering about Mr Rafiel. She had never expected to see him again after she had returned to England and she never *had* seen him again. Yet in some queer way she could at any moment have felt she was in touch with him. If he had approached her or had suggested that they meet again, feeling perhaps a bond because of a life that had been saved between them, or of some other bond. A bond—

"Surely," said Miss Marple, aghast at an idea that had come into her mind, "there can't be a bond of *ruthlessness* between us?" Was she, Jane Marple—could she ever be—ruthless? "D'you know," said Miss Marple to herself, "it's extraordinary, I never thought about it before. I believe, you know, I *could* be ruthless . . ."

The door opened and a dark, curly head was popped in. It was Cherry, the welcome successor to Miss Bishop—Miss Knight.

"Did you say something?" said Cherry.

"I was speaking to myself," said Miss Marple, "I just wondered if I could ever be ruthless."

"What, you?" said Cherry. "Never! You're kindness itself."

"All the same," said Miss Marple, "I believe I *could* be ruthless if there was due cause."

"What would you call due cause?"

"In the cause of justice," said Miss Marple.

"You did have it in for little Gary Hopkins I must say," said Cherry. "When you caught him torturing his cat that day. Never knew you had it in you to go for anyone like that! Scared him stiff, you did. He's never forgotten it."

"I hope he hasn't tortured any more cats."

"Well, he's made sure you weren't about if he did," said Cherry. "In fact I'm not at all sure as there isn't other boys as got scared. Seeing you with your wool and the pretty things you knits and all that—anyone would think you were gentle as a lamb. But there's times I could say you'd behave like a lion if you was goaded into it."

Miss Marple looked a little doubtful. She could not quite see herself in the rôle in which Cherry was now casting her. Had she ever—she paused on the reflection, recalling various moments;—there had been intense irritation with Miss Bishop—Knight. (Really, she must *not* forget names in this way.) But her irritation had shown itself in more or less ironical remarks. Lions, presumably, did not use irony. There was nothing ironical about a lion. It sprang. It roared. It used its claws, presumably it took large bites at its prey.

"Really," said Miss Marple, "I don't think I have ever behaved *quite* like that."

Walking slowly along her garden that evening with the usual feelings of vexation rising in her, Miss Marple considered the point again. Possibly the sight of a plant of snapdragons recalled it to her mind. Really, she had *told* old George again and again that she only wanted sulphur-coloured antirrhinums, *not* that rather ugly purple shade that gardeners always seemed so fond of. "Sulphur yellow," said Miss Marple aloud.

Someone the other side of the railing that abutted on the lane past her house turned her head and spoke.

"I beg your pardon? You said something?"

"I was talking to myself, I'm afraid," said Miss Marple, turning to look over the railing.

This was someone she did not know, and she knew most people in St Mary Mead. Knew them by sight even if not personally. It was a thickset woman in a shabby but tough tweed skirt, and wearing good country shoes. She wore an emerald pullover and a knitted woollen scarf.

"I'm afraid one does at my age," added Miss Marple.

"Nice garden you've got here," said the other woman.

"Not particularly nice now," said Miss Marple. "When I could attend to it myself—"

"Oh I know. I understand just what you feel. I suppose you've got one of those—I have a lot of names for them, mostly very rude—elderly chaps who say they know all about gardening. Sometimes they do, sometimes they don't know a thing about it. They come and have a lot of cups of tea and do a little very mild weeding. They're quite nice, some of them, but all the same it does make one's temper rise." She added, "I'm quite a keen gardener myself."

"Do you live here?" asked Miss Marple, with some interest.

"Well, I'm boarding with a Mrs Hastings. I think I've heard her speak of you. You're Miss Marple, aren't you?"

"Oh yes."

"I've come as a sort of companion-gardener. My name is Bartlett, by the way. Miss Bartlett. There's not really much to do there," said Miss Bartlett. "She goes in for annuals and all that. Nothing you can really get your teeth into." She opened her mouth and showed her teeth when making this remark. "Of course I do a few odd jobs as well. Shopping, you know, and things like that. Anyway, if you want any time put in here, I could put in an hour or two for you. I'd say I might be better than any chap you've got now."

"That would be easy," said Miss Marple. "I like flowers best. Don't care so much for vegetables."

"I do vegetables for Mrs Hastings. Dull but necessary. Well, I'll be getting along." Her eyes swept over Miss Marple from head to foot, as though memorizing her, then she nodded cheerfully and tramped off.

Mrs Hastings? Miss Marple couldn't remember the name of any Mrs Hastings. Certainly Mrs Hastings was not an old friend. She had certainly never been a gardening chum. Ah, of course, it was probably those newly built houses at the end of Gibraltar Road. Several families had moved in in the last year. Miss Marple sighed, looked again with annoyance at the antirrhinums, saw several weeds which she yearned to root up, one or two exuberant suckers she would like to attack with her secateurs, and finally, sighing, and manfully resisting temptation, she made a detour round by the lane and returned to her house. Her mind recurred again to Mr Rafiel. They had been, he and she,—what was the title of that book they used to quote so much when she was young? *Ships that pass in the night.* Rather apt it was really, when she came to think of it. Ships that pass in the night . . . It was in the night that she had gone to him to ask—no, to demand—help. To insist, to say no time must be lost. And he had agreed, and put things in train at once! Perhaps she *had* been rather lion-like on that occasion? No. No, that was quite wrong. It had not been anger she had felt. It had been insistence on something that was absolutely imperative to be put in hand at once. And he'd understood.

Poor Mr Rafiel. The ship that had passed in the night had been an interesting ship. Once you got used to his being rude, he might have been quite an agreeable man? No! She shook her head. Mr Rafiel could never have been an agreeable man. Well, she must put Mr Rafiel out of her head.

Ships that pass in the night, and speak each other in passing;
Only a signal shown and a distant voice in the darkness.

She would probably never think of him again. She would look out perhaps to see if there was an obituary of him in *The Times*. But she did not think it was very likely. He was not a very well known character, she thought. Not famous. He had just been very rich. Of course, many people did have obituaries in the paper just because they were very rich; but she thought that Mr Rafiel's richness would possibly not have been of that kind. He had not been prominent in any great industry, he had not been a great financial genius, or a noteworthy banker. He had just all his life made enormous amounts of money . . .

2. *Code Word Nemesis*

i

IT WAS about a week or so after Mr Rafiel's death that Miss Marple picked up a letter from her breakfast tray, and looked at it for a moment before opening it. The other two letters that had come by this morning's post were bills, or just possibly receipts for bills. In either case they were not of any particular interest. This letter might be.

A London postmark, typewritten address, a long, good quality envelope. Miss Marple slit it neatly with the paper knife she always kept handy on her tray. It was headed, Messrs Broadribb and Schuster, Solicitors and Notaries Public, with an address in Bloomsbury. It asked her, in suitable courteous and legal phraseology, to call upon them one day in the following week, at their office, to discuss a proposition that might be to her advantage. Thursday, the 24th was suggested. If that date was not convenient, perhaps she would let them know what date she would be likely to be in London in the near future. They added that they were the solicitors to the late Mr Rafiel, with whom they understood she had been acquainted.

Miss Marple frowed in some slight puzzlement. She got up rather more slowly than usual, thinking about the letter she had received. She was escorted downstairs by Cherry, who was meticulous in hanging about in the hall so as to make sure that Miss Marple did not come to grief walking by herself down the staircase, which was of the old-fashioned kind which turned a sharp corner in the middle of its run.

"You take very good care of me, Cherry," said Miss Marple.

"Got to," said Cherry, in her usual idiom. "Good people are scarce."

"Well, thank you for the compliment," said Miss Marple,

arriving safely with her last foot on the ground floor.

"Nothing the matter, is there?" asked Cherry. "You look a bit rattled like, if you know what I mean."

"No, nothing's the matter," said Miss Marple. "I had rather an unusual letter from a firm of solicitors."

"Nobody is suing you for anything, are they?" said Cherry, who was inclined to regard solicitors' letters as invariably associated with disaster of some kind.

"Oh no, I don't think so," said Miss Marple. "Nothing of that kind. They just asked me to call upon them next week in London."

"Perhaps you've been left a fortune," said Cherry, hopefully.

"That, I think, is *very* unlikely," said Miss Marple.

"Well, you never know," said Cherry.

Settling herself in her chair, and taking her knitting out of its embroidered knitting bag, Miss Marple considered the possibility of Mr Rafiel having left her a fortune. It seemed even more unlikely than when Cherry had suggested it. Mr Rafiel, she thought, was not that kind of a man.

It was not possible for her to go on the date suggested. She was attending a meeting of the Women's Institute to discuss the raising of a sum for building a small additional couple of rooms. But she wrote, naming a day in the following week. In due course her letter was answered and the appointment definitely confirmed. She wondered what Messrs Broadribb and Schuster were like. The letter had been signed by J. R. Broadribb who was, apparently, the senior partner. It was possible, Miss Marple thought, that Mr Rafiel *might* have left her some small memoir or souvenir in his will. Perhaps some book on rare flowers that had been in his library and which he thought would please an old lady who was keen on gardening. Or perhaps a cameo brooch which had belonged to some great-aunt of his. She amused herself by these fancies. They were only fancies, she thought, because in either case it would merely be a case of the Executors—if these lawyers were the Executors—forwarding her by post any such object. They would not have wanted an interview.

"Oh well," said Miss Marple, "I shall know next Tuesday."

ii

"Wonder what she'll be like," said Mr Broadribb to Mr Schuster, glancing at the clock as he did so.

"She's due in a quarter of an hour," said Mr Schuster. "Wonder if she'll be punctual?"

"Oh, I should think so. She's elderly, I gather, and much more punctilious than the young scatter-brains of to-day."

"Fat or thin, I wonder?" said Mr Schuster.

Mr Broadribb shook his head.

"Didn't Rafiel ever describe her to you?" asked Mr Schuster.

"He was extraordinarily cagey in everything he said about her."

"The whole thing seems very odd to me," said Mr Schuster. "If we only knew a bit more about what it all meant . . ."

"It might be," said Mr Broadribb thoughtfully, "something to do with Michael."

"What? After all these years? Couldn't be. What put that into your head? Did he mention—"

"No, he didn't mention anything. Gave me no clue at all as to what was in his mind. Just gave me instructions."

"Think he was getting a bit eccentric and all that towards the end?"

"Not in the least. Mentally he was as brilliant as ever. His physical ill-health never affected his brain, anyway. In the last two months of his life he made an extra two hundred thousand pounds. Just like that."

"He had a *flair*," said Mr Schuster with due reverence. "Certainly, he always had a flair."

"A great financial brain," said Mr Broadribb, also in a tone of reverence suitable to the sentiment. "Not many like him, more's the pity."

A buzzer went on the table. Mr Schuster picked up the receiver. A female voice said,

"Miss Jane Marple is here to see Mr Broadribb by appointment."

Mr Schuster looked at his partner, raising an eyebrow for an affirmative or a negative. Mr Broadribb nodded.

"Show her up," said Mr Schuster. And he added, "Now we'll see."

Miss Marple entered a room where a middle-aged gentleman with a thin, spare body and a long rather melancholy face rose to greet her. This apparently was Mr Broadribb, whose appearance somewhat contradicted his name. With him was a rather younger middle-aged gentleman of definitely more ample proportions. He had black hair, small keen eyes and a tendency to a double chin.

"My partner, Mr Schuster," Mr Broadribb presented.

"I hope you didn't feel the stairs too much," said Mr Schuster. "Seventy if she is a day—nearer eighty perhaps," he was thinking in his own mind.

"I always get a little breathless going upstairs."

"An old-fashioned building this," said Mr Broadribb apologetically. "No lift. Ah well, we are a very long established firm and we don't go in for as many of the modern gadgets as perhaps our clients expect of us."

"This room has very pleasant proportions," said Miss Marple, politely.

She accepted the chair that Mr Broadribb drew forward for her. Mr Schuster, in an unobtrusive sort of way, left the room.

"I hope that chair is comfortable," said Mr Broadribb. "I'll pull that curtain slightly, shall I? You may feel the sun a little too much in your eyes."

"Thank you," said Miss Marple, gratefully.

She sat there, upright as was her habit. She wore a light tweed suit, a string of pearls and a small velvet toque. To himself Mr Broadribb was saying, "The Provincial Lady. A good type. Fluffy old girl. May be scatty—may not. Quite a shrewd eye. I wonder where Rafiel came across her. Somebody's aunt, perhaps, up from the country?" While these thoughts passed through his head, he was making the kind of introductory small talk relating to the weather, the unfortunate effects of late frosts early in the year and such other remarks as he considered suitable.

Miss Marple made the necessary responses and sat placidly awaiting the opening of preliminaries to the meeting.

"You will be wondering what all this is about," said Mr

Broadribb, shifting a few papers in front of him and giving her a suitable smile. "You've heard, no doubt, of Mr Rafiel's death, or perhaps you saw it in the paper."

"I saw it in the paper," said Miss Marple.

"He was, I understand, a friend of yours."

"I met him first just over a year ago," said Miss Marple. "In the West Indies," she added.

"Ah. I remember. He went out there, I believe, for his health. It did him some good, perhaps, but he was already a very ill man, badly crippled, as you know."

"Yes," said Miss Marple.

"You knew him well?"

"No," said Miss Marple, "I would not say that. We were fellow visitors in a hotel. We had occasional conversations. I never saw him again after my return to England. I live very quietly in the country, you see, and I gather that he was completely absorbed in business."

"He continued transacting business right up—well, I could almost say right up to the day of his death," said Mr Broadribb. "A very fine financial brain."

"I am sure that was so," said Miss Marple. "I realized quite soon that he was a—well, a very remarkable character altogether."

"I don't know if you have any idea—whether you've been given any idea at some time by Mr Rafiel—as to what this proposition is that I have been instructed to put up to you?"

"I cannot imagine," said Miss Marple, "what possible kind of proposition Mr Rafiel might have wanted to put up to me. It seems most unlikely."

"He had a very high opinion of you."

"That is kind of him, but hardly justified," said Miss Marple. "I am a very simple person."

"As you no doubt realize, he died a very rich man. The provisions of his Will are on the whole fairly simple. He had already made dispositions of his fortune some time before his death. Trusts and other beneficiary arrangements."

"That is, I believe, very usual procedure nowadays," said Miss Marple, "though I am not at all cognizant of financial matters myself."

"The purpose of this appointment," said Mr Broadribb, "is that I am instructed to tell you that a sum of money has been laid aside to become yours absolutely at the end of one year, but conditional on your accepting a certain proposition, with which I am to make you acquainted."

He took from the table in front of him a long envelope. It was sealed. He passed it across the table to her.

"It would be better, I think, that you should read for yourself of what this consists. There is no hurry. Take your time."

Miss Marple took her time. She availed herself of a small paper knife which Mr Broadribb handed to her, slit up the envelope, took out the enclosure, one sheet of typewriting, and read it. She folded it up again, then re-read it and looked at Mr Broadribb.

"This is hardly very definite. Is there no more definite elucidation of any kind?"

"Not so far as I am concerned. I was to hand you this, and tell you the amount of the legacy. The sum in question is twenty thousand pounds free of legacy duty."

Miss Marple sat looking at him. Surprise had rendered her speechless. Mr Broadribb said no more for the moment. He was watching her closely. There was no doubt of her surprise. It was obviously the last thing Miss Marple had expected to hear. Mr Broadribb wondered what her first words would be. She looked at him with the directness, the severity that one of his own aunts might have done. When she spoke it was almost accusingly.

"That is a very large sum of money," said Miss Marple.

"Not quite so large as it used to be," said Mr Broadribb (and just restrained himself from saying, "Mere chicken feed nowadays").

"I must admit," said Miss Marple, "that I am amazed. Frankly, quite amazed."

She picked up the document and read it carefully through again.

"I gather you know the terms of this?" she said.

"Yes. It was dictated to me personally by Mr Rafiel."

"Did he not give you any explanation of it?"

"No, he did not."

"You suggested, I suppose, that it might be better if he did," said Miss Marple. There was a slight acidity in her voice now.

Mr Broadribb smiled faintly.

"You are quite right. That is what I did. I said that you might find it difficult to—oh, to understand exactly what he was driving at."

"Very remarkable," said Miss Marple.

"There is no need, of course," said Mr Broadribb, "for you to give me an answer now."

"No," said Miss Marple, "I should have to reflect upon this."

"It is, as you have pointed out, quite a substantial sum of money."

"I am old," said Miss Marple. "Elderly, we say, but old is a better word. Definitely old. It is both possible and indeed probable that I might not live as long as a year to earn this money, in the rather doubtful case that I *was* able to earn it?"

"Money is not to be despised at any age," said Mr Broadribb.

"I could benefit certain charities in which I have an interest," said Miss Marple, "and there are always people. People whom one wishes one could do a little something for but one's own funds do not admit of it. And then I will not pretend that there are not pleasures and desires—things that one has not been able to indulge in or to afford—I think Mr Rafiel knew quite well that to be able to do so, quite unexpectedly, would give an elderly person a great deal of pleasure."

"Yes, indeed," said Mr Broadribb. "A cruise abroad, perhaps? One of these excellent *tours* as arranged nowadays. Theatres, concerts—the ability to replenish one's cellars."

"My tastes would be a little more moderate than that," said Miss Marple. "Partridges," she said thoughtfully, "it is very difficult to get partridges nowadays, and they're very expensive. I should enjoy a partridge—a whole partridge—to myself, very much. A box of *marrons glacés* are an expensive taste which I cannot often gratify. Possibly a visit to the opera. It means a car to take one to Covent Garden and back, and the expense of a night in a hotel. But I must not indulge in idle chat," she said. "I will take this back with me and reflect upon it. Really, what on earth made Mr Rafiel—you have no idea *why* he should have suggested this particular proposition, and why he should think that I could be of service to him in any way? He must have known that it was over a year, nearly two years since he had seen me and that I might have got much more feeble than I have, and much more unable to exercise such small talents as I might have. He was taking a risk. There are other people surely much better qualified to undertake an investigation of this nature?"

"Frankly, one would think so," said Mr Broadribb, "but he selected *you*, Miss Marple. Forgive me if this is idle curiosity but have you had—oh, how shall I put it?—any connection with crime or the investigation of crime?"

"Strictly speaking I should say no," said Miss Marple. "Nothing professional, that is to say. I have never been a probation officer or indeed sat as a magistrate on a Bench or been connected in any way with a detective agency. To explain to you, Mr Broadribb, which I think is only fair for me to do and which I think Mr Rafiel ought to have done, to explain it in any way all I can say is that during our stay in the West Indies, we both, Mr Rafiel and myself, had a certain connection with a crime that took place there. A rather unlikely and perplexing murder."

"And you and Mr Rafiel solved it?"

"I should not put it quite like that," said Miss Marple. "Mr Rafiel, by the force of his personality, and I, by putting together one or two obvious indications that came to my notice, were successful in preventing a second murder just as it was about to take place. I could not have done it alone, I was physically far too feeble. Mr Rafiel could not have done it alone, he was a cripple. We acted as allies, however."

"Just one other question I should like to ask you, Miss Marple. Does the word 'Nemesis' mean anything to you?"

"*Nemesis*," said Miss Marple. It was not a question. A very slow and unexpected smile dawned on her face. "Yes," she said, "it does mean something to me. It meant something to me and it meant something to Mr Rafiel. I said it to him, and he was much amused by my describing myself by that name."

Whatever Mr Broadribb had expected it was not that. He looked at Miss Marple with something of the same astonished surprise that Mr Rafiel had once felt in a bedroom by the Caribbean sea. A nice and quite intelligent old lady. But really—Nemesis!

"You feel the same, I am sure," said Miss Marple.

She rose to her feet.

"If you should find or receive any further instructions in this matter, you will perhaps let me know, Mr Broadribb. It seems to me extraordinary that there should not be *something* of that kind. This leaves me entirely in the dark really as to what Mr Rafiel is asking me to do or try to do."

"You are not acquainted with his family, his friends, his—"

"No. I told you. He was a fellow traveller in a foreign part of the world. We had a certain association as allies in a very mystifying matter. That is all." As she was about to go to the door she turned suddenly and said: "He had a secretary, Mrs Esther Walters. Would it be infringing etiquette if I asked if Mr Rafiel left her fifty thousand pounds?"

"His bequests will appear in the press," said Mr Broadribb. "I can answer your question in the affirmative. Mrs Walters's name is now Mrs Anderson, by the way. She has re-married."

"I am glad to hear that. She was a widow with one daughter, and she was a very adequate secretary, it appears. She understood Mr Rafiel very well. A nice woman. I am glad she has benefited.'

That evening, Miss Marple, sitting in her straightbacked chair, her feet stretched out to the fireplace where a small wood fire was burning owing to the sudden cold spell which, as is its habit, can always descend on England at any moment selected by itself, took once more from the long envelope the document delivered to her that morning. Still in a state of partial unbelief she read, murmuring the words here and there below her breath as though to impress them on her mind.

> "To Miss Jane Marple, resident in the village of St Mary Mead.
>
> This will be delivered to you after my death by the good offices of my solicitor, James Broadribb. He is the man I employ for dealing with such legal matters as fall in the field of my private affairs, not my business activities. He is a sound and trustworthy lawyer. Like the majority of the human race he is susceptible to the sin of curiosity. I have not satisfied his curiosity. In some respects this matter will remain between

you and myself. Our code word, my dear lady, is Nemesis. I don't think you will have forgotten in what place and in what circumstances you first spoke that word to me. In the course of my business activities over what is now quite a long life, I have learnt one thing about a man whom I wish to employ. He has to have a flair. A flair for the particular job I want him to do. It is not knowledge, it is not experience. The only word that describes it is *flair*. A natural gift for doing a certain thing.

You, my dear, if I may call you that, have a natural *flair* for justice, and that has led to your having a natural *flair* for crime. I want you to investigate a certain crime. I have ordered a certain sum to be placed so that if you accept this request and as a result of your investigation this crime is properly elucidated, the money will become yours absolutely. I have set aside a year for you to engage on this mission. You are not young, but you are, if I may say so, tough. I think I can trust a reasonable fate to keep you alive for a year at least.

I think the work involved will not be distasteful to you. You have a natural genius, I should say, for investigation. The necessary funds for what I may describe as working capital for making this investigation will be remitted to you during that period, whenever necessary. I offer this to you as an alternative to what may be your life at present.

I envisage you sitting in a chair, a chair that is agreeable and comfortable for whatever kind or form of rheumatism from which you may suffer. All persons of your age, I consider, are likely to suffer from some form of rheumatism. If this ailment affects your knees or your back, it will not be easy for you to get about much and you will spend your time mainly in knitting. I see you, as I saw you once one night as I rose from sleep disturbed by your urgency, in a cloud of pink wool.

I envisage you knitting more jackets, head scarves and a good many other things of which I do not know the name. If you prefer to continue knitting, that is your decision. If you prefer to serve the cause of justice, I hope that you may at least find it interesting.

Let justice roll down like waters
And righteousness like an everlasting stream.
Amos."

3. *Miss Marple Takes Action*

i

MISS MARPLE read this letter three times—then she laid it aside and sat frowning slightly while she considered the letter and its implications.

The first thought that came to her was that she was left with a surprising lack of definite information. Would there be any further information coming to her from Mr Broadribb? Almost certainly she felt that there would be no such thing. That would not have fitted in with Mr Rafiel's plan. Yet how on earth could Mr Rafiel expect her to do anything, to take any course of action in a matter about which she knew nothing. It was intriguing. After a few minutes more for consideration, she decided that Mr Rafiel had meant it to be intriguing. Her thoughts went back to him, for the brief time that she had known him. His disability, his bad temper, his flashes of brilliance, of occasional humour. He'd enjoy, she thought, teasing people. He had been enjoying, she felt, and this letter made it almost certain, baffling the natural curiosity of Mr Broadribb.

There was nothing in the letter he had written to her to give her the slightest clue as to what this business was all about. It was no help to her whatsoever. Mr Rafiel, she thought, had very definitely not meant it to be of any help. He had had—how could she put it?—other ideas. All the same, she could not start out into the blue knowing nothing. This could almost be described as a crossword puzzle with no clues given. There would *have* to be clues. She would *have* to know what she was wanted to do, where she was wanted to go, whether she was to solve some problem sitting in her armchair and laying aside her knitting needles in order to concentrate better. Or did Mr Rafiel intend her to take a plane or a boat to the West Indies or to South

America or to some other specially directed spot? She would either have to find out for herself what it was she was meant to do, or else she would have to receive definite instructions. He might think she had sufficient ingenuity to guess at things, to ask questions, to find out that way? No, she couldn't quite believe *that*.

"If he does think that," said Miss Marple aloud, "he's gaga. I mean, he was gaga before he died."

But she didn't think Mr Rafiel would have been gaga.

"I shall receive instructions," said Miss Marple. "But what instructions and when?"

It was only then that it occurred to her suddenly that without noticing it she had definitely accepted the mandate. She spoke aloud again, addressing the atmosphere.

"I believe in eternal life," said Miss Marple. "I don't know exactly where you are, Mr Rafiel, but I have no doubt that you are *somewhere*—I will do my best to fulfil your wishes."

ii

It was three days later when Miss Marple wrote to Mr Broadribb. It was a very short letter, keeping strictly to the point.

"Dear Mr Broadribb,

I have considered the suggestion you made to me and I am letting you know that I have decided to accept the proposal made to me by the late Mr Rafiel. I shall do my best to comply with his wishes, though I am not at all assured of success. Indeed, I hardly see how it is possible for me to be successful. I have been given no direct instructions in his letter and have not been—I think the term is briefed—*in any way*. If you have any further communication you are holding for me which sets out definite instructions, I should be glad if you will send it to me, but I imagine that as you have not done so, that is not the case.

I presume that Mr Rafiel was of sound mind and disposition when he died? I think I am justified in asking if there has been recently in his life any criminal affair in which he might possibly have been interested, either in the course of his business or in his personal relations. Has he ever expressed to you any anger or dissatisfaction with some notable miscarriage of justice about which he felt strongly? If so, I think I should be justified in asking you to let me know about it. Has any relation or connection of his suffered some hardship, lately been the victim of some unjust dealing, or what might be considered as such?

I am sure you will understand my reasons for asking these things. Indeed, Mr Rafiel himself may have expected me to do so."

iii

Mr Broadribb showed this to Mr Schuster, who leaned back in his chair and whistled.

"She's going to take it on, is she? Sporting old bean," he said. Then he added, "I suppose she knows something of what it's all about, does she?"

"Apparently not," said Mr Broadribb.

"I wish we did" said Mr Schuster. "He was an odd cuss."

"A difficult man," said Mr Broadribb.

"I haven't got the least idea,' said Mr Schuster, "have you?"

"No, I haven't," said Mr Broadribb. He added, "He didn't want me to have, I suppose."

"Well, he's made things a lot more difficult by doing that. I don't see the least chance that some old pussy from the country can interpret a dead man's brain and know what fantasy was plaguing him. You don't think he was leading her up the garden path? Having her on? Sort of joke, you know. Perhaps he thinks that she thinks she's the cat's whiskers at solving village problems, but he's going to teach her a sharp lesson——"

"No," said Mr Broadribb, "I don't quite think that. Rafiel wasn't that type of man."

"He was a mischievous devil sometimes," said Mr Schuster.

"Yes, but not—I think he was serious over this. *Something* was worrying him. In fact I'm quite sure something was worrying him."

"And he didn't tell you what it was or give you the least idea?"

"No, he didn't."

"Then how the devil can he expect——' Schuster broke off.

"He can't really have expected anything to come of this," said Mr Broadribb. "I mean, how is she going to set about it?"

"A practical joke, if you ask me."

"Twenty thousand pounds is a lot of money."

"Yes, but if he knows she can't do it?"

"No," said Mr Broadribb. "He wouldn't have been as unsporting as all that. He must think she's got a chance of doing or finding out whatever it is."

"And what do we do?"

"Wait," said Mr Broadribb. "Wait and see what happens next. After all, there has to be some development."

"Got some sealed orders somewhere, have you?"

"My dear Schuster," said Mr Broadribb, "Mr Rafiel had implicit trust in my discretion and in my ethical conduct as a lawyer. Those sealed instructions are to be opened only under certain circumstances, none of which has yet arisen."

"And never will," said Mr Schuster.

That ended the subject.

iv

Mr Broadribb and Mr Schuster were lucky in so much as they had a full professional life to lead. Miss Marple was not so fortunate. She knitted and she reflected and she also went out for walks, occasionally remonstrated with by Cherry for so doing.

"You know what the doctor said. You weren't to take too much exercise."

"I walk very slowly," said Miss Marple, "and I am not doing anything. Digging, I mean, or weeding, I just—well, I just put one foot in front of the other and wonder about things."

"What things?" asked Cherry, with some interest.

"I wish I knew," said Miss Marple, and asked Cherry to bring her an extra scarf as there was a chilly wind.

"What's fidgeting her, that's what I would like to know," said

Cherry to her husband as she set before him a Chinese plate of rice and a concoction of kidneys. "Chinese dinner," she said.

He husband nodded approval.

"You get a better cook every day," he said.

"I'm worried about her," said Cherry. "I'm worried because she's worried a bit. She had a letter and it stirred her all up."

"What she needs is to sit quiet," said Cherry's husband. "Sit quiet, take it easy, get herself new books from the library, get a friend or two to come and see her."

"She's thinking out something," said Cherry. "Sort of plan. Thinking out how to tackle something, that's how I look at it."

She broke off the conversation at this stage and took in the coffee tray and put it down by Miss Marple's side.

"Do you know a woman who lives in a new house somewhere here, she's called Mrs Hastings?" asked Miss Marple. "And someone called Miss Bartlett, I think it is, who lives with her——"

"What—do you mean the house that's been all done up and repainted at the end of the village? The people there haven't been there very long. I don't know what their names are. Why do you want to know? They're not very interesting. At least I shouldn't say they were."

"Are they related?" asked Miss Marple.

"No. Just friends, I think."

"I wonder why——" said Miss Marple, and broke off.

"You wondered why what?"

"Nothing," said Miss Marple. "Clear my little hand desk, will you, and give me my pen and the notepaper. I'm going to write a letter."

"Who to?" said Cherry, with the natural curiosity of her kind.

"To a clergyman's sister," said Miss Marple. "His name is Canon Prescott."

"That's the one you met abroad, in the West Indies, isn't it? You showed me his photo in your album."

"Yes,"

"Not feeling bad, are you? Wanting to write to a clergyman and all that?"

"I'm feeling extremely well," said Miss Marple, "and I am

anxious to get busy on something. It's just possible Miss Prescott might help."

> "Dear Miss Prescott," wrote Miss Marple, "I hope you have not forgotten me. I met you and your brother in the West Indies, if you remember, at St Honoré. I hope the dear Canon is well and did not suffer much with his asthma in the cold weather last winter.
>
> I am writing to ask you if you can possibly let me have the address of Mrs Walters—Esther Walters—whom you may remember from the Caribbean days. She was secretary to Mr Rafiel. She did give me her address at the time, but unfortunately I have mislaid it. I was anxious to write to her as I have some horticultural information which she asked me about but which I was not able to tell her at the time. I heard in a round-about way the other day that she had married again, but I don't think my informant was very certain of these facts. Perhaps you know more about her than I do.
>
> I hope this is not troubling you too much. With kind regards to your brother and best wishes to yourself,
>
> Yours sincerely,
>
> Jane Marple."

Miss Marple felt better when she had despatched this missive.

"At least," she said, "I've started *doing* something. Not that I hope much from this, but still it might help."

Miss Prescott answered the letter almost by return of post. She was a most efficient woman. She wrote a pleasant letter and enclosed the address in question.

> "I have not heard anything directly about Esther Walters," she said, "but like you I heard from a friend that they had seen a notice of her re-marriage. Her name now is, I believe, Mrs Alderson or Anderson. Her address is Winslow Lodge, near Alton, Hants. My brother sends his best wishes to you. It is sad that we live so far apart. We in the north of England and you south of London. I hope that we may meet on some occasion in the future.
>
> Yours sincerely,
>
> Joan Prescott."

"Winslow Lodge, Alton," said Miss Marple, writing it down. "Not so far away from here, really. No. Not so far away. I could—I don't know what would be the best method—possibly one of Inch's taxis. Slightly extravagant, but if anything results from it, it could be charged as expenses quite legitimately. Now do I write to her beforehand or do I leave it to chance? I think it would be better really, to leave it to chance. Poor Esther. She could hardly remember me with any affection or kindliness."

Miss Marple lost herself in a train of thought that arose from her thoughts. It was quite possible that her actions in the Caribbean had saved Esther Walters from being murdered in the not far distant future. At any rate, that was Miss Marple's belief, but probably Esther Walters had not believed any such thing. "A nice woman," said Miss Marple, uttering the words in a soft tone aloud, "a very nice woman. The kind that would so easily marry a bad lot. In fact, the sort of woman that would marry a murderer if she were ever given half a chance. I still consider," continued Miss Marple thoughtfully, sinking her voice still lower, "that I probably saved her life. In fact, I am almost sure of it, but I don't think she would agree with that point of view. She probably dislikes me very much. Which makes it more difficult to use her as a source of information. Still, one can but try. It's better than sitting here, waiting, waiting, waiting."

Was Mr Rafiel perhaps making fun of her when he had written that letter? He was not always a particularly kindly man—he could be very careless of people's feelings.

"Anyway," said Miss Marple, glancing at the clock and deciding that she would have an early night in bed, "when one thinks of things just before going to sleep, quite often ideas come. It may work out that way."

"Sleep well?" asked Cherry, as she put down an early morning tea tray on the table at Miss Marple's elbow.

"I had a curious dream," said Miss Marple.

"Nightmare?"

"No, no, nothing of that kind. I was talking to someone, not anyone I knew very well. Just talking. Then when I looked, I saw it wasn't that person at all I was talking to. It was somebody else. Very odd."

"Bit of a mix up," said Cherry, helpfully.

"It just reminded me of something," said Miss Marple, "or rather of someone I once knew. Order Inch for me, will you? To come here about half past eleven."

Inch was part of Miss Marple's past. Originally the proprietor of a cab, Mr Inch had died, been succeeded by his son "Young Inch", then aged forty-four, who had turned the family business into a garage and acquired two aged cars. On his decease the garage acquired a new owner. There had been since then Pip's Cars, James's Taxis and Arthur's Car Hire—old inhabitants still spoke of Inch.

"Not going to London, are you?"

"No, I'm not going to London. I shall have lunch perhaps in Haslemere."

"Now what are you up to now?" said Cherry, looking at her suspiciously.

"Endeavouring to meet someone by accident and make it seem purely natural," said Miss Marple. "Not really very easy, but I hope that I can manage it."

At half past eleven the taxi waited. Miss Marple instructed Cherry.

"Ring up this number, will you, Cherry? Ask if Mrs Anderson is at home. If Mrs Anderson answers or if she is going to come to the telephone, say a Mr Broadribb wants to speak to her. You," said Miss Marple, "are Mr Broadribb's secretary. If she's out, find out what time she will be in."

"And if she is in and I get her?"

"Ask what day she could arrange to meet Mr Broadribb at his office in London next week. When she tells you, make a note of it and ring off."

"The things you think of! Why all this? Why do you want *me* to do it?"

"Memory is a curious thing," said Miss Marple. "Sometimes one remembers a voice even if one hasn't heard it for over a year."

"Well, Mrs What's-a-name won't have heard mine at any time, will she?"

"No," said Miss Marple. "That is why *you* are making the call."

Cherry fulfilled her instruction. Mrs Anderson was out shopping, she learned, but would be in for lunch and all the afternoon.

"Well, that makes things easier," said Miss Marple. "Is Inch here? Ah yes. Good morning, Edward," she said, to the present driver of Arthur's taxis whose actual name was George. "Now this is where I want you to go. It ought not to take, I think, more than an hour and a half."

The expedition set off.

4. *Esther Walters*

ESTHER WALTERS came out of the Supermarket and went towards where she had parked her car. Parking grew more difficult every day, she thought. She collided with somebody, an elderly woman limping a little who was walking towards her. She apologized, and the other woman made an exclamation.

"Why, indeed, it's—surely—it's Mrs Walters, isn't it? Esther Walters? You don't remember me, I expect. Jane Marple. We met in the hotel in St Honoré, oh—quite a long time ago. A year and a half."

"Miss Marple? So it is, of course. Fancy seeing you!"

"How very nice to see you. I am lunching with some friends near here but I have to pass back through Alton later. Will you be at home this afternoon? I should so like to have a nice chat with you. It's so nice to see an old friend."

"Yes, of course. Any time after 3 o'clock."

The arrangement was ratified.

"Old Jane Marple," said Esther Anderson, smiling to herself. "Fancy her turning up. I thought she'd died a long time ago."

Miss Marple rang the bell of Winslow Lodge at 3.30 precisely. Esther opened the door to her and brought her in.

Miss Marple sat down in the chair indicated to her, fluttering a little in the restless manner that she adopted when slightly flustered. Or at any rate, when she was seeming to be slightly flustered. In this case it was misleading, since things had happened exactly as she had hoped they would happen.

"It's so nice to see you," she said to Esther. "So very nice to see you again. You know, I do think things are so very odd in this world. You hope you'll meet people again and you're quite sure you will. And then time passes and suddenly it's all such a surprise."

"And then," said Esther, "one says it's a small world, doesn't one?"

"Yes, indeed, and I think there *is* something in that. I mean, it does *seem* a very large world and the West Indies are such a very long way away from England. Well, I mean, of course, I might have met you anywhere. In London or at Harrods. On a railway station or in a bus. There are so many possibilities."

"Yes, there are a lot of possibilities," said Esther. "I certainly shouldn't have expected to meet you just here because this isn't really quite your part of the world, is it?"

"No. No, it isn't. Not that you're really so very far from St Mary Mead where I live. Actually, I think it's only about twenty-five miles. But twenty-five miles in the country, when one hasn't got a car—and of course I couldn't afford a car, and anyway, I mean, I can't drive a car—so it wouldn't be much to the point, so one really only does see one's neighbours on the bus route, or else go by taxi from the village."

"You're looking wonderfully well," said Esther.

"I was just going to say *you* were looking wonderfully well, my dear. I had no idea you lived in this part of the world."

"I have only done so for a short time. Since my marriage, actually.

"Oh, I didn't know. How interesting. I suppose I must have missed it. I always do look down the marriages."

"I've been married four or five months," said Esther. "My name is Anderson now."

"Mrs Anderson," said Miss Marple. "Yes. I must try and remember that. And your husband?"

It would be unnatural, she thought, if she did not ask about the husband. Old maids were notoriously inquisitive.

"He is an engineer," said Esther. "He runs the Time and Motion Branch. He is," she hesitated—"a little younger than I am."

"Much better," said Miss Marple immediately. "Oh, much better, my dear. In these days men age so much quicker than women. I know it used not to be said so, but actually it's true. I mean, they get more things the matter with them. I think, perhaps, they worry and work too much. And then they get high blood pressure or low blood pressure or sometimes a little heart trouble. They're rather prone to gastric ulcers, too. I don't think *we* worry so much, you know. I think we're a tougher sex."

"Perhaps we are," said Esther.

She smiled now at Miss Marple, and Miss Marple felt reassured. The last time she had seen Esther, Esther had looked as though she hated her and probably she had hated her at that moment. But now, well now, perhaps, she might even feel slightly grateful. She might have realized that she, herself, might even have been under a stone slab in a respectable churchyard, instead of living a presumably happy life with Mr Anderson.

"You look very well," she said, "and very gay."

"So do you, Miss Marple."

"Well, of course, I am rather older now. And one has so many ailments. I mean, not desperate ones, nothing of that kind, but I mean one has always some kind of rheumatism or some kind of ache and pain somewhere. One's feet are not what one would like feet to be. And there's usually one's back or a shoulder or painful hands. Oh, dear, one shouldn't talk about these things. What a very nice house you have."

"Yes, we haven't been in it very long. We moved in about four months ago."

Miss Marple looked round. She had rather thought that that was the case. She thought, too, that when they had moved in they had moved in on quite a handsome scale. The furniture was expensive, it was comfortable, comfortable and just this side of luxury. Good curtains, good covers, no particular artistic taste displayed, but then she would not have expected that. She thought she knew the reason for this appearance of prosperity. She thought it had come about in the strength of the late Mr Rafiel's handsome legacy to Esther. She was glad to think that Mr Rafiel had not changed his mind.

"I expect you saw the notice of Mr Rafiel's death," said Esther, speaking almost as if she knew what was in Miss Marple's mind.

"Yes. Yes, indeed I did. It was about a month ago now, wasn't it? I was so sorry. Very distressed really, although, well, I suppose one knew—he almost admitted it himself, didn't he? He hinted several times that it wouldn't be very long. I think he was quite a brave man about it all, don't you?"

"Yes, he was a very brave man, and a very kind one really," said Esther. "He told me, you know, when I first worked for him, that he was going to give me a very good salary but that I would have to save out of it because I needn't expect to have anything more from him. Well, I certainly didn't expect to have *anything* more from him. He was very much a man of his word, wasn't he? But apparently he changed his mind."

"Yes," said Miss Marple. "Yes. I am very glad of that. I thought perhaps—not that he, of course, said anything—but I wondered."

"He left me a very big legacy," said Esther. "A surprisingly large sum of money. It came as a very great surprise. I could hardly believe it at first."

"I think he wanted it to be a surprise to you. I think he was perhaps that kind of man," said Miss Marple. She added: "Did he leave anything to—oh, what was his name?—the man attendant, the nurse-attendant?"

"Oh, you mean Jackson? No, he didn't leave anything to Jackson, but I believe he made him some handsome presents in the last year."

"Have you ever seen anything more of Jackson?"

"No. No, I don't think I've met him once since the time out in the islands. He didn't stay with Mr Rafiel after they got back to England. I think he went to Lord somebody who lives in Jersey or Guernsey."

"I would like to have seen Mr Rafiel again," said Miss Marple. "It seems odd after we'd all been mixed up so. He and you and I and some others. And then, later, when I'd come home, when six months had passed—it occurred to me one day how closely associated we had been in our time of stress, and yet how little I really knew about Mr Rafiel. I was thinking it only the other day, after I'd seen the notice of his death. I wished I could know a little more. Where he was born, you know, and his parents. What they were like. Whether he had any children, or nephews or cousins or any family. I would so like to know."

Esther Anderson smiled slightly. She looked at Miss Marple and her expression seemed to say "Yes, I'm sure you always want to know everything of that kind about everyone you meet". But she merely said:

"No, there was really only one thing that everyone *did* know about him."

"That he was very rich," said Miss Marple immediately. "That's what you mean, isn't it? When you know that someone is very rich, somehow, well, you don't ask any more. I mean you don't ask to *know* any more. You say 'He is very rich' or you say 'He is enormously rich,' and your voice just goes down a little because it's so impressive, isn't it, when you meet someone who *is* immensely rich."

Esther laughed slightly.

"He wasn't married, was he?" asked Miss Marple. "He never mentioned a wife."

"He lost his wife many years ago. Quite soon after they were married, I believe. I believe she was much younger than he was—I think she died of cancer. Very sad."

"Had he children?"

"Oh yes, two daughters, and a son. One daughter is married and lives in America. The other daughter died young, I believe. I met the American one once. She wasn't at all like her father. Rather a quiet, depressed looking young woman." She added, "Mr Rafiel never spoke about the son. I rather think that there had been trouble there. A scandal or something of that kind. I believe he died some years ago. Anyway—his father never mentioned him."

"Oh dear. That was very sad."

"I think it happened quite a long time ago. I believe he took off for somewhere or other abroad and never came back—died out there, wherever it was."

"Was Mr Rafiel very upset about it?"

"One wouldn't know with him," said Esther. "He was the kind of man who would always decide to cut his losses. If his son turned out to be unsatisfactory, a burden instead of a blessing, I think he would just shrug the whole thing off. Do what was necessary perhaps in the way of sending him money for support, but never thinking of him again."

"One wonders," said Miss Marple. "He never spoke of him or said anything?"

"If you remember, he was a man who never said anything

much about personal feelings or his own life."

"No. No, of course not. But I thought perhaps, you having been—well, his secretary for so many years, that he might have confided any troubles to you."

"He was not a man for confiding troubles," said Esther. "If he had any, which I rather doubt. He was wedded to his business, one might say. He was father to his business and his business was the only kind of son or daughter that he had that mattered, I think. He enjoyed it all, investment, making money. Business coups——"

"Call no man happy until he is dead——" murmured Miss Marple, repeating the words in the manner of one pronouncing them as a kind of slogan, which indeed they appeared to be in these days, or so she would have said.

"So there was nothing especially worrying him, was there, before his death?"

"No. Why should you think so?" Esther sounded surprised.

"Well, I didn't actually think so," said Miss Marple, "I just wondered because things do worry people more when they are—I won't say getting old—because he really wasn't old, but I mean things worry you more when you are laid up and can't do as much as you did and have to take things easy. Then worries just come into your mind and make themselves *felt*."

"Yes, I know what you mean," said Esther. "But I don't think Mr Rafiel was like that. Anyway," she added, "I ceased being his secretary some time ago. Two or three months after I met Edmund."

"Ah yes. Your husband. Mr Rafiel must have been very upset at losing you."

"Oh I don't think so," said Esther lightly. "He was not one who would be upset over that sort of thing. He'd immediately get another secretary—which he did. And then if she didn't suit him he'd just get rid of her with a kindly golden handshake and get somebody else, till he found somebody who suited him. He was an intensely sensible man always."

"Yes. Yes, I can see that. Though he could lose his temper very easily."

"Oh, he enjoyed losing his temper," said Esther. "It made a bit of drama for him, I think."

"Drama," said Miss Marple thoughtfully. "Do you think—I have often wondered—do you think that Mr Rafiel had any particular interest in criminology, the study of it, I mean? He—well, I don't know. . . "

"You mean because of what happened in the Caribbean?" Esther's voice had gone suddenly hard.

Miss Marple felt doubtful of going on, and yet she must somehow or other try and get a little helpful knowledge.

"Well, no, not because of that, but afterwards, perhaps, he wondered about the psychology of these things. Or he got interested in the cases where justice had not been administered properly or—oh, well . . ."

She sounded more scatty every minute.

"Why should he take the least interest in anything of that kind? And don't let's talk about that horrible business in St Honoré."

"Oh no, I think you are *quite* right. I'm sure I'm very sorry. I was just thinking of some of the things that Mr Rafiel sometimes *said*. Queer turns of phrase, sometimes, and I just wondered if he had any theories, you know . . . about the causes of crime?"

"His interests were always entirely financial," said Esther shortly. "A really clever swindle of a criminal kind might have interested him, nothing else——"

She was looking coldly still at Miss Marple.

"I am sorry," said Miss Marple apologetically. "I—I shouldn't have talked about distressing matters that are fortunately past. And I must be getting on my way," she added. "I have got my train to catch and I shall only just have time. Oh dear, what did I do with my bag—oh yes, here it is."

She collected her bag, umbrella and a few other things, fussing away until the tension had slightly abated. As she went out of the door, she turned to Esther who was urging her to stay and have a cup of tea.

"No thank you, my dear, I'm so short of time. I'm very pleased to have seen you again and I do offer my best congratulations and hopes for a very happy life. I don't suppose you will be taking up any post again now, will you?"

"Oh, some people do. They find it interesting, they say. They get bored when they have nothing to do. But I think I shall rather enjoy living a life of leisure. I shall enjoy my legacy, too, that Mr Rafiel left me. It was very kind of him and I think he'd want me—well, to enjoy it even if I spent it in what he'd think of perhaps as a rather silly, female way! Expensive clothes and a new hair-do and all that. He'd have thought that sort of thing very silly." She added suddenly, "I was very fond of him, you know. Yes, I was quite fond of him. I think it was because he was a sort of challenge to me. He was difficult to get on with, and therefore I enjoyed managing it."

"And managing him?"

"Well, not quite managing him, but perhaps a little more than he knew I was."

Miss Marple trotted away down the road. She looked back once and waved her hand—Esther Anderson was still standing on the doorstep, and she waved back cheerfully.

"I thought this might have been something to do with her or something she knew about," said Miss Marple to herself. "I think I'm wrong. No. I don't think she's concerned in this business, whatever it is, *in any way*. Oh dear, I feel Mr Rafiel expected me to be much *cleverer* than I am being. I think he expected me to put things together—but what things? And what do I do next, I wonder?" She shook her head.

She had to think over things very carefully. This business had been, as it were, left to her. Left to her to refuse, to accept, to understand what it was all about? Or *not* to understand anything, but to go forward and hope that some kind of guidance might be given to her. Occasionally she closed her eyes and tried to picture Mr Rafiel's face. Sitting in the garden of the hotel in the West Indies, in his tropical suit; his bad-tempered corrugated face, his flashes of occasional humour. What she really wanted to know was what had been in his mind when he worked up this scheme, when he set out to bring it about. To lure her into accepting it, to persuade her to accept it, to—well, perhaps one should say—to bully her into accepting it. The third was much the most likely, knowing Mr Rafiel. And yet, take it that he had wanted something done and he had chosen her, settled upon her to do it. Why? Because she had suddenly come into his mind? But why should she have come into his mind?

She thought back to Mr Rafiel and the things that had

occurred at St Honoré. Had perhaps the problem he had been considering at the time of his death sent his mind back to that visit to the West Indies? Was it in some way connected with someone who had been out there, who had taken part or been an onlooker there and was that what had put Miss Marple into his mind? Was there some link or some connection? If not, why should he suddenly think of her? What was it about her that could make her useful to him, in any way at all. She was an elderly, rather scatty, quite ordinary person, physically not very strong, mentally not nearly as alert as she used to be. What had been her special qualifications, if any? She couldn't think of any. Could it possibly have been a bit of *fun* on Mr Rafiel's part? Even if Mr Rafiel had been on the point of death he might have wanted to have some kind of joke that suited his peculiar sense of humour.

She could not deny that Mr Rafiel could quite possibly wish to have a joke, even on his death-bed. Some ironical humour of his might be satisfied.

"I must," said Miss Marple to herself firmly, "I *must* have some qualification for something." After all, since Mr Rafiel was no longer in this world, he could not enjoy his joke at first hand. What qualifications *had* she got? "What qualities have I got that could be useful to anyone for *anything*?" said Miss Marple.

She considered herself with proper humility. She was inquisitive, she asked questions, she was the sort of age and type that could be expected to ask questions. That was one point, a possible point. You could send a private detective round to ask questions, or some psychological investigator, but it was true that you could much more easily send an elderly lady with a habit of snooping and being inquisitive, of talking too much, of wanting to find out about things, and it would seem perfectly natural.

"An old pussy," said Miss Marple to herself. "Yes, I can see I'm quite recognizable as an old pussy. There are so many old pussies, and they're all so much alike. And, of course, yes, I'm very ordinary. An ordinary rather scatty old lady. And that of course is very good *camouflage*. Dear me, I wonder if I'm thinking on the right lines. I do, sometimes, know what people are *like*. I mean, I know what people are like, because they remind me of certain other people I have known. So I know some of their faults and some of their virtues. I know what kind of people *they* are. There's that."

She thought again of St Honoré and the Hotel of the Golden Palm. She had made one attempt to enquire into the possibilities of a link, by her visit to Esther Walters. That had been definitely non-productive, Miss Marple decided. There didn't seem any further link leading from there. Nothing that would tie up with his request that Miss Marple should busy herself with something, the nature of which she still had no idea!

"Dear me," said Miss Marple, "what a tiresome man you are, Mr Rafiel!" She said it aloud and there was definite reproach in her voice.

Later, however, as she climbed into bed and applied her cosy hot water bottle to the most painful portion of her rheumatic back, she spoke again—in what might be taken as a semi-apology.

"I've done the best I could," she said.

She spoke aloud with the air of addressing one who might easily be in the room. It is true he might be anywhere, but even then there might be some telepathic or telephonic communication, and if so, she was going to speak definitely and to the point.

"I've done all I could. The best according to my limitations, and I must now leave it up to *you*.'

With that she settled herself more comfortably, stretched out a hand, switched off the electric light, and went to sleep.

5. *Instructions from Beyond*

i

IT WAS some three or four days later that a communication arrived by the second post. Miss Marple picked up the letter, did what she usually did to letters, turned it over, looked at the stamp, looked at the handwriting, decided that it wasn't a bill and opened it. It was typewritten.

"Dear Miss Marple,

By the time you read this I shall be dead and also buried. *Not* cremated, I am glad to think. It has always seemed to me unlikely that one would manage to rise up from one's handsome bronze vase full of ashes and haunt anyone if one wanted so to do! Whereas the idea of rising from one's grave and haunting anyone is quite possible. Shall I want to do that? Who knows. I might even want to communicate with *you*.

By now my solicitors will have communicated with you and will have put a certain proposition before you. I hope you will have accepted it. If you have not accepted it, don't feel in the least remorseful. It will be your choice.

This should reach you, if my solicitors have done what they were told to do and, if the posts have done the duty they are expected to perform, on the 11th of the month. In two days from now you will receive a communication from a travel bureau in London. I hope what it proposes will not be distasteful to you. I needn't say more. I want you to have an open mind. Take care of yourself. I think you will manage to do that. You are a very shrewd person. The best of luck and may your guardian angel be at your side looking after you. You may need one.

Your affectionate friend,

J. B. Rafiel."

"Two days!" said Miss Marple.

She found it difficult to pass the time. The Post Office did their duty and so did the Famous Houses and Gardens of Great Britain.

"Dear Miss Jane Marple,

Obeying instructions given us by the late Mr Rafiel we send you particulars of our Tour No 37 of the Famous Houses and Gardens of Great Britain which starts from London on Thursday next—the 17th.

If it should be possible for you to come to our office in London, our Mrs Sandbourne who is to accompany the tour, will be very glad to give you all particulars and to answer all questions.

Our tours last for a period of two to three weeks. This particular tour, Mr Rafiel thinks, will be particularly acceptable to you as it will visit a part of England which as far as he knows you have not yet visited, and takes in some really very attractive scenery and gardens. He has arranged for you to have the best accommodation and all the luxury available that we can provide.

Perhaps you will let us know which day would suit you to visit our office in Berkeley Street?"

Miss Marple folded up the letter, put it in her bag, noted the telephone number, thought of a few friends whom she knew, rang up two of them, one of whom had been for tours with the Famous Houses and Gardens, and spoke highly of them, the other one had not been personally on a tour but had friends who had travelled with this particular firm and who said everything was very well done, though rather expensive, and not too exhausting for the elderly. She then rang up the Berkeley Street number and said she would call upon them on the following Tuesday.

The next day she spoke to Cherry on the subject.

"I may be going away, Cherry," she said. "On a Tour."

"A Tour?" said Cherry. "One of these travel tours? You mean a package tour abroad?"

"Not abroad. In this country," said Miss Marple. "Mainly visiting historic buildings and gardens."

"Do you think it's all right to do that at your age? These things can be very tiring, you know. You have to walk miles sometimes."

"My health is really very good," said Miss Marple, "and I have always heard that in these tours they are careful to provide restful intervals for such people who are not particularly strong."

"Well, be careful of yourself, that's all," said Cherry. "We don't want you falling down with a heart attack, even if you are looking at a particularly sumptuous fountain or something. You're a bit old, you know, to do this sort of thing. Excuse me saying it, it sounds rude, but I don't like to think of you passing out because you've done too much or anything like that."

"I can take care of myself," said Miss Marple, with some dignity.

"All right, but you just be careful," said Cherry.

Miss Marple packed a suitable bag, went to London, booked a room at a modest hotel—("Ah, Bertram's Hotel," she thought in her mind, "what a wonderful hotel *that* was! Oh dear, I must forget all those things, the St George is quite a pleasant place.") At the appointed time she was in Berkeley Street and was shown in to the office where a pleasant women of about thirty-five rose to meet her, explained that her name was Mrs Sandbourne and that she would be in personal charge of this particular tour.

"Am I to understand," said Miss Marple, "that this trip is in my case——" she hesitated.

Mrs Sandbourne, sensing slight embarrassment, said:

"Oh yes, I ought to have explained perhaps better in the letter we sent you. Mr Rafiel has paid all expenses."

"You *do* know that he is dead?" said Miss Marple.

"Oh yes, but this was arranged before his death. He mentioned that he was in ill health but wanted to provide a treat for a very old friend of his who had not had the opportunity of travelling as much as she could have wished."

ii

Two days later, Miss Marple, carrying her small overnight bag, her new and smart suitcase surrendered to the driver, had boarded a most comfortable and luxurious coach which was taking a north-westerly route out of London; she was studying the passenger list which was attached to the inside of a handsome brochure giving details of the daily itinerary of the coach, and various information as to hotels and meals, places to be seen, and occasional alternatives on some days which, although the fact was not stressed, actually intimated that one choice of itinerary was for the young and active and that the other choice would be peculiarly suitable for the elderly, those whose feet hurt them, who suffered from arthritis or rheumatism and who would prefer to sit about and *not* walk long distances or up too many hills. It was all very tactful and well arranged.

Miss Marple read the passenger list and surveyed her fellow passengers. There was no difficulty about doing this because the other fellow passengers were doing much the same themselves. They were surveying her, amongst others, but nobody as far as Miss Marple could notice was taking any particular interest in her.

Mrs Riseley-Porter
Miss Joanna Crawford
Colonel and Mrs Walker
Mr and Mrs H. T. Butler
Miss Elizabeth Temple
Professor Wanstead
Mr Richard Jameson
Miss Lumley
Miss Bentham
Mr Caspar
Miss Cooke
Miss Barrow
Mr Emlyn Price
Miss Jane Marple

There were four elderly ladies. Miss Marple took note of them first so, as it were, to clear them out of the way. Two were travelling together. Miss Marple put them down as about seventy. They could roughly be considered as contemporaries of her own. One of them was very definitely the complaining type, one who would want to have seats at the front of the coach or else would make a point of having them at the back of the coach. Would wish to sit on the sunny side or could only bear to sit on the shady side. Who would want more fresh air, or less fresh air. They had with them travelling rugs and knitted scarves and quite an assortment of guide books. They were slightly crippled and often in pain from feet or backs or knees but were nevertheless of those whom age and ailments could not prevent from enjoying life while they still had it. Old pussies, but definitely *not* stay-at-home old pussies. Miss Marple made an entry in the little book she carried.

Fifteen passengers not including herself, or Mrs Sandbourne. And since she had been sent on this coach tour, one at least of those fifteen passengers must be of importance in some way. Either as a source of information or someone concerned with the law or a law case, or it might even be a murderer. A murderer who might have already killed or one who might be preparing to kill. Anything was possible, Miss Marple thought, with Mr Rafiel! Anyway, she must make notes of these people.

On the right-hand page of her notebook, she would note down who might be worthy of attention from Mr Rafiel's point of view and on the left she would note down or cross off those who could only be of any interest if they could produce some useful information for her. Information, it might be, that they did not even know they possessed. Or rather that even if they possessed it, they did not know it could possibly be useful to her or to Mr Rafiel or to the law or to Justice with a capital 'J'. At the back of her little book, she might this evening make a note or two as to whether anyone had reminded her of characters she had known in the past at St Mary Mead and other places. Any similarities might make a useful pointer. It had done so on other occasions.

The other two elderly ladies were apparently separate travellers. Both of them were about sixty. One was a well preserved, well dressed woman of obvious social importance in her own mind, but probably in other people's minds as well. Her voice was loud and dictatorial. She appeared to have in tow a niece, a girl of about eighteen or nineteen who addressed her as Aunt Geraldine. The niece, Miss Marple noted, was obviously well accustomed to coping with Aunt Geraldine's bossiness. She was a competent girl as well as being an attractive one.

Across the aisle from Miss Marple was a big man with square shoulders and a clumsy-looking body, looking as though he had been carelessly assembled by an ambitious child out of chunky bricks. His face looked as though nature had planned it to be round but the face had rebelled at this and decided to achieve a square effect by developing a powerful jaw. He had a thick head of greyish hair and enormous bushy eyebrows which moved up and down to give point to what he was saying. His remarks seemed mainly to come out in a series of barks as though he was a talkative sheepdog. He shared his seat with a tall dark foreigner who moved restlessly in his seat and gesticulated freely. He spoke a most peculiar English, making occasional remarks in French and German. The bulky man seemed quite capable of meeting these onslaughts of foreign language, and shifted obligingly to either French or German. Taking a quick glance at them again, Miss Marple decided that the bushy eyebrows must be Professor Wanstead and the excitable foreigner was Mr Caspar.

She wondered what it was they were discussing with such animation, but was baffled by the rapidity and force of Mr Caspar's delivery.

The seat in front of them was occupied by the other woman of about sixty, a tall woman, possibly over sixty, but a woman who would have stood out in a crowd anywhere. She was still a very handsome woman with dark grey hair coiled high on her head, drawn back from a fine forehead. She had a low, clear, incisive voice. A personality, Miss Marple thought. Someone! Yes, she was decidedly someone. "Reminds me," she thought to herself, "of Dame Emily Waldron." Dame Emily Waldron had been the Principal of an Oxford College and a notable scientist, and Miss Marple having once met her in her nephew's company, had never quite forgotten her.

Miss Marple resumed her survey of the passengers. There

were two married couples, one American, middle-aged, amiable, a talkative wife and a placidly agreeing husband. They were obviously dedicated travellers and sightseers. There was also an English middle-aged couple whom Miss Marple noted down without hesitation as a retired military man and wife. She ticked them off from the list as Colonel and Mrs Walker.

In the seat behind her was a tall, thin man of about thirty with a highly technical vocabulary, clearly an architect. There were also two middle-aged ladies travelling together rather further up the coach. They were discussing the brochure and deciding what the tour was going to hold for them in the way of attractions. One was dark and thin and the other was fair and sturdily built and the latter's face seemed faintly familiar to Miss Marple. She wondered where she had seen or met her before. However, she could not recall the occasion in mind. Possibly someone she had met at a cocktail party or sat opposite to in a train. There was nothing very special about her to remember.

Only one more passenger remained for her to appraise, and this was a young man, possibly of about nineteen or twenty. He wore the appropriate clothes for his age and sex; tight black jeans, a polo necked purple sweater and his head was an outsize rich mop of non-disciplined black hair. He was looking with an air of interest at the bossy woman's niece, and the bossy woman's niece also, Miss Marple thought, was looking with some interest at him. In spite of the preponderance of elderly pussies and middle-aged females there were, at any rate, two *young* people among the passengers.

They stopped for lunch at a pleasant riverside hotel, and the afternoon sightseeing was given over to Blenheim. Miss Marple had already visited Blenheim twice before, so she saved her feet by limiting the amount of sight-seeing indoors and coming fairly soon to the enjoyment of the gardens and the beautiful view.

By the time they arrived at the hotel where they were to stay the night, the passengers were getting to know each other. The efficient Mrs Sandbourne still brisk and unwearied by her duties in directing the sight-seeing, did her part very well; creating little groups by adding anyone who looked as if they were left out to one or other of them, murmuring. "You *must* make Colonel Walker describe his garden to you. Such a wonderful collection of fuchsias he has." With such little sentences she drew people together.

Miss Marple was now able to attach names to all the passengers. Bushy eyebrows turned out to be Professor Wanstead, as she had thought, and the foreigner was Mr Caspar. The bossy woman was Mrs Riseley-Porter and her niece was called Joanna Crawford. The young man with the hair was Emlyn Price and he and Joanna Crawford appeared to be finding out that certain things in life, such as decided opinions, they had in common, on economics, art, general dislikes, politics and such topics.

The two eldest pussies graduated naturally to Miss Marple as a kindred elderly pussy. They discussed happily arthritis, rheumatism, diets, new doctors, remedies both professional, patent, and reminiscences of old wives' treatments which had had success where all else failed. They discussed the many tours they had been on to foreign places in Europe; hotels, travel agencies and finally the County of Somerset where Miss Lumley and Miss Bentham lived, and where the difficulties of getting suitable gardeners could hardly be believed.

The two middle-aged ladies travelling together turned out to be Miss Cooke and Miss Barrow. Miss Marple still felt that one of these two, the fair one, Miss Cooke, was faintly familiar to her, but she still could not remember where she had seen her before. Probably it was only her fancy. It might also be just fancy that she could not help feeling that Miss Barrow and Miss Cooke appeared to be avoiding her. They seemed rather anxious to move away if she approached. That, of course, *might* be entirely her imagination.

Fifteen people, one of whom at least must matter in some way. In casual conversation that evening she introduced the name of Mr Rafiel, so as to note if anyone reacted in any way. Nobody did.

The handsome woman was identified as Miss Elizabeth Temple, who was the retired Headmistress of a famous girls' school. Nobody appeared to Miss Marple likely to be a murderer, except possibly Mr Caspar, and that was probably foreign prejudice. The thin young man was Richard Jameson, an architect.

"Perhaps I shall do better to-morrow," said Miss Marple to herself.

iii

Miss Marple went to bed definitely tired out. Sight-seeing was pleasant but exhausting, and trying to study fifteen or sixteen people at once and wondering as you did so which of them could possibly be connected with a murder, was even more exhausting. It had a touch of such unreality about it that one could not, Miss Marple felt, take it seriously. These seemed to be all perfectly nice people, the sort of people who go on cruises and on tours and all the rest of it. However, she took another quick and cursory glance at the passenger list, making a few little entries in her notebook.

Mrs Riseley-Porter? *Not* connected with crime. Too social and self-centred.

Niece, Joanna Crawford? The same? But very efficient.

Mrs Riseley-Porter, however, might have information of some kind which Miss Marple might find had a bearing on matters. She must keep on agreeable terms with Mrs Riseley-Porter.

Miss Elizabeth Temple? A personality. Interesting. She did not remind Miss Marple of any murderer she'd ever known. "In fact," said Miss Marple to herself, "she really radiates integrity. *If* she had committed a murder, it would be a very popular murder. Perhaps for some noble reason or for some reason that she thought noble?" But that wasn't satisfactory either. Miss Temple, she thought, would always know what she was doing and why she was doing it and would not have any silly ideas about nobility when merely evil existed. "All the same," said Miss Marple, "she's *someone* and she might—she just *might* be a person Mr Rafiel wanted me to meet for some reason." She jotted down these thoughts on the right hand side of her notebook.

She shifted her point of view. She had been considering a possible murderer—what about a prospective victim? Who was a possible victim? No one very likely. Perhaps Mrs Riseley-Porter might qualify—rich—rather disagreeable. The efficient niece might inherit. She and the anarchistic Emlyn Price might combine in the cause of anti-capitalism. Not a very credible idea, but no other feasible murderee seemed to offer.

Professor Wanstead? An interesting man, she was sure. Kindly, too. Was he a scientist or was he medical? She was not as yet sure, but she put him down on the side of science. She herself knew nothing of science, but it seemed not at all unlikely.

Mr and Mrs Butler? She wrote them off. Nice Americans. No connections with anyone in the West Indies or anyone she had known. No, she didn't think that the Butlers could be relevant.

Richard Jameson? That was the thin architect. Miss Marple didn't see how architecture could come into it, though it might, she supposed. A priest's hole, perhaps? One of the houses they were going to visit might have a priest's hole which would contain a skeleton. And Mr Jameson, being an architect, would know just where the priest's hole was. He might aid her to discover it, or she might aid him to discover it and then they would find a body. "Oh really," said Miss Marple, "what nonsense I am talking and thinking."

Miss Cooke and Miss Barrow? A perfectly ordinary pair. And yet she'd certainly seen one of them before. At least she'd seen Miss Cooke before. Oh well, it would come to her, she supposed.

Colonel and Mrs Walker? Nice people. Retired Army folk. Served abroad mostly. Nice to talk to, but she didn't think there'd be anything for her there.

Miss Bentham and Miss Lumley? The elderly pussies. Unlikely to be criminals, but, being elderly pussies, they might know plenty of gossip, or have some information, or might make some illuminating remark even if it happened to come about in connection with rheumatism, arthritis or patent medicine.

Mr Caspar? Possibly a dangerous character. Very excitable. She would keep him on the list for the present.

Emlyn Price? A student presumably. Students were very violent. Would Mr Rafiel have sent her on the track of a student? Well, it would depend perhaps on what the student had done or wished to do or was going to do. A dedicated anarchist, perhaps.

"Oh dear," said Miss Marple, suddenly exhausted, "I *must* go to bed."

Her feet ached, her back ached and her mental reactions were not, she thought, at their best. She slept at once. Her sleep was enlivened by several dreams.

One where Professor Wanstead's bushy eyebrows fell off because they were not his own eyebrows, but false ones. As she woke again, her first impression was that which so often follows dreams, a belief that the dream in question had solved everything. "Of course," she thought, "of *course*!" His eyebrows were false and that solved the whole thing. *He* was the criminal.

Sadly, it came to her that nothing was solved. Professor Wanstead's eyebrows coming off was of no help at all.

Unfortunately now, she was no longer sleepy. She sat up in bed with some determination.

She sighed and slipped on her dressing-gown, moved from her bed to an upright chair, took a slightly larger notebook from her suitcase and started work.

"The project I have undertaken," she wrote, "is connected certainly with crime of some kind. Mr Rafiel has distinctly stated that in his letter. He said I had a *flair* for justice and that necessarily included a flair for crime. So crime is involved, and it is presumably not espionage or fraud or robbery, because such things have never come my way and I have no connection with such things, or knowledge of them, or special skills. What Mr Rafiel knows of me is only what he knew during the period of time when we were both in St Honoré. We were connected there with a murder. Murders as reported in the press have never claimed my attention. I have never read books on criminology as a subject or really been interested in such a thing. No, it has just happened that I have found myself in the vicinity of murder rather more often than would seem normal. My attention has been directed to murders involving friends or acquaintances. These curious coincidences of connections with special subjects seem to happen to people in life. One of my aunts, I remember, was on five occasions shipwrecked and a friend of mine was what I believe is officially called accident-prone. I know some of her friends refused to ride in a taxi with her. She had been in four taxi accidents and three car accidents and two railway accidents. Things like this seem to happen to certain people for no appreciable reason. I do not like to write it down but it does appear that murders seem to happen, not to me myself, thank goodness, but seem to happen in my vicinity."

Miss Marple paused, changed her position, put a cushion in her back, and continued:

"I must try to make as logical a survey as I can of this project which I have undertaken. My instructions, or my 'briefing' as naval friends of mine put it, are so far quite inadequate. Practically non-existent. So I must ask myself one clear question. What is all this *about*? Answer! *I do not know*. Curious and interesting. An odd way for a man like Mr Rafiel to go about things, especially when he was a successful business and financial operator. He wants me to guess, to employ my instinct, to observe and to obey such directions as are given to me or are hinted to me.

"So: Point 1. Direction will be given me. Direction from a dead man. Point 2. What is involved in my problem is *justice*. Either to set right an injustice or to avenge evil by bringing it to justice. This is in accord with the code word Nemesis given to me by Mr Rafiel.

"After explanations of the principle involved, I received my first factual directive. It was arranged by Mr Rafiel before his death that I was to go on Tour No 37 of Famous Houses and Gardens. Why? That is what I have to ask myself. Is it for some geographical or territorial reason? A connection or a clue? Some particular famous house? Or something involving some particular garden or landscape connected? This seems unlikely. The more likely explanation lies in the *people* or one of the people on this particular coach party. None of them is known to me personally, but one of them at least must be connected with the riddle I have to solve. Somebody among our group is connected or concerned with a murder. Somebody has information or a special link with the victim of a crime, or someone personally is himself or herself a murderer. A murderer as yet unsuspected."

Miss Marple stopped here suddenly. She nodded her head. She was satisfied now with her analysis so far as it went.

And so to bed.

Miss Marple added to her notebook.

"Here endeth the First Day."

6. *Love*

THE FOLLOWING morning they visited a small Queen Anne Manor House. The drive there had not been very long or tiring. It was a very charming-looking house and had an interesting history as well as a very beautiful and unusually laid out garden.

Richard Jameson, the architect, was full of admiration for the structural beauty of the house and being the kind of young man who is fond of hearing his own voice, he slowed down in nearly every room that they went through, pointing out every special moulding or fireplace, and giving historical dates and references. Some of the group, appreciative at first, began to get slightly restive, as the somewhat monotonous lecturing went on. Some of them began to edge carefully away and fall behind the party. The local caretaker, who was in charge, was not himself too pleased at having his occupation usurped by one of the sightseers. He made a few efforts to get matters back into his own hands but Mr Jameson was unyielding. The caretaker made a last try.

"In this room, ladies and gentlemen, the White Parlour, folks call it, is where they found a body. A young man it was, stabbed with a dagger, lying on the hearthrug. Way back in seventeen hundred and something it was. It was said that the Lady Moffatt of that day had a lover. He came through a small side door and up a steep staircase to this room through a loose panel there was to the left of the fireplace. Sir Richard Moffatt, her husband, you see, was said to be across the seas in the Low Countries. But he come home, and in he came unexpectedly and caught 'em there together."

He paused proudly. He was pleased at the response from his audience, glad of a respite from the architectural details which they had been having forced down their throats.

"Why, isn't that just too romantic, Henry?" said Mrs Butler in her resonant trans-Atlantic tones. "Why, you know, there's quite an *atmosphere* in this room. I feel it. I certainly can feel it."

"Mamie is very sensitive to atmospheres," said her husband proudly to those around him. "Why, once when we were in an old house down in Louisiana . . ."

The narrative of Mamie's special sensitivity got into its swing and Miss Marple and one or two others seized their opportunity to edge gently out of the room and down the exquisitely moulded staircase to the ground floor.

"A friend of mine," said Miss Marple to Miss Cooke and Miss Barrow who were next to her, "had a most nerve-racking experience only a few years ago. A dead body on their library floor one morning."

"One of the family?" asked Miss Barrow. "An epileptic fit?"

"Oh no, it was a murder. A strange girl in evening dress. A blonde. But her hair was dyed. She was really a brunette; and—oh . . ." Miss Marple broke off, her eyes fixed on Miss Cooke's yellow hair where it escaped from her headscarf.

It had come to her suddenly. She knew why Miss Cooke's face was familiar and she knew where she had seen her before. But when she had seen her then, Miss Cooke's hair had been dark—almost black. And now it was bright yellow.

Mrs Riseley-Porter, coming down the stairs, spoke decisively as she pushed past them and completed the staircase and turned into the hall.

"I really cannot go up and down any more of those stairs," she declared, "and standing around in these rooms is very tiring. I believe the gardens here, although not extensive, are quite celebrated in horticultural circles. I suggest we go there without loss of time. It looks as though it might cloud over before long. I think we shall get rain before the morning is out."

The authority with which Mrs Riseley-Porter could enforce her remarks had its usual result. All those near at hand or within hearing followed her obediently out through french doors in the dining-room into the garden. The gardens had indeed all that Mrs Riseley-Porter had claimed for them. She herself took possession firmly of Colonel Walker and set off briskly. Some of the others followed them, others took paths in the opposite direction.

Miss Marple herself made a determined bee-line for a garden seat which appeared to be of comfortable proportions as well as of artistic merit. She sank down on it with relief, and a sigh matching her own was emitted by Miss Elizabeth Temple as she followed Miss Marple and came to sit beside her on the seat.

"Going over houses is always tiring," said Miss Temple. "The most tiring thing in the world. Especially if you have to listen to an exhaustive lecture in each room."

"Of course, all that we were told is very interesting," said Miss Marple, rather doubtfully.

"Oh, do you think so?" said Miss Temple. Her head turned slightly and her eyes met those of Miss Marple. Something passed between the two women, a kind of *rapport*—of understanding tinged with mirth.

"Don't you?" asked Miss Marple.

"No," said Miss Temple.

This time the understanding was definitely established between them. They sat there companionably in silence. Presently Elizabeth Temple began to talk about gardens, and this garden in particular. "It was designed by Holman," she said, "somewhere about 1800 or 1798. He died young. A pity. He had great genius."

"It is so sad when anyone dies young," said Miss Marple.

"I wonder," said Elizabeth Temple.

She said it in a curious, meditative way.

"But they miss so much," said Miss Marple. "So many things."

"Or escape so much," said Miss Temple.

"Being as old as I am now," said Miss Marple, "I suppose I can't help feeling that early death means missing things."

"And I," said Elizabeth Temple, "having spent nearly all my life amongst the young, look at life as a period in time complete in itself. What did T. S. Eliot say: *The moment of the rose and the moment of the yew tree are of equal duration.*"

Miss Marple said, "I see what you mean . . . A life of whatever length is a complete experience. But don't you—" she hesitated, "—ever feel that a life could be incomplete because it has been cut unduly short?"

"Yes, that *is* so."

Miss Marple said, looking at the flowers near her, "How beautiful peonies are. That long border of them—so proud and yet so beautifully fragile."

Elizabeth Temple turned her head towards her.

"Did you come on this trip to see the houses or to see gardens?" she asked.

"I suppose really to see the houses," said Miss Marple, "I shall enjoy the gardens most, though, but the houses—they will be a new experience for me. Their variety and their history, and the beautiful old furniture and the pictures." She added: "A kind friend gave me this trip as a gift. I am very grateful. I have not seen very many big and famous houses in my life."

"A kind thought," said Miss Temple.

"Do you often go on these sight-seeing tours?" asked Miss Marple.

"No. This is not for me exactly a sight-seeing tour."

Miss Marple looked at her with interest. She half opened her lips to speak but refrained from putting a question. Miss Temple smiled at her.

"You wonder why I am here, what my motive is, my reason. Well, why don't you make a guess?"

"Oh, I wouldn't like to do that," said Miss Marple.

"Yes, do do so." Elizabeth Temple was urgent. "It would interest me. Yes, really interest me. Make a guess."

Miss Marple was silent for quite a few moments. Her eyes looked at Elizabeth Temple steadily, ranging over her thoughtfully in her appraisement. She said,

"This is not from what I know about you or what I have been told about you. I know that you are quite a famous person and that your school is a very famous one. No. I am only making my guess from what you look like. I should—write you down as a pilgrim. You have the look of one who is on a pilgrimage."

There was a silence and then Elizabeth said.

"That describes it very well. Yes. I am on a pilgrimage."

Miss Marple said after a moment or two,

"The friend who sent me on this tour and paid all my expenses, is now dead. He was a Mr Rafiel, a very rich man. Did you by any chance know him?"

"Jason Rafiel? I know him by name, of course. I never knew him personally, or met him. He gave a large endowment once to an educational project in which I was interested. I was very grateful. As you say, he was a very wealthy man. I saw the notice of his death in the papers a few weeks ago. So he was an old friend of yours?"

"No," said Miss Marple. "I had met him just over a year ago abroad. In the West Indies. I never knew much about him. His life or his family or any personal friends that he had. He was a great financier but otherwise, or so people always said, he was a man who was very reserved about himself. Did you know his family or anyone . . ." Miss Marple paused. "I often wondered, but one does not like to ask questions and seem inquisitive."

Elizabeth was silent for a minute—then she said:

"I knew a girl once . . . A girl who had been a pupil of mine at Fallowfield, my school. She was no actual relation to Mr Rafiel, but she *was* at one time engaged to marry Mr Rafiel's son."

"But she didn't marry him?" Miss Marple asked.

"No."

"Why not?"

Miss Temple said,

"One might hope to say—like to say—because she had too much sense. He was not the type of a young man one would want anyone one was fond of to marry. She was a very lovely girl and a very sweet girl. I don't know why she didn't marry him. Nobody has ever told me." She sighed and then said, "Anyway, she died . . ."

"Why did she die?" said Miss Marple.

Elizabeth Temple stared at the peonies for some minutes. When she spoke she uttered one word. It echoed like the tone of a deep bell—so much so that it was startling.

"Love!" she said.

Miss Marple queried the word sharply. "Love?"

"One of the most frightening words there is in the world," said Elizabeth Temple.

Again her voice was bitter and tragic.

"Love . . ."

7. *An Invitation*

MISS MARPLE decided to miss out on the afternoon's sightseeing. She admitted to being somewhat tired and would perhaps give a miss to an ancient church and its 14th-century glass. She would rest for a while and join them at the tea-room which had been pointed out to her in the main street. Mrs Sandbourne agreed that she was being very sensible.

Miss Marple, resting on a comfortable bench outside the tea-room, reflected on what she planned to do next and whether it would be wise to do it or not.

When the others joined her at tea-time it was easy for her to attach herself unobtrusively to Miss Cooke and Miss Barrow and sit with them at a table for four. The fourth chair was occupied by Mr Caspar whom Miss Marple considered as not sufficiently conversant with the English language to matter.

Leaning across the table, as she nibbled a slice of Swiss roll, Miss Marple said to Miss Cooke,

"You know, I am *quite* sure we have met before. I have been wondering and wondering about it—I'm not as good as I was at remembering faces, but I'm sure I have met you somewhere."

Miss Cooke looked kindly but doubtful. Her eyes went to her friend, Miss Barrow. So did Miss Marple's. Miss Barrow showed no signs of helping to probe the mystery.

"I don't know if you've ever stayed in my part of the world," went on Miss Marple, "I live in St Mary Mead. Quite a small village, you know. At least, not so small nowadays, there is so much building going on everywhere. Not very far from Much Benham and only twelve miles from the coast at Loomouth."

"Oh," said Miss Cooke, "let me see. Well, I know Loomouth quite well and perhaps——"

Suddenly Miss Marple made a pleased exclamation.

"Why, of *course*! I was in my garden one day at St Mary Mead and you spoke to me as you were passing by on the footpath. You said you were staying down there, I remember, with a friend——"

"Of course," said Miss Cooke. "How stupid of me. I do remember you now. We spoke of how difficult it was nowadays to get anyone—to do gardening, I mean—anyone who was any *use*."

"Yes. You were not living there, I think? You were staying with someone."

"Yes, I was staying with . . . with . . ." for a moment Miss Cooke hesitated, with the air of one who hardly knows or remembers a name.

"With a Mrs Sutherland, was it?" suggested Miss Marple.

"No, no, it was . . . er . . . Mrs——"

"Hastings," said Miss Barrow firmly as she took a piece of chocolate cake.

"Oh yes, in one of the new houses," said Miss Marple.

"Hastings," said Mr Caspar unexpectedly. He beamed. "I have been to Hastings—I have been to Eastbourne, too." He beamed again. "Very nice—by the sea."

"Such a coincidence," said Miss Marple, "meeting again so soon—such a small world, isn't it?"

"Oh, well, we are all so fond of gardens," said Miss Cooke vaguely.

"Flowers very pretty," said Mr Caspar. "I like very much——" he beamed again.

"So many rare and beautiful shrubs," said Miss Cooke.

Miss Marple went full speed ahead with a gardening conversation of some technicality—Miss Cooke responded. Miss Barrow put in an occasional remark.

Mr Caspar relapsed into smiling silence.

Later, as Miss Marple took her usual rest before dinner, she conned over what she had collected. Miss Cooke *had* admitted being in St Mary Mead. She *had* admitted walking past Miss Marple's house. Had agreed it was quite a coincidence. Coincidence? thought Miss Marple meditatively, turning the word over in her mouth rather as a child might do to a certain lollipop to decide its flavour. Was it a coincidence? Or had she had some reason to come there? Had she been *sent* there? Sent there—for what reason? Was that a ridiculous thing to imagine?

"Any coincidence," said Miss Marple to herself, "is *always* worth noticing. You can throw it away later if it *is* only a coincidence."

Miss Cooke and Miss Barrow appeared to be a perfectly normal pair of friends doing the kind of tour, which according to them, they did every year. They had been on an Hellenic cruise last year and a tour of bulbs in Holland the year before, and Northern Ireland the year before that. They seemed perfectly pleasant and ordinary people. But Miss Cooke, she thought, had for a moment looked as though she were about to disclaim her visit to St Mary Mead. She had looked at her friend, Miss Barrow, rather as though she were seeking instruction as to what to say. Miss Barrow, was presumably the senior partner——

"Of course, really, I may have been imagining all these things," thought Miss Marple. "They may have no significance whatever."

The word danger came unexpectedly into her mind. Used by Mr Rafiel in his first letter—and there had been some reference to her needing a guardian angel in his second letter. Was she going into danger in this business?—and why? From whom?

Surely not from Miss Cooke and Miss Barrow. Such an ordinary-looking couple.

All the same Miss Cooke *had* dyed her hair and altered her style of hairdressing. Disguised her appearance as much as she could, in fact. Which was odd, to say the least of it! She considered once more her fellow travellers.

Mr Caspar, now, it would have been much easier to imagine that *he* might be dangerous. Did he understand more English than he pretended to do? She began to wonder about Mr Caspar.

Miss Marple had never quite succeeded in abandoning her Victorian view of foreigners. One never *knew* with foreigners. Quite absurd, of course, to feel like that—she had many friends from various foreign countries. All the same . . .? Miss Cooke, Miss Barrow, Mr Caspar, that young man with the wild hair—Emlyn Something—a revolutionary—a practising anarchist? Mr and Mrs Butler—such nice Americans—but perhaps—too good to be true?

"Really," said Miss Marple, "I *must* pull myself together."

She turned her attention to the itinerary of their trip. Tomorrow, she thought, was going to be rather strenuous. A morning's sight-seeing drive, starting rather early: a long, rather athletic walk on a coastal path in the afternoon. Certain interesting marine flowering plants—It would be tiring. A tactful suggestion was appended. Anyone who felt like a rest could stay behind in their Hotel, the Golden Boar, which had a very pleasant garden or could do a short excursion which would only take an hour, to a beauty spot nearby. She thought perhaps that she would do that.

But though she did not know it then, her plans were to be suddenly altered.

As Miss Marple came down from her room in the Golden Boar the next day after washing her hands before luncheon, a woman in a tweed coat and skirt came forward rather nervously and spoke to her.

"Excuse me, are you Miss Marple—Miss Jane Marple?"

"Yes, that is my name," said Miss Marple, slightly surprised.

"My name is Mrs Glynne. Lavinia Glynne. I and my two sisters live near here and—well, we heard you were coming, you see——"

"You heard I was coming?" said Miss Marple with some slight surprise.

"Yes. A very old friend of ours wrote to us—oh, quite some time ago, it must have been three weeks ago, but he asked us to make a note of this date. The date of the Famous Houses and Gardens Tour. He said that a great friend of his—or a relation, I'm not quite sure which—would be on that tour."

Miss Marple continued to look surprised.

"I'm speaking of a Mr Rafiel," said Mrs Glynne.

"Oh! Mr Rafiel," said Miss Marple—"You—you know that—"

"That he died? Yes. So sad. Just after his letter came. I think it must have been certainly very soon after he wrote to us. But we felt a special *urgency* to try to do what he had asked. He suggested, you know, that perhaps you would like to come and stay with us for a couple of nights. This part of the tour is rather strenuous. I mean, it's all right for the young people, but it is very trying for anyone older. It involves several miles of walking and a certain amount of climbing up difficult cliff paths and places. My sisters and I would be so very pleased if you could come and stay in our house here. It is only ten minutes' walk from the Hotel and I'm sure we could show you many interesting things locally."

Miss Marple hesitated a minute. She liked the look of Mrs Glynne, plump, good-natured, and friendly though a little shy. Besides—here again must be Mr Rafiel's instructions—the next step for her to take? Yes, it must be so.

She wondered why she felt nervous. Perhaps because she was now at home with the people in the tour, felt part of the group although as yet she had only known them for three days.

She turned to where Mrs Glynne was standing, looking up at her anxiously.

"Thank you—it is most kind of you. I shall be very pleased to come."

8. *The Three Sisters*

MISS MARPLE stood looking out of a window. Behind her, on the bed, was her suitcase. She looked out over the garden with unseeing eyes. It was not often that she failed to see a garden she was looking at, in either a mood of admiration or a mood of criticism. In this case it would presumably have been criticism. It was a neglected garden, a garden on which little money had been spent possibly for some years, and on which very little work had been done. The house, too, had been neglected. It was well proportioned, the furniture in it had been good furniture once, but had had little in late years of polishing or attention. It was not a house, she thought, that had been, at any rate of late years, loved in any way. It lived up to its name: The Old Manor House. A house, built with grace and a certain amount of beauty, lived in once, cherished. The daughters and sons had married and left and now it was lived in by Mrs Glynne who, from a word she had let fall when she showed Miss Marple up to the bedroom appointed to her, had inherited it with her sisters from an uncle and had come here to live with her sisters after her husband had died. They had all grown older, their incomes had dwindled, labour had been more difficult to get.

The other sisters, presumably, had remained unmarried, one older, one younger than Mrs Glynne, two Miss Bradbury-Scotts.

There was no sign of anything which belonged to a child in the house. No discarded ball, no old perambulator, no little chair or a table. This was just a house with three sisters.

"Sounds very Russian," murmured Miss Marple to herself. She did mean The Three Sisters, didn't she? Chekhov, was it? or Dostoievsky? Really, she couldn't remember. Three sisters. But these would certainly not be the kind of three sisters who were yearning to go to Moscow. These three sisters were presumably, she was almost sure they were, content to remain where they were. She had been introduced to the other two who had come, one out of the kitchen and one down a flight of stairs, to welcome her. Their manners were well bred and gracious. They were what Miss Marple would have called in her youth by the now obsolete term 'ladies'—and what she once recalled calling: 'decayed ladies'. Her father had said to her.

"No, dear Jane, *not decayed*. Distressed gentlewomen."

Gentlewomen nowadays were not so liable to be distressed. They were aided by Government or by Societies or by a rich relation. Or, perhaps—someone like Mr Rafiel. Because, after all, that was the whole point, the whole reason for her being here wasn't it? Mr Rafiel had arranged all this. He had taken, Miss Marple thought, a good deal of trouble about it. He had known presumably, some four or five weeks before his death, just when that death was likely to be, give and take a little, since doctors were usually moderately optimistic, knowing from experience that patients who ought to die within a certain period very often took an unexpected lease of life and lingered on, still doomed, but obstinately declining to take the final step. On the other hand, hospital nurses when in charge of patients, had, Miss Marple thought from her experience, always expected the patients to be dead the next day, and were much surprised when they were not. But in voicing their gloomy views to Doctor, when he came, they were apt to receive in reply as the doctor went out of the hall door, a private aside of, "Linger a few weeks yet, I shouldn't wonder." Very nice of Doctor to be so optimistic, Nurse would think, but surely Doctor was wrong. Doctor very often wasn't wrong. He knew that people who were in pain, helpless, crippled, even unhappy, still liked living and wanted to live. They would take one of Doctor's pills to help them pass the night, but they had no intention of taking a few more than necessary of Doctor's pills, just in order to pass the threshold to a world that they did not as yet know anything about!

Mr Rafiel. That was the person Miss Marple was thinking about as she looked across the garden with unseeing eyes. Mr Rafiel? She felt now that she was getting a little closer to understanding the task laid upon her, the project suggested to her. Mr

Rafiel was a man who made plans. Made them in the same way that he planned financial deals and take-overs. In the words of her servant, Cherry, he had had a problem. When Cherry had a problem, she often came and consulted Miss Marple about it.

This was a problem that Mr Rafiel could not deal with himself, which must have annoyed him very much, Miss Marple thought, because he could usually deal with any problem himself and insisted on doing so. But he was bed-ridden and dying. He could arrange his financial affairs, communicate with his lawyers, with his employees and with such friends and relations as he had, but there was something or someone that he had not arranged for. A problem he had not solved, a problem he still wanted to solve, a project he still wanted to bring about. And apparently it was not one that could be settled by financial aid, by business dealings, by the services of a lawyer.

"So he thought of me," said Miss Marple.

It still surprised her very much. Very much indeed. However, in the sense she was now thinking of it, his letter had been quite explicit. He had thought she had certain qualifications for doing something. It had to do, she thought once again, with something in the nature of crime or affected by crime. The only other thing he knew about Miss Marple was that she was devoted to gardens. Well it could hardly be a gardening problem that he wanted her to solve. But he might think of her in connection with crime. Crime in the West Indies and crimes in her own neighbourhood at home.

A crime—where?

Mr Rafiel had made arrangements. Arrangements, to begin with, with his lawyers. They had done their part. At the right interval of time they had forwarded to her his letter. It had been, she thought, a well considered and well thought out letter. It would have been simpler, certainly, to tell her exactly what he wanted her to do and why he wanted it. She was surprised in a way that he had not, before his death, sent for her, probably in a somewhat peremptory way and more or less lying on what he would have assured her was his death-bed, and would then have bullied her until she consented to do what he was asking her. But no, that would not really have been Mr Rafiel's way, she thought. He *could* bully people, none better, but this was not a case for bullying, and he did not wish either, she was sure, to appeal to her, to beg her to do him a favour, to urge her to redress a wrong. No. That again would not have been Mr Rafiel's way. He wanted, she thought, as he had probably wanted all his life, to pay for what he required. He wanted to pay her and therefore he wanted to interest her enough to enjoy doing certain work. The pay was offered to intrigue her, not really to tempt her. It was to arouse her interest. She did not think that he had said to himself, "Offer enough money and she'll leap at it" because, as she knew very well herself, the money sounded very agreeable but she was not in urgent need of money. She had her dear and affectionate nephew who, if she was in straits for money of any kind, if she needed repairs to her house or visits to a specialist or special treats, dear Raymond would always provide them. No. The sum he offered was to be exciting. It was to be exciting in the same way as it was exciting when you had a ticket for the Irish Sweep. It was a fine big sum of money that you could never achieve by any other means except luck.

But all the same, Miss Marple thought to herself, she would need some luck as well as hard work, she would require a lot of thought and pondering and possibly what she was doing might involve a certain amount of danger. But she'd got to find out herself what it was all about, he wasn't going to tell her, partly perhaps because he did not want to influence her? It is hard to tell anyone about something without letting slip your own point of view about it. It could be that Mr Rafiel had thought that his own point of view might be wrong. It was not very like him to think such a thing, but it could be possible. He might suspect that his judgment, impaired by illness, was not quite as good as it used to be. So she, Miss Marple, his agent, his employee, was to make her own guesses, come to her own conclusions. Well, it was time she came to a few conclusions now. In other words, back to the old question, *what was all this about?*

She had been directed. Let her take that first. She had been directed by a man who was now dead. She had been directed away from St Mary Mead. Therefore, the task whatever it must be, could not be attacked from there. It was not a neighbourhood problem, it was not a problem that you could solve just by looking through newspaper cuttings or making enquiries, not, that is, until you found what you had to make enquiries about. She had been directed, first to the lawyer's office, then to read a letter—two letters—in her home, then to be sent on a pleasant and well run tour round some of the Famous Houses and Gardens of Great Britain. From that she had come to the next stepping stone. The house she was in at this moment. The Old Manor House, Jocelyn St Mary, where lived Miss Clotilde Bradbury-Scott, Mrs Glynne and Miss Anthea Bradbury-Scott. Mr Rafiel had arranged that, arranged it beforehand. Some weeks before he died. Probably it was the next thing he had done after instructing his lawyers and after booking a seat on the tour in her name. Therefore, she was in this house for a purpose. It might be for only two nights, it might be longer. There might be certain things arranged which would lead her to stay longer or she would be asked to stay longer. That brought her back to where she stood now.

Mrs Glynne and her two sisters. They must be concerned, implicated in whatever this was. She would have to find out what it was. The time was short. That was the only trouble. Miss Marple had no doubt for one moment that she had the capacity to find out things. She was one of those chatty, fluffy old ladies whom other people expect to talk, to ask questions that were, on the face of it, merely gossipy questions. She would talk about her childhood and that would lead to one of the sisters talking about theirs. She'd talk about food she had eaten, servants she had had, daughters and cousins and relations, travel, marriages, births and—yes—deaths. There must be no show of special interest in her eyes when she heard about a death. Not at all. Almost automatically she was sure she could come up with the right response such as, "Oh dear me, how *very* sad!" She would have to find out relationships, incidents, life stories, see if any suggestive incidents would pop up, so to speak. It might be some incidents in the neighbourhood, not directly concerned with these three people. Something they could know about, talk about, or were pretty sure to talk about. Anyway, there would be *something* here, some clue, some pointer. The second day from now she would rejoin the tour unless she had by that time some indication that she was *not* to rejoin the tour. Her mind swept from the house to the coach and the people who had sat in it. It might be that what she was seeking had been there in the coach, and would be there again when she rejoined it. One person, several people, some innocent, (some not so innocent), some long past story. She frowned a little, trying to remember something. Something that had flashed in her mind that she had thought: Really I am sure—of what had she been sure?

Her mind went back to the three sisters. She must not be too long up here. She must unpack a few modest needs for two nights, something to change into this evening, night clothes, sponge bag, and then go down and rejoin her hostesses and make pleasant talk. A main point had to be decided. Were the three sisters to be her allies or were the three sisters enemies? They might fall into either category. She must think about that carefully.

There was a tap on the door and Mrs Glynne entered.

"I do hope you will be quite comfortable here. Can I help you to unpack? We have a very nice woman who comes in but she is only here in the morning. But she'll help you with anything."

"Oh no, thank you," said Miss Marple. "I only took out just a few necessities."

"I thought I'd show you the way downstairs again. It's rather a rambling house, you know. There are two staircases and it does make it a little difficult. Sometimes people lose their way."

"Oh, it's very kind of you," said Miss Marple.

"I hope then you will come downstairs and we will have a glass of sherry before lunch."

Miss Marple accepted gratefully and followed her guide down the stairs. Mrs Glynne, she judged, was a good many years younger than she herself was. Fifty, perhaps. Not much more. Miss Marple negotiated the stairs carefully, her left knee was always a little uncertain. There was, however, a banister at one side of the stairs. Very beautiful stairs they were, and she remarked on them.

"It is really a very lovely house," she said. "Built I suppose in the 1700's. Am I right?"

"1780," said Mrs Glynne.

She seemed pleased with Miss Marple's appreciation. She took Miss Marple into the drawing-room. A large graceful room. There were one or two rather beautiful pieces of furniture. A Queen Anne desk and a William and Mary oyster-shell bureau.

There were also some rather cumbrous Victorian settees and cabinets. The curtains were of chintz, faded and somewhat worn, the carpet was, Miss Marple thought, Irish. Possibly a Limerick Aubusson type. The sofa was ponderous and the velvet of it much worn. The other two sisters were already sitting there. They rose as Miss Marple came in and aproached her, one with a glass of sherry, the other directing her to a chair.

"I don't know whether you like sitting rather high? So many people do."

"I do," said Miss Marple. "It's so much easier. One's back, you know."

The sisters appeared to know about the difficulties of backs. The eldest of the sisters was a tall handsome woman, dark with a black coil of hair. The other one might have been a good deal younger. She was thin with grey hair that had once been fair hanging untidily on her shoulders and a faintly wraith-like appearance. She could be cast successfully as a mature Ophelia, Miss Marple thought.

Clotilde, Miss Marple thought, was certainly no Ophelia, but she would have made a magnificent Clytemnestra—she could have stabbed a husband in his bath with exultation. But since she had never had a husband, that solution wouldn't do. Miss Marple could not see her murdering anyone else but a husband—and there had been no Agamemnon in this house.

Clotilde Bradbury-Scott, Anthea Bradbury-Scott, Lavinia Glynne. Clotilde was handsome, Lavinia was plain but pleasant-looking, Anthea had one eyelid which twitched from time to time. Her eyes were large and grey and she had an odd way of glancing round to right and then to left, and then suddenly in a rather strange manner, behind her over her shoulder. It was as though she felt someone was watching her all the time. Odd thought Miss Marple. She wondered a little about Anthea.

They sat down and conversation ensued. Mrs Glynne left the room, apparently for the kitchen. She was, it seemed, the active domestic one of the three. The conversation took a usual course. Clotilde Bradbury-Scott explained that the house was a family one. It had belonged to her great-uncle and then to her uncle and when he had died it was left to her and her two sisters who had joined her there.

"He only had one son, you see," explained Miss Bradbury-Scott, "and he was killed in the war. We are really the last of the family, except for some very distant cousins."

"A beautifully proportioned house," said Miss Marple. "Your sister tells me it was build about 1780."

"Yes, I believe so. One could wish, you know, it was not quite so large and rambling."

"Repairs too," said Miss Marple, "come very heavy nowadays."

"Oh yes, indeed," Clotilde sighed. "And in many ways we have had to let a lot of it just fall down. Sad, but there it is. A lot of the outhouses, for instance, and a greenhouse. We had a very beautiful big greenhouse."

"Lovely muscat grapevine in it," said Anthea. "And Cherry Pie used to grow all along the walls outside. Yes, I really regret that very much. Of course, during the war one could not get any gardeners. We had a very young gardener and then he was called up. One does not of course grudge that, but all the same it was impossible to get things repaired and so the whole greenhouse fell down.

"So did the little conservatory near the house."

Both sisters sighed, with the sighing of those who have noted time passing, and times changing—but not for the better.

There was a melancholy here in this house, thought Miss Marple. It was impregnated somehow with sorrow—a sorrow that could not be dispersed or removed since it had penetrated too deep. It had sunk in . . . She shivered suddenly.

9. *Polygonum Baldschuanicum*

THE MEAL was conventional. A small joint of mutton, roast potatoes, followed by a plum tart with a small jug of cream and rather indifferent pastry. There were a few pictures round the dining-room wall, family pictures, Miss Marple presumed, Victorian portraits without any particular merit, the sideboard was large and heavy, a handsome piece of plum-coloured mahogany. The curtains were of dark crimson damask and at the big mahogany table ten people could easily have been seated.

Miss Marple chatted about the incidents of the tour in so far as she had been on it. As this, however, had only been three days, there was not very much to say.

"Mr Rafiel, I suppose, was an old friend of yours?" said the eldest Miss Bradbury-Scott.

"Not really," said Miss Marple. "I met him first when I was on a cruise to the West Indies. He was out there for his health, I imagine."

"Yes, he had been very crippled for some years," said Anthea.

"Very sad," said Miss Marple. "Very sad indeed. I really admired his fortitude. He seemed to manage to do so much work. Every day, you know, he dictated to his secretary and was continually sending off cables. He did not seem to give in at all kindly to being an invalid."

"Oh no, he wouldn't," said Anthea.

"We have not seen much of him of late years," said Mrs Glynne. "He was a busy man, of course. He always remembered us at Christmas very kindly."

"Do you live in London, Miss Marple?" asked Anthea.

"Oh no," said Miss Marple. "I live in the country. A very small place half way between Loomouth and Market Basing.

About twenty-five miles from London. It used to be a very pretty old-world village but of course like everything else, it is becoming what they call developed nowadays." She added, "Mr Rafiel, I suppose, lived in London? At least I noticed that in the St Honoré hotel register his address was somewhere in Eaton Square, I think, or was it Belgrave Square?"

"He had a country house in Kent," said Clotilde. "He used to entertain there, I think, sometimes. Business friends, mostly you know, or people from abroad. I don't think any of us ever visited him there. He nearly always entertained us in London on the rare occasions when we happened to meet."

"It was very kind of him," said Miss Marple, "to suggest to you that you should invite me here during the course of this tour. Very thoughtful. One wouldn't really have expected a busy man such as he must have been to have had such kindly thoughts."

"We have invited before friends of his who have been on these tours. On the whole they are very considerate the way they arrange these things. It is impossible, of course, to suit everybody's taste. The young ones naturally wish to walk, to make long excursions, to ascend hills for a view, and all that sort of thing. And the older ones who are not up to it, remain in the hotels, but hotels round here are not really at all luxurious. I am sure you would have found to-day's trip and the one to St Bonaventure to-morrow also, very fatiguing. To-morrow I believe there is a visit to an island, you know, in a boat and sometimes it can be very rough."

"Even going round houses can be very tiring," said Mrs Glynne.

"Oh, I know," said Miss Marple. "So much walking and standing about. One's feet get very tired. I suppose really I ought not to take these expeditions, but it is such a temptation to see beautiful buildings and fine rooms and furniture. All these things. And of course some splendid pictures."

"And the gardens," said Anthea. "You like gardens, don't you?"

"Oh yes," said Miss Marple, "specially the gardens. From the description in the prospectus I am really looking forward very much to seeing some of the really finely kept gardens of the historic houses we have still to visit." She beamed round the table.

It was all very pleasant, very natural, and yet she wondered why for some reason she had a feeling of strain. A feeling that there was something unnatural here. But what did she mean by unnatural? The conversation was ordinary enough consisting mainly of platitudes. She herself was making conventional remarks and so were the three sisters.

The Three Sisters, thought Miss Marple once again considering that phrase. Why did anything thought of in threes somehow seem to suggest a sinister atmosphere? The Three Sisters. The Three Witches of Macbeth. Well, one could hardly compare these three sisters to the three witches. Although Miss Marple had always thought at the back of her mind that the theatrical producers made a mistake in the way in which they produced the three witches. One production which she had seen, indeed, seemed to her quite absurd. The witches had looked more like pantomime creatures with flapping wings and ridiculously spectacular steeple hats. They had danced and slithered about. Miss Marple remembered saying to her nephew, who was standing her this Shakespearean treat, "You know, Raymond, my dear, if *I* were ever producing this splendid play I would make the three witches *quite* different. I would have them three ordinary, normal old women. Old Scottish women. They wouldn't dance or caper. They would look at each other rather slyly and you would feel a sort of menace just behind the ordinariness of them."

Miss Marple helped herself to the last mouthful of plum tart and looked across the table at Anthea. Ordinary, untidy, very vague-looking, a bit scatty. Why should she feel that Anthea was sinister?

"I am imagining things," said Miss Marple to herself. "I mustn't do that."

After luncheon she was taken on a tour of the garden. It was Anthea who was deputed to accompany her. It was, Miss Marple thought, rather a sad progress. Here, there had once been a well kept, though certainly not in any way an outstanding or remarkable, garden. It had had the elements of an ordinary Victorian garden. A shrubbery, a drive of speckled laurels, no doubt there had once been a well kept lawn and paths, a kitchen garden of about an acre and a half, too big evidently for the three sisters who lived here now. Part of it was unplanted and had gone largely to weeds. Ground elder had taken over most of the flower beds and Miss Marple's hands could hardly restrain themselves from pulling up the vagrant bindweed asserting its superiority.

Miss Anthea's long hair flapped in the wind, shedding from time to time a vague hairpin on the path or the grass. She talked rather jerkily.

"*You* have a very nice garden, I expect," she said.

"Oh, it's a very small one," said Miss Marple.

They had come along a grass path and were pausing in front of a kind of hillock that rested against the wall at the end of it.

"Our greenhouse," said Miss Anthea, mournfully.

"Oh yes, where you had such a delightful grapevine."

"Three vines," said Anthea. "A Black Hamburg and one of those small white grapes, very sweet, you know. And a third one of beautiful muscats."

"And a heliotrope, you said."

"Cherry Pie," said Anthea.

"Ah yes, Cherry Pie. Such a lovely smell. Was there any bomb trouble round here? Did that—er—knock the greenhouse down?"

"Oh no, we never suffered from anything of that kind. This neighbourhood was quite free of bombs. No, I'm afraid it just fell down from decay. We hadn't been here so very long and we had no money to repair it, or to build it up again. And in fact, it wouldn't have been worth it really because we couldn't have kept it up even if we did. I'm afraid we just let it fall down. There was nothing else we could do. And now you see, it's all grown over."

"Ah that, completely covered by—what is that flowering creeper just coming into bloom?"

"Oh yes. It's quite a common one," said Anthea. "It begins with a P. Now what is the name of it," she said doubtfully. "Poly something, something like that."

"Oh yes. I think I do know the name. Polygonum Baldschuanicum. Very quick growing, I think, isn't it? Very useful really if one wants to hide any tumbledown building or anything ugly of that kind."

The mound in front of her was certainly thickly covered with the all-enveloping green and white flowering plant. It was, as Miss Marple well knew, a kind of menace to anything else that wanted to grown. Polygonum covered everthing, and covered it in a remarkably short time.

"The greenhouse must have been quite a big one," she said.

"Oh yes—we had peaches in it, too—and nectarines." Anthea looked miserable.

"It looks really very pretty now," said Miss Marple in a consoling tone. "Very pretty little white flowers, aren't they?"

"We have a very nice magnolia tree down this path to the left," said Anthea. "Once I believe there used to be a very fine border here—a herbaceous border. But that again one cannot keep up. It is too difficult. Everything is too difficult. Nothing is like it used to be—it's all spoilt—everywhere."

She led the way quickly down a path at right-angles which ran along a side wall. Her pace had increased. Miss Marple could hardly keep up with her. It was, thought Miss Marple, as though she were deliberately being steered away from the Polygonum mound by her hostess. Steered away as from some ugly or displeasing spot. Was she ashamed perhaps that the past glories no longer remained? The Polygonum certainly was growing with extraordinary abandonment. It was not even being clipped or kept to reasonable proportions. It made a kind of flowery wilderness of that bit of the garden.

She almost looks as though she was running away from it, thought Miss Marple, as she followed her hostess. Presently her attention was diverted to a broken down pig-sty which had a few rose tendrils round it.

"My great-uncle used to keep a few pigs," explained Anthea, "but of course one would never dream of doing anything of that kind nowadays, would one? Rather too noisome, I am afraid. We have a few floribunda roses near the house. I really think floribundas are such a great answer to difficulties."

"Oh, I know," said Miss Marple.

She mentioned the names of a few recent productions in the rose line. All the names, she thought, were entirely strange to

Miss Anthea.

"Do you often come on these tours?"

The question came suddenly.

"You mean the tours of houses and of gardens?"

"Yes. Some people do it every year."

"Oh I couldn't hope to do that. They're rather expensive, you see. A friend very kindly gave me a present of this to celebrate my next birthday. So kind."

"Oh. I wondered. I wondered *why* you came. I mean—it's bound to be rather tiring, isn't it? Still, if you usually go to the West Indies, and places like that . . ."

"Oh, the West Indies was the result of kindness, too. On the part of a nephew, that time. A dear boy. So very thoughtful for his old aunt."

"Oh, I see. Yes, I see."

"I don't know what one would do without the younger generation," said Miss Marple. "They are so kind, are they not?"

"I—I suppose so. I don't really know. I—we haven't—any young relations."

"Does your sister, Mrs Glynne, have any children? She did not mention any. One never likes to ask."

"No. She and her husband never had any children. It's as well perhaps."

"And what do you mean by that?" Miss Marple wondered as they returned to the house.

10. *"Oh! Fond, Oh! Fair, The Days That Were"*

i

AT HALF past eight the next morning there was a smart tap on the door, and in answer to Miss Marple's "Come in" the door was opened and an elderly woman entered, bearing a tray with a teapot, a cup and a milk jug and a small plate of bread and butter.

"Early morning tea, ma'am," she said cheerfully. "It's a nice day, it is. I see you've got your curtains drawn back already. You've slept well then?"

"Very well indeed," said Miss Marple, laying aside a small devotional book which she had been reading.

"Well, it's a lovely day, it is. They'll have it nice for going to the Bonaventure Rocks. It's just as well you're not doing it. It's cruel on the legs, it is."

"I'm really very happy to be here," said Miss Marple. "So kind of Miss Bradbury-Scott and Mrs Glynne to issue the invitation."

"Ah well, it's nice for them too. It cheers them up to have a bit of company come to the house. Ah, it's a sad place nowadays, so it is."

She pulled the curtains at the window rather more fully, pushed back a chair and deposited a can of hot water in the china basin.

"There's a bathroom on the next floor," she said, "but we think it's better always for someone elderly to have their hot water here, so they don't have to climb the stairs."

"It's very kind of you, I'm sure—you know this house well?"

"I was here as a girl—I was the housemaid then. Three servants they had—a cook, a housemaid—a parlour-maid—kitchen maid too at one time. That was in the old Colonel's time.

Horses he kept too, and a groom. Ah, those were the days. Sad it is when things happen the way they do. He lost his wife young, the Colonel did. His son was killed in the war and his only daughter went away to live on the other side of the world. Married a New Zealander she did. Died having a baby and the baby died too. He was a sad man living alone here, and he let the house go—it wasn't kept up as it should have been. When he died he left the place to his niece Miss Clotilde and her two sisters, and she and Miss Anthea came here to live—and later Miss Lavinia lost her husband and came to join them——" she sighed and shook her head. "They never did much to the house —couldn't afford it—and they let the garden go as well——"

"It all seems a great pity," said Miss Marple.

"And such nice ladies as they all are, too—Miss Anthea is the scatty one, but Miss Clotilde went to university and is very brainy—she talks three languages—and Mrs Glynne, she's a very nice lady indeed. I thought when she came to join them as things might go better. But you never know, do you, what the future holds? I feel sometimes, as though there was a doom on this house."

Miss Marple looked enquiring.

"First one thing and then another. The dreadful plane accident—in Spain it was—and everybody killed. Nasty things, aeroplanes—I'd never go in one of them. Miss Clotilde's friends were both killed, they were husband and wife—the daughter was still at school, luckily, and escaped, but Miss Clotilde brought her here to live and did everything for her. Took her abroad for trips—to Italy and France, treated her like a daughter. She was such a happy girl—and a very sweet nature. You'd never dream that such an awful thing could happen."

"An awful thing. What was it? Did it happen here?"

"No, not here, thank God. Though in a way you might say it *did* happen here. It was here that she met him. He was in the neighbourhood—and the ladies knew his father, who was a very rich man, so he came here to visit—that was the beginning——"

"They fell in love?"

"Yes, she fell in love with him right away. He was an attractive-looking boy, with a nice way of talking and passing the time of day. You'd never think—you'd never think for one moment——" she broke off.

"There was a love affair? And it went wrong? And the girl committed suicide?"

"Suicide?" The old woman stared at Miss Marple with startled eyes.

"Whoever now told you *that*? Murder it was, bare-faced murder. Strangled and her head beaten to pulp. Miss Clotilde had to go and identify her—she's never been quite the same since. They found her body a good thirty miles from here—in the scrub of a disused quarry. And it's believed that it wasn't the first murder he'd done. There had been other girls. Six months she'd been missing. And the police searching far and wide. Oh! A wicked devil he was—a bad lot from the day he was born or so it seems. They say nowadays as there are those as can't help what they do—not right in the head, and they can't be held responsible. I don't believe a word of it! Killers are killers. And they won't even hang them nowadays. I know as there's often madness as runs in old families—there was the Derwents over to Brassington—every second generation one or other of them died in the loony bin—and there was old Mrs Paulett; walked about the lanes in her diamond tiara saying she was Marie Antoinette until they shut her up. But there wasn't anything really wrong with her—just silly like. But this boy. Yes, he was a devil right enough."

"What did they do to him?"

"They'd abolished hanging by then—or else he was too young. I can't remember it all now. They found him guilty. It may have been Bostol or Broadsand—one of those places beginning with 'B' as they sent him to."

"What was the name of the boy?"

"Michael—can't remember his last name. It's ten years ago that it happened—one forgets. Italian sort of name—like a picture. Someone who paint pictures—Raffle, that's it——"

"Michael Rafiel?"

"What's right! There was a rumour as went about that his father being so rich got him wangled out of prison. An escape like the Bank Robbers. But I think as that was just talk——"

So it had not been suicide. It had been murder. "Love!"

Elizabeth Temple had named as the cause of a girl's death. In a way she was right. A young girl had fallen in love with a killer—and for love of him had gone unsuspecting to an ugly death.

Miss Marple gave a little shudder. On her way along the village street yesterday she has passed a newspaper placard: EPSOM DOWNS MURDER, SECOND GIRL'S BODY DISCOVERED, YOUTH ASKED TO ASSIST POLICE.

So history repeated itself. An old pattern—an ugly pattern. Some lines of forgotten verse came haltingly into her brain:

Rose white youth, passionate, pale,
A singing stream in a silent vale,
A fairy prince in a prosy tale,
Oh there's nothing in life so finely frail
As Rose White Youth.

Who was there to guard Youth from Pain and Death? Youth who could not, who had never been able to, guard itself. Did they know too little? Or was it that they knew too much? And therefore thought they knew it all.

ii

Miss Marple, coming down the stairs that morning, probably rather earlier than she had been expected, found no immediate sign of her hostesses. She let herself out at the front door and wandered once round the garden. It was not because she'd really enjoyed this particular garden. It was some vague feeling that there was something here that she ought to notice, something that would give her some idea, or that had given her some idea only she had not—well, frankly, she had not been bright enough to realize just what the bright idea had been. Something she ought to take note of, something that had a bearing.

She was not at the moment anxious to see any of the three sisters. She wanted to turn a few things over in her mind. The new facts that had come to her through Janet's early tea chat.

A side gate stood open and she went through it to the village street and along a line of small shops to where a steeple poked up announcing the site of the church and its churchyard. She pushed open the lych-gate and wandered about among the graves, some dating from quite a while back, some by the far wall later ones, and one or two beyond the wall in what was obviously a new enclosure. There was nothing of great interest among the older tombs. Certain names recurred as they do in villages. A good many Princes of village origin had been buried. Jasper Prince, deeply regretted. Margery Prince, Edgar and Walter Prince, Melanie Prince, 4 years old. A family record. Hiram Broad—Ellen Jane Broad, Eliza Broad, 91 years.

She was turning away from the latter when she observed an elderly man moving in slow motion among the graves, tidying up as he walked. He gave her a salute and a "good morning".

"Good morning," said Miss Marple. "A very pleasant day."

"It'll turn to rain later," said the old man.

He spoke with the utmost certainty.

"There seem to be a lot of Princes and Broads buried here," said Miss Marple.

"Ah yes, there've always been Princes here. Used to own quite a bit of land once. There have been Broads a good many years, too."

"I see a child is buried here. Very sad when one sees a child's grave."

"Ah, that'll be little Melanie that was. Mellie, we called her. Yes, it was a sad death. Run over, she was. Ran out into the street, went to get sweets at the sweet shop. Happens a lot nowadays with cars going through at the pace they do."

"It is sad to think," said Miss Marple, "that there are so many deaths all the time. And one doesn't really notice it until one looks at the inscriptions in the churchyard. Sickness, old age, children run over, sometimes even more dreadful things. Young girls killed. Crimes, I mean."

"Ah, yes, there's a lot of that about. Silly girls, I call most of 'em. And their mums haven't got time to look after them properly nowadays—what with going out to work so much."

Miss Marple rather agreed with his criticism, but had no wish to waste time in agreement on the trend of the day.

"Staying at The Old Manor House, aren't you?" the old man asked. "Come here on the coach tour I saw. But it got too much for you, I suppose. Some of those that are gettin' on can't always take it."

"I *did* find it a little exhausting," confessed Miss Marple, "and a very kind friend of mine, a Mr Rafiel, wrote to some friends of his here and they invited me to stay for a couple of nights."

The name, Rafiel, clearly meant nothing to the elderly gardener.

"Mrs Glynne, and her two sisters have been very kind," said Miss Marple. "I suppose they've lived here a long time?"

"Not so long as that. Twenty years maybe. Belonged to old Colonel Bradbury-Scott, The Old Manor House did. Close on seventy he was when he died."

"Did he have any children?"

"A son what was killed in the war. That's why he left the place to his nieces. Nobody else to leave it to."

He went back to his work among the graves.

Miss Marple went into the church. It had felt the hand of a Victorian restorer, and had bright Victorian glass in the windows. One or two brasses and some tablets on the walls was all that was left of the past.

Miss Marple sat down in an uncomfortable pew and wondered about things.

Was she on the right track now. Things were connecting up—but the connections were far from clear.

A girl had been murdered—(actually several girls had been murdered)—suspected young men (or "youths" as they were usually called nowadays) had been rounded up by the police, to "assist them in their enquiries". A common pattern. But this was all old history, dating back ten or twelve years. There was nothing to find out—now, no problems to solve. A tragedy labelled Finis.

What could be done by her? What could Mr Rafiel possibly want her to do?

Elizabeth Temple . . . She must get Elizabeth Temple to tell her more. Elizabeth had spoken of a girl who had been engaged to be married to Michael Rafiel. But was that really so? That fact did not seem to be known to those in The Old Manor House.

A more familiar version came to Miss Marple's mind—the kind of story that had been reasonably frequent in her own village. Starting as always, "Boy meets girl". Developing in the usual way——

"And then the girl finds she is pregnant," said Miss Marple to herself, "and she tells the boy and she wants him to marry her. But he, perhaps, doesn't want to marry her—he has never had any idea of marrying her. But things may be made difficult for him in this case. His father, perhaps, won't hear of such a thing. Her relations will insist that he 'does the right thing'. And by now he is tired of the girl—he's got another girl perhaps. And so he takes a quick brutal way out—strangles her, beats her head to a pulp to avoid identification. It fits with his record—a brutal sordid crime—*but* forgotten and done with."

She looked round the church in which she was sitting. It looked so peaceful. The reality of Evil was hard to believe in. A *flair* for Evil—that was what Mr Rafiel had attributed to her. She rose and walked out of the church and stood looking round the churchyard again. Here, amongst the gravestones and their worn inscriptions no sense of Evil moved in her.

Was it Evil she had sensed yesterday at The Old Manor House? That deep depression of despair, that dark desperate grief. Anthea Bradbury-Scott, her eyes gazing fearfully back over *one* shoulder, as though fearing some presence that stood there—always stood there—behind her.

They knew something, those Three Sisters, but what was it that they knew?

Elizabeth Temple, she thought again. She pictured Elizabeth Temple with the rest of the coach party, striding across the downs at this moment, climbing up a steep path and gazing over the cliffs out to sea.

To-morrow, when she rejoined the tour, she would get Elizabeth Temple to tell her more.

Miss Marple retraced her steps to The Old Manor House, walking rather slowly because she was by now tired. She could not really feel that her morning had been productive in any way. So far The Old Manor House had given her no distinctive ideas of any kind, a tale of a past tragedy told by Janet, but there were always past tragedies treasured in the memories of domestic workers and which were remembered quite as clearly as all the happy events such as spectacular weddings, big entertainments and successful operations or accidents from which people had recovered in a miraculous manner.

As she drew near the gate she saw two female figures standing there. One of them detached itself and came to meet her. It was Mrs. Glynne.

"Oh, there you are," she said. "We wondered, you know. I thought you must have gone out for a walk somewhere and I did so hope you wouldn't overtire yourself. If I had known you had come downstairs and gone out, I would have come with you to show anything there is to show. Not that there is very much."

"Oh, I just wandered around," said Miss Marple. "The churchyard, you know, and the church. I'm always very interested in churches. Sometimes there are very curious epitaphs. Things like that. I make quite a collection of them. I suppose the church here was restored in Victorian times?"

"Yes, they did put in some rather ugly pews, I think. You know, good quality wood, and strong and all that, but not very artistic."

"I hope they didn't take away anything of particular interest."

"No, I don't think so. It's not really a very old church."

"There did not seem to be many tablets or brasses or anything of that kind," agreed Miss Marple.

"You are quite interested in ecclesiastical architecture?"

"Oh, I don't make a study of it or anything like that, but of course in my own village, St Mary Mead, things do rather revolve round the church. I mean, they always have. In my young days, that was so. Nowadays of course it's rather different. Were you brought up in this neighbourhood?"

"Oh, not really. We lived not very far away, about thirty miles or so. At Little Herdsley. My father was a retired serviceman—a Major in the Artillery. We came over here occasionally to see my uncle—indeed to see my great-uncle before him. No. I've not even been here very much of late years. My other two sisters moved in after my uncle's death, but at that time I was still abroad with my husband. He only died about four or five years ago."

"Oh, I see."

"They were anxious I should come and join them here and really, it seemed the best thing to do. We had lived in India for some years. My husband was still stationed there at the time of his death. It is very difficult nowadays to know where one would wish to—should I say, put one's roots down."

"Yes, indeed. I can quite see that. And you felt, of course, that you had roots here since your family had been here for a long time."

"Yes. Yes, one did feel that. Of course, I'd always kept up with my sisters, had been to visit them. But things are always very different from what one thinks they will be. I have bought a small cottage near London, near Hampton Court, where I spend a good deal of my time, and I do a little occasional work for one or two charities in London."

"So your time is fully occupied. How wise of you."

"I have felt of late that I should spend more time here, perhaps. I've been a little worried about my sisters."

"Their health?" suggested Miss Marple. "One *is* rather worried nowadays, especially as there is not really anyone competent whom one can employ to look after people as they become rather feebler or have certain ailments. So much rheumatism and arthritis about. One is always so afraid of people falling down in the bath or an accident coming down stairs. Something of that kind."

"Clotilde has always been very strong," said Mrs Glynne. "Tough, I should describe her. But I am rather worried sometimes about Anthea. She is vague, you know, very vague indeed. And she wanders off sometimes—and doesn't seem to know where she is."

"Yes, it is sad when people worry. There is so much to worry one."

"I don't really think there is much to worry Anthea."

"She worries about income tax, perhaps, money affairs," suggested Miss Marple.

"No, no, not that so much but—oh, she worries so much about the garden. She remembers the garden as it used to be, and she's very anxious, you know, to—well, to spend money in putting things right again. Clotilde has had to tell her that really one can't afford that nowadays. But she keeps talking of the hot-houses, the peaches that used to be there. The grapes—and all that."

"And the Cherry Pie on the walls?" suggested Miss Marple, remembering a remark.

"Fancy your remembering that. Yes. Yes, it's one of the things one does remember. Such a charming smell, heliotrope. And such a nice name for it, Cherry Pie. One always remembers that. And the grapevine. The little, small, early sweet grapes. Ah well, one must not remember the past too much."

"And the flower borders too, I suppose," said Miss Marple.

"Yes. Yes, Anthea would like to have a big well kept herbaceous border again. Really *not* feasible now. It is as much as one can do to get local people who will come and mow the lawns every fortnight. Every year one seems to employ a different firm. And Anthea would like pampas grass planted again. And the Mrs Simpkin pinks. White, you know. All along the stone edge border. And a fig tree that grew just outside the greenhouse. She remembers all these and talks about them."

"It must be difficult for you."

"Well, yes. Arguments, you see, hardly appeal in any way. Clotilde, of course, is very downright about things. She just refuses point-blank and says she doesn't want to hear another word about it."

"It is difficult," said Miss Marple, "to know how to take things. Whether one should be firm. Rather authoritative. Perhaps, even, well, just a little—a little *fierce*, you know, or whether one should be sympathetic. Listen to things and perhaps hold out hopes which one knows are not justified. Yes, it's difficult."

"But it's easier for me because you see I go away again, and then come back now and then to stay. So it's easy for me to pretend things may be easier soon and that something may be done. But really, the other day when I came home and I found that Anthea had tried to engage a most expensive firm of landscape gardeners to renovate the garden, to build up the greenhouses again—which is *quite* absurd because even if you put vines in they would not bear for another two or three years.

Clotilde knew nothing about it and she was extremely angry when she discovered the estimate for this work on Anthea's desk. She was really quite unkind."

"So many things are difficult,' said Miss Marple.

It was a useful phrase which she used often.

"I shall have to go rather early to-morrow morning, I think," said Miss Marple. "I was making enquiries at the Golden Boar where I understand the coach party assembles to-morrow morning. They are making quite an early start. Nine o'clock, I understand."

"Oh dear. I hope you will not find it too fatiguing."

"Oh, I don't think so. I gather we are going to a place called—now wait a minute, what was it called?—Stirling St Mary. Something like that. And it does not seem to be very far away. There's an interesting church to see on the way and a castle. In the afternoon there is a quite pleasant garden, not too many acres, but some special flowers. I feel sure that after this very nice rest that I have had here, I shall be quite all right. I understand now that I would have been very tired if I had had these two days of climbing up cliffsides and all the rest of it."

"Well, you must rest this afternoon, so as to be fresh for to-morrow," said Mrs Glynne, as they went into the house. "Miss Marple has been to visit the church," said Mrs Glynne to Clotilde.

"I'm afraid there is not very much to see," said Clotilde. "Victorian glass of a most hideous kind, I think myself. No expense spared. I'm afraid my uncle was partly to blame. He was very pleased with those rather crude reds and blues."

"Very crude. Very vulgar, I always think," said Lavinia Glynne.

Miss Marple settled down after lunch to have a nap, and she did not join her hostesses until nearly dinner time. After dinner a good deal of chat went on until it was bedtime. Miss Marple set the tone in remembrances . . . Remembrances of her own youth, her early days, places she had visited, travels or tours she had made, occasional people she had known.

She went to bed tired, with a sense of failure. She had learned nothing more, possibly because there was nothing more to learn. A fishing expedition where the fish did not rise—possibly because there were no fish there. Or it could be that she did not know the right bait to use?

11. Accident

MISS MARPLE'S tea was brought at seven-thirty the following morning so as to allow her plenty of time to get up and pack her few belongings. She was just closing her small suitcase when there was a rather hurried tap on the door and Clotilde came in, looking upset.

"Oh dear, Miss Marple, there is a young man downstairs who has called to see you. Emlyn Price. He is on the tour with you and they sent him here."

"Of course, I remember him. Yes. Quite young?"

"Oh yes. Very modern-looking, and a lot of hair and all that, but he has really come to—well, to break some bad news to you. There has been, I am sorry to say, an accident."

"An accident?" Miss Marple stared. "You mean—to the coach? There has been an accident on the road? Someone has been hurt?"

"No. No, it was not the coach. There was no trouble there. It was in the course of the expedition yesterday afternoon. There was a great deal of wind you may remember, though I don't think that had anything to do with it. People strayed about a bit, I think. There is a regular path, but you can also climb up and go across the downs. Both ways lead to the Memorial Tower on the top of Bonaventure—where they were all making for. People got separated a bit and I suppose, really, there was no one actually guiding them or looking after them which, perhaps, there ought to have been. People aren't very sure-footed always and the slope overhanging the gorge is very steep. There was a bad fall of stones or rocks which came crashing down the hillside and knocked someone out on the path below."

"Oh dear," said Miss Marple, "I am sorry. I am most terribly sorry. Who was it who was hurt?"

"A Miss Temple or Tenderdon, I understand."

"Elizabeth Temple," said Miss Marple. "Oh dear, I am sorry. I talked to her a good deal. I sat in the next seat to her on the coach. She is, I believe, a retired schoolmistress, a very well known one."

"Of course," said Clotilde, "I know her quite well. She was Headmistress of Fallowfield, quite a famous school. I'd no idea she was on this tour. She retired as Headmistress, I think a year or two ago, and there is a new, rather young Headmistress there now with rather advanced progressive ideas. But Miss Temple is not very old, really, she's about sixty, I should think, and very active, fond of climbing and walking and all the rest of it. This really seems *most* unfortunate. I hope she's not badly hurt. I haven't heard any details yet."

"This is quite ready now," said Miss Marple, snapping down the lid of her suitcase. "I will come down at once and see Mr Price."

Clotilde seized the suitcase.

"Let me. I can carry this perfectly. Come down with me, and be careful of the stairs."

Miss Marple came down. Emlyn Price was waiting for her. His hair was looking even wilder than usual and he was wearing a splendid array of fancy boots and a leather jerkin and brilliant emerald green trousers.

"Such an unfortunate business," he said, seizing Miss Marple's hand. "I thought I'd come along myself and—well, break it to you about the accident. I expect Miss Bradbury-Scott has told you. It's Miss Temple. You know. The school dame. I don't know quite what she was doing or what happened, but some stones, or rather boulders, rolled down from above. It's rather a precipitous slope and it knocked her out and they had to take her off to hospital with concussion last night. I gather she's rather bad. Anyway, the tour for to-day is cancelled and we are stopping on here to-night."

"Oh dear," said Miss Marple, "I am sorry. I'm very sorry."

"I think they've decided not to go on to-day because they really have to wait and see what the medical report is, so we are proposing to spend one more night here at the Golden Boar and to rearrange the tour a little, so that perhaps we shall miss out altogether going to Grangmering which we were going to do to-morrow, and which is not very interesting really, or so they say. Mrs Sandbourne has gone off early to the hospital to see how things are this morning. She's going to join us at the Golden Boar for coffee at 11 o'clock. I thought perhaps you'd like to come along and hear the latest news."

"I'll certainly come along with you," said Miss Marple. "Of course. At once."

She turned to say goodbye to Clotilde and Mrs Glynne who had joined her.

"I must thank you so much," she said. "You have been so kind and it has been so delightful to have these two nights here. I feel so rested and everything. Most unfortunate this has occurred."

"If you would like to spend another night," said Mrs Glynne, "I am sure——" She looked at Clotilde.

It occurred to Miss Marple, who had as sharp a sideways glance as anyone could desire, that Clotilde had a slightly disapproving look. She almost shook her head, though it was such a small movement that it was hardly noticeable. But she was, Miss Marple thought, hushing down the suggestion that Mrs Glynne was making.

". . . although of course I expect it would be nicer for you to be with the others and to——"

"Oh yes, I think it would be better," said Miss Marple. "I shall know then what the plans are and what to do about things, and perhaps I could be of help in some way. One never knows. So thank you again very much. It will not be difficult, I expect, to get a room at the Golden Boar." She looked at Emlyn, who said reassuringly,

"That'll be all right. Several rooms have been vacated to-day. They won't be full at all. Mrs Sandbourne, I think, has booked for all the party to stay there to-night, and to-morrow we shall see—well, we shall see how this all goes on."

Good-byes were said again and thanks. Emlyn Price took Miss Marple's belongings and started out at a good striding pace.

"It's really only just round the corner, and then the first street to the left," he said.

"Yes, I passed it yesterday, I think. Poor Miss Temple. I do hope she's not badly hurt."

"I think she is rather," said Emlyn Price. "Of course, you know what doctors are, and hospital people. They say the same thing always: 'as well as can be expected'. There's no local hospital—they had to take her to Carristown which is about eight miles away. Anyway, Mrs Sandbourne will be back with the news by the time we've fixed you up at the hotel."

They got there to find the tour assembled in the coffee room and coffee and morning buns and pastries were being served. Mr and Mrs Butler were talking at the moment.

"Oh, it's just too, too tragic this happening," said Mrs Butler. "Just too upsetting, isn't it? Just when we were all so happy and enjoying everything so much. Poor Miss Temple. And I always thought she was very sure-footed. But there, you know, you never can tell, can you, Henry?"

"No, indeed," said Henry. "No, indeed. I am wondering really—yes, our time's very short you know—whether we hadn't better—well, give up this tour at this point here. Not continue with it. It seems to me that there's bound to be a bit of difficulty resuming things until we know definitely. If this was—well—I mean, if this should be so serious that it could prove fatal, there might—well—I mean there might have to be an inquest or something of that kind."

"Oh Henry, don't say dreadful things like that!"

"I'm sure," said Miss Cooke, "that you are being a little too pessimistic, Mr Butler. I am sure that things couldn't be as serious as that."

In his foreign voice Mr Caspar said: "But yes, they are serious. I hear yesterday. When Mrs Sandbourne talk on telephone to doctor. It is very, very serious. They say she has concussion bad—very bad. A special doctor he is coming to look at her and see if he can operate or if impossible. Yes—it is all very bad."

"Oh dear," said Miss Lumley. "If there's any doubt, perhaps we ought to go home, Mildred. I must look up the trains, I think." She turned to Mrs Butler. "You see, I have made arrangements about my cats with the neighbours, and if I was delayed a day or two it might make great difficulties for *everyone*."

"Well, it's no good our working ourselves up too much," said Mrs Riseley-Porter, in her deep, authoritative voice. "Joanna, put this bun in the waste-paper basket, will you? It is really quite uneatable. Most unpleasant jam. But I don't want to leave it on my plate. It might make for bad feeling."

Joanna got rid of the bun. She said:

"Do you think it would be all right if Emlyn and I went out for a walk? I mean, just saw something of the town. It's not much good our sitting about here, making gloomy remarks, is it? We can't *do* anything."

"I think you'd be very wise to go out," said Miss Cooke.

"Yes, you go along," said Miss Barrow before Mrs Riseley-Porter could speak.

Miss Cooke and Miss Barrow looked at each other and sighed, shaking their heads.

"The grass was very slippery," said Miss Barrow. "I slid once or twice myself, you know, on that very short turf."

"And the stones, too," said Miss Cooke. "Quite a shower of small stones fell down just as I was turning a corner on the path. Yes, one struck me on the shoulder quite sharply."

Tea, coffee, biscuits and cakes despatched, everyone seemed somewhat dissociated and ill at ease. When a catastrophe has occurred, it is very difficult to know what is the proper way to meet it. Everyone had given their view, had expressed surprise and distress. They were now awaiting news and at the same time had a slight hankering after some form of sight-seeing, some interest to carry them through the morning. Lunch would not be served until one o'clock and they really felt that to sit around and repeat their same remarks would be rather a gloomy business.

Miss Cooke and Miss Barrow rose as one woman and explained that it was necessary for them to do a little shopping. One or two things they needed, and they also wished to go to the post office and buy stamps.

"I want to send off one or two postcards. And I want to enquire about postal dues on a letter to China," said Miss Barrow.

"And I want to match some wools," said Miss Cooke. "And

also it seemed to me there was rather an interesting building on the other side of the Market Square."

"I think it would do us all good to get out," said Miss Barrow.

Colonel and Mrs Walker also rose, and suggested to Mr and Mrs Butler that they too might go out and see what there was to see. Mrs Butler expressed hopes of an antique shop.

"Only I don't really mean a real antique shop. More what you would call a junk shop. Sometimes you can pick up some really interesting things there."

They all trooped out. Emlyn Price had already sidled to the door and disappeared in pursuit of Joanna without troubling to use conversation to explain his departure. Mrs Riseley-Porter, having made a belated attempt to call her niece back, said she thought that at least the lounge would be rather more pleasant to sit in. Miss Lumley agreed—Mr Caspar escorted the ladies with the air of a foreign equerry.

Professor Wanstead and Miss Marple remained.

"I think myself," said Professor Wanstead, addressing Miss Marple, "that it would be pleasant to sit outside the Hotel. There is a small terrace giving on the street. If I might persuade you?"

Miss Marple thanked him and rose to her feet. She had hardly exchanged a word so far with Professor Wanstead. He had several learned looking books with him, one of which he was usually perusing, even in the coach he continued to try and read.

"But perhaps you too want to shop," he said. "For myself, I would prefer to wait somewhere peacefully for the return of Mrs Sandbourne. It is important, I think, that we should know exactly what we are in for."

"I quite agree with you, as to that," said Miss Marple. "I did a certain amount of walking round the town yesterday and I don't feel any necessity to do so again to-day. I'd rather wait here in case there is anything I can do to help. Not that I suppose there is, but one never knows."

They moved together through the hotel door and round the corner to where there was a little square of garden with a raised stone walk close to the wall of the hotel and on which there were various forms of basket chairs. There was no one there at the moment so they sat down. Miss Marple looked thoughtfully at her vis-à-vis. At his corrugated and wrinkled face, his bushy brows, his luxuriant head of grey hair. He walked with a slight stoop. He had an interesting face, Miss Marple decided. His voice was dry and caustic, a professional man of some kind, she thought.

"I am not wrong, am I," said Professor Wanstead. "You *are* Miss Jane Marple?"

"Yes, I am Jane Marple."

She was slightly surprised, though for no particular reason. They had not been long enough together for people to be identified by the other travellers. The last two nights she had not been with the rest of the party. It was quite natural.

"I thought so," said Professor Wanstead, "from a description I have had of you."

"A description of me?" Miss Marple was again slightly surprised.

"Yes, I had a description of you—" he paused for a moment. His voice was not exactly lowered, but it lost volume, although she could still hear it quite easily. "—from Mr Rafiel."

"Oh," said Miss Marple, startled. "From Mr Rafiel."

"You are surprised?"

"Well, yes, I am rather."

"I don't know that you should be."

"I didn't expect——" began Miss Marple and then stopped.

Professor Wanstead did not speak. He was merely sitting, looking at her intently. In a minute or two, thought Miss Marple to herself, he will say to me, "What symptoms exactly, dear lady? Any discomfort in swallowing? Any lack of sleep? Digestion in good order?" She was almost sure now that he was a doctor.

"When did he describe me to you? That must have been——"

"You were going to say some time ago—some weeks ago. Before his death—that is so. He told me that you would be on this tour."

"And he knew that you would be on it too—that you were going on it."

"You can put it that way," said Professor Wanstead. "He said," he continued, "that you would be travelling on this tour, that he had in fact arranged for you to be travelling on this tour."

"It was very kind of him," said Miss Marple. "Very kind indeed. I was most surprised when I found he'd booked me. Such a treat. Which I could not have afforded for myself."

"Yes," said Professor Wanstead. "Very well put." He nodded his head as one who applauds a good performance by a pupil.

"It is sad that it has been interrupted in this fashion," said Miss Marple. "Very sad indeed. When I am sure we were all enjoying ourselves so much."

"Yes," said Professor Wanstead. "Yes, very sad. And unexpected, do you think, or not unexpected?"

"Now what do you mean by that, Professor Wanstead?"

His lips curled in a slight smile as he met her challenging look.

"Mr Rafiel," he said, "spoke to me about you at some length, Miss Marple. He suggested that I should be on this tour with you. I should in due course almost certainly make your acquaintance, since members in a tour inevitably do make each other's acquaintance, though it usually takes a day or two for them to split up, as it were, into possible groupings led by similar tastes or interests. And he further suggested to me that I should, shall we say, keep on eye on you."

"Keep an eye on me?" said Miss Marple, showing some slight displeasure. "And for what reason?"

"I think reasons of protection. He wanted to be quite sure that nothing should happen to you."

"Happen to me? What should happen to me, I should like to know?"

"Possibly what happened to Miss Elizabeth Temple," said Professor Wanstead.

Joanna Crawford came round the corner of the hotel. She was carrying a shopping basket. She passed them, nodding a little, she looked towards them with slight curiosity and went on down the street. Professor Wanstead did not speak until she had gone out of sight.

"A nice girl," he said, "at least I think so. Content at present to be a beast of burden to an autocratic aunt, but I have no doubt will reach the age of rebellion fairly soon."

"What did you mean by what you said just now?" said Miss Marple, uninterested for the moment in Joanna's possible rebellion.

"That is a question which, perhaps, owing to what has happened we shall have to discuss."

"You mean because of the accident?"

"Yes. If it was an accident."

"Do you think it *wasn't* an accident?"

"Well, I think it's just possible. That's all."

"I don't of course know anything about it," said Miss Marple, hesitating.

"No. You were absent from the scene. You were—shall I put it this way—were you just possibly on duty elsewhere?"

Miss Marple was silent for a moment. She looked at Professor Wanstead once or twice and then she said:

"I don't think I know exactly what you mean."

"You are being careful. You are quite right to be careful."

"I have made it a habit," said Miss Marple.

"To be careful?"

"I should not put it exactly like that, but I have made a point of being always ready to disbelieve as well as believe anything that is told to me."

"Yes, and you are quite right too. You don't know anything about me. You know my name from the passenger list of a very agreeable tour visiting castles and historic houses and splendid gardens. Possibly the gardens are what will interest you most."

"Possibly."

"There are other people here too who are interested in gardens."

"Or profess to be interested in gardens."

"Ah," said Professor Wanstead. "You have noticed that."

He went on, "Well, it was my part, or at any rate to begin with, to observe you, to watch what you were doing, to be near at hand in case there was any possibility of—well, we might call it roughly—dirty work of any kind. But things are slightly altered now. You must make up your mind if I am your enemy or your ally."

"Perhaps you are right," said Miss Marple. "You put it very clearly but you have not given me any information about yourself yet on which to judge. You were a friend, I presume, of the late Mr Rafiel?"

"No," said Professor Wanstead, "I was not a friend of Mr

Rafiel. I had met him once or twice. Once on a committee of a hospital, once at some other public event. I knew about him. He, I gather, also knew about me. If I say to you, Miss Marple, that I am a man of some eminence in my own profession, you may think me a man of bounding conceit."

"I don't think so," said Miss Marple. "I should say, if you say that about yourself, that you are probably speaking the truth. You are, perhaps, a medical man."

"Ah. You are perceptive, Miss Marple. Yes, you are quite perceptive. I have a medical degree, but I have a speciality too. I am a pathologist and psychologist. I don't carry credentials about with me. You will probably have to take my word up to a certain point, though I can show you letters addressed to me, and possibly official documents that might convince you. I undertake mainly specialist work in connection with medical jurisprudence. To put it in perfectly plain everyday language, I am interested in the different types of criminal brain. That has been a study of mine for many years. I have written books on the subject, some of them violently disputed, some of them which have attracted adherence to my ideas. I do not do very arduous work nowadays, I spend my time mainly writing up my subject, stressing certain points that have appealed to me. From time to time I come across things that strike me as interesting. Things that I want to study more closely. This I am afraid must seem rather tedious to you."

"Not at all," said Miss Marple. "I am hoping perhaps, from what you are saying now, that you will be able to explain to me certain things which Mr Rafiel did not see fit to explain to me. He asked me to embark upon a certain project but he gave me no useful information on which to work. He left me to accept it and to proceed, as it were, completely in the dark. It seemed to me extremely foolish of him to treat the matter in that way."

"But you accepted it?"

"I accepted it. I will be quite honest with you. I had a financial incentive."

"Did that weigh with you?"

Miss Marple was silent for a moment and then she said slowly,

"You may not believe it, but my answer to that is, 'Not really'."

"I am not surprised. But your interest was aroused. That is what you are trying to tell me."

"Yes. My interest was aroused. I had known Mr Rafiel not well, casually, but for a certain period of time—some weeks in fact—in the West Indies. I see you know about it, more or less."

"I know that that was where Mr Rafiel met you and where—shall I say—you two collaborated."

Miss Marple looked at him rather doubtfully. "Oh," she said, "he said that, did he?" She shook her head.

"Yes, he did," said Professor Wanstead. "He said you had a remarkable flair for criminal matters."

Miss Marple raised her eyebrows as she looked at him.

"And I suppose that seems to you most unlikely," she said. "It surprises you."

"I seldom allow myself to be surprised at what happens," said Professor Wanstead. "Mr Rafiel was a very shrewd and astute man, a good judge of people. He thought that you, too, were a good judge of people."

"I would not set myself up as a good judge of people," said Miss Marple. "I would only say that certain people remind me of certain other people that I have known, and that therefore I can presuppose a certain likeness between the way they would act. If you think I know all about what I am supposed to be doing here, you are wrong."

"By accident more than design," said Professor Wanstead, "we seem to have settled here in a particularly suitable spot for discussion of certain matters. We do not appear to be over-looked, we cannot easily be overheard, we are not near a window or a door and there is no balcony or window overhead. In fact, we can talk."

"I should appreciate that," said Miss Marple. "I am stressing the fact that I am myself completely in the dark as to what I am doing or supposed to be doing. I don't know why Mr Rafiel wanted it that way."

"I think I can guess that. He wanted you to approach a certain set of facts, of happenings, unbiased by what anyone would tell you first."

"So you are not going to tell me anything either?" Miss Marple sounded irritated. "Really!" she said, "there are limits."

"Yes," said Professor Wanstead. He smiled suddenly. "I agree with you. We must do away with some of these limits. I am going to tell you certain facts that will make certain things fairly clear to you. You in turn may be able to tell me certain facts."

"I rather doubt it," said Miss Marple. "One or two rather peculiar indications perhaps, but indications are not facts."

"Therefore——" said Professor Wanstead, and paused.

"For goodness' sake, tell me something," said Miss Marple.

12. *A Consultation*

"I'M NOT going to make a long story of things. I'll explain quite simply how I came into this matter. I act as confidential adviser from time to time for the Home Office. I am also in touch with certain institutions. There are certain establishments which, in the event of crime, provide board and lodging for certain types of criminal who have been found guilty of certain acts. They remain there at what is termed Her Majesty's pleasure, sometimes for a definite length of time and in direct association with their age. If they are below a certain age they have to be received in some place of detention specially indicated. You understand that, no doubt."

"Yes, I understand quite well what you mean."

"Usually I am consulted fairly soon after whatever the—shall we call it—crime has happened, to judge such matters as treatment, possibilities in the case, prognosis favourable or unfavourable, all the various words. They do not mean much and I will not go into them. But occasionally also I am consulted by a responsible Head of such an institution for a particular reason. In this matter I received a communication from a certain Department which was passed to me through the Home Office. I went to visit the Head of this institution. In fact, the Governor responsible for the prisoners or patients or whatever you like to call them. He was by way of being a friend of mine. A friend of fairly long standing though not one with whom I was on terms of great intimacy. I went down to the institution in question and the Governor laid his troubles before me. They referred to one particular inmate. He was not satisfied about this inmate. He had certain doubts. This was the case of a young man or one who had been a young man, in fact little more than a boy, when he came there. That was now several years ago. As time went on, and after the present Governor had taken up his own residence there (he had not been there at the original arrival of this prisoner), he became worried. Not because he himself was a professional man, but because he was a man of experience of criminal patients and prisoners. To put it quite simply, this had been a boy who from his early youth had been completely unsatisfactory. You can call it by what term you like. A young delinquent, a young thug, a bad lot, a person of diminished responsibility. There are many terms. Some of them fit, some of them don't fit, some of them are merely puzzling. He was a criminal type. That was certain. He had joined gangs, he had beaten up people, he was a thief, he had stolen, he had embezzled, he had taken part in swindles, he had initiated certain frauds. In fact, he was a son who would be any father's despair.'

"Oh, I see," said Miss Marple.

"And what do you see, Miss Marple?"

"Well, what I think I see is that you are talking of Mr Rafiel's son."

"You are quite right. I am talking of Mr Rafiel's son. What do you know about him?"

"Nothing," said Miss Marple. "I only heard—and that was yesterday—that Mr Rafiel had a delinquent, or unsatisfactory, if we like to put it mildly, son. A son with a criminal record. I know very little about him. Was he Mr Rafiel's only son?"

"Yes, he was Mr Rafiel's only son. But Mr Rafiel also had two daughters. One of them died when she was fourteen, the elder daughter married quite happily but had no children."

"Very sad for him."

"Possibly," said Professor Wanstead. "One never knows. His wife died young and I think it possible that *her* death saddened him very much, though he was never willing to show it. How much he cared for his son and daughters I don't know. He provided for them. He did his best for them. He did his best for his son, but what his feelings were one cannot say. He was not an easy man to read that way. I think his whole life and interest lay in his profession of making money. It was the making of it, like all great financiers, that interested him. Not the actual money which he secured by it. That, as you might say, was sent out like a good servant to earn more money in more interesting and unexpected ways. He enjoyed finance. He loved finance. He thought of very little else.

"I think he did all that was possible for his son. He got him out of scrapes at school, he employed good lawyers to get him released from Court proceedings whenever possible, but the final blow came, perhaps presaged by some earlier happenings. The boy was taken to Court on a charge of assault against a young girl. It was said to be assault and rape and he suffered a term of imprisonment for it, with some leniency shown because of his youth. But later, a second and really serious charge was brought against him."

"He killed a girl," said Miss Marple. "Is that right? That's what I heard."

"He lured a girl away from her home. It was some time before her body was found. She had been strangled. And afterwards her face and head had been disfigured by some heavy stones or rocks, presumably to prevent her identity being made known."

"Not a very nice business," said Miss Marple, in her most old-ladylike tone.

Professor Wanstead looked at her for a moment or two.

"You describe it that way?"

"It is how it seems to me," said Miss Marple. "I don't like that sort of thing. I never have. If you expect me to feel sympathy, regret, urge an unhappy childhood, blame bad environment; if you expect me in fact to weep over him, this young murderer of yours, I do not feel inclined so to do. I do not like evil beings who do evil things."

"I am delighted to hear it," said Professor Wanstead. "What I suffer in the course of my profession from people weeping and gnashing their teeth, and blaming everything on some happening in the past, you would hardly believe. If people knew the bad environments that people have had, the unkindness, the difficulties of their lives and the fact that nevertheless they can come through unscathed, I don't think they would so often take the opposite point of view. The misfits are to be pitied, yes, they are to be pitied if I may say so for the genes with which they are born and over which they have no control themselves. I pity epileptics in the same way. If you know what genes are——"

"I know, more or less," said Miss Marple. "It's common knowledge nowadays, though naturally I have no exact chemical or technical knowledge."

"The Governor, a man of experience, told me exactly why he was so anxious to have my verdict. He had felt increasingly in his experience of this particular inmate that, in plain words, the boy was *not* a killer. He didn't think he was the type of a killer, he was like no killer he had ever seen before, he was of the opinion that the boy was the kind of criminal type who would never go straight no matter what treatment was given to him, would never reform himself; and for whom nothing in one sense of the word could be done, but at the same time he felt increasingly certain that the verdict upon him had been a wrong one. He did not believe that the boy had killed a girl, first strangled her and then disfigured her after rolling her body into a ditch. He just couldn't bring himself to believe it. He'd looked over the facts of the case, which seemed to be fully proved. This boy had known the girl, he had been seen with her on several different occasions before the crime. They had presumably slept together and there were other points. His car had been seen in the neighbourhood. He himself had been recognized and all the rest of it. A perfectly fair case. But my friend was unhappy about it, he said. He was a man who had a very strong feeling for justice. He wanted a different opinion. He wanted, in fact, not the police side which he knew, he wanted a professional medical view. That was my field, he said. My line of country entirely. He wanted me to see this young man and talk with him, visit him, make a professional appraisal of him and give him my opinion."

"Very interesting," said Miss Marple. "Yes, I call that very interesting. After all, your friend—I mean your Governor—was a man of experience, a man who loved justice. He was a man whom you'd be willing to listen to. Presumably then, you did listen to him."

"Yes," said Professor Wanstead, "I was deeply interested. I saw the subject, as I will call him, I approached him from several different attitudes. I talked to him, I discussed various changes likely to occur in the law. I told him it might be possible to bring down a lawyer, a Queen's Counsel, to see what points there might be in his favour, and other things. I approached him as a friend but also as an enemy so that I could see how he responded to different approaches, and I also made a good many physical tests, such as we use very frequently nowadays. I will not go into those with you because they are wholly technical."

"Then what did you think in the end?"

"I thought," said Professor Wanstead, "I thought my friend was likely to be right. I did not think that Michael Rafiel was a murderer."

"What about the earlier case you mentioned?"

"That told against him, of course. Not in the jury's mind, because of course they did not hear about that until after the judge's summing up, but certainly in the judge's mind. It told against him, but I made a few enquiries myself afterwards. He had assaulted a girl. He had conceivably raped her, but he had not attempted to strangle her and in my opinion—I have seen a great many cases which come before the Assizes—it seemed to me highly unlikely that there was a very definite case of rape. Girls, you must remember, are far more ready to be raped nowadays than they used to be. Their mothers insist, very often, that they should call it rape. The girl in question had had several boy-friends who had gone further than friendship. I did not think it counted very greatly as evidence against him. The actual murder case—yes, that was undoubtedly murder—but I continued to feel by all tests, physical tests, mental tests, psychological tests, none of them accorded with this particular crime."

"Then what did you do?"

"I communicated with Mr Rafiel. I told him that I would like an interview with him on a certain matter concerning his son. I went to him. I told him what I thought, what the Governor thought, that we had no evidence, that there were no grounds of appeal, at present, but that we both believed that a miscarriage of justice had been committed. I said I thought possibly an enquiry might be held, it might be an expensive business, it might bring out certain facts that could be laid before the Home Office, it might be successful, it might not. There might be something there, some evidence if you looked for it. I said it would be expensive to look for it but I presumed that would make no difference to anyone in his position. I had realized by that time that he was a sick man, a very ill man. He told me so himself. He told me that he had been in expectation of an early death, that he'd been warned two years ago that death could not be delayed for what they first thought was about a year, but later they realised that he would last rather longer because of his unusual physical strength. I asked him what he felt about his son."

"And what did he feel about his son?" asked Miss Marple.

"Ah, you want to know that. So did I. He was, I think, extremely honest with me even if—"

"—even if rather ruthless?" said Miss Marple.

"Yes, Miss Marple. You are using the right word. He was a ruthless man, but he was a just man and an honest man. He said, 'I've known what my son was like for many years. I have not tried to change him because I don't believe that anyone could change him. He is made a certain way. He is crooked. He's a bad lot. He'll always be in trouble. He's dishonest. Nobody, nothing could make him go straight. I am well assured of that. I have in a sense washed my hands of him. Though not legally or outwardly; he has always had money if he required it. Help legal or otherwise if he gets into trouble. I have done always what I could do. Well, let us say if I had a son who was a spastic, who was sick, who was epileptic, I would do what I could for him. If you have a son who is sick morally, shall we say, and for whom there is no cure, I have done what I could also. No more and no less. What can I do for him now?' I told him that it depended what he wanted to do. 'There's no difficulty about that,' he said. 'I am handicapped but I can see quite clearly what I want to do. I want to get him vindicated. I want to get him released from confinement. I want to get him free to continue to lead his own life as best he can lead it. If he must lead it in further dishonesties, then he must lead it that way. I will leave provision for him, to do for him everything that can be done. I don't want him suffering, imprisoned, cut off from his life because of a perfectly natural and unfortunate mistake. If somebody else, some other man killed that girl, I want the fact brought to light and recognized. I want justice for Michael. But I am handicapped. I am a very ill man. My time is measured now not in years or months but in weeks.'

"Lawyers, I suggested—I know a firm— He cut me short. 'Your lawyers will be useless. You can employ them but they will be useless. I must arrange what I can arrange in such a limited time.' He offered me a large fee to undertake the search for the truth and to undertake everything possible with no expense spared. 'I can do next to nothing myself. Death may come at any moment. I empower you as my chief help, and to assist you at my request I will try to find a certain person.' He wrote down a name for me. Miss Jane Marple. He said 'I don't want to give you her address. I want you to meet her in surroundings of my own choosing,' and he then told me of this tour, this charming, harmless, innocent tour of historic houses, castles and gardens. He would provide me with a reservation on it ahead for a certain date. 'Miss Jane Marple,' he said, 'will also be on that tour. You will meet her there, you will encounter her casually, and thus it will be seen clearly to be a casual meeting.'

"I was to choose my own time and moment to make myself known to you, if I thought it advisable; or not to make myself known to you if I thought that that would be the better way. You have already asked me if I or my friend, the Governor, had any reason to suspect or know of any other person who might have been guilty of the murder. My friend the Governor certainly suggested nothing of the kind, and he had already taken up the matter with the police officer who had been in charge of the case. A most reliable detective-superintendent with very good experience in these matters."

"No other man was suggested? No other friend of the girl's? No other former friend who might have been supplanted?"

"There was nothing of that kind to find. I asked him to tell me a little about you. He did not however consent to do so. He told me you were elderly. He told me that you were a person who knew about people. He told me one other thing." he paused.

"What's the other thing?" said Miss Marple. "I have some natural curiosity, you know. I really can't think of any other advantage I conceivably could have. I am slightly deaf. My eyesight is not quite as good as it used to be. I cannot really think that I have any advantages beyond the fact that I may, I suppose, seem rather foolish and simple, and am in fact, what used to be called in rather earlier days an 'old pussy'. I *am* an old pussy. Is that the sort of thing he said?"

"No," said Professor Wanstead. "What he said was he thought you had a very fine sense of evil."

"Oh," said Miss Marple. She was taken aback.

Professor Wanstead was watching her.

"Would you say that was true?" he said.

Miss Marple was quiet for quite a long time. At last she said,

"Perhaps it is. Yes, perhaps. I have at several different times in my life been apprehensive, have recognized that there was evil in the neighbourhood, the surroundings, that the environment of someone who was evil was near me, connected with what was happening."

She looked at him suddenly and smiled.

"It's rather, you know," she said, "like being born with a very keen sense of smell. You can smell a leak of gas when other people can't do so. You can distinguish one perfume from another very easily. I had an aunt once," continued Miss Marple thoughtfully, "who said she could smell when people told a lie. She said there was quite a distinctive odour came to her. Their noses twitched, she said, and then the smell came. I don't know if it was true or not, but—well, on several occasions she was quite remarkable. She said to my uncle once, 'Don't, Jack, engage that young man you were talking to this morning. He was telling you lies the whole time he was talking.' That turned out to be quite true."

"A sense of evil," said Professor Wanstead. "Well, if you do sense evil, tell me. I shall be glad to know. I don't think I have a particular sense of evil myself. Ill-health, yes, but not—not evil up here." He tapped his forehead.

"I'd better tell you briefly how I came into things now," said Miss Marple. "Mr Rafiel, as you know, died. His lawyers asked me to come and see them, apprised me of his proposition. I received a letter from him which explained nothing. After that I heard nothing more for some little time. Then I got a letter from the company who run these tours saying that Mr Rafiel before his death had made a reservation for me knowing that I should enjoy a trip very much, and wanting to give it me as a surprise present. I was very astonished but took it as an indication of the first step that I was to undertake. I was to go on this tour and presumably in the course of the tour some other indication or hint or clue or direction would come to me. I think it did. Yesterday, no, the day before, I was received on my arrival here by three ladies who live at an old manor house here and who very kindly extended an invitation to me. They had heard from Mr Rafiel, they said, who had written some time before his death, saying that a very old friend of his would be coming on this tour and would they be kind enough to put her up for two or three days as he thought she was not fit to attempt the particular ascent of this rather difficult climb up the headland to where there was a memorial tower which was the principal event of yesterday's tour."

"And you took that also as an indication of what you were to do?"

"Of course," said Miss Marple. "There can be no other reason for it. He was not a man to shower benefits for nothing, out of compassion for an old lady who wasn't good at walking up hills. No. He *wanted* me to go there."

"And you went there? And what then?"

"Nothing," said Miss Marple. "Three sisters."

"Three weird sisters?"

"They ought to have been," said Miss Marple, "but I don't think they were. They didn't seem to be anyway. I don't know yet. I suppose they may have been—they may be, I mean. They seem ordinary enough. They didn't belong to this house. It had belonged to an uncle of theirs and they'd come here to live some years ago. They are in rather poor circumstances, they are amiable, not particularly interesting. All slightly different in type. They do not appear to have been well acquainted with Mr Rafiel. Any conversation I have had with them appears to yield nothing."

"So you learnt nothing during your stay?"

"I learnt the facts of the case you've just told me. Not from them. From an elderly servant, who started her reminiscences dating back to the time of the uncle. She knew of Mr Rafiel only as a name. But she was eloquent on the theme of the murder, it had all started with the visit here of a son of Mr Rafiel's who was a bad lot, of how the girl had fallen in love with him and that he'd strangled the girl, and how sad and tragic and terrible it all was.

'With bells on', as you might say," said Miss Marple, using a phrase of her youth. "Plenty of exaggeration, but it was a nasty story, and she seemed to believe that the police view was that this hadn't been his only murder."

"It didn't seem to you to connect up with the three weird sisters?"

"No, only that they'd been the guardians of the girl—and had loved her dearly. No more than that."

"They might know something—something about another man?"

"Yes—that's what we want, isn't it? The other man—a man of brutality, who wouldn't hesitate to bash in a girl's head after he'd killed her. The kind of man who could be driven frantic with jealousy. There are men like that."

"No other curious things happened at The Old Manor?"

"Not really. One of the sisters, the youngest I think, kept talking about the garden. She sounded as though she was a very keen gardener, but she couldn't be because she didn't know the names of half the things. I laid a trap or two for her, mentioning special rare shrubs and saying did she know it? and yes, she said, wasn't it a wonderful plant? I said it was not very hardy and she agreed. But she didn't know anything about plants. That reminds me——"

"Reminds you of what?"

"Well, you'll think I'm just silly about gardens and plants, but I mean one does *know* things about them. I mean, I know a few things about birds and I know some things about gardens."

"And I gather that it's not birds but gardens that are troubling you."

"Yes. Have you noticed two middle-aged women on this tour? Miss Barrow and Miss Cooke."

"Yes. I've noticed them. Pair of middle-aged spinsters travelling together."

"That's right. Well, I've found out something odd about Miss Cooke. That is her name, isn't it? I mean it's her name on the tour."

"Why—has she got another name?"

"I think so. She's the same person who visited me—I won't say visited me exactly, but she was outside my garden fence in St

Mary Mead, the village where I live. She expressed pleasure at my garden and talked about gardening with me. Told me she was living in the village and working in somebody's garden, who'd moved into a new house there. I rather think," said Miss Marple, "yes, I rather think that the whole thing was lies. There again, she knew nothing about gardening. She pretended to but it wasn't true."

"Why do you think she came there?"

"I'd no idea at the time. She said her name was Bartlett—and the name of the woman she said she was living with began with 'H', though I can't remember it for the moment. Her hair was not only differently done but it was a different colour and her clothes were of a different style. I didn't recognize her at first on this trip. Just wondered why her face was vaguely familiar. And then suddenly it came to me. Because of the dyed hair. I said where I had seen her before. She admitted that she'd been there—but pretended that she, too, hadn't recognized *me*. All lies."

"And what's your opinion about all that?"

"Well, one thing certainly—Miss Cooke (to give her her present name) came to St Mary Mead just to have a look at me—so that she'd be quite sure to be able to recognize me when we met again——"

"And why was that felt to be necessary?"

"I don't know. There are two possibilities. I'm not sure that I like one of them very much."

"I don't know," said Professor Wanstead, "that I like it very much either."

They were both silent for a minute or two, and then Professor Wanstead said——

"I don't like what happened to Elizabeth Temple. You've talked to her during this trip?"

"Yes, I have. When she's better I'd like to talk to her again—she could tell me—us—things about the girl who was murdered. She spoke to me of this girl—who had been at her school, who had been going to marry Mr Rafiel's son—but didn't marry him. Instead she died. I asked how or why she died—and she answered with the word 'Love'. I took it as meaning a suicide—but it was murder. Murder through jealousy would fit. Another man. Some other man we've got to find. Miss Temple may be able to tell us who he was."

"No other sinister possibilities?"

"I think, really, it is casual information we need. I see no reason to believe that there is any sinister suggestion in any of the coach passengers—or any sinister suggestion about the people living in The Old Manor House. But one of these three sisters may have known or remembered something that the girl or Michael once said. Clotilde used to take the girl abroad. Therefore, she may know of something that occurred on some foreign trip perhaps. Something that the girl said or mentioned or did on some trip. Some man that the girl met. Something which has nothing to do with The Old Manor House here. It is difficult because only by talking, by casual information, can you get any clue. The second sister, Mrs Glynne married fairly early, has spent time, I gather, in India and in Africa. She may have heard of something through her husband, or through her husband's relations, through various things that are unconnected with The Old Manor House here although she has visited it from time to time. She knew the murdered girl presumably, but I should think she knew her much less well than the other two. But that does not mean that she may not know some significant *facts* about the girl. The third sister is more scatty, more localized, does not seem to have known the girl as well. But still, she too *may* have information about possible lovers—or boyfriends—seen the girl with an unknown man. That's her, by the way, passing the Hotel now."

Miss Marple, however occupied by her tête-à-tête, had not relinquished the habits of a lifetime. A public thoroughfare was always to her an observation post. All the passers-by, either loitering or hurrying, had been noticed automatically.

"Anthea Bradbury-Scott—the one with the big parcel. She's going to the post office, I suppose. It's just round the corner, isn't it?"

"Looks a bit daft to me," said Professor Wanstead, "all that floating hair—grey hair too—a kind of Ophelia of fifty."

"I thought of Ophelia too, when I first saw her. Oh dear, I wish I knew what I ought to do next. Stay here at the Golden Boar for a day or two, or go on with the coach tour. It's like looking for a needle in a haystack. If you stick your fingers in it long enough, you ought to come up with something—even if one does get pricked in the process."

13. *Black and Red Check*

i

MRS SANDBOURNE returned just as the party was sitting down to lunch. Her news was not good. Miss Temple was still unconscious. She certainly could not be moved for several days.

Having given the bulletin, Mrs Sandbourne turned the conversation to practical matters. She produced suitable time tables of trains for those who wished to return to London and proposed suitable plans for the resumption of the tour on the morrow or the next day. She had a list of suitable short expeditions in the near neighbourhood for this afternoon—small groups in hired cars.

Professor Wanstead drew Miss Marple aside as they went out of the dining-room——

"You may want to rest this afternoon. If not, I will call for you here in an hour's time. There is an interesting church you might care to see——?"

"That would be very nice," said Miss Marple.

ii

Miss Marple sat quite still in the car that had come to fetch her. Professor Wanstead had called for her at the time he had said.

"I thought you might enjoy seeing this particular church. And a very pretty village, too," he explained. "There's no reason really why one should not enjoy the local sights when one can."

"It's very kind of you, I'm sure," Miss Marple had said.

She had looked at him with that slightly fluttery gaze of hers.

"*Very* kind," she said. "It just seems—well, I don't want to say it seems heartless, but well, you know what I mean."

"My dear lady, Miss Temple is not an old friend of yours or anything like that. Sad as this accident has been."

"Well," said Miss Marple again, "this is very kind of you."

Professor Wanstead had opened the door of the car and Miss Marple got into it. It was, she presumed, a hired car. A kindly thought to take an elderly lady to see one of the sights of the neighbourhood. He might have taken somebody younger, more interesting and certainly better looking. Miss Marple looked at him thoughtfully once or twice as they drove through the village. He was not looking at her. He was gazing out of his own window.

When they had left the village behind and were on a second class country road twisting round the hillside, he turned his head and said to her,

"We are not going to a church, I am afraid."

"No," said Miss Marple, "I thought perhaps we weren't."

"Yes, the idea would have come to you."

"Where are we going, may I ask?"

"We are going to a hospital, in Carristown."

"Ah yes, that was where Miss Temple was taken?"

It was a question, though it hardly needed to be one.

"Yes," he said. "Mrs Sandbourne saw her and brought me back a letter from the Hospital Authorities. I have just finished talking to them on the telephone."

"Is she going on well?"

"No. Not going on very well."

"I see. At least—I hope I don't see," said Miss Marple.

"Her recovery is very problematical but there is nothing that can be done. She may not recover consciousness again. On the other hand she may have a few lucid intervals."

"And you are taking *me* there? Why? I am not a friend of hers, you know. I only just met her for the first time on this trip."

"Yes, I realize that. I'm taking you there because in one of the lucid intervals she has had, she asked for you."

"I see," said Miss Marple. "I wonder why she should ask for *me*, why she should have thought that I—that I could be useful in any way to her, or do anything. She is a woman of perception.

In her way, you know, a great woman. As Headmistress of Fallowfield she occupied a prominent position in the educational world."

"The best girls' school there is, I suppose?"

"Yes. She was a great personality. She was herself a woman of considerable scholarship. Mathematics were her speciality, but she was an 'all round'—what I should call an educator. Was interested in education, what girls were fitted for, how to encourage them. Oh, many other things. It is sad and very cruel if she dies," said Miss Marple. "It will seem such a waste of a life. Although she had retired from her Headmistress-ship she still exercised a lot of power. This accident——" She stopped. "Perhaps you do not want us to discuss the accident?"

"I think it is better that we should do so. A big boulder crashed down the hillside. It has been known to happen before though only at very long divided intervals of time. However, somebody came and spoke to me about it," said Professor Wanstead.

"Came and spoke to you about the accident? Who was it?"

"The two young people. Joanna Crawford and Emlyn Price."

"What did they say?"

"Joanna told me that she had the impression there was someone on the hillside. Rather high up. She and Emlyn were climbing up from the lower main path, following a rough track that wound round the curve of the hill. As they turned a corner she definitely saw, outlined against the skyline, a man or a woman who was trying to roll a big boulder forward along the ground. The boulder was rocking—and finally it started to roll, at first slowly and then gathering speed down the hillside. Miss Temple was walking along the main path below, and had come to a point just underneath it when the boulder hit her. If it was done deliberately it might not, of course, have succeeded; it might have missed her—but it did succeed. If what was being attempted was a deliberate attack on the woman walking below it succeeded only too well."

"Was it a man or a woman they saw?" asked Miss Marple.

"Unfortunately, Joanna Crawford could not say. Whoever it was, was wearing jeans or trousers, and had on a lurid polo-neck pullover in red and black checks. The figure turned and moved out of sight almost immediately. She is inclined to think it was a man but cannot be certain."

"And she thinks, or you think, that it was a deliberate attempt on Miss Temple's life?"

"The more she mulls it over, the more she thinks that that was exactly what it was. The boy agrees."

"You have no idea who it might have been?"

"No idea whatever. No more have they. It might be one of our fellow travellers, someone who went for a stroll that afternoon. It might be someone completely unknown who knew that the coach was making a halt here and chose this place to make an attack on one of the passengers. Some youthful lover of violence for violence's sake. Or it might have been an enemy."

"It seems very melodramatic if one says 'a secret enemy'," said Miss Marple.

"Yes, it does. Who would want to kill a retired and respected Headmistress? That is a question we want answered. It is possible, faintly possible that Miss Temple herself might be able to tell us. She might have recognized the figure above her or she might more likely have known of someone who bore her ill-will for some special reason."

"It still seems unlikely."

"I agree with you," said Professor Wanstead. "She seems a totally unlikely person to be a fit victim of attack, but yet when one reflects, a Headmistress knows a great many people. A great many people, shall we put it this way, have passed through her hands."

"A lot of girls you mean have passed through her hands."

"Yes. Yes, that is what I meant. Girls and their families. A Headmistress must have knowledge of many things. Romances, for instance, that girls might indulge in, unknown to their parents. It happens, you know. It happens very often. Especially in the last ten or twenty years. Girls are said to mature earlier. That is physically true, though in a deeper sense of the word, they mature late. They remain childish longer. Childish in the clothes they like to wear, childish with their floating hair. Even their mini skirts represent a worship of childishness. Their Baby Doll nightdresses, their gymslips and shorts—all children's fashions. They wish *not* to become adult—*not* to have to accept our kind of responsibility. And yet like all children, they want to be *thought* grown up, and free to do what they think are grown up things. And that leads sometimes to tragedy and sometimes to the aftermath of tragedy."

"Are you thinking of some particular case?"

"No. No, not really. I'm only thinking—well, shall we say letting possibilities pass through my mind. I cannot believe that Elizabeth Temple had a *personal* enemy. An enemy ruthless enough to wish to take an opportunity of killing her. What I do think—" he looked at Miss Marple, "—would you like to make a suggestion?"

"Of a possibility? Well, I think I know or guess what you *are* suggesting. You are suggesting that Miss Temple knew something, knew some fact or had some knowledge that would be inconvenient or even dangerous to somebody if it was known."

"Yes, I do feel exactly that."

"In that case," said Miss Marple, "it seems indicated that there is someone on our coach tour who recognized Miss Temple or knew who she was, but who perhaps after the passage of some years was not remembered or might even not have been recognized by Miss Temple. It seems to throw it back on our passengers, does it not?" she paused. "That pullover you mentioned—red and black checks, you said?"

"Oh yes? The pullover——" He looked at her curiously. "What was it that struck you about that?"

"It was very noticeable," said Miss Marple. "That is what your words led me to infer. It was very mentionable. So much so that the girl Joanna mentioned it specifically."

"Yes. And what does that suggest to you?"

"The trailing of flags," said Miss Marple thoughtfully. "Something that will be seen, remembered, observed, recognized."

"Yes." Professor Wanstead looked at her with encouragement.

"When you describe a person you have seen, seen not close at hand but from a distance, the first thing you will describe will be their clothes. Not their faces, not their walk, not their hands, not their feet. A scarlet tam-o'-shanter, a purple cloak, a bizarre leather jacket, a pullover of brilliant reds and blacks. Something very recognizable, very noticeable. The object of it being that when that person removes that garment, gets rid of it, sends it by post in a parcel to some address, say, about a hundred miles away, or thrusts it in a rubbish bin in a city or burns it or tears it up or destroys it, she or he will be the one person modestly and rather drably attired who will not be suspected or looked at or thought of. It must have been *meant*, that scarlet and black check jersey. Meant so that it will be recognized again though actually it will never again be seen on that particular person."

"A very sound idea," said Professor Wanstead. "As I have told you," continued the Professor, "Fallowfield is situated not very far from here. Sixteen miles, I think. So this is Elizabeth Temple's part of the world, a part she knows well with people in it that she also might know well."

"Yes. It widens the possibilities," said Miss Marple. "I agree with you," she said presently, "that the attacker is more likely to have been a man than a woman. That boulder, if it was done with intent, was sent on its course very accurately. Accuracy is more a male quality than a female one. On the other hand there might easily have been someone on our coach, or possibly in the neighbourhood, who saw Miss Temple in the street, a former pupil of hers in past years. Someone whom she herself might not recognize after a period of time. But the girl or woman would have recognized her, because a Headmaster or Headmistress of over sixty is not unlike the same Headmaster or Headmistress at the age of fifty. She is recognizable. Some woman who recognized her former mistress and also knew that her mistess knew something damaging to her." She sighed. "I myself do not know this part of the world at all. Have you any particular knowledge of it?"

"No," said Professor Wanstead. "I could not claim a personal knowledge of this part of the country. I know something, however, of various things that have happened in this part of the world entirely because of what you have told me. If it had not been for my acquaintanceship with you and the things you have told me I should have been more at sea than I am.

"What are you yourself actually doing here? You do not know. Yet you were sent here. It was deliberately arranged by Rafiel that you should come here, that you should take this coach tour, that you and I should meet. There have been other places where we have stopped or through which we have passed, but special arrangements were made so that you should actually stay for a couple of nights here. You were put up with former friends of his who would not have refused any request he made. Was there a reason for that?"

"So that I could learn certain facts that I had to know," said Miss Marple.

"A series of murders that took place a good many years ago?" Professor Wanstead looked doubtful. "There is nothing unusual in that. You can say the same of many places in England and Wales. These things seem always to go in a series. First a girl found assaulted and murdered. Then another girl not very far away. Then something of the same kind perhaps twenty miles away. The same pattern of death.

"Two girls were reported missing from Jocelyn St Mary itself, the one that we have been discussing whose body was found six months later, many miles away and who was last seen in the company of Michael Rafiel——"

"And the other?"

"A girl called Nora Broad. *Not* a 'quiet girl with no boy-friends'. Possibly with one boy-friend too many. Her body was never found. It will be—one day. There have been cases when twenty years have passed," said Wanstead. He slowed down: "We have arrived. This is Carristown, and here is the Hospital."

Shepherded by Professor Wanstead, Miss Marple entered. The Professor was obviously expected. He was ushered into a small room where a woman rose from a desk.

"Oh yes," she said, "Professor Wanstead. And—er—this is—er——" She hesitated slightly.

"Miss Jane Marple," said Professor Wanstead. "I talked to Sister Barker on the telephone."

"Oh yes. Sister Barker said that she would be accompanying you."

"How is Miss Temple?"

"Much the same, I think. I am afraid there is not much improvement to report." She rose. "I will take you to Sister Barker."

Sister Barker was a tall, thin woman. She had a low, decisive voice and dark grey eyes that had a habit of looking at you and looking away almost immediately, leaving you with the feeling that you had been inspected in a very short space of time, and judgment pronounced upon you.

"I don't know what arrangements you have in mind," said Professor Wanstead.

"Well, I had better tell Miss Marple just what we have arranged. First I must make it clear to you that the patient, Miss Temple, is still in a coma with very rare intervals. She appears to come to occasionally, to recognize her surroundings and to be able to say a few words. But there is nothing one can do to stimulate her. It has to be left to the utmost patience. I expect Professor Wanstead has already told you that in one of her intervals of consciousness she uttered quite distinctly the words 'Miss Jane Marple'. And then: '*I want to speak to her. Miss Jane Marple.*' After that she relapsed into unconsciousness. Doctor thought it advisable to get in touch with the other occupants of the coach. Professor Wanstead came to see us and explained various matters and said he would bring you over. I am afraid that all we can ask you to do is to sit in the private ward where Miss Temple is, and perhaps be ready to make a note of any words she should say, if she does regain consciousness. I am afraid the prognosis is not very helpful. To be quite frank, which is better I think, since you are not a near relative and are unlikely to be disturbed by this information, Doctor thinks that she is sinking fast, that she may die without recovering consciousness. There is nothing one can do to relieve the concussion. It is important that someone should hear what she says and Doctor thinks it advisable that she should not see too many people round her if she regains consciousness. If Miss Marple is not worried at the thought of sitting there alone, there will be a nurse in the room, though not obviously so. That is, she will not be noticed from the bed, and will not move unless she's asked for. She will sit in a corner of the room shielded by a screen." She added, "We have a police official there also, ready to take down anything. The Doctor thinks it advisable that he also should not be noticed by Miss Temple. One person alone, and that possibly a person she *expects* to see, will not alarm her or make her lose knowledge of what she wants to say to you. I hope this will not be too difficult a thing to ask you?"

"Oh no," said Miss Marple, "I'm quite prepared to do that. I have a small notebook with me and a Biro pen that will not be in evidence. I can remember things by heart for a very short time, so I need not appear to be obviously taking notes of what she says. You can trust my memory and I am not deaf—not deaf in the real sense of the word. I don't think my hearing is quite as good as it used to be, but if I am sitting near a bedside, I ought to be able to hear anything she says quite easily even if it is whispered. I am used to sick people. I have had a good deal to do with them in my time."

Again the lightning glance of Sister Barker went over Miss Marple. This time a faint inclination of the head showed satisfaction.

"It is kind of you," she said, "and I am sure that if there is any help you can give, we can rely on you to give it. If Professor Wanstead likes to sit in the waiting-room downstairs, we can call him at any moment if it should be necessary. Now, Miss Marple, perhaps you will accompany me."

Miss Marple followed Sister along a passage and into a small well appointed single room. In the bed there, in a dimly-lighted room since the blinds were half drawn, lay Elizabeth Temple. She lay there like a statue, yet she did not give the impression of being asleep. Her breath came uncertainly in slight gasps. Sister Barker bent to examine her patient, motioned Miss Marple into a chair beside the bed. She then crossed the room to the door again. A young man with a notebook in his hand came from behind the screen there.

"Doctor's orders, Mr Reckitt," said Sister Barker.

A nurse also appeared. She had been sitting in the opposite corner of the room.

"Call me if necessary, Nurse Edmonds," said Sister Barker, "and get Miss Marple anything she may need."

Miss Marple loosened her coat. The room was warm. The nurse approached and took it from her. Then she retired to her former position, Miss Marple sat down in the chair. She looked at Elizabeth Temple thinking, as she had thought before when looking at her in the coach, what a fine shaped head she had. Her grey hair drawn back from it, fitted her face in a perfect cap-like effect. A handsome woman, and a woman of personality. Yes, a thousand pities, Miss Marple thought, a thousand pities if the world was going to lose Elizabeth Temple.

Miss Marple eased the cushion at her back, moved the chair a fraction of an inch and sat quietly to wait. Whether to wait in vain or to some point, she had no idea. Time passed. Ten minutes, twenty minutes, half an hour, thirty-five minutes. Then suddenly, quite unexpectedly as it were, a voice came. Low, but distinct, slightly husky. None of the resonance it had once held. "Miss Marple."

Elizabeth Temple's eyes were open now. They were looking at Miss Marple. They looked competent, perfectly sensible. She was studying the face of the woman who was sitting by her bed, studying her without any sign of emotion, of surprise. Only, one would say, of scrutiny. Fully conscious scrutiny. And the voice spoke again.

"Miss Marple. You are Jane Marple?"

"That is right. Yes," said Miss Marple, "Jane Marple."

"Henry often spoke of you. He said things about you."

The voice stopped. Miss Marple said with a slight query in her voice,

"Henry?"

"Henry Clithering, an old friend of mine—very old friend."

"An old friend of mine too," said Miss Marple. "Henry Clithering."

Her mind went back to the many years she had known him, Sir Henry Clithering, the things he had said to her, the assistance he had asked from her sometimes, and the assistance that she had asked from him. A very old friend.

"I remembered your name. On the passenger list. I thought it must be you. You could help. That's what he—Henry, yes—would say if he were here. You might be able to help. To find out. It's important. Very important although—it's a long time ago now—a—long—time—ago."

Her voice faltered a little, her eyes half closed. Nurse got up, came across the room, picked up a small glass and held it to Elizabeth Temple's lips. Miss Temple took a sip, nodded her head dismissively. Nurse put down the glass and went back to her chair.

"If I can help, I will," said Miss Marple. She asked no further questions.

Miss Temple said, "Good," and after a minute or two, again, "Good."

For two or three minutes she lay with her eyes closed. She might have been asleep or unconscious. Then her eyes opened again suddenly.

"Which," she said, "which of them? That's what one has got to know. Do you know what I am talking about?"

"I think so. A girl who died—Nora Broad?" A frown came quickly to Elizabeth Temple's forehead.

"No, no, no. The other girl. Verity Hunt."

There was a pause and then, "Jane Marple. You're old—older than when he talked about you. You're older, but you can still find out things, can't you?"

Her voice became slightly higher, more insistent.

"You can, can't you? Say you can. I've not much time. I know that. I know it quite well. One of them, but which? Find out. Henry would have said you can. It may be dangerous for you—but you'll find out, won't you?"

"With God's help, I will," said Miss Marple. It was a vow.

"Ah."

The eyes closed, then opened again. Something like a smile seemed to try and twitch the lips.

"The big stone from above. The Stone of Death."

"Who rolled that stone down?"

"Don't know. No matter—only—Verity. Find out about Verity. Truth. Another name for truth, Verity."

Miss Marple saw the faint relaxation of the body on the bed. There was a faintly whispered: "Goodbye. Do your best . . ."

Her body relaxed, the eyes closed. The nurse came again to the bedside. This time she took up the pulse, felt it, and beckoned to Miss Marple. Miss Marple rose obediently and followed her out of the room.

"That's been a big effort for her," said the nurse. "She won't regain consciousness again for some time. Perhaps not at all. I hope you learnt something?"

"I don't think I did," said Miss Marple, "but one never knows, does one."

"Did you get anything?" asked Professor Wanstead, as they went out to the car.

"A name," said Miss Marple. "Verity. Was that the girl's name?"

"Yes. Verity Hunt."

Elizabeth Temple died an hour and a half later. She died without regaining consciousness.

14. *Mr Broadribb Wonders*

"SEEN *The Times* this morning?" said Mr Broadribb to his partner, Mr Schuster.

Mr Schuster said he couldn't afford *The Times*, he took the *Telegraph*.

"Well, it may be in that, too," said Mr Broadribb. "In the deaths. Miss Elizabeth Temple, D.Sc."

Mr Schuster looked faintly puzzled.

"Headmistress of Fallowfield. You've heard of Fallowfield, haven't you?"

"Of course," said Schuster. "Girls' school. Been going for fifty years or so. First class, fantastically expensive. So she was the headmistress of it, was she? I thought the headmistress had resigned some time ago. Six months at least. I'm sure I read about it in the paper. That is to say there was a bit about the new headmistress. Married woman. Youngish. Thirty-five to forty. Modern ideas. Give the girls lessons in cosmetics, let 'em wear trouser suits. Something of that kind."

"Hum," said Mr Broadribb, making the noise that solicitors of his age are likely to make when they hear something which elicits criticism based on long experience. "Don't think she'll ever make the name that Elizabeth Temple did. Quite someone, she was. Been there a long time, too."

"Yes," said Mr Schuster, somewhat uninterested. He wondered why Broadribb was so interested in defunct schoolmistresses.

Schools were not really of particular interest to either of the two gentlemen. Their own offspring were now more or less disposed of. Mr Broadribb's two sons were respectively in the Civil Service and in an oil firm, and Mr Schuster's rather younger progeny were at different universities where both of them respectively were making as much trouble for those in authority as they possibly could do. He said,

"What about her?"

"She was on a coach tour," said Mr Broadribb.

"Those coaches," said Mr Schuster. "I wouldn't let any of my relations go on one of those. One went off a precipice in Switzerland last week and two months ago one had a crash and twenty were killed. Don't know who drives these things nowadays."

"It was one of those Country Houses and Gardens and Objects of Interest in Britain—or whatever they call it—tours," said Mr Broadribb. "That's not quite the right name, but you know what I mean."

"Oh yes, I know. Oh the—er—yes that's the one we sent Miss What's-a-name on. The one old Rafiel booked."

"Miss Jane Marple was on it."

"She didn't get killed too, did she?" asked Mr Schuster.

"Not so far as I know," said Mr Broadribb. "I just wondered a bit, though."

"Was it a road accident?"

"No. It was at one of the beauty spot places. They were walking on a path up a hill. It was a stiff walk. Up a rather steep hill with boulders and things on it. Some of the boulders got loose and came rushing down the mountainside. Miss Temple was knocked out and taken to hospital with concussion and died——"

"Bad luck," said Mr Schuster, and waited for more.

"I only wondered," said Mr Broadribb, "because I happened to remember that—well, that Fallowfield was the school where the girl was at."

"What girl? I don't really know what you're talking about, Broadribb."

"The girl who was done in by young Michael Rafiel. I was just recalling a few things which might seem to have some slight connection with this curious Jane Marple business that old Rafiel was so keen on. Wish he'd told us more."

"What's the connection?" said Mr Schuster.

He looked more interested now. His legal wits were in process of being sharpened, to give a sound opinion on whatever it was that Mr Broadribb was about to confide to him.

"That girl. Can't remember her last name now. Christian name was Hope or Faith or something like that. Verity, that was her name. Verity Hunter, I think it was. She was one of that series of murdered girls. Found her body in a ditch about thirty miles away from where she'd gone missing. Been dead six months. Strangled apparently, and her head and face had been bashed in—to delay recognition, they thought, but she *was* recognized all right. Clothes, handbag, jewellery nearby—some mole or scar. Oh yes, she was identified quite easily——"

"Actually, she was the one the trial was all about, wasn't she?"

"Yes. Suspected of having done away with perhaps three other girls during the past year, Michael was. But evidence wasn't so good in the other deaths—so the police went all out on this one—plenty of evidence—bad record. Earlier cases of assault and rape. Well, we all know what rape is nowadays. Mum tells the girl she's got to accuse the young man of rape even if the young man hasn't had much chance, with the girl at him all the time to come to the house while mum's away at work, or dad's gone on holiday. Doesn't stop badgering him until she's forced him to sleep with her. Then, as I say, mum tells the girl to call it rape. However, that's not the point," said Mr Broadribb. "I wondered if things mightn't tie up a bit, you know. I thought this Jane Marple business with Rafiel might have something to do with Michael."

"Found guilty, wasn't he? And given a life sentence?"

"I can't remember now—it's so long ago. Or did they get away with a verdict of diminished responsibility?"

"And Verity Hunter or Hunt was educated at that school. Miss Temple's school? She wasn't still a schoolgirl though, was she, when she was killed? Not that I can remember."

"Oh no. She was eighteen or nineteen, living with relations or friends of her parents, or something like that. Nice house, nice people, nice girl by all accounts. The sort of girl whose relations always say 'she was a very quiet girl, rather shy, didn't go about with strange people and had no boy-friends.' Relations never know what boy-friends a girl has. The girls take mighty good care of that. And young Rafiel was said to be very attractive to girls."

"Never been any doubt that he did it?" asked Mr Schuster.

"Not a scrap. Told a lot of lies in the witness box, anyway. His Counsel would have done better not to have let him give evidence. A lot of his friends gave him an alibi that didn't stand up, if you know what I mean. All his friends seemed to be fluent liars."

"What's your feeling about it, Broadribb?"

"Oh, I haven't got any feelings," said Mr Broadribb, "I was just wondering if this woman's death might tie up."

"In what way?"

"Well, you know—about these boulders that fall down cliff sides and drop on top of someone. It's not always in the course of nature. Boulders usually stay where they are, in my experience."

15. *Verity*

"VERITY," SAID Miss Marple.

Elizabeth Margaret Temple had died the evening before. It had been a peaceful death. Miss Marple, sitting once more amidst the faded chintz of the drawing-room in The Old Manor House, had laid aside the baby's pink coat which she had previously been engaged in knitting and had substituted a crocheted purple scarf. This half-mourning touch went with Miss Marple's early Victorian ideas of tactfulness in face of tragedy.

An inquest was to be held on the following day. The vicar had been approached and had agreed to hold a brief memorial service in the church as soon as arrangements could be made. Undertakers suitably attired, with proper mourning faces, took general charge of things in liaison with the police. The inquest was to take place on the following morning at 11 o'clock. Members of the coach tour had agreed to attend the inquest. And several of them had chosen to remain on so as to attend the church service also.

Mrs Glynne had come to the Golden Boar and urged Miss Marple to return to The Old Manor House until she finally returned to the tour.

"You will get away from all the reporters."

Miss Marple had thanked all three sisters warmly and had accepted.

The coach tour would be resumed after the memorial service, driving first to South Bedestone, thirty-five miles away, where there was a good class hotel which had been originally chosen for a stopping place. After that the tour would go on as usual.

There were, however, as Miss Marple had considered likely,

certain persons who were disengaging themselves and returning home, or were going in other directions and not continuing on the tour. There was something to be said in favour of either decision. To leave what would become a journey of painful memories, or to continue with the sight-seeing that had already been paid for and which had been interrupted only by one of those painful accidents that may happen on any sight-seeing expedition. A lot would depend, Miss Marple thought, on the outcome of the inquest.

Miss Marple, after exchanging various conventional remarks proper to the occasion with her three hostesses, had devoted herself to her purple wool and had sat considering her next line of investigation. And so it was that with her fingers still busy, she had uttered the one word, "Verity". Throwing it as one throws a pebble into a stream, solely to observe what the result—if any—would be. Would it mean something to her hostesses? It might or it might not. Otherwise, when she joined the members of the tour at their hotel meal this evening, which had been arranged, she would try the effect of it there. It had been, she thought to herself, the last word or almost the last word that Elizabeth Temple had spoken. So therefore, thought Miss Marple, (her fingers still busy because she did not need to look at her crocheting, she could read a book or conduct a conversation while her fingers, though slightly crippled with rhematism, would proceed correctly through their appointed movements). So therefore, "Verity".

Like a stone into a pool, causing ripples, a splash, something? Or nothing. Surely there would be a reaction of one sort or another. Yes, she had not been mistaken. Although her face registered nothing, the keen eyes behind her glasses had watched three people in a simultaneous manner as she had trained herself to do for many years now, when wishing to observe her neighbours either in church, mothers' meetings, or at other public functions in St Mary Mead when she had been on the track of some interesting piece of news or gossip.

Mrs Glynne had dropped the book she was holding and had looked across towards Miss Marple with slight surprise. Surprise, it seemed, at the particular word coming from Miss Marple, but not surprised really to hear it.

Clotilde reacted differently. Her head shot up, she leant forward a little, then she looked not at Miss Marple but across the room in the direction of the window. Her hands clenched themselves, she kept very still. Miss Marple, although dropping her head slightly as though she was not looking any more, noted that her eyes were filling with tears. Clotilde sat quite still and let the tears roll down her cheeks. She made no attempt to take out a handkerchief, she uttered no word. Miss Marple was impressed by the aura of grief that came from her.

Anthea's reaction was different. It was quick, excited, almost pleasurable.

"Verity? Verity, did you say? Did you know her? I'd no idea. It is Verity Hunt you mean?"

Lavinia Glynne said, "It's a Christian name?"

"*I* never knew anyone of that name," said Miss Marple, "but I *did* mean a Christian name. Yes. It is rather unusual, I think. Verity." She repeated it thoughtfully.

She let her purple wool ball fall and looked round with the slightly apologetic and embarrassed look of one who realizes she has made a serious *faux pas*, but not sure why.

"I—I am so sorry. Have I said something I shouldn't? It was only because . . ."

"No, of course not," said Mrs Glynne. "It was just that it is—it is a name we know, a name with which we have—associations."

"It just came into my mind," said Miss Marple, still apologetic, "because, you know, it was poor Miss Temple who said it. I went to see her, you know, yesterday afternoon. Professor Wanstead took me. He seemed to think that I might be able to—to—I don't know if it's the proper word—to *rouse* her, in some way. She was in a coma and they thought—not that I was a friend of hers at any time, but we had chatted together on the tour and we often sat beside each other, as you know, on some of the days and we had talked. And he thought perhaps I might be of some use. I'm afraid I wasn't though. Not at all. I just sat there and waited and then she did say one or two words, but they didn't seem to mean anything. But finally, just when it was time for me to go, she did open her eyes and looked at me—I don't know if she was mistaking me for someone—but she did say that word. Verity! And, well of course it stuck in my mind, especially with her passing away yesterday evening. It must have been someone or something that she had in her mind. But of course it might just mean—well, of course it might just mean Truth. That's what verity means, doesn't it?"

She looked from Clotilde to Lavinia to Anthea.

"It was the Christian name of a girl we knew," said Lavinia Glynne. "That is why it startled us."

"Especially because of the awful way she died," said Anthea.

Clotilde said in her deep voice, "Anthea! there's no need to go into these details."

"But after all, everyone knows quite well about her," said Anthea. She looked towards Miss Marple. "I thought perhaps you might have known about her because you knew Mr Rafiel, didn't you? Well, I mean, he wrote to us about you so you must have known him. And I thought perhaps—well, he'd mentioned the whole thing to you."

"I'm so sorry," said Miss Marple, "I'm afraid I don't quite understand what you're talking about."

"They found her body in a ditch," said Anthea.

There was never any holding Anthea, Miss Marple thought, not once she got going. But she thought that Anthea's vociferous talk was putting additional strain on Clotilde. She had taken out a handkerchief now in a quiet, non-committal way. She brushed tears from her eyes and then sat upright, her back very straight, her eyes deep and tragic.

"Verity," she said, "was a girl we cared for very much. She lived here for a while. I was very fond of her——"

"And she was very fond of you," said Lavinia.

"Her parents were friends of mine," said Clotilde. "They were killed in a plane accident."

"She was at school at Fallowfield," explained Lavinia. "I suppose that was how Miss Temple came to remember her."

"Oh I see," said Miss Marple. "Where Miss Temple was headmistress, is that it? I have heard of Fallowfield often, of course. It's a very fine school, isn't it?"

"Yes," said Clotilde. "Verity was a pupil there. After her parents died she came to stay with us for a time while she could decide what she wanted to do with her future. She was eighteen or nineteen. A very sweet girl and a very affectionate and loving one. She thought perhaps of training for nursing, but she had very good brains and Miss Temple was very insistent that she ought to go to university. So she was studying and having coaching for that when—when this terrible thing happened."

She turned her face away.

"I—do you mind if we don't talk about it any more just now."

"Oh, of course not," said Miss Marple. "I'm so sorry to have impinged on some tragedy. I didn't know. I—I haven't heard . . . I thought—well I mean . . ." She became more and more incoherent.

That evening she heard a little more. Mrs Glynne came to her bedroom when she was changing her dress to go out and join the others at the hotel.

"I thought I ought to come and explain a little to you," said Mrs Glynne, "about—about the girl Verity Hunt. Of course you couldn't know that our sister Clotilde was particularly fond of her and that her really horrible death was a terrible shock. We never mention her if we can help it, but—I think it would be easier if I told you the facts completely and you will understand. Apparently Verity had, without our knowledge, made friends with an undesirable—a more than undesirable—it turned out to be a dangerous—young man who already had a criminal record. He came here to visit us when he was passing through once. We knew his father very well." She paused. "I think I'd better tell you the whole truth if you don't know, and you don't seem to. He was actually Mr Rafiel's son, Michael——"

"Oh dear," said Miss Marple, "not—not—I can't remember his name but I do remember hearing that there was a son—and, that he hadn't been very satisfactory."

"A little more than that," said Mrs Glynne. "He'd always given trouble. He'd been had up in court once or twice for various things. Once assaulting a teenager—other things of that type. Of course I consider myself that the magistrates are too lenient with that kind of thing. They don't want to upset a young man's university career. And so they let them off with a—I forget what they call it—a suspended sentence, something of that kind. If these boys were sent to gaol at once it would perhaps warn them off that type of life. He was a thief, too. He had forged cheques, he pinched things. He was a thoroughly bad lot. We were friends of his mother's. It was lucky for her, I think, that she died young before she had time to be upset by the way her son was turning out. Mr Rafiel did all he could, I think. Tried to find suitable jobs for the boy, paid fines for him and things like that. But I think it was a great blow to him, though he pretended to be more or less indifferent and to write it off as one of those things that happen. We had, as probably people here in the village will tell you, we had a bad outbreak of murders and violence in this district. Not only here. They were in different parts of the country, twenty miles away, sometimes fifty miles away. One or two, it's suspected by the police, were nearly a hundred miles away. But they seemed to centre more or less on this part of the world. Anyway, Verity one day went out to visit a friend and—well, she didn't come back. We went to the police about it, the police sought for her, searched the whole countryside but they couldn't find any trace of her. We advertised, they advertised, and they suggested that she'd gone off with a boy-friend. Then word began to get round that she had been seen with Michael Rafiel. By now the police had their eye on Michael as a possibility for certain crimes that had occurred, although they couldn't find any direct evidence. Verity was said to have been seen, described by her clothing and other things, with a young man of Michael's appearance and in a car that corresponded to a description of his car. But there was no further evidence until her body was discovered six months later, thirty miles from here in a rather wild part of wooded country, in a ditch covered with stones and piled earth. Clotilde had to go to identify it—it was Verity all right. She'd been strangled and her head beaten in. Clotilde has never quite got over the shock. There were certain marks, a mole and an old scar and of course her clothes and the contents of her handbag. Miss Temple was very fond of Verity. She must have thought of her just before she died."

"I'm sorry," said Miss Marple. "I'm really very, very sorry. Please tell your sister that I didn't know. I had no idea."

16. *The Inquest*

MISS MARPLE walked slowly along the village street on her way towards the market place where the inquest was to take place in the old-fashioned Georgian building which had been known for a hundred years as the Curfew Arms. She glanced at her watch. There was still a good twenty minutes before she need be there. She looked into the shops. She paused before the shop that sold wool and babies' jackets, and peered inside for a few moments. A girl in the shop was serving. Small woolly coats were being tried on two children. Further along the counter there was an elderly woman.

Miss Marple went into the shop, went along the counter to a seat opposite the elderly woman, and produced a sample of pink wool. She had run out, she explained, of this particular brand of wool and had a little jacket she needed to finish. The match was soon made, some more samples of wool that Miss Marple had admired, were brought out for her to look at, and soon she was in conversation. Starting with the sadness of the accident which had just taken place. Mrs Merrypit, if her name was identical with that which was written up outside the shop, was full of the importance of the accident, and the general difficulties of getting local governments to do anything about the dangers of footpaths and public rights of way.

"After the rain, you see, you get all the soil washed off and then the boulders get loose and then down they comes. I remember one year they had three falls—three accidents there was. One boy nearly killed, he was, and then later that year, oh six months later, I think, there was a man got his arm broken, and the third time it was poor old Mrs Walker. Blind she was and pretty well deaf too. She never heard nothing or she could have got out of the way, they say. Somebody saw it and they called out to her, but they was too far away to reach her or to run to get her. And so she was killed."

"Oh how sad," said Miss Marple, "how tragic. The sort of thing that's not easily forgotten, is it."

"No indeed. I expect the Coroner'll mention it to-day."

"I expect he will," said Miss Marple. "In a terrible way it seems quite a natural thing to happen, doesn't it, though of course there are accidents sometimes by pushing things about, you know. Just pushing, making stones rock. That sort of thing."

"Ah well, there's boys as be up to anything. But I don't think I've even seen them up that way, fooling about,"

Miss Marple went on to the subject of pullovers. Bright coloured pullovers.

"It's not for myself," she said, "it's for one of my great-nephews. You know, he wants a polo-necked pullover and very bright colours he'd like."

"Yes, they do like bright colours nowadays, don't they?" agreed Mrs Merrypit. "Not in jeans. Black jeans they like. Black or dark blue. But they like a bit of brightness up above."

Miss Marple described a pullover of check design in bright colours. There appeared to be quite a good stock of pullovers and jerseys, but anything in red and black did not seem to be on display, nor even was anything like it mentioned as having been lately in stock. After looking at a few samples Miss Marple prepared to take her departure, chatting first about the former murders she had heard about which had happened in this part of the world.

"They got the fellow in the end," said Mrs Merrypit. "Nice-looking boy, hardly have thought it of him. He'd been well brought up, you know. Been to university and all that. Father was very rich, they say. Touched in the head, I suppose. Not that they sent him to Broadway, or whatever the place is. No, they didn't do that, but I think myself he must have been a mental case—there was five or six other girls, so they said. The police had one after another of the young men round hereabouts to help them. Geoffrey Grant they had up. They were pretty sure it was him to begin with. He was always a bit queer, ever since he was a boy. Interfered with little girls going to school, you know. He used to offer them sweets and get them to come down the lanes with him and see the primroses, or something like that. Yes, they had very strong suspicions about him. But it wasn't him. And then there was another one. Bert Williams, but he'd been far away on two occasions, at least—what they call an alibi so it couldn't be him. And then at last it came to this—what's-'is-name, I can't remember him now. Luke I think his name was—no Mike something. Very nice-looking, as I say, but he had a bad record. Yes, stealing, forging cheques, all sorts of things like that. And two what-you-call 'em paternity cases, no, I don't mean that, but you know what I mean. When a girl's going to have a baby. You know and they make an order and make the fellow pay. He'd got two girls in the family way before this."

"Was this girl in the family way?"

"Oh yes, she was. At first we thought when the body was found it might have been Nora Broad. That was Mrs Broad's niece, down at the mill shop. Great one for going with the boys, she was. She'd gone away missing from home in the same way. Nobody knew where she was. So when this body turned up six months later they thought at first it was her."

"But it wasn't?"

"No—someone quite different."

"Did her body ever turn up?"

"No. I suppose it might some day, but they think on the whole it was pushed into the river. Ah well, you never know, do you? You never know what you may dig up off a ploughed field or something like that. I was taken once to see all that treasure. Luton Loo was it—some name like that? Somewhere in the East Counties. Under a ploughed field it was. Beautiful. Gold ships and Viking ships and gold plate, enormous great platters. Well, you never know. Any day you may turn up a dead body or you may turn up a gold platter. And it may be hundreds of years old like that old plate was, or it may be a three- or four-years-old body, like Mary Lucas who'd been missing for four years, they say. Somewhere near Reigate she was found. Ah well, all these things! It's a sad life. Yes, it's a very sad life. You never know what's coming."

"There was another girl who'd lived here, wasn't there?" said Miss Marple, "Who was killed."

"You mean the body they thought was Nora Broad's but it wasn't? Yes. I've forgotten her name now. Hope, it was, I think. Hope or Charity. One of those sort of names, if you know what I mean. Used to be used a lot in Victorian times but you don't hear them so much nowadays. Lived at the Manor House, she did. She'd been there for some time after her parents were killed."

"Her parents died in an accident, didn't they?"

"That's right. In a plane going to Spain or Italy, one of those places."

"And you say she came to live here? Were they relations of hers?"

"I don't know if they were relations, but Mrs Glynne as she is now, was I think a great friend of her mother's or something that way. Mrs Glynne, of course, was married and gone abroad but Miss Clotilde—that's the eldest one, the dark one—she was very fond of the girl. She took her abroad, to Italy and France and all sorts of places, and she had her trained a bit of typewriting and shorthand and that sort of thing, and art classes too. She's very arty, Miss Clotilde is. Oh, she was mighty fond of the girl. Broken-hearted she was when she disappeared. Quite different to Miss Anthea——"

"Miss Anthea is the youngest one, isn't she?"

"Yes. Not quite all there, some people say. Scatty like, you know, in her mind. Sometimes you see her walking along, talking to herself, you know, and tossing her head in a very queer way. Children get frightened of her sometimes. They say she's a bit queer about things. I don't know. You hear everything in a village, don't you? The great-uncle who lived here before, he was a bit peculiar too. Used to practise revolver shooting in the garden. For no reason at all so far as anyone could see. Proud of his marksmanship, he said he was, whatever marksmanship is."

"But Miss Clotilde is not peculiar?"

"Oh no, she's clever, she is. Knows Latin and Greek, I believe. Would have liked to go to university but she had to look after her mother who was an invalid for a long time. But she was very fond of Miss—now, what was her name?—Faith perhaps.

She was very fond of her and treated her like a daughter. And then along comes this young what's-his-name, Michael I think it was—and then one day the girl just goes off without saying a word to anyone. I don't know if Miss Clotilde knew as she was in the family way."

"But you knew," said Miss Marple.

"Ah well, I've got a lot of experience. I usually know when a girl's that way. It's plain enough to the eye. It's not only the shape, as you might say, you can tell by the look in their eyes and the way they walk and sit, and the sort of giddy fits they get and sick turns now and again. Oh yes, I thought to myself, here's another one of them. Miss Clotilde had to go and identify the body. Nearly broke her up, it did. She was like a different woman for weeks afterwards. Fairly loved that girl, she did."

"And the other one—Miss Anthea?"

"Funnily enough, you know, I thought she had a kind of pleased look as though she was—yes, just pleased. Not nice, eh? Farmer Plummer's daughter used to look like that. Always used to go and see pigs killed. Enjoyed it. Funny things go on in families."

Miss Marple said goodbye, saw she had another ten minutes to go and passed on to the post office. The post office and general store of Jocelyn St Mary was just off the Market Square.

Miss Marple went into the post office, bought some stamps, looked at some of the postcards and then turned her attention to various paper back books. A middle-aged woman with rather a vinegary face presided behind the postal counter. She assisted Miss Marple to free a book from the wire support in which the books were.

"Stick a bit sometimes, they do. People don't put them back straight, you see."

There was by now no one else in the shop. Miss Marple looked with distaste at the jacket of the book, a naked girl with blood-stained markings on her face and a sinister-looking killer bending over her with a blood-stained knife in his hand.

"Really," she said, "I don't like these horrors nowadays."

"Gone a bit too far with some of their jackets, haven't they," said Mrs Vinegar. "Not everyone as likes them. Too fond of violence in every way, I'd say nowadays."

Miss Marple detached a second book. "*Whatever Happened to Baby Jane*," she read. "Oh dear, it's a sad world one lives in."

"Oh yes, I know. Saw in yesterday's paper, I did, some woman left her baby outside a supermarket and then someone else comes along and wheels it away. And all for no reason as far as one can see. The police found her all right. They all seem to say the same things, whether they steal from a supermarket or take away a baby. Don't know what came over them, they say."

"Perhaps they really don't," suggested Miss Marple.

Mrs Vinegar looked even more like vinegar.

"Take me a lot to believe that, it would."

Miss Marple looked round—the Post Office was still empty. She advanced to the window.

"If you are not too busy, I wonder if you could answer a question of mine," said Miss Marple. "I have done something extremely stupid. Of late years I make so many mistakes. This was a parcel addressed to a charity. I send them clothes—pullovers and children's woollies, and I did it up and addressed it and it was sent off—and only this morning it came to me suddenly that I'd made a mistake and written the wrong address. I *don't* suppose any list is kept of the addresses of parcels—but I thought someone might have just happened to remember it. The address I meant to put was The Dockyard and Thames Side Welfare Association."

Mrs Vinegar was looking quite kindly now, touched by Miss Marple's patent incapacity and general state of senility and dither.

"Did you bring it yourself?"

"No, I didn't—I'm staying at The Old Manor House—and one of them, Mrs Glynne, I think—said she or her sister would post it. Very kind of her——"

"Let me see now. It would have been on Tuesday, would it? It wasn't Mrs Glynne who brought it in, it was the youngest one, Miss Anthea."

"Yes, yes I think that was the day——"

"I remember it quite well. In a good sized dress box—and moderately heavy, I think. But not what you said, Dockyard Association—I can't recall anything like that. It was the Reverend Mathews—The East Ham Women and Children's

Woollen Clothing Appeal."

"Oh yes," Miss Marple clasped her hands in an ecstasy of relief. "How clever of you—I see now how I came to do it. At Christmas I *did* send things to the East Ham Society in answer to a special appeal for knitted things, so I must have copied down the wrong address. Can you just repeat it?" She entered it carefully in a small notebook.

"I'm afraid the parcel's gone off, though——"

"Oh yes, but I can write, explaining the mistake and ask them to forward the parcel to the Dockyard Association instead. Thank you *so* much."

Miss Marple trotted out.

Mrs Vinegar produced stamps for her next customer, remarking in an aside to a colleague—"Scatty as they make them, poor old creature. Expect she's always doing that sort of thing."

Miss Marple went out of the Post Office and ran into Emlyn Price and Joanna Crawford.

Joanna, she noticed, was very pale and looked upset.

"I've got to give evidence," she said. "I don't know—what will they ask me? I'm so afraid. I—I don't like it. I told the police sergeant, I told him what I thought we saw."

"Don't you worry, Joanna," said Emlyn Price. "This is just a coroner's inquest, you know. He's a nice man, a doctor, I believe. He'll just ask you a few questions and you'll say what you saw."

"You saw it too," said Joanna.

"Yes, I did," said Emlyn. "At least I saw there was someone up there. Near the boulders and things. Now come on, Joanna."

"They came and searched our rooms in the hotel," said Joanna. "They asked our permission but they had a search warrant. They looked in our rooms and among the things in our luggage."

"I think they wanted to find that check pullover you described. Anyway, there's nothing for you to worry about. If you'd had a black and scarlet pullover yourself you wouldn't have talked about it, would you. It was black and scarlet, wasn't it?"

"I don't know," said Emlyn Price. "I don't really know the colours of things very well. I think it was a sort of bright colour. That's all I know."

"They didn't find one," said Joanna. "After all, none of us have very many things with us. You don't when you go on a coach travel. There wasn't anything like that among anybody's things. I've never seen anyone—of our lot, I mean, wearing anything like that. Not so far. Have you?"

"No, I haven't, but I suppose—I don't know that I should know if I *had* seen it," said Emlyn Price. "I don't always know red from green."

"No, you're a bit colour blind, aren't you," said Joanna. "I noticed that the other day."

"What do you mean, you noticed it."

"My red scarf. I asked if you'd seen it. You said you'd seen a green one somewhere and you brought me the red one. I'd left it in the dining-room. But you didn't really know it was red."

"Well, don't go about saying I'm colour blind. I don't like it. Puts people off in some way."

"Men are more often colour blind than women," said Joanna. "It's one of those sex-link things," she added, with an air of erudition. "You know, it passes through the female and comes out in the male."

"You make it sound as though it was measles," said Emlyn Price. "Well, here we are."

"You don't seem to mind," said Joanna, as they walked up the steps.

"Well, I don't really. I've never been to an inquest. Things are rather interesting when you do them for the first time."

Dr Stokes was a middle-aged man with greying hair and spectacles. Police evidence was given first, then the medical evidence with technical details of the concussion injuries which had caused death. Mrs Sandbourne gave particulars of the coach tour, the expedition as arranged for that particular afternoon, and particulars of how the fatality had occurred. Miss Temple, she said, although not young, was a very brisk walker. The party were going along a well known footpath which led round the curve of a hill which slowly mounted to the old Moorland Church originally built in Elizabethan times, though repaired and added to later. On an adjoining crest was what was called the

Bonaventure Memorial. It was a fairly steep ascent and people usually climbed it at different pace from each other. The younger ones very often ran or walked ahead and reached their destination much earlier than the others. The elderly ones took it slowly. She herself usually kept at the rear of the party so that she could, if necessary, suggest to people who were tired that they could, if they liked, go back. Miss Temple, she said, had been talking to a Mr and Mrs Butler. Miss Temple, though she was over sixty, had been slightly impatient at their slow pace and had out-distanced them, had turned a corner and gone on ahead rather rapidly, which she had done often before. She was inclined to get impatient if waiting for people to catch up for too long, and preferred to make her own pace. They had heard a cry ahead, and she and the others had run on, turned a curve of the pathway and found Miss Temple lying on the ground. A large boulder detached from the hillside above where there were several others of the same kind, must, they had thought, have rolled down the hillside and struck Miss Temple as she was going along the path below. A most unfortunate and tragic accident.

"You had no idea there was anything but an accident?"

"No, indeed. I can hardly see how it could have been anything but an accident."

"You saw no one above you on the hillside?"

"No. This is the main path round the hill but of course people do wander about over the top. I did not see anyone that particular afternoon."

Then Joanna Crawford was called. After particulars of her name and age Dr Stokes asked,

"You were not walking with the remainder of the party?"

"No, we had left the path. We'd gone round the hill a little higher up the slope."

"You were walking with a companion?"

"Yes. With Mr Emlyn Price."

"There was no one else actually walking with you?"

"No. We were talking and we were looking at one or two of the flowers. They seemed of rather an uncommon kind. Emlyn's interested in botany."

"Were you out of sight of the rest of the party?"

"Not all the time. They were walking along the main path—some way below us, that is."

"Did you see Miss Temple?"

"I think so. She was walking ahead of the others, and I think I saw her turn a corner of the path ahead of them after which we didn't see her because the contour of the hill hid her."

"Did you see someone walking above you on the hillside?"

"Yes. Up amongst a good many boulders. There's a sort of great patch of boulders on the side of the hill."

"Yes," said Dr Stokes, "I know exactly the place you mean. Large granite boulders. People call them the Wethers, or the Grey Wethers sometimes."

"I suppoe they might look like sheep from a distance but we weren't so very far away from them."

"And you saw someone up there?"

"Yes. Someone was more or less in the middle of the boulders, leaning over them.'

"Pushing them, do you think?"

"Yes. I thought so, and wondered why. He seemed to be pushing at one on the outside of the group near the edge. They were so big and so heavy I would have thought it was impossible to push them. But the one he or she was pushing seemed to be balanced rather like a rocking stone."

"You said first *he*, now you say *he* or *she*, Miss Crawford. Which do you think it was?"

"Well, I thought—I suppose—I suppose I thought it was a man, but I wasn't actually thinking at the time. It was—he or she was—wearing trousers and a pullover, a sort of man's pullover with a polo neck."

"What colour was the pullover?"

"Rather a bright red and black in checks. And there was longish hair at the back of a kind of beret, rather like a woman's hair, but then it might just as well have been a man's."

"It certainly might," said Dr Stokes, rather drily. "Identifying a male or female figure by their hair is certainly not easy these days." He went on, "What happened next?"

"Well, the stone began to roll over. It sort of toppled over the edge and then it began to gain speed. I said to Emlyn, 'Oh it's going to go right over down the hill.' Then we heard a sort of crash as it fell. And I think I heard a cry from below but I might have imagined it."

"And then?"

"Oh, we ran on up a bit and round the corner of the hill to see what had happened to the stone."

"And what did you see?"

"We saw the boulder below on the path with a body underneath it—and people coming running round the corner."

"Was it Miss Temple who uttered the cry?"

"I think it must have been. It might have been one of the others who was catching up and turned the corner. Oh! it was—it was horrible."

"Yes, I'm sure it was. What had happened to the figure you'd seen above? The man or woman in the red and black pullover? Was that figure still there among the stones?"

"I don't know. I never looked up there. I was—I was busy looking at the accident, and running down the hill to see if one could do anything. I did just look up, I think, but there wasn't anyone in sight. Only the stones. There were a lot of contours and you could lose anyone quite easily from view."

"Could it have been one of your party?"

"Oh, no. I'm sure it wasn't one of us. I would have known because, I mean, one would have known by their clothes. I'm sure nobody was wearing a scarlet and black pullover."

"Thank you, Miss Crawford."

Emlyn Price was called next. His story was practically a replica of Joanna's.

There was a little more evidence which did not amount to much.

The Coroner brought in that there was not sufficient evidence to show how Elizabeth Temple had come to her death, and adjourned the inquest for a fortnight.

17. *Miss Marple Makes a Visit*

AS THEY walked back from the inquest to the Golden Boar hardly anyone spoke. Professor Wanstead walked beside Miss Marple, and since she was not a very fast walker, they fell slightly behind the others.

"What will happen next?" Miss Marple asked at last.

"Do you mean legally or to us?"

"I suppose both," said Miss Marple, "because one will surely affect the other."

"It will be presumably a case of the police making further enquiries, arising out of the evidence given by those two young people."

"Yes,"

"Further enquiry will be necessary. The inquest was bound to be adjourned. One can hardly expect the Coroner to give a verdict of accidental death."

"No, I understand that." She said, "What did you think of their evidence?"

Professor Wanstead directed a sharp glance from under his beetling eyebrows.

"Have you any ideas on the subject, Miss Marple?" His voice was suggestive. "Of course," said Professor Wanstead, "we knew beforehand what they were going to say."

"Yes."

"What you mean is that you are asking what I thought about them themselves, their feelings about it."

"It was interesting," said Miss Marple. "Very interesting. The red and black check pullover. Rather important, I think, don't you? Rather striking?"

"Yes, exactly that."

He shot again that look at her under his eyebrows. "What

does it suggest to you exactly?"

"I think," said Miss Marple. "I think the description of that might give us a valuable clue."

They came to the Golden Boar. It was only about half past twelve and Mrs Sandbourne suggested a little refreshment before going in to luncheon. As sherry and tomato juice and other liquors were being consumed, Mrs Sandbourne proceeded to make certain announcements.

"I have taken advice," she said, "both from the Coroner and Inspector Douglas. Since the medical evidence has been taken fully, there will be at the church a funeral memorial service tomorrow at eleven o'clock. I'm going to make arrangements with Mr Courtney, the local vicar, about it. On the following day it will be best, I think, to resume our tour. The programme will be slightly altered, since we have lost three days, but I think it can be reorganized on rather simpler lines. I have heard from one or two members of our party that they would prefer to return to London, presumably by rail. I can quite understand the feelings lying behind this, and would not like to try and influence you in any way. This death has been a very sad occurrence. I still cannot help but believe that Miss Temple's death *was* the result of an accident. Such a thing has happened before on that particular pathway, though there do not appear in this case to have been any geological or atmospherical conditions causing it. I think a good deal more investigation will have to be made. Of course, some hiker on a walking tour—that kind of thing—may have been pushing about boulders quite innocently, not realizing that there was a danger for someone walking below in what he or she was doing. If so, if that person comes forward, the whole thing may be cleared up quite quickly, but I agree one cannot take that for granted at present. It seems unlikely that the late Miss Temple could have had any enemy, or anyone who wished her harm of any kind. What I should suggest is, that we do not discuss the accident any further. Investigations will be made by the local authorities whose business it is. I think we will probably all like to attend the memorial service in the church tomorrow. And after that, on continuing the tour, I hope that it may distract our minds from the shock we have had. There are still some very interesting and famous houses to see and some very beautiful scenery also."

Luncheon being announced shortly after that, the subject was not discussed any further. That is to say, not openly. After lunch, as they took coffee in the lounge, people were prone to get together in little groups, discussing their further arrangements.

"Are you continuing on the tour?" asked Professor Wanstead of Miss Marple.

"No," said Miss Marple. She spoke thoughtfully. "No. I think—I think that what has happened inclines me to remain here a little longer."

"At the Golden Boar or at The Old Manor House?"

"That rather depends as to whether I receive any further invitation to go back to The Old Manor House. I would not like to suggest it myself because my original invitation was for the two nights that the tour was to have stayed here originally. I think possibly it would be better for me to remain at the Golden Boar."

"You don't feel like returning to St Mary Mead?"

"Not yet," said Miss Marple. "There are one or two things I could do here, I think. One thing I have done already." She met his enquiring gaze. "If you are going on," she said, "with the rest of the party, I will tell you what I have put in hand, and suggest a small side-line of enquiry that might be helpful. The other reason that I wish to stay here I will tell you later. There are certain enquiries—local enquiries—that I want to make. They may not lead anywhere so I think it as well not to mention them now. And you?"

"I should like to return to London. I have work there waiting to be done. Unless, that is, I can be helpful to you here?"

"No," said Miss Marple, "I do not think so at present. I expect you have various enquiries of your own that you wish to put in hand."

"I came on the tour to meet you, Miss Marple."

"And now you have met me and know what I know, or practically all that I know, you have other enquiries to put in hand. I understand that. But before you leave here, I think there are one or two things—well, that might be helpful, might give a result."

"I see. You have ideas."

"I am remembering what you said."

"You have perhaps pinned down the smell of evil?"

"It is difficult," said Miss Marple, "to know exactly what something wrong in the atmosphere really means."

"But you do feel that there is something wrong in the atmosphere?"

"Oh yes. Very clearly."

"And especially since Miss Temple's death which, of course, was not an accident, no matter what Mrs Sandbourne hopes."

"No," said Miss Marple, "It was not an accident. What I don't think I have told you is that Miss Temple said to me once that she was on a pilgrimage."

"Interesting," said the Professor. "Yes, interesting. She didn't tell you what the pilgrimage was, to where or to whom?"

"No," said Miss Marple, "if she'd lived just a little longer and not been so weak, she might have told me. But unfortunately, death came a little too soon."

"So that you have not any further ideas on that subject."

"No. Only a feeling of assurance that her pilgrimage was put an end to by malign design. Someone wanted to stop her going wherever she was going, or stop her going to whomever she was going to. One can only hope that chance or Providence may throw light on that."

"That's why you're staying here?"

"Not only that," said Miss Marple. "I want to find out something more about a girl called Nora Broad."

"Nora Broad." He looked faintly puzzled.

"The other girl who disappeared about the same time as Verity Hunt did. You remember you mentioned her to me. A girl who had boy-friends and was, I understand, very *ready* to *have* boy-friends. A foolish girl, but attractive apparently to the male sex. I think," said Miss Marple, "that to learn a little more about her might help me in my enquiries."

"Have it your own way, Detective-Inspector Marple," said Professor Wanstead.

The service took place on the following morning. All the members of the tour were there. Miss Marple looked round the church. Several of the locals were there also. Mrs Glynne was there and her sister Clotilde. The youngest one, Anthea, did not attend. There were one or two people from the village also, she thought. Probably not acquainted with Miss Temple but there out of a rather morbid curiosity in regard to what was now spoken of by the term "foul play". There was, too, an elderly clergyman; in gaiters, well over seventy, Miss Marple thought, a broad-shouldered old man with a noble mane of white hair. He was slightly crippled and found it difficult both to kneel and to stand. It was a fine face, Miss Marple thought, and she wondered who he was. Some old friend of Elizabeth Temple, she presumed, who might perhaps have come from quite a long distance to attend the service?

As they came out of the church Miss Marple exchanged a few words with her fellow travellers. She knew now pretty well who was doing what. The Butlers were returning to London.

"I told Henry I just couldn't go on with it," said Mrs Butler. "You know—I feel all the time that any minute just as we might be walking round a corner, someone, you know, might shoot us or throw a stone at us. Someone who has got a down perhaps on the Famous Houses of England."

"Now then, Mamie, now then," said Mr Butler, "don't you let your imagination go as far as that!"

"Well, you just don't know nowadays. What with hijackers about and kidnapping and all the rest of it, I don't feel really protected anywhere."

Old Miss Lumley and Miss Bentham were continuing with the tour, their anxieties allayed.

"We've paid very highly for this tour and it seems a pity to miss anything just because this very sad accident has happened. We rang up a very good neighbour of ours last night, and they are going to see to the cats, so we don't need to worry."

It was going to remain an accident for Miss Lumley and Miss Bentham. They had decided it was more comfortable that way.

Mrs Riseley-Porter was also continuing on the tour. Colonel and Mrs Walker were resolved that nothing would make them miss seeing a particularly rare collection of fuchsias in the garden due to be visited the day after tomorrow. The architect, Jameson, was also guided by his wish to see various buildings of special interest for him. Mr Caspar, however, was departing by rail, he said. Miss Cooke and Miss Barrow seemed undecided.

"Pretty good walks round here," said Miss Cooke. "I think we'll stay at the Golden Boar for a little. That's what you're going to do, isn't it, Miss Marple?"

"I really think so," said Miss Marple. "I don't feel quite equal to going on travelling and all that. I think a day or two's rest would be helpful to me after what's happened."

As the little crowd dispersed, Miss Marple took an unostentatious route of her own. From her handbag she took out a leaf torn from her notebook on which she had entered two addresses. The first, a Mrs Blackett, lived in a neat little house and garden just by the end of the road where it sloped down towards the valley. A small neat woman opened the door.

"Mrs Blackett?"

"Yes, yes, ma'am, that's my name."

"I wonder if I might just come in and speak to you for a minute or two. I have just been to the service and I am feeling a little giddy. If I could just sit down for a minute or two?"

"Dear me, now, dear me. Oh, I'm sorry for that. Come right in ma'am, come right in. That's right. You sit down here. Now I'll get you a glass of water—or maybe you'd like a pot of tea?"

"No, thank you," said Miss Marple, "a glass of water would put me right."

Mrs Blackett returned with a glass of water and a pleasurable prospect of talking about ailments and giddiness and other things.

"You know, I've got a nephew like that. He oughtn't to be at his age, he's not much over fifty but now and then he'll come over giddy all of a sudden and unless he sits down at once—why you don't know, sometimes he'll pass out right on the floor. Terrible, it is. Terrible. And doctors, they don't seem able to do anything about it. Here's your glass of water."

"Ah," said Miss Marple, sipping, "I feel much better."

"Been to the service, have you, for the poor lady as got done in, as some say, or accident as others. I'd say it's accident every time. But these inquests and coroners, they always want to make things look criminal, they do."

"Oh yes," said Miss Marple. "I've been so sorry to hear of a lot of things like that in the past. I was hearing a great deal about a girl called Nora. Nora Broad, I think."

"Ah, Nora, yes. Well, she was my cousin's daughter. Yes. A long while ago, that was. Went off and never come back. These girls, there's no holding them. I said often, I did, to Nancy Broad—that's my cousin—I said to her, 'You're out working all day' and I said 'What's Nora doing? You know she's the kind that likes the boys. Well,' I said, 'there'll be trouble. You see if there isn't.' And sure enough, I was quite right."

"You mean——?"

"Ah, the usual trouble. Yes, in the family way. Mind you, I don't think as my cousin Nancy knew about it yet. But of course, I'm sixty-five and I know what's what and I know the way a girl looks and I think I know who it was, but I'm not sure. I might have been wrong because he went on living in the place and he was real cut up when Nora was missing."

"She went off, did she?"

"Well, she accepted a lift from someone—a stranger. That's the last time she was seen. I forget the make of the car now. Some funny name it had. An Audit or something like that. Anyway, she'd been seen once or twice in that car. And off she went in it. And it was said it was that same car that the poor girl what got herself murdered used to go riding in. But I don't think as that happened to Nora. If Nora'd been murdered, the body would have come to light by now. Don't you think so?"

"It certainly seems likely," said Miss Marple. "Was she a girl who did well at school and all that?"

"Ah no, she wasn't. She was idle and she wasn't too clever at her books either. No. She was all for the boys from the time she was twelve years old onwards. I think in the end she must have gone off with someone or other for good. But she never let anyone know. She never sent as much as a postcard. Went off, I think, with someone as promised her things. You know. Another girl I knew—but that was when I was young—went off with one of them Africans. He told her as his father was a Shake. Funny sort of word, but a shake I think it was. Anyway it was somewhere in Africa or in Algiers. Yes, in Algiers it was. Somewhere there. And she was going to have all sorts of wonderful things. He had six camels, the boy's father, she said and a whole troop of horses and she was going to live in a wonderful house, she was, with carpets hanging up all over the walls, which seems a funny place to put carpets. And off she went. She came back again three years later. Yes. Terrible time, she'd had. Terrible. They lived in a nasty little house made of earth. Yes, it was. And nothing much to eat except what they call cos-cos which I always thought was lettuce, but it seems it isn't. Something more like semolina pudding. Oh terrible it was. And in the end he said she was no good to him and he'd divorce her. He said he'd only got to say 'I divorce you' three times, and he did and walked out and somehow or other, some kind of Society out there took charge of her and paid her fare home to England. And there she was. Ah, but that was about thirty to forty years ago, that was. Now Nora, that was only about seven or eight years ago. But I expect she'll be back one of these days, having learnt her lesson and finding out that all these fine promises didn't come to much."

"Had she anyone to go to here except her—her mother—your cousin, I mean? Anyone who——"

"Well, there's many as was kind to her. There was the people at The Old Manor House, you know. Mrs Glynne wasn't there then, but Miss Clotilde, she was always one to be good to the girls from school. Yes, many a nice present she's given Nora. She gave her a very nice scarf and a pretty dress once. Very nice, it was. A summer frock, a sort of foulard silk. Ah, she was very kind, Miss Clotilde was. Tried to make Nora take more interest in her schooling. Lots of things like that. Advised her against the way she was going on because, you see—well, I wouldn't like to say it, not when she's my cousin's child though, mark you, my cousin is only one who married my boy cousin, that is to say—but I mean it was something terrible the way she went on with all the boys. Anyone could pick her up. Real sad it is. I'd say she'll go on the streets in the end. I don't believe she has any future but that. I don't like to say these things, but there it is. Anyway, perhaps it's better than getting herself murdered like Miss Hunt did, what lived at The Old Manor House. Cruel, that was. They thought she'd gone off with someone and the police, they was busy. Always asking questions and having the young men who'd been with the girl, up to help them with their enquiries and all that. Geoffrey Grant there was, Billy Thompson, and the Langfords' Harry. All unemployed—with plenty of jobs going if they'd wanted to take them. Things usedn't to be like that when I was young. Girls behaved proper. And the boys knew they'd got to work if they wanted to get anywhere."

Miss Marple talked a little more, said that she was now quite restored, thanked Mrs Blackett, and went out.

Her next visit was a girl who was planting out lettuces.

"Nora Broad? Oh, *she* hasn't been in the village for years. Went off with someone, she did. She was a great one for boys. I always wondered where she'd end up. Did you want to see her for any particular reason?"

"I had a letter from a friend abroad," said Miss Marple, untruthfully. "A very nice family and they were thinking of engaging a Miss Nora Broad. She'd been in some trouble, I think. Married someone who was rather a bad lot and had left her and gone off with another woman, and she wanted to get a job looking after children. My friend knew nothing about her, but I gathered she came from this village. So I wondered if there was anyone here who could—well, tell me something about her. You went to school with her, I understand?"

"Oh yes, we were in the same class, we were. Mind you, I didn't approve of all Nora's goings-on. She was boy mad, she was. Well, I had a nice boy-friend myself that I was going steady with at the time, and I told her she'd do herself no good going off with every Tom, Dick and Harry that offered her a lift in a car or took her along to a pub where she told lies about her age, as likely as not. She was a good mature girl as looked a lot older than she was."

"Dark or fair?"

"Oh, she had dark hair. Pretty hair it was. Always loose like, you know, as girls do."

"Were the police worried about her when she disappeared?"

"Yes. You see, she didn't leave no word behind. She just went out one night and didn't come back. She was seen getting into a car and nobody saw the car again and nobody saw her. Just at that time there'd been a good many murders, you know. Not specially round here, but all over the country. The police, they were rounding up a lot of young men and boys. Thought as Nora might be a body at the time we did. But not she. She was all right. I'd say as likely as not she's making a bit of money still in London or one of these big towns doing a strip-tease, something of that kind. That's the kind she was."

"I don't think," said Miss Marple, "that if it's the same person, that she'd be very suitable for my friend."

"She'd have to change a bit if she was to be suitable," said the girl.

18. *Archdeacon Brabazon*

WHEN MISS MARPLE, slightly out of breath and rather tired, got back to the Golden Boar, the receptionist came out from her pen and across to greet her.

"Oh, Miss Marple, there is someone here who wants to speak to you. Archdeacon Brabazon."

"Archdeacon Brabazon?" Miss Marple looked puzzled.

"Yes. He's been trying to find you. He had heard you were with this tour and he wanted to talk to you before you might have left or gone to London. I told him that some of them were going back to London by the later train this afternoon, but he is very, very anxious to speak to you before you go. I have put him in the television lounge. It is quieter there. The other is very noisy just at this moment."

Slightly surprised, Miss Marple went to the room indicated. Archdeacon Brabazon turned out to be the elderly cleric whom she had noticed at the memorial service. He rose and came towards her.

"Miss Marple. Miss Jane Marple?"

"Yes, that is my my name. You wanted——"

"I am Archdeacon Brabazon. I came here this morning to attend the service for a very old friend of mine, Miss Elizabeth Temple."

"Oh yes?" said Miss Marple. "Do sit down."

"Thank you, I will. I am not quite as strong as I was." He lowered himself carefully into a chair.

"And you——"

Miss Marple sat down beside him.

"Yes," she said, "you wanted to see me?"

"Well, I must explain how that comes about. I'm quite aware

that I am a complete stranger to you. As a matter of fact I made a short visit to the hospital at Carristown, talking to the matron before going on to the church here. It was she who told me that before she died Elizabeth had asked to see a fellow member of the tour. Miss Jane Marple. And that Miss Jane Marple had visited her and sat with her just a very, very short time before Elizabeth died."

He looked at her anxiously.

"Yes," said Miss Marple, "that is so. It surprised me to be sent for."

"You are an old friend of hers?"

"No," said Miss Marple. "I only met her on this tour. That's why I was surprised. We had expressed ideas to each other, occasionally sat next to each other in the coach, and had struck up quite an acquaintanceship. But I was surprised that she should have expressed a wish to see me when she was so ill."

"Yes. Yes, I can quite imagine that. She was, as I have said, a very old friend of mine. In fact, she was coming to see me, to visit me. I live in Fillminster, which is where your coach tour will be stopping the day after to-morrow. And by arrangement she was coming to visit me there, she wanted to talk to me about various matters about which she thought I could help her."

"I see," said Miss Marple. "May I ask you a question? I hope it is not too intimate a question."

"Of course, Miss Marple. Ask me anything you like."

"One of the things Miss Temple said to me was that her presence on the tour was *not* merely because she wished to visit historic homes and gardens. She described it by a rather unusual word to use, as a pilgrimage."

"Did she," said Archdeacon Brabazon. "Did she indeed now? Yes, that's interesting. Interesting and perhaps significant."

"So what I am asking you is, do you think that the pilgrimage she spoke of was her visit to you?"

"I think it must have been," said the Archdeacon. "Yes, I think so."

"We had been talking," said Miss Marple, "about a young girl. A girl called Verity."

"Ah yes. Verity Hunt."

"I did not know her surname. Miss Temple, I think, mentioned her only as Verity."

"Verity Hunt is dead," said the Archdeacon. "She died quite a number of years ago. Did you know that?"

"Yes," said Miss Marple. "I knew it. Miss Temple and I were talking about her. Miss Temple told me something that I did not know. She said she had been engaged to be married to the son of a Mr Rafiel. Mr Rafiel is, or again I must say was, a friend of mine. Mr Rafiel has paid the expenses of this tour out of his kindness. I think, though, that possibly he wanted—indeed, intended—me to meet Miss Temple on this tour. I think he thought she could give me certain information."

"Certain information about Verity?"

"Yes."

"That is why she was coming to me. She wanted to know certain facts."

"She wanted to know," said Miss Marple, "why Verity broke off her engagement to marry Mr Rafiel's son."

"Verity," said Archdeacon Brabazon, "did *not* break off her engagement. I am certain of that. As certain as one can be of anything."

"Miss Temple did not know that, did she?"

"No. I think she was puzzled and unhappy about what happened and was coming to me to ask me why the marriage did not take place."

"And why did it not take place?" asked Miss Marple. "Please do not think that I am unduly curious. It's not idle curiosity that is driving me. I too am on—not a pilgrimage—but what I should call a mission. I too want to know why Michael Rafiel and Verity Hunt did not marry."

The Archdeacon studied her for a moment or two.

"You are involved in some way," he said. "I see that."

"I am involved," said Miss Marple, "by the dying wishes of Michael Rafiel's father. He asked me to do this for him."

"I have no reason not to tell you all I know," said the Archdeacon slowly. "You are asking me what Elizabeth Temple would have been asking me, you are asking me something I do not know myself. Those two young people, Miss Marple, intended to marry. They had made arrangements to marry. I was going to marry them. It was a marriage, I gather, which was being kept secret. I knew both these young people. I knew that dear child Verity from a long way back. I prepared her for confirmation, I used to hold services in Lent, for Easter, on other occasions, in Elizabeth Temple's school. A very fine school it was, too. A very fine woman she was. A wonderful teacher with a great sense of each girl's capabilities—for what she was best fitted for in studies. She urged careers on girls she thought would relish careers, and did not force girls that she felt were not really suited to them. She was a great woman and a very dear friend. Verity was one of the most beautiful children—girls, rather—that I have come across. Beautiful in mind, in heart, as well as in appearance. She had the great misfortune to lose her parents before she was truly adult. They were both killed in a charter plane going on a holiday to Italy. Verity went to live when she left school with a Miss Clotilde Bradbury-Scott whom you know, probably, as living here. She had been a close friend of Verity's mother. There are three sisters, though the second one was married and living abroad, so there were only two of them living here. Clotilde, the eldest one, became extremely attached to Verity. She did everything possible to give her a happy life. She took her abroad once or twice, gave her art lessons in Italy and loved and cared for her dearly in every way. Verity, too, came to love her probably as much as she could have loved her own mother. She depended on Clotilde. Clotilde herself was an intellectual and well educated woman. She did not urge a university career on Verity, but this I gather was really because Verity did not really yearn after one. She preferred to study art and music and such subjects. She lived here at The Old Manor House and had, I think, a very happy life. She always seemed to be happy. Naturally, I did not see her after she came here since Fillminster where I was in the cathedral, is nearly sixty miles from here. I wrote to her at Christmas and other festivals, and she remembered me always with a Christmas card. But I saw nothing of her until the day came when she suddenly turned up, a very beautiful and fully grown young woman by then, with an attractive young man whom I also happened to know slightly, Mr Rafiel's son, Michael. They came to me because they were in love with each other and wanted to get married."

"And you agreed to marry them?"

"Yes, I did. Perhaps, Miss Marple, you may think that I should not have done so. They had come to me in secret, it was obvious. Clotilde Bradbury-Scott, I should imagine, had tried to discourage the romance between them. She was well within her rights in doing so. Michael Rafiel, I will tell you frankly, was not the kind of husband you would want for any daughter or relation of yours. She was too young really, to make up her mind, and Michael had been a source of trouble ever since his very young days. He had been had up before junior courts, he had had unsuitable friends, he had been drawn into various gangster activities, he'd sabotaged buildings and telephone boxes. He had been on intimate terms with various girls, had maintenance claims which he had had to meet. Yes, he was a bad lot with the girls as well as in other ways, yet he was extremely attractive and they fell for him and behaved in an extremely silly fashion. He had served two short jail sentences. Frankly, he had a criminal record. I was acquainted with his father, though I did not know him well, and I think that his father did all that he could—all that a man of his character could—to help his son. He came to his rescue, he got him jobs in which he might have succeeded. He paid up his debts, paid out damages. He did all this. I don't know——"

"But he could have done more, you think?"

"No," said the Archdeacon, "I've come to an age now when I know that one must accept one's fellow human beings as being the kind of people and having the kind of, shall we say in modern terms, genetic make-up which gives them the characters they have. I don't think that Mr Rafiel had affection for his son, a great affection at any time. To say he was reasonably fond of him would be the most you could say. He gave him no love. Whether it would have been better for Michael if he had had love from his father, I do not know. Perhaps it would have made no difference. As it was, it was sad. The boy was not stupid. He had a certain amount of intellect and talent. He could have done well if he had wished to do well, and had taken the trouble. But he was by nature—let us admit it frankly—a delinquent. He had certain qualities one appreciated. He had a sense of humour, he was in various ways generous and kindly. He would stand by a friend, help a friend out of a scrape. He treated his girl-friends badly, got them into trouble as the local saying is, and then more or less abandoned them and took up with somebody else. So there I was faced with those two and—yes—I agreed to marry them. I told Verity, I told her quite frankly, the kind of boy she wanted to marry. I found that he had not tried to deceive her in any way. He'd told her that he'd always been in trouble with the police, and in every other way. He told her that he was going, when he married her, to turn over a new leaf. Everything would be changed. I warned her that that would not happen, he would not change. People do not change. He might *mean* to change. Verity, I think, knew that almost as well as I did. She admitted that she knew it. She said, 'I know what Mike is like. I know he'll probably always be like it, but I love him. I may be able to help him and I may not. But I'll take that risk.' And I will tell you this, Miss Marple. I know—none better, I have done a lot with young people, I have married a lot of young people and I have seen them come to grief, I have seen them unexpectedly turn out well—but I know this and recognize it. I know when a couple are really in love with each other. And by that I do not mean just sexually attracted. There is too much talk about sex, too much attention is paid to it. I do not mean that anything about sex is wrong. That is nonsense. But sex cannot take the place of love, it goes *with* love but it cannot succeed by itself. To love means the words of the marriage service. For better, for worse, for richer for poorer, in sickness and in health. That is what you take on if you love and wish to marry. Those two loved each other. To love and to cherish until death do us part. And that," said the Archdeacon, "is where my story ends. I cannot go on because *I do not know what happened*. I only know that I agreed to do as they asked, that I made the necessary arrangements; we settled a day, an hour, a time, a place. I think perhaps that I was to blame for agreeing to the secrecy."

"They didn't want anyone to know?" said Miss Marple.

"No. Verity did not want anyone to know, and I should say most certainly Mike did not want anyone to know. They were afraid of being stopped. To Verity, I think, besides love, there was also a feeling of escape. Natural, I think, owing to the circumstances of her life. She had lost her real guardians, her parents, she had entered on her new life after their death, at an age when a schoolgirl arrives at having a 'crush' on someone. An attractive mistress. Anything from the games mistress to the mathematics mistress, or a prefect or an older girl. A state that does not last for very long, is merely a natural part of life. Then from that you go on to the next stage when you realize that what you want in your life is what complements yourself. A relationship between a man and a woman. You start then to look about you for a mate. The mate you want in life. And if you are wise, you take your time, you have friends, but you are looking, as the old nurses used to say to children, for Mr Right to come along. Clotilde Bradbury-Scott was exceptionally good to Verity, and Verity, I think, gave her what I should call hero-worship. She was a personality as a woman. Handsome, accomplished, interesting. I think Verity adored her in an almost romantic way and I think Clotilde came to love Verity as though she were her own daughter. And so Verity grew to maturity in an atmosphere of adoration, lived an interesting life with interesting subjects to stimulate her intellect. It was a happy life, but I think little by little she was conscious—conscious without knowing she was conscious, shall we say—of a wish to escape. Escape from being loved. To escape, she didn't know into what or *where*. But she did know after she met Michael. She wanted to escape to a life where male and female come together to create the next stage of living in this world. But she knew that it was impossible to make Clotilde understand how she felt. She knew that Clotilde would be bitterly opposed to her taking her love for Michael seriously. And Clotilde, I fear, was right in her belief . . . I know that now. He was not a husband that Verity ought to have taken or had. The road that she started out on led not to life, not to increased living and happiness. It led to shock, pain, death. You see, Miss Marple, that I have a grave feeling of guilt. My motives were good, but I didn't know what I ought to have known. I knew Verity, *but I didn't know Michael*. I understood Verity's wish for secrecy because I knew what a strong personality Clotilde Bradbury-Scott had. She might have had a strong enough influence over Verity to persuade her to give up the marriage."

"You think then that that was what she did do? You think

Clotilde told her enough about Michael to persuade her to give up the idea of marrying him?"

"No, I do *not* believe that. I still do not. Verity would have told me if so. She would have got word to me."

"What did actually happen on that day?"

"I haven't told you that yet. The day was fixed. The time, the hour and the place, and I waited. Waited for a bride and bridegroom who didn't come, who sent no word, no excuse, *nothing*. I didn't know why! I never *have* known why. It still seems to me unbelievable. Unbelievable, I mean, not that they did not come, that could be explicable easily enough, but that they sent no word. Some scrawled line of writing. And that is why I wondered and hoped that Elizabeth Temple, before she died, might have told *you* something. Given you some message perhaps for me. If she knew or had any idea that she was dying, she might have wanted to get a message to me."

"She wanted information *from* you," said Miss Marple. "That, I am sure, was the reason she was coming to you."

"Yes. Yes, that is probably true. It seemed to me, you see, that Verity would have said nothing to the people who could have stopped her, Clotilde and Anthea Bradbury-Scott, but because she had always been very devoted to Elizabeth Temple—and Elizabeth Temple had had great influence over her—it seems to me that she would have written and given her information of some kind."

"I think she did," said Miss Marple.

"Information, you think?"

"The information she gave to Elizabeth Temple," said Miss Marple, "was this. That she was going to marry Michael Rafiel. Miss Temple knew that. It was one of the things she said to me. She said: 'I knew a girl called Verity who was going to marry Michael Rafiel' and the only person who could have told her that was Verity herself. Verity must have written to her or sent some word to her. And then when I said 'Why didn't she marry him?' she said: 'She died'."

"Then we come to a full stop," said Archdeacon Brabazon. He sighed. "Elizabeth and I know no more than these two facts. Elizabeth, that Verity was going to marry Michael. And I that those two were going to marry, that they had arranged it and that they were coming on a settled day and time. And I waited for them, but there was no marriage. No bride, no bridegroom, no word."

"And you have no idea what happened?" said Miss Marple.

"I do not for one minute believe that Verity or Michael definitely parted, broke off."

"But *something* must have happened between them? Something that opened Verity's eyes perhaps, to certain aspects of Michael's character and personality, that she had not realized or known before."

"That is not a satisfying answer because still she would have let me know. She would not have left me waiting to join them together in holy matrimony. To put the most ridiculous side of it, she was a girl with beautiful manners, well brought up. She would have sent word. No. I'm afraid that only one thing could have happened."

"Death?" said Miss Marple. She was remembering that one word that Elizabeth Temple had said which had sounded like the deep tone of a bell.

"Yes." Archdeacon Brabazon sighed. "Death."

"Love," said Miss Marple thoughtfully.

"By that you mean——" he hesitated.

"It's what Miss Temple said to me. I said 'What killed her?' and she said 'Love' and that love was the most frightening word in the world. The most frightening word."

"I see," said the Archdeacon. "I see—or I think I see."

"What is your solution?"

"Split personality," he sighed. "Something that is not apparent to other people unless they are technically qualified to observe it. Jekyll and Hyde are real, you know. They were not Stevenson's invention as such. Michael Rafiel was a—must have been schizophrenic. He had a dual personality. I have no medical knowledge, no psycho-analytic experience. But there must have been in him the two parts of two identities. One, a well-meaning, almost lovable boy, a boy perhaps whose principal attraction was his wish for happiness. But there was also a second personality, someone who was forced by some mental deformation perhaps—something we as yet are not sure of—to kill—not an enemy, but the person he loved, and so he killed

Verity. Not knowing perhaps *why* he had to or *what* it meant. There are very frightening things in this world of ours, mental quirks, mental disease or deformity of a brain. One of my parishioners was a very sad case in point. Two elderly women living together, pensioned. They had been friends in service together somewhere. They appeared to be a happy couple. And yet one day one of them killed the other. She sent for an old friend of hers, the vicar of her parish, and said: 'I have killed Louisa. It is very sad,' she said, 'but I saw the devil looking out of her eye and I knew I was being commanded to kill her.' Things like that make one sometimes despair of living. One says why? and how? and yet one day knowledge will come. Doctors will find out or learn just some small deformity of a chromosome or gene. Some gland that overworks or leaves off working."

"So you think that's what happened?" said Miss Marple.

"It *did* happen. The body was not found, I know, for some time afterwards. Verity just disappeared. She went away from home and was not seen again . . ."

"But it must have happened *then*—that very day——"

"But surely at the trial——"

"You mean after the body was found, when the police finally arrested Michael?"

"He had been one of the first, you know, to be asked to come and give assistance to the police. He had been seen about with the girl, she had been noticed in his car. They were sure all along that he was the man they wanted. He was their first suspect, and they never stopped suspecting him. The other young men who had known Verity were questioned, and one and all had alibis or lack of evidence. They continued to suspect Michael, and finally the body was found. Strangled and the head and face disfigured with heavy blows. A mad frenzied attack. He wasn't sane when he struck those blows. Mr Hyde, let us say, had taken over"

Miss Marple shivered.

The Archdeacon went on, his voice low and sad. "And yet, even now sometimes, I hope and feel that it was some other young man who killed her. Someone who was definitely mentally deranged, though no one had any idea of it. Some stranger, perhaps, whom she had met in the neighbourhood. Someone whom she had met by chance, who had given her a lift in a car, and then——" He shook his head.

"I suppose that *could* have been true," said Miss Marple.

"Mike made a bad impression in court," said the Archdeacon. "Told foolish and senseless lies. Lies as to where his car had been. Got his friends to give him impossible alibis. He was frightened. He said nothing of his plan to marry. I believe his Counsel was of the opinion that that would tell against him—that she might have been forcing him to marry her and that he didn't want to. It's so long ago now, I remember no details. But the evidence was dead against him. He was guilty—and he looked guilty.

"So you see, do you not, Miss Marple, that I'm a very sad and unhappy man. I made the wrong judgment, I encouraged a very sweet and lovely girl to go to her death, because I did not know enough of human nature. I was ignorant of the danger she was running. I believed that if she had had any fear of him, any sudden knowledge of something evil in him, she would have broken her pledge to marry him and have come to me and told me of her fear, of her new knowledge of him. But nothing of that ever happened. Why *did* he kill her? Did he kill her because perhaps he knew she was going to have a child? Because by now he had formed a tie with some other girl and did not want to be forced to marry Verity? I can't believe it. Or was it some entirely different reason. Because *she* had suddenly felt a fear of him, a knowledge of danger from him, and had broken off her association with him? Did that rouse his anger, his fury, and did that lead him to violence and to killing her? One does not know."

"You do not know?" said Miss Marple, "but you *do* still know and believe one thing, don't you?"

"What do you mean exactly by 'believe'? Are you talking from the religious point of view?"

"Oh no," said Miss Marple, "I didn't mean that. I mean, there seems to be in you, or so I feel it, a very strong belief that those two loved each other, that they meant to marry, and that *something* happened that prevented it. Something that ended in her death, but you still really believe that they *were* coming to you to get married that day?"

"You are quite right, my dear. Yes, I cannot help still believing in two lovers who wished to get married, who were ready to take each other for better, for worse, for richer or poorer, in sickness and in health. She loved him and she would have taken him for better or for worse. As far as she had gone, she took him for worse. It brought about her death."

"You must go on believing as you do," said Miss Marple. "I think, you know, that *I* believe it too."

"But then what?"

"I don't know yet," said Miss Marple. "I'm not sure, but I think Elizabeth Temple did know or was beginning to know what happened. A frightening word, she said. *Love*. I thought when she spoke that what she meant was that because of a love affair Verity committed suicide. Because she found out something about Michael, or because something about Michael suddenly upset her and revolted her. But it couldn't have been suicide."

"No," said the Archdeacon, "that couldn't be so. The injuries were described very fully at the trial. You don't commit suicide by beating in your own head."

"Horrible!" said Miss Marple. "Horrible! And you couldn't do that to anyone you loved even if you had to kill 'for love', could you? If he'd killed her, he couldn't have done it that way. Strangling—perhaps, but you wouldn't beat in the face and the head that you loved." She murmured, "Love, love—a frightening word."

19. Goodbyes Are Said

THE COACH was drawn up in front of the Golden Boar on the following morning. Miss Marple had come down and was saying goodbye to various friends. She found Mrs Riseley-Porter in a state of high indignation.

"Really, girls nowadays," she said. "No vigour. No stamina."

Miss Marple looked at her enquiringly.

"Joanna, I mean. My niece."

"Oh dear. Is she not well?"

"Well, she says not. I can't see anything much the matter with her. She says she's got a sore throat, she feels she might have a temperature coming on. All nonsense, I think."

"Oh, I'm very sorry," said Miss Marple. "Is there anything I can do? Look after her?"

"I should leave her alone, if I were you," said Mrs Riseley-Porter. "If you ask me, it's all an excuse."

Miss Marple looked enquiringly at her once more.

"Girls are so silly. Always falling in love."

"Emlyn Price?" said Miss Marple.

"Oh, so you've noticed it too. Yes, they're really getting to a stage of spooning about together. I don't much care for him anyway. One of these long-haired students, you know. Always going on demos or something like that. Why can't they say demonstration properly? I hate abbreviations. And how am *I* going to get along. Nobody to look after me, collect my luggage, take it in, take it out. Really. I'm paying for this complete trip and everything."

"I thought she seemed so attentive to you," said Miss Marple.

"Well, not the last day or two. Girls don't understand that people have to have a little assistance when they get to middle age. They seem to have some absurd idea—she and the Price boy—of going to visit some mountain or some landmark. About a seven or eight mile walk there and back."

"But surely if she has a sore throat and a temperature . . ."

"You'll see, as soon as the coach is gone the sore throat will get better and the temperature will go down," said Mrs Riseley-Porter. "Oh dear, we've got to get on board now. Oh, goodbye, Miss Marple, it's nice to have met you. I'm sorry you're not coming with us."

"I'm very sorry myself," said Miss Marple, "but really you know, I'm not so young and vigorous as you are, Mrs Riseley-Porter, and I really feel after all the—well, shock and everything else the last few days, I really must have a complete twenty-four hours' rest."

"Well, hope to see you somewhere in the future."

They shook hands. Mrs Riseley-Porter climbed into the coach.

A voice behind Miss Marple's shoulder said:

"*Bon Voyage* and Good Riddance."

She turned to see Emlyn Price. He was grinning.

"Was that addressed to Mrs Riseley-Porter?"

"Yes. Who else."

"I'm sorry to hear that Joanna is under the weather this morning."

Emlyn Price grinned at Miss Marple again.

"She'll be all right," he said, "as soon as that coach is gone."

"Oh really!" said Miss Marple, "do you mean——?"

"Yes, I do mean," said Emlyn Price. "Joanna's had enough of that aunt of hers, bossing her around all the time."

"Then you are not going in the coach either?"

"No. I'm staying on here for a couple of days. I'm going to get around a bit and do a few excursions. Don't look so disapproving, Miss Marple. You're not really as disapproving as all that, are you?"

"Well," said Miss Marple, "I have known such things happen in my own youth. The excuses may have been different, and I think we had less chance of getting away with things than you do now."

Colonel and Mrs Walker came up and shook Miss Marple

warmly by the hand.

"So nice to have known you and had all those delightful horticultural talks." said the Colonel. "I believe the day after tomorrow we're going to have a real treat, if nothing else happens. Really, it's too sad, this very unfortunate accident. I must say I think myself it *is* an accident. I really think the Coroner was going beyond everything in his feelings about this."

"It seems very odd," said Miss Marple, "that nobody has come forward, if they were up on top there, pushing about rocks and boulders and things, that they haven't come forward to say so."

"Think they'll be blamed, of course," said Colonel Walker. "They're going to keep jolly quiet, that's what they're going to do. Well, goodbye. I'll send you a cutting of that Magnolia highdownensis and one of the Mahonia japonica too. Though I'm not quite sure if it would do as well where you live."

They in turn got into the coach. Miss Marple turned away. She turned to see Professor Wanstead waving to the departing coach. Mrs Sandbourne came out, said goodbye to Miss Marple and got in the coach and Miss Marple took Professor Wanstead by the arm.

"I want you," she said. "Can we go somewhere where we can talk?"

"Yes. What about the place where we sat the other day?"

"Round here there's a very nice verandah place, I think."

They walked round the corner of the hotel. There was some gay horn-blowing, and the coach departed.

"I wish, in a way, you know," said Professor Wanstead, "that you weren't staying behind. I'd rather have seen you safely on your way in the coach." He looked at her sharply. "Why are you staying here? Nervous exhaustion or something else?"

"Something else," said Miss Marple. "I'm not particularly exhausted, though it makes a perfectly natural excuse for somebody of my age."

"I feel really I ought to stay here and keep an eye on you."

"No," said Miss Marple, "there's no need to do that. There are other things you ought to be doing."

"What things?" He looked at her. "Have you got ideas or knowledge?"

"I think I have knowledge, but I'll have to verify it. There are certain things that I can't do myself. I think you will help to do them because you're in touch with what I refer to as the authorities."

"Meaning Scotland Yard, Chief Constables and the Governors of Her Majesty's Prisons?"

"Yes. One or other or all of them. You might have the Home Secretary in your pocket, too."

"You certainly do have ideas! Well, what do you want me to do?"

"First of all I want to give you this address."

She took out a notebook and tore out one page and handed it to him.

"What's this? Oh yes, well known charity, isn't it?"

"One of the better ones, I believe. They do a lot of good. You send them clothes," said Miss Marple, "children's clothes and women's clothes. Coats. Pullovers, all those sort of things."

"Well, do you want me to contribute to this?"

"No, it's an appeal for charity, it's a bit of what belongs to what we're doing. What you and I are doing."

"In what way?"

"I want you to make enquiries there about a parcel which was sent from here two days ago, posted from this post office."

"Who posted it—did you?"

"No," said Miss Marple. "No. But I assumed responsibility for it."

"What does that mean?"

"It means," said Miss Marple, smiling slightly, "that I went into the post office here and I explained rather scattily and—well, like the old pussy I am—that I had very foolishly asked someone to take a parcel for me and post it, and I had put the wrong address on it. I was very upset by this. The post-mistress very kindly said she remembered the parcel, but the address on it was not the one I was mentioning. It was this one, the one I have just given to you. I explained that I had been very foolish and written the wrong address on it, confusing it with another one I sometimes send things to. She told me it was too late to do anything about it now because the parcel, naturally, had gone off. I said it was quite all right, that I would send a letter to the particular charity to which the parcel had been sent, and explain that it had been addressed to them by mistake. Would they very kindly forward it on to the charity that I had meant to receive it."

"It seems rather a roundabout way."

"Well," said Miss Marple, "one has to *say* something. I'm not going to do that at all. *You* are going to deal with the matter. We've got to know what's inside that parcel! I have no doubt you can get means."

"Will there be anything inside the parcel to say who actually sent it?"

"I rather think not. It may have a slip of paper saying 'from friends' or it may have a fictitious name and address--something like Mrs Pippin, 14 Westbourne Grove and if anyone made enquiries there, there'd be no person of such a name living there."

"Oh. Any other alternatives?"

"It might possibly, most unlikely but possible have a slip saying 'From Miss Anthea Bradbury-Scott'—"

"Did she——?"

"She took it to the post," said Miss Marple.

"And you had asked her to take it there?"

"Oh no," said Miss Marple. "I hadn't asked anyone to post anything. The first I saw of the parcel was when Anthea passed the garden of the Golden Boar where you and I were sitting talking, carrying it."

"But you went to the post office and represented that the parcel was yours."

"Yes," said Miss Marple, "which was quite untrue. But post offices are careful. And, you see, I wanted to find out where it had been sent."

"You wanted to find out if such a parcel had been sent, and if it had been sent by one of the Bradbury-Scotts—or especially Miss Anthea?"

"I knew it would be Anthea," said Miss Marple, "because we'd seen her."

"Well?" He took the paper from her hand. "Yes, I can set this in motion. You think this parcel will be interesting?"

"I think the contents of it might be quite important."

"You like keeping your secrets, don't you?" said Professor Wanstead.

"Not exactly secrets," said Miss Marple, "they are only *probabilities* that I am exploring. One does not like to make definite assertions unless one has a little more definite knowledge."

"Anything else?"

"I think—I think that whoever's in charge of these things, ought to be warned that there might be a second body to be found."

"Do you mean a second body connected with the particular crime that we have been considering? A crime that took place ten years ago?"

"Yes," said Miss Marple. "I'm quite sure of it, as a matter of fact."

"Another body. Whose body?"

"Well," said Miss Marple, "it's only my idea so far."

"Any idea where this body is?"

"Oh! Yes," said Miss Marple, "I'm quite sure I know where it *is*, but I have to have a little more time before I can tell you that."

"What kind of a body? Man's? Woman's? Child's? Girl's?"

"There's another girl who is missing," said Miss Marple. "A girl called Nora Broad. She disappeared from here and she's never been heard any more of. I think her body might be in a particular place."

Professor Wanstead looked at her.

"You know, the more you say, the less I like leaving you here," he said. "Having all these ideas—and possibly doing something foolish—either—" He stopped.

"Either it's all nonsense?—" said Miss Marple.

"No, no, I didn't mean that. But either you know too much—which might be dangerous . . . I think I am going to stay here to keep an eye on you."

"No, you're not," said Miss Marple. "You've got to go to London and set certain things moving."

"You spoke as though you knew a good deal, Miss Marple."

"I think I do know a good deal now. But I have got to be sure."

"Yes, but if you make sure, that may be the last thing you do make sure of! We don't want a third body. Yours."

"Oh, I'm not expecting anything like that," said Miss Marple.

"There might be danger, you know, if any of your ideas are right. Have you suspicions of any one particular person?"

"I think I have certain knowledge as to one person. I have got to find out—I have got to stay here. You asked me once if I felt an atmosphere of evil. Well, that atmosphere is here all right, an atmosphere of evil, of danger if you like—of great unhappiness, of fear . . . I've got to do something about that. The best I can do. But an old woman like me can't do very much."

Professor Wanstead counted under his breath. 'One—two—three—four——"

"What are you counting?" asked Miss Marple.

"The people who left in the coach. Presumably you're not interested in them, since you've let them go off and you're staying here."

"Why should I be interested in them?"

"Because you said Mr Rafiel had sent you in the coach for a particular reason and sent you on this tour for a particular reason and sent you to The Old Manor House for a particular reason. Very well then. The death of Elizabeth Temple ties up with someone in the coach. Your remaining here ties up with The Old Manor House."

"You're not quite right," said Miss Marple. "There are connections between the two. I want someone to tell me things."

"Do you think you can make anyone tell you things?"

"I think I might. You'll miss your train if you don't go soon."

"Take care of yourself," said Professor Wanstead.

"I mean to take care of myself."

The door into the lounge opened and two people came out. Miss Cooke and Miss Barrow.

"Hullo," said Professor Wanstead, "I thought you'd gone off with the coach."

"Well, we changed our minds at the last moment," said Miss Cooke cheerfully. "You know we've just discovered that there are some very agreeable walks near here and there are one or two places I'm very anxious to see. A church with a very unusual Saxon font. Only four or five miles away and quite easily reached by the local bus, I think. You see, it's not only houses and gardens. I'm very interested in church architecture."

"So am I," said Miss Barrow. "There's also Finley Park which is a very fine piece of horticultural planting not far from here. We really thought that it would be much pleasanter to stay here for a day or two."

"You're staying here at the Golden Boar?"

"Yes. We were fortunate enough to be able to get a very nice double room. Really a better one than the one we have had for the last two days."

"You will miss your train," said Miss Marple again.

"I wish," said Professor Wanstead, "that you——"

"I shall be quite all right," said Miss Marple urgently. "Such a kind man," she said, as he disappeared round the side of the house, "who really takes so much care of me—I might be a great-aunt of his or something like that."

"It's all been a great shock, hasn't it," said Miss Cooke. "Perhaps you may like to come with us when we go to visit St Martins in the Grove."

"You're very kind," said Miss Marple, "but I don't think today I feel quite strong enough for expeditions. Perhaps tomorrow if there is anything interesting to see."

"Well, we must leave you then."

Miss Marple smiled at them both and went into the Hotel.

20. *Miss Marple Has Ideas*

HAVING HAD lunch in the dining-room, Miss Marple went out on the terrace to drink her coffee. She was just sipping her second cup when a tall, thin figure came striding up the steps, and approached her, speaking rather breathlessly. She saw it was Anthea Bradbury-Scott.

"Oh, Miss Marple, we've only just heard, you know, that you didn't go with the coach, after all. We thought you were going on with the tour. We had no idea you were staying on here. Both Clotilde and Lavinia sent me here to say we do so hope you will come back to The Old Manor House and stay with us. I'm sure it will be nicer for you to be there. There are so many people coming and going here always, especially over a weekend and things like that. So we'd be very, very glad—we really would—if you would come back to us."

"Oh, that's very kind of you," said Miss Marple. "Really very kind, but I'm sure—I mean, you know it was just a two-day visit. I meant originally to go off with the coach. I mean, after the two days. If it hadn't been for this very, very tragic accident but—well, I really felt I couldn't go on any longer. I thought I must have at least, well at least one night's rest."

"But I mean it would be so much better if you came to us. We'd try and make you comfortable."

"Oh, there's no question of that," said Miss Marple. "I was extremely comfortable staying with you. Oh yes, I did enjoy it very much. Such a beautiful house. And all your things are so nice. You know, your china and glass and furniture. It's such a pleasure to be in a home and not a hotel."

"Then you must come with me now. Yes, you really must. I could go and pack your things for you."

"Oh—well, that's very kind of you. I can do that myself."

"Well, shall I come and help you?"

"That would be very kind," said Miss Marple.

They repaired to her bedroom where Anthea, in a somewhat slap-dash manner, packed Miss Marple's belongings together. Miss Marple, who had her own ways of folding things, had to bite her lip to keep an air of complacency on her face. Really, she thought, she can't fold *anything* properly.

Anthea got hold of a porter from the hotel and he carried the suitcase round the corner and down the street to The Old Manor House. Miss Marple tipped him adequately and, still uttering fussy little speeches of thanks and pleasure, rejoined the sisters.

"The Three Sisters!" she was thinking, "Here we are again." She sat down in the drawing-room, and closed her eyes for a minute, breathing rather fast. She appeared to be somewhat out of breath. It was only natural, she felt at her age, and after Anthea and the hotel porter had set a fast pace. But really she was trying to acquire through her closed eyes what the feeling was she had on coming into this house again. Was something in it sinister? No, not so much sinister as unhappy. Deep unhappiness. So much so it was almost frightening.

She opened her eyes again and looked at the two other occupants of the room. Mrs Glynne had just come in from the kitchen, bearing an afternoon tea tray. She looked as she had looked all along. Comfortable, no particular emotions or feelings. Perhaps almost too devoid of them, Miss Marple thought. Had she accustomed herself through perhaps a life of some stress and difficulty, to show nothing to the outer world, to keep a reserve and let no-one know what her inner feelings were?

She looked from her to Clotilde. She had a Clytemnestra look, as she had thought before. She had certainly not murdered her husband for she had never had a husband to murder and it seemed unlikely that she had murdered the girl to whom she was said to have been extremely attached. That, Miss Marple was quite sure was true. She had seen before how the tears had welled from Clotilde's eyes when the death of Verity had been mentioned.

And what about Anthea? Anthea had taken that cardboard box to the post office. Anthea had come to fetch her. Anthea—

she was very doubtful about Anthea. Scatty? Too scatty for her age. Eyes that wandered and came back to you. Eyes that seemed to see things that other people might not see, over your shoulder. She's frightened, thought Miss Marple. Frightened of something. What was she frightened of? Was she perhaps a mental case of some kind? Frightened perhaps of going back to some institution or establishment where she might have spent part of her life. Frightened of those two sisters of hers feeling that it was unwise for her to remain at liberty? Were they uncertain, those two, what their sister Anthea might do or say?

There was *some* atmosphere here. She wondered, as she sipped the last of her tea, what Miss Cooke and Miss Barrow were doing. Had they gone to visit that church or was that all talk, meaningless talk. It was odd. Odd the way they had come and looked at her at St Mary Mead so as to know her again on the coach, but not to acknowledge that they had ever seen or met her before.

There were quite a lot of difficult things going on. Presently Mrs Glynne removed the tea tray, Anthea went out into the garden and Miss Marple was left alone with Clotilde.

"I think," said Miss Marple, "that you know an Archdeacon Brabazon, do you not?"

"Oh yes," said Clotilde, "he was in church yesterday at the service. Do you know him?"

"Oh no," said Miss Marple, "but he did come to the Golden Boar and he came and spoke to me there. I gather he had been to the hospital and was enquiring about poor Miss Temple's death. He wondered if Miss Temple had sent any message to him. I gather she was thinking of paying him a visit. But of course I told him that although I did go there in case I could do anything, there was nothing that could be done except sit by poor Miss Temple's bed. She was unconscious, you know. I could have done nothing to help her."

"She didn't say—say anything—any explanation of what had happened?" asked Clotilde.

She asked without much interest. Miss Marple wondered if she felt more interest than she expressed, but on the whole she thought not. She thought Clotilde was busy with thoughts of something quite different.

"Do you think it *was* an accident?" Miss Marple asked, "or do you think there is something in that story that Mrs Riseley-Porter's niece told. About seeing someone pushing a boulder."

"Well, I suppose if those two said so, they must have seen it."

"Yes. They both said so, didn't they," said Miss Marple, "though not quite in the same terms. But perhaps that's quite natural."

Clotilde looked at her curiously.

"You seem to be intrigued by that."

"Well, it seems so very unlikely," said Miss Marple, "an unlikely story, unless——"

"Unless what?"

"Well, I just wondered," said Miss Marple.

Mrs Glynne came into the room again.

"You just wondered what?" she asked.

"We're talking about the accident, or non-accident," said Clotilde.

"But who——"

"It seems a very odd story that they told," said Miss Marple again.

"There's something about this place," said Clotilde suddenly. "Something about this atmosphere. We never got over it here. Never. Never since—since Verity died. It's years but it doesn't go away. A shadow's here." She looked at Miss Marple. "Don't you think so too? Don't you feel a shadow here?"

"Well, I'm a stranger," said Miss Marple. "It's different for you and your sisters who've lived here and who knew the dead girl. She was, I gather, as Archdeacon Brabazon was saying—a very charming and beautiful girl."

"She was a lovely girl. A dear child too," said Clotilde.

"I wish I'd known her better," said Mrs Glynne. "Of course I was living abroad at that time. My husband and I came home on leave once, but we were mostly in London. We didn't come down here often."

Anthea came in from the garden. She was carrying in her hand a great bunch of lilies.

"Funeral flowers," she said. "That's what we ought to have here today, isn't it? I'll put them in a great jar. Funeral flowers," and she laughed suddenly. A queer, hysterical little giggle.

"Anthea," said Clotilde, "don't—don't do that. It's not—it's not right."

"I'll go and put them in water," said Anthea, cheerfully. She went out of the room.

"Really," said Mrs Glynne, "Anthea! I do think she's——"

"She's getting worse," said Clotilde.

Miss Marple adopted an attitude of not listening or hearing. She picked up a small enamel box and looked at it with admiring eyes.

"She'll probably break a vase now," said Lavinia.

She went out of the room. Miss Marple said.

"You are worried about your sister, about Anthea?"

"Well yes, she's always been rather unbalanced. She's the youngest and she was rather delicate as a girl. But lately, I think, she's got definitely worse. She hasn't got any idea, I think, of the gravity of things. She has these silly fits of hysteria. Hysterical laughter at things one ought to be serious about. We don't want to—well, to send her anywhere or—you know. She ought to have treatment, I think, but I don't think she would like to go away from home. This is her home, after all. Though sometimes it's—it's very difficult."

"All life is difficult sometimes," said Miss Marple.

"Lavinia talks of going away," said Clotilde. "She talks of going to live abroad again. At Taormina. I think. She was there with her husband a lot and they were very happy. She's been at home with us now for many years, but she seems to have this longing to get away and to travel. Sometimes I think—sometimes I think she doesn't like being in the same house as Anthea."

"Oh dear," said Miss Marple. "Yes, I have heard of cases like that where these difficulties do arise."

"She's afraid of Anthea," said Clotilde. "Definitely afraid of her. And really, I keep telling her there's nothing to be afraid of. Anthea's just rather silly at times. You know, has queer ideas and says queer things. But I don't think there's any danger of her—well, I mean of—oh, I don't know what I mean. Doing anything dangerous or strange or queer."

"There's never been any trouble of that kind?" enquired Miss Marple.

"Oh no. There's never been anything. She gets nervous fits of temper sometimes and she takes rather sudden dislikes to people. She's very jealous, you know, over things. Very jealous of a lot of—well, fuss being made over different people. I don't know. Sometimes I think we'd better sell this house and leave it altogether."

"It is sad for you, isn't it," said Miss Marple. "I think I can understand that it must be very sad for you living here with the memory of the past."

"You understand that, do you? Yes, I can see that you do. One cannot help it. One's mind goes back to that dear, lovable child. She was like a daughter to me. She was the daughter, anyway, of one of my best friends. She was very intelligent too. She was a clever girl. She was a good artist. She was doing very well with her art training and designing. She was taking up a good deal of designing. I was very proud of her. And then—this wretched attachment, this terrible mentally afflicted boy."

"You mean Mr Rafiel's son, Michael Rafiel?"

"Yes. If only he'd never come here. It just happened that he was staying in this part of the world and his father suggested he might look us up and he came and had a meal with us. He could be very charming, you know. But he always had been a sad delinquent, a bad record. He'd been in prison twice, and a very bad history with girls. But I never thought that Verity . . . just a case of infatuation. I suppose it happens to girls of that age. She was infatuated with him. Thought of nothing else, wouldn't hear a word against him. Insisted that everything that had happened to him had not been his fault. You know the things girls say. 'Everyone is against him,' that's what they always say. Everyone's against him. Nobody made allowances for him. Oh, one gets tired of hearing these things said. Can't one put a little sense into girls?"

"They have not usually very much sense, I agree," said Miss Marple.

"She wouldn't listen. I—I tried to keep him away from the house. I told him he was not to come here any more. That of course was stupid. I realized that afterwards. It only meant that she went and met him outside the house. I don't know where. They had various meeting places. He used to call for her in his car at an agreed spot and bring her home late at night. Once or twice he didn't bring her home until the next day. I tried to tell them it must stop, that it must all cease, but they wouldn't listen. Verity wouldn't listen. I didn't expect him to, of course."

"She intended to marry him?" asked Miss Marple.

"Well, I don't think it ever got as far as that. I don't think he ever wanted to marry her or thought of such a thing."

"I am very sorry for you," said Miss Marple. "You must have suffered a lot."

"Yes. The worst was having to go and identify the body. That was some time after—after she'd disappeared from here. We thought of course that she'd run away with him and we thought that we'd get news of them some time. I knew the police seemed to be taking it rather seriously. They asked Michael to go to the police station and help them with enquiries and his account of himself didn't seem to agree with what local people were saying.

"Then they found her. A long way from here. About thirty miles away. In a kind of ditch hedgy spot down an unfrequented lane where anyone hardly ever went. Yes, I had to go and view the body in the mortuary. A terrible sight. The cruelty, the force that had been used. What did he want to do that to her for? Wasn't it enough that he strangled her? He strangled her with her own scarf. I can't—I can't talk about it any more. I can't bear it, I can't bear it."

Tears rained suddenly down her face.

"I'm sorry for you," said Miss Marple. "I'm very, very sorry."

"I believe you are." Clotilde looked at her suddenly. "And even you don't know the worst of it?"

"In what way?"

"I don't know—I don't know about Anthea."

"What do you mean about Anthea?"

"She was so queer at that time. She was—she was very jealous. She suddenly seemed to turn against Verity. To look at her as though she hated her. Sometimes I thought—I thought perhaps—oh no, it's an awful thing to think, you can't think that about your own sister—she did once attack someone. You know, she used to get these storms of rage. I wondered if it *could* have been—oh, I mustn't say such things. There's no question of any such thing. Please forget what I've said. There's nothing in it, nothing at all. But—but—well, she's not quite normal. I've got to face that. When she was quite young queer things happened once or twice—with animals. We had a parrot. A parrot that said things, silly things that parrots do say and she wrung its neck and I've never felt the same since. I've never felt that I could trust her. I've never felt *sure*. I've never felt—oh, goodness, I'm getting hysterical, too."

"Come, come," said Miss Marple, "don't think of these things."

"No. It's bad enough to know—to know that Verity died. Died in that horrible way. At any rate, other girls are safe from that boy. Life sentence he got. He's still in prison. They won't let him out to do anything to anyone else. Though why they couldn't bring it in as some mental trouble—diminished responsibility—one of these things they use nowadays. He ought to have gone to Broadmoor. I'm sure he wasn't responsible for anything that he did."

She got up and went out of the room. Mrs. Glynne had come back and passed her sister in the doorway.

"You mustn't pay any attention to Clotilde," she said. "She's never quite recovered from that ghastly business years ago. She loved Verity very much."

"She seems to be worried about your other sister."

"About Anthea? Anthea's all right. She's—er—well, she's scatty, you know. She's a bit—hysterical. Apt to get worked up about things, and she has queer fancies, imagination sometimes. But I don't think there's any need for Clotilde to worry so much. Dear me, who's that passing the window?"

Two apologetic figures suddenly showed themselves in the French window.

"Oh do excuse us," said Miss Barrow, "we were just walking round the house to see if we could find Miss Marple. We had heard she'd come here with you and I wonder—oh, there you are, my dear Miss Marple. I wanted to tell you that we didn't get to that church after all this afternoon. Apparently it's closed for cleaning, so I think we shall have to give up any other expedition to-day and go on one to-morrow. I do hope you don't mind us coming in this way. I did ring at the front-door bell but it didn't seem to be ringing."

"I'm afraid it doesn't sometimes," said Mrs Glynne. "You know, it's rather temperamental. Sometimes it rings and sometimes it doesn't. But do sit down and talk to us a little. I'd no idea that you hadn't gone with the coach."

"No, we thought we would do a little sight-seeing round here, as we had got so far, and going with the coach would really be rather—well, rather painful after what has happened just a day or two ago."

"You must have some sherry," said Mrs Glynne.

She went out of the room and presently returned. Anthea was with her, quite calm now, bringing glasses and a decanter of sherry, and they sat down together.

"I can't help wanting to know," said Mrs Glynne, "what really is going to happen in this business. I mean of poor Miss Temple. I mean, it seems so very impossible to know what the police think. They still seem to be in charge, and I mean the inquest being adjourned, so obviously they are not satisfied. I don't know if there's anything in the nature of the wound."

"I shouldn't think so," said Miss Barrow. "I mean a blow on the head, bad concussion—well, I mean that came from the boulder. The only point is, Miss Marple, if the boulder rolled itself down or somebody rolled it."

"Oh," said Miss Cooke, "but surely you can't think that—who on earth would want to roll a boulder down, do that sort of thing? I suppose there are always hooligans about. You know, some young foreigners or students. I really wonder, you know, whether—well——"

"You mean," said Miss Marple, "you wondered if that someone was one of our fellow travellers."

"Well, I—I didn't say that," said Miss Cooke.

"But surely," said Miss Marple, "we can't help—well thinking about that sort of thing. I mean, there must be some explanation. If the police seem sure it wasn't an accident, well then it must have been done by somebody and—well, I mean, Miss Temple was a stranger to this place here. It doesn't seem as if anyone could have done it—anyone local I mean. So it really comes back to—well, I mean, to all of us who were in the coach, doesn't it?"

She gave a faint, rather whinnying old lady's laugh.

"Oh surely!"

"No, I suppose I ought not to say such things. But you know, really crimes are very interesting. Sometimes the most extraordinary things have happened."

"Have you any definite feeling yourself, Miss Marple? I should be interested to hear," said Clotilde.

"Well, one does think of possibilities."

"Mr Caspar," said Miss Cooke. "You know, I didn't like the look of that man from the first. He looked to me—well, I thought he might have something to do with espionage or something. You know, perhaps come to this country to look for atomic secrets or something."

"I don't think we've got any atomic secrets round here." said Mrs Glynne.

"Of course we haven't," said Anthea. "Perhaps it was someone who was following her. Perhaps it was someone who was tracking her because she was a criminal of some kind."

"Nonsense," said Clotilde. "She was the Headmistress retired, of a very well known school, she was a very fine scholar. Why should anyone be trying to track *her* down?"

"Oh, I don't know. She might have gone peculiar or something."

"I'm sure," said Mrs Glynne, "that Miss Marple has some ideas."

"Well, I have some ideas," said Miss Marple. "It seems to me that—well, the only people that could be . . . Oh dear, this is so difficult to say. But I mean there are two people who just spring into one's mind as possibilities logically I mean, I don't think that it's really so at all because I'm sure they're both very nice people, but I mean there's nobody else really logically who could be suspected, should I say."

"Who do you mean? This is very interesting."

"Well, I don't think I ought to say such things. It's only a—a sort of wild conjecture."

"Who do you think might have rolled the boulder down? Who do you think could have been the person that Joanna and Emlyn Price saw?"

"Well, what I did think was that—that perhaps they hadn't seen anybody."

"I don't quite understand," said Anthea, "they hadn't seen anybody?"

"Well, perhaps they might have made it all up."

"What—about seeing someone?"

"Well, it's possible, isn't it."

"Do you mean as a sort of joke or a sort of unkind idea? What *do* you mean?"

"Well, I suppose—one does hear of young people doing very extraordinary things nowadays," said Miss Marple. "You know, putting things in horses' eyes, smashing Legation windows and attacking people. Throwing stones at people, and it's usually being done by somebody young, isn't it? And they were the only young people, weren't they?"

"You mean Emlyn Price and Joanna might have rolled over that boulder?"

"Well, they're the only sort of obvious people, aren't they?" said Miss Marple.

"Fancy!" said Clotilde. "Oh, I should never have thought of that. But I see—yes, I just see that there could be something in what you say. Of course, I don't know what those two were like. I haven't been travelling with them."

"Oh, they were very nice," said Miss Marple. "Joanna seemed to me a particularly—you know, capable girl."

"Capable of doing anything?" asked Anthea.

"Anthea," said Clotilde, "do be quiet."

"Yes. Quite capable," said Miss Marple. "After all, if you're going to do what may result in murder, you'd have to be rather capable so as to manage not to be seen or anything."

"They must have been in it together, though," suggested Miss Barrow.

"Oh yes," said Miss Marple. "They were in it together and they told roughly the same story. They are the—well, they are the obvious suspects, that's all I can say. They were out of sight of the others. All the other people were on the lower path. They could have gone up to the top of the hill, they could have rocked the boulder. Perhaps they didn't mean to kill Miss Temple specially. They may have meant it just as a—well, just a piece of anarchy or smashing something or someone—anyone in fact. They rolled it over. And then of course they told the story of seeing someone there. Some rather peculiar costume or other which also sounds very unlikely and—well, I oughtn't to say these things but I *have* been thinking about it."

"It seems to me a very interesting thought," said Mrs Glynne. "What do you think, Clotilde?"

"I think it's a possibility. I shouldn't have thought of it myself."

"Well," said Miss Cooke, rising to her feet, "we must be going back to the Golden Boar now. Are you coming with us, Miss Marple?"

"Oh no," said Miss Marple. "I suppose you don't know. I've forgotten to tell you. Miss Bradbury-Scott very kindly asked me to come back and stay another night—or two nights—here."

"Oh, I see. Well, I'm sure that'll be very nice for you. Much more comfortable. They seem rather a noisy lot that have arrived at the Golden Boar this evening."

"Won't you come round and have some coffee with us after dinner?" suggested Clotilde. "It's quite a warm evening. We can't offer you dinner because I'm afraid we haven't got enough in the house, but if you'll come in and have some coffee with us . . ."

"That would be very nice," said Miss Cooke. "Yes, we will certainly avail ourselves of your hospitality."

21. *The Clock Strikes Three*

MISS COOKE and Miss Barrow arrived very promptly at 8.45. One wore beige lace and the other one a shade of olive green. During dinner Anthea had asked Miss Marple about these two ladies.

"It seems very funny of them," she said, "to want to stay behind."

"Oh, I don't think so," said Miss Marple. "I think it is really quite natural. They have a rather exact plan, I imagine."

"What do you mean by a plan?" asked Mrs Glynne.

"Well, I should think they are always prepared for various eventualities and had a plan for dealing with them."

"Do you mean," said Anthea, with some interest, "do you mean that they had a plan for dealing with murder?"

"I wish," said Mrs Glynne, "that you wouldn't talk of poor Miss Temple's death as murder."

"But of course it's murder," said Anthea. "All I wonder is who wanted to murder her? I should think probably some pupil of hers at the school who always hated her and had it in for her."

"Do you think hate can last as long as that?" asked Miss Marple.

"Oh, I should think so. I should think you could hate anyone for years."

"No," said Miss Marple, "I think hate would die out. You could try and keep it up artificially, but I think you would fail. It's not as strong a force as love," she added.

"Don't you think that Miss Cooke or Miss Barrow or both of them might have done the murder?"

"Why should they?" said Mrs Glynne. "Really, Anthea! They seemed very nice women to me."

"*I* think there's something rather mysterious about them," said Anthea. "Don't you, Clotilde?"

"I think perhaps you're right," said Clotilde. "They seemed to me to be slightly artificial, if you know what I mean."

"*I* think there's something very sinister about them," said Anthea.

"You've got such an imagination always," said Mrs Glynne. "Anyway, they were walking along the bottom path, weren't they? You saw them there, didn't you?" she said to Miss Marple.

"I can't say that I noticed them particularly," said Miss Marple. "In fact, I had no opportunity of doing so."

"You mean——?"

"She wasn't there," said Clotilde. "She was here in our garden."

"Oh, of course. I forgot."

"A very nice, peaceful day it was," said Miss Marple. "I enjoyed it very much. Tomorrow morning I would like to go out and look again at that mass of white flowers coming into bloom at the end of the garden near that raised up mound. It was just beginning to come out the other day. It must be a mass of bloom now. I shall always remember that as part of my visit here, you know."

"I hate it," said Anthea. "I want it taken away. I want to build up a greenhouse again there. Surely if we save enough money we can do that, Clotilde?"

"We'll leave that alone," said Clotilde. "I don't want that touched. What use is a greenhouse to us now? It would be years before grapes would bear fruit again."

"Come," said Mrs Glynne, "we can't go on arguing over that. Let us go into the drawing-room. Our guests will be coming shortly for coffee."

It was then that the guests had arrived. Clotilde brought in the tray of coffee. She poured out the cups and distributed them. She placed one before each guest and then brought one to Miss Marple. Miss Cooke leaned forward.

"Oh, do forgive me, Miss Marple, but really, do you know, I shouldn't drink that if I were you. Coffee, I mean, at this time of night. You won't sleep properly."

"Oh, do you think so?" said Miss Marple. "I am quite used to coffee in the evening."

"Yes, but this is very strong, good coffee. I should advise you not to drink it."

Miss Marple looked at Miss Cooke. Miss Cooke's face was very earnest, her fair, unnatural-looking hair flopped over one eye. The other eye blinked slightly.

"I see what you mean," said Miss Marple. "Perhaps you are right. You know something, I gather, about diet."

"Oh yes, I make quite a study of it. I had some training in nursing, you know, and one thing and another."

"Indeed." Miss Marple pushed the cup away slightly. "I suppose there is no photograph of this girl?" she asked. "Verity Hunt, or whatever her name was? The Archdeacon was talking about her. He seemed to have been very fond of her."

"I think he was. He was fond of all young people," said Clotilde.

She got up, went across the room and lifted the lid of a desk. From that she brought a photograph and brought it over for Miss Marple to see.

"That was Verity," she said.

"A beautiful face," said Miss Marple. "Yes, a very beautiful and unusual face. Poor child."

"It's dreadful nowadays," said Anthea, "these things seem happening the whole time. Girls going out with every kind of young man. Nobody taking any trouble to look after them."

"They have to look after themselves nowadays," said Clotilde, "and they've no idea of how to do it, heaven help them!"

She stretched out a hand to take back the photograph from Miss Marple. As she did so her sleeve caught the coffee cup and knocked it to the floor.

"Oh dear!" said Miss Marple. "Was that my fault? Did I jog your arm?"

"No," said Clotilde, "it was my sleeve. It's rather a floating sleeve. Perhaps you would like some hot milk, if you are afraid to take coffee?"

"That would be very kind," said Miss Marple. "A glass of hot milk when I go to bed would be very soothing indeed, and always gives one a good night."

After a little more desultory conversation, Miss Cooke and Miss Barrow took their departure. A rather fussy departure in which first one and then the other came back to collect some article they'd left behind. A scarf, a handbag and a pocket handkerchief.

"Fuss, fuss, fuss," said Anthea, when they had departed.

"Somehow," said Mrs Glynne, "I agree with Clotilde that those two don't seem *real*, if you know what I mean," she said to Miss Marple.

"Yes," said Miss Marple. "I *do* rather agree with you. They *don't* seem very real. I have wondered about them a good deal. Wondered, I mean, why they came on this tour and if they were really enjoying it. And what was their reason for coming."

"And have you discovered the answers to all those things?" asked Clotilde.

"I think so," said Miss Marple. She sighed. "I've discovered the answers to a lot of things," she said.

"Up to now I hope you've enjoyed yourself," said Clotilde.

"I am glad to have left the tour now," said Miss Marple. "I don't think I should have enjoyed much more of it."

"No. I can quite understand that."

Clotilde fetched a glass of hot milk from the kitchen and accompanied Miss Marple up to her room.

"Is there anything else I can get you?" she asked. "Anything at all?"

"No, thank you," said Miss Marple. "I have everything I want. I have my little night bag here, you see, so I need not do any more unpacking. Thank you," she said, "it is very kind of you and your sisters to put me up again tonight."

"Well, we couldn't do much less, having had Mr Rafiel's letter. He was a very thoughtful man."

"Yes," said Miss Marple, "the kind of man who—well, thinks of everything. A good brain, I should think."

"I believe he was a very noted financier."

"Financially and otherwise, he thought of a lot of things," said Miss Marple. "Ah well, I shall be glad to get to bed. Good-night, Miss Bradbury-Scott."

"Shall I send you breakfast up in the morning, you'd like to have it in bed?"

"No, no, I wouldn't put you out for the world. No, no, I would rather come down. A cup of tea, perhaps, would be very nice, but I want to go out in the garden. I particularly want to see that mound all covered with white flowers, so beautiful and so triumphant——"

"Good-night," said Clotilde, "sleep well."

ii

In the hall of The Old Manor House the grandfather clock at the bottom of the stairs struck two o'clock. The clocks in the house did not all strike in unison and some of them indeed, did not strike at all. To keep a house full of antique clocks in working order was not easy. At three o'clock the clock on the first floor landing struck a soft-chimed three o'clock. A faint chink of light showed through the hinge of the door.

Miss Marple sat up in bed and put her fingers on the switch of the electric lamp by her bed. The door opened very softly. There was no light outside now but the soft footstep came through the door into the room. Miss Marple switched the light on.

"Oh," she said, "it's you, Miss Bradbury-Scott. Is there anything special?"

"I just came to see if you wanted anything," said Miss Bradbury-Scott.

Miss Marple looked at her. Clotilde had on a long purple robe. What a handsome woman she was, thought Miss Marple. Her hair framing her forehead, a tragic figure, a figure of drama. Again Miss Marple thought of Greek plays. Clytemnestra again.

"You're sure there is nothing I can bring you?"

"No, thank you," said Miss Marple. "I'm afraid," she said apologetically, "that I have not drunk my milk."

"Oh dear, why not?"

"I did not think it would be very good for me," said Miss Marple.

Clotilde stood there, at the foot of the bed, looking at her.

"Not wholesome, you know," said Miss Marple.

"Just what do you mean by that?" Clotilde's voice was harsh now.

"I think you know what I mean," said Miss Marple. "I think you've known all the evening. Perhaps before that."

"I have no idea what you are talking about."

"No?" There was a faint satirical note to the questioning monosyllable.

"I am afraid the milk is cold now. I will take it away and get you some hot."

Clotilde stretched out a hand and took the glass of milk from the bedside.

"Don't trouble yourself," said Miss Marple. "Even if you brought it me, I should not drink it."

"I really cannot understand the point of what you're saying. Really," said Clotilde, looking at her. "What a very extraordinary person you are. What sort of a woman are you? Why are you talking like this? Who are you?"

Miss Marple pulled down the mass of pink wool that encircled her head, a pink wool scarf of the same kind that she had once worn in the West Indies.

"One of my names," she said, "is Nemesis."

"Nemesis? And what does that mean?"

"I think you know," said Miss Marple. "You are a very well educated woman. Nemesis is long delayed sometimes, but it comes in the end."

"What are you talking about?"

"About a very beautiful girl whom you killed," said Miss Marple.

"Whom I killed? What do you mean?"

"I mean the girl Verity."

"And why should I kill her?"

"Because you loved her," said Miss Marple.

"Oh course I loved her. I was devoted to her. And she loved me."

"Somebody said to me not very long ago that love was a very frightening word. It *is* a frightening word. You loved Verity very much. She meant everything in the world to you. She was devoted to you until something else came into her life. A different kind of love came into her life. She fell in love with a boy, a young man. Not a very suitable one, not a very good specimen, not anyone with a good record, but she loved him and he loved her and she wanted to escape. To escape from the burden of the bondage of love she was living in with you. She wanted a normal woman's life. To live with the man of her choice, to have children by him. She wanted marriage and the happiness of normality."

Clotilde moved. She came to a chair and sat down in it, staring at Miss Marple.

"So," she said, "you seem to understand very well."

"Yes, I do understand."

"What you say is quite true. I shan't deny it. It doesn't matter if I do or do not deny it."

"No," said Miss Marple, "you are quite right there. It will not matter."

"Do you know at all—can you imagine—how I have suffered?"

"Yes," said Miss Marple, "I can imagine it. I've always been able to imagine things."

"Did you imagine the agony, the agony of thinking, of knowing you are going to lose the thing you love best in the world. And I was losing it to a miserable, depraved delinquent. A man unworthy of my beautiful, splendid girl. I had to stop it. I had to—I had to."

"Yes," said Miss Marple. "Sooner than let the girl go, you killed her. Because you loved her, you killed her."

"Do you think I could ever do a thing like that? Do you think I could strangle the girl I loved? Do you think I could bash her face in, crush her head to a pulp? Nothing but a vicious, depraved man would do a thing like that."

"No," said Miss Marple, "you wouldn't do that. You loved her and you would not be able to do that."

"Well then, you see, you are talking nonsense."

"You didn't do that to her. The girl that happened to was not the girl you loved. Verity's here still, isn't she? She's here in the garden. I don't think you strangled her. I think you gave her a drink of coffee or milk, you gave her a painless overdose of sleeping stuff. And then when she was dead, you took her out into the garden, you pulled aside the fallen bricks of the greenhouse, and you made a vault for her there, under the floor with the bricks, and covered it over. And then the polygonum was planted there and has flowered ever since, growing bigger and stronger every year. Verity has remained here with you. You never let her go."

"You fool! You crazy old fool! Do you think you are ever going to get away to tell this story?"

"I think so," said Miss Marple. "I'm not quite sure of it. You are a strong woman, a great deal stronger than I am."

"I'm glad you appreciate that."

"And you wouldn't have any scruples," said Miss Marple. "You know one doesn't stop at one murder. I have noticed that in the course of my life and in what I have observed of crime. You killed two girls, didn't you. You killed the girl you loved and you killed a different girl."

"I killed a silly little tramp, an adolescent tart. Nora Broad. How did you know about her?"

"I wondered," said Miss Marple. "I didn't think from what I saw of you that you could have borne to strangle and disfigure the girl you loved. But another girl disappeared also about that time, a girl whose body has never been found. But I thought that the body *had* been found, only they hadn't known that the body was Nora Broad's. It was dressed in Verity's clothes, it was identified as Verity by the person who would be the first applied to, the person who knew her better than anyone else. You had to go and say if the body found was the body of Verity. You recognized it. You said that that dead body was Verity's."

"And why should I do that?"

"Because you wanted the boy who had taken Verity away from you, the boy whom Verity had loved and who had loved Verity, you wanted him tried for murder. And so you hid that second body in a place where it would not be too easily discovered. When that was discovered, it would be thought to be the wrong girl. You would make sure that it was identified in the way you wanted. You dressed it in Verity's clothes, put her handbag there; a letter or two, a bangle, a little cross on a chain—you disfigured her face.

"A week ago you committed a third murder, the murder of Elizabeth Temple. You killed her because she was coming to this part of the world, and you were afraid of what she might have known, from what Verity might have written to her or told her, and you thought that if Elizabeth Temple got together with Archdeacon Brabazon, they might with what they both knew come at some appraisal of the truth. Elizabeth Temple must not be allowed to meet the Archdeacon. You are a very powerful woman. You could have rolled that boulder down the hillside. It must have taken some doing, but you are a very strong woman."

"Strong enough to deal with you," said Clotilde.

"I don't think," said Miss Marple, "that you will be allowed to do that."

"What do you mean, you miserable, shrivelled up old woman?"

"Yes," said Miss Marple, "I'm an elderly pussy and I have very little strength in my arms or my legs. Very little strength anywhere. But I am in my own way an emissary of justice."

Clotilde laughed, "And who'll stop me from putting an end to you?"

"I think," said Miss Marple, "my guardian angel."

"Trusting to your guardian angel, are you?" said Clotilde, and laughed again.

She advanced towards the bed.

"Possibly two guardian angels," said Miss Marple. "Mr Rafiel always did things on a lavish scale."

Her hand slipped under the pillow and out again. In it was a whistle which she put to her lips. It was something of a sensation in whistles. It had the shrill fury which would attract a policeman from the end of a street. Two things happened almost simultaneously. The door of the room opened. Clotilde turned. Miss Barrow was standing in the doorway. At the same moment the large wardrobe hanging cupboard opened and Miss Cooke stepped out of it. There was a grim air of professionalism about them both which was very noticeable, in contrast to their pleasant social behaviour a little earlier in the evening.

"Two guardian angels," said Miss Marple happily. "Mr Rafiel has done me very proud! as one used to say."

22. *Miss Marple Tells Her Story*

"WHEN DID you find out," asked Professor Wanstead, "that those two women were private agents accompanying you for your protection?"

He leaned forward in his chair looking thoughtfully at the white-haired old lady who sat in an upright position in the chair opposite him. They were in an official Government building in London, and there were four other persons present.

An official from the Public Prosecutor's Office; the Assistant Commissioner of Scotland Yard, Sir James Lloyd, the Governor of Manstone Prison, Sir Andrew McNeil. The fourth person was the Home Secretary.

"Not until the last evening," said Miss Marple. "I wasn't actually sure until then. Miss Cooke had come to St Mary Mead and I found out fairly quickly that she was not what she represented herself to be, which was a woman knowledgeable in gardening who had come there to help a friend with her garden. So I was left with the choice of deciding what her real object had been, once she had acquainted herself with my appearance, which was obviously the only thing she could have come for. When I recognized her again on the coach, I had to make up my mind if she was accompanying the tour in the rôle of guardianship, or whether those two women were enemies enlisted by what I might call the other side.

"I was only really sure that last evening when Miss Cooke prevented me by very distinct words of warning, from drinking the cup of coffee that Clotilde Bradbury-Scott had just set down in front of me. She phrased it very cleverly, but the warning was clearly there. Later, when I was wishing those two good-night, one of them took my hand in both of hers giving me a particularly friendly and affectionate handshake. And in doing so she passed something into my hand, which, when I examined it later, I found to be a high-powered whistle. I took it to bed with me, accepted the glass of milk which was urged upon me by my hostess, and wished her good-night, being careful not to change my simple and friendly attitude."

"You didn't drink the milk?"

"Of course not," said Miss Marple. "What do you take me for?"

"I beg your pardon," said Professor Wanstead. "It surprises me that you didn't lock your door."

"That would have been quite the wrong thing to do," said Miss Marple. "I wanted Clotilde Bradbury-Scott to come in. I wanted to see what she would say or do. I thought it was almost certain that she *would* come in when sufficient time had elapsed, to make sure that I had drunk the milk, and was in an unconscious sleep from which presumably I would not have woken up again."

"Did you help Miss Cooke to conceal herself in the wardrobe?"

"No. It was a complete surprise when she came out of that suddenly. I suppose," said Miss Marple thoughtfully, thinking it over, "I suppose she slipped in there just when I had gone down the passage to the—er—to the bathroom."

"You knew the two women were in the house?"

"I thought they would be at hand somewhere after they'd given me the whistle. I do not think it was a difficult house to which to gain access, there were no shuttered windows or burglar alarms or anything of that kind. One of them came back on the pretext of having left a handbag and a scarf. Between them they probably managed to leave a window unfastened, and I should imagine they came back into the house almost as soon as they left it, while the inhabitants inside were going up to bed."

"You took a big risk, Miss Marple."

"I hoped for the best," said Miss Marple. "One cannot go through life without attracting certain risks if they are necessary."

"Your tip about the parcel dispatched to that charity, by the way, was entirely successful. It contained a brand new brightly coloured man's polo-necked jumper in scarlet and black checks.

Most noticeable. What made you think of that?"

"Well," said Miss Marple, "that was really very simple. The description that Emlyn and Joanna gave of the figure they had seen made it seem almost certain that these very bright coloured and noticeable clothes were *meant* to be noticed, and that therefore it would be very important that they should not be hidden locally or kept among the person's own belongings. They must be got out of the way as soon as could be. And really there is only one way successfully of disposing of something. That is through the general post. Anything in the nature of clothes can be very easily dispatched to charities. Think how pleased the people who collect winter garments for Unemployed Mothers, or whatever the name of the charity would be to find a nearly brand new woollen jumper. All I had to do was to find out the address where it had been sent."

"And you *asked* them that at the post office?" The Home Secretary looked slightly shocked.

"Not directly, of course. I mean, I had to be a little flustered and explain how I'd put the wrong address on some clothes that I was sending to a charity and could they by any chance tell me if the parcel one of my hostesses had brought up there, had been sent off. And a very nice woman there did her best and remembered that it was *not* the address I was hoping it had been sent to, and she gave me the address that she *had* noted. She had no suspicion, I think, that I had any wish for the information apart from being—well, rather muddle-headed, elderly, and very worried about where my parcel of worn clothes had gone."

"Ah," said Professor Wanstead, "I see you are an actress, Miss Marple, as well as an avenger." Then he said, "When did you first begin to discover what had happened ten years ago?"

"To begin with," said Miss Marple, "I found things very difficult, almost impossible. In my mind I was blaming Mr Rafiel for not having made things clear to me. But I see now that he'd been very wise not to do so. Really, you know, he *was* extraordinarily clever. I can see why he was such a big financier and made so much money so easily. He laid his plans so well. He gave me just enough information in small packets each time. I was, as it were, directed. First my guardian angels were alerted to note what I looked like. Then I was directed on the tour and to the people on it."

"Did you suspect, if I may use that word, anyone on the tour at first?"

"Only as possibilities."

"No feeling of evil?"

"Ah, you have remembered that. No, I did not think there was any definite atmosphere of evil. I was not told who my contact was there, but *she* made herself known to *me*."

"Elizabeth Temple?"

"Yes. It was like a searchlight," said Miss Marple, "illuminating things on a dark night. So far, you see, I had been in the dark. There were certain things that must be, must logically be, I mean, because of what Mr Rafiel had indicated. There must be somewhere a victim and somewhere a murderer. Yes, a killer was indicated because that was the only liaison that had existed between Mr Rafiel and myself. There had been a murder in the West Indies. Both he and I had been involved in it and all he knew of me was my connection with that. So it could not be any other type of crime. And it could not, either, be a casual crime. It must be a deliberate crime. It must be, and show itself definitely to be the handiwork of someone who had accepted evil. Evil instead of good. There seemed to be two victims indicated. There must be someone who had been killed and there must be clearly a victim of injustice. A victim who had been accused of a crime he or she had not committed. So now, while I pondered these things, I had no light upon them until I talked to Miss Temple. She was very intense, very compelling. There came the first link which I had with Mr Rafiel. She spoke of a girl she had known, a girl who had once been engaged to Mr Rafiel's son. Here then was my first ray of light. Presently she also told me that the girl had not married him. I asked why not and she said 'because she died'. I asked then how she had died, what had killed her, and she said very strongly, very compellingly—I can hear her voice still, it was like the sound of a deep bell—she said *Love*. And she said after that 'the most frightening word there can be is Love'. I did not know then exactly what she meant. In fact the first idea that came to me was that the girl had committed suicide as a result of an unhappy love affair. It can happen often enough, and a very sad tragedy it is when it does happen. That was the most I knew then. That and the fact that the journey she herself was engaged upon was no mere pleasure tour. She was going, she told me, on a pilgrimage. She was going to some place or to some person. I did not learn then who the person was, that only came later."

"Archdeacon Brabazon?"

"Yes. I had no idea then of his existence. But from then on I felt that the chief characters—the chief actors—in the drama, whichever way you like to put it, were not on the tour. They were not members of the coach party. I hesitated just for a short time, hesitated over some particular persons. I hesitated, considering Joanna Crawford and Emlyn Price."

"Why fix on them?"

"Because of their youth," said Miss Marple. "Because youth is so often associated with suicide, with violence, with intense jealousy and tragic love. A man kills his girl—it happens. Yes, my mind went to them but it did not seem to me there was any association there. No shadow of evil, of despair, of misery. I used the idea of them later as a kind of false pointer when we were drinking sherry at The Old Manor House that last evening. I pointed out how they could be the most easy suspects in the death of Elizabeth Temple. When I see them again," said Miss Marple, punctiliously, "I shall apologize to them for having used them as useful characters to distract attention from my real ideas."

"And the next thing was the death of Elizabeth Temple?"

"No," said Miss Marple. "Actually the next thing was my arrival at The Old Manor House. The kindness of my reception and taking up my stay there under their hospitable roof. That again had been arranged by Mr Rafiel. So I knew that I must go there, but not for what reason I was to go there. It might be merely a place where more information would come to me to lead me onwards in my quest. I am sorry," Miss Marple said suddenly becoming her normal apologetic and slightly fussy self, "I am talking at much too great a length. I really must not inflict on you all that I thought and . . ."

"Please go on," said Professor Wanstead. "You may not know it but what you are telling me is particularly interesting to me. It ties up with so much I have known and seen in the work I do. Go on giving me what you felt."

"Yes, go on," said Sir Andrew McNeil.

"It *was* feeling," said Miss Marple. "It wasn't really, you know, logical deduction. It was based on a kind of emotional reaction or susceptibility to—well, I can only call it atmosphere."

"Yes," said Wanstead, "there is atmosphere. Atmosphere in houses, atmosphere in places, in the garden, in the forest, in a public house, in a cottage."

"The three sisters. That is what I thought and felt and said to myself when I went into The Old Manor House. I was so kindly received by Lavinia Glynne. There's something about the phrase—the three sisters—that springs up in your mind as sinister. It combines with the three sisters in Russian literature, the three witches on Macbeath's heath. It seemed to me that there was an atmosphere there of sorrow, of deep felt unhappiness, also an atmosphere of fear and a kind of struggling different atmosphere which I can only describe as an atmosphere of normality."

"Your last word interests me," said Wanstead.

"It was due, I think, to Mrs Glynne. She was the one who came to meet me when the coach arrived and explained the invitation. She was an entirely normal and pleasant woman, a widow. She was not very happy, but when I say she was not very happy it was nothing to do with sorrow or deep unhappiness, it was just that she had the wrong atmosphere for her own character. She took me back with her and I met the other two sisters. The next morning I was to hear from an aged housemaid who brought my early morning tea, a story of past tragedy, of a girl who had been killed by her boy-friend. Of several other girls in the neighbourhood who'd fallen victims to violence, or sexual assault. I had to make my second appraisal. I had dismissed the people in the coach as not being personally concerned in my search. Somewhere still there was a killer. I had to ask myself if one of the killers could be here. Here in this house where I had been sent, Clotilde, Lavinia, Anthea. Three names of three weird sisters, three happy—unhappy—suffering—frightened—what were they? My attention was caught first by Clotilde. A tall, handsome woman. A personality. Just as Elizabeth Temple had been a personality. I felt that here where the field was limited, I must at least sum up what I could about the three sisters. Three Fates. Who could be the killer? What kind of a killer? What kind of a killing? I could feel then rising up rather slowly, rather slowly like a miasma does, an atmosphere. I don't think there is any other word that expresses it except evil. Not necessarily that any one of these three was evil, but they were certainly living in an atmosphere where evil had happened, had left its shadow or was still threatening them. Clotilde, the eldest, was the first one I considered. She was handsome, she was strong, she was, I thought, a woman of intense emotional feeling. I saw her, I will admit, as a possible Clytemnestra. I had recently," Miss Marple dropped into her everyday tones, "been taken very kindly to a Greek play performed at a well-known boys' public school not far from my home. I had been very, very impressed by the acting of the Agamemnon and particularly the performance of the boy who had played Clytemnestra. A very remarkable performance. It seemed to me that in Clotilde I could imagine a woman who could plan and carry out the killing of a husband in his bath."

For a moment Professor Wanstead had all he could do to repress a laugh. It was the seriousness of Miss Marple's tone. She gave him a slight twinkle from her eyes.

"Yes, it sounds rather silly, does it not, said like that? But I could *see* her that way, playing that part, that is to say. Very unfortunately, she had no husband. She had never had a husband, and therefore did not kill a husband. Then I considered my guide to the house. Lavinia Glynne. She seemed an extremely nice, wholesome and pleasant woman. But alas, certain people who have killed have produced much that effect on the world round them. They have been charming people. Many murderers have been delightful and pleasant men and people have been astonished. They are what I call the respectable killers. The ones who would commit murder from entirely utilitarian motives. Without emotion, but to gain a required end. I didn't think it was very likely and I should be highly surprised if it was so, but I could not leave out Mrs Glynne. She had had a husband. She was a widow and had been a widow for some years. It could be. I left it at that. And then I came to the third sister. Anthea. She was a disquieting personality. Badly co-ordinated, it seemed to me, scatter-brained, and in a condition of some emotion which I thought on the whole was fear. She was frightened of something. Intensely frightened of something. Well, that could fit in too. If she had committed a crime of some kind, a crime which she had thought was finished with and past, there might have been some recrudescence, some raising up of old problems, something perhaps connected with the Elizabeth Temple enquiries; she might have felt fear that an old crime would be revived or discovered. She had a curious way of looking at you, and then looking sharply from side to side over one shoulder as though she saw something standing behind her. Something that made her afraid. So she too was a possible answer. A possibly slightly mentally unhinged killer who could have killed because she considered herself persecuted. Because she was afraid. These were only ideas. They were only a rather more pronounced assessment of possibilities that I had already gone through on the coach. But the atmosphere of the house was on me more than ever. That next day I walked in the garden with Anthea. At the end of the principal grass path was a mound. A mound created by the falling down of a former greenhouse. Owing to a lack of repairs and of gardeners at the end of the war it had fallen into disuse, come to pieces, bricks had been piled up surmounted with earth and turf, and had been planted with a certain creeper. A creeper well known when you want to hide or cover some rather ugly piece of building in your garden. Polygonum it is called. One of the quickest flowering shubs which swallows and kills and dries up and gets rid of everything it grows over. It grows over everything. It is in a way a rather frightening plant. It has beautiful white flowers, it can look very lovely. It was not yet in bloom but it was going to be. I stood there with Anthea, and she seemed to be desperately unhappy over the loss of the greenhouse. She said it had had such lovely grapes, it seemed to be the thing she remembered most about the garden when she had been a child there. And she wanted, she wanted desperately to have enough money so as to dig up the mound, level the ground and rebuild the greenhouse and stock it with muscat grapes and peaches as the old greenhouse had been. It was a terrible nostalgia for the past she was feeling. It was more than that. Again, very clearly, I felt an atmosphere of fear. Something about the mound made her frightened. I couldn't then think what it was. You know the next thing that happened. It was Elizabeth Temple's death and there was no doubt, from the story told by Emlyn Price and Joanna Crawford, that there could be only one conclusion. It was not accident. It was deliberate murder.

"I think it was from then on," said Miss Marple "that I knew. I came to the conclusion there had been three killings. I heard the full story of Mr Rafiel's son, the delinquent boy, the ex-jailbird and I thought that he was all those things, but none of them showed him as being a killer or likely to be a killer. All the evidence was against him. There was no doubt in anyone's mind that he had killed the girl whose name I had now learned as being Verity Hunt. But Archdeacon Brabazon put the final crown on the business, as it were. He had known those two young people. They had come to him with their story of wanting to get married and he had taken it upon himself to decide that they should get married. He thought that it was not perhaps a wise marriage, but it was a marriage just was justified by the fact that they both loved each other. The girl loved the boy with what he called a true love. A love as true as her name. And he thought that the boy, for all his bad sexual reputation, had truly loved the girl and had every intention of being faithful to her and trying to reform some of his evil tendencies. The Archdeacon was not optimistic. He did not, I think, believe it would be a thoroughly happy marriage, but it was to his mind what he called a necessary marriage. Necessary because if you love enough you will pay the price, even if the price is disappointment and a certain amount of unhappiness. But one thing I was quite sure of. That disfigured face, that battered-in head could not have been the action of a boy who really loved the girl. This was not a story of sexual assault. In this love affair the love was rooted in tenderness. I was ready to take the Archdeacon's word for that. But I knew, too, that I'd got the right clue, the clue that was given me by Elizabeth Temple. She had said that the cause of Verity's death was Love—one of the most frightening words there is.

"It was quite clear then," said Miss Marple. "I think I'd

known for some time really. It was just the small things that hadn't fitted in, but now they did. They fitted in with what Elizabeth Temple had said. The cause of Verity's death. She had said first the one word 'Love' and then that 'Love could be the most frightening word there was'. It was all mapped out so plainly then. The overwhelming love that Clotilde had had for this girl. The girl's hero-worship of her, dependency on her, and then as she grew a little older, her normal instincts came into play. She wanted Love. She wanted to be free to love, to marry, to have children. And along came the boy that she could love. She knew that he was unreliable, she knew he was what was technically called a bad lot, but that," said Miss Marple, in a more ordinary tone of voice, "is not what puts any girl off a boy. No. Young women like bad lots. They always have. They fall in love with bad lots. They are quite sure they can change them. And the nice, kind, steady, reliable husbands got the answer, in my young days, that one would be 'a sister to them' which never satisfied them at all. Verity fell in love with Michael Rafiel, and Michael Rafiel was prepared to turn over a new leaf and marry this girl and was sure he would never wish to look at another girl again. I don't say this would have been a happy-ever-after thing, but it was, as the Archdeacon said quite surely, it *was* real love. And so they planned to get married. And I think Verity wrote to Elizabeth and told her that she was going to marry Michael Rafiel. It was arranged in secret because I think Verity did realize that what she was doing was essentially an escape. She was escaping from a life that she didn't want to live any longer, from someone whom she loved very much but not in the same way she loved Michael. And she would not be allowed to do so. Permission would not be willingly given, every obstacle would be put in their way. So, like other young people, they were going to elope. There was no need for them to fly off to Gretna Green, they were of sufficiently mature age to marry. So she appealed to Archdeacon Brabazon, her old friend who had confirmed her—who was a real friend. And the wedding was arranged, the day, the time, probably even she bought secretly some garment in which to be married. They were to meet somewhere, no doubt. They were to come to the rendezvous separately. I think he came there, but she did *not* come. He waited perhaps. Waited and then tried to find out, perhaps, why she didn't come. I think then a message may have been given him, even a letter sent him, possibly in her forged handwriting, saying she had changed her mind. It was all over and she was going away for a time to get over it. I don't know. But I don't think he ever dreamt of the real reason of why she hadn't come, of why she had sent no word. He hadn't thought for one moment that she had been deliberately, cruelly, almost madly perhaps, destroyed. Clotilde was not going to lose the person she loved. She was not going to let her escape, she was not going to let her go to the young man whom she herself hated and loathed. She would keep Verity, keep her in her own way. But what I could not believe was—I did not believe that she'd strangled the girl and had then disfigured her face. I don't think she could have borne to do that. I think that she had re-arranged the bricks of the fallen greenhouse and piled up earth and turf over most of it. The girl had already been given a drink, an over-dose of sleeping draught probably. Grecian, as it were, in tradition. One cup of hemlock—even if it wasn't hemlock. And she buried the girl there in the garden, piled the bricks over her and the earth and the turf——"

"Did neither of the other sisters suspect it?"

"Mrs Glynne was not there then. Her husband had not died and she was still abroad. But Anthea was there. I think Anthea did know *something* of what went on. I don't know that she suspected death at first, but she knew that Clotilde had been occupying herself with the raising up of a mound at the end of the garden to be covered with flowering shrubs, to be a place of beauty. I think perhaps the truth came to her little by little. And then Clotilde, having accepted evil, done evil, surrendered to evil, had no qualms about what she would do next. I think she enjoyed planning it. She had a certain amount of influence over a sly, sexy little village girl who came to her cadging for benefits now and then. I think it was easy for her to arrange one day to take the girl on a picnic or an expedition a good long way away. Thirty or forty miles. She'd chosen the place beforehand, I think. She strangled the girl, disfigured her, hid her under turned earth, leaves and branches. Why should anyone ever suspect her of doing any such thing? She put Verity's handbag there and a little chain Verity used to wear round her neck and possibly dressed her in clothes belonging to Verity. She hoped the crime would not be found out for some time but in the meantime she spread abroad rumours of Nora Broad having been seen about in Michael's car, going about with Michael. Possibly she spread a story that Verity had broken off the engagement to be married because of his infidelity with this girl. She may have said anything and I think everything she said she enjoyed, poor lost soul."

"Why do you say 'poor lost soul', Miss Marple?"

"Because," said Miss Marple, "I don't suppose there can be any agony so great as what Clotilde has suffered all this time—ten years now—living in eternal sorrow. Living, you see, with the thing she *had* to live with. She had kept Verity, kept her there at The Old Manor House, in the garden, kept her there for ever. She didn't realize at first what that meant. Her passionate longing for the girl to be alive again. I don't think she ever suffered from remorse. I don't think she had even that consolation. She just suffered—went on suffering year after year. And I know now what Elizabeth Temple meant. Better perhaps than she herself did. Love *is* a very terrible thing. It is alive to evil, it can be one of the most evil things there can be. And she had to live with that day after day, year after year. I think, you know, that Anthea was frightened of that. I think she knew more clearly the whole time what Clotilde had done and she thought that Clotilde knew that she knew. And she was afraid of what Clotilde might do. Clotilde gave that parcel to Anthea to post, the one with the pullover. She said things to me about Anthea, that she was mentally disturbed, that if she suffered from persecution or jealousy Anthea might do anything. I think—yes—that in the not so distant future—something might have happened to Anthea—an arranged suicide because of a guilty conscience——"

"And yet you are sorry for that woman?" asked Sir Andrew. "Malignant evil is like cancer—a malignant tumour. It brings suffering."

"Of course," said Miss Marple.

"I suppose you have been told what happened that night," said Professor Wanstead, "after your guardian angels had removed you?"

"You mean Clotilde? She had picked up my glass of milk, I remember. She was still holding it when Miss Cooke took me out of the room. I suppose she—drank it, did she?"

"Yes. Did you know that might happen?"

"I didn't think of it, no, not at the moment. I suppose I could have known it if I'd thought about it."

"Nobody could have stopped her. She was so quick about it, and nobody quite realized there was anything wrong in the milk."

"So she drank it."

"Does that surprise you?"

"No, it would have seemed to her the natural thing to do, one can't really wonder. It had come by this time that she wanted to escape—from all the things she was having to live with. Just as Verity had wanted to escape from the life that she was living there. Very odd, isn't it, that the retribution one brings on oneself fits so closely with what has caused it."

"You sound sorrier for her than you were for the girl who died."

"No," said Miss Marple, "it's a different kind of being sorry. I'm sorry for Verity because of all that she missed, all that she was so near to obtaining. A life of love and devotion and service to the man she had chosen, and whom she truly loved. Truly and in all verity. She missed all that and nothing can give that back to her. I'm sorry for her because of what she *didn't* have. But she escaped what Clotilde had to suffer. Sorrow, misery, fear and a growing cultivation and imbibing of evil. Clotilde had to live with all those. Sorrow, frustrated love which she could never get back, she had to live with the two sisters who suspected, who were afraid of her, and she had to live with the girl she had kept there."

"You mean Verity?"

"Yes. Buried in the garden, buried in the tomb that Clotilde had prepared. She was *there* in The Old Manor House and I think Clotilde *knew* she was there. It might be that she even saw her or thought she saw her, sometimes when she went to pick a spray of polygonum blossom. She must have felt very close to Verity then. Nothing worse could happen to her, could it, than that? Nothing worse. . ."

23. *End Pieces*

"THAT OLD lady gives me the creeps," said Sir Andrew McNeil, when he had said goodbye and thanks to Miss Marple.

"So gentle—and so ruthless," said the Assistant Commissioner.

Professor Wanstead took Miss Marple down to his car which was waiting, and then returned for a few final words.

"What do you think of her, Edmund?"

"The most frightening woman I ever met," said the Home Secretary.

"Ruthless?" asked Professor Wanstead.

"No, no, I don't mean that but—well, a very frightening woman."

"Nemesis," said Professor Wanstead thoughtfully.

"Those two women," said the P.P.D. man, "you know, the security agents who were looking after her, they gave a most extraordinary description of her that night. They got into the house quite easily, hid themselves in a small downstairs room until everyone went upstairs, then one went into the bedroom and into the wardrobe and the other stayed outside the room to watch. The one in the bedroom said that when she threw open the door of the wardrobe and came out, there was the old lady sitting up in bed with a pink fluffy shawl round her neck and a perfectly placid face, twittering away and talking like an elderly school marm. They said she gave them quite a turn."

"A pink fluffy shawl," said Professor Wanstead. "Yes, yes, I do remember——"

"What do you remember?"

"Old Rafiel. He told me about her, you know, and then he laughed. He said one thing he'd never forget in all his life. He said it was when one of the funniest scatter-brained old pussies he'd ever met came marching into his bedroom out in the West Indies, with a fluffy pink scarf round her neck, telling him he was to get up and do something to prevent a murder. And he said, 'What on earth do you think you're doing?' And she said she was Nemesis. Nemesis! He could not imagine anything less like it, he said. I like the touch of the pink woolly scarf," said Professor Wanstead, thoughtfully, "I like that, very much."

ii

"Michael," said Professor Wanstead, "I want to introduce you to Miss Jane Marple, who's been very active on your behalf."

The young man of thirty-two, looked at the white-haired, rather dicky old lady with a slightly doubtful expression.

"Oh—er—" he said, "well, I guess I have heard about it. Thanks very much."

He looked at Wanstead.

"It's true, is it, they're going to give me a free pardon or something silly like that?"

"Yes. A release will be put through quite soon. You'll be a free man in a very short time."

"Oh." Michael sounded slightly doubtful.

"It will take a little getting used to, I expect," said Miss Marple kindly.

She looked at him thoughtfully. Seeing him in retrospect as he might have been ten years or so ago. Still quite attractive—though he showed all the signs of strain. Attractive, yes. Very attractive, she thought he would have been once. A gaiety about him then, there would have been, and a charm. He'd lost that now, but it would come back perhaps. A weak mouth and attractively shaped eyes that could look you straight in the face, and probably had been always extremely useful for telling lies that you really wanted to believe. Very like—who was it?—she dived into past memories—Jonathan Birkin, of course. He had sung in the choir. A really delightful baritone voice. And how fond the girls had been of him! Quite a good job he'd had as clerk in Messrs Gabriel's firm. A pity there had been that little matter of the cheques.

"Oh," said Michael. He said, with even more embarrassment, "It's been very kind of you, I'm sure, to take so much trouble."

"I've enjoyed it," said Miss Marple. "Well, I'm glad to have met you. Goodbye. I hope you've got a very good time coming to you. Our country is in rather a bad way just now, but you'll probably find some job or other that you might quite enjoy doing."

"Oh yes. Thanks, thanks very much. I—I really am very grateful, you know."

His tone sounded still extremely unsure about it.

"It's not me you ought to be grateful to," said Miss Marple, "you ought to be grateful to your father."

"Dad? Dad never thought much of me."

"Your father, when he was a dying man, was determined to see that you got justice."

"Justice." Michael Rafiel considered it.

"Yes, your father thought Justice was important. He was, I think, a very just man himself. In the letter he wrote me asking me to undertake this proposition, he directed me to a quotation:

'Let Justice roll down like waters
And Righteousness like an everlasting stream.'"

"Oh! What's it mean? Shakespeare?"

"No, the Bible—one has to think about it—I had to."

Miss Marple unwrapped a parcel she had been carrying.

"They gave me this," she said. "They thought I might like to have it—because I had helped to find out the truth of what had really happened. I think, though, that you are the person who should have first claim on it—that is if you really want it. But maybe you do *not* want it——"

She handed him the photograph of Verity Hunt that Clotilde Bradbury-Scott had shown her once in the drawing-room of The Old Manor House.

He took it—and stood with it, staring down on it. . . . His face changed, the lines of it softened, then hardened. Miss Marple watched him without speaking. The silence went on for some little time. Professor Wanstead also watched—he watched them both, the old lady and the boy.

It came to him that this was in some way a crisis—a moment that might affect a whole new way of life.

Michael Rafiel, sighed—he stretched out and gave the photograph back to Miss Marple.

"No, you are right, I do not want it. All that life is gone—she's gone—I can't keep her with me. Anything I do now has got to be new—going forward. You—" he hesitated, looking at her—'You understand?"

"Yes," said Miss Marple—"I understand—I think you are right. I wish you good luck in the life you are now going to begin."

He said goodbye and went out.

"Well," said Professor Wanstead, "not an enthusiastic young man. He could have thanked you a bit more enthusiastically for what you did for him."

"Oh, that's quite all right," said Miss Marple. "I didn't expect him to do so. It would have embarrassed him even more. It is, you know," she added, "very embarrassing when one has to thank people and start life again and see everything from a different angle and all that. I think he might do well. He's not bitter. That's the great thing. I understand quite well why that girl loved him——"

"Well, perhaps he'll go straight this time."

"One rather doubts that," said Miss Marple. "I don't know that he'd be able to help himself unless—of course," she said, "the great thing to hope for is that he'll meet a really nice girl."

"What I like about you," said Professor Wanstead, "is your delightfully practical mind."

iii

"She'll be here presently," said Mr Broadribb to Mr Schuster.

"Yes. The whole thing's pretty extraordinary, isn't it?"

"I couldn't believe it at first," said Broadribb. "You know, when poor old Rafiel was dying, I thought this whole thing was—well, senility or something. Not that he was old enough for that."

The buzzer went. Mr Schuster picked up the phone.

"Oh, she's here, is she? Bring her up," he said. "She's come," he said. "I wonder now. You know, it's the oddest thing I ever heard in my life. Getting an old lady to go racketing round the countryside looking for she doesn't know what. The police think, you know, that that woman committed not just one murder but three. Three! I ask you! Verity Hunt's body was under the mound in the garden, just as the old lady said it was. She hadn't been strangled and the face was not disfigured."

"I wonder the old lady herself didn't get done in," said Mr Broadribb. "Far too old to be able to take care of herself."

"She had a couple of detectives, apparently, looking after her."

"What, *two* of them?"

"Yes, I didn't know that."

Miss Marple was ushered into their room.

"Congratulations, Miss Marple," said Mr Broadribb rising to greet her.

"Very best wishes. Splendid job," said Mr Schuster, shaking hands.

Miss Marple sat down composedly on the other side of the desk.

"As I told you in my letter," she said, "I think I have fulfilled the terms of the proposition that was made to me. I have succeeded in what I was asked to do."

"Oh I know. Yes, we've heard already. We've heard from Professor Wanstead and from the legal department and from the police authorities. Yes, it's been a splendid job, Miss Marple. We congratulate you."

"I was afraid," said Miss Marple, "that I would not be able to do what was required of me. It seemed so very difficult, almost impossible at first."

"Yes indeed. It seems quite impossible to me. I don't know how you did it, Miss Marple."

"Oh well," said Miss Marple, "it's just perseverance, isn't it, that leads to things."

"Now about the sum of money we are holding. It's at your disposal at any time now. I don't know whether you would like us to pay it into your bank or whether you would like to consult us possibly as to the investment of it? It's quite a large sum."

"Twenty thousand pounds," said Miss Marple. "Yes, it is a very large sum by my way of thinking. Quite extraordinary," she added.

"If you would like an introduction to our brokers, they could give you possibly some ideas about investing."

"Oh, I don't want to invest any of it."

"But surely it would be——"

"There's no point in saving at my age," said Miss Marple. "I mean the point of this money—I'm sure Mr Rafiel meant it that way—is to enjoy a few things that one thought one never would have the money to enjoy."

"Well, I see your point of view," said Mr Broadribb. "Then your instructions would be that we pay this sum of money into your bank?"

"Middleton's Bank, 132 High Street, St Mary Mead," said Miss Marple.

"You have a deposit account, I expect. We will place it to your deposit account?"

"Certainly not," said Miss Marple. "Put in into my current account."

"You don't think——"

"I do think," said Miss Marple. "I want it in my current account."

She got up and shook hands.

"You could ask your bank manager's advice, you know, Miss Marple. It really is—one never knows when one wants something for a rainy day."

"The only thing I shall want for a rainy day will be my umbrella," said Miss Marple.

She shook hands with them both again.

"Thank you so much, Mr Broadribb. And you too, Mr Schuster. You've been so kind to me, giving me all the information I needed."

"You really want that money put into your current account?"

"Yes," said Miss Marple. "I'm going to spend it, you know. I'm going to have some fun with it."

She looked back from the door and she laughed. Just for one moment Mr Schuster, who was a man of more imagination than Mr Broadribb, had a vague impression of a young and pretty girl shaking hands with the vicar at a garden party in the country. It was, as he realized a moment later, a recollection of his own youth. But Miss Marple had, for a minute, reminded him of that particular girl, young, happy, going to enjoy herself.

"Mr Rafiel would have liked me to have fun," said Miss Marple.

She went out of the door.

"Nemesis," said Mr Broadribb. "That's what Rafiel called her. Nemesis! Never seen anybody less like Nemesis, have you?"

Mr Schuster shook his head.

"It must have been another of Mr Rafiel's little jokes," said Mr Broadribb.